The Revolutions Trilogy

Also by John Banville

Long Lankin

Nightspawn

Birchwood

Mefisto

The Book of Evidence

Ghosts

Athena

The Untouchable

Eclipse

JOHN BANVILLE

The Revolutions Trilogy

DOCTOR COPERNICUS

KEPLER

THE NEWTON LETTER

PICADOR

This omnibus edition published 2000 by Picador
an imprint of Macmillan Publishers Ltd
25 Eccleston Place, London SW1W 9NF
Basingstoke and Oxford
Associated companies throughout the world
www.macmillan.com

Dr Copernicus first published in Great Britain 1976 by Martin Secker & Warburg Ltd
First published by Picador 1999
Kepler first published in Great Britain 1981 by Martin Secker & Warburg Ltd
First published by Picador 1999
The Newton Letter first published in Great Britain 1982 by Martin Secker & Warburg Ltd
First published by Picador 1999

ISBN 0 330 37345 5

1 3 5 7 9 8 6 4 2

A CIP catalogue record for this book is available from the British Library.

Typeset by SetSystems Ltd, Saffron Walden, Essex
Printed and bound in Great Britain by
Mackays of Chatham plc, Chatham, Kent

Contents

DOCTOR COPERNICUS

1

KEPLER

283

THE NEWTON LETTER

501

EUROPE IN 1500
200 miles
300 kilometres
NORTH SEA
BALTIC SEA
Copenhagen
Königsberg
EAST PRUSSIA
Danzig
PRUSSIA (ROYAL)
Hamburg
Bremen
SAXONY
Berlin
Vistula
INSET MAP 2
Warsaw
HOLY ROMAN EMPIRE
Wittenberg
Elbe
Rhine
Brussels
Cologne
POLAND
Oder
Cracow
Prague
Nuremberg
Seine
Danube
FRANCE
Vienna
Buda (Ofen)
Pest
Berne
HUNGARY
Milan
VENICE
Venice
Turin
Rhône
Genoa
INSET MAP 1
Belgrade
Florence
OTTOMAN EMPIRE
PAPAL STATES
ADRIATIC SEA
MEDITERRANEAN
Corsica (to Genoa)
NAPLES (to Spain)
Rome
N
Sardinia (to Spain)
BALTIC SEA
Frisches Haff
Königsberg
EAST PRUSSIA
Frauenburg
Danzig
Elbing
ERMLAND
Heilsberg
PRUSSIA (ROYAL)
Allenstein
(Teutonic Knights)
Kulm
Torun
Vistula
Włocławek
100 miles
200 kilometres
Warsaw
50 miles
70 kilometres
Lake Garda
Padua
Venice
Ferrara
Bologna

DOCTOR COPERNICUS

IN MEMORIAM

DOUGLAS SYNNOTT

You must become an ignorant man again
And see the sun again with an ignorant eye
And see it clearly in the idea of it.

– Wallace Stevens,
'Notes Toward a Supreme Fiction'

I

Orbitas Lumenque

At first it had no name. It was the thing itself, the vivid thing. It was his friend. On windy days it danced, demented, waving wild arms, or in the silence of evening drowsed and dreamed, swaying in the blue, the goldeny air. Even at night it did not go away. Wrapped in his truckle bed, he could hear it stirring darkly outside in the dark, all the long night long. There were others, nearer to him, more vivid still than this, they came and went, talking, but they were wholly familiar, almost a part of himself, while it, steadfast and aloof, belonged to the mysterious outside, to the wind and the weather and the goldeny blue air. It was a part of the world, and yet it was his friend.

Look, Nicolas, look! See the big tree!

Tree. That was its name. And also: the linden. They were nice words. He had known them a long time before he knew what they meant. They did not mean themselves, they were nothing in themselves, they meant the dancing singing thing outside. In wind, in silence, at night, in the changing air, it changed and yet was changelessly the tree, the linden tree. That was strange.

Everything had a name, but although every name was nothing without the thing named, the thing cared nothing for its name, had no need of a name, and was itself only. And then there were the names that signified no substantial thing, as linden and tree signified that dark dancer. His mother asked him who did he love the best. Love did not dance, nor tap the window with frantic fingers, love had no leafy arms to shake, yet when she spoke that name that named nothing, some impalpable but real thing within him responded as if to a summons, as if it had heard its name spoken. That was very strange.

He soon forgot about these enigmatic matters, and learned to talk as others talked, full of conviction, unquestioningly.

The sky is blue, the sun is gold, the linden tree is green. Day is light, it ends, night falls, and then it is dark. You sleep, and in the morning wake again. But a day will come when you will not wake. That is death. Death is sad. Sadness is what happiness is not. And so on. How simple it all was, after all! There was no need even to think about it. He had only to be, and life would do the rest, would send day to follow day until there were no days left, for him, and then he would go to Heaven and be an angel. Hell was under the ground.

Matthew Mark Luke and John
Bless the bed that I lie on
If I die before I wake
Ask holy God my soul to take

He peered from behind clasped hands at his mother kneeling beside him in the candlelight. Under a burnished coif of coiled hair her face was pale and still, like the face of the Madonna in the picture. Her eyes were closed, and her lips moved, mouthing mutely the pious lines as he recited them aloud. When he stumbled on the hard words she bore him up gently, in a wonderfully gentle voice. He loved her the best, he said. She rocked him in her arms and sang a song.

See saw Margery Daw
This little chicken
Got lost in the straw

*

He liked to lie in bed awake, listening to the furtive noises of the night all around him, the creaks and groans and abrupt muffled cracks which he imagined were the voice of the house complaining as, braced under the weight of the enormous darkness outside, it stealthily stretched and shifted the aching bones of its back. The wind sang in the chimney, the rain drummed on the roof, the linden tree tapped and tapped, tap tap tap. He was warm. In the room below his room his mother and father were talking, telling each other of their doings that day abroad in the world. How could they be so calm, and speak so softly, when surely they had such fabulous tales to recount? Their voices were like the voice of sleep itself, calling him away. There were other voices, of church-bells gravely tolling the hours, of dogs that barked afar, and of the river too, though that was not so much a voice as a huge dark liquidy, faintly frightening rushing in the darkness that was felt not heard. All called, called him to sleep. He slept.

But sometimes Andreas in the bed in the corner made strange noises and woke him up again. Andreas was his older brother: he had bad dreams.

The children played games together. There was hide and seek, and hide the linger, jack stones and giant steps, and others that had no names. Katharina, who was older than Andreas, soon came to despise such childish frivolity. Andreas too grew tired of play. He lived in his own silent troubled world from whence he rarely emerged, and when he did it was only to pounce on them, pummelling and pinching, or twisting an arm, smiling, with eyes glittering, before withdrawing again as swiftly as he had come. Barbara alone, although she was the eldest of the four, was always glad of the excuse to abandon her gawky height and chase her little brother on all fours about the floor and under the tables, grinning and growling like a happy hound all jaws and paws and raggedy fur. It was Barbara that he loved the best, really, although he did not tell anyone, even her. She was going to be a nun. She told him about God, who resembled her strangely, an amiable, loving and sad person given to losing things, and dropping things. He it was, struggling to hold aloft so much, that fumbled and let fall their mother from out his tender embrace.

That was an awful day. The house seemed full of old women and the dreary sound of weeping. His father's face, usually so stern and set, was shockingly naked, all pink and grey and shiny. Even Katharina and Andreas were polite to each other. They paced about the rooms with measured tread, emulating their elders, bowing their heads and clasping their hands and speaking in soft stiff formal voices. It was all very alarming. His mother was laid out upon her bed, her jaw bound fast with a white rag. She was utterly, uniquely still, and seemed in this unique utter stillness to have arrived at last at a true and total definition of what she was, herself, her vivid self itself. Everything around her, even the living creatures coming and going, appeared vague and unfinished compared with her stark thereness. And yet she was dead, she was no longer his mother, who was in Heaven, so they told him. But if that was so, then what was this thing that remained?

They took it away and buried it, and in time he forgot what it was that had puzzled him.

*

Now his father loomed large in his life. With his wife's death he had changed, or rather the change that her departure had wrought in the life of the household left him stranded in an old, discarded world, so that he trod with clumsy feet among the family's new preoccupations like a faintly comical, faintly sinister and exasperating ghost. The other children avoided him. Only Nicolas continued willingly to seek his company, tracking to its source the dark thread of silence that his father spun out behind him in his fitful wanderings about the house. They spent long hours together, saying nothing, each hardly acknowledging the other's presence, bathing in the balm of a shared solitude. But it was only in these pools of quiet that they were at ease together, and thrust into unavoidable contact elsewhere they were as strangers.

Despite the helplessness and pain of their public encounters, the father clung obstinately to his dream of a hearty man-to-man communion with his son, one that the town of Torun would recognise and approve. He explained the meaning of money. It was more than coins, O much more. Coins, you see, are only for poor people, simple people, and for little boys. They are only a kind of picture of the real thing, but the real thing itself you cannot see, nor put in your pocket, and it does not jingle. When

I do business with other merchants I have no need of these silly bits of metal, and my purse may be full or empty, it makes no difference. I give my word, and that is sufficient, because my word is money. Do you see? He did not see, and they looked at each other in silence helplessly, baffled, and inexplicably embarrassed.

Nevertheless once a week they sallied forth from the big house in St Anne's Lane to display to the town the impregnable eternal edifice that is the merchant and his heir. The boy performed his part as best he could, and gravely paced the narrow streets with his hands clasped behind his back, while his insides writhed in an agony of shame and self-consciousness. His father, sabred, black-hatted, wagging an ornate cane, was a grotesque caricature of the vigorous bluff businessman he imagined himself to be. The garrulous greetings – *Grüss Gott, mein-herr!* fine day! how's trade? – that he bestowed on friend and stranger alike in a booming public voice, fell clumsily about the streets, a horrible hollow crashing. When he paused to speak to an acquaintance, his sententiousness and grating joviality made the boy suck his teeth and grind one heel slowly, slowly, into the ground.

'And this is Nicolas, he is my youngest, but he has a nose already for the business, have you not, hey, what do you say, young scamp?'

He said nothing, only smiled weakly and turned away, seeking the consolation of poplars, and the great bundles of steely light above the river, and brass clouds in a high blue sky.

They made their way along the wharf, where Nicolas's fearful soul ventured out of hiding, enticed by the uproar of men and ships, so different from the inane babbling back there in the streets. Here was not a world of mere words but of glorious clamour and chaos, the big black barrels rumbling and thudding, winch ropes humming, the barefoot loaders singing and swearing as they trotted back and forth under their burdens across the thrumming gangplanks. The boy was entranced, prey to terror and an awful glee, discerning in all this haste and hugeness the prospect of some dazzling, irresistible annihilation.

His father too was nervous of the river and the teeming wharves, and hurried along in silence now, with his head bent and shoulders hunched, seeking shelter. The house of Koppernigk & Sons stood back from the quayside and contemplated with obvious satisfaction the frantic hither and thithering of trade below its windows; under that stony gaze even the unruly Vistula lay down meekly and flowed away. In the dusty offices, the cool dim caverns of the warehouses, the boy watched, fascinated and appalled, his father put on once more the grimacing mask of the man of consequence, and a familiar mingling of contempt and pity began to ache again within him.

Yet secretly he delighted in these visits. An obscure hunger fed its fill here in this tight assured little world. He wandered dreamily through the warren of pokey offices, breathing the crumbly odours of dust and ink, spying on inky dusty grey old men crouched with their quills over enormous ledgers. Great quivering blades of sunlight smote the air, the clamour of the quayside stormed the windows, but nothing could shake the stout twin pillars of debit and credit on which the house was balanced. Here was harmony. In the furry honeybrown gloom of the warehouses his senses reeled, assailed by smells and colours and textures, of brandy and vodka snoozing in casks, of wax and pitch, and tight-packed tuns of herring, of timber and corn and an orient of spices. Burnished sheets of copper glowed with a soft dark flame in their tattered wraps of sacking and old ropes, and happiness seemed a copper-coloured word.

It was from this metal that the family had its name, his father said, and not from the Polish *coper*, meaning horseradish, as some were spiteful enough to suggest. Horseradish indeed! Never forget, ours is a distinguished line, merchants and magistrates and ministers of Holy Church – patricians all! Yes, Papa.

*

The Koppernigks had originated in Upper Silesia, from whence in 1396 one Niklas Koppernigk, a stonemason by trade, had moved to Cracow and taken Polish citizenship. His son, Johannes, was the founder of the merchant house that in the late 1450s young Nicolas's father was to transfer to Torun in Royal Prussia. There, among the old German settler families, the Koppernigks laboured long and diligently to rid themselves of Poland and all things Polish. They were not entirely successful; the children's German was still tainted with a southern something, a faint afterglow of boiled cabbage as it were, that had troubled their mother greatly during her brief unhappy life. She was a Waczelrodt. The Waczelrodts it is true were Silesians just like the Koppernigks, having their name from the village of Weizenrodau near Schweidnitz, but apart from that they were something quite different from the Koppernigks: no stonemasons there, indeed no. There had been Waczelrodts among the aldermen and councillors of Münsterburg in the thirteenth century, and, a little later, of Breslau. Towards the end of the last century they had arrived in Torun, where they had soon become influential, and were among the governors of the Old City. Nicolas's maternal grandfather had been a wealthy man, with property in the town and also a number of large estates at Kulm. The Waczelrodts were connected by marriage with the Peckaus of Magdeburg and the von Allens of Torun. They had also, of course, married into the Koppernigks, late of Cracow, but that was hardly a connection that one would wish to boast of, as Nicolas's Aunt Christina Waczelrodt, a very grand and formidable lady, had often pointed out.

'Remember,' his mother told him, 'you are as much a Waczelrodt as a Koppernigk. Your uncle will be Bishop one day. Remember!'

*

Father and son returned weary and disgruntled from their outings, and parted quickly, with faces averted, the father to nurse in solitude his disappointment and unaccountable sense of shame, the son to endure the torment of Andreas's baiting.

'And how was business today, brother, eh?'

Andreas was the rightful heir, being the elder son. The notion elicited from his father one of his rare brief barks of laughter.

'That wastrel? Ho no. Let him go for the Church, where his Uncle Lucas can find a fat prebend for him.' And Andreas gnawed his knuckles, and slunk away.

Andreas hated his brother. His hatred was like a kind of anguish, and Nicolas sometimes fancied he could hear it, a high-pitched excruciating whine.

'The Turk is coming, little brother, he has invaded the south.' Nicolas turned pale. Andreas smirked. 'O yes, it is true, you know, believe me. Are you afraid? Nothing will stop the Turk. He impales his prisoners, they say. A big sharp stake right up your bum – like *that!* Ha!'

They walked to school and home again together. Andreas chose to be elaborately indifferent to Nicolas's meek presence beside him, and whistled through his teeth, and considered the sky, slowed up his pace abruptly to scrutinise some fascinating thing floating in a sewer or quickened it to lurch in mockery behind an unsuspecting cripple, so that, try as he might to anticipate these sudden checks and advances, Nicolas was forced to dance, smiling a puppet's foolish fixed smile, on the end of his capricious master's invisible leash. And the harder he tried to efface himself the fiercer became Andreas's scorn.

'You, creepy – do not creep behind me always!'

Andreas was handsomely made, very tall and slender, dark, fastidious, cold. Running or walking he moved with languorous negligent grace, but it was in repose that he appeared most lovely, standing by a window lost in a blue dream, with his pale thin face lifted up to the light like a perfect vase, or a shell out of the sea, some exquisite fragile thing. He had a way when addressed directly of frowning quickly and turning his head away; then, poised thus, he seemed shaped in his beauty by the action of an ineradicable distress within him. In the smelly classrooms and the corridors of St John's School he floundered, a vulnerable aetherial creature brought low in an alien element, and the masters roared in his face and beat him, their stolid souls enraged by this enigma, who learned nothing, and trailed home to endure in silence, with his face turned away, the abuse of a disappointed father.

Gaiety took him like a falling sickness, and sent him whinnying mad through the house with his long limbs wildly spinning. These frantic fits of glee were rare and brief, and ended abruptly with the sound of something shattering, a toy, a tile, a windowpane. The other children cowered then, as the silence fluttered down.

He chose for friends the roughest brutes of boys St John's could offer. They gathered outside the school gates each afternoon for fights and farting contests and other fun. Nicolas dreaded that bored malicious crowd. Nepomuk Müller snatched his cap and pranced away, brandishing the prize aloft.

'Here, Nepomuk, chuck it here!'

'Me, Müller, me!'

The dark disc sailed here and there in the bitter sunlight, sustained in flight it seemed by the wild cries rising around it. A familiar gloom invaded Nicolas's soul. If only he could be angry! Red rage would have flung him into the game, where even the part of victim would have been preferable to this contemptuous detachment. He waited morose and silent outside the ring of howling boys, drawing patterns on the ground with the toe of his shoe.

The cap came by Andreas and he reached up and plucked it out of the air, but instead of sending it on its way again instanter he paused, seeking as always some means of investing the game with a touch of grace. The others groaned.

'O come on, Andy, throw it!'

He turned to Nicolas and smiled his smile, and began to measure up the distance separating them, making feints like a rings player, taking careful aim.

'Watch me land it on his noggin.'

But catching Nicolas's eye he hesitated again, and frowned, and then with a surly defiant glance over his shoulder at the others he stepped forward and offered the cap to his brother. 'Here,' he murmured, 'take it.' But Nicolas looked away. He could cope with cruelty, which was predictable. Andreas's face darkened. 'Take your damned cap, you little snot!'

They straggled homeward, wrapped in a throbbing silence. Nicolas, sighing and sweating, raged inwardly in fierce impotence against Andreas, who was so impressively grown-up in so many ways, and yet could be so childish sometimes. That with the cap had been silly. *You must not expect me to understand you, even though I do!* He did not quite know what that meant, but he thought it might mean that the business of the cap had not really been silly at all. O, it was hopeless! There were times such as this when the muddle of his feelings for Andreas took on the alarming aspect of hatred.

They were no longer heading homeward. Nicolas halted.

'Where are we going?'

'Never mind.'

But he knew well where they were going. Their father had forbidden them to venture by themselves beyond the walls. Out there was the New Town, a maze of hovels and steaming alleys rife with the thick green stench of humankind. That was the world of the poor, the lepers and the Jews, the renegades. Nicolas feared that world. His flesh crawled at the thought of it. When he was dragged there by Andreas, who revelled in the low life, the hideousness rolled over him in choking slimy waves, and he seemed to drown. 'Where are we going? We are not to go down there! You know we are not supposed to go down there. Andreas.'

But Andreas did not answer, and went on alone down the hill, whistling, toward the gate and the drawbridge, and gradually the distance made of him a crawling crablike thing. Nicolas, abandoned, began discreetly to cry.

*

The room was poised, weirdly still. A fly buzzed and boomed tinily against the diamond panes of the window. On the floor a dropped book was surreptitiously shutting itself page by page, slowly. The beady eager eye of a mirror set in a gilt sunburst on the far wall contained another room in miniature, and another doorway in which there floated a small pale frightened face gaping aghast at the image of that stricken creature swimming like an eyelash come detached on the rim of the glass. Look! On tiptoe teetering by the window he hung, suspended from invisible struts, an impossibly huge stark black puppet, clawing at his breast, his swollen face clenched in terrible hurt.

And here comes a chopper
To chop off his
head

He dropped, slack bag-of-bones, and with him the whole room seemed to collapse.

'*Children, your father is dead, of his heart.*'

*

The reverberations of that collapse persisted, muted but palpable, and the house, bruised and raw from the shedding of tears, seemed to throb hugely in pain. Grief was the shape of a squat grey rodent lodged in the heart.

The more fiercely this grief-rat struggled the clearer became Nicolas's thinking, as if his mind, horrified by that squirming thing down there, were scrambling higher and higher away from it into rarer and rarer heights of chill bright air. His mother's death had puzzled him, yet he had looked upon it as an accident, in dimensions out of all proportion to the small flaw in the machine that had caused it. This death was different. The machine seemed damaged now beyond repair. Life, he saw, had gone horribly awry, and nothing they had told him could explain it, none of the names they had taught him could name the cause. Even Barbara's God withdrew, in a shocked silence.

*

Uncle Lucas, Canon Waczelrodt, travelled post-haste from Frauenburg in Ermland when the news reached him of his brother-in-law's death. The affairs of the Chapter of Canons at Frauenburg Cathedral were as usual in disarray, and it was not a good time to be absent for a man with his eye on the bishopric. Canon Lucas was extremely annoyed – but then, his life was a constant state of vast profound annoyance. The ravages wrought by the unending war between his wilfulness and a recalcitrant world were written in nerveknots on the grey map of his face, and his little eyes, cold and still above the nose thick as a hammerhead, were those of the lean sentinel that crouched within the fleshy carapace of his bulk. He did not like things as they were, but luckily for things he had not yet decided finally how they should be. It was said that he had never in his life been known to laugh.

His coming was the boom of a bronze gong marking the entry of a new order into the children's lives.

He strode about the house sniffing after discrepancies, with the four of them trotting in his wake like a flock of frightened mice, twittering. Nicolas was mesmerised by this hard, fascinatingly ugly, overbearing manager of men. His cloak, flying out behind him, sliced the air ruthlessly, as once Nicolas had seen him on the magistrate's bench in the Town Hall slicing to shreds the arguments of whining plaintiffs. In the strange, incomprehensible and sometimes cruel world of adults, Uncle Lucas was the most adult of all.

'Your father in his will has delivered you his children into my care. It is not a responsibility that I welcome, yet it is my duty to fulfil his wishes. I shall speak to each of you in turn. You will wait here.'

He swept into the study and shut the door behind him. The children sat on a bench in the sanded hall outside, picking at their fingernails and sighing. Barbara began quietly to weep. Andreas tapped his feet on the floor in time to the rhythm of his worried thoughts. Sweat sprang out on Nicolas's skin, as always when he was upset. Katharina nudged him.

'You will be sent away, do you know that?' she whispered. 'O yes, far far away, to a place where you will not have Barbara to protect you. Far, far away.'

She smiled. He pressed his lips tightly together. He would not cry for her.

The time went slowly. They listened intently to the tiny

sounds within, the rustle of papers, squeak of a pen, and once a loud grunt, of astonishment, so it sounded. Andreas announced that he was not going to sit here any longer doing nothing, and stood up, but then sat down again immediately when the door flew open and Uncle Lucas came out. He looked at them with a frown, as if wondering where it was that he had seen them before, then shook his head and withdrew again. The flurry of air he had left behind him in the hall subsided.

At last the summons came. Andreas went in first, pausing at the doorway to wipe his damp hands on his tunic and fix on his face an ingratiating leer. In a little while he came out again, scowling, and jerked his thumb at Nicolas.

'You next.'

'But what did he say to you?'

'Nothing. We are to be sent away.'

O!

Nicolas went in. The door snapped shut behind him like a mouth. Uncle Lucas was sitting at the big desk by the window with the family papers spread before him. He reminded Nicolas of a huge implacable frog. A panel of the high window stood open on a summer evening full of white clouds and dusty golden light.

'Sit, child.'

The desk was raised upon a dais, and when he sat on the low stool before it he could see only his uncle's head and shoulders looming above him like a bust of hard grey grainy stone. He was frightened, and his knees would not stay still. The voice addressing him was a hollow booming noise directed less at him than at an idea in Uncle Lucas's mind called vaguely Child, or Nephew, or Responsibility, and Nicolas could distinguish only the meaning of the words and not the sense of what was being said. His life was being calmly wrenched apart at the joints and reassembled unrecognisably in his uncle's hands. He gazed intently upward through the window, and a part of him detached itself and floated free, out into the blue and golden air. *Włocławek.* It was the sound of some living thing being torn asunder . . .

The interview was at an end, yet Nicolas still sat with his hands gripping his knees, quaking but determined. Uncle Lucas looked up darkly from the desk. 'Well?'

'Please sir, I am to be a merchant, like my father.'

'What do you say, boy? Speak up.'

'Papa said that one day I should own the offices and the warehouses and all the ships and Andreas would go for the Church because you would find a place for him but I would stay here in Torun to tend the business, Papa said. You see,' faintly, 'I do not think I really want to go away.'

Uncle Lucas blinked. 'What age are you, child?'

'Ten years, sir.'

'You must finish your schooling.'

'But I am at St John's.'

'Yes yes, but you will leave St John's! Have you not listened? You will go to the Cathedral School at Włocławek, you and your brother both, and after that to the University of Cracow, where you will study canon law. Then you will enter the Church. I do not ask you to understand, only to obey.'

'But I want to stay here, please sir, with respect.'

There was a silence. Uncle Lucas gazed at the boy without expression, and then the great head turned, like part of an immense engine turning, to the window. He sighed.

'Your father's business has failed. Torun has failed. The trade has gone to Danzig. He timed his death well. These papers, these so-called accounts: I am appalled. It is a disgrace, such incompetence. The Waczelrodts made him, and this is how he repays us. The house will be retained, and there will be some small annuities, but the rest must be sold off. I have said, child, that I do not expect you to understand, only to obey. Now you may go.'

Katharina was waiting for him in the hall. 'I told you: far far away.'

*

The evening waned. He would not, could not weep, and his face, aching for tears, pained him. Anna the cook fed him sugar cakes and hot milk in the kitchen. He sat under the table. That was his favourite place. The last of the day's sunlight shone through the window on copper pots and polished tiles. Outside, the spires of Torun dreamed in summer and silence. Everywhere he looked was inexpressible melancholy. Anna leaned down and peered at him in his lair.

'Aye, master, you'll be a good boy now, eh?'

She grinned, baring yellowed stumps of teeth, and nodded and nodded. The sun withdrew stealthily, and a cloud the colour of a bruise loomed in the window.

'What is canon law, Anna, do you know?'

Barbara was to be sent to the Cistercian Convent at Kulm. He thought of his mother. The future was a foreign country; he did not want to go there.

'*Ach ja*, you be a good boy, *du*, *Knabe*.'

*

The wind blew on the day that he left, and everything waved and waved. The linden tree waved. Goodbye!

* * *

Dearest Sister:

I am sorry that I did not write to you before. Are you happy at the Convent? I am not happy here. I am not very unhappy. I miss you & Katharina & our house. The Masters here are very Cross. I have learned Latin very well & can speak it very well. We learn Geometry also which I like very much. There is one who is named Wodka but he calls himself Abstemius. We think that is very funny. There is another by name Caspar Sturm. He teaches Latin & other things. Does Andreas write to you? I do not see him very often: he goes with older fellows. I am very Lonely. It is snowing here now & very Cold. Uncle Lucas came to visit us. He did not remember my name. He tested me in Latin & gave me a Florin. He did not give Andreas a Florin. The Masters were afraid of him. They say he is to be the Bishop soon in Ermland. He did not say anything to me of that matter. I must go to Vespers now. I like Music: do you? I say Prayers for you & for everyone. We are going home for Christmas-tide: I mean to Torun. I hope that you are well. I hope that you will write to me soon & then I will write to you again.

Your Loving Brother:
Nic: Koppernigk

*

He was not very unhappy. He was waiting. Everything familiar had been taken away from him, and all here was strange. The school was a whirling wheel of noise and violence at the still centre of which he cowered, dizzy and frightened, wondering at the poise of those swaggering fellows with their rocky knuckles and terrible teeth, who knew all the rules, and never stumbled, and ignored him so completely. And even when the wheel slowed down, and he ventured out to the very rim, still he felt that he was living only half his life here at Włocławek, and that the other, better half was elsewhere, mysteriously. How otherwise to explain the small dull ache within him always, the achc that a severed limb leaves throbbing like an imprint of itself upon the emptiness dangling from the stump? In the cold and the dark at five in the mornings he rose in the mewling dormitory, aware that somewhere a part of him was turning languidly into a deeper lovelier sleep than his hard pallet would ever allow. Throughout his days that other self crossed his path again and again, always in sunlight, always smiling, taunting him with the beauty and grace of a phantom existence. So he waited, and endured as patiently as he could the mean years, believing that someday his sundered selves must meet in some far finer place, of which at moments he was afforded intimations, in green April weather, in the enormous wreckage of clouds, or in the aetherial splendours of High Mass.

He found curiously consoling the rigours of discipline and study. They sustained him in those times when the mind went dead, after he had been trounced by the band of bullies that were

Andreas's friends, or flogged for a minor misdemeanor, or when memories of home made him weep inside.

Lessons commenced at seven in the Great Hall after matins. At that grey hour nothing was real except discomfort, and there was neither sleep nor waking but a state very like hallucination between the two. The clatter and crack of boots on floorboards were the precise sounds that in the imagination chilled bones were making in their stiff sockets. Slowly the hours passed, sleep withdrew, and the morning settled down to endure itself until noon, when there was dinner in the refectory and then what they called play for an hour. The afternoons were awful. Time slackened to a standstill as the orbit of the day yawned out into emptiness in a long, slow, eccentric arc. The raucous babble of a dozen classes ranged about the room clashed in the stale thickening air, and the masters bellowed through the din in mounting desperation, and by evening the school, creeping befuddled toward sleep, knew that another such day was not to be borne. But day followed day with deathly inevitability, into weeks distinguished one from the next only by the dead caesura of the sabbath.

He learned with ease, perhaps too easily. The masters resented him, who swallowed down their hard-won knowledge in swift effortless draughts. It was as if they were not really teaching him, but were merely confirming what he knew already. Dimly he saw how deeply he thus insulted them, and so he feigned dull-wittedness. He watched certain of his classmates, and learned from them, to whom it came quite naturally, the knack of letting his lower lip hang and his eyes glaze over when some complexity held up the progress of a lesson; and sure enough the masters softened toward him, and at length to his relief began to ignore him.

But there were some not so easily fooled.

*

Caspar Sturm was a Canon of the Chapter of Włocławek Cathedral, to which the school was attached. He taught the *trivium* of logic and grammar and Latin rhetoric. Tall and lean, hard, dark, death-laden, he stalked through the school like a wolf, always alone, always seemingly searching. He was famous in the town for his women and his solitary drinking bouts. He feared neither God nor the Bishop, and hated many things. Some said he had killed a man once long ago, and had entered the Church to atone for his sin: that was why he had not taken Holy Orders. There were other stories too, that he was the King of Poland's bastard, that he had gambled away an immense fortune, that he slept in sheets of scarlet silk. Nicolas believed it all.

The school feared Canon Sturm and his moods. Some days his classes were the quietest in the hall, when the boys sat mute and meek, transfixed by his icy stare and the hypnotic rhythm of his voice; at other times he held riotous assembly, stamping about and waving his arms, roaring, laughing, leaping among the benches to slash with the whip he always carried at the fleeing shoulders of a miscreant. His fellow teachers eyed him with distaste as he pranced and yelled, but they said nothing, even when his antics threatened to turn their classes too into bedlam. Their forbearance was an acknowledgment of his wayward brilliance – or it might have been only that they too, like the boys, were afraid of him.

He chose his favourites from among the dullards of the school, hulking fellows bulging with brawn and boils who sprawled at their desks and grinned and guffawed, basking in the assurance of his patronage. He looked on them with a kind of warm contempt. They amused him. He cuffed and pummelled them merrily, and with cruel shafts of wit exposed their irredeemable ignorance, making them squirm before the class in stuttering sullen shame; yet still they loved him, and were fiercely loyal.

On Nicolas he turned a keen and quizzical eye. The boy blushed and bowed his head, embarrassed. There was something indecent in the way Caspar Sturm looked at him, gently but firmly lifting aside the mask and delving into the soft palpitating core of his soul. Nicolas clenched his fists, and a drop of sweat trickled down his breastbone. *You must not understand me!* The master rarely addressed him directly, and when he did there settled around them a private silence fraught with cloying unspeakable intimacies that neither would think of attempting to speak, and Canon Sturm stepped back and nodded curtly, as if he had satisfied himself once again of the validity of a conclusion previously reached.

'And here is Andreas, elder scion of the house of Koppernigk! Come, dolt, what can you tell us now of Tullius's rules for the art of memory, eh?'

*

He learned with ease, perhaps too easily: his studies bored him. Only now and then, in the grave cold music of mathematics, in the stately march of a Latin line, in logic's hard bright lucid, faintly frightening certainties, did he dimly perceive the contours of some glistening ravishing thing assembling itself out of blocks of glassy air in a clear blue unearthly sky, and then there thrummed within him a coppery chord of perfect bliss.

'Herr Sturm Herr Sturm!' the class cried, 'a conundrum, Herr Sturm!'

'What! Are we here to learn or to play games?'

'Ach, Herr Sturm!'

'Very well, very well. Regard:

'In a room there are 3 men, A & B who are blindfold, & C who is blind. On a table in this room there are 3 black hats & 2 white hats, 5 hats in all. A 4th man enters: call him D. He, D, places a hat on each of the heads of A & B & C, and the 2 remaining hats he hides. Now D removes the blindfold from A, who thus can see the hats that B & C are wearing, but not the hat that he himself wears, nor the 2 hats that are hidden. D asks A if he can say what colour is the hat that he, A, is wearing? A ponders, and answers:

' "No."

'Now D removes the blindfold from B, who thus can see the hats that A & C are wearing, but not the hat that he himself wears, nor the two hats that are hidden. D asks B if he can say what colour is the hat that he, B, is wearing? B ponders, hesitates, and answers:

'"No."

'Now: D cannot remove the blindfold from C, who does not wear a blindfold, and can see no hats at all, not white nor black, not worn nor hidden, for C, as said, is blind. D asks C if he can say what colour is the hat that he, C, is wearing? C ponders, smiles, and answers:

'"Yes!"

'—Well, gentlemen,' said Canon Sturm, 'what is the colour of the blind man's hat, and how does he know it?'

The glass blocks sailed in silence through the bright air, and locked. Done!

Harmonia.

'Well, young Koppernigk? You have solved it?'

Startled, Nicolas ducked his head and began scribbling feverishly on his slate. He was hot all over, and sweating, aghast to think that his face might have betrayed him, but despite all that he was ridiculously pleased with himself, and had to concentrate very hard on the thought of death in order to keep from grinning.

'Come, man,' the Canon muttered. 'Have you got it?'

'Not yet, sir, I am working on it sir.'

'Ah. You are working on it.'

And Caspar Sturm stepped back, and nodded curtly.

*

And then there was Canon Wodka. Nicolas walked with him by the river. It was the Vistula, the same that washed in vain the ineradicable mire of Torun – that is, the name was the same, but the name meant nothing. Here the river was young, as it were, a bright swift stream, while there it was old and weary. Yet it was at once here and there, young and old at once, and its youth and age were separated not by years but leagues. He murmured aloud the river's name and heard in that word suddenly the concepts of space and time fractured.

Canon Wodka laughed. 'You have a clerkly conscience, Nicolas.' It was true: what the world took for granted he found a source of doubt and fear. He would not have had it otherwise. The Canon's smile faltered, and he glanced at the boy timidly, tenderly, out of troubled eyes. 'Beware these enigmas, my young friend. They exercise the mind, but they cannot teach us how to live.'

Canon Wodka was an old man of thirty. He was startlingly ugly, a squat fat waddling creature with a globular head and pockmarked face and tiny wet red mouth. His hands were extraordinary things, brown and withered like the claws of a bat. Only his eyes, disconsolate and bright, revealed the sad maimed soul within. To the school he was a figure of rare fun, and Canon Sturm's boys loved to follow him at a lurch down the corridors, mocking his preposterous gait. Even his name, so perfectly inapt, conspired to make a clown of him, a role to which he seemed to have resigned himself, for it was in irony that he had taken the name Abstemius, and when thus addressed would sometimes cross his eyes and let his great head loll about in a travesty of drunkenness. Nicolas suspected that the Canon, despite his admonition, derived from the intricacies of pure playful thought the only consolation afforded by a life that he had never quite learned how to live.

He taught the *quadrivium* of arithmetic and geometry, astronomy and music theory. He was a very bad teacher. His was not the disciplined mind that his subjects required. It was too excitable. In the midst of a trigonometrical exposition he would go scampering off after Zeno's arrow, which will never traverse the 100 ells that separate the target from the bow because first it must fly 50 ells, and before that 25, and before that 12½, and so on to infinity, where it comes to a disgruntled kind of halt. But the farther that the arrow did not go the nearer Nicolas drew to this poor fat laughable master. They became friends, cautiously, timidly, with many checks and starts, unwilling to believe in their good fortune, but friends they did become, and even when one day in the airy silence of the organ loft in the cathedral Canon Wodka put one of his little withered claws on Nicolas's leg, the boy stared steadily off into the gloom under the vaulted ceiling and began to talk very rapidly about nothing, as if nothing at all were happening.

In their walks by the river the Canon sketched the long confused history of cosmology. At first he was reluctant to implant new ideas in a young mind that he considered too much concerned already with abstractions, but then the wonder of the subject possessed him and he was whirled away into stammering starry heights. He spoke of the oyster universe of the Egyptians in which the Earth floated on a bowl of bitter waters beneath a shell of glair, of the singing spheres of the Greeks, Pythagoras and Herakleides, of the Church Fathers whose Earth was a temple walled with air, and then of the Gnostic heresiarchs and their contention that the world was the work of fallen angels. Last of all he explained Claudius Ptolemy's theory of the heavens, formulated in Alexandria thirteen centuries before and still held by all men to be valid, by which the Earth stands immobile at the centre of all, encircled eternally in grave majestic dance by the Sun and the lesser planets. There were so many names, so many notions, and Nicolas's head began to whirl. Canon Wodka glanced at him nervously and put his finger to his own lips to silence himself, and presently began to speak earnestly, like one doing penance, of the glory of God and the unchallengeable dogma of Mother Church, and of the joys of orthodoxy.

But Nicolas hardly listened to all that. He knew nothing yet of scruples such as those besetting his friend. The firmament sang to him like a siren. Out there was unlike here, utterly. Nothing that he knew on earth could match the pristine purity he imagined in the heavens, and when he looked up into the limitless blue he saw beyond the uncertainty and the terror an intoxicating, marvellous grave gaiety.

Together they made a sundial on the south wall of the cathedral. When they had finished they stood and admired in silence this beautiful simple thing. The shadow crept imperceptibly across the dial as the day waned, and Nicolas shivered to think that they had bent the enormous workings of the universe to the performance of this minute and insignificant task.

'The world,' he said, 'is all an engine, then, after all, no more than that?'

Canon Wodka smiled. 'Plato in the *Timaeus* says that the universe is a kind of animal, eternal and perfect, whose life is lived entirely within itself, created by God in the form of a globe, which is the most pleasing in its perfection and most like itself of all figures. Aristotle postulated as an explanation of planetary motion a mechanism of fifty-five crystalline spheres, each one touching and driving another and all driven by the primary motion of the sphere of the fixed stars. Pythagoras likened the world to a vast lyre whose strings as it were are the orbits of the planets, which in their intervals sing beyond human hearing a perfect harmonic scale. And all this, this crystalline eternal singing being, *this* you call an engine?'

'I meant no disrespect. Only I am seeking a means of understanding, and belief.' He hesitated, smiling a little sheepishly at the lofty sound of that. 'Herr Wodka – Herr Wodka, what do you believe?'

The Canon opened wide his empty arms.

'I believe that the world is *here*,' he said, 'that it exists, and that it is inexplicable. All these great men that we have spoken of, did they believe that what they proposed exists in reality? Did Ptolemy believe in the strange image of wheels within wheels that he postulated as a true picture of planetary motion? Do *we* believe in it, even though we say that it is true? For you see, when we are dealing with these matters, truth becomes an ambiguous concept. In our own day Nicolas Cusanus has said that the universe is an infinite sphere whose centre is nowhere. Now this is a *contradictio in adjecto*, since the notions of sphere and infinity cannot sensibly be put together; yet how much more strange is the Cusan's universe than those of Ptolemy or Aristotle? Well, I leave the question to you.' He smiled again, ruefully. 'I think it will give you much heartache.' And later, as they walked across the cathedral close at dusk, the Canon halted, suddenly struck, and touched the boy lightly in excitement with a trembling hand. 'Consider this, child, listen: all theories are but names, *but the world itself is a thing.*'

In the light of evening, the gathering gloom, it was as if a sibyl had spoken.

*

On Saturdays in the fields outside the walls of the town Caspar Sturm instructed the school in the princely art of falconry. The hawks, terrible and lovely, filled the sunny air with the clamour of tiny deaths. Nicolas looked on in a mixture of horror and elation. Such icy rage, such intentness frightened him, yet thrilled him too. The birds shot into the kill like bolts from a bow, driven it seemed by a seeled steely anguish that nothing would assuage. Compared with their vivid presence all else was vague and insubstantial. They were absolutes. Only Canon Sturm could match their bleak ferocity. At rest they stood as still as stone and watched him with a fixed tormented gaze; even in flight their haste and brutal economy seemed bent to one end only, to return with all possible speed to that wrist, those silken jesses, those eyes. And their master, object of such terror and love, grew leaner, harder, darker, became something other than he was. Nicolas watched him watching his creatures and was stirred, obscurely, shamefully.

'Up sir! Up!' A heron shrieked and fell out of the air. 'Up!' Monstrous hawklike creatures were flying on invisible struts and wires across a livid sky, and there was a great tumult far off, screams and roars, and howls of agony or of laughter, that came to him from that immense distance as a faint terrible twittering. Even when he woke and lay terror-stricken in a stew of sweat the dream would not end. It was as if he had tumbled headlong into some beastly black region of the firmament. He pulled at that blindly rearing lever between his legs, pulled at it and pulled, pulling himself back into the world. Dimly he sensed someone near him, a dark figure in the darkness, but he could not care, it was too late to stop, and he shut his eyes tight. The hawks bore down upon him, he could see their great black gleaming wings, their withered claws and metallic talons, their cruel beaks agape and shrieking without sound, and under that awful onslaught his self shrank together into a tiny throbbing point. For an instant everything stopped, and all was poised on the edge of darkness and a kind of exquisite dying, and then he arched his back like a bow and spattered the sheets with his seed.

He sank down and down, far, far down, and sighed. The beasts were all banished, and his inner sky was empty now and of a clear immaculate blue, and despite the guilt and the grime and the smell like the smell of blood and milk and decayed flowers, he felt afar a faint mysterious chiming that was at once everywhere and nowhere, that was a kind of infinite music.

He opened his eyes. In moonlight Andreas's pale thin unforgiving face floated above him, darkly grinning.

*

Now he became an insubstantial thing, a web of air rippling in red winds. He felt that he had been flayed of a vital protective skin. His surfaces ached, flesh, nails, hair, the very filaments of his eyes, yearning for what he could not name nor even properly imagine. At Mass he spied down from the choir loft on the women of the town kneeling in the congregation below him. They were hopelessly corporeal creatures. Even the youngest and daintiest of them in no way matched the shimmering singing spirits that flew at him out of the darkness of his frantic nights. Nor was there any comfort to be had from the snivelling smelly little boys that came trailing their blankets through the dormitory, offering themselves in return for the consolation of a shared bed. What he sought was something other than ordinary flesh, was something made of light and air and marvellous grave gaiety.

Snow fell, and soothed the raw wound he had opened with his own hands. For three days it stormed in eerie silence, and then, on the fourth, dawn found the world transformed. It was in the absence of things that the change lay; the snow itself was hardly a presence, was rather a nothing where before there had been something, a pavement, a headstone, a green field, and the eye, lost in that white emptiness, was led irresistibly to the horizon that seemed immeasurably farther off now than it had ever been before.

Nicolas carried his numbed and lightened spirit up the winding stairs of the tower where Canon Wodka had his observatory, a little circular cell with a single window that opened out like a trapdoor on the sky. All tended upward here, so that the tower itself seemed on the point of flight. He climbed the seven wooden steps to the viewing platform, and as his head emerged into the stinging air he felt for a moment that he might indeed continue upward effortlessly, up and up, and he grew dizzy. The sky was a dome of palest glass, and the sun sparkled on the snow, and everywhere was a purity and brilliance almost beyond bearing. Through the far clear silence above the snowy fields and the roofs of the town he heard the bark of a fox, a somehow perfect sound that pierced the stillness like a gleaming needle. A flood of foolish happiness filled his heart. All would be well, O, all would be well! The infinite possibilities of the future awaited him. That was what the snow meant, what the fox said. His young soul swooned, and slowly, O, slowly, he seemed to fall upward, into the blue.

* * *

In his fourth year at the University of Cracow he was ordered by Uncle Lucas to return at once to Torun: the Precentor of the Frauenburg Chapter was dying, and Uncle Lucas, now Bishop of the diocese, was bent on securing the post for his youngest nephew. Nicolas made the long journey northwards alone through a tawny sad September. He was twenty-two. He carried little away with him from the Polish capital. Memories still haunted him of certain spring days in the city when the wind sang in the spires and washes of sunlight swept through the streets, and the heart, strangely troubled by clouds and birds and the voices of children, became lost and confused in surroundings that yesterday had seemed irreproachably familiar.

Andreas and he had lodged with Katharina and her husband, Gertner the merchant. Nicolas disliked that smug stolid household. Womanhood and early marriage had not changed his sister much. She was still, behind the mask of the young matron, a feline calculating child, cruel and greedy, tormented by an implacable discontent. Nicolas suspected her of adultery. She and Andreas fought as fiercely as ever they had done as children, but there was palpable between them now a new accord, forged by the sharing of secrets concealed from husband and brother alike. They united too in baiting Nicolas. His anxieties amused them, his shabbiness, his studiousness, his risible sobriety – amused them, yes, but disturbed them too, obscurely. He suffered their jibes in silence, smiling meekly, and saw, not without a certain satisfaction of which he tried but failed to feel ashamed, that indifference was the weapon that wounded them most sorely.

*

True, he had learned a great deal in Poland. After four years his head was packed with great granite blocks of knowledge; but knowledge was not perception. His mind, already venturing apprehensively along certain perilous and hitherto untrodden paths, required a lightness and delicacy of atmosphere, a sense of air and space, that was not to be had at Cracow. It was significant, he realised later, that the college on first sight had reminded him of nothing so much as a fortress, for it was, despite its pretensions, the main link in the defences thrown up by scholasticism against the tide of new ideas sweeping in from Italy, from England, and from Rotterdam. In his first year there he witnessed pitched bloody battles in the streets between Hungarian scholastics and German humanists. Although these student brawls seemed to him senseless and even comical, he could not help but see, in the meeting under the lowering mass of Wawel Rock of flaxen-haired northerners and the Magyars with their sullen brows and muddy complexions, something made tangible of that war of minds being waged across the continent.

The physical world was expanding. In their quest for a sea route to the Indies the Portuguese had revealed the frightening immensity of Africa. Rumours from Spain spoke of a vast new world beyond the ocean to the west. Men were voyaging out to all points of the compass, thrusting back the frontiers everywhere. All Europe was in the grip of an inspired sickness whose symptoms were avarice and monumental curiosity, the thirst for conquest and religious conversion, and something more, less easily defined, a kind of irresistible gaiety. Nicolas too was marked with the rosy tumours of that plague. His ocean was within him. When he ventured out in the frail bark of his thoughts he was at one with those crazed mariners on their green sea of darkness, and the visions that haunted him on his return from *terra incognita* were no less luminous and fantastic than theirs.

Yet the world was more, and less, than the fires and ice of lofty speculation. It was also his life and the lives of others, brief, painladen, irredeemably shabby. Between the two spheres of thought and action he could discern no workable connection. In this he was out of step with the age, which told him heaven and earth in his own self were conjoined. The notion was not seriously to be entertained, however stoutly he might defend it out of loyalty to the humanist cause. There were for him two selves, separate and irreconcilable, the one a mind among the stars, the other a worthless fork of flesh planted firmly in earthy excrement. In the writings of antiquity he glimpsed the blue and gold of Greece, the blood-boltered majesty of Rome, and was allowed briefly to believe that there had been times when the world had known an almost divine unity of spirit and matter, of purpose and consequence: was it this that men were searching after now, across strange seas, in the infinite silent spaces of pure thought?

Well, if such harmony had ever indeed existed, he feared deep down, deep beyond admitting, that it was not to be regained.

*

He took humanities, and also theology, as Uncle Lucas had directed. His studies absorbed him wholly. His ways became the set ways of the scholar. Old before his time, detached, desiccated and fussy, he retreated from the world. He spoke Latin now more readily than German.

And yet it was all a deeply earnest play-acting, a form of ritual by which the world and his self and the relation between the two were simplified and made manageable. Scholarship transformed into docile order the hideous clamour and chaos of the world outside himself, endistanced it and at the same time brought it palpably near, so that, as he grappled with the terrors of the world, he was terrified and yet also miraculously tranquil. Sometimes, though, that tranquil terror was not enough; sometimes the hideousness demanded more, howled for more, for risk, for blood, for sacrifice. Then, like an actor who has forgotten his lines, he stood paralysed, staring aghast into a black hole in the air.

He believed in action, in the absolute necessity for action. Yet action horrified him, tending as it did inevitably to become violence. Nothing was stable: politics became war, law became slavery, life itself became death, sooner or later. Always the ritual collapsed in the face of the hideousness. The real world would not be gainsaid, being the true realm of action, but he must gainsay it, or despair. That was his problem.

*

Amongst the things he wished to forget from Cracow was his encounter with Professor Adalbert Brudzewski, the mathematician and astronomer. The memory of that mad mangled afternoon, however, was the ghost of a persistent giant with huge hairy paws that for years came at him again and again, laughing and bellowing, out of a crimson miasma of embarrassment and shame. It would not have been so bad if only Andreas had not been there to witness his humiliation. By rights he should not have been there: he had shown no interest whatever in Brudzewski or his classes until, after weeks of wheedling and grovelling, Nicolas had at last won a grudging invitation to the Professor's house – to his *house*! – and then he had announced in that languid way of his that he would go along too, since he had nothing better to do that day. Yet Nicolas made no protest, only shrugged, and frowned distractedly to show how little he cared in the matter, while in his imagination a marvellously haughty version of himself turned and told his brother briefly but with excoriating accuracy what a despicable hound he was.

*

Professor Brudzewski's classes were rigorous and very exclusive, and were, as the Professor himself was fond of pointing out, one of the main bases on which the university's impeccable reputation rested. Although he was of course a Ptolemeian, his recent cautious but by no means hostile commentary on Peurbach's planetary theory had raised some eyebrows among his fellow academics – brows which, however, he immediately caused to knit again into their wonted, lamentably low state by means of a few good thumps in defence of Ptolemaic dogma, delivered with malicious relish to the more prominent temples of suspect scholarship. The Peurbachs of the present day might come and go, but Ptolemy was unassailable on his peak, and Professor Brudzewski was there to say so, as often and as strenuously as he deemed it necessary so to do.

Nicolas had read everything the Professor had ever written on the Ptolemaic theory. Out of all those weary hours of wading through the dry sands of a sealed mind there had been distilled one tiny precious drop of pearly doubt. He could no longer remember where or when he had found the flaw, along what starry trajectory, on which rung of those steadily ascending ladders of tabular calculation, but once detected it had brought the entire edifice of a life's work crashing down with slow dreamlike inevitability. *Professor Brudzewski knew that Ptolemy was gravely wrong.* He could not of course admit it, even to himself; his investment was too great for that. This failure of nerve explained to Nicolas how it was that a mathematician of the first rank could stoop into deceit in order, in Aristotle's words, *to save the phenomena*, that is, to devise a theory grounded firmly in the old reactionary dogmas that yet would account for the observed motions of the planets. There were cases, such as the wildly eccentric orbit of Mars, that the general Ptolemaic theory could not account for, but faced with these problems the Professor, like his Alexandrian *magister* before him, leant all the weight of his prodigious skill upon the formulae until they buckled into conformity.

At first Nicolas was ashamed on the Professor's behalf. Then the shame gave way to compassion, and he began to regard the misfortunate old fellow with a rueful, almost paternal tenderness. He would help him! Yes, he would become a pupil, and in the classroom take him gently in hand and show him how he might admit his folly and thereby make amends for the years of stubbornness and wilful blindness. And there would be another but very different book, perhaps the old man's last, the crowning glory of his life, *Tractatus contra Ptolemaeus*, with a brief acknowledgment to the student – so young! so brilliant! – whose devastating arguments had been the thunderbolt that had struck down the author on his blithe blind way to Damascus. O yes. And though the text itself be forgotten, as surely it would be, generations of cosmologists as yet unborn would speak of the book with reverence as marking the first public appearance – so characteristically modest! – of one of the greatest astronomers of all time. Nicolas trembled, drunk on these mad visions of glory. Andreas glanced at him and smirked.

'You are sweating, brother, I can smell you from here.'

'I do not have your calm, Andreas. I worry. I very much want to hear him lecture.'

'Why? This stargazing and so forth, what good is it?'

Nicolas was shocked. What good? – the only certain good! But he could not say that, and contented himself with a smile of secret knowing. They passed under the spires of St Mary's Church. Spring had come to Cracow, and the city today seemed somehow airborne, an intricate aetherial thing of rods and glass flying in sunlight through pale blue space. Andreas began to whistle. How handsome he was, after all, how dashing, in his velvet tunic and plumed cap, with his sword in its ornate scabbard swinging at his side. He had carried intact into manhood the frail heartbreaking beauty of his youth. Nicolas touched him tenderly on the arm.

'I am interested in these things, you see,' he said, 'that is all.'

He had done his brother no wrong that he could think of, yet he seemed to be apologising; it was a familiar phenomenon.

'You are interested – of course you are,' Andreas answered. 'But I imagine you are not entirely unmindful either that our dear uncle is watching our progress closely, eh?'

Nicolas nodded gloomily. 'So: you think I am trying by being zealous to outflank you in his favour.'

'What else should I think? You did not want me to come with you today.'

'You were not invited!'

'Pah. You must understand, brother, that I know you, I know how you plot and scheme behind my back. I do not hate you for it, no – I only despise you.'

'Andreas.'

But Andreas had begun to whistle again, merrily.

*

Professor Brudzewski lived in a big old house in the shadow of St Mary's. The brothers were shown into the hall and left to wait, ringed round by oppressive pillars of silence stretching up past the gallery to the high ceiling with its faded frescos. They looked about them blandly, as if to impress on someone watching them the innocence of their intentions, only to discover with a start that they were indeed being watched by a dim figure behind the screens to the left. They turned away hurriedly, and heard at their backs a soft mad laugh and footsteps retreating.

They waited for a long time, apparently forgotten, while the hall came gradually to weird life around them. At first it was a matter of doors flying open to admit disembodied voices that shredded the silence, before closing again slowly with a distinct but inexplicable air of menace. Then, when they had wearied of assuming an expectant smile at each unfinished entrance, the voices began to be followed through the doorways by their owners, an oddly distracted, anonymous assortment of persons who did not stay, however, but merely passed through in small tight groups of two or three, murmuring, on their absorbed way elsewhere. These enigmatic pilgrims were to cross Nicolas's path throughout that day without ever giving up the secret of their mysterious doings.

The steward returned at last, a soft fat pale pear-shaped creature with a tiny voice and paddle feet and an immaculately bald white skull. He crooked a dainty finger at the brothers and led them into an adjoining room full of sudden sunlight from a high window. Briefly they glimpsed, as they entered by one door, a smiling girl in a green gown going out by another, leaving behind her trembling on the bright air an image of blurred beauty. Professor Brudzewski peered at them dubiously and said:

'Ah!'

He had a long yellowish face with a little pointed grey beard clenched under the lower lip like a fang. His back was so grievously bent that his loose black robe, fastened tight at the throat, hung down to the floor curtainwise. Through a vent at the side was thrust a gnarled claw in which there was fixed, as a peg into a socket, the stout black stick that alone it seemed prevented him from collapsing in a little heap of dust and drapery and dry bones. This seeming frailty was deceptive: he was a quick-tempered cold old body who disliked the world, and tolerated it at best, or, when it made so bold as to accost him face to face, lashed out at it with high-pitched furious loathing.

There was a silence; it was plainly apparent that he had no idea who his guests were, and hardly cared. Nicolas felt his smile curdle into a sickly smirk. He could think of nothing to say. Andreas, clutching the hilt of his sword – which both brothers at once, wincing, suddenly remembered he was forbidden by college rules to wear in public – stepped forward with a clank.

'*Magister!* this is my brother, Nicolas Koppernigk, whom you know, of course; I am Andreas of that name. We come in humility to this veritable Olympus. Ha ha. Our uncle, Doctor Lucas Waczelrodt, Bishop of Ermland, sends greetings.'

'Yes yes, quite so,' the Professor muttered. 'Quite so.' He had not been listening. He looked past them with a frown to the doorway where three gentlemen had entered quietly, and stood now in a huddle, whispering. One was tall and thin, another short and fat, and the third, whose back was turned, was a middling sort with warts. They had a look about them of conspirators. Professor Brudzewski began to make a whirring noise under his breath. Abruptly he excused himself, set off rapidly crabwise for the door through which the green girl had gone, mumbled something that the brothers did not catch, and vanished. The conspirators hesitated, exchanging looks and hopping agitatedly from foot to foot, and then all together in a rush plunged after him, almost knocking over in their haste the steward returning with two incongruously jolly foaming mugs of beer, which he tenderly bestowed upon the guests in silence, with a mournful smile. Cloudshadow swooped into the room like a great dark bird.

After that for a long time the brothers drifted slowly about the house, somewhat dazed, jostled by flotsam. A strange distraught little man in cloak and hose with an absurd feather in his hat waylaid them in a corridor and launched without preamble into a bitter invective against the incompetence of the Chaldean cosmographers, who he seemed to feel had injured him personally in some mysterious way. Andreas slipped off, leaving Nicolas to stand alone, smiling and nodding helplessly, under a fine spray of spittle. At last the little man wound down, and, panting, departed, nodding furious approval of his own arguments. Nicolas turned, and turning caught at the edge of a canted mirror blazing with reflected sunlight a glimpse of green, that smile again, that girl! and all at once he knew her to be an emblem of light and elusive loveliness, a talisman whose image he might hold up against the malignant chaos of this ramshackle afternoon.

He hurried down the corridor, following the mirror's burning gaze, and turned a corner to find no girl, only the black stooped figure of the Professor tapping his way toward him.

'Ah, you!' the old man said peevishly. 'Where have you been?' He frowned. 'Were there not two of you? Well, no matter.'

Nicolas launched forth at once upon the speech that for days he had been preparing. He stammered and sweated, beside himself in his eagerness to impress. Pythagoras! Plato! Nicolas Cusanus! The names of the glorious dead rolled out of his mouth and crashed together in the narrow corridor like great solid stone spheres. He hardly knew what he was saying. He felt that he had become entangled in the works of some dreadful yet farcical, inexorable engine. Herakleides! Aristotle! Regiomontanus! Bang! Crash! Clank! The Professor watched him carefully, as if studying a novel and possibly snappish species of rodent.

'Ptolemy, young man – you make no mention of Ptolemy, who has after all, as is well known, resolved for us the mysteries of the universe.'

'Yes but but but *magister*, if I may say, is it not true, has it not been suggested, that there are certain, how shall I say, certain dispositions of the phenomena that nothing in Ptolemy will explain?'

The Professor smiled a wan and wintry smile, and tapped on the oaken tiles with his stick as if searching for a flaw in the floor.

'And what,' he murmured, 'might these inexplicable phenomena be?'

'O but I do not say that there are such mysteries, no no,' Nicolas answered hastily. 'I am asking rather.'

This would not do, this faint-heartedness, it would not do at all. What was required now was a clear and fearless exposition of his views. But what were his views? And could they be spoken? It was one thing to know that Ptolemy had erred, and that planetary science since his time had been a vast conspiracy aimed at saving the phenomena, but it was quite another to put that knowledge into words, especially in the presence of a prime conspirator.

The orbit of the afternoon had brought him back to his

starting point in the hall. He was confused, and growing desperate. Things were not at all as he had imagined they would be. The little man with the feather in his cap, scourge of the Chaldeans, passed them by with a fierce look.

He could only say what was not, and not what was; he could only say: this is false, and that is false, ergo that other must be true of which as yet I can discern only the blurred outline.

'It seems to me, *magister*, that we must revise our notions of the nature of things. For thirteen hundred years astronomers have been content to follow Ptolemy without question, *like credulous women*, as Regiomontanus says, but in all that time they have not been able to discern or deduce the principal thing, namely the shape of the universe and the unchanging symmetry of its parts.'

The Professor said: 'Hum!' and flung open the door on the sunlit room and the high window. This time there was alas no green girl, only the ubiquitous trio of conspirators, each with a hand on another's shoulder – *Soft! See who comes!* – watching. The Professor advanced, shaking his head.

'I fail to understand you,' he growled. 'The principal thing, you claim, is to, what was it? to discern the shape of the universe and its parts. I do not understand that. How is it to be done? We are here and the universe, so to speak, is there, and between the two there is no sensible connection, surely?'

The room was high and wide, with rough white walls above half panelling, a ceiling with arched black beams and a checkered stone floor. There was a table and four severe chairs, and on the table a burnished copper bowl brimming with rose petals. A plaster relief on one wall depicted three naked women joined hand to shoulder in a sinuous circular dance of giving, receiving and returning. Below them on the floor a pearwood chest stood smugly shut, opposite an antique hour-glass-shaped iron stove with a brass canopy. The conspirators began imperceptibly to advance. The window's stippled diamond panes gave on to a little courtyard and a stunted cherry tree in bloom. Suddenly Nicolas was appalled by the blank anonymity of surfaces, the sullen, somehow resentful secretiveness of unfamiliar things whose contours have been rubbed and shaped by the action of unknown lives. Doubtless for others this room was strung with a shimmering web of exquisitely exact significances, perhaps it was so even for these three peculiar persons edging stealthily forward; but not for Nicolas. He thought: what can we know that is not of ourselves?

'Paracelsus says,' he said, 'that in the scale of things man occupies the centre, that he is the measure of all things, being the point of equilibrium between that which is great and that which is small.'

Professor Brudzewski was staring at him.

'Paracelsus? Who is this? He is mad, surely. *God* is the measure of all things, and only *God* can comprehend the world. What you seem to suggest, young man, with your *principal thing*, smacks of blasphemy therefore.'

'Blablablasphemy?' Nicolas bleated. 'Surely not. Did you yourself not say that in Ptolemy we find the solution to the mysteries of the universe?'

'That was a manner of speaking, no more.'

The door behind them opened and Andreas entered softly. Nicolas squirmed, drenched with sweat. The conspirators, without seeming to move, were yet bearing down upon him inexorably. He felt a dismayed sense of doom, like one who hears the ice shattering behind him as he careers with slow, mad inevitability out into the frozen lake.

'But *magister*, you said—!'

'Yes yes yes yes, quite – I know what I said.' The old man glared at the floor, and gave it a whack with his stick – take *that*, you! 'Listen to me: you are confusing astronomy with philosophy, or rather that which is called philosophy today, by that Dutchman, and the Italians and their like. You are asking our science to perform tasks which it is incapable of performing. Astronomy does not describe the universe as it is, but only as we observe it. That theory is correct, therefore, which accounts for our observations. Ptolemy's theory is perfectly, almost perfectly valid insofar as pure astronomy is concerned, *because it saves the phenomena*.

This is all that is asked of it, and all that can be asked, in reason. It does not discern your principal thing, for that is not to be discerned, and the astronomer who claims otherwise will be hissed off the stage!'

'Are we to be content then,' Nicolas cried, 'are we to be content with mere abstractions? Columbus has proved that Ptolemy was mistaken as to the dimensions of the Earth; shall we ignore Columbus?'

'An ignorant sailor, and a Spaniard. Pah!'

'He has *proved* it, sir—!' He lifted a hand to his burning brow; calm, he must keep calm. The room seemed full of turbulence and uproar, but it was only the tumult within him dinning in his ears. Those three were still advancing steadily, and Andreas was at his back doing he did not wish to imagine what. The Professor swung himself on his stick in a furious circle around the table, so stooped now that it appeared he might soon, like some fabulous serpent, clamp his teeth upon his own nether regions and begin to devour himself in his rage. Nicolas, gobbling and clucking excitedly, pursued him at a hesitant hop.

'Proof?' the old man snapped. 'Proof? A ship sails a certain distance and returns, and the captain comes ashore and agitates the air briefly with words; you call this *proof*? By what immutable standards is this a refutation of Ptolemy? You are a nominalist, young man, and you do not even know it.'

'I a nominalist – *I*? Do you not merely say the name of Ptolemy and imagine that all contrary arguments are thus refuted? No no, *magister*; I believe not in names, but in things. I believe that the physical world is amenable to physical investigation, and if astronomers will do no more than sit in their cells counting upon their fingers then they are shirking their responsibility!'

The Professor halted. He was pale, and his head trembled alarmingly on its frail stalk of neck, yet he sounded more puzzled than enraged when he said:

'Ptolemy's theory saves the phenomena, I have said so already; what other responsibility should it have?'

Tell him. *Tell him*.

'Knowledge, *magister*, must become perception. The only acceptable theory is that one which *explains* the phenomena, which explains . . . which . . .' He stared at the Professor, who had begun to shake all over, while out of his pinched nostrils there came little puffs of an extraordinary harsh dry noise: he was laughing! Suddenly he turned, and pointed with his stick and asked:

'What do you say, young fellow? Let us hear your views.'

Andreas leaned at ease by the window with his arms folded and his face lifted up to the light. A handful of rain glistened on the glass, and a breeze in silence shook the blossoms of the cherry tree. The unutterable beauty of the world pierced Nicolas's sinking heart. His brother pondered a moment, and then with the faintest of smiles said lightly:

'I say, *magister*, that we must hold fast to sanity and Aristotle.'

It meant nothing, of course, but it sounded well; O yes, it sounded well. Professor Brudzewski nodded his approval.

'Ah yes,' he murmured. 'Just so.' He turned again to Nicolas. 'I think you have been too much influenced by our latterday upstarts, who imagine that they can unravel the intricacies of God's all-good creation. You spoke of Regiomontanus: I studied under that great man, and I can assure you that he would have scorned these wild notions you have put forth today. You question Ptolemy? Mark this: to him who thinks that the ancients are not to be entirely trusted, the gates of our science are certainly closed. He will lie before those gates and spin the dreams of the deranged about the motion of the eighth sphere, and he will get what he deserves for believing that he can lend support to his own hallucinations by slandering the ancients. Therefore take this young man's sound advice, and hold fast to sanity.'

Nicolas in his dismay felt that he must be emitting a noise, a thin piercing shriek like that of chalk on slate. There was a distinct sensation of shock at the base of his spine, as if he had sat down suddenly without looking on the spot from whence a chair had been briskly removed. The three conspirators, crowding at his shoulder, regarded him with deep sadness. They were at once solicitous and sinister. The one with the warts kept his face turned away, unable to look full upon such folly. Andreas, laughing silently, said softly in his brother's ear:

'*Bruder, du hast in der Scheisse getreppen.*'

And the fat conspirator giggled. Behind the screens in the hall the secret watcher waited. It was of course – of course! – the green girl. The Professor peered at her balefully, and turning to the brothers he sighed and said:

'Gentlemen, you must forgive me my daughter. The wench is mad.'

He shook his stick at her and she retreated, harlequinned by crisscross shadows, pursued by the conspirators scurrying on tiptoe, twittering, to the stairs, where the little man in the plumed hat waited among other, vaguer enigmas. All bowed and turned, ascended slowly into the gloom, and vanished.

Professor Brudzewski impatiently bade the brothers good day – but not before he had invited Andreas to attend his lectures. Grey rain was falling on Cracow.

'What? – spend my mornings listening to that old cockerel droning on about the planets and all that? Not likely, brother; I have better things to do.'

*

Nicolas arrived in Torun at September's end. The house in St Anne's Lane received him silently, solicitously, like a fellow mourner. Old Anna and the other servants were gone now, and there was a new steward in charge, a surly fellow, one of the Bishop's men. He followed Nicolas about the house with a watchful suspicious eye. The sunny autumn day outside was all light and distance, and above the roofs and spires a cloud, a ship in air, sailed gravely at the wind's pace across a sky immensely high and blue. The leaves of the linden were turning.

'Build a fire, will you. I am cold.'

'Yes, master. His Grace your uncle gave me to understand that you would not be staying?'

'No, I shall not be staying.'

Uncle Lucas came that evening, in a black rage. He greeted Nicolas with a glare. The Frauenburg Precentor had been crass enough to die in an uneven-numbered month, when the privilege of filling Church appointments in the See of Ermland passed by Church law from the Bishop to the Pope.

'So we may forget it, nephew: I am not loved at Rome. Ach!' He beat the air vainly with his fists. 'Another week, that was all! However, we must be charitable. God rest his soul.' He fastened his little black eyes on Nicolas. 'Well, have you lost your tongue?'

'My Lord—'

'Pray, do not grovel! You took no degree at Cracow. Four years.'

'It was you that summoned me away, my Lord. I had not completed my studies.'

'Ah.' The Bishop paced about a moment, nodding rapidly, with his hands clasped behind his back. 'Hmm. Yes.' He halted. 'Let me give you some advice, nephew. Rid yourself of this rebellious streak, if you wish to remain in my favour. *I will not have it!* Do you understand?' Nicolas bowed his head meekly, and the Bishop grunted and turned away, disappointed it seemed with so easy a victory. He hoisted up his robe and thrust his backside to the fire. 'Steward! Where is the whore-son? Which reminds me: I suppose your wastrel brother is also kicking his heels in Poland waiting for me to find him a soft post? What a family, dear God! It is from the father, of course. Bad blood there. And you, wretch, look at you, cowering like a kicked dog. You hate me, but you have not the courage to say it – O yes, it's true, I know. Well, you will be rid of me soon enough. There will be other posts at Frauenburg. Once I have secured you a prebend you will be off my hands, and my accounts, and after that I care not a whit what you do, I shall have fulfilled my responsibility. Take my advice and go to Italy.'

'It—?'

'—Or wherever, it's no matter, so long as it is somewhere far off. And take your brother with you: I do not want him within an ass's roar of my affairs. Well, man, what are you grinning at?'

Italy!

* * *

ON EASTER DAY in 1496 Canon Nicolas and his brother marched forth from Cracow's Florian Gate in the company of a band of pilgrims. There were holy men and sinners, monks, rogues, mountebanks and murderers, poor peasants and rich merchants, widows and virgins, mendicant knights, scholars, pardoners and preachers, the hale and the halt, the blind, the deaf, the quick and the dying. Royal banners fluttered in the sunlight against an imperial blue sky, and the royal trumpeters blew a brassy blast, and from high upon the fortress walls the citizens with cheers and a wild waving of caps and kerchiefs bade the wayfarers farewell, as down the dusty road into the plain they trudged. Southwards they were bound, over the Alps to Rome, the Holy City.

'He could have got us a couple of nags,' Andreas grumbled, 'damned skinflint, instead of leaving us to walk like common peasants.'

Nicolas would not have cared had Bishop Lucas forced them to crawl to Italy. He was, for the first time in his life, so it seemed to him, free. A post had been found for him at last at Frauenburg; the Chapter at the Bishop's direction had granted him immediate leave of absence, and he had departed without delay for Cracow. He found that city strangely altered, no longer the forlorn gloomy terminus he had known during his university years, but a bustling waystation cheerful with travellers and loud with the uproar of foreign tongues. To be sure, the change was not in the city but in him, the traveller, who noticed now what the student had ignored, yet he chose to see his new regard for this proud cold capital as a sign that he had at last grown up into himself and his world, that he was at last renouncing the past and turning his face toward an intrepid manhood; it was all nonsense, of course, he knew it; but still, he was allowed for a few days at least to feel mature, and worldly-wise, and significant.

His newfound self-esteem, however tentative it was and prone to collapse into self-mockery, infuriated Andreas. No undemanding canonry had been secured for him. Wherever he turned Bishop Lucas's black shadow fell upon him like a blight. He was not going to Italy – he was being sent. And he had not even been provided with a horse to lift him above the common throng.

'I am almost thirty, and still he treats me like a child. What have I ever done to deserve his contempt? What have I done?'

He glared at Nicolas, daring him to answer, and then turned his face away, grinding his teeth in rage and anguish. Nicolas was embarrassed, as always in the presence of another's public pain. He wanted to walk away very quickly, he even imagined himself fleeing with head down, muttering, waving his arms like one pursued by a plague of flies, but there was nowhere to go that would be free of his brother's anger and pain.

Andreas laughed.

'And you, brother,' he said softly, 'feeding off me, eating me alive.'

Nicolas stared at him. 'I do not understand you.'

'O get away, get away! You sicken me.'

And so, lashed together by thongs of hatred and frightful love, they set out for Italy.

*

They equipped themselves with two stout staffs, good heavy jackets lined with sheepskin against the Alpine cold, a tinderbox, a compass, four pounds of sailor's biscuit and a keg of salt pork. The gathering of these provisions afforded them a deep childish satisfaction. Andreas found in the Italian swordsmith's near the cathedral an exquisitely tooled dagger with a retracting blade that at the touch of a concealed lever sprang forward with an evil click. This ingenious weapon he kept in a sheath sewn for the purpose inside his bootleg. It made him feel wonderfully dangerous. Bartholemew Gertner, Katharina's husband, sold them a mule, and cheated them only a little on the deal, since they were family, after all. A taciturn and elderly beast, this mule carried their baggage readily enough, but would not bear the indignity of a rider, as they quickly discovered.

Nicolas could have bought them a pair of horses. Before leaving Frauenburg he had drawn lavishly on his prebend. But he kept his riches secret, and sewed the gold into the lining of his cloak, because he did not wish to embarrass his penniless brother, so he told himself.

Andreas gazed gloomily southwards. 'Like common pig peasants!'

Forth from St Florian's Gate they marched into the great plain, behind them the cheering and the brassy blare of trumpets, before them the long road.

*

The weather turned against them. Near Braclav a windstorm rose without warning out of the plain and came at them like a great dark animal, howling. The inns were terrible, crawling with lice and rogues and poxed whores. At Graz they were fed a broth of tainted meat and suffered appalling fluxions; at Villach the bread was weevilled. A child died, fell down on the road screaming, clenched in agony, while its mother stood by and bawled.

Their number shrank steadily day by day, for many who had left with them from Cracow had been, like the brothers, merely travellers seeking protection and companionship on their way to Silesia or Hungary or South Germany, and by the time they reached the Carnic Alps they were no more than a dozen adults and some children, and even of that small band less than half were pilgrims. Old Felix, the holy man, smote the ground with his staff and inveighed against those worldly ones in their midst who were exploiting God's protection on this holy journey; it was their impiety that had led them all to misfortune. He was a stooped emaciated ancient with a long white beard. On the women especially he fixed his burning eyes.

'It is sin that has brought us to this pass!'

Krack the murderer grinned.

'Ah give it a rest, grandpa.'

He was a jolly fellow, Krack, and useful too, for he knew well the ways of the road, and could truss and roast a pilfered chicken very prettily. He was convinced that they were all fugitives like him, using the pilgrimage as a handy camouflage for flight. Their dogged protests of innocence hurt his feelings: had he not regaled them readily enough with the details of his own moment of glory? 'Bled like a pig he did, howling murder and God-a-mercy. He was tough, I tell you, the old bugger – slit from ear to ear and still clutching his few florins as if they was his ballocks I was tearing off. Jesus!'

The men squabbled among themselves, and once there broke out a desperate fight with fists and cudgels in which a knife with a spring blade played no small part. There was trouble too with the womenfolk. A young girl, a crazed creature mortally diseased who lay at night with whatever man would have her, was set upon by the other women and beaten so severely that she died soon after. They left her for the wolves. Her ghost followed them, filling their nights with visions of blood and ruin.

And then one rainy evening as they were crossing a high plateau under a sulphurous lowering sky a band of horsemen wheeled down on them, yelling. They were unlovely ruffians, tattered and lean, deserters from some distant war. 'Good holy Jesus poxed fucking Christ!' Krack muttered, gaping at them, and slapped his leg and laughed. They were old comrades of his, apparently. Their leader was a redheaded Saxon giant with an iron hook where his right hand had once been.

'We are crusaders, see,' this Rufus roared, his carroty hair whipping in the yellow wind, 'off to fight the infidel Turk. We need food and cash for the long journey before us. When you reach Rome you may tell the Pope you met with us: we're his men, fighting his cause, and he'll return with interest the donations you're going to make to us. Right, lads?' His fellows laughed heartily. 'Now then, let's have you. Food I say, and whatever gold you've got, and anyone who tries to cheat us will have his tripes cut out.'

Old Felix stepped forward.

'We are but poor pilgrims, friend. If you take what little we have you must answer to God for our deaths, for *certes* we shall not leave these mountains alive.'

Rufus grinned. 'Offer up a prayer, dad, and Jesus might send manna from heaven.'

The old man shakily lifted his staff to strike, but Rufus with a great laugh drew his sword and ran him through the guts, and he sank to his knees in a torrent of blood, bellowing most terribly. Rufus wiped his sword on his sleeve and looked about. 'Any other arguments? No?'

His men went among the travellers then like locusts, leaving them only their boots and a few rags to cover their backs. The brothers watched in silence their mule being driven off. Nicolas's suspiciously weighty cloak was ripped asunder, and the hoard of coins spilled out. Andreas looked at him.

'Friends,' cried Rufus, 'many thanks, and God go with you.'

They mounted up, but paused and muttered among themselves, grinning, and then dismounted again and raped the woman and two young boys. It took a long time for all those heaps of wriggling white flesh to be skewered, screaming, in the mud. Old Felix died as night fell, lying supine on the ground in the rain with his horny bare feet splayed, like a large wooden effigy, crying: Ah! Ah! Krack, waving a cheery farewell, had gone off with his friends. Andreas said:

'All that money, and not a word; you cunt.'

*

They would have perished surely, every one, had they not next day at dawn chanced upon a monastery perched on a rock high above a verdant valley. An old monk tending a vegetable garden outside the walls dropped his hoe and fled in terror at the sight of these walking dead who lifted up their frozen arms and mewled eerily. They could themselves hardly believe that they had survived. The night had been a kind of silvery icy death. They had spent it climbing blindly and in frantic haste, like possessed things, up the rocky slopes, watched by a huge impassive moon. Dawn had come in a flash of cold fire.

The monks of St Bernard received them kindly. One of the young boys died. Andreas, still brooding on that hidden trove of gold, would not speak to his brother. Nicolas passed his days out of doors, tramping the mountain paths in a monk's cloak and cowl, telling himself stories, muttering Latin verse, imagining Italy, trying to purge himself of the memory of rain and screaming, of rags stiff with brown blood, of Krack's smile. This country was unreal, this fiery icy Ultima Thule. He could not get his bearings here, everything was too big or too small, those impossible glittering mountains, the tiny blue flowers in the valley. Even the weather was strange, vast bluish brittle days of Alpine spring, fierce sun all light and little heat, transparent skies pierced by snowy peaks. The mountain goats clattered off with bells jangling at his approach, frightened by this staring alpenstocked dark parcel of pain and loathing. There was no forgetting. At night he was plagued by dreams whose sombre afterglow contaminated his waking hours, hung about him like a darkening of the air. He began to detect in everything signs of secret life, in flowers, mountain grasses, the very stones underfoot, all living, all somehow in agony. Thunderclouds flew low across the sky like roars of anguish on their way to being uttered elsewhere.

It was not the sufferings of the maimed and dead that pained him, but the very absence of that pain; he could not forget those terrible scenes, the blood and mud, the bundles of squirming flesh, but, remembering, he felt nothing, nothing, and this emptiness horrified him.

*

At Bologna, where they were to enrol at the university, the brothers parted company with the remnants of the pilgrimage. The representative at Rome of the Frauenburg Chapter, Canon

Bernhard Schiller, had travelled north to meet them. He was a small grey cautious man.

'Well, gentlemen,' he snapped, 'welcome to Italy. You are late arriving. I hope you had a pleasant journey, for certainly it was a leisurely one.'

They gazed at him. Andreas laughed. He said:

'We have no money.'

'What!' The Canon's grey face turned greyer. In the end, however, he agreed to advance them a hundred ducats. 'Understand, this is not my money, nor the Church's either; it is your uncle's. I have written to him today informing him of this transaction, and demanding an immediate refund.' He permitted himself a bleak smile. 'I trust you have ready for him a satisfactory explanation of your poverty? And why, may I ask, are you got up in this monkish garb? Have you been gambling with clerics? A perilous pastime. Well, it is no business of mine. Good day.'

Andreas watched with bitter amusement as Nicolas carefully counted his share of the ducats.

'Better get it sewed up quick, brother.'

* * *

AT TWILIGHT through hot crowded noxious streets he strode, speculating furiously on the true dimensions of the universe. Dark glossy heads and almond eyes turned to follow him with curiosity and amusement as he flew past. Bologna was a city of grotesques and madmen, yet he did not go unnoticed, with his long cloak and stark fanatic face. What did he care for their opinion, this noisy, stupid people! Italy had been a great disappointment; he hated it, the heat, the stale inescapable smell, the infantile uproar, the indolence, the corruption, the disorder. He had imagined a proud blue sunlit, serene land. Hawkers shrieked in his face, wheedling and bullying, thrusting at him their wine, their sweetmeats, their blinded singing birds. A fat buffoon with a head like a gobbet of raw meat, jiggling a string of stinking sausages, opened the wet red hole of his mouth and crowed: *Bello*, *professore*, *bello, bello!* A leprous beggar extended a fingerless hand and whined. He fled around a corner and was struck full tilt by a blinding blast of light. The setting sun sat on the city wall, flanked by a pair of robbers freshly hung that morning, black blots against the gold. Suddenly he yearned for those still pale pearly, limpid northern evenings full of silence and clouds. Vile vapours rose up from below. He had stepped in dogmerd.

With a sinking heart he heard his name called from the courtyard of a tavern close by, but when he made to hurry on he was prevented by a grinning drab, black as pitch, who planted herself in his path, smacking her blubber lips. A roar of tipsy laughter gushed out of the tavern.

'Come join us, brother, in a cup of wine,' Andreas called. He sat with a band of blades, good Germans all, his friends. 'See, fellows, how pale and gaunt he looks. You are too much at the books.'

They regarded him merrily, delighted with him, provider of fine sport. One said:

'Too much at the rod, more like.'

'Aye, been galloping the maggot, have you, Canon?'

'Bashing the venerable bishop, eh?'

'Haw haw.'

'O sit down!' Andreas snapped, flushed and petulant; drink did not agree with him very well. Nicolas had often wondered at his brother's uncanny knack of gathering about him the same friends wherever he went. The names varied, and the faces a little, but otherwise they were the same at Torun or Cracow or here in Bologna, idlers and whoremasters, pretender poets, rich men's sons with too much money, bullyboys all. There was of course this difference, that they got progressively older. Among this present lot there was not a one under thirty. Perennial students! Nicolas smiled wryly to himself: he was not so young that he could afford to scoff at others. Yet he *was* different, he knew it, a different species; why else did he fit so ill among them, perched here on the edge of this bench, hugging himself in a transport of embarrassment and repugnance, grinning like an idiot?

'Tell us, brother, who was that fair wench we spied you with just now? Likely you were discussing the motions of the spheres? Venus rising and suchlike?' Nicolas shrugged and squirmed, simpering foolishly; he was no match for his brother at this kind of cutting banter. Andreas turned to the others with his languorous smile. 'He is very hot on stargazing, you know, the pearly orbs, the globes of night, and so forth.'

A pimply fellow with straw-coloured locks and a wispy beard, the son of a Swabian count, took his sharp little nose out of his pintpot and leaned across the table seriously, and seriously said:

'Canon, have you heard tell of the unfortunate astronomer who got his sums mixed, and ended up with two planets where there should have been only one? Why, he made a ballocks of the orbit of Mars!'

There was more hawing and hohoing then, and more wine, and landlord! landlord! come fellow, a bowl of your best stewed tripe, for blind me but I have a longing for innards tonight. They left off baiting Nicolas. He was a poor foil for their wit, a poor punchbag. The last light of evening faded and the night came on apace, and stars, hesitant and dainty, glimmered in the trellis of vineleaves above their heads. A boy with a bunch of smoking tapers went among the tables. Here comes our young Prometheus, bringer of fire. What a sweet arse he has, look where he bends; here, boy, a ducat for your favours. The child backed off, smiling in fright. Music swelled in the street, wild caterwauling of fifes and the rattle of kettledrums, and a band of minstrels entered the courtyard in search of free wine. Nicolas grew dizzy in the noise and the smoke of the shaking rushlight. He drank. The Tuscan red was dark and tawny as old blood. Andreas mounted the table, wild-eyed and unsteady, roaring of freedom and rebirth, the new age, *l'uomo nuovo*. He staggered, clutching the air, and fell with a scream and a clatter into his brother's lap. Nicolas, suddenly stricken by sad helpless love, rocked in his arms this slack damp drunken lump, this grotesque babe, who leaned out over the table and gawked – *Ork!* – upon the straw-strewn floor a dollop of tripe and wine.

Later they were in a narrow ill-lit stinking street, and someone was lying in an open drain being strenuously kicked. The count's son stood by sniggering, until he was punched smartly out of the darkness by a disembodied fist and went down with a cry, gushing blood from a smashed nose. Nicolas found himself unaccountably on his knees in a low room or kind of little hut. The place was loud with grunting and moaning, and tangles of humped pale phosphorescent flesh writhed on the earthen floor. In the ghastly candlelight a woman lay on a pallet before him spreadeagled like an anatomical specimen, grinning and whimpering. She smelled of garlic and fish. He fell upon her with a moan and sank his teeth into her shoulder. It was a messy business, quickly done. Only afterwards did it strike him, when he put it to himself formally as it were, that he had at last relinquished his virginity. It had been just as he had imagined it would be.

*

Next morning he crept into the Aula Maxima bleared and crapulous, and late; his fellow students, elderly earnest young men, glared at him in disapproval and reproach. The Professor ignored him – what was a student's tardiness to Domenico Maria da Novara, astronomer, scholar of Greek, devotee of Plato and Pythagoras? Perched in his high pulpit he was as ever supremely, magisterially bored. The dry sombre voice strolled weary and indifferent through the lecture, pacing out the sentences as if they were so many ells of fallow land; only later would the significance and peculiar brilliance of his thought be made manifest, when their notes exploded slowly, like an unfolding myriad-petalled flower, in the mean rooms and minds of his students. He was a cold queer fastidious man, tall and swart, in his middle years, with a cruel face like a sharp dark blade. At Bologna, where it was not uncommon for an arrogant lecturer to be humbled by a hail of brickbats, or even run through by a playful rapier, Novara commanded universal fear and respect.

'Koppernigk – a word, if I might.' Nicolas halted in alarm. The class had ended, and the last of his fellows were shuffling out of the hall. He tried to smile, and leering waited, sick-shotten, quaking. The Professor descended thoughtfully from the pulpit, and on the last step stopped and looked at him. 'I am told that you have been putting about some, how shall I say, some curious ideas. Is it so, hmm?'

'Forgive me, *maestro*, I do not understand.'

'No?' Novara smiled thinly. They walked together down a sunlit corridor. Narrow stone arches to their right gave on to a paved courtyard and a marble statue with one arm raised in mysterious hieratic greeting; jagged shadows bristled under their feet. The Professor went on: 'I mean of course astronomical ideas, speculations on the shape and size of the universe, that kind of thing. I am interested, you understand. They tell me that you have expressed doubts on certain parts of the Ptolemaic doctrine of planetary motion?'

'I have taken part, it is true, in some discussions, in the taverns, but I have done no more than echo what has been said already, many times, by you yourself among others.' Novara pursed his lips and nodded. Something seemed to amuse him. Nicolas said: 'I do not believe that I have anything original to say. I am a dabbler. And I am not well this morning,' he finished wanly.

They strolled in silence for a time. The corridor was loud with the tramp of students, who eyed with furtive speculation this ill-assorted pair. Novara brooded. Presently he said:

'But your ideas on the dimensions of the universe, the intervals between planets, these seem to me original, or at least to promise great originality.' Nicolas wondered uneasily how the man could have come to hear of these things. His encounter with Brudzewski in Cracow had taught him discretion. He had admitted taking part in tavern talk, but surely he had never been more than a silent sharer? Who then knew enough of his thinking to betray him? The Professor watched him sidelong with a calculating look. 'What interests me,' he said, 'is whether or not you have the mathematics to support your theories?' There was of course one only who could have betrayed him; well, no matter. He was both pained and pleased, as if he had been caught in the commission of a clever crime. The few notions he had managed to put into words, gross ungainly travesties of the inexpressibly elegant concepts blazing in his brain, were suddenly made to seem far finer things than he had imagined by the attentions of the authoritative Novara.

'*Maestro*, I am no astronomer, nor a mathematician either.'

'Yes.' The Professor smiled again. 'You are a dabbler, as you say.' He seemed to think that he had made a joke. Nicolas grinned greyly. They came out on the steps above the sunny piazza. The bells of San Pietro began to ring, a great bronze booming high in the air, and flocks of pigeons blossomed into the blue above the golden domes. Novara mused dreamily on the crowds below in the square, and then abruptly turned and with what passed in him for animation said:

'Come to my house, will you? Come today. There are some people I think you might be interested to meet. Shall we say at noon? Until noon, then. *Vale*.' And he went off quickly down the steps.

Well what—?

*

'Well, what happened?' Andreas asked.

'Where?'

'At Novara's!'

'O, that.' They sat in the dining-hall of the German *natio*, where they lodged; it was evening, and beyond the grimy windows the Palazzo Communale brooded in late sunlight. The hall was crowded with crop-headed Germans at feed. Nicolas's head pained him. 'I do not know what Novara wants with me, I am not his kind at all. There were some others there, Luca Guarico, Jacob Ziegler, Calcagnini the poet—'

Andreas whistled softly. 'Well well, I am impressed. The cream of Italy's intellectuals, eh?' He smirked. '—And you, brother.'

'And I, as you say. Andreas, have you been putting about those few things I told you of my ideas on astronomy?'

'Tell me what happened at Novara's.'

'—Because I wish you would not; I would rather you would not do that.'

'Tell me.'

*

He was shown into a courtyard with orange bushes in earthenware pots; a fountain plashed, playing a faint cool music. The guests were gathered on the terrace, lolling elegantly on couches and dainty cane chairs, sipping white wine from long-stemmed goblets of Murano crystal and lazily conversing. Nicolas was reminded of those cages of pampered quail that were to be seen hanging from the porticoes of the better houses of the city. Diffident, ill at ease, acutely aware of his raw-boned Prussian gracelessness, he stood mute and nervously smiling as the Professor introduced him. Novara was very much the patrician here, with his fine town house behind him. He affected a scissors-shaped lorgnon with which he made much play. This article, together with the brilliant light, the pools of violet shadow on the terrace, the sparkling glass, the watermusic and the perfume of the orange bushes, contrived to create an air of theatre. Elbing. Elbing? Nicolas wondered vaguely why he should suddenly have thought of that far northern town.

How did he like Italy? The climate, ah yes. And what subjects was he studying here? Indeed? There was a silence, and someone coughed behind gloved fingers. Their duty done, they turned back to the conversation that evidently his arrival had interrupted. Celio Calcagnini, a willowy person no longer in the first flower of youth, said languidly:

'The question, then, is what can be achieved? Bologna is not Firenze, and I think we all agree that our Don John Bentivoglio is not, and never could be, a Magnifico.' All softly laughed and shook their heads; the jibe against the Duke of Bologna seemed to be a familiar one. 'And yet, my friends,' the poet continued, 'we must work with the material to hand, however poor it is. The wise man knows that compromise is sometimes the only course –

this is an excellent vintage, Domenico, by the way. I envy your cellar.'

Novara, leaning at ease against a white pillar, lifted his glass and bowed sardonically. A sleek black hound, which Nicolas with a start noticed now for the first time, lay at the Professor's feet, sphinxlike, panting, with a fanged ferocious grin. Jacob Ziegler, astronomer of some repute and author of a recent much-admired work on Pliny, was a dark and brooding lean young blade with a pale long face and flashing eyes and a pencil-line moustache. He was exquisitely if a trifle foppishly attired in rubious silk and calfskin; a wide-brimmed velvet hat lay beside him like a great soft black exotic bird. The cane chair on which he sat crackled angrily as he leaned forward and cried:

'Compromise! Caution! *I tell you we must act!* Times do not change of themselves, but are changed by the actions of men. Bologna is not Firenze, just so; but what is Firenze? A town of fat shopkeepers besotted by soft living.' He glanced darkly at Calcagnini, who raised his eyebrows mildly and toyed with the stem of his wineglass. 'They gobble up art and science as they would sugared marchpane, and congratulate themselves on their culture and liberality. Culture? Pah! And their artists and their scientists are no better. A gang of panders, theirs is the task of supplying the pretty baubles to mask the running sores of the poxed courtesan that is their city. Why, I should a thousand times rather we were the outcasts that we are than be as they, pampered adorners of decadence!'

'Decadence,' Novara softly echoed, gingerly tasting the word. Calcagnini looked up.

'A pretty speech, Jacob,' he said, smiling, 'but I think I resent your imputations. Compromise likes me no better than it does you, yet I know that there is a time for everything, for caution and for action. If we move now we can only make our state worse than it already is. And come to that, what, pray, would you have us do? The Bentivoglio rule in this city is unshakeable. There is peace here, while all Italy is in turmoil I know, I know you would not call it peace, but besottedness. Yet call it what you will, our citizens, like their fellows in Firenze, are well fed and therefore well content to leave things just as they are. That is the equation; it is as simple as that. You may harangue them all you wish, berate them for their decadence, but they will only laugh at you – that is, so long as you are no more than a crazy astronomer with your head in the clouds. Come down to earth and meddle in their affairs, then it will be another matter. Fra Girolamo, the formidable Savonarola, was cherished for a time by Firenze. The city writhed in holy ecstasy under his lash, until he began to frighten them, and then – why, then they burnt him. You see? No no, Jacob, there will be no *autos da fe* in Bologna.'

Ziegler pouted, and a pretty flush spread upward from his cheeks to his pale forehead. 'Are you comparing us to that mad monk, that *creature*, who castigated Plato as a source of immorality? He deserved burning, I say!'

Calcagnini smiled again tolerantly.

'No, my dear Jacob,' he murmured, 'of course I make no such comparison. I am merely trying to demonstrate to you that precipitate and rash action on our part can lead us straight to ruin.'

'—And further,' Ziegler continued hotly, 'why do you assume that the power of the Bentivoglios can be challenged only from within Bologna's walls?'

The hound shut its jaws with a wet snap and rose and loped leanly away. There was an awkward silence. Ziegler glared about him haughtily, flushed and defiant. 'Well?' he asked, of no one in particular. Novara frowned at him with pursed lips, and very slightly shook his head in wordless mild reproof. A scrawny individual, rejoicing in the name of Nono, laughed squeakily.

'L-let us hear the results of L-Luca's l-l-labours!' he ventured brightly. The others paid no heed to him, being engrossed in disapproving silently of whatever indiscretion it was that the unrepentant Ziegler had committed, and Nono turned unhappily to Nicolas and said, very loudly and deliberately, as if addressing a stone-deaf idiot: 'H-he has made a horosc-sc-scope of Cesare, you see. *Il Valentino*, as he is called, ha ha.' Nicolas nodded, smiling hugely, miming extravagant gratitude and encouragement. 'Bo-Bo-Borgia, that is,' Nono finished lamely, and frowned, searching it seemed for that last elusive word, the stammerer's obsession, that surely would make all come marvellously clear.

Novara stirred. 'Yes, Luca, tell us, what do the stars say of our young prince?'

Luca Guarico, he of the large head and hooked nose of a decayed Caesar, sighed fatly, and fatly shrugged. He was fat; he was that kind of fat that conjures up, in the goggling imaginations of thin fastidious men such as Nicolas, hideous and irresistible visions of quaking copulations, and monstrous labours in water closets, and helpless tears at the coming undone of a shoe buckle. He thrashed about briefly on the couch where he sat, and panting brought out from beneath his robes a wrinkled scrap of parchment.

'There is little to tell,' he wheezed. 'Had I the facts it would be easy, but I have not. A long life, certainly; good fortune at first, as befits—' he smiled gloomily '—the Pope's bastard. After his thirtieth year there will come a falling off, but that is not clear. He will conduct a victorious campaign in Lombardy and the Romagna, as that Sforza bitch will learn to her cost. He should beware the French, if Mars is to be trusted.' He shrugged again apologetically and put away the parchment. 'So.'

'O brilliant, brilliant,' Ziegler muttered, plucking fiercely at his moustache. Guarico looked at him. Calcagnini hastened to say:

'Jacob, you are so fiery today! As Luca has told us, he has not the necessary facts – and indeed we may ask, who can know the facts concerning that strange and secretive dynasty?'

Bland smiles were exchanged. Novara said:

'But Luca, do you have nothing that touches on our concerns?'

'I can tell you this,' the fat man answered, and looked about him dourly, 'this I can tell you: he will never sit on the throne of Peter.'

There was the sense of a slow soft crash, and Ziegler sniggered bitterly.

'Well then,' Novara murmured, 'there is nothing for us there.'

Suddenly they all relaxed, and looked at Nicolas, a little bashfully it seemed, like players awaiting his applause. He stared back blankly, baffled. He felt he must have missed something of deep significance. The servants carried on to the terrace small silver trays of choice comestibles, flaked game in aspic, chunks of melon, translucent cuts of the spiced ham of the region. He picked, not without a faint concealed amusement, at a portion of cold quail. The sun had shifted out of the square of sky above the courtyard, and the light there no longer crackled harshly, but was a solid cube of hot bluish brilliance. He was acutely aware of his foreignness, and longed for the cold north. This was not his world, this heat, these strident passions, this stale flat air that sat so heavily in his lungs, like someone else's breath; nothing touched him here, and he touched nothing. He was a little Prussia in the midst of Italy. An olive-skinned young dandy sitting opposite was eyeing him peculiarly, with a kind of knowing insolence.

Having eaten, the company retired from the terrace to a cool blue high-ceilinged lavish room, with an open archway at one end, and at the other wide windows giving on to a hazy sunlit distance of shimmering cypresses and olive-green hills. An air of expectancy was palpable, and presently the desultory talk stopped abruptly on the entrance of a strange distraught emaciated person with a lyre. He seemed the luckless bearer of a burden of intolerable knowledge, a seer cursed with unspeakable secrets. He stood by patiently, his blurred gaze fixed on some inner vision, while the servants reverently arranged a bank of cushions for him in the centre of the floor, then he settled himself with great care, crossing his pathetically skinny ankles, and began to sing in a weird piping voice. A breeze stirred the silken drapes at the windows, and billows of pale pearly light swayed across the shining floor. The black dog returned and lay down throbbing at Novara's feet with wet jaws agape. Nicolas felt vaguely alarmed, for what reason he did not know. The song was a sustained sinuous incomprehensible cry that the anguished singer seemed to spin out of his very substance, slowly, painfully, a thin silver thread of sound rippling and weaving hypnotically above the soft dark plashing of the lyre. The company sat rapt, listening with such intensity that it appeared they were in some way assisting in the making of this unearthly music.

At length the song ended, and the singer gazed about him with a lost forsaken look, fretfully fingering the lank yellow strands of his hair. The others rose and went to him quickly, cooing and whispering, solicitous as women. He was given a beaker of wine to drink but took only a sip, and then was helped away, mumbling and sighing. The room was left limp and somehow satiated, as after a debauch. Novara rose, and with a glance invited Nicolas to follow him. Together they went out under the archway with the black dog padding softly behind them. The singer sat alone in an antechamber, ravaged and desolate in the midst of a great light. He looked at them blankly out of his strange pale yellowish eyes, and could not answer when Novara spoke to him, and only shook his head a little and turned away. But he smiled at the dog knowingly, as one conspirator to another. They passed on, and Nicolas asked:

'What is he? Is he ill?'

Novara lifted the lorgnon and looked at him searchingly.

'You do not know? Did you not recognise that music? It was an Orphic hymn to the Sun. He knew Ficino, you see, at the Academy in Firenze. He is not ill, not with what you or I understand as illness. The ancient knowledge to which he is heir consumes him fiercely. Great passion, great wisdom, these cannot be lightly borne by mortal men.'

Nicolas nodded, and said no more. All this was fraught with deep meaning, it seemed; it meant little to him.

They entered the library and walked among the cases of precious manuscripts and incunabula and priceless first editions from Germany and Venice. Novara caressed with his fingertips tenderly the polished spines. He was abstracted, and said little. A bent blade of sunlight from a narrow window clove the gloom. The silence throbbed. Novara produced a tiny gold key with which he unlocked a pearwood chest that Nicolas vaguely felt he had seen somewhere before. Here was the heart of the library, its true treasure, rare and exquisite copies of the *Corpus Hermeticum* along with Marsilio Ficino's translations and a host of commentaries and glosses. The Professor began gravely to expatiate on the celestial mysteries. He spoke of decans and angels, of talismans and sympathetic magic, of the *spiritus mundi* that rules the world in secret. A change came over him and he spoke as one possessed. He was, it seemed, something of a magus.

'Do you believe, Herr Koppernigk?' he asked suddenly.

'I do not know what I believe, *maestro*.'

'Ah.'

Nicolas had already heard of the strange aetherial philosophy of this Thrice-Great Hermes, Trismegistus the Egyptian, wherein the universe is conceived as a vast grid of dependencies and sympathetic action controlled by the seven planets, or Seven Governors as Trismegistus called them. It was all altogether too raddled with cabalistic obscurities for Nicolas's sceptical northern soul, yet he found deeply and mysteriously moving the gnostic's dreadful need to discern in the chaos of the world a redemptive universal unity.

'The link that bound all things was broken by the will of God,' Novara cried. 'That is what is meant by the fall from grace. Only after death shall we be united with the All, when the body dissolves into the four base elements of which it is made, and the spiritual man, the soul free and ablaze, ascends through the seven crystal spheres of the firmament, shedding at each stage a part of his mortal nature, until, shorn of all earthly evil, he shall find redemption in the Empyrean and be united there with the world soul that is everywhere and everything and eternal!' He fixed on Nicolas his burning gaze. 'Is this not what you yourself have been saying, however differently you say it, however different your terms? Ah yes, my friend, yes, I think you do believe!'

Nicolas smiled nervously and turned away, alarmed by this man's sudden tentacled intensity. It was mad, all mad! yet when he imagined that fiery soul flying upward, aching upward into light, a nameless elation filled him, and that word glowed in his head like a talisman, that greatest of all words: *redemption*.

'I believe in mathematics,' he muttered, 'nothing more.'

At that suddenly the Professor checked himself, his fire abated, and he was once again his former urbane studied self. 'Exactly, my dear fellow,' he said, smiling, 'just my point!' And he touched his guest lightly on the shoulder and led him back to join the waiting company.

Luca Guarico, squatting on a delicate ebony and velvet couch, shifted his vast bulk to make a little space beside him which he patted with a pudgy hand in roguish invitation, and Nicolas had no choice but to lower himself with a shiver into the faintly perfumed puddle of warmth that the fat man had left behind him. Novara paced the floor deep in thought, tapping the folded lorgnon against a thumbnail. No one spoke. Nicolas suspected that Guarico was watching him, and he would not turn for fear of what frightful intimacies he might be forced to share by meeting those pinkish porcine eyes. The insolent dandy who had stared at him before was now deep in whispered dark confabulation with two others of his kind. Celio Calcagnini sighed a brief bored melody and considered the ceiling, peeling off his immaculate white linen gloves finger by finger. The fiery Ziegler gnawed his nails in a furious abstraction. Nicolas was suddenly beset out of the blue by a sense of general absurdity. He rose hastily, propelled to his feet by the force of a soft fart inadvertently let slip by Guarico, and at that moment Novara turned to him and said: 'Herr Koppernigk . . .' He stopped, perplexed, finding his guest apparently on the point of fleeing. Nicolas leered apologetically and slowly subsided, while just above his head he fancied he could hear rumblings of muffled celestial merriment. 'Herr Koppernigk,' Novara continued, 'I feel I am not wrong in thinking that you are one of us at heart. You have realised by now, of course, that this is no mere aimless gathering of friends; we are, you may say, men with a purpose. We marked how closely you attended to that brief exchange between Celio here and our dear impetuous Jacob, and so we suspect that you have some little notion of the nature of our purpose?'

'O yes,' Nicolas said brightly, quite at a loss; finding himself stared at he beat an immediate retreat. 'That is to say I feel I understand—'

'Yes yes, I see.' Novara waved a languid hand and resumed his pacing. 'Let me explain. I say we have a purpose, but from this you must not imagine that you have stumbled upon a nest of conspirators. No doubt in the north they tell terrible tales of us here in Italy, but I assure you, we have no stilettos under our cloaks, no poisons secreted in our signet rings. We are, simply, a group of men dissatisfied with the state of things, *frightened* by the state of things. The world, my dear friend, is flying headlong to disaster, driven thither by the corruption that is all too evident in Church and State. There is the decay of the aristocracy, and along with it the collapse of the manorial system. There is the diminution of the standards of education, so that mere tradesmen's sons are now allowed into our greatest univ . . .' He caught Nicolas's eye, and winced. 'Ahem. In short, Herr *von* Koppernigk, there is the decadence of the age. Decadence. Ah. Is it not greatly to be feared? Is it not a plague, is it not worse than war? For decadence is the attendant midwife at a brute birth, and the beast that is being born, here, now, in this very city, is – I shudder to say it—'

'He m-means,' piped Nono, eager as the clever boy in the classroom, 'the c-concept of lullul lullul lu-liberty!'

Novara looked at him coldly. 'Just so,' he said, and turned away.

Calcagnini was still dreamily considering the ceiling, where pink plaster cherubs rioted in buttocky abandon.

'Ah, liberty,' he murmured, smacking his lips delicately, 'that *fearful* word.' For the first time that day he turned his cool sardonic gaze directly on Nicolas, and smiled. 'You see, my dear sir, we believe that when the people are allowed to entertain notions of individual freedom – nay when they are encouraged to it! – then begins the swift decline of civilised values.'

At that for some reason Guarico chortled. Nicolas's heart sank into a quay of gloom. He was tired, he wanted to be elsewhere. His glass was full again, and already he had drunk too much. He shook his head and mumbled dully:

'I do not understand.'

'The point is—' Novara began, but once again he was interrupted, this time by Ziegler who lunged forward and jabbed a trembling finger at Nicolas's breastbone, crying:

'The point is that the rot can be stopped! Yes yes, it can be stopped by a few determined men, a few good minds – *we*, sir, we can stop it!'

'How, pray?' Nicolas snapped. He disliked intensely this rabid young man, whose face under the force of his passion had turned a kind of furious purple.

'Jacob,' Novara said softly. 'Calm now, calm.' He turned to Nicolas. 'You see how strongly our feelings run? How should it be otherwise? We are, as Jacob has already remarked, outcasts in this city. O there is no conspiracy against us, no pressures are brought to bear on us, we are free to come and go, to congregate, to hatch plots even, if we wish; we are—' he shrugged '—free. But what does it signify, this objectless freedom? Only that we are not feared, because the times themselves ensure that men such as we shall not be heeded. In a bad age the wise man is scorned.' He paused in his pacing and looked about him at the company with a fond melancholy smile. 'Regard us, sir: we are scholars, we are philosophers and scientists and poets, but we are not activists. Yet now, here in Bologna and throughout Italy and all Europe, action is necessary. Who will act if we do not? As Platonists we know that justice and good government are possible only when power rests in the hands of the philosophers. Therefore we must have power. How are we to achieve it? Herr Koppernigk, let me be specific: we seek—' Calcagnini stirred nervously, but Novara disregarded him '—we seek, sir, firstly union between our city state and Rome, and beyond that, O far beyond that, a Europe united under papal rule. A new, strong and united Holy Roman Empire – that is our aim, no less than that.'

Nicolas blinked. Calcagnini coughed drily.

'I think, Domenico,' he murmured, 'I think you have forgotten a most important thing.' He looked at Nicolas. 'We seek, yes, a Europe united, *but only under a Pope of our making.* His Holiness Alexander will not do, he will not do at all.' A ripple of bitter amusement passed through the room. Novara nodded.

'Of course,' he said, not without a trace of irritation, and bowed to the poet, 'a most important point assuredly. A Pope, yes, of our making. We have even considered candidates; does that surprise you, Herr Koppernigk? We are in earnest, you see. We have for instance considered Alexander's bastard Cesare. Luca's horoscope, however, is not encouraging, and tends to confirm the grave doubts we have for some time been entertaining in that quarter. I think we must look elsewhere.' And he looked with a smile upon Nicolas, who after a moment's reflection sat upright suddenly and said:

'O but you cannot imagine that I – I mean, surely not!'

They stared at him, and then Novara laughed somewhat uneasily.

'Ah,' he said, 'a joke; I see. I did not at first – very droll, yes.'

Calcagnini joined his fingers at the tips and tapped that spire thoughtfully against his pursed lips, saying:

'We thought: What if we should discover that there is in Bologna a young churchman from the north, a scientist, whose uncle is Bishop of a Prussian princedom and a voice of no little significance in the affairs of Europe? And what if we should discover further that this young scientist is a thinker of potential greatness? Would he not be, to use a cold word, useful? These are strange times. The world is yielding up its secrets to those who know how to look for them. What if it should come to our ears that this young man has been cautiously expounding the outlines of a planetary theory which, if proved, should compel us to reconsider our conception of the nature of the physical world?

We said: What if we were to provide for this astronomer certain facilities – a villa in the quiet of the provinces, say, and ample funds to enable him to spend two or three years in study and research – if, in short, we were to provide him with the means of perfecting this new theory of his? Now the Church, as we all know, is free apparently to indulge in all manner of fleshly vices, but it is not free to indulge in speculations that run contrary to dogma: for dogma is unassailable. And whose is the task of ensuring the inviolability of dogma? Why, it is the Pope's! Now, what if our young astronomer, at the end of this two or three years of seclusion, should travel to Prussia and present to his uncle the proofs of his new theory? It is well known that the Bishop of Ermland is no friend of Rome's, and especially not of Alexander, this bloated Borgia despot. Does it not seem likely that within a short time all Europe would be rife with reports of this new and apparently blasphemous theory? And Alexander would be forced to act. But the Bishop of Ermland is not the only enemy that the Pope has; his enemies are legion. In that battle, then, between a theory mathematically verified and vouched for beyond all doubt, and a bad Pope, who, we wondered, would be likely to win? It seemed to us that the only possible outcome would be a new conclave of the College of Cardinals; and thus the cause of the Church would be served, and our cause, and also of course, Herr Koppernigk, yours. These are questions, you understand, that we have been putting to ourselves for some time past. We hoped that you might be able to help us to find the answers. Hmm?'

But Nicolas was engrossed in the wonderfully ridiculous image of himself and Bishop Lucas deep in dark discussion of a plot to bring down the Pope, and he said only:

'Sir, you do not know my uncle.'

It was a poor reply to such a speech, but it hardly mattered, for the company, strangely, had lost all interest in him. The dandy and his friends, amid shrieks of laughter, were trying to force the hound to drink a goblet of wine. Novara stood by the window gazing vacantly at the far hills. Nicolas was reminded of an audience grown bored with a play. The singer had crept back into their midst with a tentative uncertain grin, no longer the mysterious priestly figure that their attentions had made him seem before, but a soulful, sad, unloved and unlovely weird madman. Guarico had fallen asleep. Calcagnini smiled blearily, nodding. He was drunk. They were all drunk. Nicolas rose to go. The scrawny Nono, giggling and stammering and trembling all over, crept after him and made an inept and farcical attempt at seduction.

*

Andreas pushed his platter away and belched sourly. A scullion passed by their table, lugging a steaming urn, and he turned to watch her joggling haunches. Dreamily he said:

'They are all *Italians*, of course,' and he smiled at his brother suddenly, icily. 'Yes, bumboys all.'

Nicolas went no more to Novara's house, and stayed away from his lectures. By Christmastide he had left Bologna for ever.

* * *

THE CITY CROUCHED, sweating in fright, under the sign of the brooding bull. Talk of portents was rife. Blood rained from the sky at noon, at night the deserted streets shook with the thunder of unearthly hoofbeats and weird cries filled the air. A woman at Ostia come to her time brought forth an issue of rats. Some said it was the reign of Antichrist, and that the end was nigh. In February the Pope's son Cesare returned victorious from the Romagna and rode in triumph with his army through the cheering streets. He was clad for the occasion all in black, with a collar of gold blazing at his throat. The entire army likewise was draped in black. It seemed, in the brumous yellowy light of that winter day, that the Lord of Darkness himself had come forth to be acclaimed by the delirious mob.

This was Rome, in the jubilee year of 1500.

*

The brothers had moved south to the capital on the instructions of Uncle Lucas: they were to act as unofficial ambassadors of the Frauenburg Chapter at the jubilee celebrations. It was a nebulous posting. They performed during that year only one duty that could have been considered in any way connected with diplomacy, when they dined at the Vatican as guests of a minor papal official, a smooth foxy cleric with a disconcerting wall-eyed stare, who desired, as far as the brothers could ascertain from his elaborately veiled insinuations, to be reassured that Bishop Lucas's loyalty to Rome was in no danger of being transferred to the King of Poland; and they might have made a serious blunder, inexperienced as they were in matters of such delicacy, had not the grey and cautious Canon Schiller, the representative of the Frauenburg Chapter, been there to guide them with astutely timed and enthusiastically administered kicks under the table.

It was with Schiller that they lodged, in a gloomy villa on the damp side of a hill near the Circo Massimo, where the food was stolidly Prussian and the air heavy with the odour of sanctity. Nicolas glumly accepted the discipline and arid rituals of the house; from his schooldays on he had been accustomed to that kind of thing, and expected nothing better. Andreas, however, chafed under Canon Schiller's watchful eye, in which there was reflected, all the way from Prussia, the light of a far fiercer, icier gaze. Lately he had become more morose than ever, his rages were redder, his fits of melancholia less and less amenable to the curative pleasures of student life. What had once in him been fecklessness was now a thirst for small destructions; his gay cynicism had turned into something very like despair. He complained vaguely of being ill. His face was drawn and pallid, eyes shot with blood, his breathing oddly thin and papery. He began to frequent the booths of astrologers and fortune tellers of the worst kind. Once even he asked Nicolas to cast his horoscope, which Nicolas, appalled at the idea, refused to do, pleading not very convincingly a lack of skill. Uncle Lucas had secured a canonry at Frauenburg for Andreas, and for a time his finances flourished, but he was soon penniless again, and, worse, in the hands of the Jews. Nicolas watched helplessly his brother's life disintegrate; it was like witnessing the terrible slow fall into the depths of a once glorious marvellously shining angel.

Yet Andreas loved Rome. In that wicked wolf-suckled city his peculiar talents came briefly to full flower, nourished by the pervading air of menace and intrigue. He spoke the language of these scheming worldly churchmen, and it was not long before he had found his way into the cliques and cabals that abounded at the papal court. In the eyes of the world he was a firebrand, brilliant, careless, and hedonistic, destined for great things. Schiller cautioned him on the manner of his life. He paid no heed. He was by then treading waters deeper than that Canon could conceive of. But he was out over jagged reefs, and his light was being extinguished; he was drowning.

Nicolas detested the capital. It reminded him of an old tawny lion dying in the sun, on whose scarred and smelly pelt the lice bred and feverishly fed in final frantic carnival. He was shocked by what he saw of the workings of the Church. God had been deposed here, and Rodrigo Borgia ruled in his place. On Easter Sunday two hundred thousand pilgrims knelt in St Peter's Square to receive the blessing of the Pope; Nicolas was there, pressed about by the poor foolish faithful who sighed and swayed like a vast lung, lifting their faces trustingly toward the hot sun of spring. He wondered if perhaps the tavern prophets were right, if this was the end, if here today a last terrible blessing was being administered to the city and the world.

In July Lucrezia Borgia's husband, Alfonso Duke of Bisceglie, was savagely attacked on the steps of St Peter's; Cesare was behind the outrage, so it was whispered. The rumours seemed confirmed some weeks later when *Il Valentino's* man, Don Michelotto, broke into Alfonso's sickroom in the Vatican and throttled the Duke in his bed. Nicolas recalled a certain strange day in Bologna, and wondered. But of course it was altogether mad to think that Novara and his friends could be in any way involved in these bloody doings, or so at least the Professor himself insisted when one day, by chance, Nicolas met him on the street near the amphitheatre of Vespasian.

'No no!' Novara whispered hoarsely, glancing nervously about. 'How can you imagine such a thing? In fact the Duke knew something of our views, and was not unsympathetic. Certainly we wished him no harm. It is too terrible, truly. And to think that we once considered this Cesare as . . . O, terrible!'

He was paying a brief visit to Rome on university business. Nicolas was shocked by his appearance. He was stooped and sallow, with dead eyes and trembling hands, hardly recognisable as the magisterial, cold and confident patrician he had lately been. He frowned distractedly and mopped his brow, tormented by the heat and the dust and the uproar of the traffic. He was dying. A slender bored young man got up in scarlet accompanied him, and stood by in insolent silence with one hand resting on his hip; his name was Girolamo. He smiled at Nicolas, who suddenly remembered where he had seen him before, and blushed and turned away only to find to his horror Novara watching him with tears in his eyes.

'You think me a fool, Koppernigk,' he said. 'You came to my house only to laugh at me – O yes, do not deny it, your brother told me how you laughed after running away from us that day. My scheming and my magic, I suppose they must have seemed foolish to you, whose concern is facts, computation, the laws of the visible world.'

Nicolas groaned inwardly. Why were people, Andreas always, now Novara, so eager that he should think well of them? What did his opinion matter? He said:

'My brother lied; he is prone to it. Why should I laugh at you? You are a greater astronomer than I.' This was horrible, horrible. 'I left your house because I knew I could be of no use to you. What part could I play in your schemes—' he could not resist it '—I, a mere tradesman's son?'

Novara nodded, grimacing. The sun rained hammerblows on him. He had the look of a wounded animal.

'You lack charity, my friend,' he said. 'You must try to understand that men have need of answers, articles of faith, myths – lies, if you will. The world is terrible and yet we are terrified to leave it: that is the paradox that hurts us so. Does anything hurt you, Koppernigk? Yours is an enviable immunity, but I wonder if it will endure.'

'I cannot help it if I am cold!' Nicolas cried, beside himself with rage and embarrassment. 'And I have done nothing to deserve your bitterness.' But Novara had lost interest, and was shuffling away. The youth Girolamo hesitated between them, glancing with a faint sardonic smile from one of them to the other. Nicolas trembled violently. It was not fair! – even if he was dying, Novara had no right to cringe like this; his task was to be proud and cold, to intimidate, not to mewl and whimper, not to be weak. It was a scandal! 'I never asked anything of you!' Nicolas howled at the other's back, ignoring the looks of the passers-by. 'It was you that approached me. *Are you listening?*'

'Yes yes,' Novara muttered, without turning. 'Just so, indeed. And now farewell. Come, Girolamo, come.'

The young man smiled languorously a last time, and with a small regretful gesture went to the Professor and took his arm. Nicolas turned and fled, with his fury clutched to him like a struggling captive wild beast. He was frightened, as if he had looked into a mirror and seen reflected there not his own face but an unspeakable horror.

He did not see Novara again. Once or twice their paths might have crossed, but time and circumstance happily intervened to keep them apart; happily, not only because Nicolas feared another painful scene, but also because he dreaded the possibility of being confronted again by the frightening image of himself he had glimpsed in the looking glass of that incomprehensible fit of naked fury. When he heard of the Professor's death he could not even remember clearly what the man had looked like; but by then he was in Padua, and everything had changed.

*

That city at first made little impression on him, he was so busy searching for habitable lodgings, performing the complicated and exasperating rituals of enrolment at the university, choosing his subjects, his professors. He had also to cope with Andreas, who by now was badly, though still mysteriously, ill, and full of spleen. Early in the summer the brothers travelled to Frauenburg, their leave of absence having expired. They had asked by letter for an extension, but Bishop Lucas had insisted that they should make the request in person. The extra leave was granted, of course, and after less than a month in Prussia they set out once more for Italy.

Nicolas paused at Kulm to visit Barbara at the convent. She had not changed much in the years since he had seen her last; in middle age she was still, for him, the ungainly girl who had played hide and seek with him long ago in the old house in Torun. Perhaps it was these childhood echoes that made their talk so stilted and unreal. There was between them still that familiar melancholy, that tender hesitant regard, but now there was something more, a faint sense of the ridiculous, of the ponderous, as if they were despite their pretensions really children playing at being grown-ups. She was, she told him, Abbess of the convent now, in succession to their late Aunt Christina Waczelrodt, but he could not grasp it. How could Barbara, his Barbara, have become a person of such consequence? She also was puzzled by the elaborate dressing-up that he was trying to pass off as his life. She said:

'You are becoming a famous man. We even hear talk of you here in the provinces.'

He shook his head and smiled. 'It is all Andreas's doing. He thinks it a joke to put it about that I am formulating in secret a revolutionary theory of the planets.'

'And are you not?'

Summer rain was falling outside, and a pallid, faintly flickering light entered half-heartedly by the streaming windows of the high hall where they sat. Even in her loose-fitting habit Barbara was all knees and knuckles and raw scrubbed skin. She looked away from him shyly. He said:

'I shall come again to see you soon.'

'Yes.'

*

When he returned to Padua he found Andreas, though sick and debilitated already from the Prussian journey, preparing to depart for Rome. 'I can abide neither your sanctimonious stink, brother, nor this cursed Paduan smugness. You will breathe easier without me to disgrace you before your pious friends.'

'I have no friends, Andreas. And I wish you would not go.'

'You are a hypocrite. Do not make me spew, please.'

However much he tried not to be, Nicolas was glad of his brother's going; now perhaps at last, relieved of the burden of Andreas's intolerable presence, he would be permitted to become the real self he had all his life wished to be.

But what was that mysterious self that had eluded him always? He could not say. Yet he was convinced that he had reached a turning point. Those first months alone in Padua were strange. He was neither happy nor sad, nor much of anything: he was neutral. Life flowed over him, and under the wave he waited, for what he did not know, unless it was rescue. He applied himself with energy to his studies. He took philosophy and law, mathematics, Greek and astronomy. It was in the faculty of medicine, however, that he surfaced at last, like a spent swimmer flying upward into light, in whose aching lungs the saving air blossoms like a great dazzling yellow flower.

*

'Signor Fracastoro?'

The young man turned, frowning. '*Si*, I am Fracastoro.'

How handsome he was, how haughty, with those black eyes, that dark narrow arrogant face; how languidly he sprawled on the bench among the twittering band of dandies, with his long legs negligently crossed. The lecture hall was putrid with the stink of a dissected corpse, the gross gouts and ganglia of which two bloodstained attendants were carting away, but he was aristocratically indifferent to that carnage, and only now and then bothered to lift to his face the perfume-soaked handkerchief whose pervasive musky scent was the unmistakable trademark of the medical student. He was dressed with casual elegance in silk and soft leather, booted and spurred, with a white linen shirt open on the frail cage of his chest; he had come late to the lecture that morning, flushed and smiling, bringing with him into the fetid hall a crisp clean whiff of horses and sweet turf and misty dawn meadows. He was all that Nicolas was not, and Nicolas, sensing imminent humiliation, cursed himself for having spoken.

'We met last year in Rome, I think,' he said. 'You were with Professor Novara.'

'O?'

Fracastoro's friends nudged each other happily, and gazed at Nicolas with bland sardonic seriousness, trying not to laugh; they too could see humiliation coming.

'Yes yes, in Rome, and before that in Bologna, at the Professor's house.' He was beginning to babble. Someone sniggered. 'I remember it well. You tried to make a drunkard of Novara's dog, ha ha. Ha.'

The young man raised an eyebrow. 'Yes? A dog, you say? Extraordinary. Certainly I do not remember that.'

Nicolas sighed. Blast you, you young prig. Life is dreadful, really. He stepped back, trying not to bow.

'A mistake,' he muttered. 'Forgive me.'

'But wait, wait,' Fracastoro said, 'this Novara, it seems to me I do know the man, vaguely.' He lifted a slender hand to his brow. 'Ah yes, a mathematician, is he not?' – much given to mysticism? Yes, I know him. Well?'

'You do not remember our meeting.'

'No; but I may do so, if I concentrate. Do you have news of the Professor?'

'No, no, I merely – it is no matter.'

'But—?'

'No matter, no matter.' And he fled, pursued by laughter.

*

They met again some days later, in the vegetable market, of all places, at dawn. Lately Nicolas had begun to suffer from sleeplessness, and went out often at night to walk about the city and bathe his feverishly spinning brain in the chill dark air. He developed a fondness for the market especially; the colours, the clamour, the heavy honeyed smell of ripeness, all conspired to cheat of its bleakness that inhuman hour before first light. He was leaning on the damp parapet of the Ponte San Giorgio, idly watching the upriver barges like great ungainly whales unloading their produce in the bluish gloom of the wharf below, when a voice said at his shoulder:

'Koppernigk, is it not?'

He was wrapped in a dun cloak, and his long fair swathe of hair was hidden under a battered old black slouch hat; even in such dull apparel he could not be less than elegant. He was smiling a little, not looking at Nicolas, but musing on the still-dark distance beyond the city walls, saying silently, as it were: come, cut me now if you wish, and so have some small revenge. But Nicolas just as silently declined the offer, and suddenly the Italian laughed softly and said:

'Nicolas Koppernigk – you see? I have been concentrating.'

Nicolas with a faint smile inclined his head in acknowledgment. 'Signor Fracastoro.'

The other looked at him directly then, and laughed again.

'O please,' he said, 'my friends call me that; *you* may call me Girolamo. Shall we walk this way a little?' They left the bridge and crossed the open piazza, where the fishwives were hurling amiable abuse from stall to stall. 'But tell me, what brings you here at this strange hour?'

Nicolas shrugged. 'I do not sleep well. And you?'

'Wine and women, I fear, keep me from my bed. I am for home now after a misspent night.' It was meant as a boast. He was at that age, not quite twenty yet, when the youth he had been and the man he was becoming both held sway at once, so that in the same breath he could slip disconcertingly from hard cold derisive cynicism into simple silliness. Now he said: 'You disappointed Novara greatly, you know, by not taking seriously his grand schemes to save the world. Ah, poor Domenico!'

They both laughed, a little spitefully, and Nicolas, suddenly stared at out of the sky by the Professor's pained reproachful eyes, said hastily:

'But they are not without significance, his preoccupations.'

'No, of course; but it is all mere talking. He is too much in love with magic, and despises action. I mean that natural magic for him is all centaurs and chimaeras. Now I, however, understand it in general as the science which applies the knowledge of hidden forms to the production of wonderful operations.' He glanced out quickly from under the downturned brim of his black hat with a candid questioning look, but it was impossible to know if he was being sincere or otherwise. 'What do you say, friend?'

But Nicolas only shrugged and murmured warily:

'Perhaps, perhaps . . .'

He did not know what to make of this young man; he did not trust him, and did not trust himself, and so determined to go cautiously, even though he could not see where trust came into it, except that he knew he did not care to be made a fool of again. It was all odd, this meeting, this dreamlike morning, these dim figures hurrying here and there and crying out in the gloom. They entered a narrow alleyway given over entirely to the trade in cagebirds. Cascades of bright mad music drenched the dark air. Coming out at the other end they found themselves abruptly in a deserted square. The sky was of a deep illyrian blue, lightening rapidly now to the east, and the towers of the city were tipped with gold.

'May I offer you breakfast?' said Fracastoro. 'My rooms are close by.'

He lived in a tumbledown palazzo near the Basilica of St Anthony, the family home of an elderly count who had long ago fled to a villa in the Dolomites for the sake of his ailing lungs. 'My uncle, you know,' he said, and winked. They ascended through the shabby splendours of gilt and tempera and stained marble statuary to the fourth floor, where a kind of rambling lair, stretching through five or six large rooms, had been scooped out of the dust and genteel wreckage deposited by years of neglect. Here, under the sagging canopy of a vast four-poster, they came upon a young man asleep in a tangle of soiled sheets. He was naked, his limbs sprawled in touchingly childish abandon, tacked down firmly, as it were, like some exotic specimen, by the enormous erection that reared grotesquely out of his jet-black bush. Fracastoro barely glanced at him, but in passing picked up a tortured shirt from the floor and flung it at his head, crying:

'Up up up! Come!'

The main room was a general disorder of books and clothes and empty wine bottles. Most of the furniture was draped in dustsheets. Here and there amidst the clutter the skeleton of a former glory was visible in richly patterned panelling and polished marble pillars, gold-embroidered drapes, an inlaid rosewood spinet delicate and tentative as a deer. Magnificent arched windows framed a triptych of the airy architecture of St Anthony's soaring motionless against an immaculate blue sky. Fracastoro looked about him, and with a shrug waved his hand in a vague helpless gesture of apology. How many generations of aristocratic breeding had been necessary, Nicolas wondered, to produce that patrician indifference and ease? He shrank back into his black cloak, a lean grey troubled soul suddenly aching with envy of this young man's confidence and carelessness, his disdain for the trivial trappings of the world. They stood a while in silence by the window, gazing out at the sunlit city and listening to the morning noises that rose to them from the street below, the rattle of cane shutters, rumbling of the watercart, the breadman's harsh cry. Nothing happened, they said nothing, but forever afterwards, even when much else had faded, Nicolas was to remember that moment with extraordinary vividness as marking the true beginning of their friendship.

There was a sound behind them, and Girolamo turned and said:

'Ah, here you are, you dreadful dog.'

It was the handsome young man from the bedroom. He stood in the doorway clad only in his shirt, scratching his head and gazing at them blearily. His name was Tadziu or Tadzio, Nicolas did not catch it clearly; it hardly mattered, since he was never to see him again. After that first morning he disappeared mysteriously, and Girolamo did not mention him save once, a long time afterwards. They spoke together rapidly now in a dialect that Nicolas did not understand, and the boy shrugged and went away. Girolamo turned to his guest with a smile. 'I must apologise: apparently there is no food. But we shall have something presently.' He began to glance idly through a disorderly mass of papers overflowing a small ornate table, looking up at Nicolas now and then with a quizzical, faintly amused expression, seeming each time about to speak but yet remaining silent. At last he laughed, and throwing up his hands said helplessly:

'I do not know what to say!'

Nicolas would not look at him; he knew what he meant.

'Nor I,' he murmured, confused and suddenly happy. 'Nor I!'

Tadziu or Tadzio returned then, with a steaming loaf of bread under his arm, and in one hand a magnum of champagne, in the other a platter covered with a napkin which Girolamo lifted gingerly to reveal a greasy mess of griddle cakes. 'O disgusting, disgusting!' he cried, laughing, and they sat down and began to eat. Girolamo's handsome young friend bent on Nicolas bitterly a dark unwavering glare. But Nicolas refused to be intimidated; he had been light-headed already from lack of sleep, but now the champagne and the warm brown stink of the bread and the griddle cakes befuddled him entirely. He was happy.

'Come,' said Girolamo, 'tell us your famous theory of the planets.'

Yes, yes, he was happy!

*

But happiness was an inadequate word for the transformation that he underwent that summer – for it was no less than a transformation. His heart thawed. A great soft inexpressible something swelled within him, and there were moments when he felt that this rapture must burst forth, that his cloak would fly open to reveal a huge grotesque foolish gaudy flower sprouting comically from his breast. It was ridiculous, but that was all right; he dared to be ridiculous. He fell in love with the city, its limpid mornings, burning noons, evenings in the piazzas loud with birds, that city fraught now with secret significances. Never again without a unique pang of anguished tenderness would he walk through the market, or stand upon the Ponte San Giorgio at dawn, or smell at the streetcorner stalls the rank humble pungency of frying griddle cakes.

Yet behind all this fine frenzy there was the fear that it could destroy him, for surely it was a kind of sickness. In his studies he thought he might find an antidote. He read Plato in the Greek, and reread Nicolas Cusanus and Ptolemy's *Almagest*, which last by now he almost knew by heart. He took up again those texts to which Novara had introduced him, and plunged once more into the thickets of the translation of Trismegistus that Ficino had made for Lorenzo de' Medici. But it was useless, he could not concentrate, and rushed out and strode through the deserted noonday streets under the throbbing plane trees, distraught and alarmed, until his legs of their own volition brought him to the Palazzo Antonini and that disordered room overlooking the basilica, where Girolamo smiled at him sleepily and said:

'Why, my friend, what is it? You look quite crazed.'

'I am too old for this, too old!'

'For what?'

'All this: you, Italy, everything. Too old!'

'An old greybeard you are, yes, of twice ten years and eight! Come, uncle, sit here. You should not go out in the sun, you know.'

'It is not the sun!'

'No; you are altogether too much a Prussian, too sceptical and cold. You must learn to treasure yourself more dearly.'

'Nonsense.'

'But—'

'Nonsense!'

Girolamo stretched himself and yawned.

'Very well, uncle,' he mumbled, 'but it is siesta time now,' and he laid his head down on the couch beside his friend and smiling fell asleep at once. Nicolas gazed at him, and wrung his hands. I am besotted with him, besotted!

*

He was captive to a willing foolishness. Those concerns that up to now he had held to be serious, and worthy of serious considerations, he had with lunatic lightheartedness abandoned; but they had not abandoned him, no, they waited in the outer darkness, gnashing their teeth, ready to come back at him and have a fourfold revenge, he knew it. He knew, but could not care. Had he not liberated himself at last from the pinched mean hegemony of the intellect? Had he not at last set free the physical man that all his life had waited within him for release? The senses now would have their day; they deserved it. Yet strangely, the body whose bonds he had cast off seemed not to know what to do with its newfound liberty. Like a starved stark loony released after years in the dungeons, it reeled about drunkenly in the unaccustomed light, sweating and dribbling, tripping over itself, a gangling spidery pale fork of flesh and fur, faintly repellent, faintly comical, wholly absurd.

Absurd, absurd: he remembered Ferrara particularly, and the day of his conferring.

*

It was for reasons of economy – or stinginess, according to Girolamo – that Nicolas chose to take his doctorate in canon law other than at Padua, for even the most solitary of graduates would find himself surrounded by hitherto unknown friends when the conferring ceremony, and more especially the lavish banquet he would be expected to provide afterwards, were at hand. Nicolas had no intention of allowing a gang of sots to stupefy themselves with drink at his expense, and therefore, although it was a far less prestigious institution than Padua, and he had never studied there, he applied for graduation to the University of Ferrara, and was accepted, and in the autumn of the year travelled south accompanied by Girolamo.

The ritual of conferring took a full week to complete. It was a horrible business. The promoter assigned to him by the college was one Alberti, a harassed apologetic canon lawyer with a limp and a wild fuzz of prematurely grey hair that stood out from his narrow skull like an exclamation of alarm. During a class of his once a student had been stabbed to death while he lectured on oblivious. Nicolas liked him; he was of the same sad endearing tribe as Abstemius of Włocławek.

'Well now, Herr Kupperdik, here is the drill. Firstly I take you before an assembly of doctors to whom you will swear that you have been through the proper course et cetera, which ha ha you have, I take it? The reverend gentlemen will set you two passages of law, and we retire together to study them. It is all a sham, of course, since I know already what the passages will be – I should be a poor promoter if I didn't, eh, Herr Kopperdyke? Anyway, after a decent absence we return, the doctors question you, they ballot, and you are made a licentiate. All that remains then is for you to take the public examination for your full doctorate, but that is merely a formality after the oral test, which as I said is really a formality also. And there you are: *Doctor Popperdink!* Nothing to it!'

But of course it was not so simple. Alberti got the set passages mixed, and coached Nicolas, with admirable diligence, in those intended for another graduate, and on the day of the inquisition Nicolas spent a frantic hour in a hot antechamber, while the doctors fretted next door, trying to memorise the new answers and at the same time block out the distracting apologies of his mortified promoter. The examiners, however, seemed to have had some experience already of Alberti's organisational powers. It was apparent that they cared less about the indifferent quality of Nicolas's performance than they did about the fact that the ritual had not been strictly adhered to. They voted, mumbling among themselves, fixed Alberti with a crushing glare, and having announced the result of the examination rose and swept away amid an outraged rustling of gowns. Nicolas, drenched with sweat, closed his eyes and lowered his burning face gently into his hands. His promoter leapt at him and began to thump him on the back in a transport of relief, almost knocking him off his chair. 'Congratulations, my dear fellow, congratulations!' Throughout, Nicolas had been able to think of one thing only: the reception he would get from Uncle Lucas if he returned to Ermland without his doctorate. 'Herr Poppernik? Are you unwell?'

Girolamo laughed, of course, when he heard of the affair, and then sat in silence, pale and distant, while Nicolas poured over him the scalding bitter brew of the day's pent-up frustration and rage. And that night along with Alberti they went down to the stews and got vilely drunk in the company of a band of shrieking whores.

The week rolled on inexorably, like a giant engine gone out of control and disintegrating, flinging bits of itself in all directions, bombarding Nicolas, the innocent bystander, with spokes and broken ratchets and gouts of thick black oil. On Sunday the contraption exploded finally, with a deafening report. Arriving at the cathedral for the conferring, he halted in the porch, horror-stricken. 'Jesus, what's this?' The place was full of students, hundreds of them, they were even squatting on the steps of the high altar. Alberti turned to him with a bland enquiring smile. 'Yes, *Doctor*?' He had taken to using that title at every opportunity, with a proprietary rib-nudging roguishness that made Nicolas want to strike him very hard with his fist.

'This crowd!' he cried. 'What does it mean? I came to Ferrara to avoid just this kind of thing!'

Alberti was puzzled; a true Italian, he thrived on crowds and clamour.

'But the students always come to hear the orations,' he said mildly. 'It is the custom.'

'God!'

Girolamo was studiously inspecting the architecture, with the solemn look of one shaking inwardly with laughter. He was got up for the occasion in a quilted scarlet doublet and tight black hose, with a long white plume to his cap; like a damned peacock, Nicolas thought bitterly. Now without turning Girolamo murmured:

'It is for the comic possibilities that they come, I imagine?'

Alberti nodded enthusiastically. '*Si, si*, the comedy, just so.'

'*God*,' Nicolas groaned again, and, wrapping his gown about him tightly, plunged up the aisle to the pulpit. On the narrow steps he trod upon the liripipe dangling from his neck and almost throttled himself. A sea of rapturous expectant faces greeted him as he peered apprehensively over the brim of the pulpit. Someone at the back of the nave whistled a piercing heraldic flourish, provoking an uproar of catcalls and applause. Nicolas fished about under his gown for the text of his oration. For one appalling moment he thought . . . but no, he had not left it behind, it was there, though in a dreadful jumble that his shaking hands at once made worse.

'*Reverendissimi . . .*'

The rest of his opening address was drowned by shouts and a stamping of feet, and he stopped, quite lost. Alberti and Girolamo, sitting below him, leaned forward with their hands cupped around their mouths and together cried: '*They cannot hear you!*' After a time some semblance of order returned, and he stuck out his neck like an enraged tortoise and hurled his text at them as if it were an execration. His argument was a defence of the canonical interdict on marriage between a widow and her brother-in-law; it was a purely formal declaration of an accepted doctrine, upon which his audience in like formality was meant to challenge him, but he suspected, rightly as it happened, that these turbulent students had no intention of playing by the rules. Even before he had finished, a dozen of them or more were on their feet, howling abuse at him and at each other amid a general hilarity. He tried to discern even some halfway sensible objection to the contents of his text, but in vain, for his tormentors were mouthing merely nonsense, or obscenities, or both at once, and like a large rag doll being fought over by children he bounced about in the pulpit, throwing up his arms, grinning, opening and closing his mouth in mute helplessness and pain. Never in his life had he known such an exquisite agony of embarrassment.

At length they lost interest in him, and as the uproar subsided and they began to look about for the entrance of a fresh victim, he scrambled shakily down from the pulpit. He was grabbed at once by a pair of burly vestrymen with cruelly barbered skulls, who marched him off smartly to a side altar and thrust him into the master's chair. There he was presented with the cap, the book and the gold ring and the graduate's diploma, and Alberti, with the lunatic intensity of a father crazed with pride, his wild hair bristling, advanced limping and planted on his cheek a tacky garlic-scented kiss of peace.

'*Ave magister!*' he cried; and then, unable to restrain himself, he added rapturously: '*Doctor* Peppernik!'

As if from a distance Nicolas looked in anguished amusement at himself, a dazed grotesque figure with cap askew, full of irredeemable foolishness, a lord of misrule propped upon a pretender's throne. Italy had done this to him, Italy and all that Italy signified. Girolamo came forward to kiss him, but he turned his cheek away.

* * *

THE WEATHER WAS BAD that spring, rain and gales for weeks and the muttering of thunder in the mountains. Great fortresses of black cloud rumbled westward ceaselessly, and Lake Garda boiled in leaden rage. This tumult in the air seemed to Nicolas an omen, though what it might signify he could not say. He arrived with Girolamo at the villa at dusk, wet and weary and dispirited. The big old timber and stone house was set among tall cypresses on a steep hill overlooking Incaffi and the lake. It had the look of money about it. There was a spacious courtyard paved with rough-cut marble, and busts of the Caesars set on marble plinths; wide stone steps swept up to a pillared entrance. He had expected something far more modest than this.

'Will your family be here?' he asked, unable to conceal his apprehension.

'Why no,' said Girolamo, 'they are in Verona. They live there. We do not agree, and so I seldom see them. This is my house.'

'O.'

The Italian laughed. 'Come now, my friend, do not look so alarmed. There will be no one here but you and I.'

'I did not think you were so—'

'—Rich? Does it trouble you?'

'No; why should it?'

'Then for God's sake stop cringing!' he snapped, and slapping his riding gloves against his thigh he turned and strode up the steps to the vestibule, where the servants were gathered to welcome their master. There was a dozen of them or more, from young girls to grey old men. They looked at Nicolas in silence stonily, and all at once he was acutely aware of his shabbiness, his cracked boots and few poor bits of baggage, the decrepit mare trying not to fall over out in the courtyard behind him. We know your kind, those eyes told him, we have seen you come and go many times before, in different versions but all essentially the same. And he wondered how many others there had been . . .

Girolamo impatiently performed his signorial duty, pacing up and down the line of attentive servants with a fixed false smile, questioning each one in turn in a detached formal voice on their health and that of their parents or children. And what news of the estate? Everything was in order? Splendid, splendid. Nicolas looked on with envy. At twenty, Girolamo had the ageless self-assurance of the aristocrat. He dropped his wet cloak and gloves on the floor, from whence they were immediately and reverently snatched up by one of the maids, and throwing himself down into a chair he motioned the steward, a bent old gouty brute, to help him off with his boots. He looked up at Nicolas and smiled faintly.

'Well, my friend?' he said.

'What?'

'*Caro Nicolo.*'

They sat down in a richly appointed dining-room to an elaborate veal and champagne supper. A candelabrum of Venetian glass glistened above their heads, its gaudy splendours reflected deep in the dark pool of the polished table on which there sailed a fleet of handcrafted gold and silver serving dishes. The room was hushed, suspended in stillness, except where their bone knives and delicate forks stabbed and sliced the silence above their plates with tiny deft ferocity. Everywhere that Nicolas looked he encountered the Fracastoro monogram, intricately graven in gold-leaf on the dishes and the cruets, woven into the napkins, even carved on the facings and reredos of the vast black marble fireplace.

'Tell me,' he said, 'how many such establishments as this do you keep up?'

'O, not many; the apartments in Verona, where my books are, and a house in Rome. And of course there is a hunting lodge in the mountains, which we must visit, if the weather clears. Why do you ask?'

'Curiosity.'

'Are you still brooding on my unsuspected wealth? It is not so great as you seem to imagine. You are too easily impressed.'

'Yes.'

'Are you glad you came here?'

'Yes.'

'Is that all you can say?'

'What would you have me say? Indeed, my liege, my humble thanks, sweet lord, I am overwhelmed.' He ground his teeth. 'Forgive me, I am tired from the journey, and out of sorts. Forgive me.'

Girolamo gazed at him mildly, more in curiosity it seemed than anger or hurt.

'No, it is my fault,' he said. 'I should not have brought you here. We were happier on neutral ground – or should I say, we were *happy*?' He smiled. 'For we are not happy now, are we?'

'Does happiness seem to you the greatest good?'

At that the Italian laughed. 'Come, Nicolas, none of your sham philosophising, not with me. Do you hate me for my wealth and privilege?'

'Hate?' He was genuinely shocked, and a little frightened. 'I do not hate you. I . . . do not hate you. I am happy to be here, in your—'

'Then do you love me?'

He was sweating. Girolamo continued to gaze at him, with fondness, and amusement, and regret.

'I am happy to be here, in your house; I am grateful, I am glad we came.' He realised suddenly that even yet they did not call each other *thou*. 'Perhaps,' he stammered, 'perhaps the weather will clear tomorrow . . .'

*

But the weather did not clear, in the world nor in the villa. Nicolas stormed, wrapped in a black silence. His rage had no one cause, not that he could discover, but bubbled up, a poisonous vapour, out of a mess of boiling emotions. He felt constantly slighted, by Girolamo, by the smirking servants, even by the villa itself, whose sumptuous sybaritic splendours reminded him that it was accustomed to entertaining aristocrats, while he was what Novara had said, a mere tradesman's son. Yet was he in reality being thus sorely scorned? Was he not, in discerning, indeed in cultivating this contempt all round him, merely satisfying some strange hunger within him? It was as if he were being driven to add more and more knots to a lash wielded by his own hand. It was as if he were beating himself into submission, cleansing himself, preparing himself: but for what? He hungered, obscenely, obscurely, as under the lash his flesh flinched, went cold and dead, and at last out of a wracked humiliated body his mind soared slowly upward, into the blue.

Now he saw at last how the plot had been hatching in secret for years, the plot that had brought him without his willing it to this moment of recognition and acceptance; or rather, he had not been brought, had not been made to move at all, but had simply stood and waited while the trivia and the foolishness were shorn away. The Church had offered him a quiet living, the universities had offered academic success, Italy had even offered love. Any or all of these gifts might have seduced him, had not the hideousness intervened to demonstrate the poverty of what they had to offer. At Frauenburg among the doddering canons he had been appalled by the stink of celibacy and clerkly caution. Ferrara had been a farce. Now Italy was making of him an anguished grimacing clown. The Church, academe, love: nothing. Seared and purified, shorn of the encumbering lumber of life, he stood at last like a solitary pine that stands in a wilderness of snow, aching upward fiercely into the sky of fire and ice that was the true concern of the essential selfhood that had eluded him always until now. Beware of these enigmas, Canon Wodka had warned him, for they cannot teach us how to live. But he did not wish to live, not by lessons that the world would teach him.

He had often before retreated into science as a refuge from the ghastliness of life; thus, he saw now, he had made a plaything of science, by demanding from it comfort and consolation. There would be no more of that, no more play. Here was no retreat, but the conscious accepting, on its own terms, of a cold harrowing discipline. Yet even astronomy was not the real issue. He had not spent his life pursuing a vision down the corridors of pain and loneliness in order merely to become a stargazer. No: astronomy was but the knife. What he was after was the deeper, the deepest thing: the kernel, the essence, the true.

*

Rain fell without cease. The world streamed. Lamps were lit at noon, and a great fire of pine logs burned day and night in the main hall. Outside, black phantom cypresses shuddered in the wind.

'The villagers have gone back to the old ways,' Girolamo said. 'Christ-come-lately is abandoned, and the ancient cults are revived. Now they are praying to Mercury to carry their appeals to the gods of fair weather.'

They were at table. They dined now four or five times a day. Eating had become a sullen joyless obsession: they fed their guts incessantly in a vain effort to dull the pangs of a hunger that no food would assuage. The tender flesh of fish was as ash in Nicolas's mouth. He was pained by Girolamo's gentle puzzled attempts to reach out to him across the chasm that had opened between them, but it was a vague pain, hardly much more than an irritant, and becoming vaguer every day. He nodded absently. 'Curious.'

'What? What is curious? Tell me.'

'O, nothing. They are praying to Mercury, you say; but I am thinking that Mercury is the Hermes of the Greeks, who in turn is the Egyptian Thoth, whose wisdom was handed down to us, through the priests of the Nile, by Hemmes Trismegistus. Therefore by a roundabout way your villagers are praying to that magus.' He looked up mildly. 'Is that not curious?'

'The fisherfolk cannot work in this weather,' Girolamo said. 'Three of their men have been lost on the lake.'

'Yes? But then fishermen are always being drowned. It is, so to speak, what they are for. All things, and all men, however humble, have their part to play in the great scheme.'

'That is somewhat heartless, surely?'

'Would you not say *honest*, rather? This sudden concern of yours comes strangely from one who lives by the labour of the common people. Look at this fish here, so impeccably prepared, so tastefully arranged: has it not occurred to you that those fishermen may have perished so that you might sit down to this splendid dinner?'

Guido, the stooped steward, paused in his quaking progress

around the table and peered at him intently. Girolamo had turned pale about the lips, but he smiled and said only:

'Do I deserve this, Nicolas, really? – Guido, you may go now, thank you.' The old man departed with a dazed look, shocked and amazed it seemed at the suggestion that his master should concern himself with *housekeeping*. Girolamo's hand trembled as he poured the wine. 'Must you make a fool of me before the servants?'

Nicolas put down his knife and laughed. 'You see? You are less anxious for the fate of fishermen than for the good opinion of your servants!'

'You twist everything I say, everything!' Suddenly the Italian's poise had collapsed entirely, and for a moment he was a spoilt petulant boy. Nicolas, intensely gratified, smiled with his teeth. He watched the other closely, with a kind of detached curiosity, wondering if he might be about to break down and weep in fury and frustration. But Girolamo did not weep, and sighed instead and murmured: 'What do you want from me, Nicolas, more than I have already given?'

'Why nothing, my dear friend, nothing at all.' But that was not true: he wanted something, he did not know precisely what, but something large, vivid, outrageous – violence perhaps, terrible insult, a hideous blood-boltered wounding that would leave them both whimpering in final irremediable humiliation. Both, yes. There must be no victor. They must destroy each other, that is, that part of each that was in the other, for only by mutual destruction would he be freed. He understood none of this, he was too crazed with rage and impatience to try to understand, nevertheless he knew it to be valid. Frantically he cast about for a further weapon to thrust into the shuddering flesh. 'My theory is almost complete, you know,' he said, shouted almost, with a kind of ghastly constricted cheerfulness.

Girolamo glanced up uneasily. 'Your theory?'

'Yes yes, my theory of planetary motion, my refutation of Ptolemy. Ptolemy . . .' He seemed to gag on the name. 'Have I not told you about it? Let me tell you about it. Ptolemy, you see—'

'Nicolas.'

'—Ptolemy, you see, misled us, or we misled ourselves, it hardly matters which, into believing that the *Almagest* is an explanation, a representation – *vorstellung*, you know the German term? – for what is real, but the truth is, the truth is that Ptolemaic astronomy is nothing so far as existence is concerned; it is only convenient for computing the nonexistent.' He paused, panting. 'What?'

Girolamo shook his head. 'Nothing. Tell me about your theory.'

'You do not believe it, do you? I mean you do not think that I am capable of formulating a theory which shall reveal the eternal truths of the universe; you do not believe that I am capable of greatness. *Do you?*'

'Perhaps, Nicolas, it is better to be good than great?'

'*You do not believe!*—'

'—I believe that if there are eternal truths, and I am not convinced of it, then they can only be known, but not expressed.' He smiled. 'And I believe that you and I should not fight.'

'You! You you you – I amuse you, do I not? I am kept for the fine sport I provide: what matter if it rain, Koppernigk will cut a merry caper and keep us in good spirits.' He had leapt up from the table, and was prancing furiously about the room in what indeed looked like a grotesque comic dervish dance of pain and loathing. 'O, he's a jolly fellow, old Koppernigk, old Nuncle Nick!' Girolamo would not look at him, and at last, trembling, he sat down again and held his face in his hands.

They were silent. Greenish rainlight draped them about. The trees beyond the window throbbed and thrashed. Presently Girolamo said:

'You wrong me, Nicolas; I have never laughed at you. We are made differently. I cannot take the world so seriously as you do. It is a lack in me, perhaps. But I am not the dunderhead you like to think me. Have you ever, once, shown even the mildest interest in *my* concerns? I am a physician, that I take seriously. My work on contagion, the spread of diseases, this is not without value. Medicine is a science of the tangible, you see. I deal with what is here, with what ails men; if I were to discover thereby one of your eternal truths, why, I think I should not notice having done it. Are you listening? I express it badly, I know, but I am trying to teach you something. But then, I suppose you cannot believe that I am capable of teaching you anything. It is no matter. Do you want to know what I am currently embarked upon? I am writing a poem – yes, a poem – dealing with the pox! But you do not want to know, do you? Remember, Nicolas, the morning we met in the market place in Padua? I told you I was returning from a debauch; not so. I had gone there to study the methods of sanitation, or I should say the lack of such, in the meat market. Yes, laugh—' It had been hardly a laugh, rather a hollow retching noise. '—How prosaic, you will say, how comic even. That is why I lied to you that morning. You wanted me to be a rake, a rich wastrel, something utterly different from yourself: a happy fool. And I obliged you. I have been lying ever since. So you see, Nicolas, you are not the only one who fears to be thought dull, who is afraid to be ridiculous.' He paused. 'Love . . .' It was as if he were turning up the word gingerly with the toe of his shoe to see what outlandish things might be squirming underneath. 'You drove Tadzio away.' There was no trace of accusation in his tone, only sadness, and a faint wonderment. Nicolas, still cowering behind his hands, ground his teeth until they ached. He was in pain, he thought it was pain, until late that night when the word was redefined for him, and *pain* took on a wholly new meaning. Girolamo's door was ajar, and there were sounds, awful, vaguely familiar. The scene was illuminated by the faint flickering light of an untrimmed lamp, and in a mirror on the far wall all was eerily repeated in miniature. Girolamo with his long legs splayed was sitting on the edge of the bed with his head thrown back and his lips open in an O of ecstasy, a grotesque and yet mysteriously lovely stranger, his blurred gaze fixed sightlessly on the shadowy ceiling. Ah! he cried softly, Ah! and suddenly his body seemed to buckle, and reaching out with frenzied fingers he grasped by the hair the serving girl kneeling before him and plunged his shuddering cock into her mouth. Look! The girl squirmed, moaning and gagging. Girolamo twined his legs about her thighs. Thus, locked together in that monstrous embrace like some hideous exhibit in a bestiary, they began to rock slowly back and forth, and with them the whole room seemed to writhe and sway crazily in the shaking lamplight. Nicolas shut his eyes. When he opened them again it was finished. Girolamo gazed at him with a look of mingled desolation and defiance, and of utter finality. The slattern turned away and spat into the darkness. Nicolas retreated, and closed the door softly.

*

Nothing less than a new and radical instauration would do, if astronomy was to mean more than itself. It was this latter necessity that had obsessed him always, and now more than ever. Astronomy was entirely sufficient unto itself: it saved the phenomena, it explained the inexistent. That was no longer enough, not for Nicolas at least. The closed system of the science must be broken, in order that it might transcend itself and its own sterile concerns, and thus become an instrument for verifying the real rather than merely postulating the possible. He considered this recognition, of the need to restate the basic function of cosmography, to be his first contribution of value to science; it was his manifesto, as it were, and also a vindication of his right to speak and be heard.

A new beginning, then, a new science, one that would be objective, open-minded, above all honest, a beam of stark cold light trained unflinchingly upon the world as it is and not as men, out of a desire for reassurance or mathematical elegance or whatever, wished it to be: that was his aim. It was to be achieved only through the formulation of a sound theory of planetary motion, he saw that clearly now. Before, he had naturally assumed that the new methods and procedures must be devised first, that they would be the tools with which to build the theory; that, of course, was to miss the essential point, namely, that the birth of the new science must be preceded by a radical act of creation. Out of nothing, next to nothing, disjointed bits and scraps, he would have to weld together an explanation of the phenomena. The enormity of the problem terrified him, yet he knew that it was that problem and nothing less that he had to solve, for his intuition told him so, and he trusted his intuition – he must, since it was all he had.

Night after night in the villa during that tempestuous spring he groaned and sweated over his calculations, while outside the storm boomed and bellowed, tormenting the world. His dazed brain reeled, slipping and skidding in a frantic effort to marshal into some semblance of order the amorphous and apparently irreconcilable fragments of fact and speculation and fantastic dreaming. He knew that he was on the point of breaking through, he knew it; time and time over he leapt up from his work, laughing like a madman and tearing his hair, convinced that he had found the solution, only to sink down again a moment later, with a stricken look, having detected the flaw. He feared he would go mad, or fall ill, yet he could not rest, for if he once let go his fierce hold, the elaborate scaffolding he had so painfully erected would fall asunder; and also, of course, should his concentration falter he would find himself sucked once more into the quag of that other unresolved problem of Girolamo.

And then at last it came to him, sauntered up behind him, as it were, humming happily, and tapped him on the shoulder, wanting to know the cause of all the uproar. He had woken at dawn out of a coma of exhaustion into an immediate, almost lurid wakefulness. It was as if the channels of his brain had been sluiced with an icy drench of water. Involuntarily he began to think at once, in a curiously detached and yet wholly absorbed fashion that was, he supposed later, a unique miraculous objectivity, of the two seemingly unconnected propositions, which he had formulated long before, in Bologna or even earlier, that were the solidest of the few building blocks he had so far laid for the foundation of his theory: that the Sun, and not Earth, is at the centre of the world, and secondly that the world is far more vast than Ptolemy or anyone else had imagined. The wind was high. Rain beat upon the window. He rose in the dawning grey gloom and lifted aside the drapes. Clouds were breaking to the east over a sullen waterscape. Calmly then it came, the solution, like a magnificent great slow golden bird alighting in his head with a thrumming of vast wings. It was so simple, so ravishingly simple, that at first he did not recognise it for what it was.

He had been attacking the problem all along from the wrong direction. Perhaps his training at the hands of cautious schoolmen was to blame. No sooner had he realised the absolute necessity for a creative leap than his instincts without his knowing had thrown up their defences against such a scandalous notion, thrusting him back into the closed system of worn-out orthodoxies. There, like a blind fool, he had sought to arrive at a new destination by travelling the old routes, had thought to create an original theory by means of conventional calculations. Now in this dawn, how or why he did not know, his brain, without his help or knowledge, as it were, had made that leap that he had not had the nerve to risk, and out there, in the silence and utter emptiness of the blue, had done all that it was necessary to do, had combined those two simple but momentous propositions and identified with impeccable logic the consequences of that combining. Of course, of course. Why had he not thought of it before? If the Sun is conceived as the centre of an immensely expanded universe, then those observed phenomena of planetary motion that had baffled astronomers for millennia became perfectly rational and necessary. Of course! The verification of the theory, he knew, would take weeks, months, years perhaps, to complete, but that was nothing, that was mere hackwork. What mattered was not the propositions, but the combining of them: *the act of creation.* He turned the solution this way and that, admiring it, as if he were turning in his fingers a flawless ravishing jewel. It was the thing itself, the vivid thing.

He crawled back to bed, exhausted now. He felt like a very worn old man. The shining clarity of a moment ago was all gone.

He needed sleep, days and days of sleep. However, no sooner had he laid down than he was up again, scrabbling eagerly at the drapes. He thrust his face against the stippled glass, peering toward the east, but the clouds had gathered again, and there was to be no sun, that day.

*

Girolamo and he said their farewells in a filthy little inn by the lakeshore; it seemed best to part on neutral ground. They could think of nothing to say, and sat in silence uneasily over an untouched jar of wine amid the reek of piss and the rancid catty stink of spilt beer. Through a tiny grimed window above their heads they watched the thunderclouds massing over the lake.

'*Caro Nicolo.*'

'My friend.'

But they were only words. Nicolas was impatient to be away. He was returning to Prussia; Italy had been used up. Go! he told himself, go now, and abruptly he rose, wearing his death's-head grin. Girolamo looked up at him with a faint smile. 'Farewell then, uncle.' And as Nicolas turned, something of the past came back, and he realised that once, not long ago, there had been nothing in the world more precious than this young man's reserved, somehow passionately detached presence by his side. He went out quickly, into the wind and the gauzy warm rain, and mounted up. Riding away from Incaffi was like riding away from Italy herself. He was leaving behind him a world that had begun and ended, that was complete, and immune to change. What had been, was still, in his memory. Someday, fleeing from some extremity of anguish or of pain, his spirit would return to this bright place and find it all intact. The ghostly voices rose up at his back. *Do thyself no harm!* they cried, *for we are all here!*

II

Magister Ludi

WATERBORNE HE COMES, at dead of night, sliding sleek on the river's gleaming back, snout lifted, sniffing, under the drawbridge, the portcullis, past the drowsing sentry. Brief scrabble of claws on the slimed steps below the wall, brief glint of a bared tooth. In the darkness for an instant an intimation of agony and anguish, and the night flinches. Now he scales the wall, creeps under the window, grinning. In the shadow of the tower he squats, wrapped in a black cloak, waiting for dawn. Comes the knocking, the pinched voice, the sly light step on the stair, and how is it that I alone can hear the water dripping at his heels?

One that would speak with you, Canon.

No! No! Keep him hence! But he will not be denied. He drags himself into the corner where night's gloom still clings, and there he hangs, watching. At times he laughs softly, at others lets fall a sob. His face is hidden in his cloak, all save the eyes, but I recognise him well enough, how would I not? He is the ineffable thing. He is ineluctable. He is the world's worst. Let me be, can't you!

*

Canon Koppernigk arrived at Heilsberg as night came on, bone-weary, wracked by fever, a black bundle slumped in the saddle of the starved nag that someone somewhere along the way had tricked him into buying. He had set out from Torun that morning, and travelled without pause all day, fearful of facing, prostrate in a rat-infested inn, the gross fancies conjured up by this sickness boiling in his blood. Now he could hardly understand that the journey was over, hardly knew where he was. It seemed to him that, borne thither on the surge and sway of waters, he had run aground on a strange dark shore. There were stars already, but no moon, and torches smoking high up on the walls. Off to the left a fire burned, tended by still figures, some squatting wrapped in cloaks and others with halberds leaning at watch. The river sucked and slopped, talking to itself as it ran. All this appeared disjointed and unreal. It was as if in his sickness he could apprehend only the weird underside of things, while the real, the significant world was beyond his fevered understanding. A rat, caught in a chance reflection of firelight from the river, scuttled up the slimed steps below the wall and vanished.

He was shaken roughly, and heard himself, as from a great distance, groan. Maximilian, his manservant, gnawing an onion, scowled up at him, mumbling.

'What? What do you say?' The servant only shrugged, and gestured toward the gate. A peasant's cart with a broken axle straddled the drawbridge. In the half-light it had the look of a huge malign frog. 'Go on, go on,' the Canon said. 'There is room enough.'

But they were forced to pass perilously close to the edge. He peered down at the glittering black water, and felt dizzy. How fast it runs! The carter was belabouring with a stick in mute fury the impassive mule standing trapped between the shafts. Max blessed the fellow gravely, and sniggered. From this hole in the gate-tower a sentry shambled sleepily forth.

'State your business, strangers.'

Max, the good German, waxed immediately indignant, to be addressed thus loutishly in the outlandish jabber of a native Prussian, a barbarian, beneath contempt. Imperiously he announced: 'Doctor Copernicus!' and made to march on. The Prussian poked him perfunctorily in the belly with his blunt lance.

'Nicolas Koppernigk,' the Canon said hastily, 'liegeman to our Lord Bishop. Let us pass now, please, good fellow, and you shall have a penny.' Max looked up at him, and he perceived, not for the first time and yet with wonder still, the peculiar mixture of love and loathing his servant bore for him.

In the deserted courtyard his horse's hoofs rang frostily and clear upon the flagstones. The hounds began to bay. He lifted his throbbing eyes to the pillared arches of the galleries, to the lowering mass of the castle keep faintly slimed with starlight, and thought how like a prison the place appeared. Heilsberg was intended to be his home now; not even Prussia itself was that, any longer.

'Max.'

'*Ja, ja,*' the servant growled, stamping off. 'I know – the Bishop must not be disturbed. I know!'

Then there were lights, and voices close by in the darkness, and a decrepit half-blind old woman came and led him inside, scolding him, not unkindly, as though he were an errant child. He had not been expected until the morrow. A fire of birchwood burned on the hearth in the great main hall, where a pallet had been laid for him. He was glad to be spared the stairs, for his limbs were liquid. The fever was mounting again, and he trembled violently. He lay down at once and pulled his cloak tight about him. Max and the old woman began to bicker. Max was jealous of her authority.

'Master, she says your nuncle must be summoned, with you sick and arriving unexpected.'

'No no,' the Canon groaned, 'please, no.' And, in a whisper, with a graveyard laugh: 'O keep him hence!'

The old woman babbled on, but he closed his eyes and she went away at last, grumbling. Max squatted beside him and began to whistle softly through his teeth.

'Max – Max I am ill.'

'Aye. I seen it coming. And I warned you. Didn't I say we should have stopped at Allenstein for the night? But you would none of it, and now you're sicker than a dog.'

'Yes yes, you were right.' Max was a good cure for self-pity. 'You were quite right.' He could not sleep. Even his hair seemed to pulse with pain. The sickness was a keepsake of Italy; he smiled wryly at the thought. Long shadows pranced like crazed things upon the walls. A dog came to sniff at him, its snout fastidiously twitching, but Max growled, and the creature pricked up its ears and loped away. Canon Koppernigk gazed into the fire. The flames sang a little song whose melody was just beyond grasping. 'Max?'

'Aye.'

Still there: a lean bundle of bones and sinew crouched in the firelight, staring narrowly at nothing. The hound returned and settled down unmolested beside them, licked its loins with relish, slept. The Canon touched the soiled coarse fur with his fingertips. Suddenly he was comforted by common things, the fire's heat, this flea-bitten dog, Max's bitter regard, and beyond these the campfire too, and the watchers about it, the peasant's cart, the poor fastidious mule, even that rat on the steps: enduring things, brutish and bloody and warm, out of which, however dark and alien the shore, the essential self assembles a makeshift home.

Later that night Bishop Lucas came and looked at him, and shook his great head gloomily. 'A fine physician I have appointed!'

*

That title meant little. He was no true medic. He had not sufficient faith in the art of healing, nor in himself as a healer. At Padua they had taught him to cut up corpses very prettily, but that would have made him a better butcher than physician. Yet he had accepted the post without protest. On returning from Italy he had gone straight to Frauenburg, thinking to take up his duties as a canon of the Chapter; but he was not ready yet for that life, Italy was too much in his blood, and having secured with ease yet another, this time indefinite, leave of absence he had drifted to Torun. Katharina and her husband, after protracted negotiations, had bought from the Bishop the old house in St Anne's Lane, and had moved there from Cracow. He should have known better than to go to them, of course. The company of his shrewish sister and her blustering mate irked him; they for their part made him less than welcome. He had engaged Max more as an ally than a servant, for he was a match indeed for that ill-tempered sullen household.

Then word came from the Bishop: Canon Nicolas was summoned at once to Heilsberg as physician-in-residence at the castle, that he might thus, however inadequately, repay the expense of his years of Italian studies.

He liked the job well enough. Medicine was a means of concealment, whereby he might come at his true concerns obliquely and by stealth: to unsuspecting eyes there was not much difference between a star table and an apothecary's prescription, a geometrical calculation and a horoscope. But although he was free to work, he felt that he was trapped at Heilsberg, trapped and squirming, a grey old rat. He was thirty-three; his teeth were going. Once life had been an intense bright dream awaiting him elsewhere, beyond the disappointment of ordinary days, but now when he looked to that place once occupied by that gorgeous golden bowl of possibilities he saw only a blurred dark something with damaged limbs swimming toward him. It was not death, but something far less distinguished. It was, he supposed, failure. Each day it came a little nearer, and each day he made its coming a little easier, for was not his work – that is, his true work, his astronomy – a process of progressive failing? He moved forward doggedly, line by painful line, calculation by defective calculation, watching in mute suspended panic his blundering pen pollute and maim those concepts that, unexpressed, had throbbed with limpid purity and beauty. It was barbarism on a grand scale. Mathematical edifices of heart-rending frailty and delicacy were shattered at a stroke. He had thought that the working out of his theory would be nothing, mere hackwork: well, that was somewhat true, for there was hacking indeed, bloody butchery. He crouched at his desk by the light of a guttering candle, and suffered: it was a kind of slow internal bleeding. Only vaguely did he understand the nature of his plight. It was not that the theory itself was faulty, but somehow it was being contaminated in the working out. There seemed to be lacking some essential connection. The universe of dancing planets was out there, and he was here, and between the two spheres mere words and figures on paper could not mediate. Someone had once said something similar: who was that, or when? What matter! He dipped his pen in ink. He bled.

And yet, paradoxically, he was happy, if that was the word. Despite the pain and the repeated disappointments, despite the emptiness of his grey life, there was not happiness anywhere in the world to compare with his rapturous grief.

But there was more to his post at Heilsberg than tending to the Bishop's boils and bowels and fallen arches: there was politics also. At sixty, and despite his numerous ailments, Bishop Lucas was far more vigorous than the nephew nearly half his age. A hard cold prince, a major man, he devoted the main part of his prodigious energies to the task of extricating Ermland from the monstrous web of European political intrigue. The Canon was not long at the castle before he discovered that, along with physician, secretary and general factotum, he was to be his uncle's co-conspirator as well. He was appalled. Politics baffled him. The ceaseless warring of states and princes seemed to him insane. He wanted no part in that raucous public world, and yet, aghast, like one falling, he watched himself being drawn into the arena.

He began to be noticed, at Prussian Diets, or on the autumn circuit of the Ermland cities, hanging back at the Bishop's side. He cultivated anonymity, yet his pale unsmiling face and drab black cloak, his silence, his very diffidence, served only to surround him with an aura of significance. Toadies and leeches sought him out, hung on his heels, waylaid him in corridors, grinning their grins, baring their sharp little teeth, imagining that they had in him a sure channel to the Bishop's favour. He took the petitions that they thrust at him on screwed-up bits of paper, and bent his ear intently to their whisperings, feeling a fool and a fraud. He could do nothing, he assured them, in a voice that even to him sounded entirely false, and realised with a sinking heart that he was making enemies across half of Europe. Pressures from all sides were brought to bear on him. His brother-in-law Bartholemew Gertner, that fervent patriot, stopped speaking to him after the Canon one day during his stay at Torun had refused to declare himself, by inclination if not strictly by birth, a true

German. Suddenly he was being called upon to question his very nationality! and he discovered that he did not know what it was. Bishop Lucas, however, resolved that difficulty straightway. 'You are not German, nephew, no, nor are you a Pole, nor even a Prussian. You are an Ermlander, simple. Remember it.'

And so, meekly, he became what he was told to be. But it was only one more mask. Behind it he was that which no name nor nation could claim. He was Doctor Copernicus.

*

Bishop Lucas knew nothing of that separate existence – or if he did, for there was little that went on at the castle without his knowledge, he chose to ignore it. He had lofty plans for his nephew. These he never spoke of openly, however, believing seemingly that they were best left to become apparent of themselves in the fullness of time, of which there was ample, he knew, for he had yet to be convinced that one day he would, like lesser men, be compelled to die. He was torn between his innate obsession with secrecy on one hand, and on the other the paramount necessity of dinning into the Canon's wilfully dull-witted skull, by main force if that would do it, the niceties of political intrigue. Diplomacy and public government were all right, any fool could conduct himself with skill and even elegance there, but the scheming and conniving by which the world was really run, these were a different matter, requiring intensive and expert coaching. But the trouble was that he did not entirely trust his nephew. The Canon sometimes had a look, hard to identify, but worrying. It was not simple stupidity, surely, that made his jaw hang thus, that misted over his rather ratty eyes with that peculiar greyish film?

'—Your head is in the clouds, nephew. Come back to earth!' The Canon started, hastily covering up the papers he had been working on, and peered over his shoulder with a wan apprehensive smile. Bishop Lucas looked at him balefully. I'll tell the dolt nothing; let him flounder! 'I said: there is a guest expected. Are you going deaf?'

'No, my lord, I heard you well enough. I shall be down presently. I have some . . . some letters to finish.'

The Bishop had turned to go, but now he came back, glowering menacingly. A born bully, he was well aware that his power over others depended on his determination to let pass no challenge, however fainthearted. 'Letters? What letters?' He was decked out all in purple, with purple gloves, and carried the mitre and staff tucked negligently under a fat arm. He was at once alarming and faintly comic. The Canon wondered uneasily why he had found it necessary personally to climb to this high room atop a windy tower merely to summon his nephew to dinner: it must be an important guest indeed. '*Now*, man – come!'

They hurried down dark stairways and rank damp passages. A storm was bellowing about the castle like a demented bull. The great entrance doors stood wide open, and in the porch a muffled faceless crowd of clerics and petty officials huddled by flickering torchlight, muttering. The night outside was a huge black spinning cylinder of wind and rain. Faintly between gusts there came the noise of riders approaching and the shrill blast of a trumpet. A ripple of excitement passed through the porch. Hoofbeats clattered across the courtyard, and suddenly dark mounted figures loomed up in the swirling darkness. Then there were many voices at once, and one that rang above all others, saying:

'Sennets and tuckets, by Christ! – and look here, a damned army awaiting us.'

The Canon heard his uncle beside him moan faintly in anger and dismay, and then they were both confronted abruptly by a stone-grey face with staring eyes and a beard streaming rain.

'Well Bishop, now that you have announced our coming to every German spy in Prussia, I suppose we can leave off this blasted disguise, eh?'

'Your majesty, forgive me, I thought—'

'Yes yes yes, enough.'

There was a scuffling in the porch, and the Canon glanced behind him to see the welcoming party with difficulty sinking to its knees in homage. Some few fell over in the crush, clutching wildly, amid stifled hilarity. Bishop Lucas juggled with the mitre and staff and proffered awkwardly the episcopal ring to be kissed. His Majesty looked at it. The Bishop whirled on his nephew and snarled:

'Bend your knee, churl, before the King of Poland!'

*

In the Hall of Knights above the nine great tables a thousand candles burned. First came hounds and torch-bearers and gaudy minstrels, and then the Bishop with his royal guest, followed by the Polish nobles, those hard-eyed horsemen, and at last the common household herd, pushing and squabbling and yelping for its dinner. A sort of silence fell as grace was offered. At the *amen* the Bishop sketched a hasty blessing on the air and ascended the dais to the *mensa princeps*, where he seated himself with the King on his right hand and the Canon on his left, and with heavy jowls sunk on his breast cast a cold eye upon the antics of the throng. He was still brooding on his humiliation in the porch. Jugglers and mountebanks pranced and leaped, spurred on by the shrieks of Toad the jester, a malignant stunted creature with a crazed fixed grin. Sandalled servants darted to and fro with fingerbowls and towels, and serving maids carried platters of smoking viands from the fire, where an uproar of cooks was toiling. A ragged cheer went up: one of the tumblers had fallen, and was being dragged away, writhing. Toad made a droll joke out of the fellow's misfortune. Then an ancient rhymester with a white beard tottered forth and launched into an epic in praise of Ermland. He was pelted with crusts of bread. Come, Toad, a song!

See how he flies up, O, pretty young thrush
  Heigh ho! sing willow
Here's a health to the bird in the bush

Clamour and meat! Brute bliss! King Sigismund laughed loud and long, clawing at his tangled black beard.

'You keep a merry table, Bishop!' he cried. His temper was

greatly improved. He had cast off his sodden disguise of linsey cloak and jerkin ('Who would mistake us for a peasant anyway!'), and was dressed now in the rough splendour of cowhide and ermine. That Jagellon head, however, lacking its crown, was still a rough-hewn undistinguished thing. Only the manner, overbearing, cruel and slightly mad, proclaimed him royal. He had made the long hard journey from Cracow to Prussia in wintertime, disguised, because he, like the Bishop, was alarmed by the resurgence of the Teutonic Knights. 'Aye, very merry.'

But Bishop Lucas was in no mood for pleasantries, and he shrugged morosely and said nothing. He was worried indeed. The Knights, once rulers of all Prussia and now banished to the East, were again, with the encouragement of Germany, pushing westward against Royal Prussia, whose allegiance to the Jagellon throne, however unenthusiastic, afforded Poland a vital foothold on the Baltic coast. At the centre of this turbulent triangle stood little Ermland, sore pressed on every side, her precarious independence gravely threatened, by Poland no less than by the Knights. Something would have to be done. The Bishop had a plan. But from the start, from that stormy arrival tonight, he had felt that things were going somehow awry. Sigismund played at being a boor, but he was no fool. He was crazed, perhaps, but cunningly so. His Ambassador was whispering in his ear. The Bishop's brow darkened.

'I am a plain man,' he growled, 'a priest. I believe in plain speaking. And I say that the Knights are a far greater threat to Poland than to our small state.'

The Ambassador left off whispering, and squirmed unhappily in his chair. The Bishop and he were old enemies. He was a sour little man with an absurd moustache and sallow high-boned cheeks: a Slav. His one secret concern was to protect his prospects of a coveted posting out of the backwoods of Ermland to Paris, city of his dreams (where within a year he was to be throttled by a berserk in a brothel).

'Yes yes, Lord Bishop,' he ventured, 'but is it not possible that we might treat with these unruly Knights in some way other than by open, and, I might add, dangerous, confrontation? I have great faith in diplomacy.' He simpered. 'It is something I am not unskilled in.'

Bishop Lucas bent on him a withering look. 'Sir, you may know diplomacy, but you do not know the Cross. They are a vile rapacious horde, and cursed of God. *Infestimmus hostis Ordinis Theutonici!* The time is not long past when they held open season against our native Prussians, and slaughtered them for sport.'

King Sigismund looked up, suddenly interested. 'Did they?' His expression grew wistful, but then he recollected himself, and frowned. 'Yes, well, for our part we see only one real threat, that is, the Turk, who is already at our southern border. What do you say of *that* vile horde, Bishop?'

It was just the opening that the Bishop needed to reveal his plan, yet, because his too intense hatred of the Knights threw him off, or because he underestimated the King and his crawling Ambassador, for whatever reason, his judgment faltered, and he bungled it.

'Is it not plain,' he snapped, 'what I have in mind? Are not the Knights, supposedly at least, a crusading order? I say send, or lure, or force them, whatever, to your southern frontiers, that they may defend those territories against the Infidel.' There was a silence. He had been too precipitate, even the Canon saw it. He began to see it himself, and hastened to retrieve the situation. 'They want to fight?' he cried, '—then let them fight, and if they are destroyed, why, the loss shall not be ours.' But he had succeeded only in making things worse, for now there arose before the horrified imaginations of the Poles the vision of a Turkish army flushed with victory, blooded as it were, swarming northwards over the mangled corpse of one of Europe's finest military machines. Ah no, no. They avoided his fiercely searching eye; they seemed almost embarrassed. Of course they had known beforehand the nature of his scheme, but knowing was not the thing. The Canon watched his uncle covertly, and wondered, not without a certain malicious satisfaction, how it came that such an expert ritualist had stumbled so clumsily – for ritual *was* the thing.

'A jolly fellow, Bishop, that fool of yours,' King Sigismund said. 'Sing up, sirrah! And let us have more wine here. This Rhenish is damned good – the only good that's ever come out of Germany, I say. Ha!'

All dutifully laughed, save the Bishop, who sat and glared before him out of a purple trance of fury and chagrin. The Ambassador eyed him craftily, and smoothly said:

'I think, my lord, that we must consider in greater detail this problem of the Knights. Your solution seems a little too – how should I say? – too simple. Destroy the Turk or be destroyed, these appear to be the only alternatives you foresee, but rather might not the Cross destroy Poland? Ah no, Bishop, I think: no.'

Bishop Lucas seemed about to bite him, but instead, plucking at himself in his agitation, he turned abruptly to the King and made to speak, but was prevented by a steward who came running and whispered urgently in his ear. 'Not now, man, not . . . what? . . . *who?*' He whirled on the Canon, the wattles of red fat at his throat wobbling. 'You! you knew of this.'

The Canon reared away in fright, shaking his head. 'Of what, my lord, knew of what?'

'The whoreson! Go to him, go, and tell him, tell him—' The table was agog. '—Tell him if he is not gone hence by dawn I'll have his poxed carcase strung up at the castle gate!'

Through passageways Canon Nicolas scurried, tripping on his robe in the darkness and moaning softly under his breath. Something from long ago, from childhood, ran in his head, over and over: *The Turk impales his prisoners! The Turk impales his prisoners!* In the flickering torchlight under the porch a dark figure waited, wrapped in a black cloak. The wind bellowed, whirled all away into the swirling tunnel of the tempest, Turks and Toad, sceptre and Cross, crusts, dust, old rags, a battered crown: all.

'You!'

'Yes, brother: I.'

* * *

BISHOP LUCAS's decline began mysteriously that night of Andreas's arrival at Heilsberg. It was not that he fell ill, or that his reason failed, but a kind of impalpable though devastating paralysis set in that was eventually to sap his steely will. The King of Poland, crapulous and monumentally irritated, would hear no more talk of the Knights, and left before morning with his henchmen, despite the weather. The Bishop stood puzzled and querulous, wracked by impotent rage and buffeted by black rain, watching his hopes for the security of Ermland depart with the royal party into storm and darkness. Of any other man it would have been said that he was growing old, that he had met his match in the King and his Ambassador, but these simple reasonings were not sufficient here. Perhaps for him also a dark something had lain in wait, whose vague form was suddenly made hideous flesh in Andreas's coming.

'Has that bitch's bastard gone yet?'

'No, my lord. My lord he is ill, you cannot send him away.'

'Cannot? Cannot I now!' He was flushed and shaken, and bobbed about in his rage like a large inflated bladder. 'Go find him, you, in whatever rathole he is skulking, and tell him, tell him – *ach!*'

The Canon climbed the tower to his cell, where his brother sat on the edge of the bed with his cloak thrown over his shoulders, eating a sausage.

'You have been speaking with the Bishop, I can see,' he said. 'You are sweating.' He laughed, a faint thin dry scraping sound. Now in the candlelight his face was horrible and horribly fascinating, worse even than it had seemed at first sight in the ill-lit porch, a ghastly ultimate thing, a mud mask set with eyes and emitting a frightful familiar voice. He was almost entirely bald above a knotted suppurating forehead. His upper lip was all eaten away on one side, so that his mouth was set lop-sidedly in what was not a grin and yet not a snarl either. One of his ears was a mess of crumbled white meat, while the other was untouched, a pinkish shell that in its startling perfection appeared far more hideous than its ruined twin. The nose was pallid and swollen, unreal, dead already, as if there, at the ravaged nostrils, Death the Jester had marked the place where when his time came he would force an entry. With such damage, the absence of blood was an unfailing surprise. 'I think, brother, our uncle loves me not.'

The Canon nodded, unable to speak. He felt sundered, as if mind and body had come apart, the one writhing here in dazed helpless horror, the other bolt upright there on the floor, a thing of sticks and straw, nodding like a fairground dummy. A dome of turbulent darkness, held aloft only by the frail flame of the candle, pressed down upon the little room. He drew up a chair and very slowly sat. He told himself that *this* was not Andreas, could not be, was a phantom out of a dream. But it was Andreas, he knew it. What surprised him was that he was not surprised: had he known all along, without admitting it, the nature of his brother's illness? Suddenly his sundered halves rushed together with a sickening smack, and he wrung his hands and cried:

'Andreas, Andreas, how have you come so low!'

His brother looked at him, amused and gratified by his distress, and lightly said:

'I had suspected, you know, that you would not fail to notice some little change in me since last we met. Have I aged, do you think? Hmm?'

'But what – what—?'

But he knew, only too well. Andreas laughed again.

'Why, it is the pox, brother, the *Morbus Gallicus*, or as your dear friend Fracastoro would have it in his famous verses, *Syphilis*, the beautiful boy struck down by the gods. A most troublesome complaint, I assure you.'

'O Christ. Andreas.'

Andreas frowned, if that was what to call this buckling of his maimed face.

'I'll have none of your pity, damn you,' he said, 'your mealy-mouthed concern. I am brought low, am I? You cringing clown. Rather I should rot with the pox than be like you, dead from the neck down. I have lived! Can you understand what that means, you, death-in-life, Poor Pol, can you? When I am dead and in the ground I shall not have been brought so low as you are now, brother!'

Into the globe of light in which they sat dim shapes were pressing, a crouched chair, the couch, a pile of books like clenched teeth, mute timid things, lifeless and yet seemingly alive, aching toward speech. The Canon looked about, unable to sustain the weight of his brother's burning eyes, and wondered vaguely if these things among which he lived had somehow robbed him of some essential presence, of something vivid and absolutely vital, in order to imbue themselves with a little vicarious life. For certainly (Andreas was right!) he was in a way dead, cold, beyond touching. Even now it was not Andreas really that he pitied, but the pity itself. That seemed to mean something. Between the object and the emotion a third something, for him, must always mediate. Yes, that meant something. He did not know what. And then it all drifted away, those paradoxical fragments of almost-insight, and he was back in the charnel house.

'Why do you hate me so?' he asked, not in anger, nor even sadness much, but wonderingly, with awe.

Andreas did not answer. He fished up from under his cloak a soiled piece of cheese, looked at it doubtfully, and put it away. 'Is there wine?' he growled. 'Give it here.' And the ghost of the imperious headstrong bright beautiful creature he had once been appeared briefly in the furry yellow light, bowed haughtily, and was gone. He produced a length of hollow reed, and turning away with the fastidious stealth of a wounded animal, inserted one end of it between his lips and sucked up a mouthful of wine. 'I suppose you think it only justice,' he mumbled, 'that I have no longer a mouth with which to drink? You always disapproved of my drinking.' He wiped his lips carefully on his wrist. 'Well, enough of this poking in the past – let us speak of present things.

So you have sold yourself to Nuncle Luke, eh? For how much, I wonder. Another fat prebend? I hear he has given you a canonry at Breslau: rich pickings there, I daresay. Still, hardly enough to buy you whole, I should have thought. Or has he promised you Ermland, the bishopric? You'll have to take Holy Orders for that. Well, say nothing, it's no matter. You'll rot here, as surely as I will, elsewhere. Perhaps I shall return to Rome. I have friends there, influence. You do not believe me, I see. But that is no matter either. What else can I tell you? – ah yes: I am a father.' Suddenly his eyes glittered, bright with spite. The Canon flinched. 'Yes, the bitch that dosed me redeemed herself somewhat by dropping a son. Imagine that, brother: a son, a little Andreas! That burns your celibate soul, doesn't it?'

O yes, it burned him, burned him badly, worse than he would ever have suspected it could do. Andreas's aim was uncanny: he felt as dry as a barren woman. He said:

'Where is he now, your son?'

Andreas took another sip of wine, and looked up, grinning in anguish. 'Hard to say where he might be; in Purgatory, I expect, seeing that he was so grossly got. He could not live, not with such parents, no.' He sighed, and glanced about the darkling room abstractedly, then groped under his cloak again and brought up this time a raw carrot with the stalk still on. 'I asked your fellow to filch me some food, and look what he brought, the dog.'

'*Max?*' the Canon yelped, 'was it Max? Did he see your . . . did he see you clearly? He will tell the Bishop how things are with you. Andreas.'

But Andreas was not listening. He let fall the carrot from his fingers, and gazed at it where it lay on the floor as if it were all hope, all happiness lost. 'Our lives, brother, are a little journey through God's guts. We are soon shat. Those hills are not hills but heavenly piles, this earth a mess of consecrated cack, in which we sink at the end.' He grinned again. 'Well, what do you say to that? Is it not a merry notion? The world as God's belly: there is an image to confound your doctors of astronomy. Come, drink some wine. Why do I hate you? But I do not. I hate the world, and you, so to speak, are standing in the way. Come, do take some wine, we might as well be drunk. How the wind blows! Listen! Ah, brother, ah, I am in pain.'

A bitter cold invaded the Canon's veins. He had emerged on the far side of grief and horror into an icy plain. He said:

'You cannot stay here, Andreas. Max will surely tell the Bishop how things are. He knows you are sick, but not how badly, how . . . how obviously. He will drive you out, he has threatened already to have you hanged. You must go now, tonight. I shall send Max with you to the town, he will find lodgings for you.' And in the same dry measured tone he added: 'Forgive me.'

Andreas had taken up his ebony cane and was leaning on it heavily, rocking back and forth where he sat. He was drunk.

'But tell me what *you* think of the world, brother,' he mumbled. 'Do you think it a worthy place? Are we incandescent angels inhabiting a heaven? Come now, say, what do you think of it?'

The Canon grimaced and shook his head. 'Nothing, I do not think. Will you go now, please?'

'*Christ!*' Andreas cried, and lifted the stick as if to strike. The Canon did not stir, and they sat thus, with the weapon trembling above them. 'Tell me, damn you! Tell me what you think!'

'I think,' Canon Koppernigk said calmly, 'that the world is absurd.'

Andreas lowered the stick, and nodded, smiling, it was almost a smile, almost blissful. 'That is what I wanted you to say. Now I shall go.'

*

He went. Max found a hole for him to hide in. The Bishop, believing, wishing to believe, that he had left the country, let it be known that he wanted to hear no more mention of him. But such rage and pain as Andreas's could not easily be erased. His coming had contaminated the castle, and some malign part of his presence persisted, a desolation, a blackening of the air. The Canon visited him once. He lay in darkness in a shuttered garret and would not speak, pretending to be asleep. The crown of his skull, all that was visible of him above the soiled blanket, scaly with scurf and old scabs and stuck with patches of scant hair, was horrid and heart-rending. Downstairs the innkeeper leered with ghastly knowing. He wiped his hands on his apron before taking the coins the Canon offered.

'You must give him better food. None of your slops, mind. Send to the castle for supplies if you must. Do not tell him that I spoke to you, that I gave you money.'

'O aye, your honour, mum's the word. And I'll do that with the prog.'

'Yes.' He looked at the cowering ingratiating fellow, and saw himself. 'Yes.'

*

Church business took him with his uncle to Cracow. For once he was glad of that long weary journey. As they travelled southwards over the Prussian plain he felt the clutch of that dread phantom in the garret weaken, and at last fall away.

In Cracow he spent at Haller's bookshop what little time the Bishop would allow him away from his secretarial duties. Haller was publishing his Latin translations from the Byzantine Greek of Simocatta's *Epistles*. It was a poor dull book. The sight of the text, mysteriously, shockingly naked on the galley proofs, nauseated him. *If thou wouldst obtain mastery over thy grief, wander among graves* . . . O! But the text was unimportant. What mattered was the dedication. He was out to woo the Bishop.

He enlisted in this delicate task the help of an old acquaintance, Laurentius Rabe, a poet and wandering scholar who had taught him briefly here at Cracow during his university days. Rabe, who affected on occasion the grandiloquent latinised name of Corvinus, was a spry old man with spindly legs and a plump chest and watery pale blue eyes. He liked to dress in black, and sported proudly still the liripipe of the graduate. He was no raven, despite the name, but resembled some small quick fastidious bird, a swallow, perhaps, or a swift. A jewel glittered at the tip of his sharp little beak.

'I would have some verses, you see,' the Canon said, 'to flatter my uncle. I should be grateful to you.'

They stood together amid the crash and clatter of the case-room at the rear of Haller's. Rabe nodded rapidly, rubbing his chilblained fingers together like bundles of dry twigs.

'Of course, of course,' he cried, in his pinched voice. 'Tell me what you require.'

'Some small thing merely, a few lines.' Canon Nicolas shrugged. 'Something, say, on Aeneas and Achates, something like that, loyalty, piety, you know. The verse is no matter—'

'O.'

'—But most importantly, you must put in some mention of astronomy. I plan to produce a small work on planetary motion, a mere outline, you understand, of something much larger that I have in train. This preliminary *commentariolus* is a modest affair, but I fear controversy among the schoolmen, and therefore I must have the support of the Bishop, you see.' He was babbling, beset by embarrassment and nervousness. He found it unaccountably obscene to speak to others of his work. 'Anyway, you know how these things go. Will you oblige me?'

Rabe was flattered, and for the moment, quite overcome, he could say nothing, and continued to nod, making faint squeaking noises under his breath. He was preparing one of his ornate speeches. The Canon had not time for that.

'Excuse me,' he said hastily, 'I must speak to Haller.' The printer approached between the benches, a big stolid silent man in a leather apron, scratching his beard with a thick thumb and studying a sheet of parchment. '*Meister* Haller, I wish to put in some verses with the dedication: can you do that?'

Haller frowned pensively, and then nodded.

'We can do that,' he said gravely.

Rabe was watching the Canon with a gentle, somewhat crestfallen questioning look.

'You have changed, my dear Koppernigk,' he murmured.

'What?'

'You have become a public man.'

'Have I? Perhaps so.' What can he mean? No matter. 'You will do this favour for me, then? I shall pay you, of course.'

He turned his attention to the galleys, and when he looked again Rabe was gone. He had the distinct, vaguely troubling impression that the old man had somehow been folded up and put neatly but unceremoniously away: closed, as it were, like a dull book. He shook his head impatiently. He had not the time to worry over trivia.

*

He had all the time in the world. There was no hurry. He knew in his heart that the Bishop would be about as much impressed with the *Commentariolus* on Doctor Copernicus's planetary theory (did it not sound somehow like the name of a patent medicine put out by some quack?) as he would be with dreary Simocatta. Or he might be so impressed as to forbid publication. The times were inauspicious. In Germany the Church was under attack, while the humanists were everywhere execrated – and translating Simocatta could be, the Canon supposed, considered a humanist pursuit, however laughable the notion seemed to him. Bishop Lucas had troubles in plenty abroad without exposing himself to the accusation of laxity in his own house. One scandalous nephew was enough.

'What am I to do with him!' he roared, drumming on his forehead with his fists. 'Come, you are my physician, advise me how to rid myself of this sickness that is your blasted brother.'

'He is sick, my lord,' Canon Nicolas said quietly. 'We must try to be charitable.'

'Charity? *Charity*? Christ in Heaven, man, don't make me spew. How can I be charitable to this . . . this . . . this defilement, this weeping sore? You have seen him: he is rotting, the beast is rotting on his feet! Jesus God, if they should hear of this scandal at Rome—'

'He tells me he has influence at the Vatican, my lord.'

'—Or in Königsberg! O!' He sat down suddenly, appalled. 'If they hear of it in Königsberg, what will they not make of it, the Knights. Something must be done. I will be rid of him, nephew, mark it, I will be rid of him.'

They were in the library, a large high cold stone hall that in former times had been the garderobe, where now the business of the castle, and all Ermland, was conducted. The furnishings were scant, some uninviting chairs, a prie-dieu, an incongruously dainty Italian table, the vast desk at the side of which the Canon sat on a low stool with pen and slate before him. One wall was draped with a vast tapestry, out of which, as from some elaborate puzzle, the Bishop's flat stern face in various disguises peered with watchful mien, while in the middle distance, incidentally as it were, was depicted the martyrdom of St Stephen. A seven-branched candelabrum shed a brownish underwater light. Nervous petty officials summoned here over the years had left their mark on the air, a vague mute sense of distress and guilt and failure. It was Bishop Lucas's favourite room. He snuffed up great lungfuls of that rank air, puffed himself up on it. In these latter days he left the library only to eat and sleep. He was safe here, while outside the pestilence raged, that plague of the spirit made tangible in Andreas's coming. They had returned from Cracow to find him entrenched at the castle, determined, with hideous cheerfulness, not to be dislodged this time. Max had made him very comfortable in his master's tower, where he passed the time waiting for their return by reading the notes and preliminary drafts of the Canon's secret book . . . A climate of doom descended on Heilsberg.

The Bishop began pacing again, a bell-like bundle of fear and frustration in his long voluminous purple robe, banging and booming angrily. He halted at the narrow mullioned window and stood staring out with his fists clasped behind him. Hoarfrost was on the glass, and a pale moon like a fat cheesy skull gleamed above a snowbound land.

'I might have him murdered,' he mused. 'Can you find me an assassin that we can trust?' He turned, glowering. 'Can you?'

Canon Nicolas closed his eyes wearily. 'My lord, your letter to King Sigismund—'

'Damn King Sigismund! I have asked you a question.'

'You are not in earnest, surely.'

'Why not? Would he not be better off dead? He is dead already, except that his black heart out of spite persists in beating.'

'Yes,' the Canon murmured, 'yes, he is dead already.'

'Just so. Therefore—'

'He is my brother!'

'—Yes, and he is my nephew, my sister's son, my blood, and I would happily see his throat cut if I knew it could be quietly done.'

'I cannot believe—'

'What? What can you not believe? He is anathema, *and I will be rid of him.*'

The Canon frowned. 'Then, Bishop, you will be rid of me also.'

His uncle slowly approached and stood over him, peering at him with interest. He seemed gratified, as if he derived a certain grim satisfaction from the thought that the long list of injuries done him by a filthy world were here being neatly rounded off.

'So you will betray me also, will you?' he said briskly. 'Well well, so it has come to this. After all I have done for you. Well. And where, pray, will you go?'

'To Frauenburg.'

'Ha! And rot there, among the cathedral mice? You are a fool, nephew.'

But the Canon was hardly listening, engrossed as he was in contemplation of this new unrecognisable self that had suddenly from nowhere risen up, waving fists in defiance and demanding an apocalypse. Yet he was calm, quite, quite calm. It was of course the logical thing to do; yes, he would leave Heilsberg, there was no avoiding that command, it sang in the wires of his blood, a great black chord. He would embrace exile, would give it all up, for Andreas. It would be the final irrefutable proof of his regard for his brother. And there would be no need for words. Yes. Yes. He looked about him, blinking, bemused by the joy and dismay warring in his confused heart. It was all so simple, after all. The Bishop threw up his hands and lumbered off.

'*Fool!*'

*

Andreas laughed. 'Fool you are, brother. Think you can escape me by hiding among the holy canons?'

'He is talking of assassination, Andreas.'

'What of it! A dagger in the throat is not the worst thing that can befall me. O go away, you. Your false concern is sickening. You would like nothing better than to see me dead. I know you, brother, I *know* you.' The Canon said nothing. What there was to say could not be said. No need for words? Ah! He turned to go, but Andreas plucked him slyly by the sleeve. 'Our nuncle will be interested to know how you have occupied yourself all these years under his patronage, do you not think?'

'I ask you, say nothing to him of this work of mine. You should not have read my papers. It is all foolery, a pastime merely.'

'O, but you are too modest. I feel it is my duty to acquaint him with these very interesting theories which you have formulated. A heliocentric universe! He will be impressed. Well, what do you say?'

'I cannot prevent you from betraying me. It hardly matters now. Heed me, Andreas, and leave Heilsberg, or he will surely do you grievous injury.'

Andreas grinned, grinding his teeth.

'You do not understand,' he said. '*I want to die!*'

'Nonsense. It is revenge that you want.'

They were startled by that, the Canon no less than Andreas, who stepped back with an offended look.

'What do you know of it?' he muttered sulkily. 'Go on, scuttle off to your pious friends at Frauenburg.' But as the Canon went down the stairs the door flew open behind him and Andreas appeared, framed against the candlelight like a dangling black spider, crying: 'Yes! Yes! I will be revenged!'

*

Canon Koppernigk set out for Frauenburg by night, a cloaked black figure slumped astride a drooping mare. He was alone. Max had elected to stay and serve Andreas. That was all right. They might try, but they would not take everything from him, no. If the sentry were to accost him now he would announce himself fiercely, would bellow his name and impress it like a seal upon the waxen darkness for all Heilsberg to hear: *Doctor Copernicus!* But the sentry was asleep.

* * *

DAY UP THERE on the Baltic broke in storms of petrified fire. He had never seen such dawns. They were excessive, faintly alarming, not at all to his taste. He had come to detest extremes. The sky here was altogether too vast, too high, and too much given to empty tempestuous displays. It was all surface. He preferred the sea, whose hidden deeps communicated a sense of enormous grey calm. But sometimes the sea too disturbed him, when by a trick of tide or light it rose up in his window, humped, slate-blue, like the back of some waterborne brute, menacing and ineluctable.

He had asked for the tower at the north-west corner of the cathedral wall. The Frauenburg Chapter thought him mad. It was a grim bare place, certainly, but it suited him. There were three whitewashed rooms set squarely one above the other. From the second floor a door led out to a kind of platform atop the wall. This would do for an observatory, affording as it did an open view of the great plain to the south, and north and west across the narrow freshwater lake called the Frisches Haff to the Baltic beyond, and of the stars by night. For furniture he had a couch to sleep on, a table, two chairs, a lectern. That second chair troubled him in its suggestion of the possibility of a guest, but he allowed it to stay, knowing that perfection is not of this world. Anyway, the desk far outweighted in garishness any number of chairs. It was his father's desk from Torun, which he had asked Katharina to let him have, as a keepsake. A big solid affair of oak, with drawers and brass fittings and a top inlaid with worn green leather, it fitted ill in that stark cell, but it was a part of the past, and in time he grew accustomed to it. He felt that to have left the rooms entirely bare would have been preferable, but he was not a fanatic. It was only that he had perceived in this grey stone tower, this least place, an image of his deepest self that furniture, possessions, comforts, only served to blur. He was after the thing itself now, the unadorned, the stony thing.

The Chapter demanded little of him. His fifteen fellow canons considered him a dull dog. They lived in the grand style, with servants and horses and estates outside the walls. His tower to them was a mark of incomprehensible and suspect humility. Yet they treated him with studied deference. He supposed they were afraid of him, of what he represented: he was, after all, the Bishop's nephew. He had not the interest to reassure them on that score. Anyway, their fright kept them at a welcome distance – the last thing he wanted was companionship. On his arrival at Frauenburg he was immediately, with indecent haste almost, appointed Visitator, a largely honorary title thrust on him in the hope apparently of mollifying for the moment the hunger for advancement that the canons imagined must be gnawing at this stark alarming newcomer. He compelled himself to attend all Chapter meetings, and sat, without ever uttering a word, listening diligently to endless talk of tithes and taxes and Church politics. Easier to bear were the daily services at the cathedral. As a canon without Holy Orders he was called on to be present, but not of course to officiate. Unlike the Chapter sessions, where his mute brooding presence was patently resented, in church his reticence was ideally matched, was absorbed even, by God's huge stony silence.

Only rarely did he travel beyond the environs of Frauenburg.

He liked the town. It was old, sleepy, safe, it reminded him of his birthplace; it was enough. Once he journeyed to Torun and called upon the Gertner household, and to Kulm to see Barbara at the convent. Neither visit was a success. Barbara and he still could not cope with each other as adults, and Katharina . . . was still Katharina. He resolved to venture forth no more, and gently refused the invitations of his colleagues to accompany them on their frequent roistering rounds of the diocese. He had at last, so it seemed to him, come to a dead halt. The waves of the world broke in storm and clamour far above the pool of stillness in which he floated.

*

But he was not left entirely unmolested. Ripples slithered down and stirred the filth at the bottom of his pool. He heard of the death of Rabe, poor Corvinus, on the very day that the copy of the Simocatta translations that he had sent to Bishop Lucas was returned, unread and unremarked, from Heilsberg. Then Max appeared one evening, sheepish and sullen; Andreas, he said, had gone back to Italy, with twelve hundred Hungarian gold florins in his belt, entrusted to him for ecclesiastical purposes by the Frauenburg Chapter.

'*What!*' The Canon stared. 'What are you saying? Was he here? When was he here?'

Max shrugged. 'Aye, he was here. They gave him the gold. He's gone off. Said I could go to the devil. Your nuncle gave him monies too, to be rid of him. A bad lot, your brother, if you'll permit me say it, master.'

The Canon sat down. 'Twelve hundred gold florins!' That was bad, but worse, far worse, was that Andreas had been in Frauenburg and no one had thought to warn him. (Warn? He turned the word this way and that, scrutinising it.)

*

He was not to have peace, that much was clear. No matter how far he fled he would be followed. Mysterious emissaries were sent to him, cunningly disguised. The most innocent-seeming stranger, or even someone he thought he knew, might suddenly by a look, a word, deliver the secret message: *beware*. He had rid his life of everything that could have brought him comfort, but evidently that was not enough, renunciation was not enough. Was passivity, then, his crime? He set himself to work on behalf of the Chapter, accepting only the most servile and distasteful of tasks. He wrote letters, collected rents, drew up reports that no one read; he rode the length and breadth of the diocese to deal with minute matters, frenziedly, like a deckhand racing about a sinking ship vainly plugging leaks that opened again as soon as they were stanched. Now the Chapter became finally convinced that he was a lunatic. He negotiated, almost on his knees, with sneering officials from Cracow and Königsberg. And he treated the sick. Even they sometimes to his horror revealed a treacherous knowing.

It was strange: the people had such faith in him. They sent him their sickest, their hopeless cases, leprous children, wasting brides, the old. He could do nothing, yet he continued doggedly to advise and admonish, making passes in the air, frowning under the weight of a wholly spurious wisdom. The more outlandish his treatment, and more grotesque the ingredients of the potions he poured down their throats, the more satisfied they seemed. Why, some even recovered! He gained quite a reputation throughout Ermland. Yet not for a moment did he doubt that he was a fake.

There was a young girl, Alicia her name, she could not have been more than fifteen, a slender delicate child. She was brought to him one day in April. The air was drenched with sun and rain, cloudshadows skimmed the bright Baltic. She wore a green gown. The tower did not know what to do with her: such loveliness was more than those grim grey stones could cope with. Her father was an over-dressed faintly ridiculous fat man, a fodder merchant and a member of the town council. He owned a wooden house within the walls and a vineyard in the suburbs. His people, he said, hailed from Lower Saxony, a fact which he seemed to consider impressive. He let it be known that he could read, and also write; he carefully avoided meeting the Canon's eye directly.

The mother was a large sad timid woman in black, with a broad pale face all puffed and wrinkled as if perpetually anticipating tears. They were both elderly. Alicia had come, they confided, a gift from God, just when they had at last given up all hope of issue; and they looked at each other shyly, in wonder, and then at their daughter with such anguished tenderness that the Canon was forced to turn away, the celibate's bitterness rising in him like bile.

'Why have you come to me?'

'She is not well, Father, we think,' the merchant answered. He hesitated, and looked to his wife. She wrung her pale heavy hands, and her lips trembled. She said:

'She has a . . . a rash, Father, and there is a flux—'

'Please, do not call me Father, I am not a priest.' He had meant to be kind, to put them at their ease, but succeeded only in intimidating them further. He was himself uneasy. He wanted to walk out quickly now and abandon this fat fodder merchant and his sorrowful wife and ailing daughter, to escape. A handful of bright rain clattered against the window. The sea sparkled. He disliked springtime, unsettling season. With a thumb and finger under her chin he lifted the child's face and studied it silently for a moment. A faint blush spread upwards from her slender inviolate throat. She was afraid of him also. Or was she? It seemed to him that he detected fleetingly in those exquisite velvety dark eyes a cold and calculating sardonic look, piercing and familiar. He stepped away from her, frowning.

'Come,' he said. The mother moaned faintly in distress and made as if to touch her daughter. Alicia did not look at her. 'Come, child, do not be afraid.'

He led her up the narrow stairs to his observatory. (The sick were suitably cowed by the astrolabe and quadrant and all those dusty tomes.) Today however it was not the patient who was the most apprehensive, but the physician. The girl's strange closed silence was disturbing. She seemed to be turned inward somehow, away from the world, as if she were the carrier of a secret that made her inner self wholly sufficient, as if she were the initiate of a cult.

'Where have you this rash, child?'

Still she said nothing, but stood a moment apparently debating within herself, then leaned down quickly and lifted up the hem of her skirts. He was not surprised; he was appalled, even frightened, yes, but not surprised. A carrier she was, certainly. Now he knew the cult into which she had been initiated. How strange: the sun was on the Baltic, the lindens were in bud, and water and air and earth trembled with the complicity of the awakening season's fire, and yet this young girl was infected. Once again he was struck by the failure of things and times to connect. The world was there, Alicia was here, and between the two the chasm yawned. She was watching him out of those blank exquisite eyes without fear or shame, but with a kind of curiosity. There, between seraphic face and that dreadful flower blossoming in secret inside her young girl's frail thighs, was yet another failure of connection.

'What man have you been with?' he asked.

She let fall the hem of her gown and with prim little swooping movements smoothed the wrinkles carefully out of the green silk.

'No man,' she said. 'I have been with no man, Father.'

'Odysseus then,' the Canon murmured, and was vaguely shocked at himself for making a joke at such a time. He could think of nothing else to say. He took her hand and felt her heart-breaking frailty. 'Ah child, child.' There was nothing to be said, nor done. The sense of his failure struck him like a hammerblow.

The parents stood as he had left them, poised, like ships becalmed, waiting for wonders. They had only to look at him and they knew. They had known already, in their hearts. The silence was frightful. The Canon said: 'I suggest—' but the merchant and his wife both began to speak at once, and then stopped in confusion. The mother was weeping effortlessly.

'There is a young man, Father,' she said. 'He wishes to marry our Alicia.' Her face suddenly crumpled, and she wailed: 'O he is a fine boy, Father!'

'We—' the merchant began, puffing up his chest, but he could not go on, and looked about the room, baffled and lost, as if searching for some solid support that he knew was not to be found, not here nor anywhere. '*We!*—'

'My sister is Abbess of the Cistercian Convent at Kulm,' the Canon said quickly. 'I can arrange for your daughter to go there. She need not take the vow, of course, unless you wish it. But the nuns will care for her, and perhaps—' Stop! Do not! '—Perhaps in time, when she is cured . . . when she . . . perhaps this young man . . . Ach!' He could bear this no longer. They knew, they all knew: the child's groin was crawling with crabs, she was poxed, she would never marry, would probably not live to be twenty, they knew that! Why then this charade? He advanced on them, and they retreated before him as if buffeted by the wind of his dismay and rage. The girl did not even glance at him. He wanted to shake her, or clasp her in his arms, to throttle her, save her, he did not know what he wanted, and he did nothing. When the door was opened a solid block of sunlight fell upon them, and all hesitated a moment, dazzled, and then mother and daughter turned away into the street. The merchant suddenly stamped his foot.

'It is witchcraft,' he gasped, 'I know it!'

'No,' the Canon said. 'There is no witchery here. Go now and comfort your wife and child. I shall write today to Kulm.'

But the merchant was not listening. He nodded distractedly, mechanically, like a large forlorn doll.

'The blame must fall somewhere,' he muttered, and for the first time looked directly at the Canon. 'It must fall somewhere!'

Yes, yes: somewhere.

*

The ripples increased in intensity, became waves. Rumours reached him that he was being talked of at Rome as the originator of a new cosmology. Julius II himself, it was said, had expressed an interest. The blame must fall somewhere: he heard again that voice on the stairs shrieking of revenge. An unassuageable constriction of fear and panic afflicted him. Yet there was nowhere further that he could flee to. Lateral drift was all that remained.

Suddenly one day God abandoned him. Or perhaps it had happened long before, and he was only realising it now. The crisis came unbidden, for he had never questioned his faith, and he felt like the bystander, stopped idly to watch a brawl, who is suddenly struck down by a terrible stray blow. And yet it could not really be called a crisis. There was no great tumult of the soul, no pain. The thing was distinguished by a lack of feeling, a numbness. And it was strange: his faith in the Church did not waver, only his faith in God. The Mass, transubstantiation, the forgiveness of sin, the virgin birth, the vivid truth of all *that* he did not for a moment doubt, but behind it, behind the ritual, there was for him now only a silent white void that was everywhere and everything and eternal.

He confessed to the Precentor, Canon von Lossainen, but more out of curiosity than remorse. The Precentor, an ailing unhappy old man, sighed and said:

'Perhaps, Nicolas, the outward forms are all that any of us can believe in. Are you not being too hard on yourself?'

'No, no; I do not think it is possible to be too hard on oneself.'

'You may be right. Should I give you absolution? I hardly know.'

'Despair is a great sin.'

'Despair? Ah.'

*

He ceased to believe also in his book. For a while, in Cracow, in Italy, he had succeeded in convincing himself that (what was it?) the physical world was amenable to physical investigation, that the principal thing could be deduced, that the thing itself could be said. That faith too had collapsed. The book by now had gone through two complete revisions, rewritings really, but instead of coming nearer to essentials it was, he knew, flying off in a wild eccentric orbit into emptiness; instead of approaching the word, the crucial Word, it was careering headlong into a loquacious silence. He had believed it possible to say the truth; now he saw that all that could be said was the saying. His book was not about the world, but about itself. More than once he snatched up this hideous ingrown thing and rushed with it to the fire, but he had not the strength to perform that ultimate act.

Then at last there came, mysteriously, a ghastly release.

It was a sulphurous windy evening in March when Katharina's steward arrived to summon him to Torun, where his uncle the Bishop was lying ill. He rode all night through storm and rain into a sombre yellowish dawn that was more like twilight. At Marienburg a watery sun broke briefly through the gloom. The Vistula was sullen. By nightfall he had reached Torun, exhausted, and almost delirious from want of sleep. Katharina was solicitous, and that told him, if nothing else would, that the situation was serious.

Bishop Lucas had been to Cracow for the wedding of King Sigismund. On the journey home he had fallen violently ill, and being then closer to Torun than Heilsberg had elected to be taken to the house of his niece. He lay now writhing in a grey sweat in the room, in the very bed where Canon Nicolas had been born and probably conceived. And indeed the Bishop, mewling in pain and mortal fright, seemed himself a great gross infant labouring toward an agonised delivery. He was torn by terrible fluxions, that felt, he said, as if he were shitting his guts: he was. The room was lit by a single candle, but a greater ghastly light seemed shed by his rage and pain. The Canon hung back in the shadows for a long time, watching the little changing tableau being enacted about the bed. Priests and nurses came and went silently. A physician with a grey beard shook his head. Katharina put a cross into her uncle's hands, but he fumbled and let it fall. Gertner picked his nails.

'*Nicolas!*'

'Yes, uncle, I am here.'

The stricken eyes sought his vainly, a shaking hand took him fiercely by the wrist. 'They have poisoned me, Nicolas. Their spies were at the palace, everywhere. O Jesus curse them! O!'

'He is raving now,' Katharina said. 'We can do nothing.'

The Canon paced about the dark house. It was changed beyond all recognition. It looked the same as it had always done, yet everything that he rapped upon with his questioning presence gave back only a dull sullen silence, as if the living soft centre of things had gone dead, had petrified. The deathwatch had conferred a lawless dispensation, and weird scenes of licence met him everywhere. In the little room that as a child he had shared with Andreas a pair of hounds, a bitch and her mate, reared up from the bed and snarled at him, baring their phosphorescent fangs in the darkness. Under a disordered table in the dining-hall he found his servant Max, and Toad, the Bishop's jester, drunk and asleep, wrapped in a grotesque embrace, each with a hand thrust into the other's lap. A stench like the stench of stagnant waters hung on the stairs. There was laughter in the servants' quarters and the sounds of stealthy merrymaking. His own fingers when he lifted them to his face smelled of rot. He sat down by a dead fire in the solar and fell into a kind of trance between sleep and waking peopled by blurred phantoms.

In the dead hour before dawn he was summoned to the sickroom. There was in the globe of light about the bed that sense of suspended animation, of a finger lifted to lips, preparatory to the entrance of the black prince. Only the dying man himself seemed unaware that the moment was at hand. He hardly stirred at all now, and yet he appeared to be frantically busy. Life had shrunk to a swiftly spinning point within him, the last flywheel turning still as the engine approached its final collapse. The Canon was prey to an unshakeable feeling of incongruousness, of being inappropriately dressed, of being, somehow, all wrong. Suddenly the Bishop's eyes flew open and stared upward with an expression of astonishment, and in a strong clear voice he cried: 'No!' and all in the sickroom went utterly still and silent, as if fearing, like children in a hiding game, that to make a sound would mean being called forth to face some dreadful forfeit. 'No! Keep him hence!' But the dark visitor would not be denied, and, battered and shapeless, an already indistinct pummelled soiled sack of pain and bafflement, Bishop Lucas Waczelrodt blundered into the darkness under the outstretched black wing of that enfolding cloak. The priest anointed his forehead with holy chrism. Katharina sobbed. Gertner looked up, frowning. The Canon turned away.

'Send at once to Heilsberg, tell them their Bishop is dead.'

The bells spoke.

*

Revolted by the pall of fake mourning put on by the house, Canon Nicolas slipped out by the servants' passageway into the garden. The morning, sparkling with sun and frost, seemed made of finely wrought glass. The garden had been let go to ruin, and it was with difficulty that memory cleared away the weeds and rubbish and restored it to what it had been once. Here were the fruit bushes, the little paved path, the sundial – yes, yes, he remembered. As a child he had played here happily, soothed and reassured by the familiarity of the ramshackle: weathered posts, smouldering bonfires, unaccountably amiable backs of houses, the gaiety of cabbages. And when he was older, how many mornings such as this had he stood here in chill brittle sunlight, rapt and trembling at the thought of the infinite possibilities of the future, dreaming of mysterious pale young women in green gowns walking through dewy grass under great trees. He passed through a gap in the tumbledown paling into the narrow lane that ran behind the gardens. Brambles sprouted here at the base of a high white wall. A faint, sweetish, not altogether unpleasant tang of nightsoil laced the air. An old woman in a black cloak with a basket of eggs on her arm passed him by, bidding him *Grüss Gott* out of a toothless mouth. An extraordinary stealthy stillness reigned, as if an event of great significance were waiting for him to be gone so that it could occur in perfect solitude. The night, the candles and the murmuring, the wracked creature dying on the bed, all that was immensely far away now, unreal. Yet it had been as much a part of the world as this sunlight and stillness, those pencil-lines of blue smoke rising unruffled into the paler blue: was all this also unreal, then? He turned, and stood for a long time gazing toward the linden tree. It was to be cut down, so Gertner had said. It was old, and in danger of falling. The Canon nodded once, smiling a little, and walked back slowly through the resurrected garden to the house.

* * *

HE COULD NOT in honesty mourn his uncle's death. There was guilt, of course, regret at the thought of opportunities lost (perhaps I wronged him?), but these were not true feelings, only empty rituals, purification rites, as it were, performed in order that the ghost might be laid; for death, he now realised, produces a sudden nothingness in the world, a hole in the fabric of the world, with which the survivors must learn to live, and whether the lost one be loved or hated makes no difference, that learning still is difficult. He was haunted for a long time by a kind of ferocious implacable absence stamped unmistakably with the Bishop's seal.

Then, inevitably, came the feeling of relief. Cautiously he tested the bars of his cage and found them not so rigid as they had been before. He even began to look a little more kindly on his work, telling himself that after all what he considered a poor flawed thing the world would surely think a wonder. He completed the *Commentariolus*, and, at once appalled and excited by his own daring, had copies made of it by a scribe in the town which he quietly distributed among the few scholars he considered sympathetic and discreet. Then, with teeth gritted, he awaited the explosion that would surely be set off by the seven axioms which together formed the basis of the theory of a sun-centred universe. He feared ridicule, refutations, abuse; most of all he feared involvement. He would be dragged out, kicking and howling, into the market place, he would be stood on a platform like a fairground exhibit and invited to expound proofs. It was ridiculous, horrible, not to be borne! Again he began to wonder if he would be well advised to destroy his work and thus have done with the whole business. But his book was all he had left – how could he burn it? Yet if they should come, sneering and snarling and bellowing for proof, smash down his door and snatch the manuscript from his hands, dear God, what then?

It was not the academics that he feared most (he felt he knew how to handle them), but the people, the poor ordinary deluded people ever on the lookout for the sign, the message, the word that would herald the imminent coming of the millennium and all that it entailed: liberty, happiness, redemption. They would seize upon his work, or a mangled version of it more like, with awful fervour, beside themselves in their eagerness to believe that what he was offering them was an explanation of the world and their lives in it. And when sooner or later it dawned upon them that they had been betrayed yet again, that here was no simple comprehensive picture of reality, no new instauration, then they would turn on him. But even that was not the point. O true, he had no wish to be reviled, but far more important than that was his wish not to mislead the people. They must be made to understand that by banishing Earth and man along with it from the centre of the universe, he was passing no judgments, expounding no philosophy, but merely stating what is the case. The game of which he was master could exercise the mind, but it would not teach them how to live.

He need not have worried. There was no explosion, no one came. There was not even a tapping at his door. The world overlooked him. It was just as well. He was relieved. He had given them the *Commentariolus*, the preface as it were, and they had taken no notice. Now he could finish writing his book in peace, unmolested by idiots. For surely they were all idiots, if they could ignore the challenge he had thrown down at their feet, idiots and cowards, that they would not see the breathtaking splendour and daring of his concepts – he would show them, yes,

yes! And sullenly, consumed by disappointment and frustration, he sat down to his desk, to show them. The great spheres wheeled in a crystal firmament in his head, and when (rarely, rarely!) he looked into the night sky, he was troubled by a vague sense of recognition that puzzled him until he remembered that it was that sky, those cold white specks of light, that had given form to his mind's world. Then the familiar feeling of dislocation assailed him as he strove in vain to discern a connection between the actual and the imagined. Inevitably, inexplicably, Andreas's ravaged face swam into view, slyly smiling – Constellation of Syphilis! – blotting out all else.

*

'One that would speak with you, Canon.'

Canon Koppernigk looked up frowning and shook his head vehemently in silent refusal. He did not wish to be disturbed. Max only shrugged, and with a brief sardonic bow withdrew. Even before his visitor appeared the Canon knew from that inimitable respectful light step on the stairs who it was. He sighed, and put away carefully into a drawer the page of manuscript on which he had been working.

'My dear Doctor, forgive me, I hope I do not disturb you?' Canon Tiedemann Giese was a good-humoured, somewhat stout, curiously babyish fresh-faced man of thirty. He had a large flaxen head, an incongruously stern hooked nose, squarish useless hands, and wide innocent eyes that managed to bestow a unique tender concern on even the least thing that they encountered. Although he came of an aristocratic line, he disapproved of the opulent lives led by his colleagues in the Chapter, a disapproval that he expressed – or paraded, as some said – by dressing always in the common style in smocks and breeches and stout sensible riding boots. His academic achievements were impressive, yet he was careful to wear his learning lightly. By some means he had got hold of a copy of the *Commentariolus*, and although he had never mentioned that work directly, he let it be known, by certain sly remarks and meaningful looks that made Canon Koppernigk flinch, that he had been won over entirely to the heliocentric doctrine. Canon Giese was one of the world's innate enthusiasts.

'Please sit,' Canon Koppernigk said, with a wintry smile. 'There is something I can do for you?'

Giese laughed nervously. He was the younger of the two by some seven years only, yet his manner in Canon Koppernigk's presence was that of a timid but eager bright schoolboy. With desperate nonchalance he said:

'Just passing, you know, and I thought I might call in to . . .'

'Yes.'

Giese's discomfited eye slid off and wandered about the cell. It was low and white, white everywhere: even the beams of the ceiling were white. On the wall behind the desk at which the Doctor sat was fixed an hourglass in a frame, his wide-brimmed hat hanging on a hook, and a wooden stand holding a few medical implements. Set in a deep embrasure, a small window with panes of bottled glass gave on to the Frisches Haff and the great arc of the Baltic beyond. The rickety door leading on to the wall was open, and out there could be seen the upright sundial and the triquetrum, a rudimentary crossbow affair over five ells tall for measuring celestial angles, a curiously distraught-looking thing standing with its frozen arms flung skywards. Was it with the aid of these poor pieces only, Giese wondered, that the Doctor had formulated his wonderful theory? A gull alighted on the windowsill, and for a moment he gazed thoughtfully at the bird's pale eye magnified in the bottled glass. (Magnified? – but no, no, a foolish notion . . .)

'I too have some interest in astronomy, you know, Doctor,' he said. 'Of course, I am merely a dabbler, you understand. But I think I know enough to recognise greatness when I encounter it, as I have done, lately.' And he leered. Canon Koppernigk's stony expression did not alter. He was really a peculiar cold closed person, difficult to touch. Giese sighed. 'Well, in fact, Doctor, there *is* a matter on which I wished to speak to you. The subject is, how shall I say, a delicate one, painful even. Perhaps you know what I am referring to? No?' He began to fidget. He was seated on a low hard chair before the Doctor's desk. It was on occasions such as this that he heartily regretted having accepted the position of Precentor of the Frauenburg Chapter, which had fallen to him on Canon von Lossainen's accession to the bishopric following the death of Lucas Waczelrodt: he was not cut out for this kind of thing, really. 'It is your brother, you see,' he said carefully. 'Canon Andreas.'

'O?'

'I know that it must be a painful subject for you, Doctor, and indeed that is why I have come to you personally, not only as Precentor, but as, I hope, a friend.' He paused. Canon Koppernigk raised one eyebrow enquiringly, but said nothing. 'The Bishop, you see, and indeed the Chapter, all feel that, well, that your brother's presence, in his lamentable condition, is not . . . that is to say—'

'Presence?' said the Doctor. 'But my brother is in Italy.'

Giese stared. 'O but no, Doctor, no; I assumed that you – have you not been told? He is here, in Frauenburg. He has been here for some days now. I assumed he would have called on you. He is not – he is not well, you know.'

*

He was not well: he was a walking horror. In the years since the Canon had seen him last he had surrendered his own form to that of his disease, so that he was no longer a man but a *memento mori* only, a shrivelled twisted hunchbacked thing on whose ruined face was fixed a death's-head grin. All this the Canon learned at second hand, for his brother kept away from him, not out of tact, of course, but because he found it amusing to haunt him from a distance, by proxy as it were, knowing how much more painful it would be that others should carry word of his disgraceful doings into the fastness of the Canon's austere white tower. He lodged at a kip down in the stews (where else would have him?), but flaunted his frightful form by day in the environs of the cathedral, where he terrified the town's children and their mothers alike; and once even, one Sunday morning, he came lurching up the central aisle during High Mass and knelt in elaborate genuflexion at the altar rails, behind which poor ailing Bishop von Lossainen sat in horror-stricken immobility on his purple throne.

It was not long, of course, until there began to be talk of black magic, of vampirism and werewolves. Crosses appeared on the doors of the town. A young girl, it was said, had been found in the hills with her throat torn open. By night a black-cloaked demon haunted the streets, and howling and eerie laughter was heard in the darkness. Toto the idiot, who had the gift of second sight, was said to have seen a huge bird with the pinched violet face of a man fly low over the roofs on All Souls' Eve, shrieking. Hysteria spread through Frauenburg like the pest, and throughout that sombre smoky autumn small groups of grimfaced men gathered at twilight on street corners and muttered darkly, and mothers called their children home early from play. The Jews outside the walls began discreetly to fortify their houses, fearing a pogrom. Things could not continue thus.

The first snow of winter was falling when the canons met in the conference hall of the chapterhouse, determined finally to resolve the situation. They had already decided privately on a course of action, but a general convocation was necessary to put an official seal upon it. The meeting had a further purpose: Canon Koppernigk had so far remained entirely aloof from the problem, as if his brother were no concern of his, and the Chapter, outraged at his silence and apparent indifference, was determined that he should be made to bear his share of responsibility. Indeed, feeling among the canons ran so high that they were no longer quite clear in their minds as to which of the brothers deserved the harsher treatment, and some were even in favour of banishing both and thus having done with that troublesome tribe for good and ever.

The Canon arrived late at the chapterhouse, wrapped up against the cold and with his wide-brimmed hat pulled low. A thin forbidding figure in black, he moved slowly down the hall and took his place at the table, removed his hat, his gloves, and having crossed himself in silence folded his hands before him and lifted his eyes to the bruisedark sky looming in the high windows. His colleagues, who had fallen silent as he entered, now stirred themselves and glanced morosely about the table, dissatisfied and obscurely disappointed; they had somehow expected something of him today, something dramatic and untoward, a yell of defiance or a grovelling plea for leniency, even threats perhaps, or a curse, but not this, this *nothingness* – why, he was hardly here at all!

Giese at the head of the table coughed, and, continuing the address that Canon Nicolas's coming had interrupted, said:

'The situation then, gentlemen, is delicate. The Bishop demands that we take action, and now even the people press for the afflicted Canon's, ah, departure. However, I would counsel against too hasty or too severe a solution. We must not exaggerate the gravity of this affair. The Bishop himself, as we know, is not well, and therefore may not be expected perhaps to take a perfectly reasoned view on these matters—'

'*Is he saying that von Lossainen has the pox?*' someone enquired in a loud whisper, and there was a subdued rumble of laughter.

'—The people, of course,' Giese continued stoutly, 'the people as ever are given to superstitious and hysterical talk, and should be ignored. We must recognise, gentlemen, that our brother, Canon Andreas, is mortally afflicted, but that he has not willed this terrible curse upon himself. We must, in short, try to be charitable. Now—' While before he had simply not looked at Canon Koppernigk, now he began elaborately and with tight-lipped sternness not to look at him, and fidgeted nervously with the sheaf of papers before him on the table. '—I have canvassed opinion generally among you, and certain proposals have emerged which are, in my opinion, somewhat extreme. However, these proposals are . . . the proposals . . . ah . . . 'Now he looked at the Canon, and blanched, and could not go on. There was silence, and then the Danziger Canon Heinrich Snellenburg, a big swarthy truculent man, snorted angrily down his nostrils and declared:

'It is proposed to break all personal connections with the leper, to demand that he account for the sum of twelve hundred gold florins entrusted to him by this Chapter, to seize his prebend and all other revenues, and to grant him a modest annuity on condition that he takes himself off from our midst immediately. That, Herr Precentor, gentlemen, is what is proposed.' And he turned his dark sullen gaze on Canon Koppernigk. 'If there are dissenting voices, let them be heard now.'

The Canon was still watching the snow swirling greyly against the window. All waited in vain for him to speak. He seemed genuinely indifferent to the proceedings, and somehow that genuineness annoyed the Chapter far more than pretence would have done, for they could at least have understood pretence. Had the man no ordinary human feelings whatever? He said nothing, only now and then drummed his fingers lightly, thoughtfully, on the edge of the table. But even if he would not speak they were yet determined to have some response of him, and so, with unspoken unanimity, they agreed that his silence should be taken as a protest. Canon von der Trank, an aristocratic German with the thin nervous look about him of a whippet, pursed up his wide pale pink lips and said:

'Whatever it is that we do, gentlemen, certainly we must do something. The matter must be dealt with, there must be a quick clean end to the present intolerable situation. The Precentor gives it as his opinion that the measures we have proposed are too extreme. He tells us that this—' his sharp fastidious nose twitched at the tip '—this *person* did not will upon himself the disease that afflicts him, yet we may ask whose will, if not his, was involved? All are aware of the nature of his malady, which he contracted in the bawdyhouses of Italy. We are urged to be charitable, but our charity and our care must be extended firstly to the faithful of this diocese: them we have the duty to protect from this outrageous source of scandal. And further, there is the reputation of this Chapter to be considered. This is the very sort of thing that the monk Luther will be delighted to hear of, so that he may add it as another strand to the whip with which he lashes the Church.

Therefore I say let us hear no more talk of charity and caution. Our duty is clear – let us perform it. The leper must be declared anathema and driven hence without delay!'

A rumble of yeas followed this address, and all with set jaws glared at Giese grimly, who squirmed, and mopped his forehead, and turned a beseeching gaze on Canon Koppernigk.

'What do you think, Doctor? Surely you wish to make some reply?'

The Canon took his eyes reluctantly from the darkling window and glanced about the table. Snellenburg, you owe me a hundred marks; von der Trank, you hate me because I am a tradesman's son and yet cleverer than you; Giese – poor Giese. What does it matter? Lately he had begun to feel that he was somehow fading, that his physical self was as it were evaporating, becoming transparent; soon there would remain only a mind, a sort of grey ghostly amoeba spinning silently in the dead air. What does it matter? He turned away. How softly the snow falls! 'I think,' he murmured, 'that it would be foolish to worry overmuch as to what Father Luther thinks of us or says. He will go the way all others of his kind have gone, and will be forgotten with the rest.'

They stared at him, nonplussed. Did he think this was some kind of religious discussion? Had he even been listening? For a long time no one spoke, and then Canon Snellenburg shrugged and said:

'Well, if the fellow's own brother will not even say a word in his defence!—'

'Please, please gentlemen,' Giese cried, as if convinced that the table was about to rise up and attack the Canon with fists. 'Please! Doctor, I wonder if you realise fully what is being proposed? The Chapter intends to strip your brother of all rights and privileges whatever, to – to cast him out, like a beggar!'

But Canon Koppernigk paid no heed. Look at them! First they blamed me because he is my brother, now they despise me because I will not defend him. Wait, Snellenburg, just wait, I will have my hundred marks of you! Just then he found an unexpected and unwanted ally, when another of the canons, one Alexander Sculteti, a scrawny fellow with a red nose, stood up and delivered himself of a rambling and disjointed defence of Canon Andreas to which nobody listened, for Sculteti was a reprobate who kept a woman and a houseful of children at his farm outside the walls, and besides, he was far from sober. Canon Koppernigk took up his hat, and wrapping his cloak about him went out into the burgeoning darkness and the snow.

*

As if he had been waiting for a signal, Andreas visited his brother for the first time on the very day that he heard of the Chapter's decision to banish him. For a man so grievously maimed he negotiated the stairs of the tower with surprising stealth, and all that could be heard of his coming was his laboured breathing and the light fastidious tapping of his stick. He was indeed in a bad way now, but what shocked the Canon most were the signs of ageing that even the damage wrought by the disease could not outweigh. The few swatches of hair remaining on his skull had turned a yellowish grey, and his eyes that had once flashed fire were weary and rheumy and querulous. His uncanny intuition, however, had not forsaken him, for he said:

'Why do you stare so, brother – did you expect me to have become whole again? I am nearing fifty, I do not have long more, thank God.'

'Andreas—'

'Do not *Andreas* me; I have heard what plans the Chapter has in store for me. And now – wait! – you are going to tell me how on your knees you pleaded my cause, spoke of my sterling work at Rome on behalf of little Ermland, how I have taken up the banner in the crusade against the Teutonic Knights passed on to me by our dear late uncle – eh, brother, eh, are you going to tell me that?'

The Canon shook his head. 'I know nothing of your doings, and so how should I plead such mitigation?'

Andreas glanced at him quickly, surprised despite himself at the coldness of his brother's tone. 'Well, it's no matter,' he growled. He eyed morosely the bare white walls. 'Still stargazing, are you, brother?'

'Yes.'

'Good, good. It's well to have some pastime.' He sat down slowly at the Canon's desk and folded his ravaged hands on the knob of his stick. His mouth, all eaten away at the corners, was fixed in a horrid leer. Extraordinary, that one could be so damaged and still live. It was spleen and spite, surely, that kept him going. He gazed through the bottled windowpanes at the blurred blue of the Baltic. 'I will not be made to go,' he said. 'I will not be kicked out, like a dog. I am a canon of this Chapter, I have rights. You cannot compel me to go, whatever you do, and you may tell the holy canons that. I shall leave Frauenburg, yes, Prussia, I shall return to Rome, happily, but only when the interdict against me is lifted, and when my prebend and all my revenues are restored. Until then I shall remain here, frightening the peasants and drinking the blood of their daughters.' Suddenly he laughed, that familiar dry scraping sound. 'I am quite flattered, you know, by this unwonted notoriety. Is it not strange, that I had to begin visibly to rot before I could win respect? Life, brother, life is very odd. And now good day; I trust you will communicate my terms to your colleagues? I feel the message will carry more weight, coming from you, who are so intimately involved in the affair.'

Max had been listening outside the door, for he entered at once unbidden, with the ghost of a grin on his lean face. At the foot of the stairs he and Andreas stopped and whispered together briefly; seemingly they had patched up their Heilsberg quarrel. The Canon shivered. He was cold.

*

The battle dragged on for three months. Chapter sessions grew more and more frantic. At one such meeting Andreas himself made an appearance, stumbled drunk into the conference hall and sat laughing among the outraged canons, mumbling and dribbling out of his ruined mouth. At length they panicked, and gave in.

The seizure of his prebend was withdrawn, and he was granted a higher annuity. On a bleak day in January he left Frauenburg forever. He did not bid his brother goodbye, at least not in any conventional way; but Max, the Canon's sometime servant, went with him, saying he was sick of Prussia, only to return again that same night, not by road, however, but floating face down on the river's back, a bloated gross black bag with a swollen purplish face and glazed eyes open wide in astonishment, grotesquely dead.

* * *

IT ROSE UP in the east like black smoke, stamped over the land like a ravening giant, bearing before it a brazen mask of the dark fierce face of Albrecht von Hohenzollern Ansbach, last Grand Master of the brotherhood of the Order of St Mary's Hospital of the Germans at Jerusalem, otherwise called the Teutonic Knights. Once again they were pushing westward, determined finally to break the Polish hold on Royal Prussia and unite the three princedoms of the southern Baltic under Albrecht's rule; once again the vice closed on little Ermland. In 1516 the Knights, backed up by gangs of German mercenaries, made their first incursions across the eastern frontier. They plundered the countryside, burnt the farms and looted the monasteries, raped and slaughtered, all with the inimitable fervent enthusiasm of an army that has had its bellyful of peace. It was not yet a fully fledged war, but a kind of sport, a mere tuning up for the real battle with Poland that was to come, and hence the bigger Ermland towns were left unmolested, for the present.

In November of that turbulent year Canon Koppernigk was appointed Land Provost, and transferred his residence to the great fortress of Allenstein, lying some twenty leagues south-east of Frauenburg in the midst of the great plain. It was an onerous and exacting post, but one with which, during the three years that he held it, he proved himself well fitted to cope. His duties included the supervision of Allenstein as well as the castle at nearby Mehlsack and the domains in those areas; he supervised also the collection of the tithes paid to the Frauenburg Chapter by the two towns and the villages and estates roundabout. At the end of each year he was required to submit to the Chapter a written report of all these affairs, a task to which he applied himself with scrupulous care and, indeed, probity.

But above all else he was responsible for ensuring that the areas under his control were fully tenanted. With the rise of the towns, the land over the previous hundred years had become steadily more and more depopulated, but now, with the Knights rampaging across the frontier, driving all before them, the exodus from the land to the urban centres had quickened alarmingly. Without tenants, so the Frauenburg Chapter reasoned, there would be no taxes, but beyond that immediate danger was the fear that the very fabric of society was unravelling. As long ago as 1494 the Prussian ordinances had imposed restrictions upon the peasants that had effectively made serfs of them – but what ordinance could hold a farmer locked to a burnt-out hovel and ravaged fields? During his three years as Provost, Canon Koppernigk dealt with seventy-five cases of resettlement of abandoned holdings, but even so he had barely scratched the surface of the problem.

Those were difficult and demoralising years for him, whose life hitherto had been lived almost entirely in the lofty empyrean of speculative science. Along with the rigours of his administrative duties came the further and far more wearying necessity of holding at arm's length, so to speak, the grimy commonplace world with which those duties brought him into unavoidable contact. For it was necessary to fend it off, lest it should contaminate his vision, lest its pervasive and, one might say, stubborn seediness should seep into the very coils of his thought and taint with earthiness the transcendent purity of his theory of the heavens. Yet he could not but feel for the plight of the people, whose pain and anguish was forever afterwards summed up for him in the memory of the corpse of a young peasant woman that he came upon in the smouldering ruins of a plundered village the name of which he did not even know. As he expressed it many years later to his friend and colleague Canon Giese: 'The wench (for indeed she was hardly more than a child) had been tortured to death by the soldiery. I shall not describe to you, my dear Tiedemann, the state in which they had left her, although the image of that poor torn thing is burned ineradicably upon my recollection. They had worked on her for hours, laboured over her with infinite care, almost with a kind of obscene love, if I may express it thus, in order to ensure her as agonising a death as it was possible for them to devise. I realised then, perhaps (to my shame I say it!) perhaps for the *first time*, the inexpendable capacity for evil which there is in man. How, I asked myself then (I ask it now!), how can we hope to be redeemed, that would do such things to our fellow creatures?'

As well as Land Provost, he was also for a time head of the *Broteamt*, or Bread Office, at Frauenburg, in which capacity he had charge over the Chapter's bakeries and the malt and corn stores, the brewery, and the great mill at the foot of Cathedral Hill. Repeatedly he held the post of Chancellor, supervising the Chapter's records and correspondence and legal paperwork. Briefly too he was *Mortuarius*, whose task it was to administer the numerous and often considerable sums willed to the Church or donated by the families of the wealthy dead.

Along with these public duties, he was being called upon in another sphere, that of astronomy, to make himself heard in the world. His fame was spreading, despite the innate humility and even diffidence which had kept him silent for so long when others far less gifted than he were agitating the air with their empty babbling. Canon Bernhard Wapowsky of Cracow University, a learned and influential man, requested of him an expert opinion on the (defective, defective!) astronomical treatise lately put out by the Nuremberger, Johann Werner, a request with which Canon Koppernigk readily complied, glad of the opportunity to take a swipe at that proud foolish fellow who had dared to question Ptolemy. Then came a letter from Cardinal Schönberg of Capua, one of the Pope's special advisers, urging the learned

Doctor to communicate in printed form his wonderful discoveries to the world. All this, of course, is not to mention the invitation that had come to him in 1514, by way of Canon Schiller in Rome (no longer the representative of the Frauenburg Chapter, but domestic chaplain to Leo X, no less), to take part in a Lateran Council on calendar reform. Canon Koppernigk refused to attend the council, however, giving as excuse his belief that such reform could not be carried out until the motions of the Sun and Moon were more precisely known. (One may remark here, that while this account – *ipse dixit*, after all! – of his unwillingness to accept what was most probably an invitation from the Pope himself, must be respected, one yet cannot, having regard to the date, and the stage at which we know the Canon's great work then was, help suspecting that the *learned Doctor*, to use Cardinal Schönberg's mode of address, was using the occasion to drop a careful hint of the revolution which, thirty years later, he was to set in train in the world of computational astronomy.)

Thus, anyway, it can be seen that, however unwillingly, he had become a public man. The Chapter was well pleased with him, and welcomed him at last as a true colleague. Some there were, it is true, who did not abandon their suspicions, remembering his extraordinary and unaccountable behaviour at the time of the distasteful affair of his outrageous brother's banishment. Among that section of the Chapter, which included of course Canons Snellenburg and von der Trank, it was never finally decided whether the Doctor should be regarded as a villain because of his connection with the *poxed Italian* (as von der Trank, his pale sharp aristocratic nose a-twitch, had dubbed Andreas), or as a cold despicable brute who would not even rise to the defence of his own brother. While that kind of thing may be dismissed as the product merely of envy and spite, nevertheless there *was* something about Canon Koppernigk – all saw it, even the kindly and all-forgiving Canon Giese – a certain lack, a transparence, as it were, that was more than the natural aloofness and other-worldliness of a brilliant scientist. It was as if, within the vigorous and able public man, there was a void, as if, behind the ritual, all was a hollow save for one thin taut cord of steely inexpressible anguish stretching across the nothingness.

*

The spring of 1519 saw the sudden collapse of the political and military situation in the southern Baltic lands. Sigismund of Poland, perhaps at last recognising the truth of Bishop Waczelrodt's contention years before that the Cross represented a very real threat to his kingdom, summoned Grand Master Albrecht to Torun for peace talks. Albrecht refused to negotiate directly, and Poland immediately mobilised and marched on Prussia. Total war seemed inevitable. The Knights now suggested that the Bishop of Ermland should mediate between themselves and Sigismund. Bishop von Lossainen's health, however, was by this time seriously in decline. The Frauenburg Chapter, therefore, knowing well that little Ermland would be the theatre for the coming war, decided that in the Bishop's stead the Precentor, Canon Tiedemann Giese, along with Land Provost Koppernigk, should travel at once to Königsberg and attempt to reconcile the warring parties.

Were the wrong men chosen for the task? Precentor Giese thought so, afterwards. He had, he supposed, gone to Königsberg too innocently, with too much trust in the essential worthiness of men, and so had failed where a hard cold scheming fellow might have succeeded. Or was it that in his heart he had known all along that the mission was doomed to failure, and this knowledge had affected his ability to negotiate? Well well, who could say? From the start he had not believed that Albrecht, although a Lutheran, could be so black as he was painted. It was said that he was irredeemably wicked, a monster, worse even than Hungary's infamous Vlad Drakulya the Impaler. But no, the good Precentor could not believe that. When he told his companion so, as they rode eastward through dawn mists along the coast at the head of their escort of Prussian mercenaries, Canon Koppernigk looked at him queerly and said:

'I would agree with you that likely he is no worse nor better than any other prince – but they are all bad.'

'You are right, Doctor, perhaps, and yet . . .'

'Well?'

'You are right, yes, quite right. Ahem.'

Precentor Giese was a little afraid of Canon Koppernigk; or perhaps that is too strong – perhaps a better word would be nervous, he was a little nervous of him, yes. There was at times a certain silent intensity, or ferocity even, about the man that alarmed those who came close to him, not that many were allowed to do so, of course, come close, that is. This morning, hunched in the saddle with his hat pulled low and his cloak wrapped about him to the nose so that only the eyes were visible, staring keenly ahead into the mist, he seemed more than ever burdened with a secret intolerable knowledge. Maybe it was this stoical air the Canon had of a man marked out for special suffering that made Giese's heart ache with sympathy and concern for his friend, if he, Giese, could call him, the Canon, a friend, as he was determined to do, justified or not.

But friendship aside, was it wise of the Chapter, Giese could not help wondering, to have sent the Canon with him on this delicate mission? He, the Canon, had always been something of a recluse, despite his public duties (which of course he fulfilled with impeccable et cetera), had always held the world at arm's length, as it were, and while this aspect of his character was not in any way a fault, indeed was only to be expected of one engaged in such important and demanding work as he was, it did mean that he was, so to say, unpractised in the subtleties of diplomacy, that he was, in fact, quite tactless, although it could be said that this very tactlessness, if that was what it was, was no more than evidence of a charming innocence and lack of guile. Well, not innocence perhaps . . . Canon Giese glanced at the dark figure in the saddle beside him: no, definitely not innocence.

O dear! The Precentor sighed. It was all very difficult.

*

They arrived at Königsberg as night came on. Their escort was allowed no further than the city gates. Albrecht's castle was a vast grim fortress on a hill. The two emissaries were led into a large white and gold hall. Crowds milled about here, soldiers, diplomats, clerics, ornate women, all going nowhere purposefully. Canon Koppernigk stood in silence waiting, wrapped in his black cloak, with his hat still on. Precentor Giese fidgeted. A band of courtiers, some armed, marched swiftly into the hall and wheeled to a halt. Grand Master Albrecht was a small quick reptile-like man with a thin dark face and pointed ears lying flat against his skull. His heavy quilted doublet and tight breeches gave him the look of a well-fed lizard. A gold medallion bearing the insignia of the Order hung by a heavy chain on his breast. (It was said that he was impotent.) He smiled briefly, displaying long yellow teeth.

'Reverend gentlemen,' he said in German, 'welcome. This way, please.'

They all turned and marched smartly out of the hall, cutting a swathe through the obsequious crowd. Candles burned in a marble corridor. Their boots crashed on the cold stone. They wheeled into a small chamber hung with maps and a huge portrait of the Grand Master standing in an heroic pose before his massed army. Albrecht sat down at an oaken desk, while his party took up positions behind him with folded arms. Flunkeys came forward bearing chairs, and Albrecht with a quick gesture invited the Canons to sit. A silken diplomat leaned down and whispered in his ear. He nodded rapidly, pursing his mouth, and then looked up and said:

'We demand an oath of allegiance from the Bishop of Ermland and the Frauenburg Chapter. Mark, this is a condition of negotiation, not of settlement. We are prepared to speak to Poland through you only when we are assured of your loyalty.' There was no bluster, no threat, only a brisk statement of fact. He was almost cheerful. He grinned. 'Well?'

Precentor Giese was astounded. He had come to negotiate,

not to take delivery of an ultimatum! He chose to disbelieve his ears.

'My dear sir,' he said, 'I fear you misunderstand the situation. Ermland is a sovereign princedom, and owes allegiance to its Prince-Bishop and clergy and none other. It was you yourself, you will recall, who requested us to mediate. Now—'

Albrecht was shaking his head.

'No no,' he said gently, 'no. It is you, I think, Herr Canon, who has misunderstood how matters are. Ermland is a small weak province. You wish to believe, or you wish *me* to believe, that you are, so to speak, an honest broker who observes matters with utter dispassion. But this war will be fought on your fields, in the streets of your towns and villages. Even if we fail to defeat Poland, as we may well fail, and even if we do not capture Royal Prussia, which is also possible I regret to say, nevertheless we shall certainly take Ermland. Sigismund will not protect you. Therefore why not join with us now and thus avoid a deal of . . . unpleasantness? Men who are anxious to win the favour of a prince present themselves to him with the possessions they value most: since you wish to win my favour in these negotiations, and since obviously you value loyalty most dearly, should you not in that case swear to be loyal to us?'

'But this is preposterous!' Giese cried, looking about him indignantly for support. He met only the cold eyes of the Grand Master's men ranged silently behind the desk. 'Preposterous,' he said again, but faintly.

Albrecht lifted his hands in a gesture of regret.

'Then there is nothing more to say,' he said. There was a silence. He turned his sardonic faintly humorous gaze now for the first time on Canon Koppernigk, and his eyes gleamed. 'Herr Canon, we are honoured by your presence. The fame of Doctor Copernicus is not unknown even in this far-flung province. We have heard of your wonderful theory of the heavens. We are eager to hear more. Perhaps you will dine with us tonight?' He waited. 'You do not speak.'

The Canon had turned somewhat pale. Giese was watching

him expectantly. Now this insolent knight would receive the kind of answer he deserved! But, in a voice so low it could be hardly heard, Canon Koppernigk said only:

'There is nothing more to say.'

Albrecht bowed his head, smiling thinly. 'I meant, of course, Herr Canon, when I said what you have just echoed, that there is nothing more to say in these – ha – negotiations. On other, more congenial topics there is surely much we can discuss. Come, my dear Doctor, let us take a glass of wine together, like civilised men.'

Then followed that curious exchange that Precentor Giese was to remember ever afterwards with puzzlement and grave misgiving. Canon Koppernigk grimaced. He seemed in some pain.

'Grand Master,' he said, 'you are contemplating waging war for the sake of sport. What is Ermland to you, or Royal Prussia? What is Poland even?'

Albrecht had been expecting something of the sort, for he answered at once:

'They are glory, Herr Doctor, they are posterity!'

'I do not understand that.'

'But you do, I think.'

'No. Glory, posterity, these are abstract concepts. I do not understand such things.'

'You, Doctor? – you do not understand abstract concepts, you who have expressed the eternal truths of the world in just such terms? Come sir!'

'I will not engage in empty discussion. We have come to Königsberg to ask you to consider the suffering that you are visiting upon the people, the greater suffering that war with Poland will bring.'

'The people?' Albrecht said, frowning. 'What people?'

'The common people.'

'Ah. The common people. But they have suffered always, and always will. It is in a way what they are for. You flinch. Herr Doctor, I am disappointed in you. The common people? – pah. What are they to us? You and I, *mein Freund*, we are lords of the earth, the great ones, the major men, the makers of supreme fictions. Look here at these poor dull brutes—' His thin dark hand took in the silent crowd behind him, the flunkeys, Precentor Giese, the painted army. '—They do not even understand what we are talking about. But *you* understand, yes, yes. The people will suffer as they have always suffered, meanly, mewling for pity and mercy, but only you and I know what true suffering is, the lofty suffering of the hero. Do not speak to me of the people! They are the brutish mask of war, but war itself is that which they in the ritual of their suffering express but can never comprehend, for their eyes are ever on the ground, while you and I look up, ever upward, into the blue! The people – peasants, soldiers, generals – they are my tool, as mathematics is yours, by which I come directly at the true, the eternal, the real. Ah yes, Doctor Copernicus, you and I – you and I! The generations may execrate us for what we do to their world, but we and those rare ones like us shall have made them what they are . . .!' He broke off then and dabbed with a silk kerchief at the corners of his thin mouth. He had a smug, drained, sated look about him, that the troubled Precentor found himself comparing to that of a trooper fastening up his breeches after a particularly brutal and gratifying rape. Canon Koppernigk, his face ashen, rose in silence and turned to go. Albrecht, in the tone he might have used to remark upon the weather, said: 'I had your uncle the Bishop poisoned, you know.' The crowd behind him stirred, and Giese, halfway up from his chair, sat down again abruptly. Canon Koppernigk faltered, but would not turn. Albrecht said lightly, almost skittishly, to his hunched black back: 'See, Doctor, how shocked they are? But *you* are not shocked, are you? Well then, say nothing. It is no matter. Farewell. We shall meet again, perhaps, when the times are better.'

As they went down the hill from the castle, borne through the gleaming darkness on a river of swaying torches, Precentor Giese, confused and pained, tried to speak to his friend, but the Doctor would not hear, and answered nothing.

*

At dead of night to the castle of Allenstein they came, a hundred men and horse, Poland's finest, bearing the standard of their king before them, thundered over the drawbridge, under the portcullis, past the drowsing sentry into the courtyard and there dismounted amidst a great clamour of hoofs and rattling sabres and the roars of Sergeant Tod, a battle-scarred tough old soldier with a heart of stoutest oak. 'Right lads!' he boomed, 'no rest for you tonight!' and dispatched them at once to the walls. 'Aw for fuck's sake, Sarge!' they groaned, but jumped to their post with alacrity, for each man knew in his simple way that they were here not only to protect a lousy castle and a pack of cringing bloody Prussians, but that the honour of Poland herself was at stake. Their Captain, a gallant young fellow, scion of one of the leading Polish families, covered with his cloak the proud glowing smile that played upon his lips as he watched them scramble by torchlight to the battlements, and then, pausing only to pinch the rosy cheek of a shy serving wench curtseying in the doorway, he hurried up the great main staircase with long-legged haste to the Crystal Hall where Land Provost Koppernigk was deep in urgent conference with his beleaguered household. He halted on the threshold, and bringing his heels together smartly delivered a salute that his commanding officer would have been proud to witness.

The Canon looked up irritably. 'Yes? What is it now? Who are you?'

'Captain Chopin, Herr Provost, at your service!'

'Captain *what*?'

'I am an officer of His Gracious Majesty King Sigismund's First Royal Cavalry, come this night from Mehlsack with one hundred of His Highness's finest troops. My orders are to defend to the last man this castle of Allenstein and all within the walls.' ('O God be praised!' cried several voices at once.) 'Our army is on the march westward and expects to engage the foe by morning. The Teutonic Knights are at Heilsberg, and are bombarding the walls of the fortress there. As you are aware, Herr Provost, they have already taken the towns of Guttstadt and Wormditt to the north. A flanking assault on Allenstein is expected hourly. These devils and their arch fiend Grand Master Albrecht must be stopped – and they shall be stopped, by God's blood! (Forgive a soldier's language, sire.) You will recall the siege of Frauenburg, how they fired the town and slaughtered the people without mercy. Only the bravery of your Prussian mercenaries prevented them from breaching the cathedral wall. Your Chapter fled to the safety of Danzig, leaving to you, Herr Provost, the defence of Allenstein and Mehlsack. However, in that regard, I must regretfully inform you now that Mehlsack has been sacked, sire, and—'

But here he was interrupted by the hasty entrance of a large dark burly man attired in the robes of a canon.

'Koppernigk!' cried Canon Snellenburg (for it is he), 'they are bombarding Heilsberg and it's said the Bishop is dead—' He stopped, catching sight of the proud young fellow standing to attention in his path. 'Who are you?'

'Captain Chopin, sire, at your—'

'Captain *who*?'

Zounds! the Captain thought, are they all deaf? 'I am an officer of His Gracious—'

'Yes yes,' said Snellenburg, waving his large hands. 'Another damned Pole, I know. Listen, Koppernigk, the bastards are at Heilsberg. They'll be here by morning. What are you going to do?'

The Land Provost looked mildly from the Canon to the Captain, at his household crouched about the table, the secretaries, whey-faced clergy, minor administrators, and then to the frightened gaggle of servants ranged expectantly behind him. He shrugged.

'We shall surrender, I suppose,' he said.

'For God's sake—!'

'Herr Provost—!'

But Canon Koppernigk seemed strangely detached from these urgent matters. He stood up from the table slowly and walked away with a look of infinite weary sadness. At the door, however, he halted, and turning to Snellenburg said:

'By the way, Canon, you owe me a hundred marks.'

'*What?*'

'Some years ago I loaned you a hundred marks – you have not forgotten, I trust? I mention it only because I thought that, if we are all to be destroyed in the morning, we should make haste to set our affairs in order, pay off old scores – I mean debts – and so forth. But do not let it trouble you, please. Captain, good night, I must sleep now.'

*

The Knights did not attack, but instead marched south-west and razed the town of Neumark. Two thousand three hundred and forty-one souls perished in that onslaught. In the first days of the new year Land Provost Koppernigk sat in what remained of Neumark's town hall, recording in his ledger, in his small precise hand, the names of the dead. It was his duty. An icy wind through a shattered casement at his back brought with it a sharp tang of smoke from the smouldering wreckage of the town. He was cold; he had never known such cold.

* * *

Frau Anna Schillings had that kind of beauty which seems to find relief in poor dress; a tall, fine-boned woman with delicate wrists and the high cheekbones typical of a Danziger, she appeared most at ease, and at her most handsome, in a plain grey gown with a laced bodice, and, perhaps, a scrap of French lace at the throat. Not for her the frills and flounces, the jewelled slippers and horned capuchons of the day. This attribute, this essential modesty of figure as well as of spirit, was now more than ever apparent, when circumstances had reduced a once lavish wardrobe to just one such gown as we have described. And it was in this very gown, with a dark cape wrapped about her shoulders against the cold, and her raven-black hair hidden under an old scarf, that she arrived in Frauenburg with her two poor mites, Heinrich and little Carla, at the beginning of that fateful year (how fateful it was to be she could not guess!), 1524.

As the physical woman prospered in misfortune, so too the spiritual found enhancement in adversity. Not for Frau Schillings the tears and tantrums with which troubles are most commonly greeted by the weaker sex. *It is life, and one must make the best of it*: such was her motto. This stoical fortitude had not always been easy to maintain: her dear Papa's early death had awakened her rudely from the happy dreaming of early girlhood; then there had been Mama's illness in the head. Nor was marriage the escape into security and happiness that she had imagined it would be. Georg . . . poor, irresponsible Georg! She could not, even now, after he had gone off with those ruffians and left her and the little ones to fend for themselves as best they might – even now she could not find it in her heart to hate him for his wanton ways. There was this to be said for him, that he had never struck her, as some husbands were only too prone to do; or at least he had never beaten her, not badly, at any rate. Yes, she said, with that gentle smile that all who knew her knew so well, yes, there are many worse than my Georg in the world! And how dashing and gay he could be, and even, yes, how loving, when he was sober. Well, he was gone now, most likely for good and ever, and she must not brood upon the past; she must make a new life for herself, and for the children.

War is a thing invented by men, and yet perhaps it is the women who suffer most in times of strife among nations. Frau Schillings had lost almost everything in the dreadful war that was supposed to have ended – her home, her happiness, even her husband. Georg was a tailor, a real craftsman, with a good sound trade among the better Danzig families. Everything had been splendid: they had nice rooms above the shop, and money enough to satisfy their modest needs, and then the babies had come, first Heinrich and, not long after, little Carla – O yes, it was, it was, splendid! But then the war broke out, and Georg got that mad notion into his head that there was a fortune to be made in tailoring for the mercenaries. She had to admit, of course, that he might be right, but it was not long before he began to talk wildly of the need to *follow the trade*, as he put it, meaning, as she realised with dismay, that they should become some kind of camp-followers, trailing along in the wake of that dreadful gang of ragamuffins that the Prussians called an army. Well she would have none of that, no indeed! She was a spirited woman, and there was more than one clash between herself and Georg on the matter; but although she was spirited, she was also a woman, and Georg, of course, had his way in the end. He shut up shop, procured a wagon and a pair of horses, and before she knew it they were all four of them on the road.

It was a disaster, naturally. Georg, poor dreamer that he was, had imagined war as a kind of stately dance in which two gorgeously (and expensively!) caparisoned armies made ritual feints at each other on crisp mornings before breakfast. The reality – grotesque, absurd, and hideously cruel – was a terrible shock. His visions of brocaded and beribboned uniforms faded rapidly. He spent his days patching breeches and bloodstained tunics. He even took to cobbling – he, a master tailor! – for the few pennies that were in it. He grew ever more morose, and began drinking again, despite all his promises. He struck Carla once, and frequently shook poor Heinrich, who was not strong, until his teeth rattled. It could not continue thus, and one morning (it was the birthday of the Prince of Peace) Frau Schillings awoke in the filthy hovel of an inn where they had lodged for the night to find that her husband had fled, taking with him the wagon and the horses, the purse with their few remaining marks, and even hers and the children's clothes – everything! The innkeeper, a venal rough brute, told her that Georg had gone off with a band of deserters led by one Krock, or Krack, some awful brutish name like that, and would she be so good now as to pay him what was owed for herself and the brats? She had no money? Well then, she would have to think of a way of paying him in kind then, wouldn't she? It is a measure of the woman's – we do not hesitate to say it – of the woman's *saintliness* that at first she did not understand what the beastly fellow was suggesting; and when he had told her precisely what he meant, she gave vent to a low scream and burst immediately into tears. Never!

As she lay upon that bed of shame, for she was forced in the end to allow that animal to have his evil way with her, she reflected bitterly that all this misfortune that had befallen her was due not to Georg's frailty, not really, but to a silly dispute between the King of Poland and that dreadful Albrecht person. How she despised them, princes and politicians, despised them all! And was she not perhaps justified? Are not our leaders sometimes open to accusations of irresponsibility on a scale far greater than ever the poor Georg Schillingses of this world may aspire to? And you may not say that this contempt was merely the bitter reaction of an empty-headed woman searching blindly for some symbol of the world of men which she might blame for wrongs partly wrought by her own lack of character, for Anna Schillings had been educated (her father had wanted a son), she could read and write, she knew something of the world of books, and could hold her own in logical debate with any man of her class. O yes, Anna Schillings had opinions of her own, and firm ones at that.

Those weeks following Georg's departure constituted the worst time that she was ever to know. How she survived that awful period we shall not describe; we draw a veil over that subject, and shall confine ourselves to saying that in those weeks she learned that there are abroad far greater and crueller scoundrels than that concupiscent innkeeper we have spoken of already.

She did survive, she did manage somehow to feed herself and the little ones, and after that terrible journey across Royal Prussia into northern Ermland, after that *via dolorosa*, she arrived, as we have said, at Frauenburg in January of 1524.

*

The best and truest friend of her youth, Hermina Hesse, was housekeeper to one of the canons of the Cathedral Chapter there. Hermina had been a high-spirited, self-willed girl, and although the years had smoothed away much of her abrasiveness, she was still a lively person, full of well-intentioned gaiety and given to gales of laughter at the slightest provocation. She had never been a beauty, it is true: her charms were rather of the homely, reassuring kind; but it was certainly *not* true to say, as some had said, that she looked and spoke like a beer waitress, that her life was a scandal and her eternal soul irretrievably lost. That kind of thing was put about by the 'stuffed shirts', as she called them (with a defiant toss of the head that was so familiar) among the Frauenburg clergy; as if *their* lives were free of taint, besotted gang of sodomites that they were! Was she to blame if the good Lord had blessed her with an abundant fruitfulness? Did they expect her to disown her twelve children? Disown them! why, she loved them just as much and more than any so-called respectable married matron could love her lawful offspring, and would have fought for them like a wildcat if anyone had dared (which no one did!) to try to take them away from her. Scandal, indeed – pah!

The two friends greeted each other with touching affection and tenderness. They had not met for . . . well, for longer than they cared to remember.

'Anna! Why Anna, what has happened?'

'O my dear,' said Frau Schillings, 'my dear, it has been so awful, I cannot tell you—!'

Hermina lived in a pleasant old white stone house on a hectacre of land some three leagues south of Frauenburg's walls. Certainly it was a well-appointed nest, but was it not somewhat isolated, Frau Schillings wondered aloud, when they had sat down in the pantry to a glass of mulled wine and fresh-baked poppyseed cake? The wine was wonderfully cheering, and the warmth of the stove, and the sight of her friend's familiar beaming countenance, comforted her greatly, so that already she had begun to feel that her agony of poverty and exile might be at an end. (And indeed it was soon to end, though not at all in the manner she expected!) Her little ones were making overtures in their shy tentative way to the children of the house. O dear! She felt suddenly near to tears: it was all so – so *nice*.

'Isolated, aye,' Hermina said darkly, breaking in upon Frau Schillings's tender reverie. 'I am as good as banished here, and that's the truth. The Canon has rooms up in the town, but I am kept from there – not by him, of course, you understand (he would not dare attempt to impose such a restriction on *me*!), but by, well, *others*. However, Anna dear, my troubles are nothing compared with yours, I think. You must tell me all. That swine Schillings left you, did he?'

Frau Schillings then related her sorry tale, in all its awful starkness, neither suppressing that which might shock, nor embellishing those details that indicated the quality of her character: in a word, she was brutally frank. She spoke in a low voice, with eyes downcast, her fine brow furrowed by a frown of concentration; and Hermina Hesse, that good, kind, plump, stout-hearted, ruddy-cheeked woman, that pillar of fortitude, that light in the darkness of a naughty world, smiled fondly to herself and thought: Dear Anna! scrupulous to a fault, as ever. And when she had heard it all, all that heart-breaking tale, she took Frau Schillings's hands in hers, and sighed and said:

'Well, my dear, I am distressed indeed to hear of your misfortune, and I only wish that there was some way that I could ease your burden—'

'O but there is, Hermina, there is!'

'O?'

Frau Schillings looked up then, with her underlip held fast in her perfectly formed small white teeth, obviously struggling to hold back the tears that were, despite her valiant efforts, welling in her dark eyes.

'Hermina,' said she, in a wonderfully steady voice, 'Hermina, I am a proud person, as you well know from the happy days of our youth, as all will know who know anything at all of me; yet now I am brought low, and I must swallow that pride. I ask you, I beg of you, please—'

'Wait,' said Hermina, patting the hands that still lay like weary turtle doves in her own, 'dear Anna, wait: I think I know what you are about to say.'

'Do you, Hermina, do you?'

'Yes, my poor child, I know. Let *me* spare you, therefore; let me say it: you want a loan.'

Frau Schillings frowned.

'O no,' she said, 'no. Why, what can you think of me, to imagine such a thing? No, actually, Hermina, dearest Hermina, I was wondering if you could spare a room for myself and the children for a week or two, just to tide us over until—'

Hermina turned away with a pained look, and began to shake her head slowly, but at just that awkward moment they were interrupted by the sound of hoofbeats outside, and presently there entered by the rickety back door Canon Alexander Sculteti, a low-sized man in black, blowing on his chilled fists and swearing softly under his breath. He was thin, and had a red nose and small watchful eyes. He caught sight of Frau Schillings and halted, glancing from her to Hermina with a look of deep suspicion.

'Who's this?' he growled, but when Hermina began to explain her friend's presence, he waved his arms impatiently and stamped away into the next room, thrusting a toddler roughly out of his path with a swipe of his boot. He was not a pleasant person, Frau Schillings decided, and certainly she had no intention of begging *him* for a place to stay. And yet, what was she to do if Hermina could not help her? Grey January weather loomed in the window. O dear! Hermina winked at her encouragingly, however, and followed the Canon into the next room, where an argument began immediately. Despite the noise that the children made (who now, having become thoroughly acquainted, seemed from the sounds to be endeavouring to push each other down the stairs, the dear little rascals), and even though she went so far as to cover her ears, she could not help hearing *some* of what was said. Hermina, although no doubt fighting hard on her friend's behalf, spoke in a low voice, while Canon Sculteti on the other hand seemed not to care who heard his unkind remarks.

'Let her stay here?' he yelled, 'so that the Bishop can be told that I have installed another tart?' (O! Frau Schillings's hands flew to her mouth to prevent her from crying out in shame and distress.) 'Woman, are you mad? I am in trouble enough with you and these damned brats. Do you realise that I am in danger not only of losing my prebend, but of being *excommunicated*? Listen, here is a plan—' He interrupted himself with a high-pitched whinny of laughter. '—Here is what to do: send her to Koppernigk—' (What was that name? Frau Schillings frowned thoughtfully . . .) '—He's in bad need of a woman, God knows. Ha!'

Summoning up all her courage, Anna Schillings rose and went straight into the room where they were arguing, and in a cold, dignified voice asked:

'Is this *Nicolas* Koppernigk that you speak of?'

Canon Sculteti, standing in the middle of the floor with his hands on his hips, turned to her with an unpleasant, sardonic grin. 'What's that, woman?'

'I could not help overhearing – you mention the name Koppernigk: is this Canon Nicolas Koppernigk? For if so, then I must tell you that he is my cousin!'

*

Yes, she was a cousin to the famous Canon Koppernigk, or Doctor Copernicus, as the world called him now. Theirs was a tenuous connection, it is true, on the distaff side, but yet it was to be the saving of Anna Schillings. She had never met the man, although she had heard talk of him in the family; there had been some scandal, she vaguely remembered, or was that to do with his brother . . .? Well, it was no matter, for who was *she* to baulk at a whiff of scandal?

Their first meeting was unpromising. Canon Sculteti took her that very night to Frauenburg (and was knave enough to make a certain suggestion on the way, which of course she spurned with the contempt it deserved); she left the children in the care of Hermina, for, as Sculteti in his coarse way put it, they did not want to frighten 'old Koppernigk' to death with the prospect of a ready-made family. The town was dark and menacing, bearing still the marks of war, burnt-out houses and crippled beggars and the smell of death. Canon Koppernigk lived in a kind of squat square fortress in the cathedral wall, a cold forbidding place, at the sight of which, in the slime of starlight, Frau Schillings's heart sank. Sculteti rapped upon the stout oak door, and presently a window above opened stealthily and a head appeared.

'Evening, Koppernigk,' Sculteti shouted. 'There is one here that would speak with you urgently.' He sniggered under his breath, and despite the excited beating of her heart, Frau Schillings noted again what a lewd unpleasant man this Canon was. 'Kin of yours!' he added, and laughed again.

The figure above spoke not a word, but withdrew silently, and after some long time they heard the sound of slow footsteps within, and the door opened slowly, and Canon Nicolas Koppernigk lifted a lighted candle at them as if he were fending off a pair of demons.

'Here we are!' said Sculteti, with false joviality. 'Frau Anna Schillings, your cousin, come to pay you a visit. Frau Schillings – Herr Canon Koppernigk!' And so saying he took himself off into the night, laughing as he went.

*

Canon Koppernigk, then in his fifty-first year, was at that time laden heavily with the responsibilities of affairs of state. On the outbreak of war between the Poles and the Teutonic Knights, the Frauenburg Chapter almost in its entirety had fled to the safety of the cities of Royal Prussia, notably Danzig and Torun; he, however, had gone into the very midst of the battlefield, so to speak, to the castle of Allenstein, where he held the post of Land Provost. Then, after the armistice of 1521, he had in April of that year returned to Frauenburg as Chancellor, charged by Bishop von Lossainen (rumours of whose death in the siege of Heilsberg had happily proved unfounded) with the task of reorganising the administration of the province of Ermland, a task that at first had seemed an impossibility, since under the terms of the armistice the Knights retained those parts of the princedom which their troops were occupying at the close of hostilities. There was also the added difficulty of the presence in the land of all manner of deserter and renegade, who spread lawlessness and disorder through the countryside. However, by the following year the Land Provost had succeeded to such a degree in restoring normalcy that his faint-hearted colleagues could consider it safe enough for them to creep out of hiding and return to their duties.

Even yet the demands of public life did not slacken, for with the death at last, in January of 1523, of Bishop von Lossainen, the Chapter was compelled to take up the reins of government of the turbulent and war-torn bishopric; once again the Chapter turned to Canon Koppernigk, and he was elected Administrator General, which post he held until October, when a new Bishop was installed. In all this time he had been working on a detailed report of the damage wrought by the war in Ermland, which he was to present as a vital document in the peace talks at Torun. Also he had drawn up an elaborate and complex treatise setting forth means whereby the debased monetary system of Prussia might be reformed, which had been requested of him by the King of Poland. Nor was he spared personal sorrow: shortly after hearing of the death at Kulm of his sister Barbara, he received news from Italy that his brother Andreas had succumbed finally to that terrible disease which for many years had afflicted him. Small wonder then, with all this, that Canon Koppernigk appeared to Frau Schillings a reserved and distracted, cold, strange, solitary soul.

On that first night, when Sculteti abandoned her as he would some ridiculous and tasteless practical joke on his doorstep, the Canon stared at her, with a mixture of horror and bafflement, as if she were an apparition out of a nightmare. He backed away from her up the dark narrow stairs, still holding the candle at arm's length like a talisman brandished in the face of a demon. In the observatory he put his desk between himself and her. For the second time that day, Frau Schillings related her tale of woe, haltingly, with many omissions this time, holding her hands clasped upon her bodice. He watched her with a kind of horrified fascination, but she could plainly see that he was not taking in the half of what she said. He seemed to her a kindly man, for all his reserve.

'I'll not mince words, Herr Canon,' she said. 'I have begged, I have whored, and I have survived; but now I have nothing left. You are my last hope. Refuse me, and I shall perish.'

'My child,' he began, and stopped, helpless and embarrassed. 'My child . . .'

Moonlight shines through the arched window; the candle flickers. The books, the couch, the desk, all crouch like enchanted creatures frozen in the midst of a secret dance, and those strange ghostly instruments lift their shrouded arms into the shadows starward, mysterious, hieratic and inexplicable things. All fade; the dark descends.

* * *

Nicholas Koppernigk, Canonicus: Frauenburg

Rev Sir: I presume to write to you, remembering our many interesting conversations of some years ago, when we met at Cracow. I was then adviser to the Polish King, & you, as I recall, were secretary to your late uncle, His Grace Bishop Waczelrodt: on whose death may I be permitted now to offer you belated condolences. I admired the man greatly (although I knew him not at all), & would hear more of his life & works. His death was indeed a tragedy for Ermland, as events have proved. I dearly hope that your many public duties do not keep you from that great task which you are embarked upon. Many wonderful reports of your theories come to me, especially from Cardinal Schönberg at Rome, whom I think you know. You are fortunate indeed to have such allies, who surely will stand you in good stead against the bellowing of ignorant schoolmen & those others that you have outraged by the daring of your concepts. For myself, I have so little power at my command that I hesitate to assure you that you have my best wishes for your great & important work, which I pray God to bless, in the name of Truth. I hesitate, as I have said: yet who can know but that even the friendship of one so humble as myself may not at some future date prove useful? The Church in these perilous days, I fear, shall not for long be able to sustain that generous liberality which hitherto She was wont to extend to Her ministers (a liberality, I might add, for which I myself have been grateful on more than one occasion!). Dark times are coming, Herr Canon: we are all under threat. However, it is my conviction that, so long as we maintain strict vigilance over our lives, & do not leave ourselves open to accusations of corruption & lewdness by the Lutherans, we shall be safe, no matter how *revolutionary* our notions. I pray you, sir, regard me as your most devoted friend.

ex Löbau, 11 November, 1532
+ Johannes Dantiscus
Bishop of Kulm

*

Tiedemann Giese, Visitator: at Allenstein

Dear Giese: I have had a letter from Dantiscus, which I enclose herewith: please tell me what you think of it, & how I should reply. I do not trust the man. He has a daughter in Spain, they say. Perhaps our own Bishop has asked him to write to me thus? I suspect a conspiracy against me. Destroy this letter, but send back the other, with your suggestions as to how I should proceed. I am not well: a catarrh of the stomach, & my bowels do not move, as usual. I think I shall not reply to him. Please say what I am to do.

ex Franenburg, 16 December, 1532
Nic: Koppernigk

*

Johannes Dantiscus, Bishop of Kulm: Löbau

I have Your Rev Lordship's letter, full of humanity & favour, in which he reminds me of that familiarity with Your Rev

Lordship which I contracted in my youth: which I know to have remained just as vigorous up to now. As for the information you required of me, how long my uncle, Lucas Waczelrodt of blessed memory, had lived: he lived 64 years, 5 months; was Bishop for 23 years; died on the last day but one of March, *anno Christi* 1512. With him came to an end a family whose insignia can be found on the ancient monuments in Torun. I recommended my obedience to Your Rev. Lordship.

ex Frauenburg, 11 April, 1533
Nic: Koppernigk: Canonicus

*

Johannes Dantiscus, Bishop of Kulm: Löbau

My Lord: I write to you on behalf of one that is dear to us both: *id est* Doctor Nicolas Copernicus, the astronomer, & Canon of this Chapter. As you are aware, the Frauenburg canons shall assemble this month for the purpose of electing a Bishop to the throne of Ermland, following the lamented death of Our Rev Lordship Mauritius Ferber. The list of candidates, decided upon, as is the custom, by His Royal Highness Sigismund of Poland, comprises four names: Canons Zimmermann, von der Trank, & Snellenburg: the fourth name you know, of course. While it is not my wish to attempt to influence the course of this lofty affair, I feel it my duty humbly to suggest that one of these names, that of Canon Heinrich Snellenburg, be removed from the list, in order to protect the Chapter from ridicule, & the Polish throne (whose interests I hold as closely to my heart as does Your Rev. Lordship) from accusations of gross misjudgment. Your Lordship knows the manner of man it is that I speak of here. Canon Snellenburg is not a great sinner: but the very pettiness of his misdemeanours (unpaid debts et cetera) surely must exclude him from consideration as a candidate for this highest of offices. Therefore I suggest that he be removed forthwith from the list, his name to be replaced by that of

Canon Nicolas Koppernigk. The Rev. Doctor, need I say, does not aspire to so high an office as the Bishopric of Ermland (and is not aware of this petition, be assured of that): yet even to name him a candidate would, I feel, & I think I am not alone in this opinion, be an indication, however subtle, of the high regard in which the Rev. Doctor is held both by the Church & the Polish throne: it would also, of course, be a means of arming him against his enemies, who are, alas, legion. Doctor Copernicus is an old man now, & in ill-health. He does not sleep well, & is plagued by hallucinations: sometimes he speaks of dark figures that hide in the corners of his room. All this indicates how he feels himself threatened & mocked by a hostile world. Your Rev. Lordship's generous praise for his great work (which even yet he refuses to publish, for fear of what reaction it may provoke!) is not universally echoed: not long ago, the Lutheran Rector of the Latin School at Elbing, one *Ludimagister* Gnapheus, ridiculed the master's astronomical ideas (or those debased versions of them that this Gnapheus in his ignorance understands) in his so-called comedy, *Morosophus*, or *The Wise Fool*, which was performed publicly in that city as a carnival farce. (However, in this respect, as the Rev. Doctor himself remarked, Master Gnapheus has obviously never heard of the divine Cusan's great work, *De docta ignorantia*, or he would have seen the irony of choosing for his scurrilous farce the title that he did!) As another example of how the Doctor is persecuted, Your Rev. Lordship will forgive me, I hope, for mentioning this absurd but painful incident: Some ten years ago, a young girl was brought to him here in order that, in his capacity as physician, he might treat her for an unspeakable disease which the child had contracted we know not how. He could do nothing, of course, for the disease was already far advanced. The girl has since died at the Cistercian Convent in Kulm, & now her father, mad with grief no doubt, has begun to put it about that the Rev. Doctor is to blame for the tragedy, for the girl said, so the father claims, that when he was examining her he cast a spell upon her, making passes with his hands & speaking a strange word that she could not understand et cetera. The accusation is absurd, of course, but Your Lordship will understand how these things go; matters have come to such a pass that the sick will no longer trust themselves to his care. However, I fear that by now I have begun to stretch Your Lordship's patience with my ramblings. Let me close by saying that, having considered all these factors which I have mentioned, Your Lordship will recognise that our beloved Canon Nicolas deserves whatever honours it may be in our power to bestow upon him – & deserves also whatever small comforts, of the spirit *or of the flesh*, that he is himself able to wrest from a cruel world.

ex Frauenburg, 10 September, 1537
Tiedemann Giese: Canonicus

*

Tiedemann Giese, Bishop of Kulm: Löbau

Lord Bishop: Disturbing reports continue to reach me regarding the Rev. Doctor & this matter of the woman, Anna Schillings. It is suggested that he keeps her as his *focaria*, & that she fulfils *all duties* attaching to such a position, being housekeeper & also concubine. I obliged you, my Lord, by substituting his name for that of Snellenburg on the King's List, despite the grave reservations which I entertained at the time, for I confess that the substitution of the name of one sinner by that of another did not recommend itself to me as a wise act: however, I did so because of the high regard I had for the Doctor's work, if not for his character. Now I think that I should have been swayed not by your arguments & entreaties, but by my own feelings. Anyway, the matter is past: I mention it only so that you may now repay this favour by speaking to him, & encouraging him to put away this woman. *He must* yield. There is more at stake now than the reputation of the Frauenburg Chapter. He maintains close friendship with Sculteti: that is bad. Admonish him that such connections & friendships are harmful to him, but do not tell him that the warning originates from me. I am sure that you know that Sculteti has taken a wife, & is suspected of atheism.

ex Heilsberg, 4 July, 1539
+ Johannes Dantiscus
Bishop of Ermland

*

Johannes Dantiscus, Bishop of Ermland: Heilsberg

My dear Lord Bishop: Doctor Nicolas is staying with us briefly here, along with a young disciple. I have spoken earnestly to the Rev Doctor on the matter, according to Your Most Rev. Lordship's wish, & have set the facts of the matter plainly before him. He seemed not a little disturbed that although he had unhesitatingly obeyed the will of Your Rev. Lordship, malicious people still bring trumped-up charges of secret meetings, & so forth. For he denies having seen that woman since he dismissed her. I have certainly ascertained that he is not as much affected as many think. Moreover, his advanced age & his neverending studies readily convince me of this, as well as the worthiness & respectability of the man: nevertheless I urged him that he should shun even the appearance of evil, & this I believe he will do. But again I think that it would be as well that Your Rev. Lordship should not put too much faith in the informer, considering that envy attaches so easily to men of worth, & is unafraid even of troubling Your Most Rev. Lordship. I commend myself et cetera.

ex Löbau, 12 August, 1539
+ Tiedemann Giese
Bishop of Kulm

*

Johannes Dantiscus, Bishop of Ermland: Heilsberg

Your Grace . . . As regards the Frauenburg wenches, Sculteti's hid for a few days in his house. She promised that she would go away together with her children. Sculteti remains in his curia with his *focaria*, who looks like a beer waitress tainted with every evil. The woman of Doctor Nicolas sent her baggage ahead to Danzig, but she herself stays on at Frauenburg . . .

ex Allenstein, 20 October, 1539
Heinrich Snellenburg: Visitator

*

Nicolas Koppernigk: Frauenburg

Sir: I write to you directly in the hope that you may be made to understand the peril into which you have delivered yourself by your stubborn refusal to yield upon the matter of the woman, Anna Schillings. Surely you realise how great are the issues at stake? If it were merely a matter of this *focaria*, I should not be so intemperate as to hound you thus, but it is more than that, much more, as you must know. On my recommendation, Canon Stanislas Hosius was nominated candidate for the office of Precentor of the Frauenburg Chapter. I shall dare to be frank, my dear Doctor: I do not like Hosius, I do not like what he represents. He is a fanatic. You & I, my friend, are children of another age, a finer & more civilised age: but that age is past. Some years ago I warned you that dark times were coming: that darkness is upon us now, & its avatars are Canon Hosius and his ilk – the inquisitors, the fanatics. I do not like him, as I have said, yet I appointed him to a canonry at Frauenburg, & would see him Precentor: for, like him or not, I must accept him. For Ermland, the future is one of two choices: this province must become either Prussian & Lutheran, or Polish & Catholic. There is no third course. The autonomy of which your uncle was the architect & guardian is about to be taken from us. The choice, then, is clear: whatever our feelings regarding Poland, we must bow to the Jagellon throne, or perish. Now, the Frauenburg Chapter, foolishly allowing itself to be misled by forces who have not the good of Ermland, nor Frauenburg, at heart, has elected the unspeakable Sculteti to be Precentor, thereby thwarting my carefully laid plans. This is intolerable. Do those damned clerics among whom you have chosen to live not realise that Sculteti is backed by that faction at the Papal Court which imagines that Ermland can be brought under the direct control of Rome? Even if this were feasible, which it is not, Rome rule would spell disaster for all of us. *We must cleave to Poland!* It is the only course. I must have Hosius: & the corollary of that need is that I must destroy Sculteti. I shall use whatever weapons against him that I can find. The scandalous manner of his life is one such weapon, perhaps the most lethal. I trust that these revelations, which I am foolish to commit to paper, will make clear why, for so many years, I have striven to force you to be rid of this woman. This shall be my last warning; ignore it, & you shall be in grave danger of going down along with Sculteti when he falls. That is all I have to say. *Vale.*

ex Heilsberg, 13 March, 1540
+ *Johannes Dantiscus*
Bishop of Ermland

*

Johannes Dantiscus, Bishop of Ermland: Heilsberg

Reverendissime in Christo Pater et Domine Clementissime! I have received Your Rev. Lordship's letter. I understand well enough Your Lordship's grace & good will toward me: which he has condescended to extend not only to me, but to other men of great excellence. It is, I believe, certainly to be attributed not to my merits, but to the well-known goodness of Your Rev. Lordship. Would that some time I should be able to deserve these things. I certainly rejoice, more than can be said, to have found such a Lord & Patron.

I have done what I neither would nor could have left undone, whereby I hope to have given satisfaction to Your Rev. Lordship's warning.

ex Frauenburg, 3 July, 1540
Your Rev Lordship's most devoted
Nicolas Copernicus

*

Tiedemann Giese, Bishop of Kulm: Löbau

My dear Tiedemann: Sculteti has been expelled from the Chapter, & banished by Royal Edict. He will go to Rome, I think, as do all outcasts. His *focaria*, the Hesse woman, has disappeared. What a lot of trouble she caused! It occurs to me that our *Frauenburg* is aptly named. I have issued yet another edict of my own against Frau Schillings, but she refuses to go. I am touched, truly, by her devotion to a sick old man, & have not the heart to make her understand that it would be altogether best if she were to go. Anyway, where would she go to? So I await, without great interest, Dantiscus's next move. Do I seem calm? I am not. I am afraid, Tiedemann, afraid of what the world will think to do to me that it has not done already: the filthy world that will not let me be, that comes after me always, a black monster, dragging its damaged wings in its wake. Ah, Tiedemann . . .

ex Frauenburg, 31 December, 1540

*

Waterborne he comes, at dead of night, sliding sleek on the river's gleaming back, snout lifted, sniffing, under the drawbridge, the portcullis, past the drowsing sentry. Brief scrabble of claws on the slimed steps below the wall, brief glint of a bared tooth. In the darkness for an instant an intimation of agony and anguish, and the night flinches. Now he scales the wall, creeps under the window, grinning. In the shadow of the tower he squats, wrapt in a black cloak, waiting for dawn. Comes the knocking, the pinched voice, the sly light step on the stair, and how is it that I alone can hear the water . . .?

III

Cantus Mundi

I, GEORG JOACHIM VON LAUCHEN, called Rheticus, will now set down the true account of how Copernicus came to reveal to a world wallowing in a stew of ignorance the secret music of the universe. There are not many who will admit that if I had not gone to him, the old fool would never have dared to publish. When I arrived in Frauenburg I was little more than a boy (a boy of genius, to be sure!), yet he recognised my brilliance, that was why he listened to me, yes. Princes of Church and State had in vain urged him to speak, but *my* arguments he heeded. To you, now, he is Copernicus, a titan, remote and unknowable, but to me he was simply Canon Nicolas, preceptor and, yes! friend. They say I am mad. Let them. What do I care for a jealous world's contumely? They drove me out, denied me my fame and honoured name, banished me here to rot in this Godforgotten corner of Hungary that they call Cassovia – yet what of it? I am at peace at last, after all the furious years. An old man now, yes, a forlorn and weary wanderer come to the end of the journey, I am past caring. But I don't forgive them! No! *The devil shit on the lot of you.*

*

My patron, the Count, is a noble gentleman. Cultured, urbane, brilliant, generous to a fault, he reminds me in many ways of myself when I was younger. We speak the same language – I mean of course the *language of gentlemen*, for in Latin it's true he is a little . . . rusty. Not like Koppernigk, whose schoolman's Latin was impeccable, while for the rest, well, his people were, after all, in trade. The Count saw in me one of his own kind, and welcomed me into the castle here (as house physician) when the others chose to forget me and the great work I have done. He dismisses with characteristic hauteur the vile slanders they fling at me, and laughs when they whisper to him behind their hands that I am mad. The Count, unfortunately, *is* mad, a little. It comes from the mother's side, I think: bad blood there without a doubt. Yes, I must exercise more caution, for he is capricious. Be less arrogant in his presence, grovel now and then, yes yes. Still, he needs me, we both know that. What, I ask, without me, would he do for the conversation, the intellectual stimulation, which save him from going altogether out of his mind? This country is populated with swineherds and witches and cretinous priests. I was a new star in his sparse firmament. Anyway, why should I worry? – the world is full of Counts, but there is only one Doctor Rheticus. It is not, the world, I mean, full of Counts, so go easy. What was I . . .? Copernicus, of course. Forty years ago – forty years! – I came to him.

Frauenburg: that hole. It clings to the Baltic coast up there at the outermost edge of the earth, and someday please God it will drop off, like a scab. My heart sank when first I beheld that grey fortress wall. It was 1539, summer supposedly, although the rain poured down, and there was a chill white wind off the sea. I remember the houses, like clenched fists, bristling within the gates. *Clenched* is the word: that was Frauenburg, clenched on its own ignorance and bitterness and Catholicism. Was it for this I had abandoned Wittenberg, the university, my friends and confraters? Not that Wittenberg was all that much better, mind you, but the meanness was different; in the corridors of the university they were still jabbering about freedom and change and redemption, parroting the Reformer's raucous squawks, but behind all that fine talk there lurked the old terror, the despair, of those who know full well and will not admit it that the world is rotten, irredeemable. In those days I believed (or had myself convinced that I did) that we were on the threshold of the New Age, and I took part with gusto in the game, and jabbered with the best of them. How could I do otherwise? At twenty-two I held the chair of mathematics and astronomy at the great University of Wittenberg. When the world favours you so early and so generously, you feel it your duty to support its pathetic fictions. I am inside the gates of Frauenburg.

*

Once inside the gates of Frauenburg, then, I went straightway to the cathedral, dragging my bags and books behind me through the sodden streets. From the cathedral I was directed to the chapterhouse, where I encountered no little difficulty in gaining entry, for they speak a barbaric dialect up there, and furthermore the doorkeeper was deaf. At length the fellow abandoned all attempt to decode my immaculate German, and grudgingly let me into a cavernous dark room where bloodstained idols, their Virgin and so forth, peered eerily out of niches in the walls. Presently there came a sort of scrabbling at the door, and an aged cleric entered crabwise, regarding me suspiciously out of the corner of a watery eye. I must have seemed a strange apparition there in the gloom, grinning like a gargoyle and dripping rain on his polished floor. He advanced apprehensively, keeping firmly between us the big oak table that stood in the middle of the room. His gaze was uncannily like that of the statues behind him: guarded, suspicious, hostile even, but ultimately indifferent. When I mentioned the name of Copernicus I thought he would take to his heels (was the astronomer then a leper even among his colleagues?), but he concealed his consternation as best he could, and merely smiled, if that twitch could be called a smile, and directed me to – where? – the cathedral. I held my temper. He frowned. I had been to the cathedral already? Ah, then he was afraid he could not help me. I asked if I might wait, in the hope that he whom I sought might in time return here. O! well, yes, yes of course, but now that he thought of it, I might perhaps enquire at the house of Canon Suchandsuch, at the other end of the town, for at this hour the Herr Doctor was often to be found there. And I was bustled out into the streets again.

Do you know what it is like up there in the grey north? Now I have nothing against rain – indeed, I think of it as a bright link between air and angels and us poor earthbound creatures – but up there it falls like the falling of dusk, darkening the world, and in that wet gloom all seems stale and flat, and the spirit aches. Even in spring there is no glorious drenching, as there is elsewhere, when April showers sweep through the air like showers of light, but only the same dull thin drip drip drip, a drizzle of tangible *accidie*, hour after hour. Yet that day I marched along regardless through those mean streets, my feet in the mire and my head swathed in a golden mist, ah yes, it has been ever thus with me: when I set my mind on something, then all else disappears, and today I could see one thing only, the historic confrontation (for already I pictured our meeting set like a jewel in the great glittering wheel of history) between von Lauchen of Rhaetia and Doctor Copernicus of Torun. But the Herr Doctor was proving damnably elusive. At the house of Canon Suchand-such (the name was Snellenburg, I remember it now), the dolt of a steward or whatever he was just looked at me peculiarly and shook his thick head slowly from side to side, as if he felt he was dealing with a large lunatic child.

I ferreted him out in the end, never mind how. I've said enough to demonstrate the lengths he would go to in order to protect himself from the world. He lived in a tower on the cathedral wall, a bleak forbidding eyrie where he perched like an old ill-tempered bird, beak and talons at the ready. I had my foot in the door before the housekeeper, Anna Schillings, his *focaria*, that bitch (more of *her* later) could slam it in my face – and I swear to God that if she had, I would have burst it in, brass studs, hinges, locks and all, with my head, for I was desperate. I dealt her a smile bristling with fangs, and she backed off and disappeared up the narrow stairs, at the head of which she presently reappeared and beckoned to me, and up there in the half dark (it's evening now) before a low arched door she abandoned me with a terrible look. I waited. The door with a squeak opened a little way. A face, which to my astonishment I recognised, peered around it cautiously, and was immediately withdrawn. There were some furtive scuffling sounds within. I knocked, not knowing what else to do. A voice bade me come in. I obeyed.

*

At my first, I mean my second – third, really – well, my first as it were *official* sight of him, I was surprised to find him smaller than I had anticipated, but I suppose I expected him to be a giant. He stood at a lectern with his hands on the open pages of a bible, I think it was a bible. Astronomical instruments were laid out on a table near him, and through the open window at his back could be seen the Baltic and the great light dome of the evening sky (rain stopped, cloud lifting, the usual). His expression was one of polite enquiry, mild surprise. I forgot the speech I had prepared. I imagine my mouth hung open. It was the same old man that had met me at the chapterhouse, that is, he was Copernicus, I mean they were one and the same – yes yes! the same, and here he was, gazing at me with that lugubrious glazed stare, pretending he had never set eyes on me before now. Ach, it depresses me still. Did he imagine I would not recognise him in this ridiculous pose, this stylised portrait of a scientist in his cell? He did not care! If his carefully composed expression was not free of a faint trace of unease, that uneasiness sprang from concern for the polish of his performance and not from any regard for me, nor from shame that his contemptible trick had been discovered. He might have been masquerading before a mirror. *Copernicus did not believe in truth.* He had no faith in truth. You are surprised? Listen—

O but really, all this is unworthy of me, of the subject. Two of the greatest minds of the age (one, at least, was great, *is* great) met that day, and I describe the momentous occasion as if it were a carnival farce. It is all gone wrong. The rain, the difficulty of finding him, that absurd pose, I did not intend to mention any of this trivia. Why is it not possible to speak of things calmly and accurately? My head aches. I could never achieve the classic style; one must have a grave turn of mind for that, a sense of the solemn pageantry of life, an absolutely unshakeable faith in the notion of order. Order! Ha! I must pause here, it is too late, too dark, to continue. The wolves are howling in the mountains. After such splendours, my God, how have I ended up in this wilderness? My head!

*

Now, where was I? Ah, I have left poor Canon Nicolas petrified all night before his lectern and his bible, posing for his portrait. He was in sixty-sixth year, an old man whose robes, cut for a younger, stouter self, hung about him in sombre folds like a kind of silt deposited by time. His face – teeth gone in the slack mouth, skin stretched tight on the high northern cheekbones – had already taken on that blurred, faded quality that is the first bloom of death. Thus must my own face appear now to others. Ah . . . He wore no beard, but the morning blade, trembling in an unsteady grip, had left unreaped on his chin and in the deep cleft above the upper lip a few stray grizzled hairs. A velvet cap sat upon his skull like a poultice. This, surely, was not that Doctor Copernicus, that great man, whom I had come to Frauenburg to find! The eyes, however, intense and infinitely clever, and filled with what I can only call an exalted cunning, identified him as the one I sought.

Nor was his observatory what I had thought it would be. I had expected something old-fashioned, it's true, a cosy little lair full of scholarly clutter, books and manuscripts, parchments crawling with complex calculations, all this draped in the obligatory membrane of vivid dust. Also, unaccountably, I had expected warmth, thick yellow warmth, like a species of inspirational cheese, in which would be embedded in his mellow old age the master, a jolly old fellow, absentminded and unworldly, but sharp, sharp, putting the finishing touches to his masterpiece preparatory to unleashing it upon an unsuspecting world. The room I was in, however, was straight out of the last century, if not the one before, and more like an alchemist's cell than the workroom of a great modern scientist. The white walls were bare as bone, the beamed ceiling too. I saw no more than a handful of books. The instruments on the table had the self-conscious look of things that have been brought out for display. The window let in a hard merciless light. And the cold! Science here was not the cheerful, confident quest for certainties that *I* knew, but the old hugger-mugger of spells and talismans and secret signs. A leering death's-head and a clutch of dried batwings would not have surprised me. The air reeked of the chill sweat of guilt.

I did not take in all this detail at once – although it was all registered in my sense of shock – for at first I was distracted by waiting for him to offer some excuse, or at least explanation, regarding our prior meeting. When I realised, to my surprise and puzzlement (remember, I did not know him yet as I was to come to know him later), that he had no intention of doing so, I knew there was nothing for it but to play, as best I could, the part of the simpering idiot that obviously he considered me to be. In the circumstances, then, something dramatic was required. I crossed the room, I *bounded* across the room, and with my face lifted in doglike veneration I genuflected before him, crying:

'*Domine praeceptor!*'

Startled, he backed away from me, mumbling under his breath and trying not to see me, but I hobbled after him, still on one knee, until a corner of the table nudged him in the rear and he jumped in fright and halted. The instruments on the table, quivering from the collision, set up a tiny racket of chiming and chattering that seemed in the sudden silence to express exactly the old man's panic and confusion. You see? You see? How can I be expected to be grave?

'Who are you?' he demanded petulantly, and did not bother to listen when I told him my name a second time. 'You are not from the Bishop, are you?' He watched me carefully.

'No, *Meister*, I know no Bishop, nor king nor prince; I am ruled only by the greatest of lords, which is science.'

'Yes yes, well, get up, will you, get up.'

I rose, and rising suddenly remembered the words of my speech, which I delivered, in one breath, at high speed. Very flowery. *Sat verbum.*

Throughout that meeting we moved in circles about the room in a slow stealthy chase, he leading, keeping well out of my reach for fear I might attempt a sudden assault, and I following hard upon his heels uttering shrill cries of adoration and entreaty, throwing my arms about and tripping over the furniture in my excitement. We communicated (communicated!) in a kind of macaronic jabber, for whereas I found German most natural, the Canon was wont to lapse into Latin, and no sooner did I join him than we found ourselves stumbling into the vernacular again. O, it was great fun, truly. He was singularly unimpressed by my academic pedigree; his face took on a look of frank horror when it dawned upon him that I was a Lutheran – holy God, one of *them*! What would the Bishop say? But hold hard, Rheticus, hold hard now, you must be fair to him. Yes, I must be fair to him. I cannot in fairness blame a timorous cleric, who desired above all *not to be noticed*, for his dread at the arrival in his tower fortress of a firebrand from Protestant Wittenberg. Three months previous to my coming, the Bishop, Dantiscus the sleek, had issued an edict ordering all Lutherans out of Ermland on pain of dispossession or even death, and shortly thereafter he was to issue another, calling for all heretical – meaning Lutheran, *natürlich* – books and pamphlets to be burned in public. A nice gentleman, Dantiscus the bookburner: I shall have some more to say of him presently.

(In fairness to *myself*, I must add that Wittenberg considered Copernicus at best a madman, at worst the Antichrist. Luther himself, in one of those famous after-dinner harangues, amid the belches and the farts, had sneered at the notion of a heliocentric universe, thus displaying once again his unfailing discernment; so also had Melanchton mocked the theory – even Melanchton, my first patron! Therefore you see that the *Meister* was less than popular where I came from, and I was granted leave of absence to visit him only because of who and what I was, and not because the Wittenberg authorities approved of the Ermlander's theories. I wanted to make that point clear, for the sake of accuracy.)

So, as I have said, he was not impressed et cetera – indeed, so unimpressed was he, that he seemed not even fully aware of my presence, for he kept on as it were sliding away from me, as though avoiding a distasteful memory, picking at his robe with agitated fingers and grimacing to himself. He was not thinking of me, but of the *consequences* of me, so to speak (*What will the Bishop say!*). I was profoundly disappointed, or rather, I was aware that something profoundly disappointing was occurring, for I myself, the essential I, was hardly there. That is not very clear. No matter. Doctor Copernicus, who before had represented for me the very spirit incarnate of the New Age, was now revealed as a cautious cold old brute obsessed with appearances and the security of his prebend. Is it possible to be disconcerted to the point of tears?

And yet there was something that told me all was not lost, that my pilgrimage might not have been in vain: it was a faint uncertainty in his look, a tiny tension, as if there were, deep within him, a lever longing to be pressed. I had brought gifts with me, fine printed editions of Ptolemy and Euclid, Regiomontanus and others, O, there must have been a dozen volumes in all, which I had had rebound (at a cost I do not care even now to recall), with his initials and a pretty monogram stamped in gold on the spines. These books I had cunningly dispersed throughout my luggage for fear of brigands, so that now when I remembered them and fell upon my bags in a final frantic burst of hope, they fell, diamonds amid ashes, out of a storm of shirts and shoes and soiled linen, and *There!* I cried, and *There!* near to tears, challenging him to find it in his cold heart to reject this ultimate token of homage.

'What are you doing?' he said. 'What are these?'

I gathered the books in my arms and struggled to my feet. 'For you – for you, *domine praeceptor*!'

Hesitantly he lifted the *Almagest* from atop the pile, and, with many a suspicious backward glance in my direction, took it to the window; I thought of an old grey rat scuttling off with a crust. He held the book close to his nose and examined it intently, sniffing and crooning, and the harsh lines of his face softened, and he smiled despite himself, biting his lip, old *pleased* grey rat, and click! I could almost hear that lever dip.

'A handsome volume,' he murmured, 'handsome indeed. And costly too, I should think. What did you say your name was, Herr . . .?'

And then, I think, I did weep. I recall tears, and more groans of adoration, and I on my knees again and he shooing me off, though with less distaste than before, I fancied. Behind him the clouds broke for a moment over the Baltic, and the sun of evening suddenly shone, a minor miracle, and I remembered that it was summer after all, that I was young, and the world was before me. I left him soon after that, with an invitation to return on the morrow, and staggered in blissful delirium into the streets, where even the leaden twilight and the filth in the sewers, the mud, the red gaping faces of the peasants, could not dampen my spirits. I found lodgings at an inn below the cathedral wall, and there partook of a nauseating dinner, that I remember in detail to this day, and, to follow, had a fat and extremely dirty, curiously androgynous whore.

* * *

I WAS UP AND ABOUT early next morning. Low sun on the Frisches Haff, the earth steaming faintly, wind freshening, the narrow streets awash with light and loud with the shrill cries of hawkers – aye, and my poor head splitting from the effects of that filthy poison which they dare to call wine. At the tower the bitch Schillings greeted me with another black look, but let me in without a word. The Canon was waiting for me in the observatory, in a state of extreme agitation. I had hardly crossed the threshold before he began to babble excitedly, and came at me waving his hands, forcing me to retreat before him. It was yesterday in reverse. I tried to make sense of what he was saying, but the fumes of last night's revels had not yet dispersed, and phlegm not blood lay sluggish in my veins, and I could grasp only a jumble of words: Kulm . . . the Bishop . . . Löbau . . . the castle . . . *venite!* We were leaving Frauenburg. We were going to Löbau, in Royal Prussia. Bishop Giese was his friend. He was Bishop of Kulm. We would stay with him at Löbau Castle. (What did it mean?) We were leaving that morning, that minute – now! I shambled off in a daze and collected my belongings from the inn, and, when I returned, the Canon was already in the street, struggling into a broken-down hired carriage. I think if I had not arrived just then he would have left without giving me a second thought. The Schillings stuck out her fierce head at the door, the Canon groaned faintly and shrank back against the fussy seat, and as we moved off the *focaria* yelled after us like a fishwife something about being gone when we returned – on hearing which, I may add, I brightened up considerably.

There is a kind of lockjaw that comes with extreme embarrassment; I fell prey to that condition as we rattled through the streets of Frauenburg that morning. I may have been young, innocent I may have been, but I could guess easily enough the reason for our haste and the manner of our departure. It was not without justification, after all, that Luther had vilified Rome for its hypocrisy and its so-called celibacy, and no doubt now Bishop Dantiscus had instituted yet another drive against indecency among his clergy, as the Catholics were forever doing in those early days of the schism, eager to display their reforming zeal to a sceptical world. Not that I cared anything for that kind of nonsense; it was not the state of affairs between Canon Nicolas and the Schillings that troubled me (it did not trouble me much, at any rate), but the spectacle of Doctor Copernicus in the street, in public, involved in a sordid domestic scene. I could not speak, I say, and turned my face away from him and gazed out with such fierce concentration at drab Ermland passing by that it might have been the wonders of the Indies I beheld. Ah, how intolerant the young are of the frailties of the old! The Canon was silent also, until we reached the plain, and then he stirred and sighed, and there was a world of weariness in his voice when he asked:

'Tell me, young man, what do they say of me at Wittenberg?'

*

That dreary Prussian plain, I remember it. Enormous clouds, rolling down from the Baltic, kept pace with us as we were borne slowly southwards, their shadows stepping hugely across the empty land. Strange silence spread for miles about us, as if everything were somehow turned away, facing off into the limitless distance, and the muted clamour of our passage – creak of axles, monotonous thudding of hoofs – could not avail against that impassive quiet, that indifference. We met not a soul on the road, if road it could be called, but once, far in the distance, a band of horsemen appeared, galloping laboriously away, soundlessly. Through the narrow slit opposite me I could see the driver's broad back bouncing and rolling, but as the hours crawled past it ceased to be a human form, and became a stone, a pillar of dust, the wing of some great bird. We passed through deserted villages where the houses were charred shells and dust blew in the streets, and the absence of the hum of human concourse was like a hole in the air itself. Thus do we voyage in dreams. Once, when I thought the Canon was asleep, I found him instead staring at me fixedly; another time when I turned to him he smiled a cunning and inexplicably alarming smile. Confused and frightened, I looked away hurriedly, out at the countryside revolving slowly around us, but there was no comfort for me there. The plain stretched away interminably, burnished by the strange brittle sunlight, and the wind sang softly. We might have been a thousand leagues from anywhere, adrift in the sphere of the fixed stars. He was still smiling, the old sorcerer, and it seemed to me that the smile said: this is my world, do you see? there is no Anna Schillings here, no gaping peasants, no bloodied statues, no Dantiscus, only the light and the emptiness, and that mysterious music high in the air which you cannot hear but which you know is there. And for the first time then I saw him whole, no longer the image of him I had carried with me from Wittenberg, but Copernicus himself – *it*self – the true thing, a cold brilliant object like a diamond (not like a diamond, but I am in a hurry), now all at once vividly familiar and yet untouchable still. It is not vouchsafed to many men to know another thus, with that awful clarity; when it comes, the vision is fleeting, the experience lasts only an instant, but the knowledge gleaned thereby remains forever. We reached Löbau, and in the flurry of arrival I felt that I was indeed waking from a dream. I waited for the Canon to acknowledge all that had happened out on the plain (whatever it was!), but he did not, would not, and I was disappointed. Well, for all I know, the old devil may have put a spell on me out there. But I shall always remember that eerie journey. Yes.

*

Löbau Castle was an enormous white stone fortress on a hill, its towers and turrets looking down over wooded slopes to the huddled roofs of the town. The air up there was crisp with the smell of spruce and pine. I might almost have been back in Germany. We drew into the courtyard and were greeted by an uproar of servants and grooms and hysterical dogs. A grizzled old fellow in a leather jerkin and patched breeches came to receive us. I took him for a steward or somesuch, but I was wrong: it was Bishop Giese himself. He greeted the Canon with grave solicitude. He hardly glanced at me, until, when he offered me the ring to kiss, I shook his hand instead, and that provoked a keen look. The two of them moved away together, the Canon shuffling slowly with bowed head, the Bishop supporting him with a gentle hand under his elbow, and the Canon groaned:

'Ah, Tiedemann, troubles, troubles . . .'

I was left to fend for myself, of course, as usual, until one of the serving lads took pity on me. He bounced up under my nose with a saucy grin smeared on his face, Raphaël he was called, hardly more than a child, a pretty fellow with an arse on him like a peach, O, I knew what he was about! – Raphaël, indeed: some angel. But I followed him willingly enough, and not without gratitude. As he scampered along before me, babbling and leering in his childish way, it occurred to me that I should have a chat with him in private, before I left, about the joys of matrimony and so on, and warn him of the tribulations in store for him if he continued to lean in the direction he so obviously leaned, at such a tender age. Had I only known what tribulations were in store for *me* on his account!

*

And so began our strange sojourn at Löbau. Throughout that long summer we remained there. The magical spell, the first touch of which I had felt out on the empty Prussian plain, settled over all that white castle on its peak, where we, as in an enchanted sleep, wandered amidst the luminous order and music of the planets, dreaming miraculous dreams. Luther had scoffed at Copernicus, calling him *the fool who wants to turn the whole science of astronomy upside down*, but Luther should have kept to theology, for in the sweat of his worst nightmare he could not have imagined what we would do during those months at Löbau. We turned the whole universe upon its head. *We*, I say *we*, for without me he would have kept silent even into the silence of the grave. He had intended to destroy his book: how many of you knew that?

How very skilfully I am telling this tale.

*

Bishop Giese. Bishop Giese was not quite the crusty old pedant I had expected. He was no gay dog, to be sure, but he was not without a certain . . . how shall I say, a certain sense of irony – better call it that than humour, for none of those northerners knows how to laugh. In his attitude toward the Canon, a blend of awe and solicitude and an occasional, helpless exasperation that yet was never less than amiable, he revealed a loyal and gentle nature. He was something of an astronomer, and possessed a bronze armillary sphere for observing equinoxes, and a mighty gnomon from England, which I envied. However, it was with an enthusiasm plainly forced that he displayed these and other instruments, and I suspect he kept them chiefly as evidence of the sincerity of his interest in the Canon's work. He was nearing sixty at the time of which I speak, had been a canon of the Frauenburg Chapter, and was destined one day to take Dantiscus's place in the Bishopric of Ermland. Of middle height, not stout but not gaunt either, he was one of those middling men who are the unacknowledged proprietors of the world. He was decent, unassuming, diligent – in short, a *good man.* I loathed him, I still do. He suffered from the ague, which he had contracted in the course of his duties somewhere in the wilds of that enormous bog which is Prussia; Canon Nicolas, playing at medicine (as I do now!), had for some time been treating him for the affliction, hence, officially at least, our presence at Löbau. But it was not on the Bishop alone that the Canon's skill was to be lavished . . .

On the evening of our arrival, after I had lain down briefly to sleep, I awoke drenched in sweat and prey to a nameless panic. My teeth chattered. I rose and for a long time wandered fitfully about the castle, wringing my hands and moaning, lost and frightened in those unfamiliar stone corridors and silent galleries. I knew, but would not acknowledge it, what this mood of mounting urgency and alarm presaged. All my life I have been subject to prolonged bouts of melancholia, which at their most severe bring with them fainting fits and crippling pains, even temporary blindness sometimes, and a host of other lesser demons to plague me. But worst of all is the heartache, the *accidie.* More than once I have near died of it, and hard to bear indeed would be the fear that at the last the ghost might abandon me in the midst of that drear dark, but, thankfully, my stars have laid in store for me an easier, finer end. The attack that came on that evening was one of the strangest that I have ever known, and was to endure, muted but always there, throughout my stay at Löbau. I have spoken already of enchantment: was it perhaps no more than the effect of viewing the events of that summer through the membrane of melancholy?

Dinner at the castle was always a wearisome and repellent

ritual, but on that first evening it was torment. The company gathered and disposed itself hierarchically in a vast hall, whose stained-glass windows trapped the late sunlight in its muddy tints and checked its rude advance into the pious gloom so beloved of popish churchmen. Amid the appalling racket of bells and music and so forth the Bishop entered, in full regalia, and took his place at the head of the highest table. Slatterns with red hands and filthy heels bore in huge trays of pork and baskets of black Prussian bread and jars of wine, and then the uproar began in earnest as the doltish priests and leering clerks stuck their snouts into the prog, gulping and snorting and belching, flinging abuse and gnawed bones at each other, filling the smoky air with shrieks of wild laughter. A bout of fisticuffs broke out at one of the lower tables. In the face of it all, the Bishop, enthroned on my left, maintained a placid mien – and why not? By the standards of the Roman Church his dining-room was a model of polite behaviour. Yes, to him, to them all, everything was just splendid, and I alone could see the ape squatting in our midst and hear his howls. Even if they had seen him, they would have taken him for a messenger from God, an archangel with steaming armpits and blue-black ballocks, and sure enough, after a few prayers directed by the company toward the ceiling, the poor brute would have been pointing a seraphic finger upward in a new annunciation (the Word made Pork!). Thus does Rome transform into ritual the horrors of the world, in order to sustain the fictions. I hate them all, Giese with his mealy-mouthed hypocrisy, Dantiscus and his bastards, but most of all of them I hate – ah but bide, Rheticus, bide! The Bishop was speaking to me, some polite rubbish as usual, but the bread was turning to clay in my mouth, and the plate of meat before me had the look of an haruspex's bowl of entrails, signifying doom. I could no longer bear to remain in that hall. I rose with a snarl, and fled.

Soulsick and weary, I lay awake for hours by the window of the rathole I had been allotted as a room. Out on the plain faint lights flickered. The sky was eerily aglow. In those northern summers true darkness never falls, and throughout the white nights a pallid twilight endures from dusk to dawn. I longed for kindly death. My eyes ached, my arsehole was clenched, my hands stank of wax and ashes. Here in this barbarous clime was no place for me. Tears filled my eyes, and flowed in torrents down my cheeks. All of my life seemed in that moment inexplicably transfigured, a blackened and useless thing, and there was no comfort for me anywhere. I held my face in my hands as if it were some poor, wounded, suffering creature, and bawled like a baby.

There came a tapping, which I heard without hearing, thinking it was the wind, or a deathwatch beetle at work, but then the door opened a little way and the Canon cautiously put in his head and peered about. He wore the same robe that he had travelled in, a shapeless black thing, but on his head now there was perched an indescribably comic nightcap with a tassle. In his trembling hand he carried a lamp, the quaking light of which sent shadows leaping up the walls like demented ghosts. He seemed surprised, and even a little dismayed, to find me awake. I suspect he had come to spy on me. He mumbled an apology and began to withdraw, but then hesitated, remembering, I suppose, that I was not after all an article of furniture, and that a living creature wide awake and weeping might think himself entitled to an explanation as to why an elderly gentleman in a funny cap should be peering into his room at dead of night. With an impatient little sigh he shuffled in and closed the door behind him, put down the lamp with exaggerated deliberation, and then, carefully averting his gaze from my tears, he spoke thus:

'Herr von Lauchen, Bishop Giese tells me you are ill, or so he thought, when you fled his table so precipitately; and therefore I have come in order to ask if I might be of some assistance. The nature of your ailment is quite plain: Saturn, malign star, rules your existence, filled, as it has been, I'm sure, with gainful study, abstract thought, and deep reflection, which feed the hungry mind, but sap the will, and lead to melancholy and dejection. Nothing will avail you, sir, until, as Ficino recommends, you entrust yourself into the care of the Three Graces, and cleave to things under their rule. First, remember, even a single yellow crocus blossom, Jupiter's golden flower, may bring relief; also, the light of Sol, of course, is good, and green fields at dawn – or anything, in fact, that's coloured green, the shade of Venus. Do this, *meinherr*, shun all things saturnine, surround yourself instead with influences conducive to health and joy and spirits fine, and illness never more shall your defences breach. Ahem . . . The Bishop seated you by his side at table: an honour, sir, extended only to the very few. To rise in haste, as you did, is a slur. Perhaps at Wittenberg you have adopted Father Luther's table manners, and hence the reason why you so disrupted the Bishop's table. But please understand that here in Prussia we do things differently. *Vale*. – The dawn comes on apace, I see.'

He waited, with head inclined, as though he fancied that his voice, of its own volition as it were, might wish to add something further; but no, he was quite done, and taking up his lamp he prepared to depart. I said:

'I shall be leaving today.'

He stopped short in the doorway and peered at me over his shoulder. 'You are leaving us, Herr von Lauchen, already?'

'Yes, *Meister*, for Wittenberg; for home.'

'O.'

He pondered this unexpected development, sinking into himself like a puzzled old snail into its carapace, and then, mumbling, he wandered away in an introspective trance, with those ghostly shadows prancing about him. Fool that I was, I should have packed my bags and fled there and then, while all the castle was abed, and left him to publish his book or not, burn it, wipe himself with it, whatever he wished. I even imagined my going, and wept again, with compassion for that stern sad figure which was myself, striding away into a chill sombre dawn. I had come to him in a prentice tunic, humbly: I, Rheticus, doctor of mathematics and astronomy at the great school of Wittenberg, and he had dodged me, ignored me, preached at me as if I were an errant choirboy. I should have gone! But I did not go. I crawled instead under the blankets and nursed my poor forlorn heart to sleep.

* * *

I CAN SEE IT NOW, of course, how cunning they were, the two of them, Giese and the Canon, cunning old conspirators; but I could not see it then. I woke late in the morning to find Raphaël beside me, with honey and hot bread and a jug of spiced wine. The food was welcome, but the mere presence of the lithesome lad would have been sufficient, for it broke a fast far crueller than belly-hunger – I mean the fasting from the company of youth and rosy cheeks and laughing eyes, which I had been forced to observe since leaving Wittenberg and coming among these greybeards. We spent a pleasant while together, and he, the shy one, twisted his fingers and shifted from foot to foot, chattering on in a vain effort to stem his blushes. At length I gave him a coin and sent him skipping on his way, and although the old gloom returned once he was gone, it was not half so leaden as before. Too late I remembered that sober talk I had determined to have with him; the matter would have to be dealt with. An establishment of clerics, all men – and Catholics at that! – was a perilous place for a boy of his . . . his youth and beauty. (I was about to say innocence, but in honesty I must not, even though I know that thereby I banish the word from the language, for if it is denied to him then it has no meaning anymore. I speak in riddles. They shall be solved. My poor Raphaël! they destroyed us both.)

*

I rose and went in search of the Canon, and was directed to the *arboretum*, a name which conjured up a pleasant image of fruit trees in flower, dappled green shade, and little leafy paths where astronomers might stroll, discussing the universe. What I found was a crooked field fastened to a hill behind the castle, with a few stunted bushes and a cabbage patch – and, need I say, no sign of the Canon. As I stamped away, sick of being sent on false chases, a figure rose up among the cabbages and hailed me. Today Bishop Giese was rigged out again in his peasant costume. The sight of those breeches and that jerkin irritated me greatly. Do these damn Catholics, I wondered, never do else but dress up and pose? His hands were crusted with clay, and when he drew near I caught a strong whiff of horse manure. He was in a hearty mood. I suppose it went with the outfit. He said:

'*Grüss Gott*, Herr von Lauchen! The Doctor informs me that you are ill. Not gravely so, I trust? Our Prussian climate is uncongenial, although here, on Castle Hill, we are spared the debilitating vapours of the plain – which are yet not so bad as those that rise from the Frisches Haff at Frauenburg, eh, *meinherr*? Ho ho. Let me look at you, my son. Well, the nature of your ailment is plain: Saturn, malign star . . .' And he proceeded to parrot verbatim the Canon's little sermon in praise of the Graces. I listened in silence, with a curled lip. I was at once amused and appalled: amused that this clown should steal the master's words and pretend they were his own, appalled at the notion, which suddenly struck me, that the Canon may not after all have been mocking me, but may have been actually serious about that fool Ficino's cabalistic nonsense! O, I know well the baleful influence which Saturn wields over my life; I know that the Graces are good; but I also know that a hectacre of crocuses would not have eased my heartsickness one whit. *Crocuses!* However, as I was to discover, the Canon neither believed nor disbelieved Ficino's theories, no more than he believed nor disbelieved the contents of any of the score or so set speeches with which he had long ago armed himself, and from which he could choose a ready response to any situation. All that mattered to him was the saying, not what was said; words were the empty rituals with which he held the world at bay. Copernicus did not believe in truth. I think I have said that before.

Giese put his soiled hand on my arm and led me along a path below the castle wall. When he had finished his dissertation on the state of my health, he paused and glanced at me with a peculiar, thoughtful look, like that of an undertaker speculatively eyeing a sick man. The last remaining patches of the morning's mist clung about us like old rags, and the slowly ascending sun shed a damp weak light upon the battlements above. The world seemed old and tired. I wanted to find the Canon, to wrest from him his secrets, to thrust fame upon his unwilling head. I wanted *action*. I was young. The Bishop said:

'You come, I believe, from Wittenberg?'

'Yes. I am a Lutheran.'

My directness startled him. He smiled wanly, and nodded his large head up and down very rapidly, as though to shake off that dreaded word I had uttered; he withdrew his hand carefully from my arm.

'Quite so, my dear sir, quite so,' he said, 'you are a Lutheran, as you admi— as you say. Now, I have no desire to dispute with you the issues of this tragic schism which has rent our Church, believe me. I might remind you that Father Luther was not the first to recognise the necessity for reform – but, be that as it may, we shall not argue. A man must live with his own conscience, in that much at least I would agree with you. So. You are a Lutheran. You admit it. There it rests. However, I cannot pretend that your presence in Prussia is not an embarrassment. It is not to me, you understand; the world pays scant heed to events here in humble Löbau. No, Herr von Lauchen, I refer to one who is dear to us both: I mean of course our *domine praeceptor*, Doctor Nicolas. It is to him that your presence is an embarrassment, and, perhaps, a danger even. But now I see I have offended you. Let me explain. You have not been long in Prussia, therefore you cannot be expected to appreciate the situation prevailing here. Tell me, are you not puzzled by the Doctor's unwillingness to give his knowledge to the world, to publish his masterpiece? It would surprise you, would it not, if I were to tell you that it is not doubt as to the validity of his conclusions that makes him hesitate, nothing like that, no – but fear. So it is, Herr von Lauchen: *fear*.'

He paused again, again we paced the path in silence. I have called Giese a fool, but that was only a term of abuse: he was no fool. We left the castle walls behind, and descended a little way the wooded slope. The trees were tall. Three rabbits fled at our approach. I stumbled on a fallen bough. The pines were silvery, each single needle adorned with a delicate filigree of beaded mist. How strange, the clarity with which I remember that moment! Thus, even as the falcon plummets, the sparrow snatches a last look at her world. Bishop Giese, laying his talons on my arm again, began to chant, I think that is the word, in Latin:

'Painful is the task I must perform, and tell to one – from Wittenberg! – of the storm of envy which surrounds our learned friend. *Meinherr*, I pray you, to my tale attend with caution and forbearance, and don't feel that in these few bare facts you see revealed a plot hatched in the corridors of Rome. This evil is the doing of one alone: do you know the man Dantiscus, Ermland's Bishop (Johannes Flachsbinder his name, a Danzig sop)? Copernicus he hates, and from jealousy these many years he has right zealously persecuted him. Why so? you ask, but to answer you, that is a task, I fear, beyond me. Why ever do the worst detest the best, and mediocrities thirst to see great minds brought low? It is the world. Besides, this son of Zelos, dimwitted churl though he be, thinks Prussia has but room for one great mind – that's his! The fellow's moon mad, *certes*. Now, to achieve his aims, and ruin our *magister*, he defames his name, puts it about he shares his bed with his *focaria*, whom he has led into foul sin to satisfy his lust. My friend, you stare, as though you cannot trust your ears. This is but one of many lies this Danziger has told! And in the eyes of all the world the Doctor's reputation is destroyed, and mocking condemnation, he believes, would greet his book. Some years ago, at Elbing, ignorant peasants jeered a waxwork figure of Copernicus that was displayed in a carnival farce. Thus Dantiscus wins, and our friend keeps silent, fearing to trust his brilliant theories to the leering mob. And so, *meinherr*, the work of twoscore years lies fallow and unseen. Therefore, I beg you, do not leave us yet. We must try to make him reconsider – *but hush! here is the Doctor now. Mind, do not say what secrets I have told you!* – Ah Nicolas, good day.'

We had left the wood and entered the courtyard by a little low postern gate. Had Giese not pointed him out, I would not have noticed the Canon skulking under an archway, watching us intently with a peculiar fixed grin on his grey face. Out of new knowledge, I looked upon him in a new light. Yes, now I could see in him (so I thought!) a man enfettered, whose every action was constrained by the paramount need for secrecy and caution, and I felt on his behalf a burning sense of outrage. I would have flung myself to my knees before him, had there not been still vivid in my mind the memory of a previous genuflection. Instead, I contented myself with a terrible glare, that was meant to signify my willingness to take on an army of Dantiscuses at his command. (And yet, behind it all, I was confused, and even suspicious: what was it exactly that they required of me?) I had forgotten my declared intention of leaving that day; in fact, I had said it merely to elicit some genuine response from that night-capped oracle in my chamber, and certainly I had not imagined that this thoughtless threat would provoke the panic which apparently it had. I determined to proceed with care – but of course, like the young fool that I was, I had no sooner decided on caution than I abandoned it, and waded headlong into the mire. I said:

'*Meister*, we must return to Frauenburg at once! I intend to make a copy of your great work, and take it to a printer that I know at Nuremberg, who is discreet, and a specialist in such books. You must trust me, and delay no longer!'

In my excitement I expected some preposterously dramatic reaction from the Canon to this naked challenge to his secretiveness, but he merely shrugged and said:

'There is no need to go to Frauenburg; the book is here.'

I said:

'But but but but but—!'

And Giese said:

'Why Nicolas—!'

And the Canon, glancing at us both with a mixture of contempt and distaste, answered:

'I assumed that Herr von Lauchen did not journey all the way from Wittenberg merely for amusement. You came here to learn of my theory of the revolutions of the spheres, did you not? Then so you shall. I have the manuscript with me. Come this way.'

We went all three into the castle, and the Canon straightway fetched the manuscript from his room. The events of the morning had moved so swiftly that my poor brain, already bemused by illness, could not cope with them, and I was in state of shock – yet not so shocked that I did not note how the old man vainly tried to appear unconcerned when he surrendered to me his life's work, that I did not feel his trembling fingers clutch at the manuscript in a momentary spasm of misgiving as it passed between us. When the deed was done he stepped back a pace, and that awful uncontrollable grin took hold of his face again, and Bishop Giese, hovering near us, gave a kind of whistle of relief, and I, fearing that the Canon might change his mind and try to snatch the thing away from me, rose immediately and made off with it to the window.

DE REVOLUTIONIBUS ORBIUM MUNDI
—for mathematicians only—

*

How to express my emotions, the strange jumble of feelings kindled within me, as I gazed upon the living myth which I held in my hands, the key to the secrets of the universe? This book for years had filled my dreams and obsessed my waking hours so completely that now I could hardly comprehend the reality, and the words in the crabbed script seemed not to speak, but to sing rather, so that the rolling grandeur of the title boomed like a flourish of celestial trumpets, to the accompaniment of the wordly fiddling of the motto with its cautious admonition, and I smiled, foolishly, helplessly, at the inexplicable miracle of this music of Heaven and Earth. But then I turned the pages, and chanced upon the diagram of a universe in the centre of which stands Sol in the splendour of eternal immobility, and the music was swept away, and my besotted smile with it, and a new and wholly unexpected sensation took hold of me. It was sorrow! sorrow that old Earth should be thus deposed, and cast out into the darkness of the firmament, there to prance and spin at the behest of a tyrannical, mute god of fire. I grieved, friends, for our diminishment! O, it was not that I did not already know that Copernicus's theory postulated a heliocentric world – everyone knew that – and anyway I had been permitted to read Melanchton's well-thumbed copy of the *Commentariolus*. Besides, as everyone also knows, Copernicus was not the first to set the Sun at the centre. Yes, I had for a long time known what this Prussian was about, but it was not until that morning at Löbau Castle that I at last realised, in a kind of fascinated horror, the full consequences of this work of cosmography. Beloved Earth! he banished you forever into darkness. And yet, what does it matter? The sky shall be forever blue, and the earth shall forever blossom in spring, and this planet shall forever be the centre of all we know. I believe it.

*

I read the entire manuscript there and then; that is not of course to say that I read every word: rather, I opened it up, as a surgeon opens a limb, and plunged the keen blade of my intellect into its vital centres, thus laying bare the quivering arteries leading to the heart. And there, in the knotted cords of that heart, I made a strange discovery . . . but more of that presently. When at last I lifted my eyes from those pages, I found myself alone. The light was fading in the windows. It was evening. The day had departed, with Giese and Copernicus, unnoticed. My brain ached, but I forced it to think, to seek out a small persistent something which had been lodging in my thoughts since morning, biding its time. It was the memory of how, when in the courtyard I challenged him to surrender the manuscript to me, Copernicus had for an instant, just for an instant only, cast off the timorous churchman's mask to reveal behind it an icy scorn, a cold, cruel arrogance. I did not know why I had remembered it, why it seemed so significant; I was not even sure that I had not imagined it; but it troubled me. *What is it they want me to do?* Go carefully, Rheticus, I told myself, hardly knowing what I meant . . .

I found Copernicus and Giese in the great hall of the castle, seated in silence in tall carved chairs on either side of the enormous hearth, on which, despite the mildness of the evening, stacked logs were blazing fiercely. The windows, set high up in the walls, let in but little of the evening's radiance, and in the gloom the robes of the two still figures seemed to flow and merge into the elaborate flutings of the thrones on which they sat, so that to my bruised perception they appeared limbless, a pair of severed heads, ghastly in the fire's crimson glow. Copernicus had put himself as close to the blaze as he could manage without risking combustion, but still he looked cold. As I entered the arc of flickering firelight, I found that he was watching me. I was weary, and incapable of subtlety, and once again I ignored my own injunction to go carefully. I held up the manuscript and said:

'I have read it, and find it is all I had expected it would be, more than I had hoped; will you allow me to take it to Nuremberg, to Petreius the printer?'

He did not answer immediately. The silence stretched out around us until it seemed to creak. At length he said:

'That is a question which we cannot discuss, yet.'

At that, as though he had been given a signal, the Bishop stirred himself and put an end to the discussion (discussion!). Had I eaten? Why then, I must! He would have Raphaël bring me supper in my room, for I should retire, it was late, I was ill and in need of rest. And, like a sleepy child, I allowed myself to be led away, too tired to protest, clutching the manuscript, babe's favourite toy, to my breast. I looked back at Copernicus, and the severed head smiled and nodded, as if to say: sleep, little one, sleep now. My room looked somehow different, but I could not say in what way, until next morning when I noticed the desk, amply stocked with writing implements and paper, which they installed without my knowing. O the cunning!

*

A thought, which I find startling, has occurred to me, viz. that I was happy at Löbau Castle, perhaps happier than I had ever been before, or would be again. Is it true? Happiness. *Happiness.* I write down the word, I stare at it, but it means nothing. Happiness; how strange. When the world, which is populated for the most part by fools and hypocrites, talks of being happy, really it is talking about no more than the gratification of hunger – hunger for love, or revenge, money, suchlike – but that cannot be what I mean. I have never loved anyone, and if I had money I would not know what to do with it. Revenge, of course, is another matter; but it will not make me *happy.* At Löbau, certainly, I knew nothing of revenge, did not even suspect that one day I would desire it. What am I talking about? I cannot understand myself, these ravings. Yet the thought will not go away. *I was happy that summer at Löbau.* It is like a kind of message, sent to me from I do not know where; a cipher. Well then, let me see if I can discover what it was that made me happy, and then maybe I shall understand what this happiness meant.

*

Quickly the days acquired a rhythm. In the mornings I was awakened by the sombre tolling of the castle bell, signifying that in the chapel the Bishop was celebrating Mass. The thought of that strange secret ritual of blood and sacrifice being enacted close at hand in the dim light of dawn was at once comical and grotesque, and yet mysteriously consoling. After Mass came Raphaël, sleepy-eyed but unfailingly gay, to feed and barber me. He was such a pleasant creature, and was happy to chatter or keep silent as my mood demanded. Even his silence was merry. I tried repeatedly to elicit from him a precise description of his duties in the Bishop's household, for it was apparent that he held a privileged position, but his answers were always vague. It occurred to me that he might be old Giese's bastard. (Perhaps he was? I hope not.) Sometimes I had him accompany me when I went forth to take the air in the woods below the walls, but after that he was banished from my side and warned not to appear again with his distracting ways till evening, for I had work to do.

The astronomer who studies the motions of the stars is surely like a blind man, who, with only the staff of mathematics to guide him, must make a great, endless, hazardous journey that winds through innumerable desolate places. What will be the result? Proceeding anxiously for a while, and groping his way with his staff, he will at some time, leaning upon it, cry out in despair to Heaven, Earth and all the gods to aid him in his anguish. Thus, day after day, for ten weeks, beset by illness and, worse, uncertainty regarding the purpose of my labours, I struggled with the intricacies of Copernicus's theory of the movements of the planets. This second reading of the manuscript was very different from the first deceptive glance, when, entranced by music, I went straight to the heart of the work, and cheerfully ignored the details. Ah, the details! Crouched at my desk, with my head in my hands, I did furious battle with them, moaning and muttering, weeping, laughing sometimes even, uncontrollably. I remember in particular the trouble caused me by the orbit of Mars, the warlord. That planet is a *cunt*! It nearly drove me insane. One day, despairing of ever comprehending the mystery of its orbit, I rose and dashed in frantic circles about the room, crashing my head against the walls. At length, when I had knocked myself near senseless, I sank to the floor with laughter booming in my ears, and a mocking voice – I swear it came from the fourth sphere itself! – roared at me: *Good, Rheticus, very good! You have found what you sought, for just as you have whirled about this room, just so does Mars whirl in the heavens!*

As if all this were not enough, I spent the evenings, when I should have been resting, locked in endless circular arguments with Copernicus, trying to persuade him to publish. These battles took place after dinner in the great hall, where a third carved throne had been provided for me before the fire. I say battles, but assaults would be a better word, for while I attacked, Copernicus merely cowered behind the ramparts of a stony silence, apparently untouchable. A remote grey figure, he sat huddled in the folds of his robe, staring before him, his jaw clenched tight as a gintrap. No matter how hot the fire, he was always cold. It was as if he generated coldness out of some frozen waste within him. Only when my pleading reached its fiercest intensity, when, beside myself with messianic fervour, I leaped to my feet and roared frantic exhortations at him, waving my arms, only then did his stolid defences show a trace of weakness. His head began to jerk from side to side, in a clockwork frenzy of refusal, while that ghastly grin spread wider and wider, and the sweat stood out on his brow, and, like a girl teasing herself with thoughts of rape, he peered down into the depths of the abyss into which I was inviting him to leap, hugging himself in horrified, panic-stricken glee. Sometimes, even, he was pressed so far that he spoke, but only in order to throw an obstacle in the path of my merciless advance, and then he was always careful to seize on some minor point of my argument, steering well clear of the main issue. Thus, when I put it to him that he had a duty to publish, if only to demonstrate the errors in Ptolemy, he shook a trembling finger at me and cried:

'We must follow the methods of the ancients! Anyone who thinks they are not to be trusted will squat forever in the wilderness outside the locked gates of our science, dreaming the dreams of the deranged about the motions of the spheres – and he will get what he deserves for thinking he can support his own ravings by slandering the ancients!'

Giese, for his part, liked to think of himself as the wise old mediator in these one-sided debates, and waded in now and again with some inane remark, which obviously he considered immensely learned and persuasive, and to which Copernicus and I attended in a painful polite silence, before continuing on as if the old clown had never opened his mouth. But he was happy enough, so long as he was allowed to say his piece, for, like all his breed, he saw no difference between words and actions, and felt that when something was said it was as good as done. He was not the only spectator on the battlefield. As the weeks went by, word spread through the castle, and even to the town and beyond, that free entertainment was being laid on each evening in the great hall, and soon we began to draw an audience of clerics and castle officials, fat burghers from the town, travelling charlatans on diplomatic missions to the See of Kulm, and God knows what all. Even the servants came creeping in to hear this wild man from Wittenberg perform. At first it disturbed me to have that faceless, softly breathing mass shifting and tittering behind me in the gloom, but I grew accustomed to it, in time. In fact, I began to enjoy myself. In the magic circle of the firelight, immured in the impregnable fortress high above the plain, I felt that I had been lifted out of the world of ordinary men into some rarefied aetherial sphere, where nothing that was soiled could touch me, where I touched nothing soiled. Outside it was summer, the peasants were working in the fields, emperors were waging wars, but here there was none of that, all that, blood and toil, things growing, slaughter and glory, bucolic pleasures, men dying – in short, life, no, none of that. For we were angels, playing an endless, celestial game. And I was happy.

—And if that is what is meant by happiness, *then I want none of it.*

* * *

I AM GETIING ON, getting on, yes indeed; I am at Löbau still. My arguments won through in the end, and although it was in his own way, to be sure, and on his own terms, Copernicus capitulated. The first hint that he was ready to negotiate in earnest came when one evening he began out of the blue to babble excitedly about a plan, which he knew, he said, would meet with my enthusiastic approval. I must not think that his unwillingness to publish his modest theories sprang from contempt for the world; indeed, as I well knew (I did?), he bore a great love for ordinary men, and had no wish to leave them in ignorance *de rerum natura* if there was any way in which he could enlighten them. Also, he had a responsibility toward science, and the improvement of scientific method. Having regard to all this, then, he proposed to draw up astronomical tables, with new rules for plotting star courses, which would be an invaluable aid not only to astronomers but also to sailors and map-makers and so forth; these, when he had prepared them, I could take to my printer at Nuremberg. However, I should understand one thing clearly, that while the computational tables would have new and accurate rules, *there would be no proofs*. He was well aware that his theory, on which the tables would be founded, would, if published, overturn the accepted notions regarding the movements of the spheres, and would therefore cause a hideous commotion, and he was not prepared *to lend his name* to the causing of such disturbance (my italics). Pythagoras held that the secrets of science must be reserved for the few, for the initiates, the wise ones, and Pythagoras was an ancient, and he was right. So: new rules, yes, *but no proofs to support them.*

This would not do, of course, and well he knew it, for as soon as I began to put forward my objections he hurriedly agreed, and said yes, it was a foolish notion, he would abandon it. (I confess that, to this day, I still do not understand why he put forward this nonsensical plan only to relinquish it at once, unless he merely wished to signal to me, in his usual roundabout way, that he was now prepared to compromise.) The subject was closed then, which small detail was not, however, going to deter Giese from voicing *his* objections, the formulation of which, I suppose, cost him a mighty effort that he was fain to see wasted.

'But Doctor,' he said, 'these tables would be an incomplete gift to the world, unless you reveal the theory on which they are based, as Ptolemy, for whom you have such high regard, was always careful to do.'

To that, Copernicus, who had once more retreated dreamily into himself, made an extraordinary answer. He said:

'The Ptolemaic astronomy is nothing, so far as existence is concerned, but it is convenient for computing the inexistent.'

But having said it, he recollected himself, and pretended, by assuming an expression meant to indicate bland innocence but which merely made him look a halfwit, that he was unaware of having put forward a notion which, if he believed it to be true, made nonsense of his life's work (for, remember, whatever they may say about it now, his theory was based entirely upon the Ptolemaic astronomy – was indeed, as he pointed out himself, no more than a revision of Ptolemy, at least in its beginnings). So profound an admission was it, that at the time I failed to grasp its full significance, and only felt its black brittle wing brush my cheek, as it were, as it flew past. However, I must have perceived that something momentous had occurred, that part of the ramparts had collapsed, for immediately I was on my feet and crying:

'Let me take the manuscript, let me go to Nuremberg. We must act now, or forever keep silent – trust me!'

He did not answer at once. It seems to me now, although I am surely mistaken, that there was a vast audience in the hall that evening, for the silence was enormous, the kind of silence which only comes when the multitude for a moment, its infantile attention captured, stops yelping and goggles with mouth agape at some gaudy, gimcrack wonder. Even Giese held his peace. Copernicus was smiling. I don't mean grinning, not that grin, but a real smile, faint, quite calm, and full of cunning. He said:

'You say that I must trust you, and of course I do, indeed I do; but the journey to Nuremberg is long, and hazardous in these times, and who can say what evils might not befall you on the way? What if you should lose the manuscript in some misadventure, if it should be stolen, or destroyed? All would be lost then, all my work. This book has been thirty years in the writing.'

What was he about? He watched me with cold amusement (I swear it was amusement!) as I wriggled like a stranded fish in my search for the correct, the only answer to the riddle he had set me. This was different to all that had gone before; this was in earnest. With great care I said:

'Then I shall make a copy of the manuscript, and take it with me, while you retain the original. That way, the safety of the book is assured, and also its publication. I see no further difficulty.'

'But you might lose the copy, might you not, and what then?

Rather, here is a plan: go now to Nuremberg, and there write down an *account* of the book from memory, which I have no doubt you could do with ease, and publish *that*.'

'But it has already been done!' I cried. 'You yourself have written an account, in the *Commentariolus*—'

'That was nothing, worse than nothing, full of errors. You must write an accurate account. You see the advantages for us both in this: your name shall gain prominence in the world of science, while the way shall have been prepared for the publication later of my book. You shall be a kind of—' he smiled again '—a kind of John the Baptist, the one who goes before.'

He had won, and he knew it. I bowed my head, signifying defeat.

'I agree,' I said. 'I shall write this account, if it is in my power.'

Ah, his smile, that little smile, how well I remember it! He said:

'This is a splendid plan, I think. Do you agree?'

'Yes, yes – but when will you publish *De revolutionibus*?'

'Well, when I consider the matter, I see no need to publish, if you ensure that your account is sufficiently comprehensive.'

'But your book? Thirty years?'

'The book is unnecessary.'

'And you intend—?'

'To destroy it.'

'*Destroy it?*'

'Why, yes.'

How simply and cheerfully it was said! How convincing it sounded!

*

Thus was conceived my *Narratio prima*, which in the thirty-six years since its publication has gained such fame (for *him*, not for me, whose work it was!). I have not given here a strictly literal account of how I was inveigled into writing it, but have contented myself with showing how cunningly he worked upon my youthful enthusiasm and my gullibility in order to achieve his own questionable ends. That nonsense about going at once to Nuremberg and writing the account from memory was only a part of the trap, of course, a condition on which he could without harm concede, and thereby appear gracious. Anyway, he had to concede, for I had no intention of leaving his side, having heard him threaten (a threat which, I confess, I did not take seriously – but still . . .) to burn his book.

I began the writing that very night. Copernicus's book is built in six parts, each part more intricate, more difficult than the one before. By that time I was thoroughly familiar with the first three, had some grasp of the fourth, and only a general idea of the last two – but I managed, I managed, and the *Narratio prima*, as you may judge, while it is not so elegant as I would wish, is yet a brilliant piece of work. Who else – I ask it in all modesty – who else could have made such a compressed, succinct account, in so short a time, of that bristling mesh of astronomical theory, who else but I? And was I aided in my herculean labours by the *domine praeceptor*? I was not! Each evening, when I had finished work for the day, he came with some flimsy excuse and took away from me the precious manuscript. Did he think I was going to eat it? And how he dithered, and fussed and fretted, and plucked at my sleeve in his nervousness, hedging me about with admonitions and prohibitions. I must not mention him by name, he said. Then how could I proceed? A theory without a theorist? Was I to claim the work as my own? Ah, *that* made him bethink himself, and he went away and thought about it for a day or two, and came back and said that if I must name him, then let me call him only *Doctor Nicolas of Torun*. Very well – what did I care? If he wanted to be dubbed Mad Kaspar, or Mandricardo the Terrible, it was all one to me. So I wrote down my title thus

> *To the Most Illustrious Dr Johannes Schöner, a First Account of the Book of Revolutions by the Most Learned & Excellent Mathematician, the Reverend Father, Doctor Nicolas of Torun, Canon of Ermland, from a Young Student of Mathematics.*

What a start it must have given old Schöner (he taught me in mathemetics and astronomy at Nuremberg) to find himself the unwitting target, so to speak, of this controversial work. The dedication was a piece of cunning, for Schöner's name could not but lend respectability to an account which, I knew, would stir up the sleeping hive of academic bees and set them buzzing. Also, for good measure, and in the hope of placating Dantiscus somewhat, I appended the *Encomium Borussiae*, that crawling piece in praise of Prussia, its intellectual giants, its wealth in amber and other precious materials, its glorious vistas of bog and slate-grey sea, which had me wracking my brain for pretty metaphors and classical allusions. And since I had decided to print at Danzig, that city being but a day's ride away, instead of at Nuremberg, and since the Mayor there, one John of Werden, had invited me to visit him, I did not let the opportunity pass to devote a few warm words to the city and the lusty Achilles that it had for Mayor.

The *Narratio prima* was completed on the 23rd of September, in 1539. By then I had returned with Copernicus to Frauenburg. Although I cannot say that I was overjoyed to find myself once more in that dreary town, I was relieved nevertheless to be away from that fool Giese, not to mention that magicked castle of Löbau. (Leaving Raphaël was another matter, of course . . .) Alone with Copernicus in his cold tower, at least the issues were clear, I mean I could see clearly the chasm that lay between his horror of change and my firm faith in progress. But I shall deal with that subject later. Did I say we were alone in the tower – how could I forget that other presence planted in our midst like some dreadful basilisk, whose sullen glare followed my every movement, whose outraged silence hung about us like a shroud? I mean Anna Schillings, frightful woman. She did not fulfil her threat to be gone when we returned, and was there waiting for us grimly, with her arms folded under that enormous chest. O no, Anna, I have not forgotten you. She cannot have been very much younger than Copernicus, but she possessed a vigour, fuelled by bitterness and spite, which belied her years. Me she loathed, with extraordinary passion; she was jealous. I would not have put it past her to try to do me in, and I confess that, faced with those bowls of greenish gruel on which she fed us, the thought of poison oftimes crossed my mind. And speaking of poisoning, I suspect Copernicus may have considered ridding himself thus of this troublesome woman: I remember watching him concocting some noisome medicine which he had prescribed for one of her innumerable obscure complaints, grinding the pestle, and grinding it, with a wistful, horrid little smile, as though he were putting out eyes. Of course, he would not have dreamed of daring so bold a solution. Anyway, most like he feared even more than the harridan herself the prospect of her ghost coming back to haunt him.

He insisted that I lodge with him in the tower. I was flattered, until I realised that he wanted me near him not for love of my company, but so that he would have an ally against the Schillings. In truth, however, I must admit I was not of much use to him in that respect. O I could handle her, no question of that, she soon learned to beware the edge of my tongue, but when she could get no good of me she redoubled her efforts on the unfortunate Copernicus, and fairly trounced him; so that my presence in fact exacerbated his problems. Whenever she drew near he winced, and sank into the carapace of his robe, as though fearing that his ears were about to be boxed. Well, I had little sympathy for him. He had only to take his courage in his hands (what a curious phrase that is) and kick her out, or poison her, or denounce her as a witch, and all would have been well. What, anyway, was the hold she had on him? Apparently he had rescued her from a knocking shop, or so they said; she was a cousin of some sort. I confess it made me feel quite nauseous to ponder the matter, but I surmised that some cuntish ritual, performed years before when they were still capable of that kind of thing, had subjected him to her will. I have seen it before, that phenomenon, men turned into slaves by the tyranny of the twat. Women. I have nothing against them, in their place, but I know that they have only to master a few circus tricks in bed and they become veritable Circes. Ach, leave it, Rheticus, leave it.

When I say I had little sympathy for him in his plight, I do not mean that I was indifferent. The *Narratio prima* was completed, and I was ready to set off for Danzig, and after Danzig it was imperative that I return to Wittenberg, for I had already overstretched my term of leave; all this would mean that I could not be back in Frauenburg before the beginning of the following summer. By then, God knows what disasters would have occurred. Copernicus was an old man, far from robust, and his will was crumbling. Dantiscus had renewed his campaign, and almost by the week now he sent letters regarding Anna Schillings, bristling with threats under a veneer of sweetness and hypocritical concern for the astronomer's reputation; each letter, I could see it in Copernicus's stricken grey countenance, further jeopardised the survival of the manuscript. I knew, remembering what Giese had said that day in the pine wood below the walls of Löbau, that when Dantiscus spoke of his duty to extirpate vice from his diocese et cetera, he was in fact speaking of something else entirely: viz. his burning jealousy of Copernicus. Would the *Meister's* nerve hold until I returned, or, alone against the Schillings's bullying and in the face of Dantiscus's threats, would he burn his book, and bolt for the safety and silence of his burrow? It was a risk I could not take. If the Schillings could not be got rid of – and I despaired early of shifting that grim mass of flesh and fury – then the one for whom she was a weapon must be persuaded that the war he was waging was already lost. (Another riddle – solution follows.) I made a last, token effort to wrest the manuscript from the old man's clutches, but he only looked at me, mournfully, accusingly, and spoke not a word; I packed my bags and bade farewell to Frauenburg.

* * *

I SHALL NOT DWELL UPON my stay at Danzig. The Mayor, mine host, Fat Jack of Werden, was a puffed-up boorish burgher, whose greatest love, next to foodstuffs, that is, was the making of sententious speeches in praise of himself. He was pleased as punch to have as his guest that most exotic of beasts, a Lutheran scholar from Germany, and he missed no opportunity of showing me off to his friends, and, more especially, to his enemies. O, I had a rollicking time in Danzig. Still, the printer to whom I brought the manuscript of the *Narratio* was a civil enough fellow, and surprisingly capable too, for a jobber, I mean, out there in the wilds. The first edition came off his presses in February of 1540. Copies were sent to Frauenburg, and also to Löbau Castle, whence Giese dispatched one to the Lutheran Duke Albrecht of East Prussia at Königsberg – a shrewd move, as I was later to discover, which nevertheless annoyed Copernicus intensely, there being an old grudge there. A piece of shrewdness of my own was well rewarded, when my good friend Perminius Gassarus, on receipt of the copy I sent him, immediately brought out a second edition at Basle, which he financed out of his own pocket, thereby sparing me no little expense. For it was a costly business, this publishing, and, despite what they may say, I got no help, not a penny, from that old skinflint at Frauenburg, for whose benefit it was all done. Remember, these volumes to the Duke et cetera were delivered gratis (although Perminius, to my secret amusement, not only repaid my gift in the manner already recorded, but also sent me a gold piece, the fool), and as well as to Giese and of course Copernicus himself, copies went also to Schöner, and Melanchton, and to many other scholars and churchmen – including Dantiscus, in whose presence, at Heilsberg Castle, I first saw my own book in print . . .

*

Yes, it was at Heilsberg that I saw the *Narratio prima* between boards for the first time. Here is how it came about. Having found the printer trustworthy, I left the completion of the work in his hands, packed my bags, said goodbye to Fat Jack and his household, and set out on the long trek to Heilsberg. I must have been out of my mind to make that hideous journey for the sake of one undeserving of the effort, whose only thanks was a peevish outburst of abuse. But as I have said more than once before, I was young then, and not half so wise as I am now. Howsoever, despite the delicate state of my health, and the foul vapours of that Prussian marsh in winter, not to mention the appalling conditions in which I had to travel (lame horses, lousy inns, so on), I reached Heilsberg at the beginning of March, not too much the worse for wear. Impetuous as ever, I went straightway to the castle and demanded to see the Bishop. I had forgotten, of course, that you do not simply walk up to these papist princelings and grasp them warmly by the arm, O no, first the formalities must be observed. Well, I shall not go into all that. Suffice it to say that it was some days before I made my way at last one morning through the gate into the vast courtyard. There I was met by a cringing cleric, a minor official with ill-shaven jowls, who inspected me with furtive sidelong glances, the tip of his chapped red nose twitching, and informed me that the Bishop had just returned from the hunt, but nevertheless had graciously agreed to receive me without further delay. As we made our way toward the sanctum, we passed by a low cart, drawn up under one of the arched stone galleries of the courtyard, on which was flung the morning's kill, a brace of boar, one of them still whimpering in agony, and a poor torn doe lying in a mess of her own guts. Whenever now I think of Dantiscus, I think first of that steaming, savaged flesh.

I had expected him to be another Giese, a pompous old fool, thick as pigshit, a petty provincial with no more style to him than an oxcart, but I was mistaken. Johannes Flachsbinder was four-and-fifty when I met him, a vigorous, striking man who wore well his weight of years. Although he was but the son of a Danzig beer brewer, he carried himself with the grace of an aristocrat. In his time he had been a soldier, scholar, a diplomat and a poet. He had travelled throughout Europe, to Araby and the Holy Land. Kings and emperors he listed among his friends, also some of the leading scientists and explorers of the age. His amorous adventures were famous, in legend as well as in his own verses, and there was hardly a corner of the civilised world that could not boast a bastard of his. A daughter, got by a Toledan noblewoman, was his favourite, so it was said, and on this brat he continued to lavish love and money, for all that Rome might say. He feared no one. At the height of the Lutheran controversy he maintained close connections with the foremost Protestants, even while the Pope himself was hurling thunderbolts at their heads. Yes, Dantiscus was a brilliant, fearless and elegant man. And a swine. And a fraud. And a lying, vindictive cunt.

In a blue and gold hall I found him, breakfasting on red wine and venison, surrounded by a gaudy crowd of huntsmen and toadies and musicians. If I thought Giese's peasant garb ridiculous, this fellow's outfit was farcical: he was clad in velvet and silk, kneeboots of soft leather, a belt inlaid with silver filigree, and – I do not lie! – a pair of close-fitting purple gloves. A prince, one of those Italian dandies, would have been daring indeed to be seen out hunting in such foppery – but a Prussian Bishop! How odd it is, the value which these Romish churchmen attach to mere show; without it, silk and so forth, they feel naked, apparently. Yet the apparel, and the music, and the Florentine splendour of the hall, could not disguise the true nature of this hard pitiless autocrat. He was a burly, thickset man, balding, with a gleaming high forehead, a great beak of a nose, and eyes of palest blue, like those of some strange vigilant bird. As I entered he rose and bowed, smiling blandly, but the glance with which he swept me was keen as a blade. His manner was warm, urbane, with just a hint of haughtiness, and all the while that he talked or listened, that faint smile continued to play about his mouth and eyes, as though some amusing, slightly ridiculous incident were taking place behind me, of which I was ignorant, and to which he was too tactful to draw attention. O, a polished fellow. He took his seat again, and, with a magisterial gesture, bade me sit beside him. He said:

'Herr von Lauchen, we are honoured. In these remote parts we are not often visited by the famous – O yes, indeed, I have heard of you, although I confess I had not imaged you to be so young. May I enquire what matter it is that brings you here to Heilsberg?'

He had kept me waiting three days for an audience: I was not impressed by his honeyed words. I bent on him a level gaze and said:

'I came, Bishop, to speak with you.'

'Ah yes? I am flattered.'

'Flattered, sir? I fail to see why you should feel so. I have not come on this journey, to this . . . this place, to flatter anyone.'

That put a dent in his urbanity. It is not every day that a Bishop is spoken to thus. His smile disappeared so swiftly, I swear I heard the swish of its going. However, he was not at a loss for long; he chuckled softly, and rising said:

'My dear sir, that suits me well! I dislike flatterers. But come now, come, and I shall show you something which I think will interest you.'

The company rose as we left the hall, and at the door Dantiscus bethought himself, and turned with an impatient frown, meant I'm sure to win my Lutheran approval, and daubed upon the air a negligent blessing. In silence we climbed up through the castle to his study, a long low room with frescoed walls, again in blue and gold, situated in a tower in the north-west wing, where a window gave on to what I realised must be the selfsame expanse of sky which Copernicus commanded from his tower way off in Frauenburg. I was startled, and for a moment quite confused, for here was the very model of an observatory that, before coming to Prussia, I had imagined Copernicus inhabiting. The place was stocked with every conceivable aid to the astronomer's art: globes of copper and bronze, astrolabes, quadrants, a kind of triquetrum of a design more intricate than I had ever seen, and, in pride of place, a representation of the universe exquisitely worked in gold rods and spheres, at which I gaped with open mouth, for it was based upon the Copernican theory as propounded in the *Commentariolus*. Dantiscus, smiling, pretended not to notice my consternation, but went to a desk by the window and from a drawer took out a book and handed it to me. Another shock: it was the *Narratio prima*, crisp as a loaf and smelling still of the presses and the binding room. Now the

Bishop could contain himself no longer, and laughed outright. I suppose my face was something to laugh at. He said:

'Forgive me, my friend, it is too bad of me to surprise you thus. I suppose this is the first you have seen of your book in print? Tiedemann Giese – whom you know, I think? – was kind enough to send me this copy. The messenger arrived with it only yesterday, but I have been through it in large part, and find it fascinating. The clarity of the work, and the firm grasp of the theory, are impressive.'

Giese! who frothed at the mouth when he spoke the name of Dantiscus; who had warned me of this man's treachery, of his plot against Copernicus and how he had for years tormented our *domine praeceptor*; this very Giese had sent, on his own initiative, this most extraordinary of gifts to our arch enemy. Why? From nowhere, the words came to my mind: *what is it they require of me?* But then I chided myself, and put away the formless suspicions that had begun to stir within me. To be sure, there must be a simple explanation. Probably old bumbling Giese, imagining himself a cunning devil, had thought the attempt to melt this hard heart worth the hiring of a messenger to carry his gift post-haste to Heilsberg. I was not a little affected by the fancy, and wondered if my first impression of Tiedemann Giese had been mistaken, if he was not, after all, a kind and thoughtful fellow, anxious only to further my *magister*'s fortunes. O Rheticus, thou dolt! The Bishop was still talking, and as he talked he moved among his instruments, laying his hands upon them lightly, as if they were the downy heads of his bastards he were caressing. He said:

'This room, you know, was once the Canon's, when he was secretary to his late uncle, my predecessor, here at Heilsberg. I am but an amateur in the noble science of astronomy, yet I possess, as you see, some few instruments, and when I came here first, and was seeking a place to house them, it seemed only fitting that I should choose this little cell, resonant as it is, surely, with echoes of the great man's thoughts. I feel I chose wisely, for these echoes, do you not think, might touch the musings of a humbler soul such as I, and perhaps inspire them?'

No, I thought nothing of the sort; the place was dead, a kind of decorated corpse; it had forgotten Copernicus, the mark of whose grey presence had been painted over with these gaudy frescoes. I said:

'Sir, I am glad you have brought up the subject of my *domine praeceptor*, Doctor Copernicus, for it is of him that I wish to speak to you.'

He paused in his pacing, and turned upon me again his keen, careful glance. He seemed about to speak, but hesitated, and instead bade me continue. I said:

'Since his Lordship, Bishop Giese, has been in communication with you, he will, perhaps, have told you that I, along with Doctor Copernicus, have spent some months past at the Bishop's palace at Löbau. What he will not have told you, I fancy, is the purpose of our visit there.' Here I turned away from him, so as not to have to meet his eyes during what came next; for I am not a good liar, it shows in my face, and I was about to lie to him. 'We travelled to Löbau, sir, to discuss in peace and solitude the imminent publication of the Doctor's book, *De revolutionibus orbium mundi*, a work which you may already have heard some mention of.'

He seemed not to notice the sarcasm of that last, for he stared at me for a moment, and then, to my astonishment and indeed alarm, he made a rush at me with outstretched arms. I confess he gave me a fright, for he was grinning like a maniac, which made that great beak of a nose of his dip most horribly, until the tip of it was almost in peril from those big bared teeth, and for an instant it seemed as though he were about to fall upon and savage me. However, he only clapped his hands upon my shoulders, crying:

'Why, sir, this is splendid news!'

'Eh?'

'How have you managed to persuade him? I may tell you, I

have for years been urging him to publish, as have many others, and without the least success, but here *you* come from Wittenberg and win him round immediately. Splendid, I say, splendid!'

He stepped back then, evidently realising that this shouting and back-slapping was not seemly behaviour for a Bishop, and smiled his little smile again, though somewhat sheepishly. I said:

'It is good to find you so apparently pleased to hear this news.'

He frowned at the coldness of my tone. 'Indeed, I am very pleased. And I say again, you are to be congratulated.'

'Many thanks.'

'Pray, no thanks are due.'

'Yet, I offer them.'

'Well then, thanks also.'

'Sir.'

'Sir.'

We disengaged, and shook our blades, but I, making a sudden advance, dealt him a bold blow.

'I have been told, however, Bishop, that Rome would not be likely to greet with great enthusiasm the making public of this work. Have I been misinformed?'

He looked at me, and gave a little laugh. He said:

'Let us have some wine, my friend.'

Thus ended the first round. I was not displeased with my performance so far; but when the wine arrived, like a fool I drank deep, and very soon I was thinking myself the greatest swordsman in the world. That wine, and the hubris it induced, I blame for my subsequent humiliation. Dantiscus said:

'My dear von Lauchen, I begin to see why you have come to Heilsberg. Can it be, you think me less than honest when I say, hearing the news you bring with you today, that I am overjoyed? O, I well know the Canon thinks I hate him, and would, though God knows why, prevent him, if I could, from publishing his book. All this, I see, he has told you. But, my friend, believe me, he is mistaken, and does me grave injustice. To these his charges, I reply just this – come, let me fill your cup – has he forgot how I, this six years past, have ever sought to have him speak, and publicise his theory? *Meinherr* von Lauchen, truth to tell, I am weary of the man, and cannot help but feel rebuffed when you arrive here and reveal that winning his agreement took but a word from you!'

I shrugged, and said:

'But what, my Lord, about this Schillings woman, eh? It's said you accuse him of taking her to bed – and she his cousin! I think, my friend, instead of love you bear him malice.'

He hung his head.

'Ah, that. Distasteful business, I agree. But, *Meinherr*, as Bishop of this See, it is my solemn duty to ensure that Mother Church's clergy shall abjure all vice. What can I do? The man insists on keeping in his house this cousin-mistress. And anyway, the matter is deeper than you know, as I, if you will listen, shall quickly show. First, the times are bad; the Church, my friend, fears all that Luther wrought, and must defend her tarnished reputation. Second, it's not the learned Doctor Nicolas at whom my shot is mainly aimed, but one Sculteti, Canon of Frauenburg also – a treacherous fellow, this one. Not only does he live in sin, but also he plots against the Church here, and puts out false reports. Besides, he's involved with the Germans – ahem! More wine? But this is not germane to my intention, which is that you should know I love the learned Doctor, and would go to any lengths to spare him pain. And please! do not think evil of our Church. All these . . . these petty matters all are due to badness in the times. They are but passing madness, and will pass, while certain to endure is the Canon's masterwork, of this I'm sure. And now, my friend, a toast: to you! to us! and to *De revolutionibus*!'

I drained my cup, and looked about me, and was vaguely surprised to find that we had left the tower, and were standing now in the open air, on a high balcony. Below us was the courtyard, filled with searing lemon-coloured light; odd foreshortened little people hurried hither and thither about their business in a most humorous fashion. Something seemed to have gone wrong with my legs, for I was leaning all off to one side.

Dantiscus, looking more than ever like a besotted Italianate princeling, was still talking. Apparently I had stopped listening some time before, for I could not understand him now very well. He said:

'Science! Progress! Rebirth! The New Age! What do you say, friend?'

I said:

'Yesh, O yesh.'

And then there was more wine, and more talk, and music and a deal of laughter, and I grew merrier and merrier, and thought what a capital fellow after all was this Dantiscus, so civilised, so enlightened; and later I was feasted amid a large noisy company, which I addressed on divers topics, such as Science! and Progress! and the New Age! and all in all made an utter fool of myself. At dawn I awoke in a strange room, with a blinding ache in my head, and longing for death. I crept away from the castle without seeing a soul, and fled Heilsberg, never to return.

What was I to think now, in sickeningly sober daylight, of this Dantiscus, who had plied me with drink and flattery, who had feasted me in his hall, who had toasted the success of a publication for which, so Giese would have it, he wished in his heart nothing but abject failure? After much argument with myself, I decided that despite all he was a scoundrel – had he not ordered a burning of books? had he not threatened Lutherans with fire and the rack? had he not hounded without mercy my *domine praeceptor*? No amount of wine, nor flattery, nor talk of progress, could obliterate those crimes. O knave! O viper! O yesh.

*

Before I leave this part of my tale, there is something more I must mention. To this day I am uncertain whether or not what I am about to relate did in reality take place. On the following day, when I was well out on my flight from Heilsberg, and was wondering, in great trepidation, if Dantiscus, finding me gone without a word, might think to send after me, and drag me back to another round of drinking and carousing, suddenly, like some great thing swooping down on me out of a sky that a moment before had been empty, there came into my head the memory, I call it a memory, for convenience, of having seen Raphaël yesterday at the castle – Raphaël, that laughing lad from Löbau! He had been in the courtyard, surrounded by that lemon-coloured sunlight and the hither and thithering figures, mounted on a black horse. How clearly I remembered him! – or imagined that I did. He had grown a little since last I had seen him, for he was at that age when boys shoot up like saplings, and was very elegantly got up in cap and boots and cape, quite the little gentleman, but Raphaël for all that, unmistakably, I would have known him anywhere, at any age. I see it still, that scene, the sunlight, and the rippling of the horse's glossy blue-black flanks, the groom's hand upon the bridle, and the slim, capped and crimson-caped, booted, beautiful boy, that scene, I see it, and wonder that such a frail tender thing survived so long, to bring me comfort now, and make me young again, here in this horrid place. Raphaël. I write down the name, slowly, say it softly aloud, and hear aetherial echoes of seraphs singing. Raphaël. I have tears still. Why was he there, so far from home? The answer, of course, was simple, viz the boy had brought my book from Löbau. Yet was there not more to it than that? I called his name, too late, for he was already at the gate, on his way home, and Dantiscus, taking me by the arm, said: *friend, you should be careful*, and gave me a strange look. What did he mean? Or did he speak, really? Did I imagine it, all of it? Was it a dream, which I am dreaming still? If that is so, if it was but a delusion spawned by a mind sodden with drink, then I say the imagining was prophetic, in a way, as I shall demonstrate, in its place.

* * *

I RETURNED HOME then to Wittenberg, only to find to my dismay that it was no longer home. How to explain this strange sensation? You know it well, I'm sure. The university, my friends and teachers, my rooms, my books, all were just as when I had left them, and yet all were changed. It was as if some subtle blight had contaminated everything I knew, the heart of everything, the essential centre, while the surface remained sound. It took me some time to understand that it was not Wittenberg that was blighted, but myself. The wizard of Frauenburg had put his spell on me, and one thing, one only thing, I knew, would set me free of that enchantment. After my ignominious flight from Heilsberg, all interest in Copernicus's work had mysteriously abandoned me, despite the lie I had told Dantiscus regarding the imaginary triumph I had scored at Löbau; for I had now no intention of continuing my campaign to force Copernicus to publish. I say that interest in his work abandoned me, and not vice versa, for thus it happened. I had no hand in it: simply, all notion of returning to Frauenburg, and joining battle with him again, all that just departed, and was as though it had never been. Had some secret sense within me perceived the peril that awaited me in Prussia? If so, that warning sense was not strong enough, for I was hardly back in Wittenberg before I found myself in correspondence with Petreius the printer. O, I was vague, and wrote that he must understand that there was no question now of publishing the main work; but I was, I said, preparing a *Narratio secunda* (which I was not), and since it would contain many diagrams and tables and suchlike taken direct from *De revolutionibus*, it was necessary that I should know what his block-cutters and type-setters were capable of in the matter of detail et cetera. However, despite all my caution and circumlocutions, Petreius, with unintentional and uncanny good aim, ignored entirely all mention of a second *Narratio*, and replied huffily that, as I should know, his craftsmen were second to none where scientific works were concerned, and he would gladly and with confidence contract to put between boards Copernicus's great treatise, of which he had heard so many reports.

Although this pompous letter angered and disturbed me, I soon came to regard it as an omen, and began again to toy with the idea of returning to Frauenburg. Not, you understand, that I was ready to go rushing off northwards once more, with cap in hand, and panting with enthusiasm, to make a fool of myself as I had done before, O no; this time if I journeyed it would be for my own purposes that I would do so, to find my lost self, as it were, and rid myself of this spell, so as to come home to my beloved Wittenberg again, and find it whole, and be at peace. Therefore, as soon as I was free, I set out with a stout heart, by post-carriage, on horseback, sometimes on foot, and arrived at Frauenburg at summer's end, 1540, and was relieved to find Copernicus not yet dead, and still in possession, more or less, of his faculties. He greeted me with a characteristic display of enthusiasm, viz a start, an owlish stare, and then a hangman's handshake. The Schillings was still with him, and Dantiscus, need I say it, was still howling for her to be gone. For a long time now he had been using Giese to transmit his threats. Sculteti, Copernicus's ally in the affair of the *focariae*, whom Dantiscus had mentioned, had it seemed been expelled by the Chapter, and had flown to Italy. This departure, along with Dantiscus's increasingly menacing behaviour, had forced Copernicus to make a last desperate effort to get rid of her, but in vain. There had been a furious argument (smashed crockery, screams, pisspots flying through windows and striking passers-by: the usual, I suppose), which had ended with the *Mädchen* packing up her belongings and sending them off, at great expense (the Canon's), to Danzig, where some remnant of her tribe kept an inn, or a bawdyhouse, I forget which. However, it seems she considered this so to speak symbolic departure a sufficiently stern rebuke to Copernicus for his ill nature, and in reality had no intention of following after her chattels, which in due time returned, like some awful ineluctable curse. So we settled down, the three of us, in our tower, where life was barely, just barely, tolerable. I kept out of the way of the Schillings, not for fear of her, but for fear of *throttling* her; between the two of us the old man cowered, mumbling and sighing and trying his best to die. Soon, I could see, he would succeed in doing that. Death was slinking up behind him, with its black sack at the ready. I would have to work quickly, if I were to snatch his book from him before he took it with him into that suffocating darkness. Yet, if his body was weakening, his mind was still capable of withholding, in an iron grip, that for which I had come: the decision to publish.

*

I stayed with him for more than a year, tormented by boredom and frustration, and an unrelenting irritation at the impossible old fool and his ways. He agreed that I might make a copy of the manuscript, and that at least was some occupation; the work might even have calmed my restless spirit, had he not insisted on reminding me every day that I must not imagine, merely because he had relented thus far, that he would go farther, and allow me to take this copy to Petreius. So that there was little more for me in this scribbling than aching knuckles, and the occasional, malicious pleasure of correcting his slips (I crossed out that nonsensical line in which he speculated on the possibility of elliptical orbits – *elliptical orbits*, for God's sake!). Various other small tasks which I performed, to relieve the tedium, included the completion of a map of Prussia, which the old man, in collaboration with the disgraced Sculteti, had begun at the request of the previous Bishop of Ermland. This, along with some other trivial things, I sent off to Albrecht, Duke of Prussia, who rewarded me with the princely sum of one ducat. So much for aristocratic patronage! However, it was not for money I had approached this Lutheran Duke, but rather in the hope that he might use on my behalf his considerable influence among German churchmen and nobles, who I feared might make trouble should I win Copernicus's consent, and appear in their midst with a manuscript full of dangerous theories clutched under my arm. The Duke, I found, was more generous with paper and ink than he had been with his ducats; he sent letters to Johann Friedrich, Elector of Saxony, and also to the University of Wittenberg, mentioning how impressed he had been with the *Narratio prima* (*clever* old Giese!), and urging that I should be allowed to publish what he called this *admirable book on astronomy*, meaning *De revolutionibus*. There was some confusion, of course; there always is. Albrecht, like Petreius, apparently had found it inconceivable that I should be so eager to publish the work of another, and therefore he assumed that I was attempting some crafty ruse whereby I hoped to put out my own theories in disguise; did I think to fool the Duke of Prussia? thought haughty Albrecht, and put down in his letters what to him was obvious: that the work was all my own. The cretin. I had no end of trouble disentangling that mess, while at the same time keeping these manoeuvres hidden from the Canon, who was wont to spit at the mention of the name of Grand Master Albrecht, as he insisted on calling him.

This was not the only little plot I had embarked upon in secret – *and* in trepidation, for I was mortally afraid that if he found out, Copernicus would burn the manuscript on the instant. Yet I had lapses, when my caution, which I had learned from him, deserted me. One day, shortly after my return to Frauenburg, I told him in a rash moment of frankness of my visit to Dantiscus. It was one of the rare occasions when I witnessed colour invade the ghastly pallor of his face. He flew into a rage, and gibbered, spraying me copiously with spit, yelling that I had no right to do such a thing, that I had *no right*! I was, he said, as bad as Giese, that damned meddler, who had sent the *Narratio prima* to Heilsberg even after he had been expressly warned not even to consider doing such a thing. What was surprising about this outburst was not so much the fury as the fear which I could plainly see, skulking behind the bluster; true, he had cause to be wary of Dantiscus, but this show of veritable terror seemed wholly excessive. What he feared, of course, although I could not know it then, was that I might have said something to Dantiscus that would ruin the plot which the Canon and Giese had been working out against me for years in secret – but wait, I am impetuous; wait.

There were other things that puzzled and surprised me. For instance, I discovered another aspect of his passion for secrecy: the Schillings knew so little of his affairs that she thought his astronomical work a mere pastime, a means of relaxing from the rigours of his true calling, which was, so she believed, medicine! And this woman shared his house, his bed!

And yet, perhaps he did regard astronomy as merely a plaything; I do not know, I do not know, I could not understand the man, I admit it. I was then, and I am still, despite my loss of faith, one of those who look to the future for redemption, I mean redemption from the world, which has nothing to do with Christ's outlandish promises, but with the genius of Man. We can do anything, overcome anything. Am I not a living proof of this? They schemed against me, tried to ruin me, and yet I won, although even yet they will not acknowledge my victory. What was I saying . . .? Yes: I look to the future, live in the future, and so, when I speak of the present, I am as it were looking backward, into what is, for me, already the past. Do you follow that? Copernicus was different, very different. If he believed that Man could redeem himself, he saw in – how shall I say – in *immobility* the only possible means toward that end. His world moved in circles, endlessly, and each circuit was a repetition exactly of all others, past and future, to the extremities of time: which is no movement at all. How, then, could I be expected to understand one whose thinking was so firmly locked in the old wornout frame? We spoke a different language – and I do not mean his Latin against my German, although that difference, now that I think about it, represents well enough the deeper thing. Once, when we were walking together on the little path within the cathedral wall, which he paced each day, gravely, at a fixed hour and a fixed pace, as though performing a penance rather than taking the air, I began to speak idly of Italy, and the blue south, where I spent my youth. He heard me out, nodding the while, and then he said:

'Ah yes, Italy; I also spent some time there, before you were born. And what times they were! It seemed as though a new world was on the point of birth. All that was strong and youthful and vigorous revolted against the past. Never, perhaps, have the social authorities so unanimously supported the intellectual movement. It seemed as though there were no conservatives left among them. All were moving and straining in the same direction, authority, society, fashion, the politicians, the women, the artists, the *umanista.* There was a boundless confidence abroad, a feverish joy. The mind was liberated from authority, was free to wander under the heavens. The monopoly of knowledge was abolished, and it was now the possession of the whole community. Ah yes.'

I was of course astonished to hear him speak thus, astonished and filled with joy, for this, *this* was that Copernicus whom I had come to Frauenburg to find, and had not found, until now; and I turned to him with tears in my eyes, and began to yelp and caper in a paroxysm of agreement with all that he had said. Too late I noticed that small grey grin, the malicious glint in his look, and realised that I had fallen, O arse over tip, into a trap. He drew back, as one draws back from a slavering lunatic, and considered me with a contempt so profound it seemed near to nauseating him. He said:

'I was speaking less than seriously, of course. Italy is the country of death. You remind me sometimes of my late brother. He also was given to jabbering about progress and renascence, the new age whose dawn was about to break. He died in his beloved Italy, of the pox.'

It was not the words, you understand, but the tone in which they were spoken, that seemed to gather up and examine briefly all that I was, before heaving it all, blood and bones and youth and tears and enthusiasm, back upon the swarming midden-heap of humanity. He did not hate me, nor even dislike me; I think he found me . . . distasteful. But what did I care? It is true, when I came to him first there was no thought in my head of fame and fortune for myself; I had one desire only, to make known to the world the work of a great astronomer. Now, however, all that had changed. I was older. He had aged me a decade in a year. No longer was I the young fool ready to fall to his knees before some manufactured hero; I had realised myself. Yet perhaps I should be grateful to him? Was it not his contempt that had forced me to look more closely at myself, that had allowed me to recognise in the end that I was a greater astronomer than he? Yes! yes! far greater. Sneer if you like, shake your empty heads all you wish, but I – *I* know the truth. Why do you think I stayed with him, endured his mockery, his pettiness, his *distaste*? Do you imagine that I enjoyed living in that bleak tower, freezing in winter and roasting in summer, shivering at night while the rats danced overhead, groaning and straining in that putrid jakes, my guts bound immovably by the mortar of his trollop's gruel, do you think I enjoyed all that? By comparison, this place where I am now in exile is very heaven.

Well then, you say, if it was so terrible, why did I remain there, why did I not flee, and leave Copernicus, wrapped in his caution and his bitterness, to sink into oblivion? Listen: I have said that I was a greater astronomer than he, *and I am*, but he possessed one precious thing that I lacked – I mean a reputation. O, he was cautious, yes, and he genuinely feared and loathed the world, but he was cunning also, and knew that curiosity is a rash which men will scratch and scratch until it drives them frantic for the cure. For years now he had eked out, at carefully chosen intervals, small portions of his theory, each one of which – the *Commentariolus*, the *Letter contra Werner*, my *Narratio* – was a grain of salt rubbed into the rash with which he had inflicted his fellow astronomers. And they had scratched, and the rash had developed into a sore that spread, until all Europe was infected, and screaming for the one thing alone that would end the plague, which was *De revolutionibus orbium mundi*, by Doctor Nicolas Copernicus, of Torun on the Vistula. And he would give them their physic; he had decided, he had decided to publish, I knew it, and he knew I knew it, but what he did not know was that, by doing so, by publishing, he would not be crowning his own reputation, but making mine. You do not understand? Only wait, and I shall explain.

*

But first I must recount some few other small matters, such as, to begin with, how in the end he came to give me his consent to publish. However, in order to illuminate that scene, as it were, I wish to record a conversation I had with him which, later, I came to realise was a summation of his attitude to science and the world, the aridity, the barrenness of that attitude. He had been speaking, I remember, of the seven spheres of Hermes Trismegistus through which the soul ascends toward redemption in the eighth sphere of the fixed stars. I grew impatient listening to this rigmarole, and I said something like:

'But your work, *Meister*, is of this world, of the here and now; it speaks to men of what they may know, and not of mysteries that they can only believe in blindly or not at all.'

He shook his head impatiently.

'No no no *no*. You imagine that my book is a kind of mirror in which the real world is reflected; but you are mistaken, you must realise that. In order to build such a mirror, I should need to be able to perceive the world whole, in its entirety and in its essence. But our lives are lived in such a tiny, confined space, and in such disorder, that this perception is not possible. There is no contact, none worth mentioning, between the universe and the place in which we live.'

I was puzzled and upset; this nihilism was inimical to all I held to be true and useful. I said:

'But if what you say is so, then how is it that we are aware of the existence of the universe, the real world? How, without perception, do we *see*?'

'Ach, Rheticus!' It was the first time he had called me by that name. 'You do not understand me! You do not understand yourself. You think that to see is to perceive, but listen, listen: *seeing is not perception!* Why will no one realise that? I lift my head and look at the stars, as did the ancients, and I say: what are those lights? Some call them torches borne by angels, others, pinpricks in the shroud of Heaven; others still, scientists such as ourselves, call them stars and planets that make a manner of machine whose workings we strive to comprehend. But do you not understand that, without perception, all these theories are equal in value. Stars or torches, it is all one, all merely an exalted naming; those lights shine on, indifferent to what we call them. My book is not science – it is a dream. I am not even sure if science is possible.' He paused a while to brood, and then went on. 'We think only those thoughts that we have the words to express, but we acknowledge that limitation only by our wilfully foolish contention that the words mean more than they say; it is a pretty piece of sleight of hand, that: it sustains our illusions wonderfully, until, that is, the time arrives when the sands have run out, and the truth breaks in upon us. Our lives—' he smiled '—are a little journey through God's guts . . .' His voice had become a whisper, and it was plain to me that he was talking to himself, but then all at once he remembered me, and turned on me fiercely, wagging a finger in my face. 'Your Father Luther recognised this truth early on, and had not the courage to face it; he tried to deny it, by his pathetic and futile attempt to shatter the form and thereby come at the content, the essence. His was a defective mind, of course, and could not comprehend the necessity for ritual, and hence he castigated Rome for its so-called blasphemy and idol-worship. He betrayed the people, took away their golden calf but gave them no tablets of the law in its place. Now we are seeing the results of Luther's folly, when the peasantry is in revolt all over Europe. You wonder why I will not publish? The people will laugh at my book, or that mangled version of it which filters down to them from the universities. The people always mistake at first the frightening for the comic thing. But very soon they will come to see what it is that I have done, I mean what they will imagine I have done, diminished Earth, made of it merely another planet among planets; they will begin to despise the world, and something will die, and out of that death will come *death*. You do not know what I am talking about, do you, Rheticus? You are a fool, like the rest . . . like myself.'

*

I remember the evening very well: sun on the Baltic, and small boats out on the Frisches Haff, and a great silence everywhere. I had just finished copying the manuscript, and had but put down the last few words when the Canon, perhaps hearing some thunderclap of finality shaking the air of the tower, came down from the observatory and hovered in my doorway, sniffing at me enquiringly. I said nothing, and only glanced at him vacantly. The evening silence was a pool of peace in which my spirits hung suspended, like a flask of air floating upon waters, and wearily, wearily, I drifted off into a waking swoon, intending only to stay a moment, to bathe for a moment my tired heart, but it was so peaceful there on that brimming bright meniscus, so still, that I could not rouse myself from this welcome kind of little death. The Canon was standing at my shoulder. The sky outside was blue and light, enormous. When he spoke, the words seemed to come, slowly, from a long way off. He said:

'*If at the foundation of all there lay only a wildly seething power which, writhing with obscure passions, produced everything that is great and everything that is insignificant, if a bottomless void never satiated lay hidden beneath all, what then would life be but despair?*'

I said:

'*I hold it true that pure thought can grasp reality, as the ancients dreamed.*'

He said:

'*Science aims at constructing a world which shall be symbolic of the world of commonplace experience.*'

I said:

'*If you would know the reality of nature, you must destroy the appearance, and the farther you go beyond the appearance, the nearer you will be to the essence.*'

He said:

'*It is of the highest significance that the outer world represents something independent of us and absolute with which we are confronted.*'

I said:

'*The death of one god is the death of all.*'

He said:

'*Vita brevis, sensus ebes, negligentiae torpor et inutiles occupationes, nos paucula scire permittent. Et aliquotiens scita excutit ab animo per temporum lapsum fraudatrix scientiae et inimica memoriae praeceps oblivio.*'

Night advanced and darkened the brooding waters of the Baltic, but the air was still bright, and in the bright air, vivid yet serene, Venus shone. Copernicus said:

'When you have once seen the chaos, you must make some thing to set between yourself and that terrible sight; and so you make a mirror, thinking that in it shall be reflected the reality of the world; but then you understand that the mirror reflects only appearances, and that reality is somewhere else, off behind the mirror; and then you remember that behind the mirror there is only the chaos. '

Dark dark dark.

I said:

'And yet, Herr Doctor, the truth must be revealed.'

'Ah, truth, that word I no longer understand.'

'Truth is that which cannot be concealed.'

'You have not listened, you have not understood.'

'Truth is certain good, that's all I know.'

'I am an old man, and you make me weary.'

'Give your agreement then, and let me go.'

'The mirror is cracking! listen! do you hear it?'

'Yes, I hear, and yet I do not fear it.'

The light of day was gone now, and that moment that is like an ending had arrived, when the eyes, accustomed to the sun, cannot yet distinguish the humbler sources of light, and darkness seems total; but still it was not dark enough for him, and he shuffled away from me, away from the window, and crawled into the shadows of the room like some poor black bent wounded thing. He said:

'The shortness of life, the dullness of the senses, the torpor of indifference and useless occupations, allow us to know but little; and in time, oblivion, that defrauder of knowledge and memory's enemy, cheats us of even the little that we knew. I am an old man, and you make me weary. What is it you require of me? The book is nothing, less than nothing. First they shall laugh, and later weep. But you require the book. It is nothing, less than nothing. I am an old man. Take it . . .'

*

That was the last I was to see of him, in this world or, I trust, in any other. I left the tower that very night, carrying with me my books and my belongings and my bitter victory. I did not remark the abruptness of this going, nor did he. It seemed the correct way. The inn to which I fled was a pigsty, but at least the air was cleaner there than in that crypt I had left, and the pigs, for all their piggishness, were alive, and snuffling happily in the good old muck. Yet, though I abandoned the tower without a thought, I found it not so easy to do the same with Frauenburg; that was August, and not until September was in did I at last depart. I spent those few final weeks kicking my heels about the town, drinking alone, too much, and whoring joylessly. Once I returned to the tower, determined to see him again, yet at a loss to know what more there was to be said; and perhaps it was as well that the Schillings planted herself in the doorway and said that the old man would not see me, that he was ill, and anyway had given her strict instructions not to let me in if I should dare to call. Even then I did not go, but waited another week, although I should have been in Wittenberg long before. What was it that held me back? Maybe I realised, however obscurely, that in leaving Prussia I would be leaving behind what I can only call a version of myself; for Frauenburg killed the best in me, my youth and my enthusiasm, my happiness, my faith, yes, faith. From that time on I believed in nothing, neither God nor Man. You ask why? You laugh, you say: poor fool, to be so affected by a sick old man's bitterness and despair; O, you say, you ask, all of you, why, and how, and wherefore, you are all so wise, but you know nothing – nothing! Listen.

* * *

I WISHED TO GO straightway to Petreius, but if I were to keep my post at Wittenberg, I needs must return there without further delay, for the authorities at the university were beginning to mutter threateningly over my unconscionably long absence. And indeed they seemed very glad to have me back, for I had hardly arrived before I was elected Dean of the faculty of mathematics! I might have been excused for thinking that it was my own brilliance that had won this honour, but I was no fool, and I knew very well that it was not me, but my connection with the Great Man of Frauenburg that they were honouring, in their cautious way. It was no matter, anyway, for I was confident that before long the goddess Fama would turn her tender gaze on me. However, the promotion imposed new tasks on me, new responsibilities, and it would be spring, I now saw, before I could find the freedom to go to Nuremberg and Petreius; might not the goddess tire before then of waiting for me? With this thought in mind, I decided to have printed immediately, there in Wittenberg, a short extract from the manuscript, which would not reveal the scope of the entire work but only hint at it. (You see how I had learned from the master?) Thus originated *De lateribus et angulis triangulorum*. It caused no little stir in the university, and even in the town itself, and helped me to squeeze out of the burghers and the clerics, and even out of Melanchton himself, several valuable letters of recommendation, which I carried with me to Nuremberg.

*

I arrived there at the beginning of May, and at once set about the printing of *De revolutionibus orbium mundi* in its entirety. Petreius's craftsmen made swift progress. I lodged in the town in the house of a certain Lutheran merchant, Johann Müller, to whom I had been recommended by Melanchton. He was a bearable fellow, this Müller: pompous, of course, like all his kind, but not unlearned – he even displayed some interest in the work on which I was engaged. Also, his beds were soft, and his wife exceeding handsome, though somewhat fat. All in all, then, I was well content at Nuremberg, and I might even say I was happy there, had not there been lodged in my black heart the ineradicable pain that was the memory of Prussia. From there not a word came, of discouragement or otherwise, until Petreius broached the subject of finance, and I told him it was not my affair, that he should send to Frauenburg. This he did, and after some weeks a reply came, not from Koppernigk, but from Bishop Giese, who said that he had just that day arrived there from Löbau, having been summoned by Anna Schillings to attend the Canon, who was, so Giese said, sick unto death. This news moved me not at all: living or dead, Koppernigk was no longer a part of my plans. True, I spent an anxious week while Petreius underwent an attack of nerves, brought on by the realisation that he would have to finance the publication of the book himself, now that the author was dying, but in the end he went ahead, a decision he was not to regret, since he fixed the price per copy, of the thousand copies that he printed, at 28 ducats 6 pfennigs, the greedy old bastard.

My plans. How cunning they were, how cold and clever, and, in the end, how easily they were brought thundering down in rubble about my ears. The first signals of impending disaster came when I had been but two months in Nuremberg. Petreius had already set up thirty-four sheets, or about two-thirds of the book, and had begun to invite into the printing house some of the leading citizens of the town, so that they might view the progress of the work, and, being impressed, advertise it abroad. Now, it seemed to me only to be expected that these men of influence should above all wish to meet me, the sponsor of this bold new theory, but, though I spent the most part of my days in the caseroom, where the sheets were proofed for their viewing, I found to my surprise, and vague alarm, that they avoided me like the plague, and some of them even fled when I made to approach them. I spoke to Petreius of it, and he shrugged, and pretended not to understand me, and would not look me in the eye. I tried to dismiss the matter, telling myself that businessmen were always in awe of scholars, fearing their learning et cetera, but it would not do: I knew that something was afoot. Then, one evening, the good Herr Müller, twisting his hands and grimacing, and looking for all the world like a reluctant hangman, came to me and said that if it suited me, and if it was not a great inconvenience, and if I would not take his words amiss, and so on and so forth – and, well, the matter was: would I kindly leave his house? He made some lame excuse for this extraordinary demand, about needing the extra room for an impending visit by some relatives, but I was in a rage by then, and was not listening, and I told him that if it suited him, and if it was not a great inconvenience, he might fuck himself, and, pausing only to inform him that I was grateful for the use of his jade of a wife, whom I had been merrily ploughing during the past weeks, I packed my bags and left, and found myself that night once again lodging at an inn. And there, shortly afterwards, Osiander visited me.

*

Andreas Osiander, theologian and scholar, a leading Lutheran, friend of Melanchton, had for some time (despite his religious affiliations!) been in correspondence with Canon Nicolas – had been, indeed, one of those like myself who had urged him to publish. He was also, I might add, a cold, cautious, humourless grey creature, and it was, no doubt, the cast of his personality which recommended him to the Canon. O yes, they were two of a kind. At first, like a fool, I imagined that he had come to pay his respects to a great astronomer (*me*, that is), and congratulate me on winning consent to publish *De revolutionibus*, but Osiander soon dispelled these frivolous notions. I was ill when he arrived. A fever of the brain, brought on no doubt by the manner of my parting from Müller, had laid me low with a burning head and aching limbs, so that when he was shown into my humble room I fancied at first that he was an hallucination. The shutters were drawn against the harsh spring light. He planted himself at the foot of my bed, his head in the shadows and bands of light through the slats of the shutters striping his puffed-up chest, so that he looked for all the world like a giant wasp. I was frightened of him even before he spoke. He had that unmistakable smell of authority about him. He looked with distaste at my surroundings, and with even deeper distaste at me, and said in his pinched voice (a drone!) that when he had been told that I was lodging here he had hardly credited it, but now, it seemed, he must believe it. Did I not realise that I was, in a manner of speaking, an ambassador of Wittenberg in this city? And did I think it fitting that the name of the very centre of Protestant learning should be associated with this . . . this *place*? I began to explain how I had been thrown out on the street by a man to whom I had been recommended by Melanchton himself, but he was not interested in that, and cut me short by enquiring if I had anything to say in my defence. Defence? My hands began to shake, from fever or fear, I could not tell which. I tried to rise from the bed, but in vain. There was something of the inquisitor about Osiander. He said:

'I have come this day from Wittenberg, whither I was summoned in connection with certain matters of which I think you are aware. Please, Herr von Lauchen, I would ask you: no protestations of injured innocence. That will only cause delay, and I wish, indeed I *intend*, to conclude this unfortunate business as swiftly as possible, to prevent the further spread of scandal. The fact is, that for a long time now, we – and I include in that others whose names I need not mention! – for a long time, I say, we have been watching your behaviour with increasing dismay. We do not expect that a man should be without blemish. However, we do expect, we *demand*, at the very least, discretion. And you, my friend, have been anything but discreet. The manner in which you comported yourself at the university was tolerated. I use the word advisedly: you were tolerated. But, that you should go to Prussia, to Ermland, that very bastion of popery, and there disgrace not only yourself, not only the reputation of your university, but your religion as well, that, *that*, Herr von Lauchen, we could not tolerate. We gave you every chance to mend your ways. When you returned from Frauenburg, we granted you one of the highest honours at our disposal, and created you Dean of your faculty; yet how did you repay us – how? You fled, sir, and abandoned behind you a living and speaking – I might say *chattering* – testimony of your pernicious indulgences! I mean, of course, the boy, whose presence fortunately was brought to our attention by the master he deserted, and we were able to silence him.'

'Boy? What boy?' But of course I knew, I knew. Already light had begun to dawn upon me. Osiander sighed heavily. He said:

'Very well, Herr von Lauchen, play the fool, if that is what you wish. You know who I mean – and I know you know. You think to win some manner of reprieve by playing on my discretion; you think that by pressing me to speak openly of these distasteful matters you will embarrass me, and force me to withdraw – is that it? You shall not succeed. The boy's name is Raphaël. He is, or was, a servant in the household of the Bishop of Kulm, Tiedemann Giese, at Löbau, where you stayed for some time, did you not, in the company of Canon Koppernigk? Your behaviour there, and your . . . your connection with this boy, was reported to us by the Bishop himself, who, I might add, was charitable enough to defend you (as did Canon Koppernigk himself!), even while you were spreading scandal and corruption throughout his household. But what I want to ask you, for my own benefit, you understand, so that I shall know – what I want to ask you is: why, *why* did you have this boy follow you across the length of Germany?'

'He did not follow me,' I said. 'He was sent.' I saw it all, yes, yes, I saw it all.

'*Sent?*' Osiander bellowed, and his wasp's wings buzzed and boomed in the gloom. 'What do you mean, sent? The boy arrived in Wittenberg in rags, with his feet bandaged. His horse had died under him. He said you told him to come to you, that you would put him to schooling, that you would make a gentleman of him. Sent? Can you not spare even a grain of compassion for this unfortunate creature whom you have destroyed, whom you could not face, and fled before he came; and do you think to save yourself by this wild and evil accusation? Sent? Who sent him, pray?'

I turned my face to the wall. 'It's no matter. You would not believe me, if I told you. I shall say only this, that I am not a sodomite, that I have been slandered and vilified, that you have been fed a pack of lies.'

He began a kind of enraged dance then, and shrieked:

'I will not listen to this! I will not listen! Do you want me to tell you what the child said, do you want to hear, do you? These are his very words, his very words, I cannot forget them, never; he said: *Every morning I brought him his food, and he made me wank him tho' I cried, and begged him to release me.* A child, sir, a child! and you put such words into his mouth, and made him do such things, and God knows what else besides. May God forgive you. Now, enough of this, enough; I have said more than I intended, more than I should. If we were in Rome no doubt you would have been poisoned by now, and spirited away, but here in Germany we are more civilised than that. There is a post at Leipzig University, the chair of mathematics. It has been arranged that you will fill it. You will pack your bags today, now, this instant, and be gone. You may – *silence*! – you may not protest, it is too late for that: Melanchton himself has ordered your removal. It was he, I might add, who decided that you should be sent to Leipzig, which is no punishment at all. Had I my way, sir, you would be driven out of Germany. And now, prepare to depart. Whatever work of yours there is unfinished here, I shall take charge of it. I am told you are engaged in the printing of an astronomical work from the pen of Canon Koppernigk? He has asked that I should oversee the final stages of this venture. For the rest, we shall put it about that, for reasons of health, you felt you must abandon the task to my care. Now go.'

'The boy,' I said, 'Raphaël: what has become of him?' I remembered him in the courtyard at Heilsberg, in his cap and cape, mounted on his black horse; just thus must he have looked as he set out from Löbau to come to me at Wittenberg.

'He was sent back to Löbau Castle, of course,' said Osiander. 'What did you expect?'

Do you know what they do to runaway servants up there in

Prussia? They nail them by the ear to a pillory, and give them a knife with which to cut themselves free. I wonder what punishment worse than that did Giese threaten the child with, to force him to follow me and tell those lies, so as to destroy me?

*

I could not at first understand why they, I mean Koppernigk and Giese, had done this to me, and I went off to exile in Leipzig thinking that surely some terrible mistake had been made. Only later, when I saw the preface which Osiander added to the book (which, when he was finished with it, was called *De revolutionibus orbium coelestium*), only then did I see how they had used me, poor shambling clown, to smuggle the work into the heart of Lutheran Germany, to the best Lutheran printer, with the precious Lutheran letters of recommendation in my fist, and how, when all that was done, they had simply got rid of me, to make way for Osiander and the *imprimatur* of his preface, which made the book safe from the hounds of Rome and Wittenberg alike. They did not trust me, you see, except to do the hackwork.

*

Did I in some way, I asked myself then, merit this betrayal? For it seemed to me inconceivable that all my labours should have been rewarded thus without some terrible sin on my part; but I could not, try as I might, find myself guilty of any sin heinous enough to bring down such judgment on my head. Throughout the book, *there is not one mention of my name*. Schönberg is mentioned, and Giese, but not I. This omission affected me strangely. It was as if, somehow, I had not existed at all during those past years. Had this been my crime, I mean some essential lack of presence; had I not been *there* vividly enough? That may be it, for all I know. Frauenburg had been a kind of death, for death is the absence of faith, I hardly know what I am saying, yet I feel I am making sense. Christ! I have waited patiently for this moment when I would have my revenge, and now I am ruining it. Why must I blame myself, search for some sin within myself, all this nonsense, why? No need of that, no need – it was all his doing, his his *his*! Calm, Rheticus.

Here is my revenge. Here it is, at last.

*

The *Book of revolutions* is a pack of lies from start to finish . . . No, that will not do, it is too, too something, I don't know. Besides, it is not true, not entirely, and truth is the only weapon I have left with which to blast his cursed memory.

The *Book of revolutions* is an engine which destroys itself, yes yes, that's better.

The *Book of revolutions* is an engine which destroys itself, which is to say that by the time its creator had completed it, by the time he had, so to speak, hammered home the last bolt, the thing was in bits around him. I admit, it took me some time to recognise this fact, or at least to recognise the full significance of it. How I swore and sweated during those summer nights at Löbau, striving to make sense of a theory wherein each succeeding conclusion or hypothesis seemed to throw doubt on those that had gone before! Where, I asked, where is the beauty and simplicity, the celestial order so confidently promised in the *Commentariolus*, where is the pure, the pristine thing? The book which I held in my hands was a shambles, a crippled, hopeless mishmash. But let me be specific, let me give some examples of where it went so violently wrong. It was, so Koppernigk tells us, a profound dissatisfaction with the theory of the motions of the planets put forward by Ptolemy in the *Almagest* which first sent him in search of some new system, one that would be mathematically correct, would agree with the rules of cosmic physics, and that would, most importantly of all, save the phenomena. O, the phenomena were saved, indeed – but at what cost! For in his calculations, not 34 epicycles were required to account for the entire structure of the universe, as the *Commentariolus* claimed, but 48 – which is 8 more at least than Ptolemy had employed! This little trick, however, is nothing, a mere somersault, compared with the one of which I am now about to speak. You imagine that Koppernigk set the Sun at the centre of the universe, don't you? He did not. The centre of the universe according to his theory is not the Sun, *but the centre of Earth's orbit*, which, as the great, the mighty, the all-explaining *Book of revolutions* admits, is situated at a point in space some three times the Sun's diameter distant from the Sun! All the hypotheses, all the calculations, the star tables, charts and diagrams, the entire ragbag of lies and half truths and self-deceptions which is *De revolutionibus orbium mundi* (or *coelestium*, as I suppose I must call it now), was assembled simply in order to prove that at the centre of all there is nothing, that the world turns upon chaos.

*

Are you stirring in your grave, Koppernigk? Are you writhing in cold clay?

*

When at last, one black night at Löbau Castle, the nature of the absurdity which he was propounding was borne in upon me, I laughed until I could laugh no more, and then I wept. Copernicus, the greatest astronomer of his age, so they said, was a fraud whose only desire was to save appearances. I laughed, I say, and then wept, and something died within me. I do not willingly grant him even this much, but grant it I must: that if his book possessed some power, it was the power to destroy. It destroyed my faith, in God and Man – but not in the Devil. Lucifer sits at the centre of that book, smiling a familiar cold grey smile. You were evil, Koppernigk, and you filled the world with despair.

He knew it, of course, knew well how he had failed, and knew that I knew it. That was why he had to destroy me, he and Giese, the Devil's disciple.

If I saw all this, his failure and so forth, even so early as the Löbau period, why then did I continue to press him so doggedly to publish? But you see, I wanted him to make known his theory simply so that I could refute it. O, an ignoble desire, certainly; I admit, I admit it freely, that I planned to make my reputation on the ruins of his. Poor fool that I was. The world cannot abide truth: men remember heliocentricity (they are already talking of the *Copernican revolution*!), but forget the defective theory on which the concept of heliocentricity is founded. It is his name that is remembered and honoured, while I am forgotten, and left to rot here in this dreadful place. What was it he said to me? – *first they will laugh, and then weep, seeing their Earth diminished, spinning upon the void* . . . He knew, he knew. They are weeping now, bowed down under the burden of despair with which he loaded them. I am weeping. I believe in nothing. The mirror is shattered. The chaos

Well I'll be damned!

Freunde! What joy! The most extraordinary, the most extraordinary thing has happened: Otho has come! O God, I believe in You, I swear it. Forgive me for ever doubting You! A disciple, at last! He will spread my name throughout the world. Now I can return to that great work, which I planned so long ago: the formulation of a *true* system of the universe, based upon Ptolemaic principles. I shall not mention, I shall not even *mention* that other name. Or perhaps I shall? Perhaps I have been unjust to him? Did he not, in his own poor stumbling way, glimpse the majestic order of the universe which wheels and wheels in mysterious ways, bringing back the past again and again, as the past has been brought back here again today? Copernicus, Canon Nicolas, *domine praeceptor*, I forgive you: yes, even you I forgive. God, I believe: resurrection, redemption, the whole thing, I believe it all. Ah! The page shakes before my eyes. This joy!

*

Lucius Valentine Otho has this day come to me from Wittenberg, to be my amanuensis, my disciple. He fell to his knees before me. I behaved perfectly, as a great scientist should. I spoke to him kindly, enquiring how things stood at Wittenberg, and of his own work and ambitions. But behind my coolness and reserve, what a tangle of emotions! Of course, this joy I felt could not be contained, and when I had enquired his age, I could not keep myself from grasping him by the shoulders and shaking him until his teeth rattled in his head, for just at that same age did I, so many years ago, come to Copernicus at Frauenburg. The past comes back, transfigured. Shall I also send a Raphaël to destroy Otho? – but come now, Rheticus, come clean. The fact is, there never was a Raphaël. I know, I know, it was dreadful of me to invent all that, but I had to find something, you see, some terrible tangible thing, to represent the great wrongs done me by Copernicus. Not a mention of my name in his book! Not a word! He would have done more for a dog. Well, I have forgiven him, and I have admitted my little joke about Raphaël and so forth. Now a new age dawns. I am no longer the old Rheticus, banished to Cassovia and gnawing his own liver in spite and impotent rage, no: I am an altogether finer thing – I am Doctor Rheticus! I am a believer. Lift your head, then, strange new glorious creature, incandescent angel, and gaze upon the world. It is not diminished! Even in that he failed. The sky is blue, and shall be forever blue, and the earth shall blossom forever in spring, and this planet shall forever be the centre of all we know. I believe it, I think. *Vale.*

IV

Magnum Miraculum

THE SUN AT DAWN, retrieving from the darkness the few remaining fragments of his life, summoned him back at last into the present. Warily he watched the room arrange itself around him: that return journey was so far, immeasurably far, that without proof he would not believe it was over. Outside, in the sky low in the east, a storm of fire raged amidst clouds, shedding light like a shower of burning arrows upon the great glittering steely arc of the Baltic. None of that was any longer wholly real, was mere melodrama, static and cold. The world had shrunk until his skull contained it entirely, and all without that shrivelled sphere was a changing series of superficial images in a void, utterly lacking in significance save on those rare occasions when a particular picture served to verify the moment, as now the fragments of his cell, picked out by the advancing dawn, were illuminated integers that traced on the surrounding gloom a constellation, a starry formula, expressing precisely, as no words could, all that was left of what he had once been, all that was left of his life. One morning, a morning much like this one, a fire fierce as the sun itself had exploded in his brain; when that dreadful glare faded everything was transfigured. Then had begun his final wanderings. It was into the past that he had travelled, for there was nowhere else to go. He was dying.

*

The sickness had come upon him stealthily. At first it had been no more than a faint dizziness at times, a step missed, a stumbling on the stairs. Then the megrims began, like claps of thunder trapped inside his skull, and for hours he was forced to lie prostrate in his shuttered cell with vinegar poultices pressed to his brow, as cascades of splintered multicoloured glass formed jagged images of agony behind his eyes. Still he persisted in denying what the physician in him knew beyond doubt to be the case, that the end had come. An attack of ague, nothing more, he told himself; I am seventy, it is to be expected. Then that morning, in the first week of April, as he had made to rise from his couch at dawn, his entire right side had pained him suddenly, terribly, as if a bag of shot, or pellets of hot quicksilver, had been emptied from his skull into his heart and pumped out from thence to clatter down the arteries of his arm, through the ribcage, into his leg. Moaning, he laid himself down again tenderly on the couch, with great solicitude, as a mother laying her child into its cradle. A spider in the dim dawnlight swarmed laboriously across the trampoline of its web strung between the ceiling beams. From without came the burgeoning clatter and crack of a horse and rider approaching. Poised on the rack of his pain he waited, calmly, almost in eagerness, for the advent of the black catastrophe. But the horseman did not stop, passed under the window, and then he understood, without surprise, but in something like disappointment, that he was not to be let go before suffering a final jest, and, instead of death, sleep, the ultimate banality, bundled him unceremoniously under its wing and bore him swiftly away.

*

It was sleep, yes, and yet more than that, an impassioned hearkening, a pausing upon a deserted shore at twilight, a last looking backward at the soon to be forsaken land, yes, yes: he was waiting yet. For what? He did not know. Mute and expectant, he peered anxiously into the sombre distance. They were all there, unseen yet palpable, all his discarded dead. A pang of longing pierced his heart. But why were they behind him? why not before? was he not on his way now at last to join that silent throng? And why did he tarry here, on this desolate brink? A brumous yellowy sky full of wreckage sank slowly afar, and the darkness welled up around him. Then he spied the figure approaching, the massive shoulders and great dark burnished face like polished stone, the wide-set eyes, the cruel mad mouth.

Who are you? he cried, striving in vain to lift his hands and fend off the apparition.

I am he whom you seek.

Tell me who you are!

As my own father I am already dead, as my own mother I still live, and grow old. I come to take you on a journey. You have much to learn, and so little time.

What? what would you teach me?

How to die.

Ah . . . Then you are Brother Death?

No. He is not yet. I am the one that goes before. I am, you may say, the god of revels and oblivion. I make men mad. You are in my realm now, for a little while. Come with me. Here begins the descent into Hell. Come.

And so speaking the god turned and started back toward the dark land.

Come!

And the dying man looked before him again, to the invisible ineluctable sea, wanting to go on, unable to go on, turning already, even against his will, turning back toward the waiting throng.

Come . . .

And as a soldier turns unwillingly away from a heart-rending vision of home and love only to meet full in the face the fatal shot, he turned and at once the great sphere of searing fire burst in his brain, and he awoke.

*

The pain was in his right side, although he seemed to know that rather than feel it, for that side was paralysed from ear to heel. Tentatively, with eyes averted, not wishing really to know, he sent out a few simple commands to arm and flank and hip, but to no avail, for the channels of communication were broken. It was as if half of him had come detached, and lay beside him now, a felled grey brute, sullen, unmoving and dangerous. Dangerous, yes: he must be wary of provoking this beast, or it would surely lift one mighty padded paw of pain and smash him. Bright April light shone in the window. He could see the Baltic, steel-blue and calm, bearing landward a ship with a black sail. Was it too much to expect that this burdensome clarity, this awareness, might have been taken from him, was it too much to expect at least that much respite? Below, Anna Schillings was stirring, setting in motion the creaky mechanism of another day. Despite the pain, he felt now most acutely a sense of anxiety and scruple, and, weirdly, a devastating embarrassment. He had not known just such a smarting dismay since childhood, when, marked out by some act or other of mischief, a dish broken, a lie told, he had stood cowering, all boltholes barred against him, in the path of the awful unavoidable engine of retribution. To be found out! It was absurd. Anna would come in a moment, with the gruel and the mulled wine, and he would be found out. Cautiously he tested his face to find if it would smile, and then, despite himself, he began quietly to blubber; it was a tiny luxury, and it made him feel better, after all.

By the time she came sighing up the stairs he had stanched his tears, but of course she sensed disaster at once. It was the stink of his shame, the stink of the child who has wet his breeches, of the maimed animal throbbing in a lair of leaves, that betrayed him. Slowly, with her face turned resolutely away, she set down on the floor beside his couch the steaming pewter mug of wine and the bowl of gruel.

'You are not risen yet, Canon?'

'It's nothing, Anna, you must not trouble yourself. I am ill.' He found it difficult to speak, the blurred words were a kind of soft stone in his mouth. 'Inform the Chapter, please, and ask Canon Giese to come.' No no, no, Giese was no longer here, but in Löbau; he must take care, she would think him in a worse way than he was if he continued raving thus. She stood motionless, with her head bowed and hands folded before her, still turned somewhat away, unwilling or unable to look full upon the calamity that had alighted in her life. She had the injured baffled look of one who has been grievously and unaccountably slighted, but above all she appeared puzzled, and entirely at a loss to know how to behave. He could sympathise, he knew the feeling: there is no place for death in the intricate workings of ordinary days. He wished he could think of something to say that would make this new disordered state of affairs seem reasonable.

'I am dying, Anna.'

He at once regretted saying it, of course. She began quietly to weep, with a reserve, a sort of circumspection, that touched him far more deeply than the expected wild wailings could have done. She went away, sniffling, and returned presently with water to wash him, and a pot for his relief. Deftly she ministered to him, speaking not a word. He admired her competence, her resilience; an admirable woman, really. Something of the old, almost forgotten fondness stirred in him. 'Anna? . . .' Still she said nothing. She had learned from him, perhaps, to distrust words, and was content to allow these tangible ministrations to express all that could not be said. Sadly and in some wonder he gazed at her. What did she signify, what did she *mean*? For the first time it struck him as odd that they had never in all the years learned to call each other *thou*.

*

Day by day the sickness waxed and waned, pummelling him, flinging him down into vast darknesses only to haul him up again into agonising light, shaking him until he seemed to hear his bones rattling, binding up his bowels tonight and on the morrow throwing open the floodgates of his orifices, leaving him to lie for hours, nauseated and helpless, in the stench of his own messes. Bright shimmering patterns of pain rippled through him, as if the sickness, like a gloating clothier, were unfurling for a finicking taste a series of progressively more subtle and exquisite rolls of silken torture. Always, unthinkingly, he had assumed that his would be a dry death, a swift clean shrivelling up, but here were fevers that lasted for days, wringing a ceaseless ooze of sweat from his burning flesh, robbing him of that precious clarity of mind that at first had seemed such a burden.

Sometimes, however, he was sufficiently clear in his thinking to be surprised and even fascinated by his own equanimity in the face of death. That moment was now at hand the terror of which had been with him always on his journey hither, present in every landscape, no matter how bright and various the scenes, like an unmoving shadow, and yet now he was not afraid: he felt only vague melancholy and regret, and a certain anxiety lest he should miss this last and surely most distinguished experience the world would afford him. He was convinced that he would be granted an insight, a vision, of profound significance, before the end. Was this why he was calm and unafraid, because this mysterious something toward which he was eagerly advancing hid from his gaze death's true countenance? And was this the explanation for the prolonging of his agony, because it was not the death agony at all, but a manner of purification, a ritual suffering to be endured before his initiation into transcendent knowledge? Although he was gone too far now to expect that he might put to living use whatever lesson he was to learn, the profundity of the experience, he believed, would not be thus diminished. Was redemption still possible, then, even in this extremity?

Searching for an answer to this extraordinary question, his fevered understanding scavenged like a ragpicker among the detritus of his life, rummaging fitfully through the disconnected bits and scraps that were left. He could find no sense of significant meaning anywhere. Sometimes, however, he sank into a calm deep dreaming wherein he wandered at peace through the fields and palaces of memory. The past was still wonderfully intact there. Amid scenes of childhood and youth he marvelled at the wealth of detail that had stayed with him through all the years, stored away like winter fruit. He visited the old house in St Anne's Lane, and walked again in quiet rapture through the streets and alleyways of the town. Here was St John's, the school gate, the boys playing in the dust. A soft golden radiance held sway everywhere, a stylised sunlight. Tenderness and longing pierced him to the core. Had he ever in reality left Torun? Perhaps that was where his real, his essential self had remained, waiting patiently for him to return, as now, and claim his true estate. And here is the linden tree, in full leaf, steadfast and lovely, the very image of summer and silence, of happiness.

But always he returned from these backward journeys weary and dispirited, with no answers. Despair blossomed in him then, a rank hideous flower. Numbed by an overdose of grog, by an unexpectedly successful blending of herbs, or by simple weariness, he withdrew altogether from the realm of life, and lay, a shapeless piece of flesh and sweat and phlegm, in the most primitive, rudimentary state of being, a dull barely-breathing almost-death. Those periods were the worst of all.

At other times the past came to his present, in the form of little creatures, gaudy homunculi who marched into the sickroom and strutted up and down beside his couch, berating him for the injuries he had done them, or perched at his shoulder and chattered, explaining, justifying, denouncing. They were at once comic and sad. Canon Wodka came, and Professor Brudzewski, Novara and the Italians, even Uncle Lucas, pompous as ever, even the King of Poland, tipsy, with his crown awry. At first he knew them to be hallucinations, but then he realised that the matter was deeper than that: they were real enough, as real as anything can be that is not oneself, that is of the outside, for had he not always believed that others are not known but invented, that the world consists solely of oneself while all else is phantom, necessarily? Therefore they had a right to berate him, for who, if not he, was to blame for what they were, poor frail vainglorious creatures, tenants of his mind, whom he had invented, whom he was taking with him into death? They were having their last say, before the end. Girolamo alone of them was silent. He stood back in the shadows some way from the couch, with that inimitable mixture of detachment and fondness, one eyebrow raised in amiable mockery, smiling. Ah yes, Girolamo, you knew me – not so well as did that other, it's true, but you did know me – and I could not bear to be known thus.

*

Where?

He had drifted down into a dreadful dark where all was silent and utterly still. He was frightened. He waited. After a long time, what seemed a long time, he saw at an immense distance a minute something in the darkness, it could not be called light, it was barely more than nothing, the absolute minimum imaginable, and he heard afar, faintly, O, faintly, a tiny shrieking, a grain of sound that was hardly anything in itself, that served only to define the infinite silence surrounding it. And then, it was strange, it was as if time had split somehow in two, as if the *now* and the *not yet* were both occurring at once, for he was conscious of watching something approaching through the dark distance while yet it had arrived, a huge steely shining bird it was, soaring on motionless outstretched great wings, terrible, O, terrible beyond words, and yet magnificent, carrying in its fearsome beak a fragment of blinding fire, and he tried to cry out, to utter the word, but in vain, for down the long arc of its flight the creature wheeled, already upon him even as it came, and branded the burning seal upon his brow.

Word!
O word!
Thou word that I lack!

And then he was once again upon that darkling shore, with the sea at his back and before him the at once mysterious and familiar land. There too was the cruel god, leading him away from the sea to where the others awaited him, the many others, the all. He could see nothing, yet he knew these things, knew also that the land into which he was descending now was at once all the lands he had known in his life, all! all the towns and the cities, the plains and woods, Prussia and Poland and Italy, Torun,

Cracow, Padua and Bologna and Ferrara. And the god also, turning upon him full his great glazed stone face, was many in one, was Caspar Sturm, was Novara and Brudzewski, was Girolamo, was more, was his father and his mother, and their mothers and fathers, was the uncountable millions, and was also that other, that ineluctable other. The god spoke:

Here now is that which you sought, that thing which is itself and no other. Do you acknowledge it?

No, no, it was not so! There was only darkness and disorder here, and a great clamour of countless voices crying out in laughter and pain and execration; he would know nothing of this vileness and chaos.

Let me die!

But the god answered him:

Not yet.

Swiftly then he felt himself borne upwards, aching upwards into the world, and here was his cell, and dawnlight on the great arc of the Baltic, and it was Maytime. He was in pain, and his limbs were dead, but for the first time in many weeks his mind was wonderfully clear. This clarity, however, was uncanny, unlike anything experienced before; he did not trust it. All round about him a vast chill stillness reigned, as if he were poised at an immense height, in an infinity of air. Could it be he had been elevated thus only in order that he might witness desolations? For he wanted no more of that, the struggle and the anguish. Was this true despair at last? If so, it was a singularly undistinguished thing.

He slept for a little while, but was woken again by Anna when she came up with the basin and the razor to shave him. Could she not leave him in peace, even for a moment! But then he chided himself for his ingratitude. She had shown him great kindness during the long weeks of his illness. The shaving, the feeding, the wiping and the washing, these were her necessary rituals that held at bay the knowledge that soon now she would be left alone. He watched her as she bustled about the couch, setting up the basin, honing the razor, painting the lather upon his sunken jaws, all the while murmuring softly to herself, a tall, too-heavy, whey-faced woman in dusty black. Lately she had begun to yell at him, this unmoving grey effigy, as she would at a deaf mute, or an infant, not in anger or even impatience, but with a kind of desperate cheerfulness, as if she believed she were summoning him back by this means from the dark brink. Her manner irritated him beyond endurance, especially in the mornings, and he mouthed angry noises, and sometimes even tried to smack at her in impotent rage. Today, however, he was calm, and even managed a lop-sided smile, although she did not seem to recognise it as such, for she only peered at him apprehensively and asked if he were in pain. Poor Anna. He stared at her in wonderment. How she had aged! From the ripe well-made woman who had arrived at his tower twenty years before, she had without his noticing become a tremulous, agitated, faintly silly matron. Had he really had such scant regard for her that he had not even attended the commonplace phenomenon of her aging? She had been his housekeeper, and, on three occasions, more than that, three strange, now wholly unreal encounters into which he had been led by desperation and unbearable self-knowledge and surrender; she had thrice, then, been more, but not much more, certainly not enough to justify Dantiscus's crass relentless hounding. Now, however, he wondered if perhaps those three nights were due a greater significance than he had been willing to grant. Perhaps, for her, they had been enough to keep her with him. For she could have left him. Her children were grown now. Heinrich, her son, had lately come out of the time of his apprenticeship in the cathedral bakery, and Carla was in service in the household of a burgher of the town. They would have supported her, if she had left him. She had chosen to remain. She had endured. Was this what she signified, what she meant? He recalled green days of hers, storms in spring and autumn moods, grievings in wintertime. He should have shown her more regard, then. Now it was too late.

'Anna.'

'Yes, Canon?'

'*Du*, Anna.'

'Yes, Herr Canon. You know that the Herr Doctor is coming today? You remember, yes? from Nuremberg?'

What was she talking about? What doctor? And then he remembered. So that was why he had been granted this final lucidity! All that, his work, the publishing and so forth, had lost all meaning. He could remember his hopes and fears for the book, but he could no longer feel them. He had failed, yes, but what did it matter? That failure was a small thing compared to the general disaster that was his life.

Andreas Osiander arrived in the afternoon. Anna, flustered by the coming of a person of such consequence, hurried up the stairs to announce him, stammering and wringing her hands in distress. The Canon remembered, too late, that he had intended to send her away during the Nuremberger's visit, for her presence under his keen disapproving nose would surely lead to all that *focaria* nonsense being started up again – not that the Canon cared any longer what Dantiscus or any of them might say or do to him, but he did not want Anna to suffer new humiliations; no, he did not want that. She had hardly announced his name before Osiander swept roughly past her and began at once to speak in his brusque overbearing fashion. Confronted however by the sight of the shrivelled figure on the couch he faltered in his speechifying and turned uncertainly to the woman hovering at the door.

'It is the palsy, Herr Doctor,' Anna said, bowing and bobbing, 'brought on by a bleeding in the brain, they say.'

'O. I understand. Well, that will be all, thank you, mistress, you may go.'

The Canon wished her to remain, but she made a soothing sign to him and went off meekly. He strained to hear her heavy step descending the stairs, a sound that suddenly seemed to him to sum up all the comfort that was left in the world, but Osiander had begun to boom at him again, and Anna departed in silence out of his life.

*

'I had not thought to find you brought so low, friend Koppernigk,' Osiander said, in a faintly accusing tone, as if he suspected that he had been deliberately misled in the matter of the other's state of health.

'I am dying, Doctor.'

'Yes. But it comes to us all in the end, and you must put yourself into God's care. Better this way than to be taken suddenly, in the night, the soul unprepared, eh?'

He was a portly arrogant man, this Lutheran, noisy, pompous and unfeeling, full of his own opinions; the Canon had always in his heart disliked him. He began to pace the floor with stately tread, his puffed-up pigeon's chest an impregnable shield against all opposition, and spoke of Nuremberg, and the printing, and his unstinting efforts on behalf of the Canon's work. Rheticus he called *that wretched creature*. Poor, foolish Rheticus! another victim sacrificed upon the altar of decorum. The Canon sighed; he should have ignored them all, Dantiscus and Giese and Osiander, he should have given his disciple the acknowledgment he deserved. What if he was a sodomite? That was not the worst crime imaginable, no worse, perhaps, than base ingratitude.

Osiander was poking about inside the capacious satchel slung at his side, and now he brought out a handsome leather-bound volume tooled in gold on the spine. The Canon craned for a closer look at it, but Osiander, the dreadful fellow, seemed to have forgotten that he was in the presence of the author, who was still living, despite appearances, and instead of bringing it at once to the couch he took the book into the windowlight, and, dampening a thumb, flipped roughly through the pages with the careless disregard of one for whom all books other than the Bible are fundamentally worthless.

'I have altered the title,' he said absently, 'as I may have informed you was my intention, substituting the word *coelestium* for *mundi*, as it seemed to me safer to speak of the *heavens*, thereby displaying distance and detachment, rather than of the *world*, an altogether more immediate term.'

No, my friend, you did not mention that, as I recall; but it is no matter now.

'Also, of course, I have attached a preface, as we agreed. It was a wise move, I believe. As I have said to you in my various letters, the Aristotelians and theologians will easily be placated if they are told that several hypotheses can be used to explain the same apparent motions, and that the present hypotheses are not proposed because they are in reality true, but because they are the most convenient to calculate the apparent composite motions.' He lifted his bland face dreamily to the window, with a smug little smile of admiration at the precision and style of his delivery. Just thus did he pose, the Canon knew, when lecturing his slack-jawed classes at Nuremberg. 'For my part,' the Lutheran went on, 'I have always felt about hypotheses that they are not articles of faith, but bases of computation, so that even if they are false it does not matter, provided that they save the phenomena . . . And in the light of this belief have I composed the preface.'

'It must not be,' the Canon said, his dull gaze turned upward toward the ceiling. Osiander stared at him.

'What?'

'It must not be: I do not wish the book to be published.'

'But . . . but it is already published, my dear sir. See, I have a copy here, printed and bound. Petreius has made an edition of one thousand, as you agreed. It is even now being distributed.'

'It must not be, I say!'

Osiander, quite baffled, pondered a moment in silence, then came and sat down slowly on a chair beside the couch and peered at the Canon with an uncertain smile. 'Are you unwell, my friend?'

The Canon, had he been able, would have laughed.

'I am dying, man!' he cried. 'Have I not told you so already? But I am not raving. I want this book suppressed. Go to Petreius, have him recall whatever volumes he has sent out. Do you understand? *It must not be!*'

'Calm yourself, Doctor, please,' said Osiander, alarmed by the paralytic's pent-up vehemence, the straining jaw and wild anguished stare. 'Do you require assistance? Shall I call the woman?'

'No no no, do nothing.' The Canon relaxed somewhat, and the trembling in his limbs subsided. There was a fever coming on, and a pain the like of which he had not known before was crashing and booming in his skull. Terror extended a thin dark tentacle within him. 'Forgive me,' he mumbled. 'Is there water? Let me drink. Thank you, you are most kind. Ah.'

Frowning, Osiander set down the water jug. He had a look now of mingled embarrassment and curiosity: he wanted to escape from the presence of this undignified dying, yet also he wished to know the reason for the old man's extraordinary change of mind. 'Perhaps,' he ventured, 'I may return later in the day, when you are less wrought, and discuss then this matter of your book?'

But the Canon was not listening. 'Tell me, Osiander,' he said, 'tell me truly, is it too late to halt publication? For I would halt it.'

'Why, Doctor?'

'You have read the book? Then you must know why. It is a failure. I failed in that which I set out to do: to discern truth, the significance of things.'

'Truth? I do not understand, Doctor. Your theory is not without flaws, I agree, but—'

'It is not the mechanics of the theory that interest me.' He closed his eyes. O burning, burning! 'The project itself, the totality . . . Do you understand? A hundred thousand words I used, charts, star tables, formulae, and yet I said nothing . . .'

He could not go on. What did it matter now, anyway? Osiander sighed.

'You should not trouble yourself thus, Doctor,' he said. 'These are scruples merely, and, if more than that, then you must realise that the manner of success you sought – or now believe that you sought! – is not to be attained. Your work, however flawed, shall be a basis for others to build upon, of this you may be assured. As to your failure to discern the true nature of things, as you put it, I think you will agree that I have accounted for such failing in my preface. Shall you hear what I have written?'

Plainly he was proud of his work, and, a born preacher, was eager to descant it. The Canon panicked: he did not want to hear, no! but he was sinking, and could no longer speak, could only growl and gnash his teeth in a frenzy of refusal. Osiander, however, took these efforts for a sign of pleased anticipation. He laid down the book, and, with the ghastly excruciated smile of one obliged to deal with a cretin, rose and thrust his hands under the Canon's armpits, and hauled him up and propped him carefully against the bank of soiled pillows as if he were setting up a target. Then, commencing his stately pacing once more, he held the book open before him at arm's length and began to read aloud in a booming pulpit voice.

'Since the novelty of the hypotheses of this work – which sets the Earth in motion and puts an immovable Sun at the centre of the universe – has already received great attention, I have no doubt that certain learned men have taken grave offence and think it wrong thus to raise disturbance among liberal disciplines, which were established long ago on a correct basis. If, however, they are willing to weigh the matter scrupulously, they will find that the author of this work has done nothing which merits blame. For it is the task of the astronomer to use painstaking and skilled observation in gathering together the history of celestial movements, and then – since he cannot by any line of reasoning discover the true causes of these movements (you mark that, Doctor?) – to conceive and devise whatever causes and hypotheses he pleases, such that, by the assumption of these causes, those same movements can be calculated from the principles of geometry for the past and for the future also. The present artist is markedly outstanding in both these respects: for it is not necessary that these hypotheses should be true, or even probable; it is enough if they provide a calculus which is consistent with the observations . . .'

The Canon listened in wonder: was it valid, this denial, this spitting-upon of his life's work? Truth or fiction . . . ritual . . .

necessary. He could not concentrate. He was in flames. Andreas Osiander, marching into windowlight and out again, was transformed at each turn into a walking darkness, a cloud of fire, a phantom, and outside too all was strangely changing, and not the sun was light and heat, the world inert, but rather the world was a nimbus of searing fire and the sun no more than a dead frozen globe dangling in the western sky.

'... For it is sufficiently clear that this art is profoundly ignorant of causes of the apparent movements. And if it constructs and invents causes – and certainly it has invented very many – nevertheless these causes are not advanced in order to convince anyone that they are true but only in order that they may posit a correct basis for calculation. But since one and the same movement may take varying hypotheses from time to time – as eccentricity and an epicycle for the motion of the Sun – the astronomer will accept above all others the one easiest to grasp. The philosopher will perhaps rather seek the semblance of truth. Neither, however, will understand or set down anything certain, unless it has been divinely revealed to him ...'

The walls of the tower had lost all solidity, were planes of darkness out of which there came now soaring on terrible wings the great steel bird, trailing flames in its wake and bearing in its beak the fiery sphere, no longer alone, but flying before a flock of others of its kind, all aflame, all gleaming and terrible and magnificent, rising out of darkness, shrieking.

'And so far as hypotheses are concerned, let no one expect anything certain from astronomy – since astronomy can offer us nothing certain – lest he mistake for truth ideas conceived for another purpose, and depart from this study a greater fool than when he came to it!'

No! O no. He flung his mute denial into the burning world. You, Andreas, have betrayed me, you ...

Andreas?

The pacing figure drew near, and swooping suddenly down pressed its terrible ruined face close to his.

You!

Yes, brother: I. We meet again.

*

Andreas laughed then, and seated himself on the chair beside the couch, laying the book on his lap under the black wing of his cloak. He was as he had been when the Canon had seen him last, a walking corpse on which the premature maggots were at work.

You are dead, Andreas, I am dreaming you.

Yes, brother, but it is I nevertheless. I am as real as you, now, for in this final place where we meet I am precisely as close to life as you are to death, and it is the same thing. I must thank you for this brief reincarnation.

What are you?

Why, I am Andreas! You have yourself addressed me thus. However, if you must have significance in all things, then we may say that I am the angel of redemption – an unlikely angel, I grant you, with dreadfully damaged wings, yet a redeemer, for all that.

You are death.

Andreas smiled, that familiar anguished smile.

O that too, brother, that too, but that's of secondary importance. But now, enough of this metaphysical quibbling, you know it always bored me. Let us speak instead, calmly, while there is still time, of the things that matter. See, I have your book . . .

Behind the dark seated smiling figure great light throbbed in the arched window, where the steel-blue Baltic's back rose like the back of some vast waterborne brute, ubiquitous and menacing. Above in the darkness under the ceiling the metal birds soared and swooped, flying on invisible struts and wires, filling the sombre air with their fierce clamour. The fever climbed inexorably upward along his veins, a molten tide. He clutched with his fingernails at the chill damp sheets under him, striving to keep hold of the world. He was afraid. This was dying, yes, this was unmistakably the distinguished thing. Minute fragments of the past assailed him: a deserted street in Cracow on a black midwinter night, an idiot child watching him from the doorway of a hovel outside the walls of Padua, a ruined tower somewhere in Poland inhabited by a flock of plumed white doves. These had been death's secret signals. Andreas, with his faint and sardonic, yet not unsympathetic smile, was watching him.

Wait, brother, it is not yet time, not quite yet. Shall we speak of your book, the reasons for your failure? For I will not dispute with you that you did fail. Unable to discern the thing itself, you would settle for nothing less; in your pride you preferred heroic failure to prosaic success.

I will accept none of this! What, anyway, do you know of these matters, you who had nothing but contempt for science, the products of the mind, all that, which I loved?

Come come: you have said that you are dreaming me, therefore you must accept what I say, since, if I am lying, it is your lies, in my mouth. And you have finished with lying, haven't you? Yes. The lies are all done with. That is why I am here, because at last you are prepared to be . . . honest. See, for example: you are no longer embarrassed in my presence. It was always your stormiest emotion, that fastidious, that panic-stricken embarrassment in the face of the disorder and vulgarity of the commonplace, which you despised.

There was movement in the room now, and the pale flickering incongruity of candles lit in daylight. Dim faceless figures approached him, mumbling. A ceremony was being enacted, a ritual at once familiar to him and strange, and then with a shock, like the shock of falling in a dream, he understood that he was being prepared for the last rites.

Do not heed it, brother, Andreas said. All that is a myth, your faith in which you relinquished long ago. There is no comfort there for you.

I want to believe.

But you may not.

Then I am lost.

No, you are not lost, for I have come to redeem you.

Tell me, then. My book . . .? my work . . .?

You thought to discern the thing itself, the eternal truths, the pure forms that lie behind the chaos of the world. You looked into the sky: what did you see?

I saw . . . the planets dancing, and heard them singing in their courses.

O no, no brother. These things you imagined. Let me tell you how it was. You set the sights of the triquetrum upon a light shining in the sky, believing that you thus beheld a fragment of reality, inviolate, unmistakable, enduring, but that was not the case. What you saw was *a light shining in the sky*; whatever it was more than that it was so only by virtue of your faith, your belief in the possibility of apprehending reality.

What nonsense is this? How else may we live, if not in the belief that we can *know*?

It is the manner of knowing that is important. We know the meaning of the singular thing only so long as we content ourselves with knowing it in the midst of other meanings: isolate it, and all meaning drains away. It is not the thing that counts, you see, only the interaction of things; and, of course, the names . . .

You are preaching despair.

Yes? Call it, rather, *redemptive* despair, or, baser still, call it acceptance. The world will not bear anything other than acceptance. Look at this chair: there is the wood, the splinters, then the fibres, then the particles into which the fibres may be broken, and then the smaller particles of these particles, and then, eventually, nothing, a confluence of aetherial stresses, a kind of vivid involuntary dreaming in a vacuum. You see? the world simply will not bear it, this impassioned scrutiny.

You would seduce me with this philosophy of happy ignorance, of slavery, abject acceptance of a filthy world? I will have none of it!

You will have none of it . . .

You laugh, but tell me this, in your wisdom: how are we to perceive the truth if we do not attempt to discover it, and to understand our discoveries?

There is no need to search for the truth. We know it already, before ever we think of setting out on our quests.

How do we know it?

Why, simple, brother: we *are* the truth. The world, and ourselves, this is the truth. There is no other, or, if there is, it is of use to us only as an ideal, that brings us a little comfort, a little consolation, now and then.

And this truth that we are, how may we speak it?

It may not be spoken, brother, but perhaps it may be . . . shown.

How? tell me how?

By accepting what there is.

And then?

There is no more; that is all.

O no, Andreas, you will not trick me. If what you say were true, I should have had to sell my soul to a vicious world, to embrace meekly the hideousness, yes – but I would not do it! This much at least I can say, that I did not sell—

—Your soul? Ah, but you did sell it, to the highest bidder. What shall we call it? – science? the quest for truth? transcendent knowledge? Vanity, all vanity, and something more, a kind of cowardice, the cowardice that comes from the refusal to accept that the names are all there is that matter, the cowardice that is true and irredeemable despair. With great courage and great effort you might have succeeded, in the only way it is possible to succeed, by disposing the commonplace, the names, in a beautiful and orderly pattern that would show, by its very beauty and order, the action in our poor world of the otherworldly truths. But you tried to discard the commonplace truths for the transcendent ideals, and so failed.

I do not understand.

But you do. We say only those things that we have the words to express: it is enough.

No!

It is sufficient. We must be content with that much.

The candleflames like burning blades pierced his sight, and the grave voice intoning the final benediction stormed above him.

Too late!—

You thought to transcend the world, but before you could aspire to that loftiness your needs must have contended with . . . well, brother, with what?

Too late! – Death's burning seal was graven upon his brow, and all that he had discarded was gone beyond retrieving. The light, O! and the terrible birds! the great burning arc beyond the window!

With me, brother! I was that which you must contend with.

You, Andreas? What was there in you? You despised and betrayed me, made my life a misery. Wherever I turned you were there, blighting my life, my work.

Just so. I was the one absolutely necessary thing, for I was there always to remind you of what you must transcend. I was the bent bow from which you propelled yourself beyond the filthy world.

I did not hate you!

There had to be a little regard, yes, the regard which the arrow bears for the bow, but never the other, the thing itself, the vivid thing, which is not to be found in any book, nor in the firmament, nor in the absolute forms. You know what I mean, brother. It is that thing, passionate and yet calm, fierce and coming from far away, fabulous and yet ordinary, that thing which is all that matters, which is the great miracle. You glimpsed it briefly in our father, in sister Barbara, in Fracastoro, in Anna Schillings, in all the others, and even, yes, in me, glimpsed it, and turned away, appalled and . . . embarrassed. Call it acceptance, call it love if you wish, but these are poor words, and express nothing of the enormity.

Too late! – For he had sold his soul, and now payment would be exacted in full. The voice of the priest engulfed him.

'*Only after death shall we be united with the All, when the body dissolves into the four base elements of which it is made, and the spiritual man, the soul free and ablaze, ascends through the seven crystal spheres of the firmament, shedding at each stage a part of his mortal nature, until, shorn of all earthly evil, he shall find redemption in the Empyrean and be united there with the world soul that is everywhere and everything and eternal!'*

Andreas slowly shook his head.

No, brother, do not heed that voice out of the past. Redemption is not to be found in the Empyrean.

Too late!—

No, Nicolas, not too late. It is not I who have said all these things today, but you.

He was smiling, and his face was healed, the terrible scars had faded, and he was again as he had once been, and rising now he laid his hand upon his brother's burning brow. The terrible birds sailed in silence into the dark, the harsh light grew soft, and the stone walls of the tower rose up again. The Baltic shone, a bright sea bearing away a ship with a black sail. Andreas brought out the book from beneath his cloak, and placing it on the couch he guided his brother's hand until the slack fingers touched the unquiet pages.

I am the angel of redemption, Nicolas. Will you come with me now?

And so saying he smiled once more, a last time, and lifted up his delicate exquisite face and turned, to the window and the light, as if listening to something immensely far and faint, a music out of earth and air, water and fire, that was everywhere, and everything, and eternal, and Nicolas, straining to catch that melody, heard the voices of evening rising to meet him from without: the herdsman's call, the cries of children at play, the rumbling of the carts returning from market; and there were other voices too, of churchbells gravely tolling the hour, of dogs that barked afar, of the sea, of the earth itself, turning in its course, and of the wind, out of huge blue air, sighing in the leaves of the linden. All called and called to him, and called, calling him away.

D.C.

NOTES

Quotations from writings other than Copernicus's:

p. 236: 'It seemed as though a new world . . . possession of the whole community.' from Henri Pirenne's *A History of Europe*, translated by Bernard Miall (New York, 1956)

p. 241: 'If at the foundation . . . but despair?' from Søren Kierkegaard's *Fear and Trembling*, translated by Walter Lowrie (Princeton, NJ, 1968)

p. 241: 'I hold it true . . . the ancients dreamed.' from Albert Einstein's Herbert Spencer Lecture, Oxford, 1933 (quoted by Jeremy Bernstein in *Einstein*, London, 1973)

p. 241: 'Science aims at . . . of commonplace experienced.' from Sir Arthur Eddington's *The Nature of the Physical World* (Cambridge, 1923).

p. 241: 'It is of the highest . . . we are confronted.' from Max Planck (quoted by Bernstein in *Einstein*, p. 156)

p. 241: 'The death of one god is the death of all.' from Wallace Stevens's 'Notes Toward a Supreme Fiction', *Collected Poems* (London, 1955)

ACKNOWLEDGMENTS

A fully comprehensive bibliography would be wholly inappropriate, and probably impossible to compile, in a work of this nature; nevertheless, there is a small number of books which, during the years of composition of *Doctor Copernicus*, have won my deep respect, and whose scholarship and vision have been of invaluable help to me, and these I must mention. I name them also as suggested further reading for anyone seeking a fuller and perhaps more scrupulously factual account of the astronomer's life and work.

The standard biography is Ludwig Prowe's *Nicolaus Copernicus* (2 vols, Berlin, 1883–4); it has not, however, been translated into English, so far as I can ascertain. Two brief and delightful accounts of the life and work are Angus Armitage's *Copernicus, Founder of Modern Astronomy* (London, 1938), and *Sun, Stand Thou Still* (London, 1947). A more technical, but very elegant and readable explication of the heliocentric theory is contained in Professor Fred Hoyle's *Nicolaus Copernicus* (London, 1973). However, the two works on which I have mainly drawn are Thomas S. Kuhn's *The Copernican Revolution* (Harvard, 1957), and Arthur Koestler's *The Sleepwalkers: A History of Man's Changing Vision of the Universe* (London, 1959). To these two beautiful, lucid and engaging books I owe more than a mere acknowledgment can repay.

For the light which they shed upon the history and thought of the period I am grateful to F. L. Carsten, whose *The Origins of Prussia* (Oxford, 1954) was extremely helpful; Frances A. Yates, who, in *Giordano Bruno and the Hermetic Tradition* (London, 1964), revealed the influences of Hermetic mysticism and Neoplatonism upon Copernicus and his contemporaries; W. P. D. Wightman's *Science in a Renaissance Society* (London, 1972), and M. E. Mallett's *The Borgias* (London, 1969).

I must emphasise, however, that any factual errors, willed or otherwise, and all questionable interpretations in this book are my own, and are in no way to be imputed to the sources listed above.

*

As well as the numerous extracts from Copernicus's own writings which I have incorporated in my text, and which I do not feel I need to identify, I have quoted from six different sources, which are identified in the Note on p. 279.

*

For their help and encouragement, I wish to thank the following: David Farrer, Dermot Keogh, Terence Killeen, Seamus McGonagle, Douglas Sealy, Maurice P. Sweeney, and the staff of Trinity College Library, Dublin. The final word of thanks must go to my wife, Janet, for her patience and fortitude, and for the benefit of her unerring judgment.

KEPLER

Preise dem Engel die Welt . . .

– R. M. Rilke, *Duino Elegies*

I

Mysterium Cosmographicum

JOHANNES KEPLER, asleep in his ruff, has dreamed the solution to the cosmic mystery. He holds it cupped in his mind as in his hands he would a precious something of unearthly frailty and splendour. O do not wake! But he will. Mistress Barbara, with a grain of grim satisfaction, shook him by his ill-shod foot, and at once the fabulous egg burst, leaving only a bit of glair and a few coordinates of broken shell.

And 0.00429

He was cramped and cold, with a vile gum of sleep in his mouth. Opening an eye he spied his wife reaching for his dangling foot again, and dealt her a tiny kick to the knuckles. She looked at him, and under that fat flushed look he winced and made elaborate business with the brim of his borrowed hat. The child Regina, his stepdaughter, primly perched beside her mother, took in this little skirmish with her accustomed mild gaze. Young Tyge Brahe appeared then, leaning down from on high into the carriage window, a pale moist melanochroid, lean of limb, limp of paw, with a sly eye.

'We are arrived, sir,' he said, smirking. That *sir*. Kepler, wiping his mouth discreetly on his sleeve, alighted on quaking legs from the carriage.

'Ah.'

The castle of Benatky confronted him, grand and impassive in the sunlit February air, more vast even than the black bulk of woe that had lowered over him all the way from Graz. A bubble of gloom rose and broke in the mud of his fuddled wits. Mästlin, even Mästlin had failed him: why expect more of Tycho the Dane? His vision swam as the tears welled. He was not yet thirty; he felt far older than that. But then, knuckling his eyes, he turned in time to witness the Junker Tengnagel, caparisoned blond brute, fall arse over tip off his rearing horse into the rutted slush of the road, and he marvelled again at the inexhaustible bounty of the world, that has always a little consolation to offer.

It was a further comfort that the grand serenity of Benatky was no more than a stony exterior: inside the gates, that gave into a cobbled courtyard, the quintet of travellers arrived in the midst of bedlam. Planks clattered, bricks crashed, masons whistled. An overburdened pack mule, ears back and muzzle turned inside out, brayed and brayed. Tyge waved a hand and said: 'The new Uraniborg!' and laughed, and, as they stooped under a sagging granite lintel, a surge of excitement, tinged with the aftertaste of his dream, rose like warm gorge in Kepler's throat. Perhaps after all he had done right in coming to Bohemia? He might do great work here, at Brahe's castle, swaddled in the folds of a personality larger far and madder than his own.

They entered a second, smaller courtyard. There were no workings here. Patches of rust-stained snow clung in crevices and on window ledges. A beam of sunlight leaned against a tawny wall. All was calm, or was until, like a thing dropped into a still pool, a figure appeared from under the shadow of an arch, a dwarf it was, with enormous hands and head and little legs and a humped back. He smiled, essaying a curtsy as they went past. Frau Barbara took Regina's hand.

'God save you, gentles,' the dwarf piped, in his miniature voice, and was ignored.

Through a studded door they entered a hall with an open fire. Figures moved to and fro in the reddish gloom. Kepler hung back, his wife behind him panting softly in his ear. They peered. Could it be they had been led into the servants' quarters? At a table by the fire sat a swarthy man with a moustache, hugely eating. Kepler's heart thumped. He had heard tell of Tycho Brahe's eccentricities, and doubtless it was one of them to dine down here, and doubtless this was he, the great man at last. It was not. The fellow looked up and said to Tycho's son: 'Eh! you are returned.' He was Italian. 'How are things in Prague?'

'Chapped,' young Tyge said, shrugging, 'chapped, I would think.'

The Italian frowned, and then: 'Ah, I have you, I have you. Ha.'

Kepler began to fidget. Surely there should have been some better reception than this. Was he being deliberately slighted, or was it just the way of aristocrats? And should he assert his presence? That might be a gross failure of tact. But Barbara would begin to nag him in a moment. Then something brushed against him and he twitched in fright. The dwarf had come quietly in, and planted himself now before the astronomer and examined with calm attention the troubled white face and myopic gaze, the frayed breeches, crumpled ruff, the hands clutching the plumed hat. 'Sir Mathematicus, I venture,' and bowed. 'Welcome, welcome indeed,' as if he were lord of the house.

'This,' said young Brahe, 'is Jeppe, my father's fool. It is a manner of sacred beast, I warn you, and can foretell the future.'

The dwarf smiled, shaking his great smooth head. 'Tut, master, I am but a poor maimed man, a nothing. But you are tardy. This long week past we have looked for you and your . . .' darting a glance at Kepler's wife '. . . baggage. Your dad is fretting.'

Tyge frowned. 'Remember, you,' he said, 'shit-eating toad, one day I will inherit you.'

Jeppe glanced after Tengnagel, who had strode straight, glowering, to the fire. 'What ails our broody friend?'

'A fall from his mount,' Tyge said, and suddenly giggled.

'Yes? The trollops were so lively then, in town?'

Mistress Barbara bridled. Such talk, and in the child's hearing! She had been for some time silently totting up against Benatky a score of particulars that totalled now a general affront. 'Johannes,' she began, three semitones in ominous ascent, but just then the Italian rose and tapped a finger lightly on young Tyge's breastbone. 'Tell him,' he said, 'your father, I regret this thing. He's angry still, and will not see me, and I can wait no more. It was no fault of mine: the beast was drunk! So you tell him, yes? Now farewell.' He went quickly out, flinging the wing of his heavy cloak across his shoulder and damping his hat on his head. Kepler looked after him. 'Jo*hann*es.' Tyge had wandered off. Tengnagel brooded. 'Come,' said the dwarf, and showed again, like something swiftly shown before being palmed, his thin sly smile. He led them up dank flights of stairs, along endless stone corridors. The castle resounded with shouts, snatches of wild singing, a banging of doors. The guest rooms were cavernous and sparsely furnished. Barbara wrinkled her nose at the smell of damp. The baggage had not been brought up. Jeppe leaned in a doorway with his arms folded, watching. Kepler retreated to the mullioned window and on tiptoe peered down upon the courtyard and the workmen and a cloaked horseman cantering toward the gates. Despite misgivings he had in his heart expected something large and lavish of Benatky, gold rooms and spontaneous applause, the attention of magnificent serious people, light and space and ease: not this grey, these deformities, the clamour and confusion of other lives, this familiar – O familiar! – disorder.

Was Tycho Brahe himself not large, was he not lavish? When at noon the summons came, Kepler, who had fallen asleep again, stumbled down through the castle to find a fat bald man ranting about, of all things, his tame elk. They entered a high hall, and sat, and the Dane was suddenly silent, staring at his guest. And then Kepler, instead of lifting his spirit sufficiently up to meet this eminence, launched into an account of his troubles. The whining note even he could hear in his voice annoyed him, but he could not suppress it. There was cause for whining, after all. The Dane of course, Kepler gloomily supposed, knew nothing of money worries and all that, these squalid matters. His vast assurance was informed by centuries of patrician breeding. Even this room, high and light with a fine old ceiling, bespoke a stolid grandeur. Surely here disorder would not dare show its leering face. Tycho, with his silence and his stare, his gleaming dome of skull and metal nose, seemed more than human, seemed a great weighty engine whose imperceptible workings were holding firmly in their courses all the disparate doings of the castle and its myriad lives.

'. . . And although in Graz,' Kepler was saying, 'I had many persons of influence on my side, even the Jesuits, yes, it was to no avail, the authorities continued to hound me without mercy, and would have me renounce my faith. You will not believe it, sir, I was forced to pay a fine of ten florins for the privilege, the *privilege*, mark you, of burying my poor children by the Lutheran rite.'

Tycho stirred and dealt his moustaches a downward thrust of forefinger and thumb. Kepler with plaintive gaze stooped lower in his chair, as if the yoke of that finger and thumb had descended upon his thin neck.

'What is your philosophy, sir?' the Dane asked.

Italian oranges throbbed in a pewter bowl on the table between them. Kepler had not seen oranges before. Blazoned, big with ripeness, they were uncanny in their tense inexorable thereness.

'I hold the world to be a manifestation of the possibility of order,' he said. Was this another fragment out of that morning's dream? Tycho Brahe was looking at him again, stonily. 'That is,' Kepler hastened, 'I espouse the natural philosophy.' He wished he had dressed differently. The ruff especially he regretted. He had intended it to make an impression, but it was too tight. His borrowed hat languished on the floor at his feet, another brave but ill-judged flourish, with a dent in the crown where he had inadvertently stepped on it. Tycho, considering a far corner of the ceiling, said:

'When I came first to Bohemia, the Emperor lodged us in Prague at the house of the late Vice Chancellor Curtius, where the infernal ringing of bells from the Capuchin monastery nearby was a torment night and day.' He shrugged. 'One has always to contend with disturbance.'

Kepler nodded gravely. Bells, yes: bells indeed would seriously disturb the concentration, though not half so seriously, he fancied, as the cries of one's children dying in agony. They had, he and this Dane, much to learn about each other. He glanced around with a smile, admiring and envious. 'But *here*, of course . . .?' The wall by which they sat was almost all a vast arched window of many leaded panes, that gave on to a prospect of vines and pasture lands rolling away into a blue pellucid distance. Winter sunlight blazed upon the Iser.

'The Emperor refers to Benatky as a castle,' Tycho Brahe said, 'but it is hardly that. I am making extensive alterations and enlargements; I intend that here will be my Bohemian Uraniborg. One is frustrated though at every turn. His majesty is sympathetic, but he cannot attend in person to every detail. The manager of the crown estates hereabouts, with whom I must chiefly deal, is not so well disposed towards me as I would wish. Mühlstein he is called, Kaspar von Mühlstein . . .' darkly measuring the name as a hangman would a neck. 'I think he is a Jew.'

A noontide bell clanged without, and the Dane wanted his breakfast. A servant brought in hot bread wrapped in napkins, and a jug from which he filled their cups with a steaming blackish stuff. Kepler peered at it and Tycho said: 'You do not know this brew? It comes from Araby. I find it sharpens the brain wonderfully.' It was casually said, but Kepler knew he was meant to be impressed. He drank, and smacked his lips appreciatively, and Tycho for the first time smiled. 'You must forgive me, Herr Kepler, that I did not come myself to greet you on your arrival in Bohemia. As I mentioned in my letter, I seldom go to Prague, unless it is to call upon the Emperor; and besides, the opposition at this time of Mars and Jupiter, as you will appreciate, encouraged me not to interrupt my work. However, I trust you will understand that I receive you now less as a guest than as a friend and colleague.'

This little speech, despite its seeming warmth, left them both obscurely dissatisfied. Tycho, about to proceed, instead looked sulkily away, to the window and the winter day outside. The servant knelt before the tiled stove feeding pine logs to the flames. The fellow had a cropped head and meaty hands, and raw red feet stuck into wooden clogs. Kepler sighed. He was, he realised, hopelessly of that class which notices the state of servants' feet. He drank more of the Arabian brew. It did clear the head, but it seemed also, alarmingly, to be giving him the shakes. He feared his fever was coming on again. It had dogged him now for six months and more, and led him, in grey dawn hours, to believe he was consumptive. Still, he appeared to be putting on fat: this cursed ruff was choking him.

Tycho Brahe turned back and, looking at him hard, asked: 'You work the metals?'

'Metals . . .?' faintly. The Dane had produced a small lacquered ointment box, and was applying a dab of aromatic salve to the flesh surrounding the false bridge of silver and gold alloy set into his damaged nose, where as a young man he had been disfigured in a duel. Kepler stared. Was he to be asked perhaps to fashion a new and finer organ to adorn the Dane's great face? He was relieved when Tycho, with a trace of irritation, said:

'I mean the alembic and so forth. You claimed to be a natural philosopher, did you not?' He had an unsettling way of ranging back and forth in his talk, as if the subjects were marked on the counters of a game which he was idly playing in his head.

'No no, alchemy is not, I am not—'

'But you make horoscopes.'

'Yes, that is, when I—'

'For payment?'

'Well, yes.' He had begun to stammer. He felt he was being forced to confess to an essential meanness of spirit. Shaken, he gathered himself for a counter-move, but Tycho abruptly shifted the direction of play again.

'Your writings are of great interest. I have read your *Mysterium cosmographicum* with attention. I did not agree with the method, of course, but the conclusions reached I found . . . significant. '

Kepler swallowed. 'You are too kind.'

'The flaw, I would suggest, is that you have based your theories upon the Copernican system.'

Instead of on yours, that is. Well, at least they were touching on the real matter now. Kepler, his fists clenched in his lap to stop them trembling, sought feverishly for the best means of proceeding at once to the essential question. He found himself, to his annoyance, hesitating. He did not trust Tycho Brahe. The man was altogether too still and circumspect, like a species of large lazy predator hunting motionless from the sprung trap of his lair. (Yet he was, in his way, a great astronomer. That was reassuring. Kepler believed in the brotherhood of science.) And besides, what *was* the essential question? He was seeking more than mere accommodation for himself and his family at Benatky. Life to him was a kind of miraculous being in itself, almost a living organism, of wonderful complexity and grace, but racked by a chronic wasting fever; he wished from Benatky and its master the granting of a perfect order and peace in which he might learn to contain his life, to still its fevered thrashings and set it to dancing the grave dance. Now, as he brooded in quiet dismay on these confusions, the moment eluded him. Tycho, pushing away the picked bones of his breakfast, began to rise. 'Shall we see you at dinner, Herr Kepler?'

'But! . . .' The astronomer was scrabbling for his hat under the table.

'You will meet some other of my assistants then, and we can discuss a redistribution of tasks, now that we are one more. I had thought of setting you the lunar orbit. However, we must first consult my man Christian Longberg, who, as you will of course understand, has a say in these matters.' They made a slow exit from the room. Tycho did not so much walk as sail, a stately ship. Kepler, pale, twisted the hat-brim in his trembling fingers. This was all mad. Friend and colleague indeed! He was being treated as if he were a raw apprentice. In the corridor Tycho Brahe bade him an absentminded farewell and cruised away. Frau Barbara was waiting for him in their rooms. She had an air always of seeming cruelly neglected, by his presence no less than by his absence. Sorrowing and expectant, she asked: 'Well?'

Kepler selected a look of smiling abstraction and tested it gingerly. 'Hmm?'

'Well,' his wife insisted, 'what happened?'

'O, we had breakfast. See, I brought you something,' and produced from its hiding place in the crown of his hat, with a conjuror's flourish, an orange. 'And I had coffee!'

Regina, who had been leaning out at the open window, turned now and advanced upon her stepfather with a faint smile. Under her candid gaze he felt always a little shy.

'There is a dead deer in the courtyard, 'she said. 'If you lean out far you can see it, on a cart. It's very big.'

'That is an elk,' said Kepler gently. 'It's called an elk. It got drunk, you know, and fell downstairs when . . .'

Their baggage had come up, and Barbara had been unpacking, and now with the glowing fruit cupped in her hands she sat down suddenly amidst the strewn wreckage of their belongings and began to weep. Kepler and the child stared at her.

'You settled nothing!' she wailed. 'You didn't even *try*.'

* * *

O FAMILIAR INDEED: disorder had been the condition of his life from the beginning. If he managed, briefly, a little inward calm, then the world without was sure to turn on him. That was how it had been in Graz, at the end. And yet that final year, before he was forced to flee to Tycho Brahe in Bohemia, had begun so well. The Archduke had tired for the moment of hounding the Lutherans, Barbara was pregnant again, and, with the Stiftsschule closed, there was ample time for his private studies. He had even softened toward the house on Stempfergasse, which at first had filled him with a deep dislike the origins of which he did not care to investigate. It was the last year of the century, and there was the relieved sense that some old foul thing was finally, having wrought much mischief, dying.

In the spring, his heart full of hope, he had set himself again to the great task of formulating the laws of world harmony. His workroom was at the back of the house, a cubbyhole off the dank flagged passage leading to the kitchen. It had been a lumber room in Barbara's late husband's time. Kepler had spent a day clearing out the junk, papers and old boxes and broken furniture, which he had dumped unceremoniously through the window into the overgrown flowerbed outside. There it still lay, a mouldering heap of compost which put forth every spring clusters of wild gentian, in memory perhaps of the former master of the house, poor Marx Müller the pilfering paymaster, whose lugubrious ghost still loitered in his lost domain.

There were other, grander rooms he might have chosen, for it was a large house, but Kepler preferred this one. It was out of the way. Barbara still had social pretensions then, and most afternoons the place was loud with the horse-faced wives of councillors and burghers, but the only sounds that disturbed the silence of his bolted lair were the querulous clucking of hens outside and the maidservant's song in the kitchen. The calm greenish light from the garden soothed his ailing eyes. Sometimes Regina came and sat with him. His work went well.

He was at last attracting some attention. Galileus the Italian had acknowledged his gift of a copy of the *Mysterium cosmographicum.* True, his letter had been disappointingly brief, and no more than civil. Tycho Brahe, however, had written to him warmly and at length about the book. Also, his correspondence with the Bavarian Chancellor Herwart von Hohenburg continued, despite the religious turmoil. All this allowed him to believe that he was becoming a person of consequence, for how many men of twenty-eight could claim such luminaries among their colleagues (he thought that not too strong a word)?

These crumbs might impress him, but others were harder to convince. He remembered the quarrel with his father-in-law, Jobst Müller. It marked in his memory, he was not sure why, the beginning of that critical period which was to end, nine months later, with his expulsion from Graz.

The spring had been bad that year, with rain and gales all through April. At the beginning of May there came an ugly calm. For days the sky was a dome of queer pale cloud, at night there was fog. Nothing stirred. It was as if the very air had congealed. The streets stank. Kepler feared this vampire weather, which affected the delicate balance of his constitution, making his brain ache and his veins to swell alarmingly. In Hungary, it was said, bloody stains were everywhere appearing on doors and walls and even in the fields. Here in Graz, an old woman, discovered one morning pissing behind the Jesuit church not far from the Stempfergasse, was stoned for a witch. Barbara, who was seven months gone, grew fretful. The time was ripe for an outbreak of plague. And it was, to Kepler, a kind of pestilence, when Jobst Müller came up from Gössendorf to stay three days.

He was a cheerless man, proud of his mill and his moneys and his Mühleck estate. Like Barbara, he too had social aspirations, he claimed noble birth and signed himself *zu Gössendorf.* Also like Barbara, though not so spectacularly as she, he was a user-up of spouses – his second wife was ailing. He accumulated wealth with a passion lacking elsewhere in his life. His daughter he looked on as a material possession, so it seemed, filched from him by the upstart Kepler.

But the visit at least served to cheer Barbara somewhat. She was glad to have an ally. Not that she ever, in Kepler's presence, complained openly about him. Silent suffering was her tactic. Kepler spent most of the three days of the visitation locked in his room. Regina kept him company. She too bore little love for Grandfather Müller. She was nine then, though small for her age, pale, with ash-blonde hair, that seemed always streaked with damp, pulled flat upon her narrow head. She was not pretty, she was too pinched and pale, but she had character. There was in her an air of completeness, of being, for herself, a precise sufficiency; Barbara was a little afraid of her. She sat in his workroom on a high stool, a toy forgotten in her lap, gazing at things – charts, chairs, the ragged garden, even at Kepler sometimes, when he coughed, or shuffled his feet, or let fall one of his involuntary little moans. Theirs was a strange sharing, but of what, he was not sure. He was the third father she had known in her short life, and she was waiting, he supposed, to see if he would prove more lasting than the previous two. Was that what they shared, then, a something held in store, for the future?

During these days she had more cause than usual to attend him. He was greatly agitated. He could not work, knowing that his wife and her father, that pair, were somewhere in the house, guzzling his breakfast wine and shaking their heads over his shortcomings. So he sat clenched at his jumbled desk, moaning and muttering, and scribbling wild calculations that were not so much mathematics as a kind of code expressing, in their violent irrationality, his otherwise mute fury and frustration.

It could not go on like that.

'We must have a talk, Johannes.' Jobst Müller let spread like a kind of sickly custard over his face one of his rare smiles. It was seldom he addressed his son-in-law by name. Kepler tried to edge away from him.

'I—I am very busy.'

That was the wrong thing to say. How could he be busy, with the school shut down? His astronomy was, to them, mere play, a mark of his base irresponsibility. Jobst Müller's smile grew sad. He was today without the wide-brimmed conical hat which he sported most times indoors and out, and he looked as if a part of his head were missing. He had lank grey hair and a bluish chin. He was something of a dandy, despite his years, and went in for velvet waistcoats and lace collars and blue knee-ribbons. Kepler would not look at him. They were on the gallery, above the entrance hall. Pale light of morning came in at the barred window behind them.

'But you might spare me an hour, perhaps?'

They went down the stairs, Jobst Müller's buckled shoes producing on the polished boards a dull descending scale of disapproval. The astronomer thought of his schooldays: now you are for it, Kepler. Barbara awaited them in the dining room. Johannes grimly noted the bright look in her eye. She knew the old boy had tackled him, they were in it together. She had been experimenting with her hair the night before (it had fallen out in great swatches after the birth of their first child), and now as they entered she whipped off the protective net, and a frizz of curls sprang up from her forehead. Johannes fancied he could hear them crackling.

'Good morning, my dear,' he said, and showed her his teeth.

She touched her curls nervously. 'Papa wants to speak to you.'

Johannes took his place opposite her at the table. 'I know.' These chairs, old Italian pieces, part of Barbara's dowry, were too tall for him, he had to stretch to touch his toes to the floor. Still, he liked them, and the other pieces, the room itself; he was fond of carved wood and old brick and black ceiling beams, all suchlike sound things, which, even if they were not strictly his own, helped to hold his world together.

'Johannes has agreed to grant me an hour of his valuable time,' Jobst Müller said, filling himself a small mug of ale. Barbara bit her lip.

'Um,' said Kepler. He knew what the subject would be. Ulrike the servant girl came paddling in with their breakfast on a vast tray. The guest from Mühleck partook of a boiled egg. Johannes was not hungry. His innards were in uproar this morning. It was a delicate engine, his gut, and the weather and Jobst Müller were affecting it. 'Damned bread is stale,' he muttered. Ulrike, in the doorway, threw him a look.

'Tell me,' said his father-in-law, 'is there sign of the Stiftsschule, ah, reopening?'

Johannes shrugged.

'The Archduke,' he said vaguely; 'you know.'

Barbara thrust a smoking platter at him. 'Take some bratwurst, Johann,' she said. 'Ulrike has made your favourite cream sauce.' He stared at her, and she hastily withdrew the plate. Her belly was so big now she had to lean forward from the shoulders to reach the table. For a moment he was touched by her sad ungainly state. He had thought her beautiful when she was carrying their first. He said morosely:

'I doubt it will be opened while he still rules.' He brightened. 'They say he has the pox, mind; if that puts paid to him there will be hope.'

'Johannes!'

Regina came in, effecting a small but palpable adjustment in the atmosphere. She shut the big oak door behind her with elaborate care, as if she were assembling part of the wall. The world was built on too large a scale for her. Johannes could sympathise.

'Hope of what?' Jobst Müller mildly enquired, scooping a last bit of white from his egg. He was all smoothness this morning, biding his time. The ale left a faint moustache of dried foam on his lip. He was to die within two years.

'Eh?' Kepler growled, determined to be difficult. Jobst Müller sighed.

'You said there would be hope if the Archduke were to . . . pass on. Hope of what, may we ask?'

'Hope of tolerance, and a little freedom in which folk may practise their faith as conscience bids them.' Ha! that was good. Jobst Müller had gone over to the papists in the last outbreak of Ferdinand's religious fervour, while Johannes had held fast and suffered temporary exile. The old boy's smoothness developed a ripple, it ran along his clenched jaw and tightened the bloodless lips. He said:

'Conscience, yes, conscience is fine for some, for those who imagine themselves so high and mighty they need not bother with common matters, and leave it to others to feed and house them and their families.'

Johannes put down his cup with a tiny crash. It was franked with the Müller crest. Regina was watching him.

'I am still paid my salary.' His face, which had been waxen with suppressed rage, reddened. Barbara made a pleading gesture, but he ignored her. 'I am held in some regard in this town, you know. The councillors – aye and the Archduke himself – acknowledge my worth, even if others do not.'

Jobst Müller shrugged. He had gathered himself into a crouch, a rat ready to fight. For all his dandified ways he gave off a faint tang of unwashed flesh.

'Fine manner they have of showing their appreciation, then,' he said, 'driving you out like a common criminal, eh?'

Johannes tore with his teeth at a crust of bread. 'I ward addowed do—' he swallowed mightily '—I was allowed to return within the month. I was the only one of our people thus singled out.'

Jobst Müller permitted himself another faint smile. 'Perhaps,' he said, with silky emphasis, 'the others did not have the Jesuits to plead for them? Perhaps their *consciences* would not allow them to seek the help of that Romish guild?'

Kepler's brow coloured again. He said nothing, but sat, throbbing, and glared at the old man. There was a lull. Barbara sniffed. 'Eat your sausage, Regina,' she said softly, sorrowfully, as if the child's fastidious manner of eating were the secret cause of all this present distress. Regina pushed her plate away, carefully.

'Tell me,' Jobst Müller said, still crouched, still smiling, 'what *is* this salary that the councillors continue to pay you for not working?' As if he did not very well know.

'I do not see—'

'They have reduced it, papa,' Barbara broke in eagerly. 'It was two hundred florins, and now they have taken away twenty-five!' It was her way, when talking against the tide of her husband's rage, to close her eyes under fluttering lids so as not to see his twitches, that ferocious glare. Jobst Müller nodded, saying:

'That is not riches, no.'

'Yes, papa.'

'Still, you know, two hundred monthly . . .'

Barbara's eyes flew open.

'Monthly?' she shrieked. 'But papa, that is *per annum*!'

'What!'

It was a fine playacting they were doing.

'Yes, papa, yes. And if it were not for my own small income, and what you send us from Mühleck, why—'

'*Be quiet*!' Johannes snarled.

Barbara jumped. 'O!' A tear squeezed out and rolled upon her plump pink cheek. Jobst Müller looked narrowly at his son-in-law.

'I have a right, surely, to hear how matters stand?' he said. 'It is my daughter, after all.'

Johannes released through clenched teeth a high piercing sound that was half howl, half groan.

'I will not have it!' he cried, 'I will not have *this* in my own house.'

'Yours?' Jobst Müller oozed.

'O papa, stop,' Barbara said.

Kepler pointed at them both a trembling finger. 'You will kill me,' he said, in the strained tone of one to whom a great and terrible knowledge has just come. 'Yes, that's what you will do, you'll kill me, between you. It's what you want. To see my health broken. You would be happy. And then you and this your spawn, who plays at being my lady wife—' too far, you go too far '—can pack off back to Mühleck, *I* know.'

'Calm yourself, sir,' Jobst Müller said. 'No one here wishes you harm. And pray do not sneer at Mühleck, nor the revenues it provides, which may yet prove your saving when the duke next sees fit to banish you, perhaps for good!'

Johannes gave a little jerk to the reins of his plunging rage.

Had he heard the hint of a deal there? Was the old goat working himself up to an offer to buy back his daughter? The idea made him angrier still. He laughed wildly.

'Listen to him, wife,' he cried; 'he is more jealous for his estates than he is for you! I may call *you* what I like, but I am not to soil the name of Mühleck by having it on my lips.'

'I will defend my daughter, young man, by deeds, not words.'

'Your daughter, *your* daughter let me tell you, needs no defending. She is seven-and-twenty and already she has put two husbands in their graves – *and* is working well on a third.' O, too far!

'Sir!'

They surged from their chairs, on the point of blows, and

stood with baleful glares locked like antlers. Into the heaving silence Barbara dropped a fat little giggle. She clapped a hand to her mouth. Regina watched her with interest. The men subsided, breathing heavily, surprised at themselves.

'He believes he is dying, you know, papa,' Barbara said, with another gulp of manic laughter. 'He says, he says he has the mark of a cross on his foot, at the place where the nails were driven into the Saviour, which comes and goes, and changes colour according to the time of day – isn't that so, Johannes?' She wrung her little hands, she could not stop. 'Although *I* cannot see it, I suppose because I am not one of your elect, or I am not clever enough, as you . . . as you always . . .' She faded into silence. Johannes eyed her for a long moment. Jobst Müller waited. He turned to Barbara, but she looked away. He said to his son-in-law:

'What sickness is it that you think has afflicted you?' Johannes growled something under his breath. 'Forgive me, I did not hear . . .?'

'*Plague*, I said.'

The old man started. 'Plague? Is there plague in the city? Barbara?'

'Of course there is not, papa. He imagines it.'

'But . . .'

Johannes looked up with a ghastly grin. 'It must start with someone, must it not?'

Jobst Müller was relieved. 'Really,' he said, 'this talk of . . . and with the child listening, really!'

Johannes turned on him again.

'How would I not worry,' he said, 'when I took my life in my hands by marrying this angel of death that you foisted on me?

Barbara let out a wail and put her hands to her face. Johannes winced, and his fury drained all away, leaving him suddenly limp. He went to her. Here was real pain, after all. She would not let him touch her, and his hands fussed helplessly above her heaving shoulders, kneading an invisible projection of her grief. 'I am a dog, Barbara, a rabid thing; forgive me,' gnawing his knuckles.

Jobst Müller watched them, this little person hovering over his big sobbing wife, and pursed his lips in distaste. Regina quietly left the room.

'O *Christ,*' Kepler cried, and stamped his foot.

* * *

HE WAS AFTER the eternal laws that govern the harmony of the world. Through awful thickets, in darkest night, he stalked his fabulous prey. Only the stealthiest of hunters had been vouchsafed a shot at it, and he, grossly armed with the blunderbuss of his defective mathematics, what chance had he? crowded round by capering clowns hallooing and howling and banging their bells whose names were Paternity, and Responsibility, and Domestgod-damnedicity. Yet O, he had seen it once, briefly, that mythic bird, a speck, no more than a speck, soaring at an immense height. It was not to be forgotten, that glimpse.

The 19th of July, 1595, at 27 minutes precisely past 11 in the morning: that was the moment. He was then, if his calculations were accurate, 23 years, 6 months, 3 weeks, 1 day, 20 hours and 57 minutes, give or take a few tens of seconds, old.

Afterwards he spent much time poring over these figures, searching out hidden significances. The set of date and time, added together, gave a product 1,652. Nothing there that he could see. Combining the integers of that total he got 14, which was twice 7, the mystical number. Or perhaps it was simply that 1652 was to be the year of his death. He would be eighty-one. (He laughed: with his health?) He turned to the second set, his age on that momentous July day. These figures were hardly more promising. Combined, not counting the year, they made a quantity whose only significance seemed to be that it was divisible by 5, leaving him the product 22, the age at which he had left Tübingen. Well, that was not much. But if he halved 22 and subtracted 5 (that 5 again!), he got 6, and it was at six that he had been taken by his mother to the top of Gallows Hill to view the comet of 1577. And 5, what did that busy 5 signify? Why, it was the number of the intervals between the planets, the number of notes in the arpeggio of the spheres, the five-tone scale of the world's music! . . . if his calculations were accurate.

He had been working for six months on what was to become the *Mysterium cosmographicum*, his first book. His circumstances were easier then. He was still unmarried, had not yet even heard Barbara's name, and was living at the Stiftsschule in a room that was cramped and cold, but his own. Astronomy at first had been a pastime merely, an extension of the mathematical games he had liked to play as a student at Tübingen. As time went on, and his hopes for his new life in Graz turned sour, this exalted playing more and more obsessed him. It was a thing apart, a realm of order to set against the ramshackle real world in which he was imprisoned. For Graz was a kind of prison. Here in this town, which they were pleased to call a city, the Styrian capital, ruled over by narrow-minded merchants and a papist prince, Johannes Kepler's spirit was in chains, his talents manacled, his great speculative gift strapped upon the rack of schoolmastering – right! yes! laughing and snarling, mocking himself – endungeoned, by God! He was twenty-three.

It was a pretty enough town. He was impressed when first he glimpsed it, the river, the spires, the castle-crowned hill, all blurred and bright under a shower of April rain. There seemed a largeness here, a generosity, which he fancied he could see even in the breadth and balance of the buildings, so different from the beetling architecture of his native Württemberg towns. The people too appeared different. They were promenaders much given to public discourse and dispute, and Johannes was reminded that he had come a long way from home, that he was almost in Italy. But it was all an illusion. Presently, when he had examined more closely the teeming streets, he realised that the filth and the stench, the cripples and beggars and berserks, were the same here as anywhere else. True, they were Protestant loonies, it was Protestant filth, and a Protestant heaven those spires sought, hence the wider air hereabout: but the Archduke was a rabid Catholic, and the place was crawling with Jesuits, and even then at the Stiftsschule there was talk of disestablishment and closure.

He, who had been such a brilliant student, detested teaching. In his classes he experienced a weird frustration. The lessons he had to expound were always, always just somewhere off to the side of what really interested him, so that he was forever holding himself in check, as a boatman presses a skiff against the run of the river. The effort exhausted him, left him sweating and dazed. Frequently the rudder gave way, and he was swept off helplessly on the flood of his enthusiasm, while his poor dull students stood abandoned on the receding bank, waving weakly.

The Stiftsschule was run in the manner of a military academy. Any master who did not beat blood out of his boys was considered lax. (Johannes did his best, but on the one occasion when he could not avoid administering a flogging his victim was a great grinning fellow almost as old as he, and a head taller.) The standard of learning was high, sustained by the committee of supervisors and its phalanx of inspectors. Johannes greatly feared the inspectors. They dropped in on classes unannounced, often in pairs, and listened in silence from the back, while his handful of pupils sat with arms folded, hugging themselves, and gazed at him, gleefully attentive, waiting for him to make a fool of himself. Mostly he obliged, twitching and stammering as he wrestled with the tangled threads of his discourse.

'You must try to be calm,' Rector Papius told him. 'You tend to rush at things, I think, forgetting perhaps that your students do not have your quickness of mind. They cannot follow you, they become confused, and then they complain to me, or . . .' he smiled '. . . or their fathers do.'

'I know, I know,' Johannes said, looking at his hands. They sat in the rector's room overlooking the central courtyard of the school. It was raining. There was wind in the chimney, and balls of smoke rolled out of the fireplace and hung in the air around them, making his eyes sting. 'I talk too quickly, and say things before I have had time to consider my words. Sometimes in the middle of a class I change my mind and begin to speak of some other subject, or realise that what I have been saying is imprecise and begin all over again to explain the matter in more detail.' He shut his mouth, squirming; he was making it worse. Dr Papius frowned at the fire. 'You see, Herr Rector, it is my *cupiditas speculandi* that leads me astray.'

'Yes,' the older man said mildly, scratching his chin, 'there is in you perhaps too much . . . passion. But I would not wish to see a young man suppress his natural enthusiasm. Perhaps, Master Kepler, you were not meant for teaching?'

Johannes looked up in alarm, but the rector was regarding him only with concern, and a touch of amusement. He was a gentle, somewhat scattered person, a scholar and physician; no doubt he knew what it was to stand all day in class wishing to be elsewhere. He had always shown kindness to this strange little man from Tübingen, who at first had so appalled the more stately members of the staff with his frightful manners and disconcerting blend of friendliness, excitability and arrogance. Papius had more than once defended him to the supervisors.

'I am not a good teacher,' Johannes mumbled, 'I know. My gifts lie in other directions.'

'Ah yes,' said the rector, coughing; 'your astronomy.' He peered at the inspectors' report on the desk before him. 'You teach *that* well, it seems?'

'But I have no students!'

'Not your fault – Pastor Zimmermann himself says here that astronomy is not everyone's meat. He recommends that you be put to teaching arithmetic and Latin rhetoric in the upper school, until we can find more pupils eager to become astronomers.'

Johannes understood that he was being laughed at, albeit gently.

'They are ignorant barbarians!' he cried suddenly, and a log fell out of the fire. 'All they care for is hunting and warring and looking for fat dowries for their heirs. They hate and despise philosophy and philosophers. They they they – they do not *deserve* . . .' He broke off, pale with rage and alarm. These mad outbursts must stop.

Rector Papius smiled the ghost of a smile. 'The inspectors?'

'The . . .?'

'I understood you to be describing our good Pastor Zimmermann and his fellow inspectors. It was of them we were speaking.'

Johannes put a hand to his brow. 'I—I meant of course those who will not send their sons for proper instruction.'

'Ah. But I think, you know, there are many among our noble families, and among the merchants also, who would consider astronomy *not* a proper subject for their sons to study. They burn at the stake poor wretches who have had less dealings with the moon than you do in your classes. I am not defending this benighted attitude to your science, you understand, but only drawing it to your attention, as it is my—'

'But—'

'—As it is my *duty* to do.'

They sat and eyed each other, Johannes sullen, the rector apologetically firm. Grey rain wept on the window, the smoke billowed. Johannes sighed. 'You see, Herr Rector, I cannot—'

'But try, will you, Master Kepler: try?'

He tried, he tried, but how could he be calm? His brain teemed. A chaos of ideas and images churned within him. In class he fell silent more and more frequently, standing stock still, deaf to the sniggering of his students, like a crazed hierophant. He traipsed the streets in a daze, and more than once was nearly run down by horses. He wondered if he were ill. Yet it was more as if he were . . . in love! In love, that is, not with any individual object, but generally. The notion, when he hit on it, made him laugh.

At the beginning of 1595 he received a sign, if not from God himself then from a lesser deity surely, one of those whose task is to encourage the elect of this world. His post at the Stiftsschule carried with it the title of calendar maker for the province of Styria. The previous autumn, for a fee of twenty florins from the public coffers, he had drawn up an astrological calendar for the coming year, predicting great cold and an invasion by the Turks. In January there was such a frost that shepherds in the Alpine farms froze to death on the hillsides, while on the first day of the new year the Turk launched a campaign which, it was said, left the whole country from Neustadt to Vienna devastated. Johannes was charmed with this prompt vindication of his powers (and secretly astonished). O a sign, yes, surely. He set to work in earnest on the cosmic mystery.

He had not the solution, yet; he was still posing the questions. The first of these was: Why are there just six planets in the solar system? Why not five, or seven, or a thousand for that matter? No one, so far as he knew, had ever thought to ask it before. It became for him the fundamental mystery. Even the formulation of such a question struck him as a singular achievement.

He was a Copernican. At Tübingen his teacher Michael Mästlin had introduced him to that Polish master's world system. There was for Kepler something almost holy, something redemptive almost, in that vision of an ordered clockwork of sun-centred spheres. And yet he saw, from the beginning, that there was a defect, a basic flaw in it which had forced Copernicus into all manner of small tricks and evasions. For while the *idea* of the system, as outlined in the first part of *De revolutionibus*, was self-evidently an eternal truth, there was in the working out of the theory an ever increasing accumulation of paraphernalia – the epicycles, the equant point, all that – necessitated surely by some awful original accident. It was as if the master had let fall from trembling hands his marvellous model of the world's working, and on the ground it had picked up in its spokes and the fine-spun wire of its frame bits of dirt and dead leaves and the dried husks of worn-out concepts.

Copernicus was dead fifty years, but now for Johannes he rose again, a mournful angel that must be wrestled with before he could press on to found his own system. He might sneer at the epicycles and the equant point, but they were not to be discarded easily. The Canon from Ermland had been, he suspected, a greater mathematician than ever Styria's calendar maker would be. Johannes raged against his own inadequacies. He might know there was a defect, and a grave one, in the Copernican system, but it was a different matter to find it. Nights he would start awake thinking he had heard the old man his adversary laughing at him, goading him.

And then he made a discovery. He realised that it was not so much in what he *had* done that Copernicus had erred: his sin had been one of omission. The great man, Johannes now understood, had been concerned only to see the nature of things demonstrated, not explained. Dissatisfied with the Ptolemaic conception of the world, Copernicus had devised a better, a more elegant system, which yet, for all its seeming radicalism, was intended only, in the schoolman's phrase, to save the phenomena, to set up a model which need not be empirically true, but only plausible according to the observations.

Then had Copernicus believed that his system was a picture of reality, or had he been satisfied that it agreed, more or less, with appearances? Or did the question arise? There was no sustained music in that old man's world, only chance airs and fragments, broken harmonies, scribbled cadences. It would be Kepler's task to draw it together, to make it sing. For truth was the missing music. He lifted his eyes to the bleak light of winter in the window and hugged himself. Was it not wonderful, the logic of things? Troubled by an inelegance in the Ptolemaic system, Copernicus had erected his great monument to the sun, in which there was embedded the flaw, the pearl, for Johannes Kepler to find.

But the world had not been created in order that it should sing. God was not frivolous. From the start he held to this, that the song was incidental, arising naturally from the harmonious relation of things. Truth itself was, in a way, incidental. Harmony was all. (Something wrong, something wrong! but he ignored it.) And harmony, as Pythagoras had shown, was the product of mathematics. Therefore the harmony of the spheres must conform to a mathematical pattern. That such a pattern existed Johannes had no doubt. It was his principal axiom that nothing in the world was created by God without a plan the basis of which is to be found in geometrical quantities. And man is godlike precisely, and only, because he can think in terms that mirror the divine pattern. He had written: The mind grasps a matter so much the more correctly the closer it approaches pure quantities as its source. Therefore his method for the task of identifying the cosmic design must be, like the design itself, founded in geometry.

Spring came to Graz and, as always, took him by surprise. He looked out one day and there it was in the flushed air, a quickening, a sense of vast sudden swooping, as if the earth had hurtled into a narrowing bend of space. The city sparkled, giving off light from throbbing window panes and polished stone, from blue and gold pools of rain in the muddied streets. Johannes kept much indoors. It disturbed him, how closely the season matched his present mood of restlessness and obscure longing. The Shrovetide carnival milled under his window unheeded, except when a comic bugle blast or the drunken singing of revellers shattered his concentration, and he bared his teeth in a soundless snarl.

Perhaps he was wrong, perhaps the world was not an ordered construct governed by immutable laws? Perhaps God, after all, like the creatures of his making, prefers the temporal to the eternal, the makeshift to the perfected, the toy bugles and bravos of misrule to the music of the spheres. But no, no, despite these doubts, no: his God was above all a god of order. The world works by geometry, for geometry is the earthly paradigm of divine thought.

Late into the nights he laboured, and stumbled through his days in a trance. Summer came. He had been working without cease for six months, and all he had achieved, if achievement it could be called, was the conviction that it was not with the planets themselves, their positions and velocities, that he must chiefly deal, but with the intervals between their orbits. The values for these distances were those set out by Copernicus, which were not much more reliable than Ptolemy's, but he had to assume, for his sanity's sake, that they were sound enough for his purpose. Time and time over he combined and recombined them, searching for the relation which they hid. Why are there just six planets? That was a question, yes. But a profounder asking was, why are there just these distances between them? He waited, listening for the whirr of wings. On that ordinary morning in July came the answering angel. He was in class. The day was warm and bright. A fly buzzed in the tall window, a rhomb of sunlight lay at his feet. His students, stunned with boredom, gazed over his head out of glazed eyes. He was demonstrating a theorem out of Euclid – afterwards, try as he might, he could not remember which – and had prepared on the blackboard an equilateral triangle. He took up the big wooden compass, and immediately, as it always contrived to do, the monstrous thing bit him. With his wounded thumb in his mouth he turned to the easel and began to trace two circles, one within the triangle touching it on its three sides, the second circumscribed and intersecting the vertices. He stepped back, into that box of dusty sunlight, and blinked, and suddenly something, his heart perhaps, dropped and bounced, like an athlete performing a miraculous feat upon a trampoline, and he thought, with rapturous inconsequence: I shall live for ever. The ratio of the outer to the inner circle was identical with that of the orbits of Saturn and Jupiter, the furthermost planets, and here, within these circles, determining that ratio, was inscribed an equilateral triangle, the fundamental figure in geometry. Put therefore between the orbits of Jupiter and Mars a square, between Mars and earth a pentagon, between earth and Venus a . . . Yes. O yes. The diagram, the easel, the very walls of the room dissolved to a shimmering liquid, and young Master Kepler's lucky pupils were treated to the rare and gratifying spectacle of a teacher swabbing tears from his eyes and trumpeting juicily into a dirty handkerchief.

* * *

AT DUSK he rode out of the forest of Schönbuch. The bright March day had turned to storm, and a tawny light was sinking in the valley. The Neckar glimmered, slate-blue and cold. He stopped on the brow of a hill and stood in the stirrups to breathe deep the brave tempestuous air. He remembered Swabia not like this, strange and fierce: was it he, perhaps, that had changed? He had new gloves, twenty florins in his purse, leave of absence from the Stiftsschule, this dappled grey mare lent him by his friend the district secretary of Styria, Stefan Speidel, and, safe in a satchel by his side, wrapped in oilskin, most precious of all, his manuscript. The book was done, he had come to Tübingen to publish it. Black rain was falling when he entered the narrow streets of the town, and lanterns flickered on the bastioned walls of Hohentübingen above him. After the annunciation of July, it had taken seven more months of labour, and the incorporation of a third dimension into his calculations, to round out his theory and complete the *Mysterium*. Night, storm, a solitary traveller, the muted magnificence of the world; a trickle of rain got under his collar, and his shoulder-blades quivered like nascent wings.

Presently he was sitting in a bed, in a low brown room at The Boar, with a filthy blanket pulled to his chin, eating oatcakes and drinking mulled wine. Rain drummed on the roof. From the tavern below there rose a raucous singing – fine hearty people, the Swabians, and prodigious topers. Many a skinful of Rhenish he himself as a student had puked up on that rush-strewn floor down there. It surprised him, how happy he was to be back in his homeland. He was downing the dregs of the jug in a final toast to Mistress Fame, that large and jaunty goddess, when the potboy banged on the door and summoned him forth. Bleared and grinning, half drunk, and still with the blanket clutched about him, he struggled down the rickety stairs. The aleroom had the look of a ship's cabin, the drinkers swaying, candlelight swinging, and, beyond the streaming windows, the heaving of the oceanic night. Michael Mästlin, his friend and sometime teacher, rose from a table to meet him. They shook hands, and found themselves grappling with an unexpected shyness. Johannes without preamble said: 'I have written my book.' He frowned at the filthy table and the leathern cups: why did things not quake at his news?

Professor Mästlin was eyeing the blanket. 'Are you ill?'

'What? No; cold, wet. I have lately arrived. You had my message? But of course, since you are here. Ha. Though my piles, forgive my mentioning it, are terrible, after that journey.'

'You don't mean to lodge here, surely? – no no, you shall stay with me. Come, lean on my arm, we must see to your bags.'

'I am not—'

'Come now, I say. You are on fire, man, and your hands, look, they're shaking.'

'I am not, I tell you, I am *not ill.*'

The fever lasted for three days. He thought he might die. Supine on a couch in Mästlin's rooms he raved and prayed, plagued by visions of gaudy devastation and travail. His flesh oozed a noxious sweat: where did it come from, so much poison? Mästlin nursed him with a bachelor's unhandy tenderness, and on the fourth morning he woke, a delicate vessel lined with glass, and saw through an angle of window above him small clouds sailing in a patch of blue sky, and he was well.

Like a refining fire the fever had rinsed him clean. He went back to his book with new eyes. How could he have imagined it was finished? Squatting in a tangle of sheets he attacked the manuscript, scoring, cutting, splicing, taking the theory apart and reassembling it plane by plane until it seemed to him miraculous in its newfound elegance and strength. The window above him boomed, buffeted by gales, and when he raised himself on an elbow he could see the trees shuddering in the college yard. He imagined washes of that eminent exhilarated air sweeping through him also. Mästlin brought him his food, boiled fish, soups, stewed lights, but otherwise left him alone now; he was nervous of this excitable phenomenon, twenty years his junior, perched on the couch in a soiled nightshirt, like an animated doll, day after day, scribbling. He warned him that the sickness might not be gone, that the feeling of clarity he boasted of might be another phase of it. Johannes agreed, for what was this rage to work, this rapture of second thoughts, if not an ailment of a kind?

But he recovered from that too, and at the end of a week the old doubts and fears were back. He looked at his remade manuscript. Was it so much better than before? Had he not merely replaced the old flaws with new ones? He turned to Mästlin for reassurance. The Professor, shying under this intensity of need, frowned into a middle distance, as if surreptitiously spying out a hole down which to bolt. 'Yes,' he said, coughing, 'yes, the idea is, ah, ingenious, certainly.'

'But do you think it is *true*?'

Mästlin's frown deepened. It was a Sunday morning. They walked on the common behind the main hall of the university. The elms thrashed under a violent sky. The Professor had a grizzled beard and a drinker's nose. He weighed matters carefully before committing them to words. Europe considered him a great astronomer. 'I am,' he announced, 'of the opinion that the mathematician has achieved his goal when he advances hypotheses to which the phenomena correspond as closely as possible. You yourself would also withdraw, I believe, if someone could offer still better principles than yours. It by no means follows that the reality immediately conforms to the detailed hypotheses of every master.'

Johannes, debilitated and ill-tempered, scowled. This was the first time he had ventured out since the fever had abated. He felt transparent. There was a whirring high in the air, and then suddenly a crash of bells that made his nerves vibrate. 'Why waste words?' he said, yelled, bells, *damn*. 'Geometry existed before the Creation, is co-eternal with the mind of God, *is God himself*. . .'

Bang.

'O!' Mästlin stared at him.

'. . . For what,' smoothly, 'exists in God that is not God himself?' A grey wind swarmed through the grass to meet him; he shivered. 'But we are mouthing quotations merely: tell me what you truly think.'

'I have said what I think,' Mästlin snapped.

'But that, forgive me, *magister*, is scholastic shilly-shally.'

'Well then, I am a schoolman!'

'You, who teaches his students – who taught *me* – the heliocentric doctrine of Copernicus, *you* a schoolman?' but turned on the professor all the same a thoughtful sidelong glance.

Mästlin pounced. 'Aha, but that was also a schoolman, *and a* saver of the phenomena!'

'He only—'

'A schoolman, sir! Copernicus respected the ancients.'

'Well then; but I do not?'

'It seems to me, young man, that you have not much respect for anything!'

'I respect the past,' Johannes said mildly. 'But I wonder if it is the business of philosophers to follow slavishly the teaching of former masters?'

He did: he wondered: was it? Raindrops like conjured coins spattered the pavestones. They gained the porch of the Aula Maxima. The doors were shut and bolted within, but there was room enough for them to shelter under the stone Platonic seal. They stood in silence, gazing out. Mästlin breathed heavily, his annoyance working him like a bellows. Johannes, oblivious of the other's anger, idly noted a flock of sheep upon the common, their lugubriously noble heads, their calm eyes, how they champed the grass with such fastidiousness, as if they were not merely feeding but performing a delicate and onerous labour: God's mute meaningless creatures, so many and various. Sometimes like this the world bore in upon him suddenly, all that which is without apparent pattern or shape, but is simply *there*. The wind tossed a handful of rooks out of the great trees. Faintly there came the sound of singing, and up over the slope of the common a ragged file of young boys marched, wading against the gale. Their song, one of Luther's stolid hymns, quavered in the tumultuous air. Kepler with a pang recognised the shapeless tunic of the seminary: thus he, once. They passed by, a tenfold ghost, and, as the rain grew heavy, broke file and scampered the last few paces, yelling, into the shelter of St Anne's chapel under the elms. Mästlin was saying: '. . . to Stuttgart, where I have business at Duke Frederick's court.' He paused, waiting for a response; his tone was conciliatory. 'I have drawn up a calendar at the Duke's bidding, and must deliver it . . .' He tried again: 'You have done similar work, of course.'

'What? O, calendars, yes; it is all a necromantic monkeyshine, though.'

Mästlin stared. 'All . . .?'

'Sortilege and star magic, all that. And yet,' pausing, 'yet I believe that the stars do influence our affairs . . .' He broke off and frowned. The past was marching through his head into a limitless future. Behind them the doors with a rattle opened a little way and a skeletal figure peered at them and immediately withdrew. Mästlin sighed. 'Will you go with me to Stuttgart or will you not!'

They set out early next day for the Württemberg capital. Kepler's humour was greatly improved, and by the time they reached the first stop, Mästlin was slumped speechless in a corner of the post coach, dazed by a three-hour disquisition on planets and periodicity and perfect forms. They intended staying in Stuttgart perhaps a week; Johannes was to remain there for six months.

He conceived a masterly plan to promote his theory of celestial geometry. 'You see,' he confided to his fellow diners at the *trippeltisch* in the Duke's palace, 'I have designed a drinking cup, about this size, which shall be a model of the world according to my system, cast in silver, with the signs of the planets cut in precious stones – Saturn a diamond, the moon a pearl, and so on – and, mark this, with a mechanism to serve through seven little taps, from the seven planets, seven different kinds of beverage!'

The company gazed at him. He smiled, basking in their silent amaze. A portly man in a periwig, whose florid features and upright bearing bespoke a *jovian imperium*, extracted a bit of gristle from his mouth and asked:

'And who, pray, is to finance this wonderful project?'

'Why, sir, his grace the Duke. That is why I am here. For I know that princes like to play with clever toys.'

'Indeed?'

A blowsy lady, with a lot of fine old lace at her throat and what looked suspiciously like a venereal herpes coming into bloom on her upper lip, leaned forward for a good look at this bizarre young man. 'Well then you must,' she said, nodding disconcertingly under the weight of her elaborate capuchon 'cultivate my husband,' and let fall an unnerving shriek of laughter. 'He is second secretary to the Bohemian ambassador, you know.'

Johannes bobbed his head in what he felt would pass for a bow in this exalted company. 'I should be most honoured to meet your husband,' and, for a final flourish, '*madame*.'

The lady beamed, and extended a hand palm upward across the table, offering him, as if it were a dish of delicacies, the florid personage in the periwig, who looked down on him and suddenly showed, like a seal of office, a mouthful of gold teeth.

'Duke Frederick, young sir,' he said, 'let me assure you, is careful with his money.'

They all laughed, as at a familiar joke, and returned to their plates. A young soldier with a moustache, dismembering a piece of chicken, eyed him thoughtfully. 'Seven different kinds of beverage, you say?'

Johannes ignored the martial manner.

'Seven, yes,' he said: '*aqua vitae* from the sun, brandy from Mercury, Venus mead, and water from the moon,' busily ticking them off on his fingers, 'Mars a vermouth, Jupiter a white wine, and from Saturn—' he tittered '—from Saturn will come only a bad old wine or beer, so that those ignorant of astronomy may be exposed to ridicule.'

'How?' The chicken leg came asunder with a thwack. Kepler's answer was a smug smile. Tellus, the Duke's chief gardener, a jolly fat fellow with a smooth bald skull whose presence at this travellers' table was the result of a recent upheaval in protocol, laughed and said: 'Caught, caught!' and the soldier reddened. He had oily brown curls that fell to the collar of his velvet surcoat.

A bird-like person stuck his head on its stalk of neck from behind the shoulder of Kepler's neighbour and quacked: 'O but, you mean to say, do you, do I understand you, that we are not to be as it were, not to be told your wonderful, ah, theory? Eh?' He laughed and laughed, mercurial and mad, waving his little hands.

'I intend,' Johannes confided, 'to recommend secrecy to the Duke. Each of the different parts of the cup shall be made by different silversmiths, and assembled later, ensuring that my *inventum* is not revealed before the proper time.'

'Your what?' his neighbour grunted, fuming abruptly, a swarthy saturnine fellow with a peasant's head – Johannes later learned he was a baron – who until now had sat as if deaf, consuming indiscriminately plate after plate of food.

'Latin,' the periwig said shortly. 'He means invention,' and bent on Kepler a look of inordinately stern rebuke.

'I mean, yes, invention . . .' Johannes said meekly. All at once he was filled with misgiving. The table and these people, and the hall behind him with its jumbled hierarchy of other tables, the scurrying servants and the uproar of the crowd at feed, all of it was suddenly a manifestation of irremediable disorder. His heart sank. A breezy request for an audience with the Duke, dashed off on the day he arrived at court, had not been replied to; now, fully a week later, the icy blast of that silence struck him for the first time. How could he have been such a fool, and entertain such high hopes?

He packed up his designs for the cosmic cup and prepared to depart for Graz immediately. Mästlin, however, calling up a last reserve of patience, held him back, urging him to draft another, more carefully considered plea. Preening, he allowed himself to be convinced. His second letter came back with eerie promptness that same evening, bearing in the margin in a broad childish hand a note inviting him to make a model of his cup, *and when we see it and decide that it is worth being made in silver, the means shall not want.* Mästlin squeezed his arm, and he, beside himself, could only smile for bliss and breathe: '*We* . . .!'

It took him a week to build the model, sitting on the cold floor of his room at the top of a windy turret with scissors and paste and strips of coloured paper. It was a pretty thing, he thought, with the planets marked in red upon sky-blue orbits. He placed it lovingly into the complex channels that would carry it to the Duke and settled down to wait. More weeks went past, a month, another and yet another. Mästlin had long since returned to Tübingen to oversee the printing of the *Mysterium*. Johannes became a familiar figure in the dull life of the court, another of those poor demented supplicants who wandered like a belt of satellites around the invisible presence of the Duke. Then a letter came from Mästlin: Frederick had requested his expert opinion in the matter. An audience was granted. Kepler was indignant: expert opinion indeed!

He was received in a vast and splendid hall. The fireplace of Italian marble was taller than he. A gauze of pale light flowed down from enormous windows. On the ceiling, itself a pendant miracle of plaster garlands and moulded heads, an oval painting depicted a vertiginous scene of angels ascending about an angry bearded god enthroned on dark air. The room was crowded, the milling courtiers at once aimless and intent, as if performing an intricate dance the pattern of which could be perceived only from above. A flunkey touched Kepler's elbow, he turned, and a delicate little man stepped up to him and said:

'You are Repleus?'

'No, yes, I—'

'Quite so. We have studied your model of the world,' smiling tenderly; 'it makes no sense.'

Duke Frederick was marvellously got up in a cloth-of-gold tunic and velvet breeches. Jewels glittered on his tiny hands. He had close-cut grey curls like many small springs and on his chin a little horn of hair. He was smooth, soft, and Johannes thought of the sweet waxen flesh of a chestnut nestled snug within the lustrous cranium of its shell. He perceived the measure of the courtiers' saraband, for here was the centre of it. He began to babble an explanation of the geometry of his world system, but the Duke lifted a hand. 'All that is very correct and interesting, no doubt, but wherein lies the significance in *general*?'

The paper model stood upon a lacquered table. Two of the orbits had come unstuck. Kepler suspected a ducal finger had been dabbling in its innards.

'There are, sir,' he said, 'only five regular perfect solids, also called the Platonic forms. They are perfect because all their sides are identical.' Rector Papius would be impressed with his patience. 'Of the countless forms in the world of three dimensions, only these five figures are perfect: the tetrahedron or pyramid, bounded by four equilateral triangles, the cube, with six squares, the octohedron with eight equilaterals, the dodecahedron, bounded by twelve pentagons, and the icosahedron, which has twenty equilateral triangles.'

'Twenty,' the Duke said, nodding.

'Yes. I hold, as you see here illustrated, that into the five intervals between the six planets of the world, these five regular solids may be . . .' He was jostled. It was the mercurial madman from the *trippeltisch*, trying to get past him to the Duke, laughing still and pursing his lips in silent apology. Johannes got an elbow into the creature's ribs and pushed. '. . . may be inscribed . . .' and *pushed* '. . . so as to satisfy precisely,' panting, 'the intervallic quantities as measured and set down by the ancients.' He smiled; that was prettily put.

The loony was pawing him again, and now he noticed that they were all here, the venereal lady, and Meister Tellus, Kaspar the soldier, and of course the periwig, and, way out at the edge of the dance, the gloomy baron. Well, what of it? He was putting them in their places. He was suddenly intensely aware of himself, young, brilliant, and somehow wonderfully fragile. 'And so, as may be seen,' he said airily, 'between the orbits of Saturn and Jupiter I have placed the cube, between those of Jupiter and Mars the tetrahedron, Mars and earth the dodecahedron, earth and Venus the icosahedron, and, look, let me show you—' pulling the model asunder like a fruit to reveal its secret core: 'between Venus and Mercury the octahedron. So!'

The Duke frowned.

'That is clear, yes,' he said, 'what you have done, and how; but, forgive me, may we ask *why*?'

'Why?' looking from the dismembered model to the little man before him; 'well . . . well because . . . '

A froth of crazy laughter bubbled at his ear.

* * *

NOTHING CAME OF the project. The Duke did agree that the cup might be cast, but promptly lost interest. The court silversmith was sceptical, and there were cries of dismay from the Treasury. Johannes returned disheartened to Graz. He had squandered half a year on a craving for princely favour. It was a lesson he told himself he must remember. Presently, though, the whole humiliating affair was driven from his thoughts by a far weightier concern.

It was one of the school inspectors, the physician Oberdorfer, who first approached him, with a stealthy smile and – could it be? – a wink, and invited him to come on a certain day to the house of Herr Georg Hartmann von Stubenberg, a merchant of the town. He went, thinking he was to be asked to draw up a nativity or another of his famous calendars. But there was no commission. He did not even meet Herr Burghermeister Hartmann, and forever after that name was to echo in his memory like the reverberation of a past catastrophe. He loitered on a staircase for an hour, clutching a goblet of thin wine and trying to think of something to say to Dr Oberdorfer. In the wide hallway below groups of people came and went, overdressed women and fat businessmen, a bishop and attendant clerics, a herd of hip-booted horsemen from the Archduke's cavalry, clumsy as centaurs. One of Hartmann's children was being married. From a farther room a string band sent music arching through the house like aimless flights of fine bright arrows. Johannes grew agitated. He had not been officially invited, and he was troubled by images of challenge and ejection. What could Oberdorfer want with him? The doctor, a large pasty man with pendulous jowls and exceedingly small moist eyes, vibrated with nervous anticipation, scanning the passing throng below and wheezing under his breath in tuneless counterpoint to the rapt silvery slitherings of the minstrels. At last he touched a finger to Kepler's sleeve. A stout young woman in blue was approaching the foot of the stairs. Dr Oberdorfer leered. 'She is handsome, yes?'

'Yes, yes,' Johannes muttered, looking hard at a point in air, afraid that the lady below might hear; 'quite, ah, handsome.'

Oberdorfer, whispering sideways like a bad ventriloquist, inclined his great trembling head until it almost rested against Kepler's ear. 'Also she is rich, so I am told.' The young woman paused, leaning down to exclaim over a pale pursed little boy in velveteen, who turned a stony face away and tugged furiously at his nurse's hand. Kepler all his life would remember that surly Cupid. 'Her father,' the doctor hissed, 'her father has estates, you know, to the south. They say he has settled a goodly fortune to her name.' His voice sank lower still. 'And of course, she is certain to have been provided for also by her . . .' faltering '. . . her late, ah, husbands.'

'Her . . .?'

'Husbands, yes.' Dr Oberdorfer briefly shut his little eyes. 'Most tragic, most tragic: she is twice a widow. And so young!'

It dawned on Johannes what was afoot. Blushing, he ascended a step in fright. The widow threw him a fraught look. The doctor said: 'Her name is Barbara Müller – née, aha, Müller.' Johannes stared at him, and he coughed. 'A little joke, forgive me. Her family is Müller – Müller zu Gössendorf – which is also by coincidence the name of her latest, late, her *last* that is, husband . . .' trailing off to an unhappy hum.

'Yes?' Johannes said faintly, fuming away from the other's aquatic eye, and then heard himself add: 'She is somewhat fat, all the same.'

Dr Oberdorfer winced, and then, grinning bravely, with elephantine roguishness he said:

'Plump, rather, Master Kepler, plump. And the winters are cold, eh? Ha. Ha ha.'

And he took the young man firmly by the elbow and steered him up the stairs, into an alcove, where there waited a sleek grim dandified man who looked Johannes up and down without enthusiasm and said: 'My dear sir,' as if he had, Jobst Müller, been rehearsing it.

So began the long, involved and sordid business of his wiving. From the start he feared the prospect of the plump young widow. Women were a foreign country, he did not speak the language. One night four years previously, on a visit to Weilderstadt, flushed with ale and wanting to reassert himself after losing heavily at cards, he had consorted with a scrawny girl, a virgin, so he was assured. That was his sole experience of love. Afterwards the drab had laughed, and tested between her little yellow teeth the coin he had given her. Yet beyond the act itself, that frantic froglike swim to the cataract's edge, he had found something touching in her skinny flanks and her frail chest, that rank rose under its furred cap of bone. She had been *smaller* than he; not so Frau Müller. No, no, he was not enthusiastic. Was he not happy as he was? Happier at least than he suspected he would be with a wife. Later, when the marrige had come to grief, he blamed a large part of the disaster on the unseemly bartering that had sold him into it.

He discovered how small a place was Graz: everyone he knew seemed to have a hand in the turbulent making of this match. Sometimes he fancied he could detect a prurient leer on the face of the town itself. Dr Oberdorfer was the chief negotiator, assisted by Heinrich Osius, a former professor of the Stiftsschule. In September these two worthies went together down to Mühleck to hear Jobst Müller's terms. The miller opened the bidding coyly, declaring himself not at all eager to see his daughter wed again. This Kepler was a poor specimen, with small means and an unpromising future. And what of his birth? Was he not the son of a profligate soldier? Dr Oberdorfer countered with a speech in praise of the young man's industry and prodigious learning. Duke Frederick of Württemberg, no less, was his patron. Then Osius, who had been brought for the benefit of his bluntness, mentioned

Mistress Barbara's state: so young, and twice a widow! Jobst Müller frowned, his jaw twitching. He was growing weary of that refrain.

The negotiators resumed confident to Graz. Then an unexpected and serious obstacle arose, when Stefan Speidel the district secretary, Kepler's friend, declared himself opposed to the match. He knew the lady, and thought she should be better provided for. Besides, as he admitted in confidence to Kepler, he wished her to marry an acquaintance of his at court, a man of rising influence. He apologised, waving a hand; you will understand, of course, Johannes? Johannes found it hard to conceal his relief. 'Well yes, Stefan, certainly, I understand, if it is a matter of your conscience, and court affairs, O completely, completely!'

The printing of the *Mysterium* progressed. Mästlin had secured the blessing of the Tübingen college senate for the work, and was supervising the setting at Gruppenbach the printers. He reported faithfully the completion of each chapter, grumbling over the expense in cash and energy. Kepler wrote him back a cheerful note pointing out that attendance at this birth would, after all, ensure the midwife's immortal fame.

Kepler was himself busy. The school authorities, incensed by his six-month absence at the Württemberg court, had followed their inspectors' advice and set him arithmetic and rhetoric classes in the upper school. These were a torment. Rector Papius, despite his half-hearted threats, had held off from increasing the young master's duties – but Papius had been summoned to the chair of medicine at Tübingen. His successor, Johannes Regius, was a stern lean Calvinist. He and Kepler were enemies from the first. Regius considered the young man disrespectful and ill-bred, and in need of taming: the pup should marry. Jobst Müller, with the sudden smack of a card player claiming a trump, agreed, for Speidel's scheme had come to nothing, and the miller of Mühleck still had a daughter on his hands. Kepler's heart sank. In February of 1597 the betrothal was signed, and on a windy day at the end of April, *sub calamitoso caelo*, Mistress Barbara Müller put off her widow's weeds and was married for the third and last time in her short life. Kepler was then aged twenty-five years, seven months and . . . but he had not the heart to compute the figures, nor the courage, considering the calamitous disposition of the stars.

The wedding feast took place, after a brief ceremony in the collegiate church, at Barbara's inherited house on the Stempfergasse. Jobst Müller, when the deal was closed and he could afford again the luxury of contempt, had declared that he would not see celebrated in his own home, before his tenants and his servants, this affront to his family's name. He had settled on Kepler a sum of cash, as well as the yield of a vineyard and an allowance for the child Regina's upbringing. Was not that enough? He sat in silence throughout the morning, scowling under the brim of his hat, morosely drunk on his own Mühleck wine. Kepler, seeing him in a sulk, squeezed a drop of bitter satisfaction from the day by calling on him repeatedly to propose a toast, to make a speech, throwing an arm about his shoulders and urging him to sing up, sing up, sir, a rousing chorus of some good old Gössendorf ballad.

Baiting his father-in-law was a way of avoiding his bride. They had hardly spoken, had hardly met, during the long months of negotiation, and today when by chance they found themselves confronting each other they were paralysed by embarrassment. She looked, he gloomily observed, radiant, that seemed the appropriate word. She was pretty, in a vacant way. She twittered. Yet when amid a chiming of uplifted glasses he pressed his palms awkwardly to her damp trembling back and kissed her for the benefit of the company, he suddenly found himself holding something unexpectedly vivid and exotic, a creature of another species, and, catching her warm spicy smell, he was excited. He began to swill in earnest then, and was soon deliriously drunk. But even that was not enough to stifle his fright.

Yet in the weeks and months that followed he was almost happy. In May the first copies of the *Mysterium* arrived from Tübingen. The slim volume pleased him enormously. His pleasure was a little tainted however by a small obscure shame, as if he had committed an indiscretion the awfulness of which had not yet been noticed by an inattentive public. This was the first blush of that patronising attitude to the book, which in later years was to make it seem the production of a heedless but inspired child that he but vaguely remembered having been. He distributed copies among selected astronomers and scholars, and a few influential Styrians that he knew, all of whom, to his indignation and dismay, proved less than deafening in their shouts of surprise and praise.

The number of volumes he had contracted to buy under the printer's terms cost him thirty-three florins. Before his marriage he could not have afforded it, but now, it seemed, he was rich. Besides the sum Jobst Müller had settled on him, his salary had been increased by fifty florins annually. That, however, was a trifle compared with his wife's fortune. He was never to succeed in her lifetime in finding out how much exactly she had inherited, but it was greater even than the most eager of matchmakers had imagined. Regina had a sum of ten thousand from her late father, Wolf Lorenz the cabinetmaker, Barbara's first casualty. If the child had that much, how much more must her mother have got? Kepler rubbed his hands, elated, and shocked at himself too.

There was another form of wealth, more palpable than cash and as quickly squandered, which was a kind of burgeoning fortune of the senses. Barbara, for all her twittering silliness, was flesh, a corporeal world, wherein he touched and found startlingly real, something that was wholly other and yet recognisable. He flared under her light, her smell, the faintly salt taste of her skin. It took time. Their first encounters were a failure. On the wedding night, in the vast four-poster in the bedroom overlooking Stempfergasse, they collided in the dark with a crunch. He felt as if he were grappling with a heavy hot corpse. She fell all over him, panting, got an elbow somehow into his chest and knocked the wind out of him, while the bed creaked and groaned like the ghost voice of its former tenant, poor dead Marx Müller, lamenting. When the union was consummated at last, she turned away and immediately fell asleep, her snores a raucous and monotonously repeated protest. It was not until many months later, when the summer was over and cold winds were blowing down from the Alps, that they at last found each other, briefly.

He remembered the evening. It was September, the trees were already beginning to turn. He had stood up from a good day's work and walked into their bedroom. Barbara was bathing in a tub before a fire of sea-coals, dreamily soaping an extended pink leg. He turned away hastily, but she looked up and smiled at him, dazed with heat. A narrow shaft of late sunlight, worn to the colour of old brass, lay aslant the bed. *Ouf!* she said, and rose in a cascade of suds and slithering water. It was the first time he had seen her entirely naked. Her head sat oddly upon this unfamiliar bare body. Aglow and faintly steaming she displayed herself, big-bummed, her stout legs braced as if to leap, a strongman's shovel-shaped beard glistening in her lap. Her breasts stared, wall-eyed and startled, the dark tips pursed. He advanced on her, his clothes falling away like flakes of shell. She rose on tiptoe to peer past him down into the street, biting her lip and laughing softly. 'Someone will see us, Johannes.' Her shoulder-blades left a damp print of wings upon the sheet. The brazen sword of sunlight smote them.

It was at once too much and not enough. They had surrendered their most intimate textures to a mere conspiracy of the flesh. It took him a long time to understand it; Barbara never did. They had so little in common. She might have tried to understand something of his work, but it was beyond her, for which she hated it. He could have tried also, could have asked her about the past, about Wolf Lorenz the wealthy tradesman, about the rumours that Marx Müller the district paymaster had embezzled state funds, but from the start these were a forbidden topic, jealously guarded by the sentinels of the dead. And so, two intimate strangers lashed together by bonds not of their making, they began to hate each other, as if it were the most natural thing in the world. Kepler turned, hesitantly, shyly, to Regina, offering her all the surplus left over from his marriage, for she represented, frozen in prototype, that very stage of knowing and regard which he had managed to miss in her mother. And Barbara, seeing everything and understanding nothing, grew fitful and began to complain, and sometimes beat the child. She demanded more and more of Kepler's time, engaged him in frantic incoherent conversations, was subject to sudden storms of weeping. One night he found her crouched in the kitchen, gorging herself on pickled fish. The following morning she fainted in his arms, nearly knocking him down. She was pregnant.

She fulfilled her term as she did everything, lavishly, with many alarms and copious tears. She became eerily beautiful, for all her bulk. It was as if she had been designed for just this state, ancient and elemental; with that great belly, those pendant breasts, she achieved a kind of ideal harmony. Kepler began to avoid her: she frightened him now more than ever. He spent the days locked in his study, tinkering with work, writing letters, going over yet again his hopelessly unbalanced accounts, lifting his head now and then to listen for the heavy tread of the goddess.

She went early into labour, blundered into it one morning with shrill cries. The waves of her pain crashed through the house, wave upon wave. Dr Oberdorfer arrived, puffing and mumbling, and heaved himself up the stairs on his black stick like a weary oarsman plying a foundering craft. It struck Kepler that the man was embarrassed, as if he had caught indulging in some base frolic this couple whose troubled destinies he had helped to entangle. Her labour lasted for two days. The rain of February fell, clouding the world without, so that there was only this house throbbing around its core of pain. Kepler trotted up and down in a fever of excitement and dismay, wringing his hands. The child was born at noon, a boy. A great blossom of heedless happiness opened up in Kepler's heart. He held the softly pulsing mite in his hands and understood that he was multiplied. 'We shall call him Heinrich,' he said, 'after my brother – but you will be a better, a finer Heinrich, won't you, yes.' Barbara, pale in her bloodied bed, stared at him emptily through a film of pain.

He drew up a horoscope. It promised all possible good, after a few adjustments. The child would be nimble and bright, apt in mathematical and mechanical skills, imaginative, diligent, charming, O, charming! For sixty days Kepler's happiness endured, then the house was pierced again by screams, miniature echoes of Barbara's lusty howls, and Oberdorfer again sculled himself up the stairs and Kepler snatched the infant in his arms and commanded it not, not to die! He turned on Barbara, she had known, all that pain had told her all was wrong, yet she had said nothing, not a word to warn him, spiteful bitch! The doctor clicked his tongue, for shame, sir, for shame. Kepler rounded on him. And you . . . you . . .! In tears, his vision splintering, he turned away, clasping the creature to him, and felt it twitch, and cough, and suddenly, as if starting in amazement, die: his son. The damp hot head lolled in his hand. What pitiless player had tossed him this tender ball of woe? He was to know other losses, but never again quite like this, like a part of himself crawling blind and mewling into death.

* * *

NOW HIS DAYS DARKENED. The child's fall had torn a hole in the fabric of things, and through this tiny rent the blackness seeped. Barbara would not be consoled. She took to hiding in shuttered rooms, in cubbyholes, even under the bedclothes, nibbling in private her bit of anguish, making not a sound except for now and then a faint dry sobbing, like the scratching of claws, that made Kepler's hair stand on end. He let her be, crouching in his own hiding, watching for what would come next. The game, which they had not realised was a game, had ended; suddenly life was taking them seriously. He remembered the first real beating he had got as a child, his mother a gigantic stranger red with rage, her fists, the startling vividness of pain, the world abruptly shifting into a new version of reality. Yes, and this was worse, he was an adult now, and the game was up.

The year turned, and winter ended. Spring would not this year fool him with false hopes. Something was being surreptitiously arranged, he could sense it, the storm assembling its ingredients from breezes and little clouds and the thrush's song. In April the young Archduke Ferdinand, ruler of all Austria, made a pilgrimage to Italy where at the shrine of Loreto, in a rapture of piety, he swore to suppress the heresy of Protestantism in his realm. The Lutheran province of Styria trembled. All summer there were threats and alarms. Troops were mobilised. By the end of September the churches and the schools had been shut down. At last the edict, long expected, was issued: Lutheran clergy and teachers must quit Austria within a week or face inquisition and possible death.

Jobst Müller hurried up from Mühleck. He had gone over to the Catholics, and expected his son-in-law to follow him without delay. Kepler snorted. I shall do nothing of the kind, sir; mine is the reformed Church, I recognise no other, and stopped himself from adding: *Here I stand!* which would have been to overdo it. And anyway, he was not so brave as his bold words would have it. The prospect of exile terrified him. Where would he go? To Tübingen? To his mother's house in Weilderstadt? Barbara with unwonted vehemence had declared she would not leave Graz. He would lose Regina then also; he would lose everything. No, no, it was unthinkable. Yet it was being thought: his bag was packed, Speidel's mare was borrowed. He would go to Mästlin in Tübingen, welcome or not. Farewell! Barbara's kiss, juicy with grief, landed in his ear. She pressed into his trembling hands little packets of florins and food and clean linen. Regina tentatively came to him, and, her face buried in his cloak, whispered something which he did not catch, which she would not repeat, which was to be for ever, for ever, a small gold link missing from his life. Floundering in a wash of tears he stumbled back and forth between house and horse, not quite knowing how, finally, to go, beating his pockets in search of a handkerchief to stanch his streaming nose and uttering faint phlegmy cries of distress. At last, dumped like a wet sack in the saddle, he was borne out of the city into a tactlessly glorious gold and blue October afternoon.

He rode north along the valley of the Mur, eyeing apprehensively the glittering snowcapped crags of the Alps looming higher the nearer he approached. The roads were busy. He fell in with another traveller, whose name was Wincklemann. He was a Jew, a lens-grinder by trade, and a citizen of Linz: a sallow wedge of face, a bit of beard and a dark ironic eye. When they came down into Linz it was raining, the Danube pock-marked steel, and Kepler was sick. The Jew, taking pity on this mournful wayfarer with his cough and his quiver and his blue fingernails, invited Kepler to come home with him and rest a day or two before turning westward for Tübingen.

The Jew's house was in a narrow street near the river. Wincklemann showed his guest the workshop, a long low room with a furnace at the back tended by a fat boy. The floor and the workbenches were a disorder of broken moulds and spilt sand and wads of oily rag, all blurred under a bluish film of grinding flour. Dropped tears of glass glittered in the gloom about their feet. A low window, giving on to damp cobbles and timbered gables and a glimpse of wharf, let in a grainy whitish light that seemed itself a process of the work conducted here. Kepler squinted at a shelf of books: Nostradamus, Paracelsus, the *Magia naturalis*. Wincklemann watched him, and smiling held aloft in a leaf-brown hand a gobbet of clouded crystal.

'Here is transmutation,' he said, 'a comprehensible magic.'

Behind them the boy bent to the bellows, and the red mouth of the furnace roared. Kepler, his head humming with fever, felt something sweep softly down on him, a shadow, vast and winged.

They climbed to the upper floor, a warren of small dim rooms where the Jew and his family lived. Wincklemann's shy young wife, pale and plump as a pigeon and half his age, served them a supper of sausage and black bread and ale. The air was weighted with a strange sweetish smell. The sons of the house, pale boys with oiled plaits, came forward solemnly to greet their father and his guest. To Kepler it seemed he had strayed into the midst of some ancient attenuated ceremony. After the meal Wincklemann brought out his tobacco pipes. It was Kepler's first smoke; a green sensation, not wholly unpleasant, spread along his veins. He was given wine lightly laced with a distillate of poppy and mandragora. Sleep that night was a plunging steed carrying him headlong through the tumultuous dark, but when he woke in the morning, a thrown rider, the fever was gone. He was puzzled and yet calm, as if some benign but enigmatic potential were being unfurled about him.

Wincklemann demonstrated the implements of his craft, the fine-honed lapstones and the grinding burrs of blued steel. He brought out examples of the glass in all its forms, from sand to polished prism. In return Kepler described his world system, the theory of the five perfect solids. They sat at the long bench under the cobwebbed window with the furnace gasping behind them, and Kepler experienced again that excitement and faintly embarrassed pleasure which he had not known since his student days at Tübingen and the first long discussions with Michael Mästlin.

The Jew had read von Lauchen's *Narratio prima* on the Copernican cosmology. The new theories puzzled and amused him.

'But do you think they are *true*?' said Kepler; the old question.

Wincklemann shrugged. 'True? This is a word I have trouble with.' He never looked so much the Jew as when he smiled. 'Maybe yes, the sun is the centre, the visible god, as Trismegistus says; but when Dr Copernic shows it so in his famous system, what I ask you do we know that is more wonderful than what we knew before?'

Kepler did not understand. 'But science,' he said, frowning, 'science is a method of knowing.'

'Of knowing, yes: but of understanding? I tell you now the difference between the Christian and the Jew, listen. You think nothing is real until it has been spoken. Everything is words with you. Your Jesus Christ is the word made flesh!'

Kepler smiled. Was he being mocked? 'And the Jew?' he said.

'An old joke there is, that at the beginning God told his chosen people everything, everything, so now we know it all – and understand nothing. Only I think it is not such a joke. There are things in our religion which may not be spoken, because to speak such ultimate things is to . . . to damage them. Perhaps it is the same with your science?'

'But . . . damage?'

'I do not know.' He shrugged. 'I am only a maker of lenses, I do not understand these theories, these systems, and I am too old to study them. But you, my friend,' and smiled again, and Kepler knew that he was being laughed at, 'you will do great things, that's plain.'

It was in Linz, under Wincklemann's amused dark gaze, that he first heard faintly the hum of that great five-note chord from which the world's music is made. Everywhere he began to see world-forming relationships, in the rules of architecture and painting, in poetic metre, in the complexities of rhythm, even in colours, in smells and tastes, in the proportions of the human figure. A fine silver string of excitement was tightening steadily within him. In the evenings he sat with his friend in the rooms above the workshop, drinking and smoking, and talking endlessly. He was well enough to travel on to Tübingen, yet made no move to go, though he was still in Austria and the Archduke's men might seize him any time. The Jew watched him out of a peculiar stillness and intensity, and sometimes Kepler, bleared with tobacco and wine, fancied that something was being slowly, lovingly drained from him, a precious impalpable fluid, by that gaze, that intent, patient watching. He thought of those volumes of Nostradamus and Albertus Magnus on the Jew's shelves, of certain silences, of murmurings behind dosed doors, of the grey blurred forms in their sealed jars he had glimpsed in a cupboard in the workshop. Was he being magicked? The notion stirred in him a confused and guilty warmth, a kind of embarrassment, like that which made him turn away from the uxorious smile the Jew sometimes wore in the presence of his young wife. Yes this, *this* was exile.

It ended. One day a messenger from Stefan Speidel came galloping to Wincklemann's door out of a stormy dawn. Kepler, barefoot and shivering, still stuffed with sleep, stood in a damp gust and with trembling fingers broke the familiar seal of the secretariat. A fleck of foam from the horse's champing jaws settled on his eyebrow. The Archduke had consented that an exception be made to the order of general banishment. He could go home again.

Later he had time to consider the ravelled mesh of influence that had saved him. The Jesuits, for their own shady reasons, were sympathetic to his work. It was through a Jesuit, Fr Grienberger of Graz, that the Bavarian Chancellor Herwart von Hohenburg, a Catholic and an amateur scholar, had first consulted him on questions of cosmology in certain ancient texts. They corresponded via the Bavarian ambassador at Prague and the Archduke Ferdinand's secretary, the Capuchin Peter Casal. And then, Herwart was the servant of Duke Maximilian, Ferdinand's cousin, and those two noblemen had studied together at Ingolstadt under Johann Fickler, a firm friend of the Jesuits and a native of Kepler's own Weilderstadt. Thus the strands of the web radiated. Why, when he thought about it, he had advocates everywhere! It worried him, obscurely.

He returned secretly disappointed. Given time, he might have made something of exile. The Stiftsschule was still closed and he was free, there was that at least. But Graz was finished for him, used up. Things were not so bad as they had been, and other exiles had quietly begun to trickle back, but still he thought it prudent to stay indoors. Barbara in November announced another pregnancy, and he retired to the innermost sanctuary of his workroom.

He began to study in earnest, consuming ancients and moderns, Plato and Aristotle, Nicholas of Cues, the Florence academicians. Wincklemann had given him a volume by the cabalist Cornelius Agrippa, whose thinking was so odd and yet so like Kepler's own. He went back to his mathematics, and honed to a fine edge that instrument which up to now he had wielded like a club. He turned to music with a new intensity; Pythagoras's laws of harmony obsessed him. As he had asked why there should be just six planets in the solar system, now he pondered the mystery of musical relationships: why does for instance the ratio 3:5 produce a harmony, but not 5:7? Even astrology, which for so long he had despised, assumed a new significance in its theory of aspects. The world abounded for him now in signature and form. He brooded in consternation on the complexities of the honeycomb, the structure of flowers, the eerie perfection of snowflakes. What had begun in Linz as an intellectual frolic was now his deepest concern.

The new year began well. At the core of this sudden rush of speculations he was at peace. Then, however, gradually, a fearful momentum gathered. The religious turmoil boiled up again, fiercer than ever. Edict followed edict, each one more severe than its predecessor. Lutheran worship in any form was banned. Children were to be baptised only by the Catholic rite and must attend only Jesuit schools. Then they moved on the books. Lutheran writings were rooted out and burned. A pall of smoke hung over the city. Threats whirred in the air, and Kepler shivered. After the burning of the books, what would there be for them but to burn the authors? Things were out of control. He felt as if, head and shoulders back and eyes starting in mortal fright, he were strapped to an uncontrollable machine hurtling faster and faster toward a precipice. The child, a girl, was born in June. She was called Susanna. He dreamed of the ocean. He had never seen it in waking life. It appeared an immense milky calm, silent, immutable and terrifying, the horizon a line of unearthly fineness, a hairline crack in the shell of the world. There was no sound, no movement, not a living creature in sight, unless the ocean itself were living. The dread of that vision polluted his mind for weeks. On a July evening the air pale and still as that phantom sea, he returned to the Stempfergasse after one of his rare ventures abroad in the frightened town, and paused before the house. There was a child playing in the street with a hoop, an old woman with a basket on her arm limping away from him on the other side, a dog in the gutter gnawing a knuckle of bone. Something in the scene chilled him, the careful innocence with which it was arranged in that limitless light, as if to give him a sly nudge. Dr Oberdorfer waited in the hall, regarding him with a lugubrious stricken stare. The infant had died. It was a fever of the brain, the same that had killed little Heinrich. Kepler stood by the bedroom window and watched the day fade, hearing vaguely Barbara's anguished cries behind him and listening in awe to his mind, of its own volition, thinking: My work will be interrupted. He carried the tiny coffin himself to the grave, besieged by visions of conflict and desolation. There were reports from the south that the Turk had massed six hundred thousand men below Vienna. The Catholic council fined him ten florins for having the funeral conducted in the Lutheran rite. He wrote to Mästlin: *No day can soothe my wife's yearning, and the word is close to my heart: O vanity . . .*

Jobst Müller came up again to Graz, demanding that Kepler convert: convert or go, and this time stay away, and he would take his daughter and Regina back with him to Mühleck. Kepler did not deign even to answer. Stefan Speidel was another visitor, a thin, cold, tight-mouthed man in black. His news from court was grim: there would be no exceptions this time. Kepler was beside himself.

'What shall I do, Stefan, what shall I *do*? And my family!' He touched his friend's chill hand. 'You were right to oppose the marriage, I do not blame you for it, you were right—'

'I know that.'

'No, Stefan, I insist . . .' He paused, letting it sink in, and distinctly heard the tiny *ping* of another cord breaking. Speidel had lent him a copy of Plato's *Timaeus* on the day they first met, in Rector Papius's rooms; he must remember to return it. 'Yes, well . . .' wearily. 'O God, what am I to do.'

'There is Tycho Brahe?' Stefan Speidel said, picking a speck of lint from his cloak and turning away, out of Kepler's life for ever.

Yes, there was Tycho. Since June he had been installed at Prague, imperial mathematician to the Emperor Rudolph, at a salary of three thousand florins. Kepler had letters from the Dane urging him to come and share in the royal beneficence. But

Prague! A world away! And yet where was the alternative? Mästlin had written to him: there was no hope of a post at Tübingen. The century approached its end. Baron Johann Friedrich Hoffmann, a councillor to the Emperor and Kepler's sometime patron, on a visit to Graz, invited the young astronomer to join his suite for the journey back to Prague. Kepler packed his bags and his wife and her daughter into a broken-down carriage, and on the first day of the new century, not unamused by the date, he set out for his new world.

It was a frightful journey. They lodged at leaky fortresses and rat-infested military outposts. His fever came on him again, and he endured the miles in a dazed semi-sleep from which Barbara in a panic would shake him, looming down like a form out of his dreams, fearing him dead. He ground his teeth. 'Madam, if you continue to disturb me like this, by God I will box your ears.' And then she wept, and he groaned, cursing himself for a mangy dog.

It was February when they arrived in Prague. Baron Hoffmann settled them at his house, fed them, advanced them monies, and even lent Kepler a hat and a decent cloak for the meeting with Tycho Brahe. But there was no sign of Tycho. Kepler detested Prague. The buildings were crooked and ill-kept, thrown together from mud and straw and undressed planks. The streets were awash with slops, the air putrid. At the end of a week Tycho's son appeared, in company with Frans Gransneb Tengnagel, drunk, the two of them, and sullen. They carried a letter from the Dane, at once formal and fulsome, expressing greasy sentiments of regret that he had not come himself to greet his visitor. Tyge and the Junker were to conduct him to Benatky, but delayed a further week for their pleasure. It was snowing when at last they set out. The castle lay twenty miles to the north of the city, in the midst of a flat flooded countryside. Kepler waited in the guest rooms through a fretful morning, and when the summons came at noon he was asleep. He descended the stony fastness of the castle in a stupor of fever and fright. Tycho Brahe was magisterial. He frowned upon the shivering figure before him and said:

'My elk, sir, my tame elk, for which I had a great love, has been destroyed through the carelessness of an Italian lout.' With a wave of a brocaded arm he swept his guest before him into the high hall where they would breakfast. They sat. '. . . Fell down a staircase at Wandsbeck Castle where they had stopped for the night, having drunk a pot of beer, he says, and broke a leg and died. My elk!'

The vast window, sunlight on the river and the flooded fields, and beyond that the blue distance, and Kepler smiled and nodded, like a clockwork toy, thinking of his dishevelled past and perilous future, and 0.00 something something 9.

II

Astronomia Nova

ENOUGH IS ENOUGH. He plunged down the steep steps and stopped, glaring about the courtyard in angry confusion. A lame groom trundling a handcart hawked and spat, two scullery maids upended a tub of suds. They would make him a clerk, by God, a helper's helper! 'Herr Kepler, Herr Kepler please, a moment . . .' Baron Hoffmann, panting unhappily, hurried down to him. Tycho Brahe remained atop the steps, strenuously indifferent, considering a far-off prospect.

'Well?' said Kepler.

The baron, rheum-eyed grey little man, displayed a pair of empty hands. 'You must give him time, you know, allow him to consider your requests.'

'*He*,' raising his voice against a sudden clamour of hounds, 'he has had a month already, more. I have stated my conditions; I ask the merest consideration. He does nothing.' And, louder again, turning to fling it up the steps: 'Nothing!' Tycho Brahe, still gazing off, lifted his eyebrows a fraction and sighed. The pack of hounds with an ululant cheer burst through a low gate from the kennels and surged across the courtyard, avid brutes with stunted legs and lunatic grins and tiny tight puce scrotums. Kepler scuttled for the steps in fright, but faltered halfway up, prevented by Tycho the Terrible. The Dane glanced down on him with malicious satisfaction, pulling on his gauntlets. Baron Hoffmann turned up to the master of Schloss Benatky a last enquiring glance and then, shrugging, to Kepler:

'You will not stay, sir?'

'I will not stay.' But his voice was unsteady.

Tengnagel and young Tyge came out, squinting in the light, sodden with the dregs of last night's drinking. They brightened, seeing Kepler in a dither. The grooms were bringing up the horses. The dogs, which had quietened, hunched with busy tongues over their parts or ruminatively cocked against the walls, were thrown into a frenzy again by the goitrous blare of a hunting horn. A haze of silvery dust unfurled its sails to the breeze and drifted lazily gatewards, a woman leaned down from a balcony, laughing, and in the sky a panel slid open and spilled upon Benatky a wash of April sunlight that turned the drifting dust to gold.

The baron went away to fetch his carriage. Kepler considered. What was left if he refused Tycho's grudging patronage? The past was gone, Tübingen, Graz, all that, gone. The Dane, thumbs hitched on his belt and fat fingers drumming the taut slope of his underbelly, launched himself down the steps. Baron Hoffmann alighted from the carriage, and Kepler, mumbling, plucked at his sleeve, 'I want to, I want . . .' mumbling.

The baron cupped an ear. 'The noise, I did not quite . . .?'

'I *want*—' a shriek '—to *apologise*.' He closed his eyes briefly. 'Forgive me, I—'

'O but there is no need, I assure you.'

'What?'

The old man beamed. 'I am happy to help, Herr Professor, in any way that I can.'

'No, no, I mean to *him*, to *him*.' And this was Bohemia, my God, repository of his highest hopes! Tycho was laboriously mounting up with the help of two straining footmen. Baron Hoffmann and the astronomer considered him doubtfully as with a grunt he toppled forward across the horse's braced back, flourishing in their faces his large leather-clad arse. The baron sighed and stepped forward to speak to him. Tycho, upright now and puffing, listened impatiently. Tengnagel and the younger Dane, downing their stirrup cups, looked on in high amusement. The squabble between Tycho and his latest collaborator had been the chief diversion of the castle since Kepler's arrival a month ago. The bugle sounded, and the hunt with Tycho in its midst moved off like a great rowdy engine, leaving behind it a brown taste of dust. Baron Hoffmann would not meet Kepler's hungry gaze. 'I will take you into Prague,' he muttered, and fairly dived into the sanctuary of his carriage. Kepler nodded dully, an ashen awfulness opening around him in the swirling air. What have I done?

They rattled down the narrow hill road. The sky over Benatky bore a livid smear of cloud, but the hunt, straggling away across the fields, was still in sunlight. Kepler silently wished them all a wasted day, and for the Dane with luck a broken neck. Barbara, wedged beside him on the narrow seat, pulsated in speechless anger and accusation (*What have you done?*). He did not wish to look at her, but neither could he watch for long the joggling view beyond the carriage window. This country roundabout of countless small lakes and perennially flooded lowlands (which Tycho in his letters had dubbed *Bohemian Venice*!) pained his poor eyesight with its fractured perspectives of quicksilver glitter and tremulous blue-grey distances.

'. . . That he will of course,' the baron was saying, 'accept an apology, only he, ah, he suggests that it be in writing.'

Kepler stared. 'He wants . . .' and eye and an elbow setting up together a devil's dance of twitches '. . . he wants a *written apology* of me?'

'That is, yes, what he indicated.' The baron swallowed, and looked away with a sickly smile. Regina at his side watched him intently, as she watched all big people, as if he might suddenly do something marvellous and inexplicable, burst into tears, or throw back his head and howl like an ape. Kepler regarded him too, thinking sadly that this man was a direct link with Copernicus: in his youth the baron had hired Valentine Otho, disciple of von Lauchen, to instruct him in mathematics. 'Also, he will require a declaration of secrecy, that is, that you will swear an oath not to reveal to . . . to others, any astronomical data he may provide you with in the course of your work. He is especially jealous, I believe, for the Mars observations. In return he will guarantee lodgings for you and your family, and will undertake to press the Emperor either to ensure the continuation of your Styrian salary, or else to grant you an allowance himself. These are his terms, Herr Kepler; I would advise you—'

'To accept? Yes, yes, I will, of course.' Why not? He was weary of standing on his dignity. The baron stared at him, and Kepler blinked: was that contempt in those watery eyes? Damn it, Hoffmann knew nothing of what it was to be poor and an outcast, he had his lands and title and his place at court. Sometimes these bland patricians sickened him.

'But what,' said Barbara, choking on it, 'what of *our* conditions, *our* demands?' No one replied. How was it, Kepler wondered, with a twinge of guilt, that her most impassioned outbursts were met always by the same glassy-eyed, throat-clearing silence. The carriage lurched into a pothole with a mighty jolt, and from without they heard the driver address a string of lush obscenities to his horse. Kepler sighed. His world was patched together from the wreckage of an infinitely finer, immemorial dwelling place; the pieces were precious and lovely, enough to break his heart, but they did not fit.

The baron's house stood on Hradcany hill hard by the imperial palace, looking down over Kleinseit to the river and the Jewish quarter, and, farther out, the suburbs of the old town. There was a garden with poplars and shaded walkways and a fishpond brimming with indolent carp. On the north, the palace side, the windows gave on to pavonian lawns and a fawn wall, sudden skies pierced by a spire, and purple pennons undulating in a cowed immensity. Once, from those windows, Kepler had been vouchsafed an unforgettable glimpse of a prancing horse and a hound rampant, ermine and emerald, black beard, pale hand, a dark disconsolate eye. That was as near as he was to come to the Emperor for a long time.

In the library the baron's wife sat at an escritoire, sprinkling chalk from an ivory horn upon a piece of parchment. She rose as they entered, and, blowing lightly on the page, glanced at them with the distant relation of a smile. 'Why Doctor – and Frau

Kepler – you have returned to us,' a faded eagle, taller than her husband but as gaunt as he, in a satin gown of metallic blue, her attention divided equally between her visitors and the letter in her hand.

'My dear,' the baron murmured, with a jaded bow.

There was a brief silence, and then that smile again. 'And Dr Brahe, is he not with you?'

'Madam,' Kepler burst out, 'I have been cruelly used by that man. He it was urged me, *pleaded* with me to come here to Bohemia; I came, and he treats me as he would a mere apprentice!'

'You have had a falling out with our good Dane?' the baroness said, suddenly giving the Keplers all her attention; 'that is unfortunate,' and Regina, catching the rustle of that silkily ominous tone, leaned forward past her mother for a good look at this impressive large blue lady.

'I set before him,' said Kepler, 'I set before him a list of some few conditions which he must meet if I was to remain and work with him, for example I deman— I asked that is for separate quarters for my family and myself (that place out there, I swear it, is a madhouse), and that a certain quantity of food—'

Barbara darted forward – 'And firewood!'

'And firewood, to be set aside expressly—'

'For our use, that's right.'

'—For our, yes, use,' blaring furiously down his nostrils. He pictured himself hitting her, felt in the roots of his teeth the sweet smack of his palm on a fat forearm. 'I asked let me see I asked, yes, that he procure me a salary from the Emperor—'

'His majesty,' the baron said hastily, 'his majesty is . . . difficult.'

'See, my lady,' Barbara warbled, 'see what we are reduced to, begging for our food. And you were so kind when we first arrived here, accommodating us . . .'

'Yes,' the baroness said thoughtfully.

'But,' cried Kepler, 'I ask you, sir, madam, are these unreasonable demands?'

Baron Hoffmann slowly sat down. 'We met upon the matter yesterday,' he said, looking at the hem of his wife's gown, 'Dr Brahe, Dr Kepler and myself.'

'Yes?' said the baroness, growing more aquiline by the moment. 'And?'

'This!' cried Barbara, a very quack; 'look at us, thrown out on the roadside!'

The baron pursed his lips. 'Hardly, *gnädige Frau,* hardly so . . . so . . . Yet it is true, the Dane is angry.'

'Ah,' the baroness murmured; 'why so?'

Drops of rain fingered the sunlit window. Kepler shrugged. '*I* do not know.' Barbara looked at him. '. . . I never said,' he said, 'that the Tychonic system is misconceived, as he charges! I . . . I merely observed of one or two weaknesses in it, caused I believe by a too hasty acceptance of doubtful premises, that a bitch in a hurry will produce blind pups.' The baroness put a hand up quickly to trap a cough, which, had he not known her to be a noble lady fully conscious of the gravity of the moment, he might have taken for a snigger. 'And anyway, it is misconceived, a monstrous thing sired on Ptolemy out of Egyptian Herakleides. He puts the earth, you see, madam, at the centre of the world, but makes the five remaining planets circle upon the sun! It works, of course, so far as appearances are concerned – but then you could put any one of the planets at the centre and still save the phenomena.'

'Save the . . .?' She turned to the baron to enlighten her. He looked away, fingering his chin.

'The phenomena, yes,' said Kepler. 'But it's all a trick our Dane is playing, aimed at pleasing the schoolmen without entirely denying Copernicus – he knows it as well as I do, and I'm damned before I will apologise for speaking the plain truth!' He surged to his feet, choking on a sudden bubble of rage. 'The thing, excuse me, the thing is simple: he is jealous of me, my grasp of our science – yes, yes,' rounding on Barbara violently, though she had made no protest, 'yes, jealous. And furthermore he is growing old, he's more than fifty—' the baroness's left eyebrow snapped into a startled arc '—and is worried for his future reputation, would have me ratify his worthless theory by forcing me to make it the basis of my work. But . . .' But there he faltered, and turned, listening. Music came from afar, the tune made small and quaintly merry by the distance. He walked slowly to the window, as if stalking some rare prize. The rain shower had passed, and the garden brimmed with light. Clasping his hands behind him and swaying gently on heel and toe he gazed out at the poplars and the dazzled pond, the drenched clouds of flowers, that jigsaw of lawn trying to reassemble itself between the stone balusters of a balcony. How innocent, how inanely lovely, the surface of the world! The mystery of simple things assailed him. A festive swallow swooped through a tumbling flaw of lavender smoke. It would rain again. Tumty tum. He smiled, listening: was it the music of the spheres? Then he turned, and was surprised to find the others as he had left them, attending him with mild expectancy. Barbara moaned softly in dismay. She knew, O she knew that look, that empty, amiably grinning mask with the burning eyes of a busy madman staring through it. She began rapidly to explain to the baron and his pernous lady that our chief worry, our chief worry is, you see . . . and Kepler sighed, wishing she would not prattle thus, like a halfwit, her tiny mouth wobbling. He rubbed his hands and advanced from the window, all business now. 'I shall,' blithely drowning Barbara's babbling, which ran on even as it sank, a flurry of bubbles out of a surprised fish-mouth – 'I shall write a letter, apologise, make my peace,' beaming from face to face as if inviting applause. The music came again, nearer now, a wind band playing in the palace grounds. 'He will summon me back, I think, yes; he will understand,' for what did any of that squabbling matter, after all? 'A new start! – may I borrow a pen, madam?'

By nightfall he had returned to Benatky. He delivered his apology, and swore an oath of secrecy, and Tycho gave a banquet, music and manic revels and the fatted calf hissing on a spit. The noise in the dining hall was a steady roar punctuated by the crimson crash of a dropped platter or the shriek of a tickled serving girl. The spring storm that had threatened all day blundered suddenly against the windows, shivering the reflected candlelight. Tycho was in capital form, shouting and swilling and banging his tankard, nose aglitter and the tips of his straw-coloured moustaches dripping. To his left Tengnagel sat with a proprietory arm about the waist of the Dane's daughter Elizabeth, a rabbity girl with close-cropped ashen hair and pink nostrils. Her mother, Mistress Christine, was a fat fussy woman whose twenty years of concubinage to the Dane no longer outraged anyone save her. Young Tyge was there too, sneering, and the Dane's chief assistant Christian Longberg, a priestly pustular young person, haggard with ambition and self-abuse. Kepler was angry again. He wanted not this mindless carousing, but simply to get his hands on – right away, now, tonight – Tycho's treasure store of planet observations. 'You set me the orbit of Mars, no let me speak, you set me this orbit, a most intractable problem, yet you give me no readings for the planet; how, I ask, let me speak please, how I ask am I to solve it, do you imagine?'

Tycho shrugged elaborately. '*De Tydske Karle*,' he remarked to the table in general, '*ere allesammen halv gale*,' and Jeppe the dwarf, squatting at his master's feet under the table, tittered.

'My father,' said Mistress Christine suddenly, 'my father went blind, you know, from swilling all his life like a pig. Take another cup of wine, Brahe dear.'

Christian Longberg clasped his hands as if about to pray. 'You expect to solve the problem of Mars, do you, Herr Kepler?' smiling thinly at the idea. Kepler realised who it was this creature reminded him of: Stefan Speidel, another treacherous prig.

'You do not think me capable of it, sir? Will you take a wager – let us say, a hundred florins?'

'O splendid,' cried young Tyge. 'An hundred florins, by Laertes!'

'Hold hard, Longberg,' Tengnagel growled. 'Best set him a certain time to do it in, or you'll wait for ever for your winnings.'

'Seven days!' said Kepler promptly, all swagger and smile without while his innards cringed. Seven days, my God. 'Yes, give me seven days free of all other tasks, and I shall do it – provided, wait,' and nervously licked his lips, 'provided I am guaranteed free and unhindered access to the observations, all of them, everything.'

Tycho scowled, seeing the trick. He had let it go too far, all the table was watching him, and besides he was drunk. Yet he hesitated. Those observations were his immortality. Twenty years of painstaking labour had gone into the amassing of them. Posterity might forget his books, ridicule his world system, laugh at his outlandish life, but not even the most heartless future imaginable would fail to honour him as a genius of exactitude. And now must he hand over everything to this young upstart? He nodded, and then shrugged again, and called for more wine, making the best of it. Kepler pitied him, briefly.

'Well then, sir,' said Longberg, his look a blade, 'we have a wager.'

A troupe of itinerant acrobats tumbled into the hall, whizzing and bouncing and clapping their hands. Seven days! A hundred florins! Hoop la.

* * *

SEVEN DAYS became seven weeks, and the enterprise exploded in his face. It had seemed so small a task, merely a matter of selecting three positions for Mars and from them defining by simple geometry the circle of the planet's orbit. He delved in Tycho's treasures, rolled in them, uttering little yelps of doggy joy. He selected three observations, taken by the Dane on the island of Hveen over a period of ten years, and went to work. Before he knew what had hit him he was staggering backwards out of a cloud of sulphurous smoke, coughing, his ears ringing, with bits of smashed calculations sticking in his hair.

All of Benatky was charmed. The castle hugged itself for glee at the spectacle of this irritating little man struck full in the face with his own boast. Even Barbara could not hide her satisfaction, wondering sweetly where they were to find the hundred florins, if you please, which Christian Longberg was howling for? Only Tycho Brahe said nothing. Kepler squirmed, asked Longberg for another week, pleaded penury and his poor health, denied that he had made any wager. Deep down he cared nothing for the insults and the laughter. He was busy.

Of course he had lied to himself, for the sake of that bet and the tricking of Tycho: Mars was not simple. It had kept its secret through millenniums, defeating finer minds than his. What was to be made of a planet, the plane of whose orbit, according to Copernicus, oscillates in space, the value for the oscillation to depend not on the sun, but on the position of the earth? A planet which, moving in a perfect circle at uniform speed, takes varying periods of time to complete identical, portions of its journey? He had thought that these and other strangenesses were merely rough edges to be sheared away before he tackled the problem of defining the orbit itself; now he knew that, on the contrary, he was a blind man who must reconstruct a smooth and infinitely complex design out of a few scattered prominences that gave themselves up, with deceptive innocence, under his fingertips. And seven weeks became seven months.

Early in 1601, at the end of their first turbulent year in Bohemia, a message came from Graz that Jobst Müller was dying, and asking for his daughter. Kepler welcomed the excuse to interrupt his work. He detached its fangs carefully from his wrist – wait there, don't howl – and walked away from it calm in the illusion of that sleek tensed thing crouching in wait, ready at the turn of a key to leap forth with the solution to the riddle of Mars clasped in its claws. By the time they reached Graz, Jobst Müller was dead.

His death provoked in Barbara a queer melancholy lassitude. She shrank into herself, curled herself up in some secret inner chamber from which there issued now and then a querulous babbling, so that Kepler feared for her sanity. The question of the inheritance obsessed her. She harped on it with ghoulish insistence, as if it were the corpse itself she was nosing at. Not that there were not grounds for her worst fears. The Archduke's interdicts against Lutherans were still in force, and when Kepler moved to convert his wife's properties into cash the Catholic authorities threatened and cheated him. Yet it was with trumpetings of acclaim that these same authorities welcomed him as a mathematician and cosmologist. In May, when it seemed the entire inheritance might be confiscated, he was invited to set up in the city's market place an apparatus of his own making through which to view a solar eclipse which he had predicted. A numerous and respectful crowd gathered to gape at the magus and his machine. The occasion was a grand success. The burghers of Graz, lifting a puzzled and watering eye from the shimmering image in his *camera obscura*, bumped him indulgently with their big bellies and told him what a brilliant fellow he was, and only afterwards did he discover that a cutpurse, taking advantage of the ecliptic gloom at noonday, had relieved him of thirty florins. It was a paltry loss compared to what was thieved from him in Styrian taxes, but it seemed to sum up best the whole bad business of their leavetaking of Barbara's homeland.

She burst into a torrent of tears on the day of their departure. She would not be comforted, would not let him touch her, but simply stood and wound out of her quivering mouth a long dark ribbon of anguish. He hovered beside her, heart raw with pity, his ape arms helplessly enfolding hoops of empty air. Graz had meant little to him in the end, Jobst Müller even less, but still he recognised well enough that grief which, under a grey sky on the Stempfergasse, ennobled for a moment his poor fat foolish wife.

Returning to Bohemia, they found Tycho and his circus in temporary quarters at the Golden Griffin inn, about to move back into the Curtius house on the Hradcany, which the Emperor had purchased for them from the vice chancellor's widow. Kepler could not credit it. What of the Capuchins' famous bells? And what of Benatky, the work and the expense that had been lavished on those reconstructions? Tycho shrugged; he thrived on waste, the majestic squandering of fortunes. His carriage awaited him under the sign of the griffin. There would be a seat in it for Barbara and the child. Kepler must walk. He panted up the steep hill of the Hradcany, talking to himself and shaking his troubled head. A troupe of imperial cavalry almost trampled him. When he gained the summit he realised he had forgotten where the house was, and when he asked the way he was given wrong directions. The sentries at the palace gate watched him suspiciously as he trotted past for the third time. The evening was hot, the sun a fat eye fixed on him with malicious glee, and he kept looking over his shoulder in the hope of catching a familiar street in the act of taking down hurriedly the elaborate scenery it had erected in order to fox him. He might have sought help at Baron Hoffmann's, but the thought of the baroness's steely gaze was not inviting. Then he turned a corner and suddenly he had arrived. A cart was drawn up before the door, and heroically encumbered figures with splayed knees were staggering up the steps. Mistress Christine leaned out of an upstairs window and shouted something in Danish, and everyone stopped for a moment and gazed up at her in a kind of stupefied, inexpectant wonder. The house had a forlorn and puzzled air. Kepler wandered through the hugely empty rooms. They led him back, as if gently to tell him something, to the entrance hall. The summer evening hesitated in the doorway, and in a big mirror a parallelogram of sunlit wall leaned at a breathless tilt, with a paler patch in it where a picture had been removed. The sunset was a flourish of gold, and in the palace gardens an enraptured blackbird was singing. Outside on the step the child Regina stood at gaze like a gilded figure in a frieze. Kepler paused in shadow, listening to his own pulsebeat. What could she see, that so engrossed her? She might have been a tiny bride watching from a window on her wedding morning. Footsteps clattered on the stairs behind him, and Mistress Christine came hurrying down clutching her skirts in one hand and brandishing a fire iron in the other. 'I will not have that man in my house!' Kepler stared at her, Regina with her head down walked swiftly past him into the house, and he turned to see a figure on a broken-down mule stop at the foot of the steps outside. He was in rags, with a bandaged arm pressed to his side like a beggar's filthy bundle of belongings. He dismounted and plodded up the steps. Mistress Christine planted herself in the doorway, but he pushed past her, looking about him distractedly. 'I went first to Benatky,' he muttered, 'the castle. No one there anymore!' The idea amused him. He sat down on a chair by the mirror and began slowly to unpack his wounded arm, lowering to the floor loop upon loop of bandage with a regularly repeated, steadily swelling bloodstain in the shape of a copper crab with a wet red ruby in its heart. The wound, a deep swordcut, was grossly infected. He studied it with distaste, pressing gingerly upon the livid surround. '*Porco Dio*,' he said, and spat on the floor. Mistress Christine threw up her hands and went away, talking to herself.

'My wife, perhaps,' said Kepler, 'would dress that for you?'

The Italian brought out from a pocket of his leather jerkin a bit of grimy rag, tore it with his teeth and wrapped the wound in it. He held up the ends to be tied. Kepler leaning down could feel the heat of the festering flesh and smell its gamey stink.

'So, they have not hanged you yet,' the Italian said. Kepler stared at him, and then, slowly lifting his eyes to the mirror, saw Jeppe standing behind him.

'Not yet, master, no,' the dwarf said, grinning. 'But what of you?'

Kepler turned to him. 'He is hurt, see: this arm . . .'

The Italian laughed, and leaning back against the mirror he fainted quietly into his own reflection.

Felix was the name he went by. His histories were various. He had been a soldier against the Turks, had sailed with the Neapolitan fleet. There was not a cardinal in Rome, so he said, that he had not pimped for. He had first encountered the Dane at Leipzig two years before, when Tycho was meandering southward towards Prague. The Italian was on the run, there had been a fight over a whore and a Vatican guard had died. He was starving, and Tycho, displaying an unwonted sense of humour, had hired him to escort his household animals to Bohemia. But the joke misfired. Tycho had never forgiven him the loss of the elk. Now, alerted by Mistress Christine, he came roaring into the hall in search of the fellow to throw him out. Kepler and the dwarf, however, had already spirited him away upstairs.

It seemed that he must die. For days he lay on a pallet in one of the big empty rooms at the top of the house, raving and cursing, mad with fever and the loss of blood. Tycho, fearing a scandal if the renegade should die in his house, summoned Michael Maier, the imperial physician, a discreet and careful man. He applied leeches and administered a purgative, and toyed wistfully with the idea of amputating the poisoned arm. The weather was hot and still, the room an oven; Maier ordered the windows sealed and draped against the unwholesome influence of fresh air. Kepler spent long hours by the sickbed, mopping the Italian's streaming forehead, or holding him by the shoulders while he puked the green dregs of his life into a copper basin, which each evening was delivered to the haruspex Maier at the palace. And sometimes at night, working at his desk, he would suddenly lift his head and listen, fancying that he had heard a cry, or not even that, but a flexure of pain shooting like a crack across the delicate dome of candlelight wherein he sat, and he would climb through the silent house and stand for a while beside the restless figure on the bed. He experienced, in that fetid gloom, a vivid and uncanny sense of his own presence, as if he had been given back for a brief moment a dimension of himself which daylight and other lives would not allow him. Often the dwarf was there before him, squatting on the floor with not a sound save the rapid unmistakable beat of his breathing. They did not speak, but bided together, like attendants at the shrine of a demented oracle.

Young Tyge came up one morning, sidled round the door with his offal-eating grin, the tip of a pink tongue showing. 'Well, here's a merry trio.' He sauntered to the bed and peered down at the Italian tangled in the sheets. 'Not dead yet?'

'He is sleeping, young master,' said Jeppe.

Tyge coughed. 'By God, he stinks.' He moved to the window, and twitching open the drapes looked out upon the great blue day. The birds were singing in the palace grounds. Tyge fumed, laughing softly.

'Well, doctor,' he said, 'what is *your* prognosis?'

'The poison has spread from the arm,' Kepler answered, shrugging. He wished the fellow would go away. 'He may not live.'

'You know the saying: those who live by the sword . . .' The rest was smothered by a guffaw. 'Ah me, how cruel is life,' putting a hand to his heart. 'Look at it, dying like a dog in a foreign land!' He turned to the dwarf. 'Tell me, monster, is it not enough to make even you weep?'

Jeppe smiled. 'You are a wit, master.'

Tyge looked at him. 'Yes, I am.' He turned away sulkily and considered the sick man again. 'I met him in Rome once, you know. He was a great whoremaster there. Although they say he prefers boys, himself. But then the Italians all are that way.' He glanced at Kepler. 'You would be somewhat too ripe for him, I think; perhaps the frog here would be more to his taste.' He went out, but paused in the doorway. 'My father, by the way, wants him well, so he may have the pleasure of kicking him down the Hradcany. You are a fine pair of little nurses. Look to it.'

He recovered. One day Kepler found him leaning by the window in a dirty shirt. He would not speak, nor even turn, as if he did not dare break off this rapt attendance upon the world that he had almost lost, the hazy distance, those clouds, the light of summer feeding on his upturned face. Kepler crept away, and when he returned that evening the Italian looked at him as if he had never seen him before, and waved him aside when he attempted to change the crusted bandage on his arm. He wanted food and drink. 'And where is the *nano*? You tell him to come, eh?'

The days that followed were for Kepler an ashen awakening from a dream. The Italian continued to look through him with blank unrecognition. What had he expected? Not love, certainly not friendship, nothing so insipid as these. Perhaps, then, a kind of awful comradeship, by which he might gain entry to that world of action and intensity, that Italy of the spirit, of which this renegade was an envoy. Life, life, that was it! In the Italian he seemed to know at last, however vicariously, the splendid and exhilarating sordidness of real life.

The Brahes, with that casual hypocrisy which Kepler knew so well, celebrated Felix's recovery as if he were the first hope of the house. He was brought down from his bare room and given a new suit, and led out, grinning, into the garden, where the family was at feed at a long table in the shade of poplar trees. The Dane sat him down at his right hand. But though the occasion started off with toasts and a slapping of backs, it began before long to ooze a drunken rancour. Tycho, ill and half drunk, brought up again the sore subject of his lost elk, but in the midst of loud vituperation fell suddenly asleep into his plate. The Italian ate like a dog, jealously and with circumspect hurry: he also knew well these capricious Danes. His arm was in a black silk sling that Tycho's daughter Elizabeth had fashioned for him. Tengnagel threatened to call him out with rapiers if he did not stay away from her, and then stood up, overturning his chair, and stalked away from the table. Felix laughed; the Junker did not know, what everyone else knew, that he had ploughed the wench already, long before, at Benatky. It was not for her that he had come back. The court at Prague was rich, presided over by a halfwit, so he had heard. Perhaps Rudolph might have use for a man of his peculiar talents? The dwarf consulted Kepler, and Kepler responded with wry amusement. 'Why, I had to wait a year myself before your master would arrange an audience for me, and I have been to the palace only twice again. What influence have I?'

'But you will have, soon,' Jeppe whispered, 'sooner than you would guess.'

Kepler said nothing, and looked away. The dwarf's prophetic powers unnerved him. Tycho Brahe suddenly woke up. 'You are wanted, sir,' said Jeppe softly.

'Yes, I want you,' Tycho growled, wiping bleared eyes.

'Well, here I am.'

But Tycho only looked at him wearily, with a kind of hapless resentment. 'Bah.' He was unmistakably a sick man. Kepler was aware of the dwarf behind him, smiling. What was it the creature saw in their collective future? A warm gale was blowing out of the sky, and the evening sunlight had an umber tinge, as if the wind had bruised it. The poplars shook. Suddenly everything seemed to him to tremble on the brink of revelation, as if these contingencies of light and weather and human doings had stumbled upon a form of almost speech. Felix was whispering to Elizabeth Brahe, making the tips of her translucent ears glow with excitement. He was to leave, this time for ever, before the year was out, no longer interested in imperial patronage, though by then Jeppe's prophecy would be fulfilled, and the astronomer would have become indeed a man of influence.

* * *

KEPLER TURNED AGAIN now to his work on Mars. Conditions around him had improved. Christian Longberg, tired of squabbling, had gone back to Denmark, and there was no more talk of their wager. Tycho Brahe too was seldom seen. There were rumours of plague and Turkish advances, and the stars needed a frequent looking to. The Emperor Rudolph, growing ever more nervous, had moved his imperial mathematician in from Benatky, but even the Curtius house was not close enough, and the Dane was at the palace constantly. The weather was fine, days the colour of Mosel wine, enormous glassy nights. Kepler sometimes sat with Barbara in the garden, or with Regina idly roamed the Hradcany, admiring the houses of the rich and watching the imperial cavalry on parade. But by August the talk of plague had closed the great houses for the season, and even the cavalry found an excuse to be elsewhere. The Emperor decamped to his country seat at Belvedere, taking Tycho Brahe with him. The sweet sadness of summer settled on the deserted hill, and Kepler thought of how as a child, at the end of one of his frequent bouts of illness, he would venture forth on tender limbs into a town made magical by the simple absence of his schoolfellows from its streets.

Mars suddenly yielded up a gift, when with startling ease he refuted Copernicus on oscillation, showing by means of Tycho's data that the planet's orbit intersects the sun at a fixed angle to the orbit of the earth. There were other, smaller victories. At every advance, however, he found himself confronted again by the puzzle of the apparent variation in orbital velocity. He fumed to the past for guidance. Ptolemy had saved the principle of uniform speed by means of the *punctum equans*, a point on the diameter of the orbit from which the velocity will appear invariable to an imaginary observer (whom it amused Kepler to imagine, a crusty old fellow, with his brass triquetrum and watering eye and smug, deluded certainty). Copernicus, shocked by Ptolemy's sleight of hand, had rejected the equant point as blasphemously inelegant, but yet had found nothing to put in its place except a clumsy combination of five uniform epicyclic motions superimposed one upon another. These were, all the same, clever and sophisticated manoeuvres, and saved the phenomena admirably. But had his great predecessors taken them, Kepler wondered, to represent the real state of things? The question troubled him. Was there an innate nobility, lacking in him, which set one above the merely empirical? Was his pursuit of the forms of physical reality irredeemably vulgar?

In a tavern on Kleinseit one Saturday night he met Jeppe and the Italian. They had fallen in with a couple of kitchen-hands from the palace, a giant Serb with one eye and a low ferrety fellow from Württemberg, who claimed to have soldiered with Kepler's brother in the Hungarian campaigns. His name was Krump. The Serb rooted in his codpiece and brought out a florin to buy a round of schnapps. Someone struck up on a fiddle, and a trio of whores sang a bawdy song and danced. Krump squinted at them and spat. 'Riddled with it, them are,' he said, 'I know them.' But the Serb was charmed, ogling the capering drabs out of his one oystrous eye and banging his fist on the table in time to the jig. Kepler ordered up another round. 'Ah,' said Jeppe. 'Sir Mathematicus is flush tonight; has my master forgot himself and paid your wages?' 'Something of that,' Kepler answered, and thought himself a gay dog. They played a hand of cards, and there was more drink. The Italian was dressed in a suit of black velvet, with a slouch hat. Kepler spotted him palming a knave. He won the hand and grinned at Kepler, and then, calling for another jig, got up and with a low bow invited the whores to dance. The candles on the tavern counter shook to the thumping of their feet. 'A merry fellow,' said Jeppe, and Kepler nodded, grinning blearily. The dance became a general rout, and somehow they were suddenly outside in the lane. One of the whores fell down and lay there laughing, kicking her stout legs in the air. Kepler propped himself against the wall and watched the goatish dancers circling in a puddle of light from the tavern window, and all at once out of nowhere, out of everywhere, out of the fiddle music and the flickering light and the pounding of heels, the circling dance and the Italian's drunken eye, there came to him the ragged fragment of a thought. False. What false? That principle. One of the whores was pawing him. Yes, he had it. *The principle of uniform velocity is false.* He found it very funny, and smiling turned aside and vomited absent-mindedly into a drain. Krump laid a hand on his shoulder. 'Listen, friend, if you puke up a little ring don't spit it out, it'll be your arsehole.' Somewhere behind him the Italian laughed. False, by Jesus, yes!

They went on to another tavern, and another. The Serb got lost along the way, and then Felix and the dwarf reeled off arm in arm with the bawds into the darkness, and Krump and the astronomer were left to stagger home up the Hradcany, falling and shouting and singing tearful songs of Württemberg their native land. In the small hours, his elusive quarters located at last, Kepler, a smouldering red eye in his mind fixed on the image of a romping whore, attempted with much shushing and chuckling to negotiate Barbara's rigid form into an exotic posture, for what precise purpose he had forgotten when he woke into a parched and anguished morning, though something of the abandoned experiment was still there in the line of her large hip and the spicy tang of her water in the earthen pot under the bed. She would not speak to him for a week.

Later that day, when the fumes of the charnel house had dispersed in his head, he brought out and contemplated, like a penniless collector with a purloined treasure, the understanding that had been given to him that the principle of uniform orbital velocity was a false dogma. It was the only, the obvious answer to the problem of Mars, of all the planets probably, and yet for two thousand years and more it had resisted the greatest of astronomy's inquisitors. And why had this annunciation been made to him, what heaven-hurled angel had whispered in his ear? He marvelled at the process, how a part of his mind had worked away in secret and in silence while the rest of him swilled and capered and lusted after poxed whores. He experienced an unwonted humility. He must be better now, behave himself, talk to Barbara and listen to her complaints, be patient with the Dane, and say his prayers, at least until the advent of new problems.

They were not long in coming. His rejection of uniform velocity threw everything into disarray, and he had to begin all over again. He was not discouraged. Here was real work, after all, fully worthy of him. Where before, in the *Mysterium*, there had been abstract speculation, was now reality itself. These were precise observations of a visible planet, coordinates fixed in time and space. They were events. It was not by chance he had been assigned the study of Mars. Christian Longberg, that jealous fool, had insisted on keeping the lunar orbit; Kepler laughed, glimpsing there too the quivering tips of angelic wings, the uplifted finger. For he knew now that Mars was the key to the secret of the workings of the world. He felt himself suspended in tensed bright air, a celestial swimmer. And seven months were becoming seventeen.

Tycho told him he was mad: uniform velocity was a principle beyond question. Next he would be claiming that the planets do not move in perfect circles! Kepler shrugged. It was the Dane's own observations that had shown the principle to be false. No no *no*, and Tycho shook his great bald head, there must be some other explanation. But Kepler was puzzled. Why should he seek another answer, when he had the correct one? There stood at the hatch of his mind an invoice clerk with a pencil and slate and a bad liver, who would allow no second thoughts. Tycho Brahe fumed away; what little chance there had been that this Swabian lunatic would solve Mars for him was gone now. Kepler plucked at him, wait, look – where is my compass, I have lost my compass – the thing was as good as done! Even assuming a variable rate of speed, to define the orbit he had only to determine the radius of its circle, the direction relative to the fixed stars of the axis connecting aphelion and perihelion, and the position on that axis of the sun, the orbital centre, and the *punctum equans*, which for the moment he would retain, as a calculating device. Of course all this could only be done by a process of trial and error, but . . . but wait! And Tycho swept away, muttering.

He made seventy attempts. At the end, out of nine hundred pages of closely written calculations, came a set of values which gave, with an error of only two minutes of arc, the correct position of Mars according to the Tychonic readings. He clambered up out of dreadful depths and announced his success to anyone who would listen. He wrote to Longberg in Denmark, demanding settlement of their wager. The fever which he had held at bay with promises and prayers took hold of him now like a demented lover. When it had spent itself, he resumed to his calculations to make a final test. It was only play, really, a kind of revelling in his triumph. He chose another handful of observations and applied them to his model. They did not fit. Arrange matters as he would, there was always an error of eight minutes of arc. He plodded away from his desk, thinking of daggers, the poison cup, a launching into empty air from a high wall of the Hradcany. And yet, in a secret recess of his heart, a crazy happiness was stirring at the prospect of throwing away all he had done so far and starting over again. It was the joy of the zealot in his cell, the scourge clasped in his hand. And seventeen months were to become seven years before the thing was done.

His overloaded brain began to throw off sparks of surplus

energy, and he conceived all kinds of quaint ingenious enterprises. He developed a method of measuring the volume of wine casks by conic section. The keeper of the Emperor's cellars was charmed. He tested his own eyesight and made for himself an elaborate pair of spectacles from lenses ground in Linz by his old friend Wincklemann. The prosaic miracle of water had always fascinated him; he set up water clocks, and designed a new kind of pump which impressed the imperial engineers. Others of his projects caused much hilarity among the Brahes. There was his design for an automatic floorsweeper, worked by suction power from a double-valved bellows attached to the implement's ratcheted wheels. He consulted the scullery maids on a plan for a laundry machine, a huge tub with paddles operated by a treadle. They ran away from him, giggling. These were amusing pastimes, but at the end of the day always there was the old problem of Mars waiting for him.

He liked to work at night, savouring the silence and the candleglow and the somehow attentive darkness, and then the dawn that always surprised him with that sense of being given a glimpse of the still new and unsullied other end of things. In the Curtius house he had burrowed into a little room on the top floor where he could lock himself away. The summer passed. Early one October morning he heard a step outside his door, and peering out spied Tycho Brahe standing in the corridor, his arms folded, gazing down pensively at his large bare feet. He was in his nightshirt, with a cloak thrown over his shoulders. Behind him, by the far wall, Jeppe the dwarf was creeping. They had the air of weary and discouraged searchers after some hopelessly lost small thing. Tycho looked up at Kepler without surprise.

'Sleep,' said the Dane, 'I do not sleep.'

As if at a signal, there arose in the sky outside a vehement clanging. Kepler turned an ear to it and smiled. 'Bells,' he said. Tycho frowned.

Kepler's room was a cramped brown box with a pallet and a stool, and a rickety table aswarm with his papers. Tycho sat down heavily, fussing at his cloak; Jeppe scuttled under the table. Rain spoke suddenly at the window: the sky was coming apart and falling on the city in undulant swathes. Kepler scratched his head and absently inspected his fingernails. He had lice again.

'You progress?' said Tycho, nodding at the jumbled papers by his elbow.

'O yes, a little.'

'And you still hold to the Copernican system?'

'It is a useful basis of computation . . .' But that was not it. 'Yes,' he said grimly, 'I follow Copernicus.'

The Dane might not have heard. He was looking away, toward the door, where on a hook there hung a mildewed court uniform, complete with sash and feathered hat, a limp ghost of the previous householder, the late vice chancellor. Under the table Jeppe stirred, muttering. 'I came to speak to you,' Tycho said. Kepler waited, but there was nothing more. He looked at the Dane's big yellow feet clinging to the floorboards like a pair of purblind animals. In his time Tycho Brahe had determined the position of a thousand stars, and had devised a system of the world more elegant than Ptolemy's. His book on the new star of 1572 had made him famous throughout Europe.

'I have made,' said Kepler, picking up his pen and looking at it with a frown, 'I have made a small discovery regarding orbital motion.'

'That it is invariable, after all?' Tycho suddenly laughed.

'No,' Kepler said. 'But the radius vector of any planet, it seems, will sweep out equal areas in equal times.' He glanced at Tycho. 'I regard this as a law.'

'Moses Mathematicus,' said Jeppe, and sniggered.

The rain was still coming down, but the clouds to the east had developed a luminous rip. There was a sudden beating of wings at the window. Kepler's steel pen, not to be outdone by the deluge outside, deposited with a parturient squeak upon his papers a fat black blot.

'Bells,' said Tycho softly.

That night he was brought home drunk from dinner at the house of Baron Rosenberg in the city, and relieved himself in the fireplace of the main hall, waking everyone with his yelling and the stench of boiled piss. He kicked the dwarf and staggered away upstairs to his bed, from which Mistress Christine, gibbering in rage, had already fled. The household was no sooner settled back to sleep than the master reared up again roaring for lights and his fool and a meal of quails' eggs and brandy. At noon next day he summoned Kepler to his bedside. 'I am ill.' He had a mug of ale in his hand, and the bed was strewn with pastry scraps.

'You should not drink so much, perhaps,' said Kepler mildly.

'Pain. Something has burst in my gut: look at that!' He pointed with grim pride to a basin of bloodied urine on the floor by Kepler's feet. 'Last night at Rosenberg's my bladder was full for three hours, I could not leave the table for fear of seeming gross. You know what these occasions are.'

'No,' said Kepler, 'I do not.'

Tycho scowled, and took a swig of ale. He looked at Kepler keenly for a moment. 'Be careful of my family, they will try to hinder you. Watch Tengnagel, he is a fool, but ambitious. Protect my poor dwarf.' He paused. 'Remember me, and all I have done for you. Do not let me seem to have lived in vain.'

Kepler ascended laughing to his room. All he has done for me! Barbara was there before him, poking among his things. He edged around her to the table and plunged into his papers, mumbling.

'How is he?' she said.

'Eh? Who?'

'Who!'

'O, it's nothing. Too much wine.'

She was silent for a moment, standing behind him with her arms folded, nursing enormities. 'How can you,' she said at last, 'how can you be so . . . so . . .'

He turned to stare at her. 'What.'

'Have you thought, have you, what will become of us when he dies?'

'Good God, woman! He was dining with his fine friends, and drank too much as always, and was too lazy to leave his chair to pee, and injured his bladder. He will be over it by tomorrow.

Permit me to know enough of doctoring to recognise mortal illness when—'

'You recognise nothing!' shrieking a fine spray of spit in his face. 'Are you alive at all, with your stars and your precious theories and your laws of this and that and and and . . .' Fat tears sprang from her eyes, her voice broke, and she fled the room.

Tycho failed rapidly. Within the week Kepler was summoned again to his chamber. It was crowded with family and pupils and court emissaries, poised and silent like a gathering in the gloom on the fringes of a dream. Tycho was enthroned in lamplight upon his high bed. The flesh hung in folds on his shrunken face, his eyes were vague. He held Kepler's hand. 'Remember me. Do not let me seem to have lived in vain.' Kepler could think of nothing to say, and grinned uncontrollably, nodding, nodding. Mistress Christine plucked at the stuff of her gown, looking about her dazedly as if trying to remember something. The dwarf, blotched with tears, made to scramble on to the bed but someone held him back. Kepler noticed for the first time that Elizabeth Brahe was pregnant. Tengnagel skulked at her shoulder. There was a commotion outside the door of the chamber and Felix burst in, spitting Italian over his shoulder at someone outside. He strode to the bed and, thrusting Kepler away, took the Dane's hand in his own. But the Dane was dead.

He was buried, after an utraquist service, in the Teynkirche in Prague. The house on the Hradcany had an air of pained surprise, as if a wing had suddenly and silently collapsed. One morning it was discovered that the Italian had departed, taking Jeppe with him, no one knew to where. Kepler considered going too; but where would he go? And then a message came from the palace informing him that he had been appointed to succeed the Dane as imperial mathematician.

* * *

EVERYONE SAID the Emperor Rudolph was harmless, if a little mad, yet when the moment had come at last for Kepler to meet him for the first time, a spasm of fright had crushed the astronomer's heart in its hot fist. That was ten months before the Dane's death. Kepler by then had been in Bohemia nearly a year, but Tycho's grand manner was impervious to hints. He only shrugged and began to hum when Kepler ventured that it was a long time to have held off from this introduction. 'His majesty is . . . difficult.'

They trundled up the Hradcany and turned in between the high walls leading to the gate. Everywhere about them lay the economy of snow: a great white and only the black ruts of the road, the no-colour wall. The sky was the colour of a hare's pelt. Their horse stumbled on packed ice, and a scolopendrine beggar scuttled forward and opened his mouth at them through the carriage window in speechless imprecation. On the wooden bridge before the gate they skated ponderously to a halt. The horse stamped and snorted, blowing cones of steam out of flared nostrils. Kepler put his head out at the window. The air was sharp as needles. The gateman, a fat fellow in furs, waddled forth from his box and spoke to the driver, then waved them on. Tycho flung him a coin.

'Ah,' said the Dane, 'ah, I detest this country.' He fussed at the sheepskin wrap about his knees. They were in the palace gardens now. Black trees glided slowly past, bare limbs thrown up as if in stark astonishment at the cold. 'Why did I ever leave Denmark?'

'Because . . .'

'Well?' staring balefully, daring him. Kepler sighed.

'I do not know. Tell me.'

Tycho transferred his gaze to the smoky air outside. 'We Brahes have ever been ill-used by royals. My uncle Jorgen Brahe saved King Frederick from drowning in the Sund at Copenhagen, and died himself in the attempt, did you know that?' He did. It was an oft-told tale. The Dane was working himself up into a fine fit of indignation. 'And yet that young brat Christian was bold enough to banish me from my island sanctuary, my fabulous Uraniborg, granted to me by royal charter when he was still a snot-nosed mewler on his nurse's knee – did you know *that*?' O he did, he did, and more. Tycho had ruled on Hveen like a despotic Turk, until even the mild King Christian could no longer countenance it. 'Ah, Kepler, the perfidy of princes!' and glared at the palace advancing to meet them through the icy light of afternoon.

They were left to wait outside the chamber of the presence. There were others there before them, dim depressed figures given to sighing, and a crossing and recrossing of legs. It was bitterly cold, and Kepler's feet were numb. His apprehension had yielded before a grey weight of boredom when the groom of the chamber, an immaculately costumed bland little man, approached swiftly and whispered to the Dane, and already there was a hot constriction in Kepler's breast, as if his lungs, getting wind a fraction before he did of the advent at last of the longed-for and dreaded moment, had snatched a quick gulp of air to cushion the shock. He needed to urinate. I think I must go and – will you excuse—?

'Do you know,' said the Emperor, 'do you know what one of our mathematici has told us: that if the digits of any double number be transposed, and the result of the transposition be subtracted from the original, or vice versa of course, depending on which is the greater value, then the remainder in all instances shall be divisible by nine. Is this not a wonderful operation? By nine, always.' He was a short plump matronly man with melancholy eyes. A large chin nestled like a pigeon in a bit of soft beard. His manner was a blend of eagerness and weary detachment. 'But doubtless you, sir, a mathematician yourself, will think it nothing remarkable that numbers should behave in what to us is a strange and marvellous fashion?'

Kepler was busy transposing and subtracting in his head. Was this perhaps a test to which all paying court for the first time were subjected? The Emperor, slackjawed and softly panting, watched him with an unnerving avidity. He felt as if he were being slowly and ruminatively devoured. 'A mathematician, I am that, your majesty, yes,' smiling tentatively. 'Nevertheless I admit that

I cannot say what is the explanation of this phenomenon . . .' He was discussing mathematics with the ruler of the Holy Roman Empire, the anointed of God and bearer of the crown of Charlemagne. 'Perhaps your majesty himself can offer a solution?'

Rudolph shook his head. For a moment he mused in silence, a forefinger palping his lower lip. Then he sighed.

'There is a magic in numbers,' he said, 'which is beyond rational explanation. You are aware of this, no doubt, in your own work? May be, even, you put to use sometimes this magic?'

'I would not attempt,' said Kepler, with a force and suddenness that startled even him, 'I would not attempt to prove anything by the mysticism of numbers, nor do I consider it possible to do so.'

In the silence that followed, Tycho Brahe, behind him, coughed.

Rudolph took his guest on a tour of the palace and its wonder rooms. Kepler was shown all manner of mechanical apparatuses, lifelike wax figures and clockwork dummies, rare coins and pictures, exotic carvings, pornographic manuscripts, a pair of Barbary apes and a huge spindly beast from Araby with a hump and a dun coat and an expression of ineradicable melancholy, vast dim laboratories and alchemical caves, an hermaphrodite child, a stone statue which would sing when exposed to the heat of the sun, and he grew dizzy with surprise and superstitious alarm. As they progressed from one marvel to the next they accumulated in their train a troupe of murmurous courtiers, delicate men and elaborate ladies, whom the Emperor ignored, but who yet depended from him, like a string of puppets; they were exquisitely at ease, yet through all their fine languor it seemed to Kepler a thread of muted pain was tightly stretched, which out of each produced, as a stroked glass will produce, a tiny note that was one with the tone of the apes' muffled cries and the androgynous child's speechless stare. He listened closely then, and thought he heard from every corner of the palace all that royal sorceror's magicked captives faintly singing, all lamenting.

They came into a wide hall with hangings and many pictures

and a magnificent vaulted ceiling. The floor was a checkered design of black and white marble tiles. Windows gazed down upon the snowbound city, of which the tiled floor was a curious echo, except that all out there seemed a jumble of wreckage under the brumous winter light. A few persons stood about, motionless as figurines, marvellously got up in yellows and sky blues and flesh tints and lace. This was the throne room. Cups of sticky brown liqueur and trays of sweetmeats were carried in. The Emperor neither ate nor drank. He seemed ill at ease here, and glanced at his throne, making little feints at it, as if it were a live thing crouching there that he must catch off guard and subdue before he might mount it.

'Do you agree,' he said, 'that men are distinguished one from another more by the influence of heavenly bodies than even by institutions and habit? Would you agree with this view, sir?'

There was something touching in this dumpy little man, with his weak mouth and haunted eyes, that avid attentiveness. And yet this was the Emperor! Was he perhaps a little deaf?

'Yes,' said Kepler, 'yes, I do agree; but casting horoscopes, all that, an unpleasant and begrimed work, your majesty.' He paused. What was this? Who had said anything of horoscopes? But Rudolph, according to the Dane, had nodded assent to Kepler's plea for an imperial stipend; he must be made to understand that a few florins annually would not purchase another wizard to add to his collection. 'Of course,' he went on, 'I believe that the stars do, yes, influence us, and that it is permissible a ruler be allowed once in a while to take advantage of such influence. But, if you will permit me, sir, there are dangers . . .' The Emperor waited, smiling vaguely and nodding, yet managing to convey a faint unmistakable chill of warning. 'I mean, your majesty, there is,' with deliberate emphasis, while Tycho Brahe raked together the ingredients of another cautionary cough, 'there is a danger if the ruler should be too much swayed by those about him who make star magic their business. I am thinking of those Englishmen, Kelley and the angel-conjuror Dee, who lately, I am told, deceived yo – your court, with their trickery.'

Rudolph had turned slowly away, still with that pained vacant smile, still nodding, and Tycho Brahe immediately jumped in and began to speak loudly of something else. Kepler was annoyed. What did they expect of him! He was no crawling courtier, to kiss hands and curtsy.

The day waned, the lamps were lit, and there was music. Rudolph took to his throne at last. It was the only seat in the room. Kepler's legs began to ache. He had expected much of this day. Everything was going wrong. Yet he had done his best to be upright and honest. Perhaps that was not what was required. In this empire of impossible ceremony and ceaseless show Johannes Kepler fitted ill. The music of the strings sighed on, an unobtrusive creaking. 'It was the predictability of astronomical events,' the Dane was saying, 'which drew me to this science, for I saw, of course, how useful such predictions would be to navigators and calendar makers, also to kings and princes . . .' but his efforts were not succeeding either, Rudolph's chin was sunk on his breast, and he was not listening. He rose and touched Kepler's arm, and walked with him to the great window. Below them the city was dissolving into the twilight. They stood in silence for a moment, gazing down upon the little lights that flickered forth here and there. All at once Kepler felt a rush of tenderness for this soft sad man, a desire to shield him from the world's wickedness.

'They tell us that you have done wonderful works,' the Emperor murmured. 'We care for such things. If there were time . . .' He sighed. 'I do not like the world. More and more I desire to transcend these . . . these . . .' His hand moved in a vague gesture toward the room behind him. 'I think sometimes I might dress in rags and go among the people. I do not see them, you know. But then, where should I find rags, here?' He glanced at Kepler with a faint apologetic smile. 'You see our difficulties.'

'Of course, certainly.'

Rudolph frowned, annoyed not at his guest it seemed but with himself. 'What was I saying? Yes: these tables which Herr Brahe wishes to draw up, you consider them a worthwhile venture?'

Kepler felt like a hamfisted juggler, diving frantically this way and that as the balls spun out of control. 'They would contain, your majesty, everything that is known in our science.'

'Facts, then, you mean, figures?'

'Everything that is known.'

'Yes?'

'The Tychonic tables will be the foundation of a new science of the sky. Herr Brahe is a great and diligent observer. The material he has amassed is a priceless treasure. The tables must be made, they shall be, and those who come after us will bless the name of any who had a hand in their making.'

'I see, I see, yes,' and coughed. 'You are an Austrian, Herr Kepler?'

'Swabia is my birthplace; but I was in Graz for some years before I—'

'Ah, Graz.'

'But I was driven out. The Archduke Ferdinand—'

'Graz,' Rudolph said again. 'Yes, our cousin Ferdinand is diligent.'

Kepler closed his eyes. His cousin, of course.

The music ceased, and a parting glass was distributed. Tycho took Kepler's arm, trying it seemed to crush it in his fist. They bowed, and backed off towards the doors that were drawing open slowly behind them. Kepler halted, frowning, and trotted forward again before the Dane could stop him, muttering under his breath. 'Nines, nines of course! Your majesty, a moment. See, sire, it is because of the nines, or I mean the tens, because we count in tens, and therefore the result will always be divisible by nine. For if we computed by nines, now, it would be eight, divisible by eight that is, and so on. You see?' sketching a triumphantly gay figure eight on the air. But the Emperor Rudolph only looked at him, with a kind of sadness, and said nothing. As they went out Tycho Brahe, sucking his teeth, turned on Kepler savagely. 'The wrong thing you say, always the wrong thing!'

In the lamplight at the gate a few absent-minded flakes of

snow were falling. The horse's hoofs rang on the cold stones, and somewhere off to the left the watch called out. At Kepler's side the Dane snorted and struggled, trying to contain the unwieldy parcel of his rage. 'Have you no sense of of of,' he gasped, 'no understanding of – of anything? Why, at times today I suspected that you were trying, *trying* to anger him.'

Kepler said nothing. He did not need Tycho to tell him how badly he had fared. Yet he could not be angry at himself, for it was not he had done the damage, but that other Kepler shambling at his heels, that demented other, whose prints upon his life were the black bruises that inevitably appeared in the places whereon Johannes the Mild had impressed no more than a faint thumb-print of protest.

'Well, it is no matter, in the end,' said Tycho wearily. 'I convinced him, despite your clumsiness, that you should work with me in compiling the tables. I am to call them the *Tabulae Rudolphinae*. He believes that those who come after us will bless his name!'

'Yes?'

'And he will grant you two hundred florins annually, though God knows if you will ever see it, he is not renowned either for generosity or promptness.'

On the bridge the carriage halted, and Kepler gazed for a long time into the illusory emptiness outside. What would be his future, bound to a protector in need of protecting? He thought of that woebegone king immured in perpetual check in his ice palace. Tycho elbowed him furiously in the ribs. 'Have you nothing to say?'

'O – thank you.' The carriage lurched forward into the darkness. 'He does not like the world.'

'What?'

'The Emperor, he told me that he does not like the world. Those were his words. I thought it strange.'

'Strange? *Strange*? Sir, you are as mad as he.'

'We are alike, yes, in ways . . .'

That night he fell ill. An insidious fever originated in the gall, and, bypassing the bowels, gained access to the head. Barbara forced him to take a hot bath, though he considered total immersion an unnatural and foolhardy practice. To his surprise the measure brought him temporary relief. The heat, however, constricted his bowels; he administered a strong purgative, and then bled himself. He decided, after careful investigation of his excrete, that he was one of those cases whose gall bladder has a direct opening into the stomach. This was an interesting discovery, though such people, he knew, are shortlived as a rule. The sky was catastrophic at that time. But he had so much still to do! The Emperor sent good wishes for his recovery. That decided him: he would not die. The fever abated at last. He felt like one of those neatly parcelled flies that adorn spiders' webs. Death was saving him up for a future feast.

Was there a lesson for him in this latest bout of illness? He was not living as he knew he should. His rational self told him he must learn continence of thought and speech, must practise grovelling. He set himself diligently to work at the Rudolphine Tables, arranging and transcribing endless columns of observations from Tycho's papers. In his heart the predictability of astronomical events meant nothing to him; what did he care for navigators or calendar makers, for princes and kings? The demented dreamer in him rebelled. He remembered that vision he had glimpsed in Baron Hoffmann's garden, and was again assailed by the mysteriousness of the commonplace. *Give this world's praise to the angel!* He had only the vaguest notion of what he meant. He recalled too the squabbling when he had come first to Tycho, the farce of that flight from Benatky and the ignominious return. Would it be likewise with Rudolph? He wrote to Mästlin: *I do not speak like I write, I do not write like I think, I do not think like I ought to think, and so everything goes on in deepest darkness.* Where did these voices come from, these strange sayings? It was as if the future had found utterance in him.

III

Dioptrice

PAUSING IN THE MIDST OF Weilderstadt's familiar streets, he looked about him in mild amaze. It was still here, the narrow houses, the stucco and the spires and the shingled roofs, that weathervane, all of it by some means still intact, unaware that his memory had long ago reduced it all to a waxwork model. The morning air was heavy with a mingled smell of bread and dung and smoke – that smell! – and everywhere a blurred clamour was trying and just failing to make an important announcement. The lindens in Klingelbrunner lane averted their sheepish gaze from the puddles of sticky buds they had shed during the night. Faces in the streets puzzled him, familiar, and yet impossibly youthful, until presently he realised that these were not his former schoolfellows, but their sons. There is the church, there the market place. Here is the house.

There was bedlam when the carriage stopped, the children tussling, the baby squealing in Barbara's lap; it seemed to Kepler a manifestation of the speechless uproar in his heart. The street door was shut, the upstairs shutters fastened. Had the magic of his long absence worked here at least, bundled it all up and disappeared it? But the door was opening already, and his brother Heinrich appeared, with his awkward grin, stooping and bobbing in a paroxysm of shyness. They embraced, both of them speaking at once, and Kepler stepped back with a quick glance at the starched tips of his winged lace collar. Regina, a young woman now, had the protesting baby in her arms, and Barbara was trying to get at Susanna to give her a smack, and Susanna, nimbly escaping, knocked over little Friedrich, who cut his knee on the step and after a moment of open-mouthed silence suddenly howled, and a black dog trotting by on the street came over and began to bark at them all in furious encouragement. Heinrich laughed, showing a mouthful of yellow stumps, and waved them in. The old woman at the fire looked over her shoulder and went off at once, muttering, into the kitchen. Kepler pretended he had not seen her.

'Well . . .!' he said, smiling all around him, and patting his pockets distractedly, as if in search of the key somewhere on his person that would unlock this tangle of emotions. It was a little low dark house, sparsely furnished. There was a yellowish smell of cat, which presently was concentrated into an enormous ginger tom thrusting itself with a kind of truculent ardour against Kepler's leg. A black pot was bubbling on the fire of thorns in the open hearth. Kepler took off his hat.

'Well!'

Heinrich shut the door and pressed his back to it, tongue-tied and beaming. The children were suddenly solemn. Barbara peered about her in surprise and distaste, and Kepler with a sinking heart recalled those stories he had spun her long ago about his forebear the famous Kaspar von Kepler and the family coat of arms. Regina alone was at ease, rocking the baby. Heinrich was trying to take her in without going so far as to look at her directly. Poor sad harmless Heinrich! Kepler felt an inner engine softly starting up; O God, he must not weep. He scowled, and stamped into the kitchen. The old woman his mother was doing something to a trussed capon on the table.

'Here you are,' he said; 'we have arrived.'

'I know it.' She did not look up from her work. 'I am not blind yet, nor deaf.' She had not changed. She seemed to him to have been like this as far back as he could remember, little and bent and old, in a cap and a brown smock. Her eyes were of the palest blue. Three grey hairs sprouted on her chin. Her hands.

* * *

LAUGHABLE, LAUGHABLE – she had only to look at him, and his velvet and fine lace and pointed boots became a jester's costume.

He was dressed only as befitted the imperial mathematician, yet why else had he carried himself with jealous care on the long journey hither, like a marvellous bejewelled egg, except to impress her? And now he felt ridiculous. Sunlight was spilling through the little window behind her, and he could see the garden, the fruit bushes and the chicken run and the broken wooden seat. The past struck him again a soft glancing blow. Out there had been his refuge from the endless rows and beatings, out there he had dawdled and dreamed, lusting for the future. His mother wiped her hands on her apron. 'Well come then, come!' as if it were he who had been delaying.

She glanced at Barbara with a sniff and turned her attention to the children.

'This is Susanna,' said Kepler, 'and here, Friedrich. Come, say God bless to your grandma.' Frau Kepler examined them as if they were for sale. Kepler was sweating. 'Susanne is seven already, and Friedrich is three or is it four, yes, four, a big boy – and,' like a fairground barker, 'here is our latest, the baby Ludwig! His godfather, you know, is Johann Georg Gödelmann, Saxony's Ambassador to the court of Prague.'

Regina stepped forward and displayed the infant.

'Very pale,' the old woman said. 'Is he sickly?'

'Of course not, of course not. You, ah, remember Regina? My . . . our . . .'

'Aye: the cabinetmaker's daughter.'

And they all, even the children, looked at the young woman in silence for a moment. She smiled.

'We are on our way from Heidelberg,' said Kepler. 'They are printing my book there. And before that we were in Frankfurt, for the fair, the book fair, I mean, in . . . in Frankfurt.'

'Books, aye,' Frau Kepler muttered, and sniffed again. She bent over the fire to stir the bubbling pot, and in the awkward silence everyone abruptly changed their places, making little lunges and sudden stops, setting Kepler's teeth on edge. He marvelled at how well the old woman managed it still, the art of puppetry! Heinrich sidled forward and stood beside her. As she straightened up she fastened a hand on his arm to steady herself, and Kepler noted, with a pang that surprised him, his brother's embarrassed smile of pride and protectiveness. Frau Kepler squinted at the fire. 'A wonder you could come to see us, you are so busy.'

Heinrich laughed. 'Now ma!' He rubbed a hand vigorously through the sparse hairs on his pate, grinning apologetically. 'Johann is a great man now, you know. I say, you must be a great man now,' as if Kepler were deaf, 'with the books and all, eh? And working for the Emperor himself!'

Barbara, sitting by the table, quietly snorted.

'O yes,' said Kepler, and turned away from his mother and her son standing side by side before him, feeling a sudden faint disgust at the spectacle of family resemblance, the little legs and hollow chests and pale pinched faces, botched prototypes of his own, if not lovely, at least completed parts. 'O yes,' he said, trying to smile but only wincing, 'I am a great man!'

* * *

EVERYONE WAS morbidly hungry, and when the capon had been dispatched they started on the bean stew from the three-legged pot. Heinrich was sent to the baker's, and came back with a sack of loaves, and buns for the children, and a flagon of wine. He had dallied in the wine shop, and his grin was crookeder than before. He tried to make Barbara take a drink, but she shook her head, turning her face away from him. She had not spoken a word since their arrival. The baby was sprawled asleep in her lap. The old woman squatted on a stool beside the fire, picking at her bowl of stew and mumbling to herself and sometimes grinning furtively. The children had been put to sit under Regina's supervision at the kitchen table. Kepler suddenly recalled a sunny Easter Sunday long ago, when his grandfather was still alive, one of those days that had lodged itself in his memory not because of any particular event, but because all the aimless parts of it, the brilliant light, the scratchy feel of a new coat, the sound of bells, lofty and mad, had made together an almost palpable shape, a great air sign, like a cloud or a wind or a shower of rain, that was beyond interpreting and yet rich with significance and promise. Was that . . . happiness? Disturbed and puzzled, he sat now sunk in thought, watching shadows move on the wine's tensed meniscus in his cup.

He had been at Maulbronn then, the last of his many schools. Chance, in the form of the impersonal patronage of the Dukes of Württemberg, had given him a fine education. At fifteen he knew Latin and Greek, and had a grasp of mathematics. The family, surprised by the changeling in their midst, said that all this learning was not good, it would ruin his health, as if his health had ever been their only concern. The truth was they saw his scholarship as somehow a betrayal of the deluded image the Keplers had of themselves then of sturdy burgher stock. That was the time of the family's finest flourishing. Grandfather Sebaldus was the mayor of Weilderstadt, and his son Harry, Kepler's father, temporarily back from his profligate wanderings, was running an inn at Ellmendingen. It was a brief heyday. The inn failed, and Harry Kepler and his family moved back to Weil, where the mayor had become entangled in the shadowy litigations which were eventually to ruin him. Before long Harry was off again, this time to the Low Countries to join the Duke of Alba's mercenaries. Johannes was never to see him again. Grandfather Sebaldus became his guardian. A red-faced fat old reprobate, he considered Johannes a fancified little get.

The house had been crowded then. His brother Heinrich was there, a clumsy inarticulate boy, and their sister Margarete, and Christoph the baby whom no one expected would live, and Sebaldus's four or five adult sons and daughters, the renegade Jesuit Sebald the younger, locked in an upstairs room and raving with the pox, Aunt Kunigund, whose loony husband was even then secretly poisoning her, and poor doomed Katharine, lover of beautiful things, now a wandering beggar. They were all of them infected with the same wild strain. And what a noise they made, packed together in that stinking little house! All his life Kepler had suffered intermittently from tinnitus, the after-echo of those years, he believed, still vibrating in his head. His bad eyesight was another souvenir, left him by the frequent boxings which every inmate of the house, even the youngest, inflicted on him when there was nothing worthier at hand to punish. Happiness? Where in all that would happiness have found a place?

* * *

REELING A LITTLE, with a mug of wine in his fist and wearing a moist conspiratorial smile, Heinrich came and crouched beside his brother's chair. 'This is a party, eh?' he wheezed, laughing. 'You should come see us more often.'

Of his surviving siblings, Kepler loved only Heinrich. Margarete was a bore, like the pastor she had married, and Christoph, a master pewterer in Leonberg, had been an insufferable prig even as a child. Still, they were innocent souls: could the same be said of Heinrich? He had the look of a happy harmless beast, the runt of the litter whom the farmer's fond-hearted wife has saved from the blade. But he had been to the wars. What unimaginable spectacles of plunder and rape had those bland brown eyes witnessed in their time? From such wonderings Kepler's mind delicately averted itself. He had peculiar need of *this* Heinrich, a forty-year-old child, eager and unlovely, and always hugely amused by a world he had never quite learned how to manage.

'You've printed up a book then – a storybook, is it?'

'No, no,' said Kepler, peering into his wine. 'I am no good at stories. It is a new science of the skies, which I have invented.' It sounded absurd. Heinrich nodded solemnly, squaring his shoulders as he prepared to plunge into the boiling sea of his brother's brilliance. '. . . And all in Latin,' Kepler added.

'Latin! Ha, and here am I, who can't even read in our own German.'

Kepler glanced at him, searching in vain for a trace of irony in that awestruck smile. Heinrich seemed relieved, as if the Latin exonerated him.

'And now I am writing another, about lenses and spyglasses, how they may be used for looking at the stars—' and then, quietly: '—How is your health now, Heinrich?'

But Heinrich pretended he had not heard. 'It's for the Emperor, is it, all these books you're writing, he pays you to write them, does he? I saw him one time, old Rudolph—'

'The Emperor is nothing,' Kepler snapped, 'an old woman unfit to rule.' Heinrich was an epileptic. 'Don't talk to me about that man!'

Heinrich looked away, nodding. Of all the ills with which he had been cursed, the falling sickness was the one he felt most sorely. Their father had tried to beat it out of him. Those scenes were among the earliest Kepler could remember, the boy stricken on the floor, the drumming heels and foam-flecked mouth, and the drunken soldier kneeling over him, raining down blows and screeching for the devil to come forth. Once he had tried to sell the child to a wandering Turk. Heinrich ran away, to Austria and Hungary, and on up to the Low Countries; he had been a street singer, a halberdier, a beggar. At last, at the age of thirty-five, he had dragged himself and his devil back here to his mother's house in Weilderstadt. 'How is it, Heinrich?'

'Ah, not bad, not bad you know. The old attacks . . .' He smiled sheepishly, and rubbed a hand again on the bald spot on his skull. Kepler passed him his empty cup. 'Let's have another fill of wine, Heinrich.'

* * *

THE CHILDREN went out to the garden. He watched them from the kitchen window as they trailed moodily among the currant bushes and the stumps of last year's cabbages. Friedrich stumbled and fell on his face in the grass. After a moment he came up again in laborious stages, a tiny fat hand, a lick of hair with a brown leaf tangled in it, a cross mouth. How can they bear it, this helpless venturing into a giant world? Susanna stood and watched him with a complacent sneer as he struggled up. There was a streak of cruelty in her. She had Barbara's looks, that puffy prettiness, the small bright mouth and discontented eyes. The boy wiped his nose on his sleeve and waded after her doggedly through the grass. A flaw in the windowpane made him a sudden swimmer, and in the eyepiece of Kepler's heart too something stretched and billowed briefly. Just when he had given up all hope of children Barbara had begun to flower with an almost unseemly abundance. He no longer had any trust, thought they would die too, like the others; the fact of their survival dazed him. Even yet he felt helpless and unwieldy before them, as if their birth had not ended the process of parturition but only transferred it to him. He was big with love.

He thought of his own father. There was not much to think of: a calloused hand hitting him, a snatch of drunken song, a broken sword rusted with what was said to be the blood of a Turk. What had driven *him*, what impossible longings had strained and kicked in his innards? And had *he* loved? What, then? The stamping of feet on the march, the brassy stink of fear and expectation on the battlefield at dawn, brute warmth and delirium of the wayside inn? What? Was it possible to love mere action, the thrill of ceaseless doing? The window reassembled itself before his brooding eyes. This was the world, that garden, his children, those poppies. I am a little creature, my horizons are near. Then, like a sudden drenching of icy water, came the thought of death, with a stump of rusted sword in its grasp.

'. . . Well, are we?'

He jumped. 'What?'

'*Ah!* do you ever listen.' The baby in her arms put forth a muffled exploratory wail. 'Are we to lodge in this . . . this house? Will there be room enough?'

'A whole family, generations, lived here once . . .'

She stared at him. She had slept briefly, sitting by the table. Her eyes were swollen and there was a livid mark on her jaw. 'Do you ever think about—' 'Yes.' '—these things, worry about them, do you?'

'*Yes*. Do I not spend every waking hour worrying and arranging and – do I not?' A lump of self-pity rose in his throat. '*What more do you want?*'

Tears welled in her eyes, and the baby, taking its cue, began to bawl. The door to the front room had the look of an ear bent avidly upon them. Kepler put a hand to his forehead. 'Let us not fight.'

The children came in from the garden, and paused, catching the pulsations in the air. The baby howled, and Barbara rocked him jerkily in a clockwork simulacrum of tenderness. Kepler turned away from her, frightening the children with his mad grin. 'Well, Susan, Friedrich: how do you like your grandma's home?'

'There is a dead rat in the garden,' Susanna said, and Barbara sobbed, and Kepler thought how all this had happened before somewhere.

* * *

YES, IT HAD ALL, all of it happened before. How was it he expected at each homecoming to find everything transformed? Was his self-esteem such as to let him think the events of his new life must have an effect, magical and redemptive, on the old life left behind him here in Weil? Look at him now. He had tricked himself out in imperial finery and come flouncing down upon his past, convinced that simply his elevation in rank would be enough to have caused the midden heap to sprout a riot of roses. And he had been hardly in the door before he realised that the trick had not worked, and now he could only stand and sweat, dropping rabbits and paper flowers from under his spangled cloak, a comic turn whom his glassy-eyed audience was too embarrassed to laugh at.

And yet Heinrich was impressed, and so too, according to him, was their mother. 'She talks about you all the time – O yes! Then she wants to know why I can't be like you. I! Well, I tell her, you know, mam, Johann is – Johann!' slapping his brother on the shoulder, wheezing, with tears in his eyes, as if it were a rare and crafty joke he had cracked. Kepler smiled gloomily, and realised that after all that was it, what burned him, that to them his achievements were something that had merely happened to him, a great and faintly ludicrous stroke of luck fallen out of the sky upon their Johann.

He climbed the narrow stairs, yawning. Had the old woman put one of her cunning potions into the wine? – or the stew, perhaps! Chuckling and yawning, and wiping his eyes, he ducked into the little back bedroom. This house had been built for the Keplers all right, everything in miniature, the low ceilings, the stools, the little bed. The floor was strewn with green rushes, and a basin of water and towels had been set out. Towels! She had not been wholly indifferent, then, to his impending visit. Afternoon sunlight was edging its way stealthily along the sill of the dingy window. Barbara was already asleep, lying on her back in the middle of the bed like a mighty effigy, a look of vague amazement on her upturned face. The baby at her side was a tiny pink fist in a bundle of swaddling. Susanna and Friedrich were crowded together in the truckle bed. Friedrich slept with his eyes not quite closed, the pupils turned up into his head and bluish moonlets showing eerily between the parted lids. Kepler leaned over him, thinking with resigned foreboding that someday surely he would be made to pay for the happiness this child had brought him. Friedrich was his favourite.

He lay for a long time suspended between sleep and waking, his hands folded on his breast. A trapped fly danced against the window pane, like a tiny machine engaged upon some monstrously intricate task, and in the distance a cow was lowing plaintively, after a calf, perhaps, that the herdsman had taken away. Strange, how comforting and homely these sounds, that yet in themselves were plangent with panic and pain. So little we feel! He sighed. Beside him the baby stirred, burbling in its sleep. The years were falling away, like loops of rope into a well. Below him there was darkness, an intimation of waters. He might have been an infant himself, now. All at once, like a statue hoving into the window of a moving carriage, Grandfather Sebaldus rose before him, younger and more vigorous than Johannes remembered having known him. There were others, a very gallery of stark still figures looking down on him. Deeper he sank. The water was warm. Then in the incarnadine darkness a great slow pulse began to beat.

* * *

CONFUSED AND WARY, not knowing where he was, he strove to hold on to the dream. As a child, when he woke like this in nameless fright, he would lie motionless, his eyelids quivering, trying to convince an imaginary watcher in the room that he was not really awake, and thus sometimes, by a kind of sympathetic magic, he would succeed in slipping back unawares into the better world of sleep. The trick would not work now.

That was what he had dreamed of, his childhood. And water. Why did he dream so often of water? Barbara was no longer beside him, and the truckle bed was empty. The sun was still in the window. He rose, groaning, and splashed his face from the basin. Then he paused, leaning thus and staring at nothing. What was he doing here, in his mother's house? And yet to be elsewhere would be equally futile. He was a bag of slack flesh in a world drained of essence. He told himself it was the wine and that troubled sleep, blurring his sense of proportion, but was not convinced. Which was the more real reality, the necessary certainties of everyday, or this bleak defencelessness?

Early one summer morning when he was a boy he had watched from the kitchen a snail crawling up the window outside. The moment came back to him now, wonderfully clear, the washed sunlight in the garden, the dew, the rosebuds on the tumbledown privy, that snail. What had possessed it to climb so high, what impossible blue vision of flight reflected in the glass? The boy had trod on snails, savouring the crack and then the soft crunch, had collected them, had raced them and traded them, but never before now had he really looked at one. Pressed in a lavish embrace upon the pane, the creature gave up its frilled grey-green underparts to his gaze, while the head strained away from the glass, moving blindly from side to side, the horns weaving as if feeling out enormous forms in air. But what had held Johannes was its method of crawling. He would have expected some sort of awful convulsions, but instead there was a series of uniform small smooth waves flowing endlessly upward along its length, like a visible heartbeat. The economy, the heedless beauty of it, baffled him.

How closely after that he began to look at things, flies and fleas, ants, beetles, that daddy-longlegs feebly pawing the window-sill at twilight, its impossible threadlike limbs, the gauzy wings with fantastical maps traced on them – what were they *for*, these mites whose lives seemed no more than a form of clumsy dying? The world shifted and flowed: no sooner had he fixed a fragment of it than it became something else. A twig would suddenly put forth sticky malevolent wings and with a shove and a drugged leap take flight; a copper and crimson leaf lying on a dappled path would turn into a butterfly, drunken, a little mad, with two staring eyes on its wings and a body the colour of dried blood. His ailing eyesight increased the confusion. The limits of things became blurred, so that he was not sure where sentient life gave way to mere vegetable being. Sunflowers, with their faces pressed to the light, were they alive, and if not, what did it mean, being alive? Only the stars he knew for certain to be dead, yet it was they, in their luminous order, that gave him his most vivid sense of life.

He shook himself now like a wet dog. A huge yawn stopped him in his tracks, prising his jaws apart until their hinges crackled, and when Regina put her head into the room she found him teetering before her with mouth agape and eyes shut tight as if he were about to burst into violent song.

* * *

HE PEERED AT HER through streaming tears and smiled.

'Mama sent me to wake you,' she said.

'Ah.'

Why was it, he wondered, that her candid gaze so pleased him always; how did she manage to make it seem a signal of support and understanding? She was like a marvellous and enigmatic work of art, which he was content to stand and contemplate with a dreamy smile, careless of the artist's intentions. To try to tell her what he felt would be as superfluous as talking to a picture. Her inwardness, which had intrigued Kepler when she was a child, had evolved into a kind of quietly splendid equilibrium. She resembled her mother not at all. She was tall and very fair, with a strong narrow face. Through her, curiously, Kepler sometimes glimpsed with admiration and regret her dead father whom he had never known. She would have been pretty, if she had considered being pretty a worthwhile endeavour. At nineteen, she was a fine Latin scholar, and even knew a little mathematics; he had tutored her himself. She had read his works, though never once had she offered an opinion, nor had he ever pressed her to.

'And also,' she said, stepping in and shutting the door behind her, 'I wanted to speak to you.'

'O yes?' he said, vaguely alarmed. A momentary awkwardness settled between them. There was nowhere to sit save the bed. They moved to the window. Below them was the garden, and beyond that a little common with an elm tree and a duck pond. The evening was bright with sunlight and drifting clouds. A man with two children by the hand walked across the common. Kepler, still not fully awake, snatched at the corner of another memory. He had sailed a paper boat once on that pond, his father had gone there with him and Heinrich on a summer evening like this, long ago . . . And just then, as if it had all been slyly arranged, the three figures stopped by the muddy margin there and, a lens slipping into place, he recognised Heinrich and Susanna and the boy. He laughed. 'Look, see who it is, I was just remem—'

'I am going to be married,' Regina said, and looked at him quickly with an intent, quizzical smile.

'Married,' he said.

'Yes. His name is Philip Ehem, he comes of a distinguished Augsburg family, and is a Representative at the court of Frederick the Elector Palatine . . .' She paused, lifting her eyebrows in wry amusement at the noise of this grand pedigree unfurling. 'I wanted to tell *you*, before . . .'

Kepler nodded. 'Yes.' He felt as if he were being worked by strings. He heard faintly the children's laughter swooping like swifts across the common. There would be a scene with Barbara if they got their feet wet. It was one of her increasingly numerous obsessions, wet feet. Beyond Regina's head a berry-black spider dangled in a far corner of the ceiling. 'Ehem, you say.'

'Yes. He is a Lutheran, of course.'

He turned his face away. 'I see.' He was jealous.

* * *

O HOW, HOW STRANGE: to be shocked at himself; horrified but not surprised. Where before was only tenderness – suspiciously weighty perhaps – and sometimes a mild objectless craving, there suddenly stood now in his heart a full-grown creature, complete in every detail and even possessed of a past, blinking in the light and tugging hesitantly at the still unbroken birthcord. It had been in him all those years, growing unnoticed towards this sudden incarnation. And what was he supposed to do with it now, this unbidden goddess come skimming up on her scallop shell out of an innocent sea? But what else was there to do, save smile crookedly and scratch his head and squint at the window, pretending to be Heinrich, and say: 'Well, married, yes, that's . . . that's . . .'

Regina was blushing.

'It will seem that we have come upon it suddenly, I know,' she said, 'and may be we have. But I – *we* – have decided, and so there seems no reason to delay.' The colour deepened on her brow. 'There is not,' a rapid mumble, 'there is not a *necessity* to hurry, as *she* will think, and no doubt say.'

'She?'

'She, yes, who will make a great commotion.'

The business was already accomplished in his head, he saw it before him like a tableau done in heraldic hues, the solemn bride and her tall grim groom, a pennant flying and the sky pouring down fat beneficent rays behind the scroll announcing *factum est!* and below, in a draughty underworld all to himself, Kepler inconsolabilis crouched with the hoof of a hunchbacked devil treading on his neck. He turned warily from the window. Regina had been watching him eagerly, but now she dropped her gaze and considered her hands clasped before her. She was smiling, amused at herself and embarrassed, but proud too, as if she had brought off some marvellous but all the same faintly ridiculous feat.

'I wanted to ask you,' she said, 'if you would—'

'Yes?' and something, before he could capture it, swooped out at her on the vibrating wings of that little word. She frowned, studying him with a closer attention; had she, O my God, felt that fevered wingbeat brush her cheek?

'You do not . . . approve?' she said.

'I I I—'

'Because I thought that you would, I hoped that you would, and that you might speak to her for me, for us.'

'Your mother? Yes yes I will speak to her, of course,' lunging past her, talking as he went, and, pausing on the stairs: 'Of course, speak to her, yes, tell her . . . tell her what?'

She peered at him in perplexity from the doorway. 'Why, that I plan to marry.'

'Ah yes. That you plan to marry. Yes.'

'I think you do not approve.'

'But of course I . . . of course . . .' and he clambered backwards down the stairs, clasping in his outstretched arms an enormous glossy black ball of sorrow and guilt.

* * *

Barbara was kneeling at the fireplace changing the baby's diaper, her face puckered against the clayey stink. Ludwig below her waved his skinny legs, crowing. She glanced over her shoulder at Kepler. 'I thought as much,' was all she said.

'You knew? But who is the fellow?'

She sighed, sitting back on her heels. 'You have met him,' she said wearily. 'You don't remember, of course. He was in Prague, you met him.'

'Ah, I remember.' He did not. 'Certainly I remember.' How tactful Regina was, to know he would have forgotten. 'But she is so young!'

'I was sixteen when I first married. What of it?' He said nothing. 'I am surprised you care.'

He turned away from her angrily, and opening the kitchen door was confronted by a hag in a black cap. They stared at each other and she backed off in confusion. There was another one at the kitchen table, very fat with a moustache, a mug of beer before her. His mother was busy at the iron stove. 'Kathar*ina*,' the first hag warbled. The fat one studied him a moment impassively and swigged her beer. The tomcat, sitting to attention on the table near her, flicked its tail and blinked. Frau Kepler did not turn from the stove. Kepler silently withdrew, and slowly, silently, closed the door.

'Heinrich—!'

'Now they're just some old dames that come to visit her, Johann.' He grinned ruefully and shoved his hands into the pockets of his breeches. 'They are company for her.'

'Tell me the truth, Heinrich. Is she . . .' Barbara had paused, leaning over the baby with a pin in her mouth; Kepler took his brother's arm and steered him to the window. 'Is she still at that old business?'

'No, no. She does a bit of doctoring now and then, but that's all.'

'My God.'

'She doesn't want for custom, Johann. They still come, especially the women.' He grinned again, and winked, letting one eyelid fall like a loose shutter. 'Only the other day there was a fellow—'

'I don't—'

'—Blacksmith he was, big as an ox, came all the way over from Leonberg, you wouldn't have thought to look at him there was anything—'

'I do not want to know, Heinrich!' He stared through the window, gnawing a thumbnail. 'My God,' he muttered again.

'Ah, there's nothing in it,' said Heinrich. 'And she's better value than your fancy physicians, I can tell you.' Resentment was making him hoarse, Kepler noted wistfully: why had such simple loyalty been denied to *him*? 'She made up a stuff for my leg that did more for it than that army doctor ever did.'

'Your leg?'

'Aye, there's a weeping wound that I got in Hungary. It's not much.'

'You must let me look at it for you.'

Heinrich glanced at him sharply. 'No need for that. She takes care of it.'

Their mother shuffled out of the kitchen. 'Now where,' she murmured, 'where did I leave that down, I wonder.' She pointed her thin little nose at Barbara. 'Have you seen it?' Barbara ignored her.

'What is it, mother,' Kepler said.

She smiled innocently. 'Why, I had it just a moment ago, and now I have lost it, my little bag of bats' wings.'

A cackling came from the kitchen, where the two hags could be seen, shrieking and hilariously shoving each other. Even the cat might have been laughing.

* * *

REGINA CAME tentatively down the stairs. 'You are not fighting over me, surely?' They looked at her blankly. Frau Kepler, grinning, scuttled back into the kitchen.

'What does she mean, bats' wings?' said Barbara.

'A joke,' Kepler snapped, 'a joke, for God's sake!'

'Bats' wings indeed. What next?'

'She's nobody's fool,' Heinrich put in stoutly, trying not to laugh.

Kepler flung himself on to a chair by the window and drummed his fingers on the table. 'We'll put up at an inn tonight,' he muttered. 'There is a place out toward Ellmendingen. And tomorrow we'll start for home.'

Barbara smiled her triumph, but had the good sense to say nothing. Kepler scowled at her. The three old women came out of the kitchen. There was a fringe of foam on the fat one's moustache. The thin one made to address the great man sunk in gloom by the window, but Frau Kepler gave her a push from the rear. 'O! hee hee, your ma, sir, I think, wants to be rid of us!'

'Bah,' Frau Kepler said, and shoved her harder. They went out. 'Well,' the old woman said, turning to her son, 'you've driven them away. Are you satisfied now?'

Kepler stared at her. 'I said not a word to them.'

'That's right.'

'You would be better off if they did not come back, the likes of that.'

'And what do you know about it?'

'I know them, I know their sort! You—'

'Ah, be quiet. What do you know, coming here with your nose in the air. We are not good enough for you, that's what it is.'

Heinrich coughed. 'Now mam. Johann is only talking to you for your own good.'

Kepler considered the ceiling. 'These are evil times, mother. You should be careful.'

'And so should you!'

He shrugged. When he was a boy he had nursed the happy notion of them all perishing cleanly and quickly some night, in an earthquake, say, leaving him free and unburdened. Barbara was watching him, Regina also.

'We had a burning here last Michaelmas,' said Heinrich, by way of changing the subject. 'By God,' slapping his knee, 'the old dame fairly danced when the fire got going. Didn't she, mam?'

'Who was it?' said Kepler.

'Damned old fool it was,' Frau Kepler put in quickly, glaring at Heinrich. 'Gave a philtre to the pastor's daughter, no less. She deserved burning, that one.'

Kepler put a hand over his eyes. 'There will be more burnings.'

His mother turned on him. 'Aye, there will! And not only here. What about that place where you are, that Bohemia, with all those papists, eh? I've heard they burn people by the bushel over there. *You* should be careful. 'She stumped off into the kitchen. Kepler followed her. 'Coming here and preaching to me,' she muttered. 'What do you know? I was healing the sick when you were no bigger than that child out there, cacking in your pants. And look at you now, living in the Emperor's pocket and drawing up magic squares for him. I dabble with the world, *you* keep your snout turned to the sky and think you're safe. Bah! You make me sick, you.'

'Mother . . .'

'Well?'

'I worry for you, mother, that's all.'

She looked at him.

* * *

ALL OUTSIDE was immanent with a kind of stealthy knowingness. He stood for a while by the fountain in the market place. The stone gargoyles had an air of suppressed glee, spouting fatly from pursed green lips as if it were an elaborate foolery they would abandon once he turned his back. Grandfather Sebaldus used to insist that one of these stone faces had been carved in his likeness. Kepler had always believed it. Familiarity rose up all round him like a snickering ghost. What did he know? Was it possible for life to go on, his own life, without his active participation, as the body's engine continues to work while the mind sleeps? As he walked now he tried to weigh himself, squinting suspiciously at his own dimensions, looking for the telltale bulge where all that secret life might be stored. The murky emotions called forth by

Regina's betrothal were only a part of it: what other extravagances had been contracted for, and at what cost? He felt somehow betrayed and yet not displeased, like an old banker ingeniously embezzled by a beloved son. A warm waft of bread assailed him as he passed by the baker's shop; the baker, all alone, was pummelling a gigantic wad of dough. From an upstairs window a servant girl flung out an exclamation of dirty water, barely missing Kepler. He glared up, and for a moment she goggled at him, then covered her mouth with her fingers and turned laughing to someone unseen behind her in the room, the son of the house, Harry Völiger, seventeen and prodigiously pimpled, creeping toward her with trembling hands . . . Kepler walked on, brooding over all those years of deceptively balanced books.

He gained the common. The evening rested here, bronzed and quietly breathing, basking like an exhausted acrobat in the afterglow of marvellous exploits of light and weather. The elm tree hung intent above its own reflection in the pond, majestically listening. The children were still here. They greeted him with sullen glances, wishing not to know him: they had been having fun. Susanna slowly ambled away with her hands clasped behind her, smiling back in a kind of blissful idiocy at a file of confused and comically worried ducklings scrambling at her heels. Friedrich tottered to the water's edge carrying a mighty rock. His shoes and stockings were soaked, and he had managed to get mud on his eyebrows. The rock struck the water with a flat smack. 'Look at the crown, papa, look look! – did you see it?'

'That's the king, all right,' said Heinrich. He had come to fetch the children back. 'He jumps up when you throw something in, and you can see his crown with all the diamonds on it. That right, Johann? I told him that.'

'I don't want to go home,' the child said, working one foot lovingly into the mud and plucking it out again with a delicious sucking sound. 'I want to stay here with Uncle Heinrich and my grandma.' His eyes narrowed thoughtfully. 'They have a pig.'

The surface of the pond smoothed down its ruffled silks. Tiny translucent flies were weaving an invisible net among the reflected branches of the elm, and skimmers dashed out from the shallows on legs so delicate they did not more than dent the surface of the water. Myriad and profligate life! Kepler sat on the grass. It had been a long day, busy with small discoveries. What was he to do about Regina? And what of his mother, dabbling still in dangerous arts? What was he to do. He remembered, as if the memory might mean something, Felix the Italian dancing with his drunken whores in a back lane on Kleinseit. The great noisome burden of things nudged him, life itself tipping his elbow. He smiled, gazing up into the branches. Was it possible, was this, was *this* happiness?

IV

Harmonice Mundi

Loretoplatz, Hradcany Hill, Prague
Ash Wednesday 1605

David Fabricius: in Friesland

Honoured friend! you may abandon your search for a new theory of Mars: it is established. Yes, my book is done, or nearly. I have spent so much pains on it that I could have died ten times. But with God's help I have held out, and I have come so far that I can be satisfied and rest assured that the *new astronomy* truly is born. If I do not positively rejoice, it is not due to any doubts as to the truth of my discoveries, but rather to a vision that has all at once opened before me of the profound effects of what I have wrought. My friend, our ideas of the world & its workings shall never be the same again. This is a withering thought, and the cause in me of a sombre & reflective mood, in keeping with the general on this day. I enclose my wife's recipe for Easter cake as promised.

You, a colleague in arms, will know how things stand with me. Six years I have been in the heat & clamour of battle, my head down, hacking at the particular; only now may I stand back to take the wider view. That I have won, I do not doubt, as I say. My concern is, what manner of victory I have achieved, and what price I & our science, and perhaps all men, will have to pay for it. Copernicus delayed for thirty years before publishing his majestic work, I believe because he feared the effect upon men's minds of his having removed this Earth from the centre of the world, making it merely a planet among planets; yet what I have done is, I think, more radical still, for I have transformed the very shape of things – I mean of course I have demonstrated that the conception of celestial form & motion, which we have held since Pythagoras, is profoundly mistaken. The announcement of this news too will be delayed, not through any Copernican bashfulness of mine, but thanks to my master the Emperor's stinginess, which leaves me unable to afford a decent printer.

My aim in the *Astronomia nova* is, to show that the heavenly machine is not a divine, living being, but a kind of clockwork (and he who believes that a clock has a soul, attributes to the work the maker's glory), insofar as nearly all the manifold motions are caused by a simple magnetic & material force, just as all the motions of the clock are caused by a simple weight. Yet, and most importantly, it is not the form or appearance of this celestial clockwork which concerns me primarily, but *the reality of it.* No longer satisfied, as I believe astronomy has been for milleniums, with the mathematical representation of planetary movement, I have sought to explain these movements *from their physical causes.* No one before me has ever attempted such a thing; no one has ever before framed his thoughts in this way.

Why, sir, you have a son! This is a great surprise to me. I put aside this letter briefly, having some pressing matters to attend to – my wife is ill again – and in the meantime from Wittenberg one Johannes Fabricius has written to me regarding certain solar phenomena, and recommending himself to me through my friendship for you, his father! I confess I am amazed, and not a little disturbed, for I have always spoken in my letters to you as to a younger man, and indeed, I wonder if I have not now and then fallen into the tone of a master addressing a pupil! You must forgive me. We should sometime have met. I think I am short of sight not only in the physical sense. Always I am being met with these shocks, when the thing before my nose turns out suddenly to be other than I believed it to be. Just so it was with the orbit of Mars. I shall write again and recount in brief the history of my struggle with that planet, It may amuse you.

Vale
Johannes Kepler

Wenzel House, Prague
November 1607

Hans Geo. Herwart von Hohenburg: at München

Entshuldigen Sie, my dear good sir, for my long delay in plying to your latest, most welcome letter. Matters at court devour my time & energies, as always. His Majesty becomes daily more capricious. At times he will forget my name, and look at me with that frown, which all who know him know so well, as if he does not recognise me at all; then suddenly will come an urgent summons, and I must scamper up to the palace with my star charts & astrological tables. For he puts much innocent faith in this starry scrying, which, as you know well, I consider a dingy business. He demands written reports upon various matters, such as for instance the nativity of the Emperor Augustus and of Mohammed, and the fate which is to be expected for the Turkish empire, and, of course, that which so exercises everyone at court these days, the Hungarian question: his brother Matthias grows ever more brazen in his pursuit of power. Also there is the tiresome matter of the so-called Fiery Trigon and the shifting of the Great Conjunction of Jupiter & Saturn, which is supposed to have marked the birth of Christ, and of Charlemagne, and, now that another 800 years have passed, everyone asks what great event impends. I ventured that this *great event* had already occurred, in the coming of Kepler to Prague: but I do not think His Majesty appreciated the witticism.

In this atmosphere, the New Star of three years past caused a mighty commotion, which still persists. There is talk, as you would expect, of universal conflagration and the Judgment Day. The least that will be settled for, it seems, is the coming of a great new king: *nova stella, novus rex* (this last a view which no doubt Matthias encourages!). Of course,

I must produce much wordage on this matter also. It is a painful & annoying work. The mind accustomed to mathematical demonstrations, on contemplating the faultiness of the foundations of astrology, resists for a long, long time, like a stubborn beast of burden, until, compelled by blows & invective, it puts its foot into the puddle.

My position is delicate. Rudolph is fast in the hands of wizards & all manner of mountebank. I consider astrology a political more than a prophetical tool, and that one should take care, not only that it be banished from the senate, but from the heads of those who would advise the Emperor in his best interests. Yet what am I to do, if he insists? He is virtually a hermit now in the palace, and spends his days alone among his toys and his pretty monsters, hiding from the humankind which he fears and distrusts, unwilling to make the simplest of decisions. In the mornings, while the groom puts his Spanish & Italian steeds through their paces in the courtyard, he sits gloomily watching from the window of his chamber, like an impotent infidel ogling the harem, and then speaks of this as his *exercise*! Yet, despite all, he is I confess far from ineffective. He seems to operate by a certain Archimedian motion, which is so gentle it barely strikes the eye, but which in the course of time produces movement in the entire mass. The court functions somehow. Perhaps it is just the nervous energy, common to all organisms, which keeps things going, as a chicken will continue to caper after its head has been cut off. (This is treasonous talk.)

My salary, need I say, is badly in arrears. I estimate that I am owed by now some 2,000 florins. I have scant hope of ever seeing the debt paid. The royal coffers are almost exhausted by the Emperor's mania for collecting, as well as by the war with the Turks and his efforts to protect his territories against his turbulent relatives. It pains me to be dependent upon the revenues from my wife's modest fortune. My hungry stomach looks up like a little dog to the master who once fed it. Yet, as ever, I am not despondent, but put my trust in God & my science. The weather here is atrocious.

Your servant, sir,
Joh: Kepler

Aedes Cramerianis, Prague
April 1608

Dr Michael Mästlin: at Tübingen

Greetings. That swine Tengnagel. I can hardly hold this pen, I am so angry. You will not credit the depths of that man's perfidy. Of course, he is no worse than the rest of the accursed Tychonic gang – only louder. A braying ass the fellow is, vain, pompous & irredeemably stupid. I will *kill* him, God forgive me. The only bright spot in all the horrid darkness of this business is that he still has not been paid, nor is he ever likely to be, the 20,000 florins (or 30 pieces of silver!) for which he sold Tycho Brahe's priceless instruments to the Emperor while the Dane was not yet cold in his grave. (He receives 1,000 florins annually as interest on the debt. This is twice the amount of my salary as Imperial Mathematician.) I confess that, when Tycho died, I quickly took advantage of the lack of circumspection on the part of the heirs, by taking his observations under my care, or, you may say (and certainly *they* do), purloining them. Who will blame me? The instruments, once the wonder of the world, are scattered across half of Europe, rusted and falling to pieces. The Emperor has forgotten them, and Tengnagel is content with his annual 5 per cent. Should I have let the same fate befall the mass of wonderfully precise & invaluable observations which Tycho devoted his lifetime to gathering?

The cause of this quarrel lies in the suspicious nature & bad manners of the Brahe family, but, on the other hand, also in my own passionate & mocking character. It must be admitted, that Tengnagel all along has had good reason for suspecting me: I was in possession of the observations, and I did refuse to hand them over to the heirs. But there is no reason for him to hound me as he does. You know that he became a Catholic, in order that the Emperor might grant him a position at court? This shows the man's character for what it is. (His lady Elizabeth goads him on – but no, I shall not speak of her.) Now he is Appellate Counsellor, and hence is able to impose his conditions on me with imperial force. He forbade me to print anything based upon his father-in-law's observations before I had completed the Rudolphine Tables; then he offered me freedom to print, provided I put his name with my own on the title pages of my works, so that he might have half the honours with none of the labour. I agreed, if he would grant me one quarter of that 1,000 florins he has from the Emperor. This was a shrewd move on my part, for Tengnagel, of course, true to his nature, considered the sum of 250 per annum too high a price to pay for immortal fame. Next, he got it into his thick head that he would himself take on the mighty task of completing the Tables. You will laugh with me, magister, for of course this is a nonsense, since the Junker has neither the ability for the task, nor the tenacity of purpose it will require. I have noticed it before, that there are many who believe they could do as well as I, nay, better, had they the time & the interest to attend the trifling problems of astronomy. I smile to hear them blowing off, all piss & wind. Let them try!

Luckily Tengnagel was vain enough to promise the Emperor that he would complete the work in four years: during which time he has sat upon the material like the dog in the manger, unable to put the treasure to use, and preventing others from doing so. His four years are now gone, and he has done nothing. Therefore I am pressing ahead with my *Astronomia nova*, the printing of which has at last begun at Vogelin's in Heidelberg. Good enough. But now the dolt insists that the book shall carry a preface written & signed by him! I dare not think what twaddle he will produce. He claims he fears I have used Tycho's observations only in order to disprove the Dane's theory of the world, but I know all he cares for is the clinking of coins. Ach, a base & poisonous fool.

K

Gutenbergplatz, Heidelberg
Midsummer Eve 1609

Helisaeus Röslin, physician-in-ordinary to Hanau-Lichtenberg: at Buchsweiler in Alsace

Ave. I have your interesting & instructive *Discurs von heutiger Zeit Beschaffenheir*, which provokes in me, along with much speculation, many pleasant & wistful memories of those fraternal debates which engaged us in our student days together at Tübingen. I intend presently to reply with a public *Antwort* on those of my points on the Nova of 1604 which you challenge with such passion & skill, but first I wish to say a few words to you in private, not only in honour of our long friendship, but also in order to clarify certain matters which I may not air in print. For my position here in Prague grows more precarious daily. The royal personage no longer trusts anyone, and is particularly watchful concerning that science which you so energetically defend, and by which he puts much store. I would prefer to say *pseudo-science*. Please destroy this letter immediatdy you have read it.

I would grant in you, my dear Röslin, the presence of an *instinctus divinus*, a special illumination in the interpretation of celestial phenomena, which, however, has nothing to do with astrological rules. After all, it is true that God sometimes allows even pure simpletons to announce strange & wonderful things. No one should deny that clever & even holy things may come out of foolery & godlessness, as out of unclean & slimy substances comes the pretty snail or the oyster, or the silkspinner out of caterpillar dirt. Even from the stinking dung heap the industrious hen may scrape a little golden grain. The majority of astrological rules I consider to be dung; as to what may be the grains worth retrieving from the heap, that is a more difficult matter.

The essence of my position is simply stated: that the heavens do something in people one sees clearly enough, but what specifically they do, remains a mystery. I believe that the *aspects*, that is the configurations which the planets form with one another, are of special significance in the lives of men. However, I hold that to speak of good & bad aspects is nonsensical. In the heavens it is not a question of good or bad: here only the categories harmonic, rhythmic, lovely, strong, weak & unarranged, are valid. The stars do not compel, they do not do away with free will, they do not decide the particular fate of an individual; but they impress on the soul a particular character. The person in the first igniting of his life receives a character & pattern of all the constellations in the heavens, or of the form of the rays flowing on to the earth, which he retains to the grave. This character creates noticeable traces in the form of the flesh, as well as in manners & gestures, inclinations & sympathies. Thus one becomes lively, good, gay; another sleepy, indolent, obscurantist; qualities which are comparable to the lovely & exact, or the extensive & unsightly configurations, and to the colours & movements, of the planets.

But upon what are based these categories, lovely & unlovely, strong & weak, et cetera? Why, upon the division of circles made by the knowable, that is constructable, regular polygons, as for instance is set out in my *Mysterium cosmographicum*; that is, the harmonic primordial relationships foreshadowed in the divine being. Thus all animated things, human & otherwise, as well as all the vegetable world, are influenced from heaven by the appropriate geometric instinct pertaining to them. All their activities are affected, individually shaped & guided by the light rays present here below and sensed by all these objects, as well as by the geometry & harmony which occurs between them by virtue of their motion, in the same way as the flock is affected by the voice of the shepherd, the horses on a wagon by the driver's shout, and the dance of the peasant by the skirl of the bagpipes. *This* is what I believe, and none of your monkeyshine will convince me otherwise.

I trust this frank German talk has not offended you, my dear Röslin. You live in my affections always, though sometimes I may snap & snarl, as is the habit of

your friend and colleague,
Johannes Kepler

Cramer Buildings, Prague
September 1609

Frau Katharina & Heinrich Kepler: at Weilderstadt

(To be read in their presence by G. Raspe, notary. Fee enclosed.)

Loved ones: I write to say that we have arrived home safely & well. Friedrich has a cough, but otherwise remains strong. Preparations for our dear Regina's wedding are already well advanced: she is wonderfully capable in matters such as these. Her intended husband is a fine & honourable man, and well set up. He came this week to pay us his respects. Of course, he has been here before, but not as a betrothed. I find him somewhat formal, and wonder if he may not prove inflexible. Everything was most polite. I have no doubt that Regina will be well treated by him, and will be happy, perhaps. They move to Pfaffenhofen in the Upper Palatinate after the wedding. There is talk of plague there.

We are still in our rooms in the old Cramer Buildings, and I think must remain here for the present. The quarters are satisfactory, for we are on the bridge, and so have the benefit of the river. The building is of stone, therefore there is less danger of fires breaking out, a thing I have always feared, as you know. Also we are situated in a good part of the city. At Wenzel College in the Old Town, where we lived before, things were very different: the streets there are bad, ill-paved and always strewn with every kind of filth, the houses are bad, roofed with straw or wattles, and there is a stink that would drive back the Turk. Our landlord here, though, is an unmannerly ruffian, and I have many differences with him, which upsets my digestion. Barbara tells me not to mind him. Why is it, I wonder, that people behave so badly toward each other? What is to be gained by fretting & fighting? I think there are some in the world who must sustain themselves by making their fellow men suffer. This is as true for the landlord who hounds his tenants, as it is for the infidel torturing his slaves to death: only the degree of evil differs, not the quality. These are the things I think about, when my duties at court and my scientific studies allow me time to think at all. Not that I do much scientific work now, for my health is not good, with frequent fevers and an inflammation of the bowel, and my mind for the most part prostrate in a pitiful frost. But I do not complain. God is good.

We move in the midst of a distinguished society here in Prague. The Imperial Counsellor and First Secretary, Johann Polz, is very fond of me. His wife & his whole family are conspicuous for their Austrian elegance and their distinguished & noble manners. It would be due to their influence, if on some future day I were to make progress in this respect, though, of course, I am still far away from it (there is a difference between being a renowned mathematician and being great in society!). Yet notwithstanding the shabbiness of my household and my low rank, I am free to come & go in the Polz house as I please – and they are considered to belong to the nobility! I have other connections. The wives of two imperial guards acted as godmothers at Susanna's baptism. Stefan Schmid, the Imperial Treasurer; Matthäus Wackher, the Court Barrister; and His Excellency Joseph Hettler, the Baden Ambassador, all stood for our Friedrich. And at the ceremonies for little Ludwig, the Counts Palatine Philip Ludwig & his son Wolfgang Wilhelm von Pfalz-Neuburg were present. So you see, we are beginning to rise in the great world! All the same, I do not forget my own people. I think of you often, and worry for your well-being. You must take care of each other, and be kind. Mother, think on my warnings when last we spoke. Heinrich, cherish your mother. And in your prayers remember

your son & brother,
Johann

(Herr Raspe, for your eyes only: watch Frau Kepler's doings, as I requested, and keep me informed. I shall pay you for these services.)

Aedes Cramerianis, Prague
March 1610

Signor Prof. Giorgio Antonio Magini: at Bologna

It is as if one had woken up to find two suns in the sky. That is only, of course, a way of putting it. Two suns would be a miracle, or magic, whereas *this* has been wrought by human eye and mind. It seems to me that there are times when, suddenly, after centuries of stagnation, things begin to flow all together as it were with astonishing swiftness, when from all sides streams spring up and join their courses, and this great confluence rushes on like a mighty river, carrying upon its flood all the broken & pathetic wreckage of our misconceptions. Thus, it is not a twelvemonth since I published my *Astronomia nova*, changing beyond recognition our notion of celestial workings: and now comes this news from Padua! Doubtless you in Italy are already familiar with it, and I know that even the most amazing things can come to seem commonplace in only a little time; for us, however, it is still new & wonderful & somewhat frightening.

Word was brought to me first by my friend Matthäus Wackher, Court Barrister & Privy Counsellor to His Majesty, who had it from the Tuscan Ambassador lately arrived here. Whackher came to see me at once. The day was bright and blustery, with a promise of spring, I will remember it always, as one remembers only a handful of days out of a lifetime. I saw, from the window of my study, the Counsellor's carriage come clattering over the bridge, and old Wackher with his head stuck out at the window, urging the driver on. Does excitement such as his that day send out before it palpable emanations? For even as I watched him coming, I felt nervous stirrings within me, though I knew nothing of what he had to tell me. I ran down and met the carriage arriving at my door. Herr Wackher was already babbling at me before I could grasp it. Galileus of Padua had turned upon the night sky a two-lensed *perspicillum* – a common Dutch spyglass, in fact – and by means of its 30-times magnification, *had discovered four new planets.*

I experienced a wonderful emotion while I listened to this curious tale. I felt moved in my deepest being. Wackher was full of joy & feverish excitement. At one moment we both laughed in our confusion, the next he continued his narrative and I listened intently – there was no end to it. We clasped hands and danced together, and Wackher's little dog, which he had brought with him, ran about in circles barking shrilly, until, overcome by our hilarity and quite beside itself, it jumped up and clasped me amorously about the leg, as dogs will, licking its lips and insanely grinning, which made us laugh the harder. Then we went inside and sat down, calmer now, over a jug of ale.

Is the report true? And if so, of what type are these newly discovered heavenly bodies? Are they companions of fixed stars, or do they belong to our solar system? Herr Wackher, though a Catholic, holds to the view of the misfortunate Bruno, that the stars are suns, infinite in number, which fill the infinite space, and Galileo's discovery, he believes, is proof of it, the four new bodies being companions of fixed stars: in other words, that it is another solar system that the Paduan has found. To me, however, as you know, an infinite universe is unthinkable. Also I consider it impossible that these are planets circling our sun, since the geometry of the world set forth in my *Mysterium* will allow of five planets in the solar system, and no more. Therefore I believe that what Galileo has seen are *moons circling other planets*, as our moon circles the earth. This is the only feasible explanation.

Perhaps you, closer to the scene of these discoveries, already have heard the correct explanation – perhaps even you have witnessed the new phenomena! Ah, to be in Italy. The Tuscan envoy, de Medici, who gave this news to Wackher, has presented to the Emperor a copy of Galileo's book. I hope soon to get my hands on it. Then we shall see!

Write, tell me all the news!
Kepler

Prague
April 1610

George Fugger, legatus imperatorius: *at Venice*

Lest silence & delay should make you believe that I agree with all you have to say in your latest letter, and since your position is peculiarly relevant in these matters, Galileo being in the employ of the Venetian Republic, I thought it prudent to interrupt my present studies and write to you straightway. Believe me, my dear Sir, I am deeply touched by your remarks regarding the claims to pre-eminence as between the Paduan & myself. However, I am not running a foot-race with him, that I should want for cheering & partisan broadcasting. Certainly, it is true what you say, that he urgently requires in these discoveries & claims of his the blessing of the Imperial Mathematician; and perhaps indeed this is, as you maintain, the only reason he has approached me. But why not? Some dozen years ago, before I was famous, and my *Mysterium* had just been published, it was *I* approaching *him*. True, he did not at that time make any great effort on my behalf. Perhaps he was too much taken up with his own work, perhaps he did not think much of my little book. Yes, I know his reputation for arrogance & ingratitude: what of it? Science, Sir, is not like diplomacy, does not progress by nods & winks & well-wrought compliments. It has always been my habit to praise what, in my opinion, others have done well. Never do I scorn other people's work because of jealousy, never do I belittle others' knowledge when I lack it myself. Likewise I never forget myself when I have done something better, or discovered something sooner. Certainly, I had hoped for much from Galileo when my *Astronomia nova* appeared, but the fact that I received nothing will not prevent me now from taking up my pen so that he should be armed against the sour-tempered critics of everything new, who consider unbelievable that which is unknown to them, and regard as terrible wickedness whatever lies beyond the customary bounds of Aristotelian philosophy. I have no wish to *pull out his feathers*, as you put it, but only to acknowledge what is of value, and question that which is doubtful.

No one, Excellency, should allow himself to be misled by the brevity & apparent simplicity of Galileo's little book. The *Sidereus nuncius* is highly significant & admirable, as even a glance through its pages will show. It is true that not everything in it is wholly original, as he claims – the Emperor himself has already turned a spyglass upon the moon! Also, others have surmised, even if they have not provided proof, that the Milky Way would, on closer inspection, dissolve into a mass of innumerable stars gathered together in clusters. Even the existence of planetary satellites (for this is, I believe, what his *four new planets* are, in fact) is not so amazing, for does not the moon circle the earth, and hence why should not the other planets have their moons? But there is a great difference between speculating on the existence of a myriad of invisible stars, and noting their positions on a map; between peering vacantly through a lens at the moon, and announcing that it is composed not of the *quinta essentia* of the schoolmen, but of matter much like that of the earth. Copernicus was not the first to hold that the sun sits at the centre of the world, but he *was* the first to build around that concept a system which would hold good mathematically, thus putting an end to the Ptolemaic age. Likewise Galileo, in this pamphlet, has set down clearly & calmly (and with a calm precision from which, I ruefully admit, I could learn much!) a vision of the world which will deliver such a blow to the belly of the Aristotelians that I think they will be winded for a long time to come.

The *Sidereus nuncius* is much talked about at court, as by now I suppose it is everywhere. (Would that the *Astronomia nova* had attracted such attention!) The Emperor graciously let me glance through his copy, but otherwise I had to contain myself as best I could until a week ago, when Galileo himself sent me the book, along with a request for my opinion on it, which I suppose he wishes to publish. The courier returns to Italy on the 19th, which leaves me juse four days in which to complete my reply. Therefore I must close now, in the hope that you will forgive my haste – and also that you will not take amiss my response above to your touching & much appreciated gestures of support for me. In these matters of science, it is a question, you see, not of the individual, but of the work. I do not like Galileo, but I must admire him.

By the way, I wonder, during your recent time in Rome, did you see or hear anything of Tycho's dwarf, and his companion, the one called Felix? I would have news of them, if you know any.

I am, Sir, your servant,
Johannes Kepler

Aedes Cramerianis, Prague
March 1611

Dr Johannes Brengger: at Kaufbeuren

Everything darkens, and we fear the worst. In the little world of our house, a great tragedy has befallen, which, in the morbid confusion of our grief, we cannot help but believe is in some way connected with the terrible events in the wider world. I think there are times when God grows weary, and then the Devil, seizing his chance, comes flying down upon us with all his fury & cruel mischievousness, wreaking havoc high & low. How far away now, my dear Doctor, seem those happier days when we corresponded with such enthusiasm & delight on the matter of our newborn science of optics! Thank you for your latest letter, but I fear I am unable at present to engage the interesting questions which you pose – another time, perhaps, I shall turn my mind upon them, and reply with the vigour they demand. I have not the heart for work now. Also much of my time is consumed by duties at court. The Emperor's eccentricities have come to seem more & more like plain insanity. He immures himself in the palace, hiding from the sight of his loathed fellow men, while in the meantime his realm falls asunder. Already his brother Matthias has dispossessed him of Austria, Hungary & Moravia, and is even now preparing to take over what is left. Throughout last summer and into the autumn, a congress of princes was held here in the city, which urged reconciliation between the brothers. Rudolph, however, despite his whimsy & his peculiarities, displays an iron stubbornness. Thinking to curb both Matthias & the princes, and also perhaps to set aside the religious freedoms wrested from him in the Royal Charter by the Lutheran Representatives here, he plotted with his kinsman Leopold, Bishop of Passau & brother to the poisonous Archduke Ferdinand of Styria, my old enemy. Leopold, of course, as vile & treacherous as the rest of his family, turned his army against us here, and has occupied part of the city. Bohemian troops massed against him, and frightful excesses by both sides are reported. Matthias, it is said, is now on his way here with an Austrian army, at the request of the Representatives – and of Rudolph himself! There can be only one result of all this, that the Emperor will lose his throne, and so I have begun to look elsewhere for a refuge. Certain influential people have urged me to come to Linz. For my own part, I cannot help but look with longing toward my native Swabia. I have sent a petition to the Duke of Wurttemberg, my sometime patron, but I have scant faith in him. Hard it is to know that one is not wanted in one's homeland! Also I have been offered Galileo's old chair at Padua, following his departure for Rome. Galileo has himself recommended me. The irony of this does not escape me. Italy – I do not relish the thought. Linz would seem, therefore, the most promising prospect. It is a narrow & provincial town, but there are people there whom I know, as well as a special friend. My wife would be happy to leave Prague, which she has never liked, and return to her native Austria. She has been most ill, with Hungarian fever & epilepsy. She bore these afflictions with fortitude, and all might have been well with her, had not our three children shortly thereafter been seized with the smallpox. The eldest one and the youngest survived, but Friedrich, our darling son, succumbed. He was six. It was a hard death. He was a fair child, a hyacinth of the morning in the first days of spring, our hope, our joy. I confess, Doctor, I fail sometimes to understand the ways of God. Even as the boy lay on his death bed, we could hear from across the city the noise of battle. How may I adequately express to you my feelings? Grief such as this is like nothing else in the world. I must close now.

Kepler

Gasthof zum Goldenen Greif, Prague
July 1611

Frau Regina Ehem: at Pfaffenhofen

O, my dear Regina! in the face of these disasters which have befallen us, words are inapt, and silence the truest expression of feelings. Nevertheless, however things stand with me, you must have an account of these past weeks. If I am clumsy or seem heartless or cold, I know you will understand that it is sorrow & shame which prevent me from expressing adequately all that I feel.

Who can say when was the real beginning of your mother's illness? Hers was a life crowded with difficulties & sadness. It is true, she never wanted for material things, however much she would blame me for my lack of success in the great world of society which it was ever her dream of entering. But to have been twice a widow by the age of 22, surely that was hard, as was the loss of our firstborn infants, and now our beloved Freidrich. Lately she had taken to secret devotions, and was never to be seen without her prayer book. Also her memory was not what it had been, and sometimes she would laugh at nothing at all, or suddenly cry out as if stricken. Her envy also had increased, and she was forever bemoaning her lot, comparing herself to the wives of councillors & petty court offficials, who seemed to move in far greater splendour than she, the wife of the Imperial Mathematician. All this was in her mind only, of course. What could I do?

Her illness of last winter, that fever & the falling sickness, frightened me greatly, but she was very brave & strong, with a determination which astonished all who knew her. The child's death in February was a terrible blow. When I returned from a visit to Linz at the end of June, I found her ill again. The Austrian troops had brought diseases into the city, and she had contracted spotted typhus, or *fleckfieber*, as they call it here. She might have fought back, but her strength was gone. Stunned by the deeds of horror of the soldiery & the sight of the bloody fighting in the city, consumed by despair of a better future and by the unquenchable yearning for her darling lost son, she finally expired, on the 3rd day of this month. As a clean smock was being put on her, at the end, her last words were to ask, Is this the dress of salvation? She remembered you in her final hours, and spoke of you often.

I am gnawed by guilt & remorse. Our marriage was blighted from the start, made as it was against our wills and under a calamitous sky. She was of a despondent & resentful nature. She accused me of laughing at her. She would interrupt my work to discuss her household problems. I may have been impatient when she went on asking me questions, but I never called her a fool, though it may have been her understanding that I considered her such, for she was very sensitive, in some ways. Lately, due to her repeated illnesses, she was deprived of her memory, and I made her angry with my reminders & admonitions, for she would have no master, and yet often was unable to cope herself. Often I was even more helpless than she, but in my ignorance persisted in the quarrel. In short, she was of an increasingly angry nature, and I provoked her, I regret it, but sometimes my studies made me thoughtless. Was I cruel to her? When I saw that she took my words to heart, I would rather have bitten off my own finger than give her further offence. As for me, not much love came my way. Yet I did not hate her. And now, you know, I have no one to talk to.

Think of me, my dear child, and pray for me. I have transferred to this inn – you remember the Golden Griffin? – for I could not abide the house. The nights are the hardest, and I do not sleep. What shall I do? I am a widower, with two young children, and all about is the turbulent disorder of war. I shall visit you, if possible. Would that you could come to see me here, but the perils would be too great. I sign myself, as in the old days,

Papa

Post scriptum. I have opened your mother's will. She left me nothing. My regards to your husband.

Kunstadt in Moravia
April 1612

Johannes Fabricius: at Wittenberg

Greetings, noble son of a noble father. You must forgive me for my long delay in replying to your numerous most welcome & fascinating letters. I have been these past months much taken up with business, both private & public. No doubt you are aware of the momentous events that have occurred in Bohemia, events which, along with all their other effects, have led to my virtual banishment from Prague. I am here at Kunstadt briefly, at the house of an old acquaintance of my late wife, a good-hearted widow woman who has offered to care for my motherless children until I have found quarters and settled in at Linz. Yes, it is Linz I am bound for, where I am to take up the post of district mathematician. You see how low I am brought.

The year that has passed has been the worst I have ever known; I pray I shall never see another such. Who would believe that so many misfortunes could befall a man in so short a time? I lost my beloved son, and then my wife. You would say, this were enough, but it seems that when disasters come, they come in dreadful armies. It was the entry of the Passau troops to Prague that brought the diseases which took from me my little son & my wife; then came the Archduke Matthias & his men, and my patron & protector was toppled from his throne: Rudolph, that poor, sad, good man! I did my best to save him. Both sides in the dispute were much influenced by star prophecies, as soldiers & statesmen always are, and, as Imperial Mathematician & Court Astronomer, my services were eagerly sought. Although in truth my best interests would have been served had I thrown in my lot with his enemies, I was loyal to my lord, and went so far as to pretend to Matthias that the stars favoured Rudolph. It was to no avail, of course. The outcome of that battle was determined before it began. Following his abdication in May, I remained at Rudolph's side. He had been good to me, despite all, and how could I abandon him? The new Emperor is not hostile to me, and only last month went so far as to confirm me in my post of mathematicus. Matthias, however, is no Rudolph; I shall be better off in Linz.

I shall be better off: so I tell myself. At least in Upper Austria there are people who value me & my work. That is more than can be said of my fellow countrymen. Perhaps you know of my efforts to return to Germany? Recently I turned again to Frederick of Württemburg, begging him to grant me, if not a professorship of philosophy, at least some humble political post, in order that I might have some peace & a little space in which calmly & quietly to pursue my studies. The Chancellor's office was not unsympathetic, and even suggested I might be put in line for the chair of mathematics at Tübingen, since Dr Mästlin is old. The Consistory, however, took a different view. They remembered that, in a former petition, I had been honest enough to warn that I could not unconditionally subscribe to the Formula of Concord. Also they dragged out the old accusation that I lean toward Calvinism. The end of it all is that I am finally rejected by my native land. Forgive me, but I hereby consign them all to the pits of Hell.

I am 41, and I have lost everything: my family, my honoured name, even my country. I face now into a new life, not knowing what new troubles await me. Yet I do not despair. I have done great work, which some day shall be recognised for its true value. My task is not yet finished. The vision of the harmony of the world is always before me, calling me on. God will not abandon me. I shall survive. I keep with me a copy of that engraving by the great Dürer of Nuremberg, which is called Knight with Death & the Devil, an image of stoic grandeur & fortitude from which I derive much solace: for this is how one must live, facing into the future, indifferent to terrors and yet undeceived by foolish hopes.

I enclose an old letter which I found unposted among my papers. It concerns matters of scientific interest, and you should have it, for I fancy it will be some little time before I have the heart to turn again to such speculations.

Your colleague,
Joh: Kepler

Prague
December 1611

Johannes Fabricius: at Wittenberg

Ah, my dear young sir, how happy I am to hear of your researches into the nature of these mysterious solar spots. Not only am I filled with admiration for the rigour & ingenuity of your investigations, but also I am carried back out of these hateful times to a happier period of my own life. Can it be only five years ago? Lucky I, who was the first in this century to have observed these spots! I say this, not in an attempt to steal your fire, if I may put it thus (nor even do I mean to join the tiresome controversy between Scheiner & Galileo over the priority of the discovery), but only to convince myself that there was a time when I could happily, and, one might say, in innocence, pursue my scientific studies, before the disasters of this terrible year had befallen me.

I first observed the phenomenon of solar spots in May of 1607. For weeks I had been earnestly observing Mercury in the evening sky. According to calculations, that planet was to enter into lower conjunction with the sun on May 29th. Since a heavy storm arose in the evening of the 27th, and it seemed to me this aspect would be the cause of such disturbance in the weather, I wondered if perhaps the conjunction should be fixed earlier. I therefore set to work to observe the sun on the afternoon of the 28th. At that time I had rooms at Wenzel College, where the Rector, Martin Bachazek, was my friend. A keen amateur, Bachazek had built a little wooden tower in one of the college lofts, and it was to there that he & I retired that day. Rays of the sun were shining through thin cracks in the shingles, and under one of these rays we held a piece of paper whereon the sun's image formed. And lo! on the shimmering picture of the sun we espied a little daub, quite black, approximately like a parched flea. Certain that we were observing a transit of Mercury, we were overcome with the greatest excitement. To prevent error, and to make sure it was not a mark in the paper itself, we kept moving the paper back & forth so that the light moved: and everywhere the little black spot appeared with the light. I drew up a report immediately, and had my colleague endorse it. I ran to the Hradcany, and sent the announcement to the Emperor by a valet, for of course this conjunction was of great interest to His Majesty. Then I repaired to the workshop of Jost Bürgi, the court mechanic. He was out, and so, with one of his assistants, I covered a window, letting the light shine through a small aperture in a tin plate. Again the little daub appeared. Again I sought verification for my report, and had Bürgi's assistant sign it. The document lies before me on my desk, and there is the signature: *Heinrich Stolle, watchmaker journeyman, my hand.* How well I remember it all!

Of course, I was wrong, as so often; it was not a transit of Mercury I had witnessed, as you know, but a sunspot. Have you, I wonder, a theory as to the origin of this phenomenon? I have witnessed it often since that day, yet I have not decided to my own satisfaction what is the explanation. Perhaps they are a form of cloud, as in our own skies, but wonderfully black and heavy, and therefore easily to be seen. Or maybe they are emanations of burning gas rising from the fiery surface? For my own part, they are of the utmost interest not in their cause, but in that, by their form & evident motion, they prove satisfactorily the rotation of the sun, which I had postulated without proof in my *Astronomia nova.* I wonder that I could do so much in that book, without the aid of the telescope, which in your work you have put to such good use.

What should we do without our science? It is, even in these dread times, a great consolation. My master Rudolph grows stranger day by day: I think he will not live. Sometimes he seems not to understand that he is no longer emperor. I do not disabuse him of this dream. How sad a place the world is. Who would not rather ascend into the clear & silent heights of celestial speculation?

Please do not take my bad example to heart, but write to me soon again. I am, Sir,

yours,
Johannes Kepler

Gasthof zum Goldenen Greif, Prague
September 1611

Frau Regina Ehem: at Pfaffenhofen

Life, so it used to seem to me, my dear Regina, is a formless & forever shifting stuff, a globe of molten glass, say, which we have been flung, and which, without even the crudest of instruments, with only our bare hands, we must shape into a perfect sphere, in order to be able to contain it within ourselves. That, so I thought, is our task here, I mean the transformation of the chaos without, into a perfect harmony & balance within us. Wrong, wrong: for our lives contain us, *we* are the flaw in the crystal, the speck of grit which must be ejected from the spinning sphere. It is said, that a drowning man sees all his life flash before him in the instant before he succumbs: but why should it be only so for death by water? I suspect it is true whatever the manner of dying. At the final moment, we shall at last perceive the secret & essential form of all we have been, of all our actions & thoughts. Death is the perfecting medium. This truth – for I believe it to be a truth – has manifested itself to me with force in these past months. It is the only answer that makes sense of these disasters & pains, these betrayals.

I will not hold you responsible, dear child, for our present differences. There are those about you, and one in particular, I know, who will not leave in peace even a bereaved & ailing man in his hour of agony. Your mother was hardly cold in her grave when that first imperious missive from your husband arrived, like a blow to the stomach, and now *you* write to me in this extraordinary fashion. This is not your tone of voice, which I remember with tenderness & love, this is not how you would speak to me, if the choice were yours. I can only believe that these words were dictated to you. Therefore, I am not now addressing you, but, through you, another, to whom I cannot bring myself to write directly. Let him prick up his ears. This squalid matter shall be cleared up to the satisfaction of all.

How can you insinuate that I am delaying in the payment of these monies? What do I care for mere cash, I, who have lost that which was more precious to me than an emperor's treasury of gold, I mean my wife & my beloved son? That my lady Barbara chose not to mention me in her will is a profound hurt, but yet I intend to carry out her wishes. Although I have not the heart at the moment to investigate thoroughly how matters stand, I know in general the state of Frau Kepler's fortune, or what remains of it. When her father died, and the Mühleck estates were divided, she possessed some 3,000 florins in properties & goods. She was therefore not so rich as we had been led to believe – but that is another matter. I went with Frau Kepler to Graz at that time, when Jobst Müller had died, and spent no little time & pains in converting her inheritance into cash. Styrian taxes then were nothing less than punitive measures against Lutherans, and we suffered heavy losses in transferring her monies out of Austria. That is why there is not now those thousands which some people think I am trying to appropriate. Our life in Bohemia had been difficult, the Emperor was not the most prompt of paymasters, and inevitably, despite Frau Kepler's extreme parsimony, calls were made from time to time upon her capital. There were her many illnesses, the fine clothes which she insisted upon, and then, she was not one to be satisfied with beans & sausages. Do you imagine that we lived on air?

Also, after my marriage, I succeeded, against great opposition, in being appointed guardian of my wife's little daughter, our dear Regina, because I loved the child, as she was then, and because I feared that among her mother's people she would be exposed to the danger of Catholicism. I had been promised by Jobst Müller, 70 florins per annum for the child's maintenance: I was never paid a penny of that allowance, nor, of course, was I permitted to touch Regina's own considerable fortune. Therefore, I am fully justified in deducting from the inheritance a just & suitable recompense. I have two children of my own to care for. My friends & patrons, the House of Fugger, will oversee the transfer to you of the remaining sum. I trust you will not accuse *them* of suspect dealing?

Johannes Kepler

Prague
December 1610

Dr Johannes Brengger: at Kaufbeuren

I have received today, from Markus Welser in Cologne, the first pages in proof of my *Dioptrice*. The printing has been delayed, and even now, when it has finally started, there is a problem with the financing of the project, and I fear it will be some long time before the work is completed. I finished it in August, and presented it at once to my patron, the Elector Ernst of Cologne, who unfortunately has proved less enthusiastic & less prompt than the author, and seems not to be in any hurry to give to the world this important work which is dedicated to him. However, I am glad to see even these few pages in print, since in my present troubled state I am grateful for the small diversion which they provide. How far away already seem those summer months, when my health looked to be improving, and I worked with such vigour. Now I am subject once more to bouts of fever, and consequently I have no energy, and am sore in spirit. Worries abound, and there are rumours of war. Yet, looking now afresh at the form of this little book, I am struck by the thought that perhaps, without realising it, I had some intimation of the troubles to come, for certainly it is a strange work, uncommonly severe & muted, wintry in tone, precise in execution. It is not like me at all.

It is a book that is not easy to understand, and which assumes not only a clever head, but also a particularly intellectual alertness & an extraordinary desire to learn the causes of things. In it I have set about clearing up the laws by which the Galilean telescope works. (I might add, that in this task I have had scant help, as you would expect, from him whose name is given to the new instrument.) It may be said, I believe, that between this book, and my *Astronomia pars optica* of 1604, I have laid the foundations of a new science.

Whereas, however, the earlier book was a gay & speculative venturing upon the nature of light and the working of lenses, the *Dioptrice* is a sober setting out of rules, in the manner of a geometry manual. O, that I could send you a copy, for I am eager to hear your opinion. Damn these penny-pinchers! It is composed of 141 rules, schematically divided into definitions, axioms, problems & propositions. I begin with the law of refraction, the expression of which, I confess, is not much less inexact than previously, although I have managed not too badly by virtue of the fact that the angles of incidence dealt with are very small. I have also set out a description of total reflection of light rays in a glass cube & threesided prism. As well, of course, I have gone more deeply than ever into the matter of lenses. In Problem 86, in which I demonstrate how, with the help of two convex lenses, visible objects can be made larger & distinct but inverted, I believe I have defined the principle upon which the astronomical telescope is based. Also, by treating of the suitable combinations of a converging lens with a diverging lens in place of a simple object lens, I have shown the way toward a large improvement upon the Galilean telescope. This will not please the Paduan, I think.

So you see, my dear Doctor, how far ahead I have pressed in our science. I think, indeed, that I have gone as far as it is possible to go, and I confess, with some regret, that I am losing interest in the subject. The telescope is a wonderfully useful instrument, and will no doubt prove of great service to astronomy. For my part, however, I grow tired rapidly of peering into the sky, no matter how wonderful the sights to be seen there. Let others map these new phenomena. My eyesight is bad. I am, I fear, no Columbus of the heavens, but a modest stay-at-home, an armchair dreamer. The phenomena with which I am already familiar are sufficiently strange & wonderful. If the new stargazers discover novel facts which will help to explain the true causes of things, fair enough; but it seems to me that the real answers to the cosmic mystery are to be found not in the sky, but in that other, infinitely smaller though no less mysterious firmament contained within the skull. In a word, my dear friend, I am old-fashioned; as I am also,

yours,
Kepler

Aedes Cramerianis, Prague
October 1610

Georg Fugger: at Venice

Let me yet again offer you my warm & sincerest thanks for your loyal support of me & my work. I thank you also for your kind words regarding my *Dissertatio cum nuncio sidero*, and your efforts to promote in Italy the views expressed in that little work. Yet, once more, I must protest at your too enthusiastic championing of me against Galileo. I do not oppose him. My *Dissertatio* does not, as you put it, *rip the mask from his face*. If you read my pamphlet with attention, you will clearly see that I have, with reservations, given my blessing to his findings. Does this surprise you? Are you, perhaps, disappointed? How, you will ask, can I be warm toward someone who will not even deign to write to me directly? But as I have said before, I am a lover of truth, and will welcome it & celebrate it, whatever quarter it may come from. Sometimes I suspect that those who concern themselves in this squabble over the reliability of Galileo's findings, may in fact care less for the objective truth, than they do for getting hold of ammunition to use against an arrogant & clever man, and who is not subtle nor sly enough to put on a false humility in order to please the general. That young clown Martin Horky, Magini's assistant, in his so-called *Refutation*, had the gall to quote me – no, to misquote me, in support of his imbecile gibes against Galileo. I lost no time in terminating my acquaintance with the young pup.

Still, I confess Galileo is difficult to love. You know, in all this time he has written to me only one letter. For the rest, for news of his further discoveries, and even for word of his reactions to my *Dissertatio* (which after all was an open letter directed to him!), I must depend on second-hand accounts from the Tuscan Ambassador here, and other suchlike. And then, how secretive & suspicious the Paduan is! When he does send me a crumb, he hides it inside the most impossible & unnecessary of disguises. For instance, last summer he sent, again through the ambassador, the following message: *Smaismirmilmepoetaleumibunenugttaurias.* At first I was amused: after all, I myself sometimes play with anagrams & word games of this sort. However, when I set about deciphering the code, I was nearly driven out of my mind. The best I could manage was a bit of barbaric Latin verse that made no sense. It was not until last month – when Galileo had heard that the Emperor himself was curious – that the solution was furnished at last: hidden in that jumble was the announcement of the discovery of what appear to be two small moons circling Saturn! Now has come another puzzle, which seems to speak of a *red spot in Jupiter which rotates mathematically.* A red spot, I ask myself, or a red herring? How is one to respond to this kind of foolery? I shall scald the fellow's ears with my next letter.

And yet, what a splendid & daring scientist he is! O, that I could journey to Italy to meet this Titan! I will not have him sneered at, you know, in my presence. You mention how Magini & the dreadful Horky (nice name for him), and even you yourself, were delighted with the passage in the *Dissertatio* in which I mention that the principle of the telescope was set out 20 years ago by della Porta, and also in my own work on optics. But Galileo has not claimed the *invention* of the instrument! Besides, these anticipations were purely theoretical, and cannot diminish Galileo's fame. For I know what a long road it is from the theoretical concept to its practical achievement, from the mention of the Antipodes in Ptolemy to Columbus's discovery of the New World, and even more from the two-lensed instruments used in this country to the instrument with which Galileo has penetrated the skies.

Let me state, then, clearly and without equivocation, that my *Dissertatio* is not the masterpiece of irony which so many take it to be (would that I possessed such subtlety!), but an open & express endorsement of Galileo's claims. Thank you for the oranges. Though I regret to say the packaging was damaged, and they had all gone bad.

Your servant, Sir,
Joh: Kepler

Prague
September 1610

Professor Gio. A. Magini: at Bologna

Excellent news, my dear sir: the Elector Ernst of Cologne, who is my patron, and who has been here throughout the summer for the Council of princes, resumed last week from a brief visit to Vienna and brought with him a telescope, the very one which Galileo had himself presented to the Archduke of Bavaria. Thus the mean-spirited Paduan is frustrated in his jealousy by the kindness of my friends & patrons. Perhaps there is justice in the world, after all.

I have had much trouble with this Galilei (his father, I think, was a finer mind: have you read him?). With his usual imperiousness, he sends through his countrymen here at court, demands that I should support him in his claims regarding Jupiter, for it seems he is not content with my *Dissertatio*, and would have me repeat myself in ever more forceful affirmations of his genius – and yet, despite my many pleas, he would not send me an instrument with which to verify his claims to my own satisfaction. He says the expense & difficulty of manufacture prevents him, but I know that he has already distributed telescopes to all & sundry. What does he fear, that he excludes me? I confess I am led to suspect that his enemies may have something, when they say he is a braggart & a charlatan. I urged him to send me the names of witnesses, who would testify that they had seen what, in the *Sidereus nuncius*, he claims to be the case. He replied that the Grand Duke of Tuscany & one other of that numerous Medici clan would vouch for him. But I ask, what good are these? The Grand Duke of Tuscany, I do not doubt, would vouch for the sanctity of the Devil, if it suited him. Where are the *scientists* who will corroborate the findings? He says he holds them incapable of identifying either Jupiter or Mars, or even the moon, and so how can they be expected to know a new planet when they see it!

Anyway, it is all over now, thanks to the Elector Ernst. From August 30th, when he returned from Vienna, I have been, with the aid of the telescope, witnessing these wonderful new phenomena with my own eyes. Wishing, unlike the Paduan, to have the support of reliable witnesses, I invited to my house Ursinus the young mathematician, along with some other notables, that we might, individually, and by secret recording, at last provide indisputable proof of Galileo's claims. To avoid error, and also to preclude any charges of complicity, I insisted that we each draw in chalk on a tablet what we had seen in the telescope, the observations afterwards to be compared. It was all very satisfactory. We got in some good wine, and a hamper of food – game pies & a string of excellent sausage – and spent a very convivial evening, though I confess that the wine, combined with my poor eyesight, led me to a strange & peculiarly coloured view of the phenomena. However, all of the results matched up, more or less, and in the following days I was able myself to check them repeatedly. He was right, that Galilei!

Ah, with what trepidation did I apply my face to that splendid instrument! How would it be, if these new discoveries should only go to prove that I was wrong in my dearly held assumptions as to the true nature of things? I need not have feared. Yes, Jupiter possesses moons; yes, there are many more stars in heaven than are visible to the unaided eye; yes, yes, the moon is made of matter similar to that of the earth: but still, the shape of reality is as it has always seemed to me. The earth occupies the most distinguished place in the universe, since it circles the sun in the middle place between the planets, and the sun in turn represents the middle place at rest in a spherical space enclosed by the fixed stars. And everything is regulated according to the eternal laws of geometry, which is one & eternal, a reflection of the mind of God. All this I have seen, and am at peace – no thanks, however, to Galileo.

These are strange & marvellous times in which we live, that such transformations are wrought in our view of the nature of things. Yet we must hold fast to that, that it is only our vision which is being expanded & altered, not the thing itself. Curious, how easy it is for us little creatures to confuse the opening of our eyes with the coming into being of a new creation: like children conceiving the world remade each morning when they wake.

Your friend, Sir,
Johannes Kepler

Cramer Buildings, Prague
April 1610

Frau Katharina & Heinrich Kepler: at Weilderstadt

Unwholesome & frightening reports have come to me, never mind by what channels, regarding your conduct, my mother. I have already spoken to you on this matter, but it seems I must do so again, and forcefully. Do you not know what is being said about you in Weil & roundabout? Even if you do not worry for your own safety, have a thought at least for your family, for my position and that of your sons & daughter. I know that Weil is a small place, and that tongues will wag whether the scandal is real, or thought up by evil minds, but all the more reason, then, to have a care. Daily now we hear of more & more burnings in Swabia. Do not deceive yourself: no one is immune to the threat of these flames.

The woman Ursula Reinbold, the glazier's wife, has put it about that once, after taking a drink at your house, she became ill with awful fluxions, and holds that you had poisoned her with a magic draught. I know she is unbalanced, and has a bad reputation, and that the illness was probably brought on by an abortion – but it is with just such people as this that stories begin, which in time take on the semblance of truth in the general mind. Others, hearing of the Reinbold woman's charge, bethink themselves that they also have cause to complain against you. There is a kind of madness which takes hold of people at times such as this, when the stars are unpropitious. What wrong, anyway, did you do the glazier's wife? She says you abused her, and now seemingly she nurses a deep hatred of our family. I am told too that Christoph has been in some way involved with her – what is the young fool about, that he consorts with the likes of her?

There is more. Beutelspacher the schoolmaster says that he also had a drink of you, and that it was this drink which caused his lameness. (What *is* this drink, in which you seem to have soused the entire town?) Bastian Meyer says you gave his wife a lotion, and after she had applied it she fell into a lingering illness & died. Christoph Frick the butcher says he suddenly felt pains in his thigh one day when he passed you by in the street. Daniel Schmid the tailor blames you for the death of his two children, because you would come into his house without cause, and whisper invocations in a strange language over the cradle. Schmid also claims that, when the children were ill, you taught his wife a prayer, to be uttered at full moon under the open sky in the churchyard, which would cure them, though they died all the same. And, wildest of all, I am told that you, Heinrich, have testifed that our mother had ridden a calf to death, and then wanted to prepare a roast from the carcase! *What is going on?* O and yes, mother, something else: a gravedigger at Eltingen says that on a visit to your father's grave, you asked the fellow to dig up the skull, so that you could have it mounted in silver & presented to me as a drinking vessel. Can this be true? Have you gone mad? Heinrich, what do you know of these matters? I am beside myself with worry. Should I come to Swabia and investigate for myself, I wonder. The business is growing serious. I pray you, mother, keep to the house, speak to no one, and above all cease this doctoring & giving of potions. I am sending this letter directly to Herr Raspe, as I shall do with all letters in future, for I am told that previously, despite my directions, you have gone to Beutelspacher, of all people, to have my letters read.

Have a care, now, I say, and pray for him who is

your loving son,
Johann

(Herr Raspe: My thanks for these informations. What am I to do? They will burn her, sure as God! Enclosed, the usual fee.)

Prague
November 1609

H. Röslin: at Buchsweiler in Alsace

Several thoughts occur to me, following your latest letter, but the majority of them I must keep to myself, for fear of angering you further. I am sorry to note the hostility of your reaction to my *Antwort auff Röslini discurs*: believe me, my friend, it was not meant as an attack *ad hominem*. My tongue, I fear, has at times a rough & uncouth edge to it, especially when I am wrought, or even when I am only excited by the subject in hand, which last is the case on this occasion. I wished in my pamphlet to define as clearly as possible my attitude to astrology. I thought I had neither condemned nor condoned this science, of which you are such an ardent champion. Did I really say, in my last letter, that it was *monkeyshine*? What comes over me, to say such things! Please, I apologise. I shall try here, as briefly & concisely as possible, to make amends and show you my true opinion in the matter.

In fact, you will be interested to hear that I am at this very time engaged in the composition of another *Answer*, this time to an attack upon astrologers! Feselius, physician-in-ordinary to the dedicatee of your own *Discurs*, has produced a weighty attack upon the whole of astrology, which he altogether repudiates. Now, will it surprise you to know that I am about to weigh in, in my latest *Antwort*, with a defence against this broadside? For of course, contrary to what you seem to think, I do not hold all of that science to be worthless. Feselius, for instance, claims that the stars & planets were put up by God only as signs for determining time, and therefore astrologers, in scrying by the stars, impute a wrong intention to the Lord. Also he argues that Copernicus's theory is contrary to reason & to Holy Scripture. (I think, in this last, you agree with him? Forgive me, my friend, I can never resist a jibe.) All this, of course, is nonsense. Feselius is a foolish &

pompous fellow, and I intend to dispatch him with a quick thrust of my sword. I mention him merely to show you that I am not wholly unsympathetic to your views.

I am interested in your contention that there is, behind the visible world, another world of magic which is hidden from us except in a few instances where we are allowed to witness magical actions at work. I cannot agree. Do you not see, Röslin, that the magic of, say, the so-called magic square is simply that numbers may be disposed in such a way as to produce wonderful configurations – but that this is the whole of it? No effects of this *magic* extend into the world. The real mystery & miracle is not that numbers have an effect upon things (which they do not!), but that they can express the nature of things; that the world, vast & various & seemingly ruled by chance, is amenable in its basic laws to the rigorous precision & order of mathematics.

It seems to me important that, not only is innate instinct excited by the heavens, but so also is the human intellect. The search for knowledge everywhere encounters geometrical relations in nature, which God, in creating the world, laid out from his own resources, so to speak. To enquire into nature, then, is to trace geometrical relationships. Since God, in his highest goodness, was not able to rest from his labours, he played with the characteristics of things, and copied himself in the world. Thus it is one of my thoughts, whether all of nature & all heavenly elegance is not symbolised in geometry. (I suppose this is the basis of all my belief.) And so, instinctively or thinkingly, the created imitates the Creator, the earth in making crystals, planets in arranging their leaves & blossoms, man in his creative activity. All this doing is like a child's play, without plan, without purpose, out of an inner impulse, out of simple joy. And the contemplating spirit finds & recognises itself again in that which it creates. Yes, yes, Röslin: all is play.

Vale
Johannes Kepler

Prague
All Souls Day 1608

Dr Michael Mästlin: at Tübingen

I have your beautiful & affecting letter, for which much thanks, though I confess it has saddened me greatly. For a long time, though I wrote to you repeatedly, I heard not a word; now suddenly, as if you have been spurred to it by resentment & irritation, comes this strange valediction. Have I *reached such a high step & distinguished position* that I could, if I wished, *look down on you*? Why, sir, what is this? You are my first teacher & patron, and, so I would like to think, my oldest friend. How would I look down on you, why should I wish to do so? You say my questions have been sometimes too subtle for your knowledge & gifts to comprehend: yet I am sure, magister, if there have been things you did not understand, the fault was mine, that my style of expression has been clumsy & unclear, or that my thoughts themselves were senseless. So you *understand only your modest craft*? On that score, I say only this: you understood the work of Copernicus at a time when others, whose names subsequently have made a great noise in the world, had not yet heard tell of the Ermlander or his theories. Come, my dear Doctor, no more of this, I will not have it!

Ah but yet, there is something in the tone of your letter which will not be gainsaid. The fault in this matter, I believe, is in my character. For it has always been thus with me, that I find it hard, despite all my efforts, to make friends, and when I do, I cannot keep them. When I meet those whom I feel I might love, I am like a little dog, with a wagging tail & lolling tongue, showing the whites of my eyes: yet sooner or later I am sure to flare up & growl. I am malicious, and bite people with my sarcasm. Why, I even like to gnaw hard, discarded things, bones & dry crusts of bread, and have always had a dog-like horror of baths, tinctures & lotions!

How, then, may I expect people to love me for what I am, since what I am is so base?

Tycho the Dane I loved, in my way, though I think he never knew it – certainly I never attempted to tell him, so busy was I in trying to bite the hand, his hand, that was feeding me. He was a great man, whose name will last for ever. Why could I not have told him that I recognised greatness in him? We fought from the start, and there was no peace between us, even on the day he died. True, he was eager for me to found my work upon his world system instead of on that of Copernicus, which was something I could not do: but could I not have dissembled, lied a little for his sake, soothed his fears? Of course, he was arrogant, and full of duplicity & malice, and treated me badly. But now I see that was his way, as mine is mine. And yet I cannot fool myself, I know that if he were to be resurrected and sent back to me now, there would be only the old squabbling. I am not expressing myself well. I am trying to explain how it is with me, that if I growl, it is only to guard what I hold precious, and that I would far rather wag my tail and be a friend to all.

You think I consider myself a lofty personage. I do not. High honours & offices I have never had. I live here on the stage of the world as a simple, private man. If I can squeeze out a portion of my salary at court, I am happy not to have to live entirely on my own means. As for the rest, I take the attitude that I serve not the Emperor, but rather the whole human race & posterity. In this confident hope, I scorn with secret pride all honours & offices, and also those things which they bestow. I count as the only honour the fact that by divine decree I have been put near the Tychonic observations.

Forgive, then, please, any slights that have been offered you in ignorance by

Your friend,
K

Wenzel House, Prague
Christmastide 1606

Hans Georg Herwart von Hohenburg: at München

Salve. This will, I fear, be but the briefest of scribbles, to wish you & your family all happiness of the season. The court is busy with preparations for the festivities, and consequently I am forgotten for the moment, and hence am allowed a little time to pursue my private studies undisturbed. Is it not strange, how, at the most unexpected of moments, the speculative faculty, having just alighted from a long & wearisome flight, will suddenly take wing again immediately, and soar to even loftier heights? Having lately completed my *Astronomia nova*, and looking forward to a year or two of much needed rest & recuperation, here I am now launching out again, with renewed fervour, upon those studies of world harmony, which I interrupted seven years ago in order to clear away the little task of founding a new astronomy!

Since, as I believe, the mind from the first contains within it the basic & essential forms of reality, it is not surprising that, before I have any clear knowledge of what the contents will be, I have already conceived the form of my projected book. It is ever thus with me: in the beginning is the shape! Hence I foresee a work divided into five parts, to correspond to the five planetary intervals, while the number of chapters in each part will be based upon the signifying quantities of each of the five regular or Platonic solids which, according to my *Mysterium*, may be fitted into these intervals. Also, as a form of decoration, and to pay my due respects, I intend that the initials of the chapters shall spell out acrostically the names of certain famous men. Of course, it is possible that, in the heat of composition, all of this grand design might be abandoned. But it will be no matter.

I have taken as my motto that phrase from Copernicus, in which he speaks of the marvellous symmetry of the world, and the harmony in the relationships of the motion & size of the planetary orbits. I ask, in what does this symmetry consist? How is it that man can perceive these relationships? The latter question is, I think, quickly solved – I have given the answer just a moment ago. The soul contains in its own inner nature the pure harmonies as prototypes or paradigms of the harmonics perceptible to the senses. And since these pure harmonics are a matter of proportion, there must be present figures which can be compared with each other: these I take to be the circle and those parts of circles which result when arcs are cut off from them. The circle, then, is something which occurs only in the mind: the circle which we draw with a compass is only an inexact representation of an idea which the mind carried as really existing in itself. In this I take issue strenuously with Aristotle, who holds that the mind is a *tabula rasa* upon which sense perceptions write. This is wrong, wrong. The mind learns all mathematical ideas & figures out of itself; by empirical signs it only remembers what it knows already. Mathematical ideas are the essence of the soul. Of itself, the mind conceives equidistance from a point, and out of that makes a picture for itself of a circle, without any sense perceptions whatever. Let me put it thusly: If the mind had never shared an eye, then it would, for the conceiving of the things situated outside itself, demand an eye and prescribe its own laws for forming it. For the recognition of quantities which is innate in the mind determines how the eye must be, and therefore the eye is so, because the mind is so, and not vice versa. Geometry was not received through the eyes: it was already there inside.

These, then, are some of my present concerns. I shall have much to say of them in the future. For now, my lady wife desires that the great astronomer issue forth into the town to purchase a fat goose.

Fröhliche Weihnachten!
Johannes Kepler

Loretoplatz, Hradcany Hill, Prague
Easter Day 1605

David Fabricius: in Friesland

As I have delayed long in my promise of a further letter, so it is right all the same that I should sit down now, on this festival of redemption, to tell you of my triumph. As, my dear Fabricius, what a foolish bird I had been! All along the solution to the mystery of the Mars orbit was in my hands, had I but looked at things correctly. Four long years had elapsed, from the time I acknowledged defeat because of that error of 8 minutes of arc, to my coming back on the problem again. In the meantime, to be sure, I had gained much skill in geometry, and had invented many new mathematical methods which were to prove invaluable in the renewed Martian campaign. The final assault took two, nearly three more years. Had my circumstances been better, perhaps I would have done it more quickly, but I was ill with an infection of the gall, and busy with the Nova of 1604, and the birth of a son. Still, the real cause of the delay was my own foolishness & shortness of sight. It pains me to admit, that even when I had solved the problem, *I did not recognise the solution for what it was.* Thus we do progress, my dear Doctor, blunderingly, in a dream, like wise but undeveloped children!

I began again by trying once more to attribute a *circular* orbit to Mars. I failed. The conclusion was, simply, that the planet's path curves inwards on both sides, and outwards again at opposite ends. This *oval* figure, I readily admit, terrified me. It went against that dogma of circular motion, to which astronomers have held since the first beginnings of our science. Yet the evidence which I had marshalled was not to be denied. And what held for Mars, would, I knew, hold also for the rest of the planets, including our own. The prospect was appalling. Who was I, that I should contemplate recasting the world? And the labour! True, I had cleared the stables of epicycles & retrograde motions and all the rest of it, and now was left with only a single cartful of dung, i.e. this oval – but what a stink it gave off! And now I must put myself between the shafts, and draw out by myself that noisome load!

After some preliminary work, I arrived at the notion that the oval was an egg shape. Certainly, this conclusion involved some geometrical sleight of hand, but I could not think of any other means of imposing an oval orbit on the planets. It all seemed to me wonderfully plausible. To find the area of this doubtful egg, I computed 180 sun–Mars distances, and added them together. This operation I repeated 40 times. And still I failed. Next, I decided that the true orbit must be somewhere between the egg shape & the circular, just as if it were a perfect ellipse. By this time, of course, I was growing frantic, and grasping at any straw.

And then a strange & wonderful thing occurred. The two sickle shapes, or moonlets, lying between the flattened sides of the oval and the ideal circular orbit, had a width at their thickest points amounting to 0.00429 of the radius of the circle. This value was oddly familiar (I cannot say why: was it a premonition glimpsed in some forgotten dream?). Now I became interested in the angle formed between the position of Mars, the sun, and the centre of the orbit, the secant of which, to my astonishment, I discovered to be 1.00429. The reappearance of this value – .00429 – showed me at once that there is a fixed relation between that angle, and the distance to the sun, which will hold good for all points on the planet's path. At last, then, I had a means of computing the Martian orbit, by using this fixed ratio.

You think that was the end of it? There is a final act to this comedy. Having tried to construct the orbit by using the equation I had just discovered, I made an error in geometry, and failed again. In despair, I threw out the formula, in order to try a new hypothesis, namely, that the orbit might be an ellipse. When I had constructed such a figure, by means of geometry, I saw of course that the two methods produced the same result, and that my equations was, in fact, *the mathematical expression of an ellipse.* Imagine, Doctor, my amazement, joy & embarrassment. I had been staring at the solution, without recognising it! Now I was able to express the thing as a law, simple, elegant, and true: *The planets move in ellipses with the sun at one focus.*

God is great, and I am his servant; as I am also,

your humble friend,
Johannes Kepler

V

Somnium

ALREADY THE LIGHT was failing when he arrived in Regensburg at last. A fine rain drifted slantwise through the November dusk, settling in a silver fur on his cloak, his breeches, the nag's lank mane. He crossed the Steinerne Brucke over the sullen surge of the Danube. Dim figures, faceless and intent, passed him by in the streets. There was an ominous hum in his ears, and his hands, clutching the greasy reins, trembled. He told himself it was fatigue and hunger: he could not afford to be ill, not now. He had come to accost the Emperor, to demand a settlement of what he was owed.

The lamps were lit in Hillebrand Billig's house. From a way off he spied the yellow windows and the taverner and his wife within. It was an image out of a dream, that light shining through the brown gloom and the rain, and folk attending his coming. The old horse clattered to a stop, coughing. Hillebrand Billig peered at him from the doorway. 'Why, sir, we did not expect you until the morrow.'

Always the same, too late or too early. He was not sure what day of the week it was.

'Well,' stamping his numbed feet, tears in his eyes from the cold, 'here I am!'

He was put to dry by the fire in the kitchen, with a platter of ham and beans and a pint-pot of punch, and a cushion for his seething piles. An elderly dog snoozed at his feet, gasping and growling in its sleep. Billig fussed around him, a large leatherclad man with a black beard. At the stove Frau Billig stood paralysed by shyness, smiling helplessly upon her saucepans. Kepler no longer remembered how or when he had come to know the couple. They seemed to have been always there, like parents. He smiled vacantly into the fire. The Billigs were twenty years younger than he. Next year would be his sixtieth.

'I am bound for Linz,' he said. He had just remembered that. There was interest on some Austrian bonds to be collected.

'But you'll bide with us a while?' said Hillebrand Billig and, with ponderous roguishness: 'The rate here, you know heh, is *cheap*.' It was his only joke. He never tired of it. 'Is that not so, Anna?'

'O yes, 'Frau Billig managed, 'you will be very welcome, Herr Doctor.'

'Thank you,' Kepler murmured. 'I must, yes, spend a few days here. I have to see the Emperor, he owes me moneys.'

The Billigs were impressed.

'His majesty will soon be returning to Prague,' said Hillebrand Billig, who prided himself on knowing about these matters. 'The congress has finished its business, I hear.'

'But I will catch him, all the same. Of course, as to whether he will be prepared to settle his account with me, that is another question.' His majesty had larger matters on his mind than the imperial mathematician's unpaid salary. Kepler sat upright suddenly, slopping his punch. The saddlebags! He rose, making for the door. 'Where is my horse, what has become of my horse?' Billig had sent it to the stables. 'But my bags, my my . . . my bags!'

'The boy will bring them.'

'O.' Kepler, moaning, turned this way and that. All of his papers were in those satchels, including a stamped and sealed imperial order for the payment of 4,000 florins from the crown's debt to him. The merest tip of something unspeakable was shown him briefly with a grin and then whisked away. Aghast, he sat down again, slowly. 'What?'

Hillebrand Billig leaned down to him, mouthing elaborately. 'I say, I will go out myself and bring them in, your bags, yes?'

'Ah.'

'Are you unwell, Doctor?'

'No no . . . thank you.'

He was trembling. He remembered out of his childhood a recurring dream, in which a series of the most terrible tortures and catastrophes was unfolded leisurely before him, while someone whom he could not see looked on, watching his reactions with amusement and an almost friendly attention. Just now that vision, whatever to call it, had been like that, the same slick flourish and the sense of muffled gloating. That was more, surely, than simply fear for his possessions? He shivered. 'Eh?' Frau Billig had spoken. 'Beg pardon, ma'am?'

'Your family,' she said, louder, smiling nervously and plucking at her apron; 'Frau Kepler, and the children?'

'O, they are very well, very well. Yes.' A faint spasm, almost a pain, passed through him. It took him a moment to identify it. Guilt! As if by now he were not familiar with *that*. 'We have lately had a wedding, you know.'

Hillebrand Billig resumed then, with rain in his beard, and set down the saddlebags on the hearth.

'Ah, good,' Kepler mumbled, 'very kind.' He put up his feet on the bags, offering his toes to the blaze: let the chilblains suffer a little too, and serve them right. 'Yes, a wedding. Our dear Regina has gone from us.' He looked up into the Billigs' puzzled silence. 'But what am I saying? I mean of course *Susan*.' He coughed, raking up an oyster. His head hummed. 'The match was made in heaven, when Venus whispered in the ear of my young assistant, Jakob Bartsch, a stargazer also, and a doctor of medicine.' And when the goddess had become discouraged, seeing what a timid specimen was this Adonis, Kepler himself had taken up her task. Pangs of guilt then, too. Such bullying! He wondered if he had done right. There was much of her mother in that girl. Poor Bartsch. 'Young Ludwig, my eldest boy, also is going for medicine.' He paused. 'And neither have I been idle: another little one, last April, a girl,' leering sheepishly at the fire. Frau Billig rattled the pots on the stove: she disapproved of his young wife. So had Regina. *It would be a marriage*, she had written to him, *if my Herr Father had no child*. A curious way of putting it. He had read much into that letter, too much. Foolish and sinful dreams. She was only hinting again about that damned inheritance. And he had replied that she might mind her own business, that he would marry when, and whom, he liked. But ah, Regina, what I could not say was that she reminded me of you.

Three times the name Susanna had occurred in his life, two daughters, one dead in infancy, one married now, and then at last a wife. Someone had been trying to tell him something. Whoever it was, was right. He had chosen her out of eleven candidates. Eleven! The comedy of it struck him only afterwards. He could no longer remember them all. There had been the widow Pauritsch of Kunstadt, who had tried to use his motherless children in plying her case, and that mother and daughter, each one eager to sell him the other, and fat Maria with her curls, the Helmhard woman who was built like an athlete, and that titled one, what was her name, a very Gorgon: all with advantages, their houses, their rich fathers, and he had chosen a penniless orphan, Susanna Reuttinger of Eferding, despite universal opposition. Even her guardian, the Baroness von Starhemberg, had considered her too lowly a match for him.

She was twenty-four the first time he met her, at the Starhembergs' house in Linz: a tall, slightly ungainly and yet handsome girl, with fine eyes. Her silence unnerved him. She spoke hardly a word that first day. He had thought she would laugh at him, a fussy middle-aged little man with weak sight, his beard already streaked with grey. Instead she attended him with a kind of tender intensity, leaning down to him her solemn grey eyes and downturned mouth. It was not that she much resembled Regina, but there was something, an air of ordered self-containment, and he was pierced. She was a cabinetmaker's daughter, like you, like you.

'Anna Maria we have called the baby,' he said, and Anna Billig consented to smile. 'A pretty name, I think.'

Seven children Susanna had borne him. The first three had died in infancy. He wondered then if he had married another Barbara Müller née Müller. She saw him think it, watching him with that sad, apprehensive gaze. Yet he suspected, and was filled with wonder at the notion, that she was not hurt by it, but only concerned for him and *his* loss, his sense of betrayal. She asked so little! She had brought him happiness. And now he had abandoned her. 'Yes,' he said, 'a pretty name.'

He closed his eyes. Waves of wind washed against the house, and beyond the noise of the rain he fancied he could hear the river. The fire warmed him. Trapped gas piped a tiny tune deep in his gut. This brute comfort made him think again of his childhood. Why? There had been precious few log fires and mugs of punch in old Sebaldus's house. But he carried within him a vision of lost peace and order, a sphere of harmony which had never been, yet to which the idea of childhood seemed an approximation. He belched, and laughed silently at the spectacle of himself, a sodden old dolt dozing in his boots, maundering over the lost years. He should fall asleep, with blubber mouth agape and dribbling, that would complete the picture. But that other roaring fire up his backside kept him awake. The dog yelped, dreaming of rats.

'Well, Billig, you tell me the electoral congress is finished its business?'

'Aye, it has. The princes have left already.'

'And about time for them to finish, they have had six months at it. Has the young rake's succession been assured?'

'They do say so, Doctor.'

'I must be quick then, eh, if I am to have satisfaction of his father?'

The Billigs laughed with him, but weakly. His heartiness, he saw, did not fool them. They were itching to know the real reason why he had fled home and family to come on this lunatic venture. He would have liked to know, himself. Satisfaction, was that what he was after? The promise of 4,000 florins was still in his bag, with the seal unbroken. This time most likely he would receive another, equally useless piece of parchment to keep it company. Three emperors he had known, poor Rudolph, the usurper Matthias his brother, and now the wheel of his misfortune had come full circle and his old enemy Ferdinand of Styria, scourge of the Lutherans, wore the crown. Kepler would never have gone near him, were it not for that unsettled debt. It was ten months to the day since he had last accosted him.

* * *

COLD IT HAD BEEN that morning, the sky like a bruised gland and a taste of metal in the air, and everything holding its breath under an astonishment of fallen snow. Soiled white boulders of ice lolled on the river. In the dark before dawn he had lain awake, listening in fright to the floes breaking before the bow, the squeaking and the groans and the sudden flurries of cracks like distant musket-fire. They docked at first light. The quayside was deserted save for a mongrel with a swollen belly chasing the slithering hawser. The bargemaster scowled at Kepler, his oniony breath defeating even the stink seeping up from the cargo of pelts in the hold. 'Prague,' he said, with a contemptuous wave, as if he had that moment manufactured the silent city rising behind him in the freezing mist. Kepler had haggled over the fare.

He had come from Ulm with the first printed copies of the *Tabulae Rudolphinae*. On the way that time also he had paused at Regensburg, where Susanna was lodging at the Billigs'. It was Christmas, and he had not seen her and the children for almost a year, yet he could not be idle. The Jesuits at Dillengen had shown him letters from their priests in China, asking for news of the latest astronomical discoveries, and now he set himself at once to composing a little treatise for the missionaries' use. The children hardly remembered him. He would stop, feeling their eyes on his back as he worked, but when he turned they would scurry off, whispering in alarm, to the safety of Anna Billig's kitchen.

He had wanted to continue on again alone, but Susanna would not have it. She was not impressed by his talk of snow-storms, the frozen river. Her vehemence startled him. 'I do not care if you are *walking* to Prague: we shall walk with you.'

'But . . .'

'But *no*,' she said, and again, more softly this time: 'But no,

Kepler dear,' and smiled. She was thinking, he supposed, that it was not good for him to be so much alone.

'How kind you are,' he mumbled, 'how kind.' Always he believed without question that others were better than he, more thoughtful, more honourable, a state of affairs for which the standing apology that was his life could not make up. His love for Susanna was a kind of inarticulate anguish choking his heart, yet it was *not enough*, not enough, like everything else that he did and was. Eyes awash, he took her hands in his, and, not trusting himself to speak further, nodded his soggy gratitude.

They lodged in Prague at The Whale by the bridge. The children were too cold to cry. The wharfinger's men rolled his precious barrel of books up from the quay, through the snow and the filth. Fortunately he had packed it with wadding and lined the staves with oilskin. The *Tables* were a handsome folio volume. Twenty years, on and off, he had devoted to that work! It contained the most of him, he knew, though not the best. His finest flights were in the *World Harmony* and the *Astronomia nova*, even the *Mysterium*, his first. He knew he had wasted too much time on the *Tables*. A year, two at the most, would have done it, when the Dane was dead and he had the observations, if he had concentrated. It might have made his fortune. Now, with everybody too busy at each other's throats to bother with such works, he would be lucky to recoup the cost of printing. Some there were who were interested still – but what did he care for converting the Chinese, and to popery at that? Sailors, though, would bless his name, explorers and adventurers. He had always liked the notion of those hardy seafarers poring over the charts and diagrams of the *Tabulae*, their piercing eyes scanning the bleached pages. It was they, not the astronomers, who made his books live. And for a moment his mind would range out over immensities, feel the blast of sun and salt wind, hear the gales howl in the rigging: he, who had not ever even seen the ocean!

He was not prepared for Prague, the new spirit that seemed abroad in the city. The court had returned from its Viennese seat for the coronation of Ferdinand's son as King of Bohemia; at first

Kepler was charmed, imagining that the age of Rudolph had returned with it. He had been afraid, coming here, and not only of the ice on the river. The war was going well for the Catholic parties, and Kepler remembered how, thirty years before, Ferdinand had hounded the Protestant heretics out of Styria. At the palace everything was bustle and an almost gay confusion, where he had expected stillness and stealth. And the clothes! The yellow capes and scarlet stockings, the brocades and the frogging and the purple ribbons; he had never seen such stuffs, even in Rudolph's time. He might have been among a spawn of Frenchmen. But it was in the clothes that he quickly saw how wrong he had been. There was no new spirit, it was all show, a frantic paying of homage not to greatness but to mere might. These reds and purples were the bloody badge of the counter-reformation. And Ferdinand had not changed at all.

If Rudolph had reminded Kepler, especially toward the end, of someone's mother come to her dotage, Ferdinand his cousin had the look of a dissatisfied wife. Pallid and paunchy, with delicate legs, he held himself off from the astronomer with a tensed preoccupied air, as if waiting for his taster to arrive and take a nibble before risking a closer approach. He was given to long unnerving silences, a trick inherited from his predecessors, dark pools in the depths of which swam the indistinct forms of suspicion and accusation. The eyes stared out like weary sentinels guarding that preposterous fat nose, their gaze blurred and pale, and Kepler felt not pierced but, rather, palped. He wondered idly if the imperial surliness might be due to a windy gut, for Ferdinand kept bringing up soft little belches, which he caught in his fingertips like a conjuror palming illusory baubles.

He managed the sickly shadow of a smile when Kepler arrived in his presence. The *Tables* pleased him: he had pretensions to learning. He summoned a secretary, and with a flourish dictated an order for 4,000 florins in acknowledgment of the astronomer's labours and to cover the expense of printing, even adding a memorandum to the effect that 7,817 florins were still owed. Kepler shifted from one foot to another, mumbling and simpering. Imperial magnanimity was always an ominous sign. Ferdinand dismissed him with a not unfriendly wave, but still he tarried.

'Your majesty,' he said, 'has been most kind, most generous. There is not only the matter of this ample grant. It betokens a noble spirit indeed, that he has maintained me in my position as mathematicus, though I profess a creed which is anathema in his realm.'

Ferdinand, startled and faintly alarmed, turned a poached eye on him. The title of imperial mathematician, which Kepler continued to hold since Rudolph's time, was by now no more than formal, but, in the midst of a confessional war, he meant to keep it. 'Yes, yes,' the Emperor said vaguely. 'Well . . .' A pause. The secretary watched Kepler with brazen amusement, biting the tip of his pen. Kepler was wondering if he had made a tactical mistake. That was the kind of petitioning, oblique and well sugared with flattery, that Rudolph had expected: but this was Ferdinand. 'Your religion,' the Emperor said, 'yes, it is, ah, an embarrassment. We understood that you were leaning toward conversion?' Kepler sighed; that old lie. He said nothing. Ferdinand's plump lower lip crept up to nibble a strand of his moustache. 'Well, it is no great matter. Every man is entitled to profess as he . . . as he . . .' He caught Kepler's eager, harried gaze, and could not bring himself to finish it. The secretary coughed, and they both turned and looked at him, and Kepler was gratified to see how quickly he wiped the smirk off his foxy face. 'But, no, it is no matter,' the Emperor said, lifting a bejewelled hand. 'The war, of course, makes difficulties. The army, and the people, look to us for guidance and example, and we must be . . . careful. You understand.'

'Yes, of course, your majesty.' He understood. There would be no place for him at Ferdinand's court. He felt, suddenly, immensely old and tired. A door at the far end of the hall opened, and a figure entered and came toward them, hands clasped behind him and head bent, considering his brilliant black hip-boots pacing the checkered marble. Ferdinand eyed him with something like distaste. 'You are still here,' he said, as if it were an ignoble trick that had been played on him. 'Doctor Kepler, General von Wallenstein, our chief commander.'

The general bowed. 'I think I know you, sir,' he said. Kepler looked at him blankly.

'He thinks he knows you,' said Ferdinand; the idea amused him.

'I think, yes, I think we have had some contact,' the general said. 'A long time ago – twenty years ago, in fact – I sent by devious routes a request to a certain stargazer in Graz, whose reputation I knew, to draw up a horoscope for me. The result was impressive: a full and uncannily accurate account of my character and doings. It was the more impressive, in that I had warned my agents not to divulge my name.'

Tall windows on the left showed them a view down the Hradcany to the snowbound city. Kepler had stood once at just this spot, before this very view, with the Emperor Rudolph, discussing the plan for the *Tabulae Rudolphinae*. How slyly things rearrange themselves! Stargazer. He remembered. 'Well, sir,' he said, smiling tentatively, 'it was not hard to find, you know, so eminent a name.'

'Ah. Then you knew it was I.' He shook his head, disappointed. 'Even so, you did wonderfully well.'

The Emperor grunted and turned morosely aside, abandoning them to each other with the air of a small boy whose ball has been taken from him by a bully. The toy had been not much prized, anyway.

'Come,' said the general, and put a hand on Kepler's arm, 'we must have a talk.'

Thus began what was to be a brief and turbulent connection. Kepler admired the neatness of the thing: he had come here to seek an Emperor's patronage, and was given instead a general. He was not ungrateful to the arranging fates. He was in need of refuge. A year ago he had said his bitter last farewell to Linz.

* * *

NOT THAT LINZ had been the worst of places. True, that town had been his despair for fourteen years, he had thought he would feel nothing but relief at leaving. Yet when the day came, a sliver of doubt got under the quick of his expectations. After all, he had his patrons there, the Starhembergs and the Tschernembls. He had friends too, Jakob Wincklemann the lens grinder, for instance. In that old obscurantist's house by the river he had spent many a merry night drinking and dreaming. And Linz had given him Susanna. It pained him that he, the imperial mathematician, should be reduced again to teaching sums to brats and the blockhead sons of merchants at a district school, yet even in that there was something, an eerie sense of being given a second chance at life, as if it were Graz and the Stiftsschule all over again.

Upper Austria was a haven for religious exiles from the west. Linz was almost a Württemberg colony. Schwarz the jurist was there, and Baltasar Gurald the district secretary, Württembergers both. Even Oberdorfer the physician turned up briefly, a corpulent and troubled ghost, with his stick and his pale eye and poisonous breath, looking not a day older than when, twenty years before, he had officiated at the deaths of Kepler's children. To show that he held no grudge, Kepler invited the doctor to stand as sponsor at the christening of Fridmar, his second surviving child by Susanna. Oberdorfer embraced his friend with tears in his eyes, gasping out his appreciation, and Kepler thought what a spectacle they must be, this old fraud, and the grizzled papa, clasped in each other's arms and blubbering beside the baby's cot.

But then also there was Daniel Hitzler. He was the chief pastor in Linz. Younger than Kepler, he had been through the same Württemberg schools; along the way he had picked up the threads of the scandalous reputation left behind by his turbulent predecessor. Kepler was flattered, for Hitzler seemed to think him a very dangerous fellow. The pastor was a cold stick, who cultivated the air of a grand inquisitor. Little signs, however, gave him away. That black cloak was too black, the beard too pointedly pointed. Kepler had used to laugh at him a little, but liked him all the same, and felt no rancour toward him, which was curious, for Hitzler was the one who had had him excommunicated.

Kepler had known all along that it would come to this. In the matter of faith he was stubborn. He could not fully agree with any party, Catholic, Lutheran or Calvinist, and so was taken for an enemy by all three. Yet he saw himself at one with all Christians, whatever they might be called, by the Christian bond of love. He looked at the war with which God was rewarding a quarrelling Germany, and knew he was in the right. He followed the Augsburg Confession, and would not sign the Formula of Concord, which he disdained as a piece of politicking, a formula of words merely, and nothing to do with faith.

Effects and consequences obsessed him. Was there a link between his inner struggles and the general confessional crisis? Could it be his private agonisings in some way provoked the big black giant that was stalking Europe? His reputation as a crypto-Calvinist had denied him a post at Tübingen, his Lutheranism had forced him out of Graz to Prague, from Prague to Linz, and soon those dreadful footfalls would be shaking the walls of Wallenstein's palace in Sagan, his last refuge. Through the winter of 1619, from his look-out in Linz, he had followed the Calvinist Frederick Palatine's doomed attempt to wrest the crown of Bohemia from the Hapsburgs. He shivered at the thought of his own connections, however tenuous, with that disaster. Had he helped to direct the giant's gimlet gaze, by allowing Regina to marry in the Palatinate, by dedicating the *Harmonice mundi* to James of England, father-in-law to the Winter King Frederick? It was as in a dream, where it slowly dawns that *you* are the one who has committed the crime. He knew that these were grossly solipsistic conceits, and yet . . .

Hitzler would not admit him to Communion unless he would agree to ratify the Formula of Concord. Kepler was outraged. 'Do you require this condition of every Communicant?'

Hitzler stared at him out of an aquatic eye, perhaps wondering if he were wading into depths wherein he might be drowned by this excitable heretic. 'I require it of *you*, sir.'

'If I were a swineherd, or a prince of the blood, would you require it?'

'You have denied the omnipresence of the body of Christ and admitted that you agree with the Calvinists.'

'There are some things, some things, mark you, on which I do not *disagree* with them. I reject the barbarous doctrine of predestination.'

'You are set apart by your action in designating the Communion as a sign for that creed which was set down in the Formula of Concord, while at the same time contradicting this sign and defending its opposite.' Hitzler fancied himself an orator. Kepler gagged.

'Pah! My argument, sir priest, is only that the preachers are become too haughty and do not abide by the old simplicity. Read the Church Fathers! The burden of antiquity shall be my justification.'

'You are neither hot nor cold, Doctor, but tepid.'

It went on for years. They met in Kepler's house, in Hitzler's, arguing into the night. They strolled by the river, Hitzler grave in his black cloak and Kepler waving his arms about and shouting, enjoying themselves despite all, and in a way playing with each other. When the Church representatives of Linz moved to dismiss Kepler from his post at the district school, and he was saved only by the influence of the barons, who approved his stand, Hitzler made no effort to help him, though he was a school inspector. The play ended there. What angered Kepler most was the hypocrisy. When he went out of the city, to the villages around, he was not refused Communion. There he found kind and simple priests, too busy curing the sick or delivering their neighbours' calves to bother with the doctrinal niceties of the Hitzlers. Kepler appealed his case to the Stuttgart Consistory. They sided against him. His last hope was to go in person to Tübingen and seek support from Matthias Hafenreffer, Chancellor of the university.

Michael Mästlin was greatly aged since Kepler had last seen him. He had a distracted air, as if his attention were all the time being called away to something more pressing elsewhere. As Kepler recounted his latest woes the old man would now and then bestir himself, furtively apologetic, striving to concentrate. He shook his head and sighed. 'Such difficulties you bring upon yourself! You are no longer a student, arguing in the taverns and shouting rebellion. Thirty years ago I heard this talk from you, and nothing has changed.'

'No,' said Kepler, 'nothing has changed, not I nor the world. Would you have me deny my beliefs, or lie and say I accept whatever is the fashion of the day, in order to be comfortable?'

Mästlin looked away, pursing his lips. In the college grounds below his window the tawny sunlight of late autumn was burnishing the trees. 'You think me an old fool and an old pander,' Mästlin said, 'but I have lived my life honestly and not without honour, as best I could. I am not a great man, nor have I attained the heights which you have – O, you may sigh, but these things are true. Perhaps it is your misfortune, and the cause of your troubles, that you did great things and made yourself prominent. The theologians will not worry if *I* flout the dogmas, but you, ah, that is a different thing.'

To that, Kepler had no reply. Presently Hafenreffer arrived. He had been Kepler's teacher here at Tübingen, and almost a friend. Kepler had never needed him before as he did now, and it made them shy of each other. If he could win the Chancellor to his side, and with him the theology faculty, the Consistory in Stuttgart would have to relent, for Tübingen was the seat of the Lutheran conscience. But Kepler saw, even before the Chancellor spoke, that his cause was lost. Matthias Hafenreffer also had aged, but with him the accumulation of years had been a refining process, honing him like a blade. He was what Hitzler played at being. His greeting was bland, but he bent on Kepler a keen glance. Mästlin was nervous of him, and began to fuss, calling plaintively for his servants. When none came, he rose himself and set out for his guests a jug of wine and a platter of bread, mumbling apologies for the poor fare. Hafenreffer smiled, eyeing the table. 'A very suitable feast, Professor.' Mästlin peered at him nervously, quite baffled. The Chancellor turned to Kepler. 'Well, Doctor, what is all this I hear?'

'That man Hitzler—'

'He is enthusiastic, yes: but scrupulous also, and a fine pastor.'

'He has denied me Communion!'

'Unless you ratify the Concord, yes?'

'In God's name, he is excluding me because of the frankness with which I recognise that in this one article, of the omnipresence of the body of Christ, the early Fathers are more conclusive than your Concord! I can name in my support Origen, Fulgentius, Vigilius, Cyril, John of . . .'

'Yes, yes, no doubt; we are aware of the breadth of your scholarship. But you incline to the Calvinist conception in the doctrine of Communion.'

'I hold it self-evident that matter is incapable of transmutation. The body and soul of Christ are in Heaven. God, sir, is not an alchemist.'

In the stillness there was the sense of phantom witnesses starting back, shocked, their hands to their mouths. Hafenreffer sighed. 'So. That is clear and honest. But I wonder, Doctor, if you have considered the implication of what you say? I mean in particular the implication that by this . . . this doctrine, you diminish the sacrament of Communion to a mere symbol.'

Kepler considered. 'I should not say *mere*. Is not the symbol something holy, being at once itself and something other, greater? It is what may also be said, may it not, of Christ himself?'

That, he supposed afterwards, decided it. The affair dragged on for another year, but in the end Hitzler won, Kepler was excommunicated, and Hafenreffer broke with him. *If you love me*, the Chancellor wrote, *then eschew this passionate excitement.* It was sound advice, but ah, without passion he would not have been who he was. He packed his bags and set out for Ulm, where the *Tabulae Rudolphinae* were to be printed.

* * *

ELSEWHERE TOO the Keplers had been attracting the gigant's bloodshot glare. In the winter of 1616, after years of muttering and threats, the Swabian authorities moved officially to try his mother for a witch. She fled to Linz with her son Christoph. Kepler was appalled. 'Why have you come? It will be taken for an admission of guilt.'

'There has been worse already,' Christoph said. 'Tell him, mother.'

The old woman looked away, sniffing.

'What worse?' Kepler asked, not really wanting to know. 'What has happened?'

'She tried to bribe the magistrate, Einhorn,' said Christoph, smoothing a wrinkle from his doublet.

Kepler groped behind him for a chair and sat down. Susanna laid a hand on his shoulder. Einhorn. All his life he had been hounded by people with names like that. 'To *bribe* him? Why? How?'

Christoph shrugged. He was fifteen years younger than the astronomer, short and prematurely stout, with a low forehead and eyes of a peculiar violet tint. He had come to Linz chiefly to see his brother sweat over the bad news. 'A wench,' he said, 'the daughter of this Reinbold woman, claims she suffered pains after our mother touched her on the arm. Einhorn was preparing a report of the matter for the chancery, and she offered him a silver cup if he would omit it. Didn't you, ma?'

'Jesus God,' said Kepler faintly. 'And what was the result?'

'Why, Einhorn was delighted, of course, since he is very thick with the Reinbold faction, and straightway reported the attempt to buy his silence, along with the other charges. It is a pretty mess.'

'We are glad to see,' Susanna said, 'that the matter is not so serious as to trouble you greatly.'

Christoph stared at her. She met him stoutly, and Kepler felt her fingers tighten on his shoulder. 'Hush, hush,' he murmured, patting her hand, 'we must not fight.'

Katharina Kepler spoke at last. 'O no, he is not much put out, for he and your sister Margarete, and her holy husband the pastor, have sworn the three of them that they will desert me willingly if I am found in the wrong. So they told the magistrate. Isn't that a fine thing.'

Christoph reddened. Kepler contemplated him sadly, but without surprise. He had never managed to love his brother.

'We have our own good names to think of,' Christoph said, thrusting his chin at them. 'What do you expect? She was warned. This past year alone in our parish they have burned a score of witches.'

'God forgive you,' Susanna said, turning away.

Christoph soon departed, muttering. The old woman stayed for nine months. It was a trying time. Old age nor her misfortunes had not dulled her sharp tongue. Kepler regarded her with rueful admiration. She had no illusions about the peril that she faced, yet he believed she was enjoying it all, in a queer way. She had never before had so much attention lavished on her. She took a lively interest in the details of her defence which Kepler was busy assembling. She did not deny the evidence against her, only challenged the interpretations being put on it. 'And I know,' she said, 'what they are after, that whore Ursula Reinbold and the rest of them, Einhorn too, they want to get their hands on my few florins when we lose the action. Reinbold owes me money, you know. I say we should ignore them, and they'll get tired of waiting.'

Kepler groaned. 'Mother, I have told you, the case has been reported to the ducal court of Württemberg. 'He did not know whether to laugh or be angry at the flicker of pride that brightened her ancient eyes. 'Far from waiting, we must press for an early hearing. It is they who are delaying, because they know how weak is their case and want more evidence. Enough damage has been done already. Why, I too am accused of dabbling in forbidden arts!'

'O yes,' she said, 'yes, you have your good name to think of.'

'For God's sake, mother!'

She turned her face away, sniffing. 'You know how it began? It was because I defended Christoph against the Reinbold bitch.'

'You told me, yes.'

She meant to tell him again. 'He was in some business with her tribe, and there was a dispute. And I defended him. And now he says he will abandon me.'

'Well, I shall not abandon you.'

He was writing off cannonades in all directions, to Einhorn and his gang, to acquaintances in the juridical faculty at Tübingen, to the court of Württemberg. The replies were evasive, and vaguely menacing. He was becoming convinced that the highest powers were conspiring to damage him through the old woman. And behind that fear was another, harder to face. 'Mother,' he ventured, squirming, 'mother tell me, truly, swear to me, that . . . that . . .'

She looked at him. 'Have you not seen me riding about the streets at night on my cat?'

The trial date was set for September, in Leonberg. Christoph, who lived there, appealed at once to the ducal court and had the proceedings transferred to the village of Güglingen. When Kepler and his mother arrived, the old woman was taken and put in chains with two keepers in an open room in the tower gate. The gaolers, merry fellows, enjoyed their job. They were being well paid, from the prisoner's own funds. Ursula Reinbold, seeing her prospective damages dwindling, demanded that the guard be reduced to one, while Christoph and his brother-in-law, Pastor Binder, reproached Kepler for allowing the expenses to mount alarmingly: he had insisted that her straw be changed daily, and that there should be a fire lit for her at night. The witnesses were heard, and the transcripts sent to Tübingen, where Kepler's friends in the law faculty decided that the evidence was such that the old woman should be questioned further under threat of torture.

It was a tawny autumn day when they led her to the chamber behind the courthouse. A breeze moved lazily over the grass, like a sweeping of invisible wings. Einhorn the magistrate was there, a wiry little man with a drop on the end of his nose, and various clerks and court officials. The party made a slow progress, for Frau Kepler was still suffering the effects of her chains. Kepler supported her, trying in vain to think of some comforting word. The strangest thoughts came into his head. On the journey from Linz he had read the *Dialogue on ancient and modern music* by Galileo's father, and now snatches of that work came back to him, like melodies grand and severe, and he thought of the wind-tossed sad singing of martyrs on their way to the stake.

They entered a low thatched shed. It was dark here after the sunlight, except in the far corner where a brazier stood throbbing, eager and intent, like a living thing. A tooth in Kepler's jaw suddenly began to ache. The air was stifling, but he felt cold. The place reminded him of a chapel, the hush, the shuffling of feet and the muffled coughs, the sense of rapt waiting. There was a hot smell, a mingling of sweat and burning coals, and something else, bitter and brassy, which was, he supposed, the stink of fear. The instruments were laid out on a low trestle table, grouped according to purpose, the thumbscrews and the gleaming knives, the burning rods, the pincers. Here were the tools of a craftsman. The torturer stepped forward, a fine tall fellow with a bushy beard, who was also the village dentist.

'*Grüss Gott*,' he said, touching a finger to his forehead, and bent a grave appraising eye upon the old woman. Einhorn coughed, releasing a sour waft of beer.

'I charge you, sir,' he said, stumbling through the formula, 'to present before this woman here arraigned the instruments of persuasion, that in God's grace she may bethink herself, and confess her crimes.' He had a wide smudged upper lip, a kind of prehensile flap; the drop at the end of his nose glittered in the glare of the brazier. Not once during all the days of the hearing had he looked Kepler in the eye. He hesitated, that lip groping blindly for words, and then stepped back a pace, colliding with one of his assistants. 'Proceed, man, proceed!'

The torturer in silence, lovingly, one by one displayed his tools. The old woman turned away.

'Look upon them!' Einhorn said. 'See, she does not weep, even now, the creature!'

Frau Kepler shook her head. 'I have wept so often in my life, I have no tears left.' Suddenly, groaning, she fell to her knees in a grotesque parody of supplication. 'Do with me as you please! Even if you pull one vein after another from my body, I would have nothing to admit.' She clasped her hands and began to wail a *paternoster*. The torturer looked about uncertainly. 'Am I required to pierce her?' he asked, taking up an iron.

'Leave it now,' said Kepler, as if calling a halt to an unruly children's game. The sentence had been that she should be threatened only. A general snuffling and muttering broke out, and everyone turned away. Einhorn scuttled off. Thus years of litigation were ended. The absurdity of the thing overwhelmed Kepler. Outside, he leaned his head against the sunwarmed brick wall and laughed. Presently he realised that he was weeping. His mother stood by, dazed and a little embarrassed, patting his shoulder. The seraph's wings of the wind swooped about them. 'Where will you go now?' Kepler said, wiping his nose.

'Well, I will go home. Or to Heumaden, to Margarete's house,' where, within a twelvemonth, in her bed, with much complaining and crying out, she was to die.

'Yes, yes, go to Heumaden.' He knuckled his eyes, peering helplessly at the trees, the sky of evening, a distant spire. He realised, with amazement, and a sick heave, that he was, yes, it was the only word, disappointed. Like the rest of them, including even, perhaps, his mother, he had wanted something to happen; not torture necessarily, but *something*, and he was disappointed. 'O God, mother.'

'There now, hush.'

By decree of the Duke of Württemberg she was declared innocent and immediately set free. Einhorn and Ursula Reinbold and the rest were directed to pay the trial costs. It was for the Keplers a great victory. Yet, mysteriously, there was a loss also.

When Kepler returned to Linz he found his old friend Winckle-mann the lens grinder gone. His house by the river was shuttered and empty, the windows all smashed. Kepler could not rid himself of the conviction that somewhere, in some invisible workshop of the world, the Jew's fate and the trial verdict had been spatch-cocked together, with glittering instruments, by the livid light of a brazier. Something, after all, had happened.

* * *

WEEKS PASSED, and months, and nothing was heard of the Jew. Kepler was drawn again and again to the little house on River Street. It was a pin-hole in the surface of a familiar world, through which, if only he could find the right way to apply his eye, he might glimpse enormities. He worked a ritual, walking rapidly twice or thrice past the shop with no more than a covert glance, and then abruptly stopping to rap on the door and wait, before giving himself up, with hands cupped about his face, to a long and inexplicably satisfying squint through the cracks in the shutters. The gloom within was peopled with vague grey shapes. If one of them someday should move! Stepping back then he would shake his head and depart slowly in seeming puzzlement.

He laughed at himself: for whose benefit was he performing this dumbshow? Did he imagine there was a conspiracy being waged against him, with spies everywhere, watching him? The idea, with which at first he had mocked himself, began to take hold. Yet even in his worst moments of fright and foreboding he did not imagine that there was any human power behind the plot. Even random phenomena may make a pattern which, out of the tension of its mere existing, will generate effects and influences. So he reasoned, and then worried all the more. A palpable enemy would have been one thing, but this, vast and impersonal . . . When he made enquiries among the Jew's neighbours he met only silence. The locksmith next door, a flaxen-haired giant with a club foot, glared at him for a long moment, his jaw working, and then turned away saying: 'We minds our own affairs down here, squire.' Kepler watched the brute clump away into his shop, and he thought of the lens-grinder's wife, plump and young, until his mind averted itself, unable to bear the possibilities.

And then one day something shifted, with an almost audible clanking of cogs and levers, and there was, as it seemed, an attempt to make good his loss.

He recognised him a long way off by his walk, that laborious stoop and swing, as if at each pace he were moulding an intricate shape out of resistant air before him and then stepping gingerly into it. Kepler suddenly remembered a crowded hall at Benatky, and the summoner coming down from his master's table and saying silkily, as so often, *you are wanted, sir*, the great head smiling up from its platter of dingy lace and one hand settling stealthily on the edge of the table like saurian jaws. But something was changed with him now. His gait was more tortured than of old, and he advanced with his face warily inclined, clutching jealously the stirrup strap of a piebald pony.

'Why, Sir Mathematicus, is it you?' palping the air with an outstretched hand. Second sight was all that was left him, his eye sockets were empty asterisks: he had been blinded.

It was sixteen years since they had last met, at Tycho's funeral in Prague. Jeppe had not aged. The blinding had drained his face of everything save a kind of childlike attentiveness, so that he seemed to be listening constantly past the immediate to something far away. He was dressed in beggar's rig. 'A disguise, of course,' he said, and snickered. He was on his way to Prague. He showed no sign of surprise at their meeting. Perhaps for him, Kepler thought, in that changeless dark, time operated differently, and sixteen years was as nothing.

They went to a tavern on the wharf. Kepler chose one where he was not known. He gave it out that he also was passing through on his way elsewhere. He was not sure why he felt the need to dissemble. Jeppe's blank face was bent upon him intently, smiling at the lie, and he blushed, as if those puckered wounds were seeing him. It was quiet in the tavern. In a corner two old men sat playing a decrepit game of dominoes. The taverner brought two mugs of ale. He looked at the dwarf with curiosity and faint disgust. Kepler's shame increased. He should have invited the creature home.

'Tengnagel is dead, you knew that?' Jeppe said. 'He did you some wrong, I think.'

'Yes, we had differences. I did not hear he had died. What of his wife, the Dane's daughter?'

The dwarf smiled and shook his head, savouring a secret joke. 'And Mistress Christine too, dead. So many of them dead, and only you and I still here, sir.' In the tavern window suddenly there loomed the rust-red sail of a schooner plying upriver. The dominoes clattered, and one of the old men mumbled an oath.

'And what of the Italian?' Kepler asked.

It seemed for a moment the dwarf had not heard, but then he said:

'I have not seen him for many years. He took me to Rome when Master Tycho was dead. What times!' It was a garish tale. Kepler saw the pines and the pillars and the stone lions, the sunlight on marble, heard the laughter of painted whores. 'He was a hard man in those days, given to duels and scuffles, a great gambler at the dice, spinning from one game to another with a sword at his side and his fool, your humble servant, sir, behind him.' He reached out a hand, groping for his mug; Kepler stealthily slid it into his grasp. 'You remember when we nursed him, sir, in the Dane's house? That wound never fully healed. He swore he could tell coming changes in the weather by it.'

'We thought he would die,' Kepler said.

The dwarf nodded. 'You had regard for him, sir, you saw his worth, as I did.'

Kepler was startled. Was it true? 'There was much life in him,' he said. 'But he is a scoundrel, for all that.'

'O yes!' There was a pause, and Jeppe suddenly laughed. 'I will tell you something to cheer you, all the same. You knew the Dane let Tengnagel marry his daughter because the wench was with child? But the brat was none of Tengnagel's doing. Felix had been there before him.'

'And did the Junker know?'

'Surely. But he would not care. His only interest was to share in the Brahe fortune. You above all, though, sir, should appreciate the joke. What Tengnagel cheated you of is now inherited by the Italian's bastard.'

'Yes,' Kepler said, 'it is a pretty notion,' and laughed, but uneasily; between the cuckold and the cuckoo there was not much to choose. He felt a familiar unease; the dwarf knew too much. 'Where is the Italian now?' he asked. 'In prison, or on the run again?'

Jeppe called for more ale, and left Kepler to pay for it.

'Why, both, in a manner of speaking,' he said. 'He could never be at peace, that one. In Rome he might have been a gentleman, for he had friends and patrons, and was favoured even by the Pope, Her Holiness Clement, as he would have it. But he drank too much and diced too much, and spoke too freely, and made enemies. In a brawl one day over the score in a game of racquets he ran a player through the throat and killed him. We fled the city, and took sail for Malta, where he thought the Knights would give us shelter. They put him in prison. He was a turbulent guest, though, as you may imagine, and after a week they were glad to let him escape.' A cat leaped with swift grace on to the counter where the taverner leaned, listening. Jeppe took a drink of ale and wiped his mouth on his sleeve. 'For months we wandered through the Mediterranean ports, with the Vatican's spies on our heels. Then we heard talk of a papal pardon, and though I warned him it was a trick he would have nothing but to return to Rome. At Port' Ercole the customs men, Spanish louts, took him for a smuggler and threw him in the cells. When they let him go at last, our ship for Rome had sailed. He stood on the beach and watched it depart, the red sail, I remember it. He wept for rage and for himself, beaten at last. His baggage had been already put aboard, and he had nothing left.'

They left the tavern. A raw wind was blowing off the river, and snowflakes whirled in the air. Kepler helped the dwarf to mount up. 'Farewell,' Jeppe said, 'we shall not meet again, I think.' The pony stamped and snuffled nervously, smelling the impending storm. Jeppe smiled, the blind face puckering. 'He died, you know, sir, on that beach at Port' Ercole, cursing God and all Spaniards. Old wounds had opened, and he had the fever. I held his hand at the end. He gave me a ducat to buy a Mass for him.'

Kepler looked away. Sorrow welled up in him, intense and amazing as tears in sleep, and as brief. 'There was much life in him,' he said.

Jeppe nodded. 'I think you envied him that, sir?'

'Yes,' with mild surprise, 'yes, I envied him that.' He gave the dwarf a florin.

'Another Mass? You are kind, sir.'

'How will you live in Prague? Will you find a position?'

'O but I have a position.'

'Yes?'

'Yes,' and smiled again. As he watched him ride slowly away through the snow, Kepler realised that he had not thought to ask who it was had blinded him. Maybe it was better not to know.

That night he had a dream, one of those involuntary great dark plots that now and then the sleeping mind will hatch, elaborate and enigmatic and full of inexplicable significance. Familiar figures appeared, sheepish and a little crazed, dream actors who had not had time to learn their parts. The Italian came forward, clad as a knight of the Rosy Cross. In his arm he carried a little gilded statue, which sprang alive suddenly and spoke. It had Regina's face. A solemn and complex ceremony was being celebrated, and Kepler understood that this was the alchemical wedding of darkness and light. He woke into the dim glow of a winter dawn. The snow was falling fast outside, the vague shadow of it moved on the wall by his bed. A strange happiness reigned in his heart, as if a problem that had been with him all his life had at last been decided; a happiness so firm and fine it was not dispelled even when he remembered that, six months before, in her twenty-seventh year, in the Palatinate, of a fever of the brain, Regina had died.

* * *

THE AFTER-IMAGE of that dream never entirely faded. Its silvery glimmer was mysteriously present in every page of his book of the harmony of the world, which he finished in a sudden frenzy in the spring of 1618. The empire was charging headlong into war, but he hardly noticed. For thirty years he had been accumulating the material and the tools for this, the final synthesis. Now, like a demented fisherman, he hauled in the lines of his net from all directions. He was entranced. Times he found himself at table, or walking the city wall in the rain, with only the vaguest recollection of how he had come there. Answering a remark of Susanna's, it would dawn on him that an hour had passed since she had spoken. At night the spinning coils of his brain blundered into a sack of sleep, and in the morning struggled out again enmeshed in the same thoughts, as if there had been no interruption. He was no longer a young man, his health was poor, and sometimes he pictured himself a thing of rags and straw dangling limply from a huge bulbous head, like those puppets he had coveted as a child, strung up by their hair in the dollmaker's shop.

The *Harmonia mundi* was for him a new kind of labour. Before, he had voyaged into the unknown, and the books he brought back were fragmentary and enigmatic charts apparently unconnected with each other. Now he understood that they were not maps of the islands of an Indies, but of different stretches of the shore of one great world. The *Harmonia* was their synthesis. The net that he was drawing in became the grid-lines of a globe. It seemed to him an apt image, for were not the sphere and the circle the very bases of the laws of world harmony? Years before, he had defined harmony as that which the soul creates by perceiving how certain proportions in the world correspond to prototypes existing in the soul. The proportions everywhere abound, in music and the movements of the planets, in human and vegetable forms, in men's fortunes even, but they are all relation merely, and inexistent without the perceiving soul. How is such perception possible? Peasants and children, barbarians, animals even, feel the harmony of the tone. Therefore the perceiving must be instinct in the soul, based in a profound and essential geometry, that geometry which is derived from the simple divisioning of circles. All that he had for long held to be the case. Now he took the short step to the fusion of symbol and object. The circle is the bearer of pure harmonies, pure harmonies are innate in the soul, and so the soul and the circle are one.

Such simplicity, such beauty. These were the qualities which sustained him through exhaustion and the periodic bouts of rage before the intractability of the material. The ancients had sought to explain harmony by the mysticism of numbers, and had foundered in complexity and worthless magic. The reason why certain ratios produce a concord and others discord is not to be found in arithmetic, however, but in geometry, and specifically in the divisioning of the circle by means of the regular polygons. There was the beauty. And the simplicity was that harmonious results are produced only by those polygons which can be constructed with the compass and ruler alone, the tools of classical geometry.

Man he would show to be truly the *magnum miraculum*. The priests and the astrologers would have it that we are nothing, clay and ash and humours. But God had created the world according to the same laws of harmony which the swineherd holds in his heart. Do the planetary aspects influence us? Yes, but the Zodiac is no truly existing arc, only an image of the soul projected upon the sky. We do not suffer, but act, are not influenced but are ourselves the influences.

These were airy heights in which he moved. He grew dizzy. His eyesight was worsening, everything he looked on trembled as if under water or smoke. Sleep became a kind of helpless tumbling through black space. Alighting from some high leap of thought, he would find Susanna shaking him in alarm, as if he were a night-walker whom she had saved from the brink.

'What is it, what?' he mumbled, thinking of fire and flood, the children dead, his papers stolen. She held his face in her hands.

'O Kepler, Kepler . . .'

Now he went all the way back to the *Mysterium*, and the theory which through the years had been his happiness and his constant hope, the incorporation of the five regular solids within the intervals of the planets. His discovery of the ellipse law in the *Astronomia nova* had dealt a blow to that idea, but a blow not heavy enough to destroy his faith. Somehow the rules of plane harmony must be made to account for the irregularities in this model of the world. The problem delighted him. The new astronomy which he had invented had destroyed the old symmetries; then he must find new and finer ones.

He began by seeking to assign to the periods of revolution of the planets the harmonic ratios dictated by musical measurement. It would not work. Next he tried to discern a harmonic series in the sizes or volumes of the planets. Again he failed. Then he sought to fit the least and greatest solar distances into a scale, examined the ratios of the extreme velocities, and of the variable periods required by each planet to rotate through a unit length of its orbit. And then at last, by the nice trick of siting the position of observation not on earth but in the sun, and from there computing the variations in angular velocities which the watcher from the sun could be expected to see, he found it. For in setting the two extremes of velocity thus observed against each other, and in combined pairs among the other planets, he derived the intervals of the complete scale, both the major and the minor keys. The heavenly motions, he could then write, are nothing but a continuous song for several voices, perceived not by the ear but by the intellect, a figured music which sets landmarks in the immeasurable flow of time.

He was not finished yet, not by a long way. In the *Mysterium* he had asked what is the connection between the time a planet takes to complete its orbit, and its distance from the sun, and had not found a satisfactory answer. Now the question came back more urgent than ever. Since the sun governs planetary motion, as he held to be the case, then that motion must be connected with the solar distances, or else the universe is a senseless and arbitrary structure. This was the darkest hour of his long night. For months he laboured over the problem, wielding the Tychonic observations like the enormous letter-wheels of a cabalist. When the solution came, it came, as always, through a back door of the mind, hesitating shyly, an announcing angel dazed by the immensity of its journey. One morning in the middle of May, while Europe was buckling on its sword, he felt the wing-tip touch him, and heard the mild voice say *I am here.*

It seemed a nothing, the merest trifle. It sat on the page with no more remarkable an air than if it had been, why, anything, a footnote in Euclid, one of Galileo's anagrams, a scrap of nonsense out of a schoolboy's bad dream, and yet it was the third of his eternal laws, and the supporting bridge between the harmonic ratios and the regular solids. It said that the squares of the periods of evolution of any two planets are to each other as the cubes of their mean distances from the sun. It was his triumph. It showed him that the discrepancies in distance which were left over after the insertion of the regular polygons between the orbits of the planets were not a defect of his calculations, but the necessary consequences of the dominant principle of harmony. The world, he understood at last, is an infinitely more complex and subtle construct than he or anyone else had imagined. He had listened for a tune, but here were symphonies. How mistaken he had been to seek a geometrically perfected, closed cosmos! A mere clockwork could be nothing beside the reality which is the most harmonic possible. The regular solids are material, but harmony is form. The solids describe the raw masses, harmony prescribes the fine structure, by which the whole becomes that which it is, a perfected work of art.

Two weeks after the formulation of that law the book was finished. He set about the printing at once, in a kind of panic, as if fire or flood, his greatest fears, or some other hobgoblin, might strike him down before he could make public his testament.

Besides, the printing was a kind of work, and how could he simply stop? The trajectory he had long ago entered on would take time to run down, would sweep him through further books, the scrag-ends of his career. And even if he had been capable of rest, rest was not permissible, for then he would have had to face, in the dreadful stillness, the demon that had started up at his back, whose hot breath was on his neck.

For years the *World Harmony* had obsessed him, a huge weight pinning him down; now he was aware of a curious feeling of lightness, of levity almost, as if he had drunk again a dose of Wincklemann's drugged wine. That was the demon. He recognised it. He had known it before, the selfsame feeling, when, in the *Astronomia nova*, he had blithely discarded years of work for the sake of an error of a few minutes of arc, not because he had been wrong all those years – though he had – but in order to destroy the past, the human and hopelessly defective past, and begin all over again the attempt to achieve perfection: that same heedless, euphoric sense of teetering on the brink while the gleeful voice at his ear whispered *jump*.

* * *

OTHER AND FAR LESS inviting precipices appeared under his feet. The world that once had seemed so wide was becoming narrower daily. The Palatinate's army had been crushed in the battle of Weisser Berg and Bohemia regained by the Catholics, but the war of the religions still raged. The Empire was ablaze and he was on the topmost storey. He could hear the flames roaring behind him, the crash of masonry and splintering timber as another staircase gave way. Before him there was only the shivered window and the sudden chill blue air. When in the autumn of 1619 the Elector Frederick and his wife Princess Elizabeth entered Prague to accept the crown offered him by the Bohemian Protestants, the *World Harmony* had been on the presses, and Kepler had had time to suppress only in a few final copies the dedication to James of England, the Princess's father.

He had not needed that connection to mark him out as suspect. Even his attacks on the brotherhood of the Rosy Cross, and his dispute with the English Rosicrucian Robert Fludd, had won him no praise: the imperial parties, so he heard, were asking what he had to hide, that he should flaunt this too enthusiastic loyalty to his Catholic Emperor Ferdinand. He despaired, he was no good at politics. He was not even sure any longer who was fighting whom in the war. The Bohemian barons had not accepted the defeat of Weisser Berg, but they were a local disturbance: now there was talk of French and even Danish involvement. Kepler was baffled. Could these far-off kingdoms really care so much for religion and the fate of little Bohemia? It must be all a conspiracy. The Rosicrucians were to blame, or the Vatican.

Presently, as he knew it would, the old wheel turned: all Lutherans were ordered out of Linz. As the Emperor's mathematician, in title at least, Kepler could hope for immunity. He gave up his pilgrimages to Wincklemann's deserted shop, and stayed away from religious services. But the invisible plotters would not be thus easily put off. His library was confiscated by the Catholic authorities. He bitterly admired the accuracy of their aim; it was a hard blow to bear. And then, it was almost comic, Lutheranism threw up a tormentor of its own in the shape of Pastor Hitzler. Kepler felt himself backed into a corner, an old, puzzled rat.

The public turmoil was matched in the darkness of his heart, where a private war was raging. He could not tell what was the cause of battle, nor what the prize that was being fought for. On one side was all that he held precious, his work, his love for wife and children, his peace of mind; on the other was that which he could not name, a drunken faceless power. Was it still, he wondered, the demon that had risen up out of the closing pages of the *Harmonia mundi*, grown fat on the world's misfortunes? That was when he began to suspect a connection between his inner ragings and Europe's war, and feared for his sanity. He fled from the battlefield into the numbing grind of the Tabulae Rudolphinae. There, among the orderly marching columns of Tycho Brahe's lifework, he could hide. But not for long. Soon that manoeuvre was exhausted. Then he embarked on the first of his strange frantic wanderings. On the road he felt easier, the clash of battle within him stilled for a while by the pains and frustration of travel. It seemed to be what the demon wanted.

He used as excuse the moneys owed him by the crown. The printing of the *Tables* would be a costly business. He set out for Vienna and Ferdinand's court. After four months of haggling there he won a grudging part settlement of 6,000 florins. The Treasury, however, cleverer and more careful than the Emperor, immediately transferred responsibility for the payment to the three towns of Nuremberg, Kempten and Memmingen. Once more Kepler set off, seeming to hear Vienna break out in general hilarity behind him. By the end of winter he had collected from the tight-fisted trinity of towns 2,000 florins. It would buy the paper for the *Tables*. The effort had exhausted him, and he turned wearily towards home.

When he got to Linz he found the city transformed into a military camp. The Bavarian garrison sent in by the Emperor was billeted everywhere. At Plank the printer's a squad of soldiers was sprawled at feed among the presses, their stink overlaying the familiar smells of ink and machine oil. All work had stopped. They watched him incuriously as he danced before them in helpless rage. He might have dropped into their midst from another planet. They were for the most part the sons of poor farmers. When the printing got under way at last they began to display a childlike interest in the work: few of them had ever seen a machine working before. They would gather about Plank's men in silent groups, staring and softly breathing like cattle at a stile. The sudden white flourish of a pulled proof never failed to call forth a collective sigh of surprise and pleasure. Later on, when the amazing fact had soaked into their understanding that Kepler was the sole cause of all this mighty effort, they turned their awed attention on to him. They would jostle to get near him at the benches or the readers' desk, trying to sift out of his talk of fonts and colophons and faces some clue to the secret of his wizardry. And occasionally they would pluck up courage enough to offer him a mug of beer or a twist of tobacco, grinning furiously at their boots and sweating. He grew accustomed to their presence, and ceased to heed them, except that now and then something spoke to him, at once faint and insistent, out of this warm noisome mass of life pressing at his back. Then he would fly into a rage again, and yell into their stunned faces, and stamp out of the shop, waving his arms.

In the spring the Lutheran peasantry revolted, sick of being harried, of being hungry, sick most of all of their arrogant Emperor. They swept across Upper Austria, delirious with success, unable to believe their own strength. By early summer they were at the walls of Linz. The siege lasted for two months. The city had been ill-prepared, and was quickly reduced to horse meat and nettle soup. Kepler's house was on the wall, and from his workroom he could look down across the moats and the suburbs where the fiercest fighting took place. How small the protagonists looked from up here, and yet how vivid their blood and their spilled guts. The smell of death bathed him about as he worked. A detachment of troops was quartered in his house. Some among them he recognised from the printing house. He had thought his children would be terrified, but they seemed to regard it all as a glorious game. One morning, in the midst of a bitter skirmish, they came to tell him that there was a dead soldier in his bed.

'Dead, you say? No, no, he is wounded merely; your mama put him there to rest.'

Cordula shook her head. Such a serious little girl! 'He is *dead*,' she said firmly. 'There is a fly in his mouth.'

Towards the end of June the peasant forces breached the wall one night and set fire to a section of streets before being repulsed. Plank's shop was destroyed, and with it all the sheets of the *Tables* so far printed. Kepler decided it was time to move. By October, the siege long since lifted and the peasants crushed, he had packed up everything that he owned and was on his way to Ulm, excommunicate and penniless, never to return.

In Ulm for a while he was almost happy. He had left Susanna and the children in Regensburg, and, alone once more after so many years, he felt as if time had magically fallen away and he was back in Graz, or Tübingen even, when life had not properly begun, and the future was limitless. The city physician Gregor Horst, an acquaintance from his Prague days, leased him a little house in Raben Alley. He found a printer one Jonas Saur. The work went well at first. He still imagined that the *Tables* would make his fortune. He spent his days in the printing house. On Saturday nights he and Gregor Horst would get quietly drunk together and argue astronomy and politics into the small hours.

But he could not be at rest for long. The old torment was rising once more in his heart. Saur the printer lived up to his name, and there were quarrels. Yet again Kepler turned his hopes toward Tübingen and Michael Mästlin; could Gruppenbach, who had printed the *Mysterium*, finish off for him the *Tables*? He wrote to Mästlin, and getting no reply he set out for Tübingen on foot. But it was February, the weather was bad, and after two days he found himself halted at a crossroads in the midst of turnip fields, exhausted and in despair, but not so far gone that he could not see, with wry amusement, how all his life was summed up in this picture of himself, a little man, wet and weary, dithering at a fork in the road. He turned back. The town council at Esslingen presented him with a horse, got from the town's home for the infirm. The beast bore him bravely enough to Ulm and then died under him. Again he saw the aptness of it, this triumphal entry, on a broken-down jade, into a city that hardly knew him. He made his peace with Jonas Saur, and at last, after twenty years, the *Tables* were hauled to completion.

Two kinsmen of Tycho Brahe called on him one day at his lodgings in Raben Alley, Holger Rosenkrands the statesman's son and the Norwegian Axel Gyldenstjern. They were on their way to England. Kepler considered. Wotton, King James's ambassador to Prague, had urged him once to come to England. Rosenkrands and Gyldenstjern would be happy to take him with them. Something held him back. How could he leave his homelands, however bad the convulsions of war? There was nothing for him but to go to Prague. He had the *Tables* at least to offer the

Emperor. It was not likely it would be enough. His time was past. Even Rudolph in his latter days had grown bored with his mathematician. But he must go somewhere, do something, and so he took himself aboard a barge bound for the capital, where, unknown to both of them, Wallenstein awaited him.

* * *

Now, baking his chilblains at Hillebrand Billig's fire, he brooded on his time in Sagan. It had been at least a refuge, where for a while he had held still, the restlessness of his heart feeding vicariously on his new master's doings. Wallenstein's world was all noise and event, a ceaseless coming and going to the accompaniment of distant cannonades and hoofbeats at midnight: as if he too were in flight from an inexorable demon of his own. Yet Kepler had never known a man who so fitted the shape and size of his allotted space. What emptiness could there be in *him*, that a stalking devil would seek for a home?

Billig was laboriously doing the tavern accounts at the kitchen table, licking his pencil and sighing. Frau Billig sat near him, darning her children's stockings. They might have been done by Dürer. A draught from the window shook the candlelight. There was the sound of the wind and the rain, the muffled roars of the Saturday night revellers in the tavern, the crackling of the fire, the old dog's snores, but beneath all a deep silence reigned, secret and inviolable, perhaps the silence of the earth itself. Why, dear Christ, did I leave home to come on this mad venture?

At first he had been wary of Wallenstein. He feared being bought for a plaything, for the general's obsession with astrology was famous. Kepler was too old and too tired to take up again that game of guesswork and dissimulation. For months he had held back, worrying at the terms Wallenstein was offering him, wanting to know what would be required of him in return. Conversation, said Wallenstein, smiling, your company, the benefit of your learning. The Emperor, with ill-concealed enthusiasm, urged him to accept the offered post, and took the opportunity to transfer on to Wallenstein the crown's considerable debt to its mathematician. Wallenstein made no protest; his blandness caused Kepler's heart to sink. Also the astronomer would be granted an annual stipend of 1,000 florins from the Sagan coffers, a house at Gitschin where the general had his palace, and the use of a printing press with sufficient paper for whatever books he might wish to publish, all this without condition or hindrance. Kepler dared to hope. Could it be, at last, could it be . . .?

It could not. Wallenstein indeed believed he had purchased a tame astrologer. In time, after many clashes, they had come to an arrangement whereby Kepler supplied the data out of which more willing wizards would work up the horoscopes and calendars. For the rest he was free to do as he wished. He saw no sign of the imperial debt being settled, nor of the printing works and the paper that had been promised. Things might have been worse. There was the house at least, and now and then he was even paid a little of his salary on account. If he was not happy, neither was he in despair. Hitzler's word came back to him: tepid. Sagan was a barbaric place, its people peculiar and cold, their dialect incomprehensible. There were few diversions. Once he travelled down to Tübingen and spent a gloriously tipsy month with old Mästlin, deaf and doddering now but merry withal. And one day Susanna came to him, with a look of mingled amusement and surprise, to announce that she was pregnant.

'By God,' he said, 'I am not so old then as I thought, eh?'

'You are not old at all, my dear, dear Kepler.'

She kissed him, and they laughed, and then were silent for a moment, a little awkward, almost embarrassed, sharing an old complicity. What a happy day that had been, perhaps the best out of all the days of that amused and respectful, ill-matched and splendid marriage.

Wallenstein lost interest in him, even his conversation. Summonses to the palace grew rare, and then ceased altogether, and Kepler's patron became a stylised and intermittent presence glimpsed now and then in the distance, beyond a prospect of trees, or down the long slope of a hill on a sunlit evening, cantering among his aides, a stiff, rhythmically nodding figure, like a sacred effigy borne in brief procession on a feast-day. And then, as if indeed some mundane deity's memory had been jogged, workmen with a cart trundled up one day and dumped at Kepler's door a great lump of machinery. It was the printing press.

Now he could work again. There was money to be made from almanacs and navigational calendars. But he was ill that winter, his stomach was bad and he suffered much from gravel and the gout. His years were weighing heavily on him. He needed a helper. In a little book sent him from Strasburg he found on the dedication page a public letter addressed to him by the author, Jakob Bartsch, offering his humble services to the imperial astronomer. Kepler was flattered, and wrote inviting the disciple to come to Sagan. Bartsch was a mixed blessing. He was young and eager, and wearied Kepler with his impossible enthusiasms. Kepler grew fond of him, all the same, and would have had fewer misgivings at his marrying into the family if Susanna, his daughter and Bartsch's bride, had not had so much of the Müller strain in her.

The young man willingly took over the drudgery of the almanacs, and Kepler was free to return to a cherished project, his dream of a journey to the moon. The larger part of that last year in Sagan he devoted to the *Somnium*. None of his books had given him such peculiar pleasure as this one. It was as if some old strain of longing and love were at last being freed. The story of the boy Duracotus, and his mother Fiolxhilda the witch, and the strange sad stunted creatures of the moon, filled him with quiet inner laughter, at himself, at his science, at the mild foolishness of everything.

'You will stay the night, then, Doctor?'

Frau Billig was watching him, her needle poised.

'Yes,' he said, 'certainly; and thank you.'

Hillebrand Billig lifted his troubled head from his accounts and laughed ruefully. 'Maybe you will help me with these figures, for I cannot manage them!'

'Aye, gladly.'

They want to know what really has brought me here, O yes they do. But then, so do I.

When he finished the *Somnium* there had been another crisis, as he had known there would be. What was it, this wanton urge to destroy the work of his intellect and rush out on crazy voyages into the real world? It had seemed to him in Sagan that he was haunted, not by a ghost but something like a memory so vivid that at times it seemed about to conjure itself into a physical presence. It was as if he had mislaid some precious small thing, and forgotten about it, and yet was tormented by the loss. Suddenly now he recalled Tycho Brahe standing barefoot outside his room while a rainswept dawn broke over the Hradcany, that forlorn and baffled look on his face, a dying man searching too late for the life that he had missed, that his work had robbed him of. Kepler shivered. Was it that same look the Billigs saw now, on his face?

Susanna had stared at him in disbelief. He would not meet her eye. 'But why, why?' she said. 'What is to be gained?'

'I must go.' There were the bonds to be seen to in Linz. Wallenstein was in disgrace, had been dismissed. The Emperor was sitting with the Diet in Regensburg, ensuring the succession of his son. 'He owes me moneys, there is business to be finished, *I must go.*'

'My dear,' Susanna said, trying if a joke would work, 'if you go, I will expect to see the Last Judgment sooner than your return.' But neither one smiled, and she let fall her hand from his.

He travelled south into wild winter weather. He took no notice of the elements. He was prepared to go on to Prague if necessary, to Tübingen – to Weilderstadt! But Regensburg was far enough. I know he will meet me here, I'll recognise him by the rosy cross on his breast, and his lady with him. Are you there? If I walk to the window now shall I see you, out there in the rain and the dark, all of you, queen and dauntless knight, and death, and the devil . . .?

'Doctor, Doctor you must go to bed now, and rest, you are ill.'

'What?'

'You are shaking . . .'

Ill? Was he? His blood sizzled, and his heart was a muffled thunder in his breast. He almost laughed: it would be just like him, convinced all his life that death was imminent and then to die in happy ignorance. But no. 'I must have been asleep.' He struggled upright in his chair, coughing, and spread unquiet hands to the fire. Show them, show them all, I'll never die. For it was not death he had come here to meet, but something altogether other. Turn up a flat stone and there it is, myriad and profligate! 'Such a dream I had, Billig, such a dream. *Es war doch so schön.*'

What was it the Jew said? Everything is told us, but nothing explained. Yes. We must take it all on trust. That's the secret. How simple! He smiled. It was not a mere book that was thus thrown away, but the foundation of a life's work. It seemed not to matter.

'Ah my friend, such dreams . . .'

The rain beat upon the world without. Anna Billig came and filled his cup with punch. He thanked her.

Never die, never die.

NOTE

The standard biographies are *Kepler*, by Max Caspar, translated and edited by C. Doris Hellman (London, 1959), and *Tycho Brahe*, by J.L.E. Dreyer (Edinburgh, 1890). I must also mention, once again, my indebtedness to, and admiration for, Arthur Koestler's *The Sleepwalkers* (London, 1959). Another work which provided me also with valuable insights into early 17th-century life and thought is *The Rosicrucian Enlightenment*, by Frances A. Yates (London, 1972).

For their help and encouragement, I wish to thank especially Don Sherman and Ruth Dunham, and my wife, Janet.

Johannes Kepler died in Regensburg on November the 15th, 1630.

THE NEWTON LETTER

To Vincent Lawrence

I seem to have been only as a boy playing on the seashore, and diverting myself in now and then finding a smoother pebble or a prettier shell than ordinary, whilst the great ocean of truth lay all undiscovered before me.

– Sir Isaac Newton

WORDS FAIL ME, Clio. How did you track me down, did I leave bloodstains in the snow? I won't try to apologise. Instead, I want simply to explain, so that we both might understand. Simply! I like that. No, I'm not sick, I have not had a breakdown. I am, you might say, I might say, in retirement from life. Temporarily.

I have abandoned my book. You'll think me mad. Seven years I gave to it – seven years! How can I make you understand that such a project is now for me impossible, when I don't really understand it myself? Shall I say, I've lost my faith in the primacy of text? Real people keep getting in the way now, objects, landscapes even. Everything ramifies. I think for example of the first time I went down to Ferns. From the train I looked at the shy back-end of things, drainpipes and broken windows, straggling gardens with their chorus lines of laundry, a man bending to a spade. Out on Killiney bay a white sail was tilted at an angle to the world, a white cloud was slowly cruising the horizon. What has all this to do with anything? Yet such remembered scraps seem to me abounding in significance. They are at once commonplace and unique, like clues at the scene of a crime. But everything that day was still innocent as the blue sky itself, so what do they prove? Perhaps just that: the innocence of things, their non-complicity in our affairs. All the same I'm convinced those drainpipes and that cloud require me far more desperately than I do them. You see my difficulty.

I might have written to you last September, before I fled, with some bland excuse. You would have understood, certainly at least you would have sympathised. But Clio, dear Cliona, you have been my teacher and my friend, my inspiration, for too long, I couldn't lie to you. Which doesn't mean I know what the truth is, and how to tell it to you. I'm confused. I feel ridiculous and melodramatic, and comically exposed. I have shinned up to this high perch and can't see how to get down, and of the spectators below, some are embarrassed and the rest are about to start laughing.

I SHOULDN'T HAVE gone down there. It was the name that attracted me. Fern House! I expected – Oh, I expected all sorts of things. It turned out to be a big gloomy pile with ivy and peeling walls and a smashed fanlight over the door, the kind of place where you picture a mad stepdaughter locked up in the attic. There was an avenue of sycamores and then the road falling away down the hill to the village. In the distance I could see the smoke of the town, and beyond that again a sliver of sea. I suppose, thinking about it, that *was* much what I expected. To look at, anyway.

Two women met me in the garden. One was large and blonde, the other a tall girl with brown arms, wearing a tattered straw sun hat. The blonde spoke: they had seen me coming. She pointed down the hill road. I assumed she was the woman of the house, the girl in the sun hat her sister perhaps. I pictured them, vigilantly silent, watching me toiling toward them, and I felt for some reason flattered. Then the girl took off her hat, and she was not a girl, but a middle-aged woman. I had got them nearly right, but the wrong way round. This was Charlotte Lawless, and the big blonde girl was Ottilie, her niece.

The lodge, as they called it, stood on the roadside at the end of the drive. Once there had been a wall and a high pillared gate, but all that was long gone, the way of other glories. The door screeched. A bedroom and a parlour, a tiny squalid kitchen, a tinier bathroom. Ottilie followed me amiably from room to room, her hands stuck in the back pockets of her trousers. Mrs Lawless waited in the front doorway. I opened the kitchen cupboard: cracked mugs and mouse-shit. There was a train back to town in an hour, I would make it if I hurried. Mrs Lawless fingered the brim of her sun hat and considered the sycamores. Of the three of us only blonde Ottilie was not embarrassed. Stepping past Charlotte in the doorway I caught her milky smell – and heard myself offering her a month's rent in advance.

*

What possessed me? Ferns was hardly that Woolsthorpe of my vague dreams, where, shut away from the pestilence of college life, I would put the final touches to my own *Principia*. Time is different in the country. There were moments when I thought I would panic, stranded in the midst of endless afternoons. Then there was the noise, a constant row, heifers bellowing, tractors growling, the dogs baying all night. Things walked on the roof, scrabbled under the floor. There was a nest of blackbirds in the lilacs outside the parlour window where I tried to work. The whole bush shook with their quarrelling. And one night a herd of something, cows, horses, I don't know, came and milled around on the lawn, breathing and nudging, like a mob gathering for the attack.

But the weather that late May was splendid, sunny and still, and tinged with sadness. I killed whole days rambling the fields. I had brought guidebooks to trees and birds, but I couldn't get the hang of them. The illustrations would not match up with the real specimens before me. Every bird looked like a starling. I soon got discouraged. Perhaps that explains the sense I had of being an interloper. Amid those sunlit scenes I felt detached, as if I myself were a mere idea, a stylised and subtly inaccurate illustration of something that was only real elsewhere. Even the pages of my manuscript, when I sat worriedly turning them over, had an unfamiliar look, as if they had been written, not by someone else, but by another version of myself.

Remember that mad letter Newton wrote to John Locke in September of 1693, accusing the philosopher out of the blue of being immoral, and a Hobbist, and of having tried to embroil him with women? I picture old Locke pacing the great garden at Oates, eyebrows leaping higher and higher as he goggles at these wild charges. I wonder if he felt the special pang which I feel reading the subscription: *I am your most humble and unfortunate servant, Is. Newton.* It seems to me to express better than anything that has gone before it Newton's pain and anguished bafflement. I compare it to the way a few weeks later he signed, with just the stark surname, another, and altogether different, letter. What happened in the interval, what knowledge dawned on him?

We have speculated a great deal, you and I, on his nervous collapse late in that summer of '93. He was fifty, his greatest work was behind him, the *Principia* and the gravity laws, the discoveries in optics. He was giving himself up more and more to interpretative study of the Bible, and to that darker work in alchemy which so embarrasses his biographers (cf. Popov *et al.*). He was a great man now, his fame was assured, all Europe honoured him. But his life as a scientist was over. The process of lapidescence had begun: the world was turning him into a monument to himself. He was cold, arrogant, lonely. He was still obsessively jealous – his hatred of Hooke was to endure, indeed to intensify, even beyond the death of his old adversary. He was—

Look at me, writing history; old habits die hard. All I meant to say is that the book was as good as done, I had only to gather up a few loose ends, and write the conclusion – but in those first weeks at Ferns something started to go wrong. It was only as yet what the doctors call a vague general malaise. I was concentrating, with morbid fascination, on the chapter I had devoted to his breakdown and those two letters to Locke. Was that a lump I felt there, a little, hard, painless lump . . .?

Mostly of course such fears seemed ridiculous. There were even moments when the prospect of finishing the thing merged somehow with my new surroundings into a grand design. I recall one day when I was in, appropriately enough, the orchard. The sun was shining, the trees were in blossom. It would be a splendid book, fresh and clean as this bright scene before me. The academies would be stunned, you would be proud of me, and Cambridge would offer me a big job. I felt an extraordinary sense of purity, of tender innocence. Thus Newton himself must have stood one fine morning in his mother's garden at Woolsthorpe, as the ripe apples dropped about his head. I turned, hearing a violent thrashing of small branches. Edward Lawless stepped sideways through a gap in the hedge, kicking a leg behind him to free a snagged trouser cuff. There was a leaf in his hair.

I had seen him about the place, but this was the first time we had met. His face was broad and pallid, his blue eyes close-set and restless. He was not a very big man, but he gave an impression of, how would I say, of volume. He had a thick short neck, and wide shoulders that rolled as he walked, as if he had constantly to deal with large soft obstacles in air. Standing beside him I could hear him breathing, like a man poised between one lumbering run and another. For all his rough bulk, though, there was in his eyes a look, preoccupied, faintly pained, like the look you see in those pearl and ink photographs of doomed Georgian poets. His flaxen hair, greying nicely at the temples, was a burnished helmet; I itched to reach out and remove the laurel leaf tangled in it. We stood together in the drenched grass, looking at the sky and trying to think of something to say. He commended the weather. He jingled change in his pocket. He coughed. There was a shout far off, and then from farther off an answering call. 'Aha,' he said, relieved, 'the rat men!' and plunged away through the gap in the hedge. A moment later his head appeared again, swinging above the grassy bank that bounded the orchard. Always I think of him like this, skulking behind hedges, or shambling across a far field, rueful and somehow angry, like a man with a hangover trying to remember last night's crimes.

I walked back along the path under the apple trees and came out on the lawn, a cropped field really. Two figures in wellingtons and long black buttonless overcoats appeared around the side of the house. One had a long-handled brush over his shoulder, the other carried a red bucket. I stopped and watched them pass before me in the spring sunshine, and all at once I was assailed by an image of catastrophe, stricken things scurrying in circles, the riven pelts, the convulsions, the agonised eyes gazing into the empty sky or through the sky into the endlessness. I hurried off to the lodge, to my work. But the sense of harmony and purpose I had felt in the orchard was gone. I saw something move outside on the grass. I thought it was the blackbirds out foraging, for the lilacs were still. But it was a rat.

In fact, it wasn't a rat. In fact in all my time at Ferns I never saw sign of a rat. It was only the idea.

*

The campus postman, an asthmatic Lapp, has just brought me a letter from Ottilie. Now I'm really found out. She says she got my address from you. Clio, Clio . . . But I'm glad, I won't deny it. Less in what she says than in the Lilliputian scrawl itself, aslant from corner to corner of the flimsy blue sheets, do I glimpse something of the real she, her unhandiness and impetuosity, her inviolable innocence. She wants me to lend her the fare to come and visit me! I can see us, staggering through the snowdrifts, ranting and weeping, embracing in our furs like lovelorn polar bears.

She came down to the lodge the day after I moved in, bringing me a bowl of brown eggs. She wore corduroy trousers and a shapeless homemade sweater. Her blonde hair was tied at the back with a rubber band. Pale eyebrows and pale blue eyes gave her a scrubbed look. With her hands thrust in her pockets she stood and smiled at me. Hers was the brave brightness of all big awkward girls.

'Grand eggs,' I said.

We considered them a moment in thoughtful silence.

'Charlotte rears them,' she said. 'Hens, I mean.'

I went back to the box of books I had been unpacking. She hesitated, glancing about. The little square table by the window was strewn with my papers. Was I writing a book, or what? – as if such a thing were hardly defensible. I told her. 'Newton,' she said, frowning. 'The fellow that the apple fell on his head and he discovered gravity?'

She sat down.

She was twenty-four. Her father had been Charlotte Lawless's brother. With his wife beside him one icy night when Ottilie was ten he had run his car into a wall – 'that wall, see, down there' – and left the girl an orphan. She wanted to go to university. To study what? She shrugged. She just wanted to go to university. Her voice, incongruous coming out of that big frame, was light and vibrant as an oboe, a singer's voice, and I pictured her, this large unlovely girl, standing in a preposterous gown before the tiered snowscape of an orchestra, her little fat hands clasped, pouring forth a storm of disconsolate song.

Where did I live in Dublin? Had I a flat? What was it like? 'Why did you come down to this dump?' I told her, to finish my book, and then frowned at the papers curling gently in the sunlight on the table. Then I noticed how the sycamores were stirring faintly, almost surreptitiously in the bright air, like dancers practising steps in their heads, and something in me too pirouetted briefly, and yes, I said, yes, to finish my book. A shadow fell in the doorway. A tow-haired small boy stood there, with his hands at his back, watching us. His ancient gaze, out of a putto's pale eyes, was unnerving. Ottilie sighed, and rose abruptly, and without another glance at me took the child's hand and departed.

I WAS BORN DOWN THERE, in the south, you knew that. The best memories I have of the place are of departures from it. I'm thinking of Christmas trips to Dublin when I was a child, boarding the train in the dark and watching through the mist of my breath on the window the frost-bound landscape assembling as the dawn came up. At a certain spot every time, I can see it still, day would at last achieve itself. The place was a river bend, where the train slowed down to cross a red metal bridge. Beyond the river a flat field ran to the edge of a wooded hill, and at the foot of the hill there was a house, not very big, solitary and square, with a steep roof. I would gaze at that silent house and wonder, in a hunger of curiosity, what lives were lived there. Who stacked that firewood, hung that holly wreath, left those tracks in the hoarfrost on the hill? I can't express the odd aching pleasure of that moment. I knew, of course, that those hidden lives wouldn't be much different from my own. But that was the point. It wasn't the exotic I was after, but the *ordinary*, that strangest and most elusive of enigmas.

Now I had another house to gaze at, and wonder about, with something of the same remote prurience. The lodge was like a sentry box. It stood, what, a hundred, two hundred yards from the house, yet I couldn't look out my window without spotting some bit of business going on. The acoustics of the place too afforded an alarming intimacy. I could clearly hear the frequent cataclysms of the upstairs lavatory, and my day began with the pips for the morning news on the radio in Charlotte Lawless's kitchen. Then I would see Charlotte herself, in wellingtons and an old cardigan, hauling out a bucket of feed to the henhouse. Next comes Ottilie, in a sleepy trance, with the child by the hand. He is off to school. He carries his satchel like a hunchback's hump. Edward is last, I am at work before I spy him about his mysterious business. It all has the air of a pastoral mime, with the shepherd's wife and the shepherd, and Cupid and the maid, and, scribbling within a crystal cave, myself, a haggard-eyed Damon.

I had them spotted for patricians from the start. The big house, Edward's tweeds, Charlotte's fine-boned slender grace that the dowdiest of clothes could not mask, even Ottilie's awkwardness, all this seemed the unmistakable stamp of their class. Protestants, of course, landed, the land gone now to gombeen men and compulsory purchase, the family fortune wasted by tax, death duties, inflation. But how bravely, how beautifully they bore their losses! Observing them, I understood that breeding such as theirs is a preparation not for squiredom itself, but for that distant day, which for the Lawlesses had arrived, when the trappings of glory are gone and only style remains. All nonsense, of course, but to me, product of a post-peasant Catholic upbringing, they appeared perfected creatures. Oh, don't accuse me of snobbery. This was something else, a fascination before the spectacle of pure refinement. Shorn of the dull encumbrances of wealth and power, they were free to be purely what they were. The irony was, the form of life their refinement took was wholly familiar to me: wellington boots, henhouses, lumpy sweaters. Familiar, but, ah, transfigured. The nicety of tone and gesture to which I might aspire, they achieved by instinct, unwittingly. Their ordinariness was inimitable.

Sunday mornings were a gala performance at Ferns. At twenty to ten, the bells pealing down in the village, a big old-fashioned motor car would feel its way out of the garage. They are off to church. An hour later they return, minus Edward, with Charlotte at the wheel. Wisps of tiny music from the radio in the kitchen come to me. Charlotte is getting the dinner ready – no, she is preparing a light lunch. Not for them surely the midday feeds of my childhood, the mighty roast, the steeped marrowfat peas, the block of runny ice-cream on its cool perch on the bathroom windowsill. Edward tramps up the hill, hands in his pockets, shoulders rolling. In front of the house he pauses, looks at the broken fanlight, and then goes in, the door shuts, the train moves on, over the bridge.

My illusions about them soon began, if not to crumble, then to modify. One day I struck off past the orchard into the lands at the back of the house. All round were the faint outlines of what must once have been an ornate garden. Here was a pond, the water an evil green, overhung by a sadness of willows. I waded among hillocks of knee-high grass, feeling watched. The day was hot, with a burning breeze. Everything swayed. A huge bumble bee blundered past my ear. When I looked back, the only sign of the house was a single chimney pot against the sky. I found myself standing on the ruins of a tennis court. A flash of reflected sunlight caught my eye. In a hollow at the far side of the court there was a long low glasshouse. I stumbled down the bank, as others in another time must have stumbled, laughing, after a white ball rolling inexorably into the future. The door of the glasshouse made a small sucking sound when I opened it. The heat was a soft slap in the face. Row upon row of clay pots on trestle tables ran the length of the place, like an exercise in perspective, converging at the far end on the figure of Charlotte Lawless standing with her back to me. She wore sandals and a wide green skirt, a white shirt, her tattered sun hat. I spoke, and she turned, startled. A pair of spectacles hung on a cord about her neck. Her fingers were caked with clay. She dabbed the back of a wrist to her forehead. I noticed the tiny wrinkles around her eyes, the faint down on her upper lip.

I said I hadn't known the hothouse was here, I was impressed, she must be an enthusiastic gardener. I was babbling. She looked at me carefully. 'It's how we make our living,' she said. I apologised, I wasn't sure for what, and then laughed, and felt foolish. There are people to whom you feel compelled to explain yourself. 'I got lost,' I said, 'in the garden, believe it or not, and then I saw you here, and . . .' She was still watching me, hanging on my words; I wondered if she were perhaps hard of hearing. The possibility was oddly touching. Or was it simply that she wasn't really listening? Her face was empty of all save a sense of something withheld. She made me think of someone standing on tiptoe behind a glass barrier, every part of her, eyes, lips, the gloves that she clutches, straining to become the radiant smile that awaits the beloved's arrival. She was all potential. On the bench where she had been working lay an open pair of secateurs, and a cut plant with purple flowers.

We went among the tables, wading through a dead and standing pool of air, and she explained her work, naming the plants, the strains and hybrids, in a neutral voice. Mostly it was plain commercial stuff, apple tree-lets, flower bulbs, vegetables, but there were some strange things, with strange pale stalks, and violent blossoms, and bearded fruit dangling among the glazed, still leaves. Her father had started the business, and she had taken it over when her brother was killed. 'We still trade as Grainger Nurseries.' I nodded dully. The heat, the sombre hush, the contrast between the stillness here and the windy tumult pressing against the glass all around us, provoked in me a kind of excited apprehension, as if I were being led, firmly, but with infinite tact, into peril. Ranked colours thronged me round, crimson, purples, and everywhere green and more green, glabrous and rubbery and somehow ferocious. 'In Holland,' she said, 'in the seventeenth century, a nurseryman could sell a new strain of tulip for twenty thousand pounds.' It had the flat sound of something read into a recorder. She looked at me, her hands folded, waiting for my comment. I smiled, and shook my head, trying to look amazed. We reached the door. The summer breeze seemed a hurricane after the silence within. My shirt clung to my back. I shivered. We walked a little way down a path under an arch of rhododendrons. The tangled arthritic branches let in scant light, and there was a smell of mossy rot reminiscent of the tang of damp flesh. Then at once, unaccountably, we were at the rear of the house. I was confused; the garden had surreptitiously taken me in a circle. Charlotte murmured something, and walked away. On the drive under the sycamores I paused and looked back. The house was impassive, except where a curtain in an open upstairs window waved frantically in the breeze. What did I expect? Some revelation? A face watching me through sky-reflecting glass, a voice calling my name? There was nothing – but something had happened, all the same.

*

The child's name was Michael. I couldn't fit him to the Lawlesses. True, he was given, like Edward, to skulking. I would come upon him in the lanes roundabout, poking in the hedge and muttering to himself, or just standing, with his hands behind him as if hiding something, waiting for me to pass by. Sitting with a book under a tree in the orchard one sunny afternoon, I looked up to find him perched among the branches, studying me. Another time, towards twilight, I spotted him on the road, gazing off intently at something below the brow of the hill where he stood. He had not heard me behind him, and I paused, wondering what it was that merited such rapt attention. Then with a pang I heard it, rising through the stillness of evening, the tinny music of a carnival in the village below.

One evening Edward stopped at the lodge on his way up from the village. He had the raw look of a man lately dragged out of bed and thrust under a cold tap, his eyes were red-rimmed, his hair lank. He hummed and hawed, scuffing the gravel of the roadside, and then abruptly said: 'Come up and have a bite to eat.' I think that was the first time I had been inside the house. It was dim, and faintly musty. There was a hurley stick in the umbrella stand, and withered daffodils in a vase on the hall table. In an alcove a clock feathered the silence and let drop a single wobbly chime. Edward paused to consult a pocket watch, frowning. In the fussy half-light his face had the grey sheen of putty. He hiccupped softly.

Dinner was in the big whitewashed kitchen at the back of the house. I had expected a gaunt dining-room, linen napkins with a faded initial, a bit of old silver negligently laid. And it was hardly dinner, more a high tea, with cold cuts and limp lettuce, and a bottle of salad cream the colour of gruel. The tablecloth was plastic. Charlotte and Ottilie were already halfway through their meal. Charlotte looked in silence for a moment at my midriff, and I knew at once I shouldn't have come. Ottilie set a place for me. The barred window looked out on a vegetable garden, and then a field, and then the blue haze of distant woods. Sunlight through the leaves of a chestnut tree in the yard was a ceaseless shift and flicker in the corner of my eye. Edward began to tell a yarn he had heard in the village, but got muddled, and sat staring blearily at his plate, breathing. Someone coughed. Ottilie pursed her lips and began to whistle silently. Charlotte with an abrupt spastic movement turned to me and in a loud voice said:

'Do you think we'll give up neutrality?'

'Give up . . .?' The topic was in the papers. 'Well, I don't know, I—'

'Yes, tell us now,' Edward said, suddenly stirring himself and thrusting his great bull head at me, 'tell us what you think, I'm very interested, we're all very interested, aren't we all very interested? A man like you would know all about these things.'

'I think we'd be very—'

'Down here of course we haven't a clue. Crowd of bog-trotters!' He grinned, snorting softly and pawing the turf.

'I think we'd be very unwise to give it up,' I said.

'And what about that power station they want to put up down there at Carnsore? Bloody bomb, blow us all up, some clown with a hangover press the wrong button, we won't need the Russians. What?' He was looking at Charlotte. She had not spoken. 'Well what's wrong with being ordinary,' he said, 'like any other country, having an army and defending ourselves? Tell me what's wrong with that.' He pouted at us, a big resentful baby.

'What about Switzerland?' Ottilie said; she giggled.

'Switzerland? *Switzerland?* Ha. Milkmen and chocolate factories, and, what was it the fellow said, cuckoo clocks.' He turned his red-rimmed gaze on me again. 'Too many damn neutrals,' he said darkly.

Charlotte sighed, and looked up from her plate at last.

'Edward,' she said, without emphasis. He did not take his eyes off me, but the light went out in his face, and for a moment I almost felt sorry for him. 'Not that I give a damn anyway,' he muttered, and meekly took up his spoon. So much for current affairs.

I cursed myself for being there, and yet I was agog. A trapdoor had been lifted briefly on dim thrashing forms, and now it was shut again. I watched Edward covertly. The sot. He had brought me here for an alibi for his drinking, or to forestall recriminations. I saw the whole thing now, of course: he was a waster, Charlotte kept the place going, everything had been a mistake, even the child. It all fitted, the rueful look and the glazed eye, the skulking, the silences, the tension, that sense I had been aware of from the beginning of being among people facing away from me, intent on something I couldn't see. Even the child's air of sullen autonomy was explained. I looked at Charlotte's fine head, her slender neck, that hand resting by her plate. Leaf-shadow stirred on the table like the shimmer of tears. How could I let her know that I understood everything? The child came in, wrapped in a white bath-towel. His hair was wet, plastered darkly on his skull. When he saw me he drew back, then stepped forward, frowning, a robed and kiss-curled miniature Caesar. Charlotte held out her hand and he went to her. Ottilie winked at him. Edward wore a crooked leer, as if a smile aimed at the centre of his face had landed just wide of the target. Michael mumbled goodnight and departed, shutting the door with both hands on the knob. I turned to Charlotte eagerly. 'Your son,' I said, in a voice that fairly throbbed, 'your son is very . . .' and then floundered, hearing I suppose the tiny tinkle of a warning bell. There was a silence. Charlotte blushed. Suddenly I felt depressed, and . . . prissy, that's the word. What did I know, that gave me the right to judge them? I shouldn't be here at all. I ate a leaf of lettuce, at my back that great rooted blossomer, before me the insistent enigma of other people. I would stay out of their way, keep to the lodge – return to Dublin even. But I knew I wouldn't. Some large lesson seemed laid out here for me.

Ottilie came with me out on the step. She said nothing, but smiled, at once amused and apologetic. And then, I don't know why, the idea came to me. Michael wasn't their child: he was, of course, hers.

THANKS FOR the latest Popov, it arrived today. Very sly you are, Cliona – but a library of Popovs would not goad me into publishing. I met him once, an awful little man with ferret eyes and a greasy suit. Reminded me of an embalmer. Which, come to think of it, is apt. I like his disclaimer: *Before the phenomenon of Isaac Newton, the historian, like Freud when he came to contemplate Leonardo, can only shake his head and retire with as much good grace as he can muster.* Then out come the syringe and the formalin. That is what I was doing too, embalming old N.'s big corpse, only I *did* have the grace to pop off before the deathshead grin was properly fixed.

Newton was the greatest genius that science has produced. Well, who would deny it? He was still in his twenties when he cracked the code of the world's working. Single-handed he invented science: before him it had all been wizardry and sweaty dreams and brilliant blundering. You may say, as Newton himself said, that he saw so far because he had the shoulders of giants to stand on: but you might as well say that without his mother and father he would not have been born, which is true all right, but what does it signify? Anyway, when he defined the gravity laws he swept away that whole world of giants and other hobgoblins. Oh yes, you can see, can't you, the outline of what my book would have been, a celebration of action, of the scientist as hero, a gleeful acceptance of Pandora's fearful disclosures, wishy-washy medievalism kicked out and the age of reason restored. But would you believe that all this, this Popovian Newton-as-the-greatest-scientist-the-world-has-known, now makes me feel slightly sick? Not that I think any of it untrue, in the sense that it is fact. It's just that another kind of truth has come to seem to me more urgent, although, for the mind, it is nothing compared to the lofty verities of science.

Newton himself, I believe, saw something of the matter in that strange summer of 1693. You know the story, of how his little dog Diamond overturned a candle in his rooms at Cambridge one early morning, and started a fire which destroyed a bundle of his papers, and how the loss deranged his mind. All rubbish, of course, even the dog is a fiction, yet I find myself imagining him, a fifty-year-old public man, standing aghast in the midst of the smoke and the flying smuts with the singed pug pressed in his arms. The joke is, it's not the loss of the precious papers that will drive him temporarily crazy, but the simple fact that *it doesn't matter.* It might be his life's work gone, the *Principia* itself, the *Opticks*, the whole bang lot, and still it wouldn't mean a thing. Tears spring from his eyes, the dog licks them off his chin. A colleague comes running, shirt-tails out. The great man is pulled into the corridor, white with shock and stumping like a peg-leg. Someone beats out the flames. Someone else asks what has been lost. Newton's mouth opens and a word like a stone falls out: *Nothing.* He notices details, early morning light through a window, his rescuer's one unshod foot and yellow toenails, the velvet blackness of burnt paper. He smiles. His fellows look at one another.

It had needed no candle flame, it was already ashes. Why else had he turned to deciphering Genesis and dabbling in alchemy? Why else did he insist again and again that science had cost him too dearly, that, given his life to live over, he would have nothing to do with physics? It wasn't modesty, no one could accuse him of that. The fire, or whatever the real conflagration was, had shown him something terrible and lovely, like flame itself. *Nothing.* The word reverberates. He broods on it as on some magic emblem whose other face is not to be seen and yet is emphatically there. For the nothing automatically signifies the everything. He does not know what to do, what to think. He no longer knows how to live.

*

There was no fiery revelation to account for *my* crisis of faith; there was not even what could properly be called a crisis. Only, I wasn't working now. The month of June went by and I had not put pen to paper. But I was no longer worried – just the opposite. It was like the passing away of a stubborn illness. You don't notice the gradual calming of the blood, the cleared head, the limbs' new strength, you are aware only of waiting quietly, confidently, for life to start up again. You won't believe me, I know: how could I drop seven years of work, just like that? Newton was my life, not these dull pale people in their tumble-down house in the hollow heart of the country. But I didn't see it as this stark alternative: things take a definite and simple shape only in retrospect. At the time I had only a sense of lateral drift. My papers lay untouched on the table by the window, turning yellow in the sunlight, when my eye fell on them I felt impatience and a vague resentment; my real attention was elsewhere, suspended, ready to give itself with a glad cry to what was coming next.

What came was unexpected.

Consider: a day in June, birds, breezes, flying clouds, the smell of approaching rain. Lunchtime. In the kitchen the stove squats in a hot sulk after its labours, the air is dense with the smoke of burnt fat. A knock. I drag open the door, cursing silently. Ottilie is standing outside with the child unconscious in her arms.

He had fallen out of a tree. A cut on his forehead was bleeding. I took him from her. He was heavier than I expected, and limp as death, it seemed he might pour through my fingers into a pale puddle on the floor. I felt fright, and a curious faint disgust. I put him on an old horsehair sofa and he coughed and opened his eyes. At first there was only the whites, then the pupils slid down, like something awful coming down in a lift. His face was translucent marble, with violet shadows under the eyes. A large bruise was growing on his forehead; the blood had thickened to a kind of jelly. He struggled up. Ottilie sat back on her heels and sighed: 'Faugh!'

I took him in my arms again and carried him to the house.

We must have looked like an illustration from a Victorian novelette, marching forward across the swallow-swept lawn: had Ottilie her hands clasped to her breast? Michael turned his face resolutely away from me. On the steps he wriggled and made me put him down. Charlotte opened the door – and for a moment seemed about to step back hurriedly and shut it again. Ottilie said: 'Oh he's all right,' and glared at the child. I left them. My lunch had congealed into its own fat.

An hour later Ottilie came to the lodge again. Yes, yes, he was fine, nothing broken, the little brat. She apologised for bringing him to me: mine had been the nearest door. 'I'm glad,' I said, not knowing quite what I meant. She shrugged. She had put on lipstick. 'I got a fright,' she said. We stood awkwardly, looking at things, like people on a railway platform trying to think of how to say a definitive goodbye. The sunlight died in the window and it began to rain. A kind of bubble swelled suddenly in my breast and I put my hands on her shoulders and kissed her. There was a fleck of dried blood on my wrist. Her lipstick tasted like something from childhood, plasticine, or penny sweets. When I stepped back she simply stood frowning, and moving her lips, as if trying to identify a mysteriously familiar taste.

'I think he dislikes me,' I said.

'What? No. He was embarrassed.'

'Do children get embarrassed?'

'Oh yes,' she said softly, and looked at me at last, 'Oh, yes.'

*

It's strange to be offered, without conditions, a body you don't really want. You feel the most unexpected things, tenderness of course, but impatience too, curiosity, a little contempt, and something else the only name for which I can find is sadness. When she took off her clothes it was as if she were not merely undressing, but performing a far more complex operation, turning herself inside out maybe, to display not breast and bum and blonde lap, but her very innards, the fragile lungs, mauve nest of intestines, the gleaming ivory of bone, and her heart, passionately labouring. I took her in my arms and felt the soft shock of being suddenly, utterly inhabited.

I was not prepared for her gentleness. At first it seemed almost a rebuff. We were so quiet I could hear the rain's whispered exclamations at the window. In the city of the flesh I travel without maps, a worried tourist: and Ottilie was a very Venice. I stumbled lost in the blue shade of her pavements. Here was a dreamy stillness, a swaying, the splash of an oar. Then, when I least expected it, suddenly I stepped out into the great square, the sunlight, and she was a flock of birds scattering with soft cries in my arms.

We lay, damp and chill as stranded fish, until her fingers at the back of my neck gave three brisk taps and she sat up. I turned on my side and gazed in a kind of fond stupor at the two folds of flesh above her hip bone. She put on her trousers and her lumpy sweater and padded into the kitchen to make tea. Our stain on the sheet was the shape of a turtle. Grey gloom settled on my heart. I was dressed when she came back. We sat on the bed, in our own faintly ammoniac smell, and drank the strong tea from cracked mugs. The day darkened, the rain was settling in.

'I suppose you think I'm a right whore,' she said.

*

It was contingency from the start, and it stayed that way. Oh, no doubt I could work up a map of our separate journeys to that bed. There would be a little stylised tree on it and a tumbling Cupid, and an X in crimson ink marking a bloodstain, and pretty slanted blue lines indicating rain. But it would be misleading, it would look like the cartography of love. What can I say? I won't deny her baroque blonde splendour touched me. I remember her hands on my neck, the violet depths of her eyes, her unexpectedly delicate pale feet, and her cries, the sudden panic of her coming, when she would clutch me to her, wet teeth bared and her eyelids fluttering, like one falling helplessly in a dream. But love?

She burrowed into my life at the lodge with stealthy determination. She brought prints clipped from glossy magazines and pinned them over the bed, film stars, Kneller's portrait of Newton, the *Primavera*. Flowers began to sprout around me in jam jars and tin cans. A new teapot appeared, and two cups, of fine bone china, each with an identical crack. One day she arrived lugging an ancient radio that she had salvaged from the garage. She played with it for hours, gliding across the stations, mouth a little open, eyes fixed on nothing, while Hungarian disc jockeys or Scots trawlermen gabbled in her ear, and the day waned, and the little green light on the tuning panel advanced steadily into the encroaching darkness.

I think more than sex, maybe even more than love, she wanted company. She talked. Sometimes I suspected she had got into bed with me so that she could talk. She laid bare the scandals of the neighbourhood: did I know the man in Pierce's pub was sleeping with his own daughter? She recounted her dreams in elaborate detail; I was never in them. Though she told me a lot about the family I learned little. The mass of names and hazy dates numbed me. It was all like the stories in a history book, vivid and forgettable at once. Her dead parents were a favourite topic. In her fantasy they were a kind of Scott and Zelda, beautiful and doomed, hair blown back and white silk scarves whipping in the wind as they sailed blithely, laughing, down the slipstream of disaster. All I could do in return was tell her about Newton, show off my arcane learning. I even tried reading aloud to her bits of that old Galileo article of mine – she fell asleep. Of course we didn't speak much. Our affair was conducted through the intermediary of these neutral things, a story, a memory, a dream.

I wondered if the house knew what was going on. The thought was obscurely exciting. The Sunday high teas became an institution, and although I was never comfortable, I confess I enjoyed the sexual freemasonry with its secret signs, the glances and the covert smiles, the way Ottilie's stare would meet and mingle with mine across the table, so intensely that it seemed there must grow up a hologram picture of a pair of tiny lovers cavorting among the tea things.

Our love-making at first was curiously innocent. Her generosity was a kind of desperate abasing before the altar of passion. She could have no privacy, wanted none, there was no part of her body that would hide from me. Such relentless giving was flattering to begin with, and then oppressive. I took her for granted, of course, except when, exhausted, or bored, she forgot about me. Then, playing the radio, brooding by the stove, sitting on the floor picking her nose with dreamy concentration, she would break away from me and be suddenly strange and incomprehensible, as sometimes a word, one's own name even, will briefly detach itself from its meaning and become a hole in the mesh of the world. She had moments too of self-assertion. Something would catch her attention and she would push me away absentmindedly as if I were furniture, and gaze off, with a loony little smile, over the brow of the hill, toward the tinny music of the carnival that only she could hear. Without warning she would punch me in the chest, hard, and laugh. One day she asked me if I had ever taken drugs. 'I'm looking forward to dying,' she said thoughtfully; 'they give you that kind of morphine cocktail.'

I laughed. 'Where did you hear that?'

'It's what they give people dying of cancer.' She shrugged. 'Everybody knows that.'

I suppose I puzzled her, too. I would open my eyes and find her staring into the misted mirror of our kisses as if watching a fascinating crime being committed. Her hands explored me with the stealthy care of a blind man. Once, gliding my lips across her belly, I glanced up and caught her gazing down with tears in her eyes. This passionate scrutiny was too much for me, I would feel something within me wrapping itself in its dirty cloak and turning furtively away. I had not contracted to be known as she was trying to know me.

*

And for the first time in my life I began to feel my age. It sounds silly, I know. But things had been happening to me, and to the world, before she was born. The years in my life of her non-being struck me as an extraordinary fact, a sort of bravura trick played on me by time. I, whose passion is the past, was discovering in her what the past means. And not just the past. Before our affair – the word makes me wince – before it had properly begun I was contemplating the end of it. You'll laugh, but I used to picture my deathbed: a hot still night, the lamp flickering and one moth bumping the bulb; and I, a wizened infant, remembering with magical clarity as the breath fails this moment in this bedroom at twilight, the breeze from the window, the sycamores, her heart beating under mine, and that bird calling in the distance from a lost, Oh utterly lost land.

'If this is not love,' she said once in that dark voice of hers, for a moment suddenly a real grown-up, 'Jesus if this isn't love then what is!'

The truth is, it seemed hardly anything – I hear her hurt laugh – until, with tact, with deference, but immovably, another, a secret sharer, came to join our somehow, always, melancholy grapplings.

MICHAEL'S BIRTHDAY was at the end of July, and there was a party. His guests were a dozen of his classmates from the village school. They were all of a type, small famished-looking creatures, runts of the litter, the girls spindle-legged and pigtailed, the boys watchful under cruel haircuts, their pale necks defenceless as a rabbit's. Why had he picked them, were they his only friends in that school? He was a blond giant among them. While Charlotte set the table in the drawing-room for their tea, Ottilie led them in party games, waving her arms and shouting, like a conductor wielding an insane orchestra. Michael hung back, stiff and sullen.

I had gone up to the house with a present for him. I was given a glass of tepid beer and left in the kitchen. Edward appeared, brandishing a hurley stick. 'We've lost a couple of the little beggars, haven't seen them, have you? Always the same, they go off and hide, and start dreaming and forget to come out.' He loitered, eyeing my glass. 'You hiding too, eh? Good idea. Here, have a decent drink.' He removed my beer to the sink and brought out tumblers and a bottle of whiskey. 'There. Cheers. Ah.'

We stood, like a couple of timid trolls, listening to the party noises coming down the hall. He leaned on the hurley stick, admiring his drink. 'How are you getting on at the lodge,' he said, 'all right? The roof needs doing – damn chilly spot in the winter, I can tell you.' Playing the squire today. He glanced sideways at me. 'But you won't be here in the winter, will you.'

I shrugged; guess again, fella.

'Getting fond of us, are you?' he said, almost coyly.

Now it was my turn to exercise the sideways glance.

'Peace,' I said, 'and quiet: that kind of thing.'

A cloud shifted, and the shadow of the chestnut tree surged toward us across the tiled floor. I had taken him from the start for a boozer and an idler, a lukewarm sinner not man enough to be a monster: could it be a mask, behind which crouched a subtle dissembler, smiling and plotting? Impossible. But I didn't like that look in his eye today. Had Ottilie been telling secrets?

'I lived there one time, you know,' he said.

'What – in the lodge?'

'Years ago. I used to manage the nurseries, when Lotte's father was alive.'

So: a fortune hunter, by god! I could have laughed.

He poured us another drink, and we wandered outside into the gravelled yard. The hot day hummed. Above the distant wood a hawk was hunting.

Lotte.

'Still doing this book of yours?' he said. 'Used to write a bit of poetry, myself.' Ah, humankind! It will never run out of surprises. 'Gave it up, of course, like everything else.' He brooded a moment, frowning, and the blue of the Dardanelles bloomed briefly in his doomy eyes. I watched the hawk circling. What did I know? Maybe at the back of a drawer somewhere there was a sheaf of poems that unleashed would ravish the world. A merry notion; I played with it. He went into the kitchen and fetched the bottle. 'Here,' handing it to me, 'you do the honours. I'm not supposed to drink this stuff at all.' I poured two generous measures. The first sign of incipient drunkenness is that you begin to hear yourself breathing. He was watching me; the blue of his eyes had become sullied. He had a way, perhaps because of that big too-heavy head, of seeming to loom over one. 'You're not married, are you?' he said. 'Best thing. Women, some of them . . .' He winced, and thrust his glass into my hand, and going to the chestnut tree began unceremoniously to piss against the trunk, gripping that white lumpy thing in his flies with the finger and thumb of a delicately arched hand, as if it were a violin bow he held. He stowed it away and took up his hurley stick. 'Women,' he said again; 'what do you think of them?'

I didn't like the way this was going, old boys together, the booze and the blarney, the pissing into the wind. In a minute we'd be swapping dirty stories. He took back his drink, and stood and watched me, beetling o'er his base. He had violence in him, he would never let it out, but it was all the more unsettling that way, clenched inside him like a fist.

'They're here to stay, I suppose,' I said, and produced a laugh that sounded like a stiff door opening. He wasn't listening.

'It's not their fault,' he said, talking to himself. 'They have to live too, get what they can, fight, claw their way. It's not their fault if . . .' He focused on me. 'Succubus! Know that word? It's a grand word, I like it.' To my horror he put an arm around my shoulder and walked me off across the gravel into the field beyond the chestnut tree. The hurley he still held dangled down by my side. There were little tufts of vulpine fur on his cheekbones and on the side of his neck behind his earlobe. His breath was bad. 'Did you see in the paper,' he said, 'that old woman who went to the Guards to complain that the man next door was boring holes in the wall and putting in gas to poison her? They gave her a cup of tea and sent her home, and a week later she was found dead, holes in the bloody wall and the fellow next door mad out of his mind, rubber tubes stuck in the wall, a total lunatic.' He batted me gently with his stick. 'It goes to show, you should listen to people, eh? What do you think?' He laughed. There was no humour in it. Instead, a waft of woe came off him that made me miss a step. What was he asking of me? – for he was asking something. And then I noticed an odd fact. He was hollow. I mean physically, he was, well, hollow. Oh, he was built robustly enough, there was real flesh under his tweeds, and bones, and balls, blood, the lot, but inside I imagined just a greyish space with nothing in it save that bit of anger, not a fist really, but just a tensed configuration, like a three-dimensional diagram of stress. Even on the surface too something was lacking, an essential lustre. He seemed covered in a fine fall of dust, like a stuffed bird in a bell jar. He had not been like this when I came here. The discovery was peculiarly gratifying. I had been a little afraid of him before. We turned back to the house. The bottle, half-empty, stood on the windowsill. I disengaged his arm and filled us another shot. 'There,' I said. 'Cheers. Ah.'

A station wagon, the back bristling with flushed children, headed down the drive. At the gate it pulled up with a shriek of brakes as a long sleek car swept in from the road and without slowing advanced upon the house. 'Jesus, Mary and Joseph,' Edward said: 'The Mittlers.' He retreated into the kitchen. The visitors were already at the front door, we heard their imperious knock and then voices in the hall.

'I'll be going,' I said.

'No you don't.' He reached out a hand to grab me, draining his glass at the same time. 'Family, interesting, come on, meet,' and with a hanged man's grimace thrust me before him down the hall.

They were in the drawing-room, a youngish woman in grey and a fat man of fifty, and two pale little girls, twins, with long blonde candle-curls and white socks.

'This is Bunny,' Edward said, 'my sister, and Tom, Tom Mittler; Dolores, here, and Alice.'

One twin pointed a thumb at the other. '*She's* Alice.'

Tom Mittler, fingering his cravat, nodded to me and mumbled something, with a fat little laugh, and then performed the curious trick of fading instantly on the spot. His wife looked me up and down with cool attention. Her skirt was severely cut, and the padded shoulders of her jacket sloped upward, like a pair of trim little wings. An impossible pillbox hat was pinned at an angle to her tight yellow curls. It was hard to tell if her outfit were the latest thing, but it gave her an antiquated look that was oddly sinister. Her mouth was carefully outlined with vermilion glaze, and looked as if a small tropical insect had settled on her face. Her eyes were blue, like Edward's, but harder. 'My name is Diana,' she said. Edward laughed. She ignored him. 'So you're the lodger?'

'I'm staying in the lodge, yes,' I said.

'Comfy there?' and that little red insect lifted its wing-tips a fraction. She turned away. 'Is there any chance of a cup of tea, Charlotte? Or is it too much trouble?'

Charlotte, poised outside our little circle, suddenly stirred herself. 'Yes, yes, I'm sorry—'

'I'll get it,' Ottilie said, and slouched out, making a face at me as she went past.

Bunny looked around, bestowing her painted smile on each of us in turn. 'Well!' she said, 'this is nice,' and extracted from her hat its long steel pin. 'But where's the birthday boy?'

'Hiding,' Edward murmured, and winked at me.

'Full of fun today,' his sister said. She looked at the hurley stick still in his hand. 'Are you coming from a game, or going to one?'

He waggled the weapon at her playfully. 'Game's just starting, old girl.'

'Haw!' Tom Mittler said, and vanished again instantly.

There was a small commotion as Ottilie brought in the tea on a rickety trolley. Michael came after her, solemnly bearing the teapot like a ciborium. At the sight of him Bunny gave a little cry and the twins narrowed their eyes and advanced; their father made a brief appearance to hand him his present, a five-pound note in a brown envelope. Bunny shrugged apologetically: 'We didn't have time to shop. Ottilie, this is lovely. Cake and all! Shall I be mother?' The visitors disposed themselves around the empty fireplace and ate with gusto, while the tenants of the house hovered uncertainly, temporarily dispossessed. Edward muttered something and went out. Bunny watched the door closing behind him and then turned eagerly to Charlotte. 'How is he?' eyes alight, dying to know, tell me tell me.

There was a moment's silence.

'Oh,' Charlotte said, 'not . . . I mean . . . all right, you know.'

Bunny put down her cup and sat, a study in sorrow and sympathy, shaking her head. 'You poor thing; you *poor* thing.' She looked up at me. 'I suppose you know about . . .?'

'*No*,' Charlotte said swiftly.

Bunny put a hand to her mouth. 'Oops, sorry.'

Edward came back bearing the whiskey bottle. 'Here we are: now, who's for a snort?' He paused, catching something in the silence. Then he shrugged. 'Well I am,' he said, 'for one. Tom: you? And I know *you* will.' He poured Mittler and me a measure each. Tom Mittler said: 'Thanky voo.' Edward lifted his glass. 'What will we drink to?'

'August the twenty-seventh,' Bunny said, quick as a flash.

They turned blank looks on her. I remembered.

'Mountbatten?' I said. One of their dwindling band of heroes, cruelly murdered. I was charmed: only *they* would dare to make a memorial of a drawing-room tea party. 'Terrible thing, terrible.'

I was soon disabused. She smiled her little smile at me. 'And don't forget Warrenpoint: eighteen paras, *and* an earl, all on the one day.'

'Jesus, Bunny,' Edward said.

She was still looking at me, amused and glittering. 'Don't mind him,' she said playfully, 'he's a West Brit, self-made. *I* think we should name a street after it, like the French do. The glorious twenty-seventh!'

I glanced at her husband, guzzling his tea. Someone had said he was a solicitor. He had a good twenty years on her. Feeling my eye on him he looked up, and smoothed a freckled hand on his scant sandy hair and said cheerfully: 'She's off!'

Bunny poured herself another cup of tea, smirking.

'It's dead men you're talking about,' Edward muttered, with the sour weariness of one doing his duty by an argument that he has long ago lost.

'There's nothing wrong with this country,' Bunny said, 'that a lot more corpses like that won't cure.' She lifted her cup daintily. 'Long live death! Is this your own cake, Charlotte? Scrumptious.'

I realised, with the unnerving clarity that always comes to me with the fifth drink, that if there were to be a sixth I would be thoroughly drunk.

One of the twins suddenly yelped in pain. 'Mammy mammy he *pinched* me!'

Michael looked at us from under sullen eyebrows, crouched

on the carpet like a sprinter waiting for the off. Bunny laughed. 'Well pinch him back!' The girl's face crumpled, oozing thick tears. Her sister watched her with interest.

'Michael,' Edward rumbled, and showed him the hurley stick. 'Do you see this . . .?'

Ottilie left to make more tea, and I followed her. Outside the kitchen windows the chestnut tree murmured softly in its green dreaming. The afternoon had begun to wane.

'Quite a lady,' I said, 'that Diana.'

Ottilie shrugged, watching the kettle. 'Bitch,' she said mildly. 'She only comes here to . . .'

'What?'

'Never mind. To gloat. You heard her with Charlotte: *you poor thing*.' She made a simpering face. 'Make you sick.'

The kettle, like a little lunatic bird, began to whistle shrilly.

'He's not that bad,' I said, 'is he, Edward?'

She did not answer. We returned to the drawing-room. A dreamy sort of silence had settled there. They sat, staring at nothing, enchanted figures in a fairy tale. Bunny glanced at us as we came in and a flicker of interest lit her hard little eyes. She would be good at ferreting out secrets. I moved away from Ottilie.

'You're quite at home, I see,' Bunny said.

'People are kind,' I answered, and tried to laugh. My legs were not working properly. Bunny lifted a quizzical eyebrow. 'That's true,' she said. She was thinking. I lost interest in her. Edward knocked the bottle against my glass. His face was ashen. His breath hit me, a warm brown cloud. I looked at Charlotte, the only dark among all these fair. She sat, back arched and shoulders erect, slim arms extended across her lap, her pale hands clasped, a gazelle. Poor thing. My heart wobbled. The bruised light of late afternoon conjured other days, their texture felt but they themselves unremembered. I seemed about to weep. Edward cracked his fingers and sat down to the scarred upright piano. He played atrociously, swaying his shoulders and crooning. Bunny tried to speak over the noise but no one listened. Michael sat in the middle of the floor, playing sternly with the toy car I had given him. I took Ottilie's hands in mine. She stared at me, beginning to laugh. We danced, stately as a pair of tipsy duchesses, round and round the faded carpet. Bunny fairly ogled us. His repertory exhausted, Edward rose and led Charlotte protesting to the piano. She fingered the keys in silence for a moment and then began hesitantly to play. It was a tiny delicate music, it seemed to come from a long way off, from inside something, and I imagined a music box, set in motion by a chance breeze, a slammed door, launching into solitary song in its forgotten spot in the corner of an attic. I stopped to watch her, the dark glossy head, the pale neck, and those hands that now, instead of Ottilie's, seemed to be in mine. Light of evening, the tall windows – Oh, a gazelle! Ottilie moved away from me, and knelt beside Michael. The toy car had fallen over drunkenly on its side, whirring. He narrowed his eyes. He had been trying all this time to break it. Edward took up the mangled thing and examined it, turning it in his thick fingers with a bleared brutish lentor. I looked at the three of them, Ottilie, the child, the ashen-faced man, and something stirred, an echo out of some old brown painting. Jesus, Mary and Joseph. They receded slowly, slowly, as if drawn away on a piece of concealed stage machinery. And then all faded, Bunny, her fat husband, their brats, the chairs, the scattered cups, all, until only Charlotte and I were left, in this moment at the end of a past that now was utterly revised. I hiccupped softly. On the piano lid there was an empty glass, a paper party hat, a browning apple core. These are the things we remember. And I remember also, with Ottilie that night moaning in my arms, feeling for the first time the presence of another, and I heard that tiny music again, and shivered at the ghostly touch of pale fingers on my face.

'What's wrong,' Ottilie said, 'what is it?'

'Nothing,' I answered, 'nothing, nothing.'

For how should I tell her that she was no longer the woman I was holding in my arms?

*

Next morning along with the hangover came inevitably the slow burn of alarm. Had I said anything, let slip some elaborate gesture? Had I made a fool of myself? I recalled Bunny smirking, the tip of her little nose twitching, but that had been when I was still with Ottilie. Even so sharp an eye surely would not have spotted my solitary brief debauch by the piano? And later, in the dark, there had been no one to see me, save Ottilie, and she did not see things like that. Like what? In every drunkenness there comes that moment of madness and euphoria when all our accumulated knowledge of life and the world and ourselves seems a laughable misapprehension, and we realise suddenly that we are a genius, or fatally ill, or in love. The fact is obvious, simple, beyond doubt: why have we not seen it before? Then we sober up and everything evaporates, and we are again what we are, a frail, feckless, ridiculous figure with a headache. But in vain I lay in bed that morning waiting for reality to readjust itself. The fact would not go away: I was in love with Charlotte Lawless.

I was astonished, of course, but there was too a familiar shiver of fright and not wholly unpleasurable disgust. It was like that moment in a childhood party game when, hot and flustered, every nerve-end an eye, you whip off the blindfold to find that the warm quarry quivering in your clasped arms is not that little girl with the dark curls and the interestingly tight bodice whose name you did not quite hear, but a fat boy, or your convulsed older sister, or just one of Auntie Hilda's mighty mottled arms. Or a middle-aged woman, emphatically married, with middle-aged hands, and wrinkles around her eyes, and the faint beginnings of a moustache, who had spoken no more than twenty words to me and who looked at me as if I were, if not transparent, then translucent at least. There it was, all the same, sitting in bed with me, still in its party frock, with an impudent smile: love.

The secret pattern of the past months was now revealed. I saw myself that first day in the doorway of the lodge offering her a month's rent, I stumbled again down the grassy bank to the glasshouse, sat in her kitchen in sunlight watching the shadows of leaves stirring by her hand. I was like an artist blissfully checking over the plan of a work that has suddenly come to him complete in every detail, touching the marvellous, still-damp construct gently here and there with the soft feelers of imagination. Ottilie a sketch, on the oboe, of the major theme to come, Edward at once the comic relief and the shambling villain of the piece, Michael a Cupid still, the subtlety of whose aim, however, I had underestimated. Even the unbroken fine summer weather was a part of the plot.

Of course there were to be times when the whole thing would seem a delusion. I would remark the fact that the actual life I led – burnt cutlets, the bathroom to be cleaned – was far from that ideal which somehow I would manage to think I was leading: the quiet scholar alone with books and pipe and lamplight, lifting melancholy eyes now and then to the glossy block of night in the window and sighing for *die ferne Geliebte*. When Ottilie came to me I saw myself as one of those tragic gentlemen in old novels who solace themselves with a shopgirl, or a little actress, a sort of semi-animate doll with childlike ways and no name, a part for which my big blonde girl was hardly fitted. But then, as suddenly as they had come, the doubts would depart, and the dream would take wing again into the empyrean, when I saw her coming up from the glasshouse with flowers in her arms, or glimpsed her lost in thought behind a tall window in which was reflected one tree and a bronze cloud. Once, listening idly to the shipping forecast on the radio, I saw her come out on the steps in the tawny light of evening and call to the child, and even still always I think of her when I hear the word *Finisterre.*

*

In moments like that you can feel memory gathering its material, beady-eyed and voracious, like a demented photographer. I don't mean the big scenes, the sunsets and car crashes, I mean the creased black-and-white snaps taken in a bad light, with a lop-sided horizon and that smudged thumb-print in the foreground. Such are the pictures of Charlotte, in my mind. In the best of them she is not present at all, someone jogged my elbow, or the film was faulty. Or perhaps she was present and has withdrawn, with a pained smile. Only her glow remains. Here is an empty chair in rain-light, cut flowers on a workbench, an open window with lightning flickering distantly in the dark. Her absence throbs in these views more powerfully, more poignantly than any presence.

When I search for the words to describe her I can't find them. Such words don't exist. They would need to be no more than forms of intent, balanced on the brink of saying, another version of silence. Every mention I make of her is a failure. Even when I say just her name it sounds like an exaggeration. When I write it down it seems impossibly swollen, as if my pen had slipped eight or nine redundant letters into it. Her physical presence itself seemed overdone, a clumsy representation of the essential she. That essence was only to be glimpsed obliquely, on the outer edge of vision, an image always there and always fleeting, like the afterglow of a bright light on the retina.

If she was never entirely present for me in the flesh, how could I make her to be there for me in the lodge, at night, in the fields on my solitary rambles? I must concentrate on things impassioned by her passing. Anything would do, her sun hat, a pair of muddied wellingtons standing splay-footed at the back door. The very ordinariness of these mementoes was what made them precious. That, and the fact that they were wholly mine. Even she would not know their secret significance. Two little heart-shaped polished patches rubbed on the inner sides of those wellingtons by her slightly knock-kneed walk. The subtle web of light and shade that played over her face through the slack straw of the brim of her hat. Who would notice such things, that did not fix on her with the close-up lens of love?

Love. That word. I seem to hear quotation marks around it, as if it were the title of something, a stilted sonnet, say, by a silver poet. Is it possible to love someone of whom one has so little? For through the mist now and then I glimpsed, however fleetingly, the fact that what I had of her was hardly enough to bear a great weight of passion. Perhaps call it concentration, then, the concentration of the painter intent on drawing the living image out of the potential of mere paint. I would make her incarnate. By the force of my unwavering, meticulous attention she would rise on her scallop shell through the waves and *be*.

I did nothing, of course, said nothing, made no move. It was a passion of the mind. I had given up all pretence of work on the book. You see the connection.

I wondered if she were aware of being so passionately watched. Now and then I thought I caught her squirming, as if she had felt my slavering breath brush her flesh. She had a way of presenting me suddenly with unbidden bits of fact, like scraps thrown down to divert the attention of a dog that she feared might bite her. She would turn her head, consider for a moment my right shoulder, or one of my hands, with that strange blank gaze, and say: My father imported that tree from South America. And I would nod pensively, frowning. I learned the oddest things from her. Why a ha-ha is so called. That Finland was the first European country to give women the vote. Occasionally I could link these obscure pronouncements to something I had said or asked days ago, but mostly they were without discernible connection. Having spoken, she would go on gazing at me for a moment longer, as if waiting for some large sign of my acknowledgment that she was solid, that, see, she knew things, like real people do – or just that she was too dry for this dangerous dog to bother biting.

I recall one Saturday, when she was driving into town to deliver stuff from the nurseries, and I asked her for a lift. It was raining, the fields a speeding blur beyond the misted windows. We were past the village when she took her foot off the pedal and let the car bump slowly to a stop. 'Puncture,' she said. But she did not get out. We looked in silence at a wild apple tree shimmering before us in the streaming windscreen. The wheels on my side had climbed the grass verge, and everything was slightly crooked. There was no puncture. A strange moment, I remember it, the rain, the sound of the rain, the worn sticky feel of the car seat. She took off her spectacles, and a strand of hair fell across her face. What was she thinking about? I did not like the way she wore her glasses on a cord, it made her look matronly. An old harridan within me suddenly muttered: *She's forty if she's a day*, and was immediately silenced. A minute went by. I rolled down my window and let in the smell of woodbine and wet earth. Charlotte rubbed the fogged windscreen with a fingertip. 'Perhaps we should go back,' she said, and then, looking at my knees: 'Edward is not well.' The sibyl had spoken. I nodded, a puzzled priest of the shrine. What was expected of me? Whatever it was I could not give it, and she turned with vague helplessness to the plants and punnets of fruit stacked on the back seat. Her eyes, what colour were her eyes? I can't remember! She started up the car. We drove on.

Thus, always, it would teeter on the brink of being something.

*

At first I was afraid I'd give the game away, snatch up her hand and kiss it, or get drunk again and fall at her feet bawling, something like that. But of course I wouldn't. I was like a young bride who has rushed home to tell hubby that the pregnancy is confirmed, only to go suddenly shy and strange at the sight of familiar things, his hat, that new sofa, the kitchen sink. In the midst of the old life I hugged this brand-new secret to my breast. It gave me a curious sense of dignity, of quiet wisdom. Is this what love is really for, to lend us a new conception of ourselves? My voice sounded softer to me, my every action seemed informed by a melancholy grandeur. My smile, faintly flecked with sadness, was a calm benediction upon the world.

I had feared too I might reveal myself before Ottilie, by showing a sudden coldness. But in fact, I was if anything fonder of her now. I even warmed toward Edward; I fairly doted (at a safe distance) on the child. They were nearer to Charlotte, in the commonplace world of breakfasts and bedtimes, than I could ever be. And they were the keepers of that most precious thing, her past. That they could not hope to achieve the proximity to her that I did, in my love, was something for which they could not be blamed, but only pitied. I spent hours, a smiling spider, weaving webs to trap them into talking about her, so that it would be always they who appeared to have brought up the subject. The hardest part was to keep them from straying on to other things. Then I was forced to take desperate action, and, elaborately casual, would jump in with: But what you were saying about Charlotte, it was interesting, did she really never have a boyfriend before Edward? And a red-hot coal of panic would briefly glow behind my breastbone when Ottilie paused, and glanced at me, struck I suppose by the incongruity of putting together such words as *Charlotte* and *boyfriend*.

Being a man with a secret was a full-time role. Sometimes I almost lost sight of the beloved herself in the luxuriant abundance of my mission. When Ottilie was in my arms I was careful not to speak, for fear of crying out the wrong name – but there were moments too when I was not sure which was the right one, moments even when the two became fused. At first I had conjured Charlotte's presence to be only a witness to the gymnastics in my narrow bed, to lean over us, Ottilie and me, with the puzzled attention of a pure spirit of the night, immune herself to the itch of the flesh yet full of tenderness for these sad mortals struggling among the sheets, but as time went on this ceased to be enough, the sprite had to fold her delicate wings, throw off her silken wisps, and, with a sigh of amused resignation, join us. Then in the moonlight my human girl's blonde hair would turn black, her fingers pale, and she would become something new, neither herself nor the other, but a third – Charlottilie!

There was a fourth, too, which was that other version of myself which stood apart, watching the phenomenon of this love and my attendant antics with a wry smile, puzzled, and at times embarrassed. He it was who continued to, I won't say love, but to value Ottilie, her gaiety and generosity, her patience, the mournful passion that she lavished on me. Was there, then, another Ottilie as well, an autochthonous companion for that other I? Were all at Ferns dividing thus and multiplying, like amoebas? In this spawning of multiple selves I seemed to see the awesome force of my love, which in turn served to convince me anew of its authenticity.

Perhaps this sense of displacement will account for the oddest phenomenon of all, and the hardest to express. It was the notion of a time out of time, of this summer as a self-contained unit separate from the time of the ordinary world. The events I read of in the newspapers were, not unreal, but only real *out there*, and irredeemably ordinary; Ferns, on the other hand, its daily minutiae, was strange beyond expressing, unreal, and yet hypnotically vivid in its unreality. There was no sense of life messily making itself from moment to moment. It had all been lived already, and we were merely tracing the set patterns, as if not living really, but remembering. As with Ottilie I had foreseen myself on my deathbed, now I saw this summer as already a part of the past, immutable, crystalline and perfect. The future had ceased to exist. I drifted, lolling like a Dead Sea swimmer, lapped round by a warm blue soup of timelessness.

I even went back to the book, in a way. I needed something on which to concentrate, an anchor in this world adrift. And what better prop for the part of hopeless lover than a big fat book? Sitting at my table before the window and the sunlit lilacs I thought of Canon Koppernigk at Frauenburg, of Nietzsche in the Engadine, of Newton himself, all those high cold heroes who renounced the world and human happiness to pursue the big game of the intellect. A pretty picture but hardly a true one. I did little real work. I struck out a sentence or two, rearranged a paragraph, corrected a few solecisms, and, inevitably, returned again to the second, and longer, of those two strange letters to Locke, the one in which N. speaks of having sought *a means of explaining the nature of the ailment, if ailment it be, which has afflicted me this summer past.* The letter seemed to me now to lie at the centre of my work, perhaps of Newton's too, reflecting and containing all the rest, as the image of Charlotte contained, as in a convex mirror, the entire world of Ferns. It is the only instance in all his correspondence of an effort to understand and express his innermost self. And something *is* expressed, understood, forgiven even, if not in the lines themselves then in the spaces between, where an extraordinary and pitiful tension throbs. He wanted so much to know what it was that had happened to him, and to say it, as if the mere saying itself would be redemption. He mentions, with unwonted calm, Locke's challenge of the absolutes of space and time and motion on which the picture of the mechanistic universe in the *Principia* is founded, and trots out again, but without quite the old conviction, the defence that such absolutes exist in God, which is all that is asked of them. But then suddenly he is talking about the excursions he makes nowadays along the banks of the Cam, and of his encounters, not with the great men of the college, but with tradesmen, the sellers and the makers of things. *They would seem to have something to tell me; not of their trades, nor even of how they conduct their lives; nothing, I believe, in words. They are, if you will understand it, themselves the things they might tell. They are all a form of saying* – and there it breaks off, the rest of that page illegible (because of a scorch mark, perhaps?). All that remains is the brief close: *My dear Doctor, expect no more philosophy from my pen. The language in which I might be able not only to write but to think is neither Latin nor English, but a language none of whose words is known to me; a language in which commonplace things speak to me; and wherein I may one day have to justify myself before an unknown judge.* Then comes that cold, that brave, that almost carven signature: *Newton.* What did he mean, what was it those commonplace things said to him, what secret did they impart? And so I sat in the shadow of lilacs, nursing an unrequitable love and reading a dead man's testament, trying to understand it.

WHATEVER I HAD FELT for Ottilie in the beginning, there was not much left now save lust, and irritation, and a kind of grudging compassion. She sensed the change, of course, and began to probe it. She came to the lodge more often, as if to test my endurance. She said she wanted to stay all night, she didn't care what they thought at the house. Then she would look at me, not listening to my excuses, only watching my eyes and saying nothing. I began cautiously to try to disengage myself. I talked a lot about freedom. Why tie ourselves down? This summer would end. She was too young to throw away the best moments of her life on a dry old scholar. Her eyes narrowed. I too wondered what I was getting at – but no, that's not true, I knew damn well. It was devious, and heartless, and horribly pleasurable. Who knows the sweet stink of power like the disenchanted lover renouncing all claim to loyalty? I pictured her known flesh soiled by some faceless other, yet gloried in the knowledge that I need only give the reins the faintest twitch and she would come running back to me, awash in her lap.

I look back on myself in those days, and I do not like what I see.

We spent hours in bed, entire afternoons seeped away into the sheets. We invented new positions, absurd variations that left us gasping, our sinews aquiver. She had me bind her hands and tie her to chairs, to the legs of the bed. We made love on the floor, against the walls. If Michael had not been liable to pop up from the undergrowth she would have dragged me naked out into the grass to do it. When she bled we devised a whole manual of compromises. No witch could have worked at her dark art more diligently than she.

Sometimes this frenzied sorcery of the senses frightened me. Squatting before her with my face in her lap, staring in silent fascination at the brownish frills and violet-tinted folds of her sex, I would suddenly feel something blundering away from me, an almost-creature of our making, damaged and in pain, dragging a blackened limb along the floor and screaming softly. It was an image of guilt, of my shame and her desperation, the simple fear that she would get pregnant, and of things too more deeply buried. Its counterpart, light to that dark, was the pale presence of a third always with us, who was my private conjuring trick. 'Look at me!' Ottilie would say, 'Look at me when we're doing it, I want you to see me!' I looked at her, that was easy. But after these bouts of ghostly troilism I hardly had the nerve to face Charlotte.

Curiously, I seemed to see Ottilie more clearly now than ever before. Receding from me, she took on the high definition of a figure seen through the wrong end of a telescope, fixed, tiny, complete in every detail. Anyway, from the first I had assumed that I understood her absolutely, so there was no need to speculate much about her. I suppose that is why I had never asked her about the child. It seems incredible to me, now, that I didn't. She could not have been more than sixteen when he was born. Who was the father – some farmhand, or a local young buck, a wandering huckster perhaps who had come to the door one day and captivated her with his patter and his wicked eye? That she was the mother I never doubted. But she said nothing, and neither did I, and as the weeks and months went on the unasked question became faded, like one of those huge highway signs so worn by being looked at that its message has gone mute.

I don't remember when it was exactly that this skeleton began to rattle its bones with a new urgency in the Lawless cupboard. It might have been the day of Michael's party, when I turned starry-eyed from the piano and saw the three of them, Ottilie and Edward and the child, posed in a north light by the window like models for the *Madonna of the Rocks*, but probably I'm being fanciful. It was later, anyway, before I began to brood in earnest, when my love for Charlotte was demanding other, grosser conspiracies to keep it company. Then everything was in flux, and anything was possible. One Sunday, for instance, Ottilie casually remarked that she had skipped the family excursion to Mass to be with me. Mass? They were *Catholics*? My entire conception of them had to be revised.

And then there was the day she played that extraordinary trick on me. She came to the lodge, out of breath and grinning slyly. Edward and Charlotte were in Dublin, Michael was at school. 'Well?' she said, hands in her pockets, shoulders hunched, smiling and swaying, imitating some film star; 'you've never seen *my* room.' We walked up the drive under the sycamores. It was an eighteenth-century day, windswept and bright, the distances all small and sharply defined, as if painted on porcelain. The trees were that dry tired green that heralds their turning. Prompted by intimations of autumnal sadness I took her hand, and remembered suddenly, vividly, as I still can, the first time she had shown herself to me naked. In the hall she stopped and looked around her at the clock, the mirror, the hurley stick in the umbrella stand. She sighed. 'I hate this place,' she said, and I kissed her open mouth with a sweet sense of sin. The sight of the child's room sobered us; we crept past. At the next door she hesitated, biting her lip, and then threw it open. The bed was a vast squat beast with curlicues and wooden knobs. There was a smell of stale clothes and face-powder. In a corner the flowered wallpaper was bubbled on a damp patch. Is there anything more cloyingly intimate than the atmosphere of other people's bedrooms? The window looked across the lawn to the lodge. 'I see you can keep an eye on me,' I said, and laughed gloomily, like a travelling salesman in a brothel. She cast a vague glance at the window. She was already halfway out of her clothes. There was a black hair on the pillow, like a tiny crack in enamel.

We lay for a long time without stirring, in silence, desireless. A parallelogram of sunlight was shifting stealthily along the floor beneath the window. Against the pale sky I watched a flock of birds wheeling silently at a great height over the fields. A memory from childhood drifted up, paused an instant, showing the gold of its lazily beating fins, and then went down again, without breaking the surface. I kissed the damp thicket of her armpit. She stroked my cheek. She began to say something, stopped. I could feel her trying it out in her head. I waited; she would say it. There are moments like that, sunlit and still, when the worst and deepest fear of the heart will drift out with the dreamy innocence of a paper skiff on a pond.

'You've lost interest,' she said, 'really, haven't you.'

A little cloud, like a white puff of smoke, appeared in the corner of the window. Summer is the shyest season.

'Why do you say that?'

She smiled. 'So you'll tell me it's not true.' She had a way of looking at me, tentative and cool, as if she had spotted a small fault in the pupil of my eyes, and were wondering whether or not she should mention it.

'It's not true.'

'Could I take that to mean, now, that you love me?'

'Oh, all this love,' I said wearily, 'I'm weary of it.'

'All what love?' pouncing, as if with the winning line of a word game.

'See that cloud?' I said. 'That's love. It comes along, drifts across the blue, and then . . .'

'Goes. '

Silence.

She sat up, hugging the sheet to her breast. 'Well,' she said briskly, 'will I tell you something?' Her face above me, foreshortened, glazed by reflected sunlight, was for a moment an oriental mask. 'This is not my room.'

'What? Then whose . . .?' She grinned. 'Jesus Christ, Ottilie!' I leapt up like a scalded cat and stood, naked and aghast, staring at her. She laughed. 'You should see your face,' she said, 'you're all red.'

'You are mad.' It was an extraordinary sensation: disgust, and a kind of panic, and, incredibly, tumescence. I turned away, scrabbling for my clothes. I felt as if I had been turned to glass, as if the world could shine through me unimpeded: as if I were now a quicksilver shadow in someone else's looking-glass fantasy. What had possessed her, to bring me here? Was I perhaps not the only one who played at plots of sexual risk and renunciation? 'I'm going for a piss,' she muttered, and flung herself from the room. I dressed, and stood at bay, breathing through my mouth in order not to smell the flat insinuating odour of other people's intimacies. All I could think of was Edward's clumsiness, the way his sausage fingers fumbled things. A book would erupt in his hands like a terrified bird, pages whirring, dustjacket flapping, while he looked away, talking over his shoulder, until the thing with a crisp crack dropped lifeless, its spine broken, and then he would peer at it with a kind of guilty puzzlement. How could I be doing this, to a man like that. Doing what? I realised I felt as I would feel if I had cuckolded him. Ottilie came back. She sat down on the side of the bed and clasped herself in her arms. 'I'm cold.'

'For Christ's sake, Ottilie—'

'Oh, what harm is it?' she said. 'They'll never know.' She looked up at me resentfully, pouting, a big naked child. 'I thought you might like to . . . here . . . that's all.'

'You're *mad*.'

'No I'm not. I know things,' slyly, 'I could tell you things.'

'What does that mean?'

'You'll have to find out for yourself, won't you? You don't know anything. You think you're so clever, but you don't know a thing.'

I slapped her face. It happened so quickly, with such a surprising, gratifying precision, that I was not sure if I had not imagined it. She sat quite still, then lifted a hand to her already reddening cheek. She began to cry, without any sound at all. 'I'm sorry,' I said. I left the room and closed the door carefully behind me, as if the slightest violence would scatter the shards of something in there shattered but still all of a precarious piece. Outside, in the ordinary light of afternoon, I still felt unreal, but at least I could breathe freely.

*

That afternoon was to contaminate everything. I looked at the others with a new surmise, full of suspicions. They were altered, the way someone you have known all your life will be altered after appearing, all menace and maniacal laughter, in a half-remembered dream. Up to now they had been each a separate entity. I hadn't thought of them as husband and wife, mother, son, niece, aunt – aunt! – but now suddenly they were a family, a closed, mysterious organism. Amazing questions occurred to me. What really did they mean to each other? What did Charlotte feel for the child? Did Edward and she resent orphan Ottilie's presence? Were the women jealous of each other, did they circle each other warily, as Edward and I did? And what did they all think of me, how did they behave when I was not there, did they talk about me? What did they see when they looked at me? – a kind of shadow, a trick of light, a ghost grown familiar of whom no one is frightened anymore? I felt a new shyness in their presence, an awkwardness. I was like an embarrassed anthropologist realising that what he had for months taken to be the ordinary muddle of tribal life is really an immense intricate ceremony, in which the tiniest gesture is foreordained and vital, in which he is the only part that does not fit.

All questions came back to the one question: why had she chosen *that* room? Impulse? A simple prank? Or did she have some intimation of the delicate dance I was doing with Charlotte in my mind (*I thought you might like to . . . here . . .*)? And if so, did Charlotte my god, did Charlotte herself suspect, did she feel when I came near something reach out and touch her timidly, the moist pale limb of my longing? There are people you cannot, will not imagine *doing* it, but now I could not stop myself speculating on the nightworld of Ferns. Why did Charlotte and Edward have no children? Which of them was . . .? The names wove a web of confusion in my mind. I began to have lurid dreams in which the four of them slipped and slithered, joining and sundering, exchanging names, faces, voices, as in some obscene surrealist fantasy. I lay in bed in the lodge and tried to imagine Edward here, younger, less besotted, watching the old man Charlotte's father, waiting for him to die, planting his claim to Ferns by seducing the daughter, perhaps on this very mattress . . . I sat up, as suddenly as I had that day in that other bed. I was sweating. The girl my fevered imaginings had put in Edward's arms was not Charlotte. Away in the woods a night bird was singing. Sixteen, for god's sake, she was only sixteen!

Impossible.

*

The weather broke. I wakened in the middle of the night to a noise of shipwreck, a smashed mast, doomed sailors crying in the wind. In the morning when I looked out the kitchen window the scenery was rearranged. The storm had brought down a tree. It lay, a great stranded corpse, in a tangle of brambles and twisted branches not a foot from the gable end of the lodge. The day had a hangdog air, mud everywhere, and granite clouds suspended over the fields. Snails crunched under my tread. The summer was over.

Edward came down the drive in a shabby raincoat and a ridiculous tweed hat. 'Some night, eh?' He peered at the fallen tree. 'By Christ that was a close one, nearly got you.' I found it hard to look him in the face, and studied his extremities instead, the brown brogues, twill trousers, the cuffs of his raincoat. Was I imagining it, or was he shrinking; his clothes seemed made for someone a shade fuller. He looked ghastly, ashen-faced and blotched by the cold. Another hard night. Where did he do his drinking? Once or twice I had seen him sloping into the hotel bar in the village, but latterly he had been keeping to the house. Perhaps he kept a cache of bottles stowed under floorboards, at the back of the linen cupboard, as domesticated drunks are said to do. Or maybe he drank openly, turning his back on Charlotte's sad gaze. 'Planted that tree myself,' he said, 'Lotte and me, one day.' He looked up, smiling sheepishly, shrugging. 'That's the summer gone.' Something came off him, a kind of mute plea. For what, for sympathy? I was afraid he would start maundering again about women, life and love. A warm gush of contempt rose like gorge in my gullet. He felt it, for he laughed, shaking his head, and said: 'You're a hard man.' For a moment I could not make out the emphasis, then I realised that *he* was sympathising with *me*. By god! I stared at him – on your knees, cur! – but he only laughed again, and turned away.

*

Going up to the house that evening, I met in the hall a large red-faced man in a blue suit. He winked at me, and ran a finger down his fly. Above our heads the lavatory was still noisily recovering from his visit. 'Bad old weather,' he said, jauntily. We went together into the drawing-room; tea was being served there in the visitor's honour. Edward leaned against the mantelpiece in his squire's outfit of tweed and twill, one hand in his trousers pocket wriggling like a conjuror's rabbit. I tried to see him as a seducer. It was surprisingly easy. Younger, hair slicked down, creeping up on her. Give us a kiss? I'll tell Charlotte. Ah you wouldn't now. Let go! Yum yum, lovely titties . . . Charlotte was looking at me in mute dismay: she had forgotten it was Sunday. Tough. Visitors were rare, I wasn't about to miss this one. She came at us quickly, her hands out, like someone stepping in to stop a fight. 'Mr Prunty is in the seed business.' I looked at Mr Prunty with interest. He winked again.

'Have a drink,' said Edward.

Charlotte turned quickly. 'The tea is ready!'

He shrugged. 'Oh, right.'

Ottilie and the child came in.

Mr Prunty was a great talker, and a great eater; his laughter made the table tremble. He was trying to buy the nurseries. I suspect he had already a hold on the Lawlesses. When business matters were mentioned he grew ponderously coy. I studied him. I had seen him before: he was a type. His money made, he was after style now, and class. He gazed upon the Lawlesses with a kind of fond indulgence. He loved them, a ripe market. There would be no stopping him. Gently, lovingly, he would relieve them of Ferns. Eventually he would become a patrician, change his name, maybe, breed a brood of pale neurotic daughters to sit in this room doing needlepoint and writing hysterical novels. 'It's a fair offer,' he said seriously, glancing round the table, a forkful of food suspended before him. 'I think it's a fair offer.' And he laughed.

They sat looking back at him, glumly, a little stupidly even, like a small band of supplicants come from the sacked city to beg for clemency before the emperor's tent. I had not spoken to Ottilie since the afternoon in the Lawlesses' bedroom. Edward coughed.

'Well—' he began.

Charlotte, who had been gazing at the large blue man with hypnotic fascination, dragged herself out of her trance.

'He's writing, you know,' she said to Mr Prunty, pointing at me, 'a book, he is. On Newton. The astronomer. '

All eyes turned to me, as if I had that moment descended from the sky into their midst.

'Is that right now,' Mr Prunty said.

Charlotte's look pleaded with me. 'Aren't you?'

I shrugged. 'I *was*.' They waited. I was blushing. 'I seem to have given it up . . .'

'Oh?' Ottilie put in, icily bright. 'And what are you doing instead?'

I would not look at her.

'Yes,' said Mr Prunty, after a pause. 'Well as I was—'

'Given it up?' Charlotte said. With her sorrowing eyes, pale heart-shaped face, those hands, she might have stepped out of a Cranach garden of dark delights.

'Like Newton,' I said. 'He gave up too.'

'Did he?'

'It's not the money that's the point,' Edward was saying, 'it's not the main thing,' and Mr Prunty, trimming the fat from a piece of ham, pursed his lips, and pretended to be trying not to smile.

'Yes,' I said, 'his work, his astronomy, everything. He was fifty; he went a little mad.'

'I didn't know that,' she said. Michael looked around cautiously and put the jammy blade of his knife into his mouth. 'Why was that?'

'Ferns is a family affair,' Edward said grumpily, 'there's a tradition here.'

'Because—'

'Stop that!' Ottilie snapped. Michael slowly removed the knife from his mouth, looking at her.

'Oh true, true,' said Mr Prunty smoothly, 'the *Graingers* have been in this house a long time.'

Charlotte, a hand to her naked throat, gave a tiny shudder. O Isaac, make haste to help me!

'Because he had to have certain absolutes,' I said, look at me, keep looking at me, 'certain absolutes of of of, of space, time, motion, to found his theories on. But space, and time, and motion,' beats, soft beats, soft heartbeats, 'can only be relative, for us, he knew that, had to admit it, had to let them go, and when they went,' O my darling, 'everything else went with them.' Ah!

A vast dark cloud sailed into the window.

'Well,' said Prunty, routed finally, 'I've made my offer, I hope you'll consider it.' My lap was damp. Charlotte, as if nothing at all had happened, turned to him coolly and said: 'Of course, thank you.'

There was some more chat, the weather, the crops, and then he left. Charlotte saw him out. 'Bloody gombeen man,' Edward said, and yawned. Under the table Ottilie's foot touched mine, retreated, and then came back without its shoe. I suppose she had caught a whiff of rut, and thought the trail led to her. Charlotte returning stopped in the doorway. 'Was that lightning?' We turned to the window expectantly. Rain, grey light, a trembling bough. Why do I remember so clearly these little scenes? Because they seemed somehow arranged, as certain street scenes, in quiet suburbs, on dreamy summer evenings, will seem arranged, that postbox, the parked van, one tree in its wire cage, and a red ball rolling innocently into the road down which the lorry is hurtling. A tremendous clap of thunder broke above our heads. 'By Christ,'

Edward said mildly. He turned to Charlotte. A glass of whiskey had appeared in his hand out of nowhere.

'Well?' he said. 'What do you think?' She shook her head. 'You'll have to sell, you know,' he said, 'sooner or later.'

There was a silence, and once again I had that sense of them all turning away from me toward some black awful eminence that only they could see.

'We,' Charlotte said, so softly I hardly heard it; '*we*, you mean.'

*

I listened to them fighting all evening long, doors slamming, the radio switched full on and as suddenly silenced, and Edward shouting between pauses in which I pictured Charlotte in tears, her face a rain-washed flower lifted imploringly to his. More than once I started to go up to the house, with some wild idea of calling him out, and then subsided helplessly, fists like caricatures clenched before me. The rain stopped, and late sunlight briefly filled the garden, and through the drenched evening an incongruous blackbird began to sing. I felt vaguely ill. A knot of nerves seethed in my stomach. At last I heard the front door bang, and the car bumped down the drive and sped towards town. I drank a glass of brandy and put myself to bed. I was still awake when there came a knock at the door. I leapt up. But it was only Ottilie. She smiled in mock timidity. 'Am I allowed to come in?' I said nothing, and poured her a brandy. She watched me, still smiling, and biting her lip. 'Listen I'm sorry,' she said, 'about the other day. It was a stupid—'

'Forget it. I'm sorry I hit you. There. Cheers.' I sat on the sofa, pressing the glass to my still heaving stomach. I nodded in the direction of the house. 'Fireworks.'

'He's drunk,' she said. She was wandering about aimlessly, looking at things, her hands thrust in her pockets. 'I had to get out. She's just sitting there, doped to the gills, doing the martyr as usual. It's hard to have sympathy all the time . . .' She looked at me: 'You know?'

The light was fading fast. She switched on a lamp, but the bulb blew out immediately, fizzing. 'Jesus,' she said wearily. She sat down at the table and thrust a hand into her hair.

'What's going on,' I said, 'are they going to sell the place?'

'They'll have to, I suppose. They're not too happy with old Prunty. He'll get it, though, he's rotten with money.'

'What will you do, then?'

'I don't know.' She chuckled, and said, in what she called her gin-and-fog voice: 'Why don't you make me an offer? – Oh don't look so frightened, I'm joking.' She rose and wandered into the bedroom. I could hear the soft slitherings as she undressed. I went and stood in the doorway. She was already in bed, sitting up and staring before her in the lamplight, her hands clasped on the blanket, like an effigy. She turned her face to me. 'Well?' Why was it that when she took off her clothes, her face always looked more naked than the rest of her?

'He's not much of a salesman,' I said.

'Edward? He was different, before.'

'Before what?'

She continued to gaze at me. I suppose I looked a little strange, eyes slitted, jaw stuck out; suspicion, anger, jealousy – jealousy! – itches I could not get at to scratch. She said: 'Why are you so interested, all of a sudden?'

'I wondered what you thought of him. You never mention him.'

'What do you want me to say? He's sad, now.'

I got into bed beside her. That blackbird was still singing, in the dark, pouring out its heedless heart. 'I'll be leaving,' I said. She was quite still. I cleared my throat. 'I said, I'll be leaving.'

She nodded. 'When?'

'Soon. Tomorrow, the weekend, I don't know.' I was thinking of Charlotte. Leaving: it was unreal.

'That's that, then.' Her face was a tear-stained blur. I took her in my arms. She was hot and damp, as if every pore were a tiny tear-duct. 'I want to tell you,' she said, after a time, 'when you hit me that day and walked out, I lay in their bed for ages making love to myself and crying. I kept thinking you'd come back, say you were sorry, get a cold cloth for my face. Stupid.'

I said: 'Who is Michael's father?'

She showed no surprise. She even laughed: was that all I could say? 'A fellow that used to work here,' she said.

'What was his name?'

'I don't remember.'

'What became of him?'

'He went away. So did the girl. And Charlotte adopted the child. She couldn't have any, herself.'

No. *No.*

'You're lying.'

But she wasn't really listening, her ear was turned to the steady trickle of misery that had started up inside her. She laid her forehead against my cheek. 'You know,' she said, 'sometimes I think you don't exist at all, that you're just a voice, a name – no, not even that, just the voice, going on. Oh god. Oh no,' furious with herself, yet powerless to stop the great wet sobs that began to shake her, 'Oh *no*,' and wailing she came apart completely in my arms, grinding her face against mine, her shoulders heaving. I was aghast, I was – no, simply say, I was surprised, that's worst of all. Behind her, darkness stood at the window, silent, gently inquisitive. She drew herself away from me, her face averted. 'I'm sorry,' she said, gasping, 'I'm sorry, but I've never given myself like this to anyone before, and it's hard,' and the sobs shook her, 'it's *hard*.'

'There there,' I said, like a fool, helplessly, 'there there.' I felt like one who has carelessly let something drop, who realises too late, with the pieces smashed all around him, how precious a thing it was, after all. A flash of lightning lit the window, and the rain started up again with a soft whoosh. She wiped her nose on the back of her hand. The tears still flowed, as if there would be no end, but she was no longer aware of them. 'I suppose you're sick and tired of me,' she said, and lay down, and turned on her side, and was suddenly asleep, leaving me alone to nurse my shock and my cold heart.

WE MUST ASSUME that Edward did go that night into town, and not to the village, as was later to be suggested. The evidence against the latter possibility is twofold. First, there was the direction in which I had heard him drive away. Had he been headed for the village, the sound of the car would have faded quickly as it dropped below the brow of the hill; instead of which, it was audible for a considerable time, a fact consistent with the motor travelling westward, along the main road, the slope of which is much less pronounced than that of the hill road, leading to the village. Second, there is the quite considerable amount of drink which, it would later be obvious, he had consumed. At that stage the publicans of the village, both in the hotel, and in the public houses with which the place is generously endowed, knew better than to serve him the endless double whiskeys which he would demand.

However, his going to town – to coin a phrase – will not account for the considerable lapse of time between closing time (11:30 pm, summer hours) and his return to Ferns at approximately 2:30 am. As to what occurred in those 'lost' hours, we can only speculate. Did he meet a friend (did he *have* any friends?) to whose house they might have repaired? The town does not boast a bawdy-house, therefore that possibility can be eliminated. The quayfront then, the parked car, its lights aglow, the radio humming forlornly to itself, and from within the darkened windscreen the stark suicidal stare? Could he have sat there, alone, for some three hours? Perhaps he slept. One would wish him that blessing.

I can't go on. I'm not a historian anymore.

The first thing I noticed when I woke was that Ottilie was gone. The bed was warm, the pillow still damp from her tears. Then I heard the car, labouring up the drive in first gear. I must have dropped back to sleep for a moment, the voices raised in the distance seemed part of a dream. Then I opened my eyes and lay listening in the darkness, my heart pounding. The silence had the quality of disaster: it was less a silence than an aftermath. I went to the window. Lights were coming on in the house, one after another, as if someone were running dementedly from switch to switch. I pulled on trousers and a sweater. The night was pitch-black and still, smelling of laurel and sodden earth. The grass tickled my bare ankles. The car was slewed across the drive, like a damaged animal, its engine running. The front door of the house stood open. There was no one to be seen.

I found Edward in the drawing-room. He was sitting unconscious on the floor with his back against the couch, his head lolling on a cushion, his hands resting palm upward at his sides. A mandala of blood-streaked vomit was splashed on the carpet between his splayed legs. The crotch of his trousers was stained where he had soiled himself. I stood and gaped at him, disgust and triumph jostling in me for position. Triumph, oh yes. Suddenly, through opposing doors, Charlotte and Ottilie swept in, like mechanical figures in a clock tower. They saw me and stopped. 'I heard voices,' I said. Charlotte blinked. She wore an old plaid dressing-gown. Her feet were bare. Less Cranach now than El Greco. We were quite still, all three, and then everyone began to speak at once.

'I couldn't get through,' Ottilie said.

Charlotte put a hand to her forehead. 'What?'

'There was no reply.'

'Oh.'

'We'll have to—'

'Did you ring the right—'

'What?'

In the hall a hand appeared on the stairs, a small bare foot, an eye.

'I'll have to go into town,' Ottilie said. 'Christ.' She looked at me. Her face was still raw from weeping. I turned away. I turned away. 'Get back to bed, you!' she cried, and the figure on the stairs vanished. She went out, slamming the door, and in a moment we heard the car depart. Gravel from the spinning tyres sprayed the window. *That wall, see, down there.* Charlotte sighed. 'She's gone for . . .' She thought a moment, frowning; '. . . for the doctor.' She walked about the room as in a dream, picking up things, holding them for a moment, as if to verify something, and then putting them down again. Edward belched, or perhaps it was a groan. She paused, and stood motionless, listening; she did not look at him. Then she went to the switch by the door and carefully, as if it were an immensely complicated and necessary operation, turned off the main lights. A lamp on a low table by the couch was still burning. She crossed the room and sat down on a high-backed chair, facing the window. It all had the look of a ritual she had performed many times before. Something, the lamplight perhaps, the curious toylike look of things, the helpless gestures meticulously performed, stirred an ancient memory in me of another room, where, a small boy, I had played with two girl cousins while above our heads adult footsteps came and went, pacing out the ceremony of someone's dying.

'Is it raining, I wonder,' Charlotte murmured. I think she had forgotten I was there. I went forward softly and stood behind her. In the black window her face was reflected. I looked down at the pale defenceless parting of her hair; in the opening of her dressing-gown I could see the gentle slope of a breast. How can I describe to you that moment, in lamplight, at dead of night, the smell of vomit mingled with the milky perfume of her hair, and that gross thing sitting there, grotesque and comic, like a murdered pavement artist, and no world around us anymore, only the vast darkness, stretching away. Everything was possible, everything was allowed, as in a mad dream. I could feel her warmth against my thighs. I looked at her reflection in the glass; my face must be there too, for her.

'Mrs Lawless,' I said, 'this can't go on, you can't be expected to put up with this.' My voice was thick, a kind of fat whine. Tell her something, tell her a fact, a fragment from the big world, a coloured stone, a bit of clouded green glass. Young men of the

Ipo tribe in the Amazon basin pledge themselves with the nail parings of their ancestors. Oh god. The first little flames of panic were nibbling at me. 'Listen,' I said, 'listen I'll give you my address, my phone number, so that if ever you want . . . if ever you need . . .' I put my hands on her shoulders, and a hot shock zipped along my nerves, as if it were not cloth, flesh and bone I were holding, but the terminals of her very being, and 'Charlotte,' I whispered, 'Oh Charlotte!' and there was a lump thick as a heart in my throat, and tears in my eyes, and the Ipo drums began to beat, and all over the rain forest lurid birds with yellow beaks and little bright black eyes were screeching.

She stirred, and turned up her face to me, blinking. 'I'm sorry,' she said, 'I wasn't listening. What did you say?'

*

We heard the car returning. So much for the wall of death. The doctor was an ill-tempered old man, still in his pyjamas, with a raincoat thrown over his shoulders. He glared at me, as if the whole affair were my fault. 'Where is he? What? Why in the name of Christ didn't you put him to bed?' Gruff, good with children, old women would dote on him. He knelt down, grunting, and felt Edward's pulse. 'Where was he drinking?'

Charlotte began distractedly to cry.

'In the village, probably,' Ottilie said. She stood, with her hands behind her, leaning back against the door, her swollen eyes shut. Michael was sitting on the stairs, watching through the banisters. Had he been there to hear me pledge my troth to poor unheeding Charlotte?

The doctor and I, with Ottilie's help, lifted Edward and hauled him up the stairs. He opened his eyes briefly and said something. The smell, the slack feel of him, was horrible.

'Let him sleep,' the doctor said, 'there's nothing to be done.' He turned to Charlotte, watching from the doorway. 'And you, Mrs Lawless, are you all right? Have you your pills?' She continued to look at Edward's head sunk in the pillows. She nodded slowly, like a child. 'Try and sleep now.' The doctor glanced, inexplicably sheepish, at Ottilie and me – good god, was he in love with Charlotte too? 'He'll be all right now. I'll come back in the morning.'

Ottilie and I went with him to the door. The night came in, smelling of wet and the distant sea. 'Can I drive you back?' I said.

Ottilie pushed past me out on the step. 'I'll do it.'

'He should be kept an eye on,' the doctor said, throwing me a parting scowl. 'He'll go down fast, after this.'

*

The gaseous light of dawn was filtering into the garden when she came back. I went outside to meet her. I had stood at the window watching for her, listening breathlessly for a sound from upstairs, afraid to leave, but fearful that she would return and find me indoors, trap me, make me drink tea and talk about the meaning of life. Even at that late stage I was still misjudging her. She came up the steps, hugging herself against the cold, and stopped, not looking at me, swinging the car key. I asked a question about the doctor, for something to say.

'Old fraud,' she said, distantly, frowning.

'Oh?'

We were wary as two strangers trapped by a downpour in a shop doorway. A seagull swaggered across the lawn, leaving green arrow-prints in the grey wet of the grass.

'Feeding her that stuff.'

She waited; my go.

'What stuff?' I felt like a straight-man.

'Valium, seconal, I don't know, some dope like that. Six months she's been on it. She's like a zombie – didn't you notice?' with a tiny flick of contempt.

'I wondered,' I said, 'yes.'

Wonder is the word all right.

A blood-red glow was swelling among the trees. I felt – I don't know. I was cold, and there was a taste of ashes in my mouth. Something had ended, with a vast soft crash.

'In northern countries they call this the wolf hour,' I said. A fact! Pity Charlotte was not there to hear me, learning the trick at last. 'What is it he has?'

'Edward?' She looked at me then, with scorn, pityingly. 'You really didn't know,' she said, 'all this time, did you.'

'Why didn't you tell me?'

She only smiled, a kind of grimace, and looked away. Yes, a foolish question. I felt briefly like a child, pressing his face against the cold unyielding pane of adult knowingness. *She* was the grown-up. I shrugged, and went down the steps. The seagull flew away, scattering its mewling cries upon the air.

THERE'S NOT MUCH left to tell. That same morning I packed as many of my belongings as I could carry and locked up the lodge. I left the key in an envelope pinned to the door. I thought of writing a note, but to whom would I have written, and what? I stood in the gateway, afraid Ottilie might see me, and come after me – I could not have borne it – taking a last brief view of the house, the sycamores, that broken fanlight they would never fix. Michael was about. He too had grown, already the lineaments of what he would someday be were discernible in the way he held himself, unbending, silent, inviolably private. He was no longer a Cupid. Not a golden bow and arrow, but a flaming sword would have suited him now. I waved to him tentatively, but he pretended not to see me. I set off down the road to the village. The sun was shining, but too bright; it would rain later. The leaves were turning. Farewell, happy fields!

A long low car came up the hill. I almost laughed: it was the Mittlers. Had Bunny turned her little nose twitching to the wind and caught a whiff of disaster? Maybe Charlotte had called them. What did I know? They passed me by with a toot on the deep-throated horn, gazing at me through the smoked glass, the four of them, like manikins. Bunny noted my bag. Before they were past she had turned to her husband, her mouth working avidly.

On the train I travelled into a mirror. There it all was, the backs of the houses, the drainpipes, a cloud out on the bay, just like the first time, only in reverse order. In the dining-car I met Mr Prunty: life will insist on tying up loose ends. He remembered my face, but not where he had seen it. 'Ferns, was it,' he cried, 'that's it!' and jabbed a finger into my chest. I was pleased. He seemed somehow right: vivid yet inconsequential, and faintly absurd. He spoke of Edward in a whisper, shaking his head. 'Has it in the gut, I believe, poor bugger – you knew that?'

'Yes,' I said, 'I know.'

Two letters awaited me at the flat, one calling me to an interview in Cambridge, the other offering me the post here. The contract is for a year only. Was I crazy to come? My surroundings are congenial. There is nothing I could wish for, except, but no, nothing. Spring is a ferocious and faintly mad season in this part of the world. At night I can hear the ice unpacking in the bay, a groaning and a tremendous deep drumming, as if something vast were being born out there. And I have heard gatherings of wolves too, far off in the frozen wastes, howling like orchestras. The landscape, if it can be called that, has a peculiar bleached beauty, much to my present taste. Tiny flowers appear on the tundra, slender and pale as the souls of dead girls. And I have seen the auroras.

*

Ottilie writes every week. I catch myself listening for the postman panting up the stairs. She once told me, at Ferns, that when she was away from me she felt as if she were missing an arm – but now I seem weighed down by an extra limb, a large awkward thing, I don't know what to do with it, where to put it, and it keeps me awake at night. She sent me a photograph. In it she is sitting on a fallen tree, in winter sunlight. Her gaze is steady, unsmiling, her hands rest on her knees; there is the line of a thigh that is inimitably hers. There is something here, in this pose, this gaze at once candid and tender, that when I was with her I missed; it is I think the sense of her essential otherness, made poignant and precious because she seems to be offering it into my keeping. She's in Dublin now. She abandoned her plan to go to university, and is working in a shop. She feels her life is *only starting*.

Of all the mental photographs I have of her I choose one. A summer night, one of those white nights of July. We had been drinking, she got up to pee. The lavatory was not working, as so often, and she had brought in from the garage, to join her other treasures, an ornate china vessel which she quaintly called the jolly-pot. I watched her squat there in the gloaming, her elbows on her knees, one hand in her hair, her eyes closed, playing a tinkling chamber music. Still without opening her eyes she came stumbling back to bed, and kneeling kissed me, mumbling in my ear. Then she lay down again, her hair everywhere, and sighed and fell asleep, grinding her teeth faintly. It's not much of a picture, is it? But she's *in* it, ineradicably, and I treasure it.

She's pregnant. Yes, the most banal ending of all, and yet the one I least expected. Wait, that's not true. I have a confession to make. That last night in bed with her, when she sobbed in my arms: I told you she went immediately to sleep, but I lied. I could not resist her tear-drenched nakedness, the passionate convulsions of her sobbing. God forgive me. I believe that was when she conceived; she thinks so too. More sentimentality, more self-delusion? Probably. But at least this delusion has a basis in fact. The child is there. The notion of this strange life, secret in its warm sea, provokes in me the desire to live – to live forever, I mean, if necessary. The future now has the same resonance that the past once had, for me. I am pregnant myself, in a way. Supernumerous existence wells up in my heart.

*

I set out to explain to you, Clio, and to myself, why I had drown'd my book. Have you understood? So much is unsayable: all the important things. I spent a summer in the country, I slept with one woman and thought I was in love with another; I dreamed up a horrid drama, and failed to see the commonplace tragedy that was playing itself out in real life. You'll ask, where is the connection between all that, and the abandoning of a book? I don't know, or at least I can't say, in so many words. I was like a man living underground who, coming up for air, is dazzled by the light and cannot find the way back into his bolt-hole. I trudge back and forth over the familiar ground, muttering. I am lost.

*

Edward survived the winter. He's very low, bedridden: *you wouldn't know him*, she says. As if I ever did. I remember one day he tried to tell me about dying. Oh not directly, of course. I can't recall what he said, what words he used. The subject was the countryside, farming, something banal. But what he was talking about, I suppose, was his sense of oneness now with all poor dumb things, a horse, a tree, a house, that suffer their lives in silence and resigned bafflement, and die unremarked. I wish I could have erected a better monument to him than I have done, in these too many pages; but I had to show you how I thought of him *then*, how I behaved, so that you would see the cruelty of it, the wilful blindness.

*

Of Charlotte she makes no mention. That was only to be expected. I brood on certain words, these emblems. *Succubus*, for instance.

*

What shall I do? Find that fissure in the rocks, clamber down again into that roomy and commodious grave? I hope not. Begin afresh, then, learn how to live up here, in the light? Something is moving under the ice. Oh, I'm not in despair, far from it. I feel the spring around me, the banality of it, the heedless power. Emotions flourish in these frozen wastes. I stop sometimes, staring at a white hill with the tender porcelain of the sky behind it, and I feel such a sense of . . . of something, I don't know. All kinds of things appear on that white screen: a house, a chestnut tree, a dark window with a face reflected in it. Oh and other things, too many to mention. These private showings seem an invitation. Go back to Ferns, move in, set up house, fulfil some grand design, with Ottilie, poor Charlotte, the two boys – for I feel it will be a boy, it must be – become a nurseryman and wear tweeds, talk about the weather, stand around chewing a straw? Impossible. All the same, I *shall* go back. And in the end, it's come to me just this moment, in the end of course I shall take up the book and finish it: such a renunciation is not of this world. Yet I'm wary. Shall I have to go off again, leaving my research, my book and everything else unfinished? Shall I awake in a few months, in a few years, broken and deceived, in the midst of new ruins?

Dublin–Iowa–Dublin
Summer 79 – Spring 81

NOTE

The 'second' Newton letter to John Locke is a fiction, the tone and some of the text of which is taken from Hugo Von Hofmannsthal's *Ein Brief* ('The Letter of Lord Chandos').